A Companion to Indian Fiction in English

A Companion to Indian Fiction in English

Editor by

Pier Paolo Piciucco

ATLANTIC

PUBLISHERS & DISTRIBUTORS (P) LTD

Published by

ATLANTIC

PUBLISHERS & DISTRIBUTORS (P) LTD

7/22, Ansari Road, Darya Ganj,
New Delhi-110002
Phones : +91-11-40775252, 23273880, 23275880, 23280451
Fax : +91-11-23285873
Web : www.atlanticbooks.com
E-mail : orders@atlanticbooks.com

Branch Office
5, Nallathambi Street, Wallajah Road,
Chennai-600002
Phones : +91-44-64611085, 32413319
E-mail : chennai@atlanticbooks.com

Printed in India at Nice Printing Press, A-33/3A, Site-IV,
Industrial Area, Sahibabad, Ghaziabad, U.P.

PREFACE

The *Companion* is the newborn in a long-established tradition of panoramic studies of Indian literature in English and the first one in this series that does not need to explain the nature of the subject being discussed, or justification for its name. The time has come to an end when compilers of critical surveys of Indian English literature had to first clarify the reasons for exploring this field, as, for instance, Meenakshi Mukherjee did in the preface to her seminal work, *The Twice Born Fiction*. Nor shall we run the risk of finding that the topic of our research is so abstruse that it is consequently mistaken for a misprint, as happened to a prominent pioneer in this field, Professor Iyengar, who in 1943 was dismayed to find that his book dealt with "Indo-Anglican" literature instead of "Indo-Anglian," as he had written in the manuscript, because in wartime without proof-reading his zealous publisher thought the author had misspelt the crucial word and possibly imagined that Iyengar would beam with joy when he found the word with the correct(ed) spelling on the published work.

Those times now appear to us so far away that we may read anecdotes such as this as "funny old stories," a sort of shared mythical heritage. At the start of the third millennium, in fact, Indian fiction in English is an internationally acknowledged literary reality. Paradoxically, what Mongia perceptively called "the Indo-chic" phenomenon has become so trendy (in the West) that the publishing industry rapidly commodified it to the extent that, as Huggan recently argued, with India being turned into a consumer product, one may even start to wonder what the real consistency of the literary output is, or where the financial operation finishes and the literary event begins. However, although we may all share concern that business interests may have taken advantage of a heightened interest towards exoticism in Western taste, it is equally true that commercial success does not necessarily imply a decline in quality nor, more importantly, that Indian fiction in English is only that which is (brilliantly) reviewed in the pages of the American and/or English newspapers.

It is surely fair to say that it is not easy task to answer that apparently trivial question, "What is Indian fiction in English today?" To start with, it is likely that an even more trivial question—"What can represent India today?"—will find that Indians themselves disagree on the answer, given the extremely composite nature of the multi-strata social reality, now characterised by a complicated mix of traditions on the one hand, and a tendency towards a more practical Westernised attitude on the other. Of course, the situation is even further complicated when the role played in this process by diasporic writers is taken into consideration, that is to say, those who are considered to be more inclined to sever the umbilical cord with the national/central culture. Therefore, while it is now widely accepted that works originally written in the other Indian national languages and then translated into English cannot (and should not) be included in this classification, as was done by some critics, questions involved in the diasporic response and its cultural challenge to the ordinary coordinates of what is called "national identity" make delimiting the borderline an arduous, at times hazardous, affair. Elements of transnational identity play a crucial role in creating responsive mongrelised forms of culture, as Nasta underscores in a recent study. Over the years, therefore, nomenclature debates in the field seem to have shifted from the meaning of the subject itself to its remote, indistinct peripheries, determining the ambiguousness analysed by Bhabha. While once it was its centrality that was under discussion, now it is its multi-coloured vastness which is being analysed.

The very act of making a choice and delimiting the terrain subject to analysis needs to be placed in this context. Given the complexity of the situation and the multifaceted nature of the simultaneous perspectives which continuously overlap, it soon became obvious to us that reaching a compromise solution taking into all the theories postulated would be far from satisfactory. Nor was our prime intent that of compiling a history of Indian fiction in English which would mirror the extravaganzas expounded by all possible theorists. Selecting novelists according to their approved "Indianness," to borrow a term from Raja Rao, would also have proved impossible because, as previously pointed out, "What can represent India today?" is a question with either a thousand different (objectionable) answers or none at all. This is why we have opted to include all authors who write in English and were born in India, regardless of where they live now or how many months a year they spend "at home." This has perforce led us to exclude all the second generation diasporic writers, in certain cases names of paramount importance like the most recent Nobel Prize winner V.S. Naipaul. Another novelist who has not been included is Ruth Prawer Jhabvala, a significant gender writer, but Polish by birth. The *Companion*, on the other hand, takes in diasporic authors who clearly chose to distance themselves from their original cultural roots, as Bharathi Mukherjee has done, for instance, or novelists such as Vikram Seth, whose *A Suitable Boy* could not be given the Sahitya Academi Prize, India's most prestigious literary award, because its author was not in possession of an Indian passport. In this sense the *Companion* displays a rich texture, full of the same idiosyncrasies and contradictions that characterise this body of literature.

Although each entry focuses on the literary output of a single writer, the *Companion* is organised in such a way that a chronological history of Indian fiction in English emerges as the reader goes from chapter to chapter. While in the book written by Iyengar the beginnings of Indian writing in English dated back to Rammohan Roy, and M.K. Naik traced the embryonic forms of prose back to the early nineteenth century, for us, so to speak, clock-hands joined palms in respectful greeting and handcuffed Indian fiction in English to history on the arrival of the mid thirties when, after a gestation lasting over a century, three Indian gentlemen accepted the challenge to create an authentic, independent tradition for Indian fiction in English, each of them unaware of being in such a good company. Similarly to what Mukherjee has also done, in fact, we have deemed it more practical to start our analysis with the advent of the three forefathers, namely Anand, Rao and Narayan; we then warmly suggest that the scholar interested in the long gestational phase refer to the well-documented and unsurpassed scrutiny it was previously subjected to by Iyengar and Naik. In a way, in fact, the *Companion* reflects current trends in terms of the material discussed but also in the choice of the issues analysed, mirroring, therefore, the focus of interest of present-day studies.

As will be evident to anyone familiar with Indian fiction in English, our choice of collaborators was based on bringing together a team of authoritative specialists. Great care was taken not only in selecting collaborators on the basis of their specialisation but also of their cultural background in relation to the author they were to discuss. The motifs and characteristics of some Indian authors could only be properly expounded by Indian scholars, and this was always taken into account. On the other hand, it is no secret that Indian fiction in English is conceived for an Anglophone readership, and this is why the *Companion* has also relied on contributions from a group of valid Western scholars as well. We have been sensitive to creating a kind of balance between these two poles, so that the number of chapters discussed by Western critics more or less equals those by Indian scholars, and we are happy to have reached this goal, too: in the chutney the *Companion* has prepared at least half of the ingredients are authentically Indian, a recipe that we hope will satisfy a good number of our gourmets.

A fundamental task of any new work of this kind is surely that of taking into account the norms, patterns and attributes in its tradition and keeping on the same path, but at the same time the new editorial project should strive to offer something fresh, actively contributing to the development of the field of studies in question. The *Companion* therefore appears on the scene with an innovative section, dedicated to synopses of novels, planned to allow readers to immediately place the authors analysed within the panorama of Indian literature in English. The synopses included mainly introduce the works written by the novelists treated at length in the previous chapters but, along with them, the reader will also find summarised works by authors who, although contributing in a significant way to the development of forms and techniques, do not feature in the first part of the book. All their most important novels are present, and fully justify their inclusion in the great tradition of Indian English novelists.

In conclusion, we should also remember that the *Companion* is the product of a minor Indian publisher or, as postcolonial critics would have it, of a peripheral third world company, kept going by a wild bunch of die-hards. The fact itself that we have been able to conclude this odyssey is material proof—should any still be needed—that Indian fiction in English has reached a position of prestige on the international scenario.

PIER PAOLO PICIUCCO

Acknowledgments

To start with, I wish to express my gratitude to the collaborators in this editorial venture, who enthusiastically joined in this project and showed great patience in following the requirements of this uncommon book.

Of course, this fruitful collaboration would have not possible without the help of K.R. Gupta, Managing Director of M/s Atlantic Publishers and Distributors, New Delhi, who created the conditions that allowed this project to grow.

I am also very grateful to Rajeshwar Mittapalli, my Indian brother, for providing unlimited assistance during the various phases of the project's development and for helping me through rainy days.

Last but not least, I wish to acknowledge my debt of gratitude to Prof. Paolo Bertinetti: he spoke to me, and by speaking he gave me a good idea.

Contents

1

R.K. Narayan

GEOFFREY KAIN

With the death of R.K. Narayan in May of 2001, India lost perhaps its most prominent literary figure. Narayan had more staying power and offered a more consistent, prolific output over more years than any of the other internationally acclaimed Indian writers of fiction in English. Narayan is often discussed as one of the three principle trailblazing Indian novelists writing in English for an international audience who emerged in the first half of the twentieth century, along with Mulk Raj Anand and Raja Rao, but only Narayan has proven so persistently present as a writer over the decades—from the publication of *Swami and Friends* in 1935 to *The World of Nagaraj* in 1990. Over these roughly sixty years Narayan has given us fourteen novels, multiple volumes of short stories, an autobiography, translations of *Mahabharata* and *Ramayana,* travel and personal essays, editorials, and reviews. It is not possible to think of Indian literature in English without recognizing the central place of Narayan's tales of life in and around the fictional south Indian town of Malgudi with its broad array of characters facing the complications in their lives and finding ways to disentangle, move beyond, or accept the lots that life has left them.

Established as he has been for so many years, Narayan did not burst on to the international literary stage. As he recalls in his autobiography *My Days,* and has been thoroughly recounted in Susan Ram and N. Ram's biography *R.K. Narayan: The Early Years, 1906-1945,* Narayan struggled through the publication of his first three novels—*Swami and Friends* (1935), *The Bachelor of Arts* (1937), and *The Dark Room* (1938)—to gain an audience that appreciated his work as much as did his English apologist and mentor Graham Greene. Narayan had committed himself to life as a writer as early as 1930, despite his family's efforts to secure for him a more stable and profitable position. He worked on his first novel while also serving as a reporter in Mysore for the Madras newspaper *The Justice,* work which importantly brought him into "close contact with a variety of men and their activities" (*My Days* 111). As he engaged in the practical work that supported him during the writing of *Swami and Friends*, Narayan was amassing the details, bits and pieces of narrative, and a perspective on the lives of common people that continued to supply inspiration and material for his fiction for many years to come.

Narayan has always been drawn to the lives of "ordinary" men and women, taking us inside the experiences of people who remind us of our own neighbours, or our siblings—or ourselves. The novels' titles often suggest this: *The Bachelor of Arts*; *The English Teacher*; *Mr. Sampath, The Printer of Malgudi*; *The Vendor of Sweets*; *The Painter of Signs*. He would take issue with this characterization, however. Although he has clearly been committed to characters from the middle and lower-middle classes, he has always bristled at the mention of the "average" person. In one of his essays published in *Indian Thought*, the journal he founded and published for just one year (1941), Narayan directly addresses the notion of "The Average Man," whom his friends have urged him to target as his audience, deciding that he does not really exist. The average man, he speculates (who always seems to be someone other than ourselves), would likely be defined by a set of particular virtues: he would be healthy/robust; very methodical; vigilant in regards to his family members; precise in his accounts; prompt in paying off his debts; industrious and honest; would send his children to an ordinary, commonplace school. He would, however, also likely have a set of "parallel defects": he would work hard because he is a drudge; he would look closely after his family because he knows nothing different; he would be law-abiding because he is prudish; he would be healthy because he is simple and not subject to the disturbances that beset a more sensitive mind; politically he would be moved by the loudest and most passionate speaker (226-27). Yet the author notes that there really is no specific "average man" to be found. Still, while Narayan dismisses the existence of this essentialized figure, a significant number of his characters are in fact suggested by the traits he provides—either in his satirical cataloguing of "parallel defects" or, more often, in a fine balance between the virtues and defects he enumerates. In fact, we find reflections—or the seeds—of a number of his central characters in another of his essays (not dated) that he titles "The Common Man" and that further suggests his careful attention to and repeated contemplation of this "breed." After listing the common man's vision of the future, based on a sequence of expectations—including undergraduate degree, position in the civil service, respectful treatment from other (more common) persons, Narayan then evokes his picture of truly common experience:

> Life just kicked about all those nice edifices of vision. His father died and our friend found himself taking his place. Four sisters to be married, three brothers to be educated, the ancestral home

> and lands submerged in mortgages [...]. His home now appeared to him as a very leaky ship which would go down any moment, and it did go down [...]. The rest of his life might be described as one grand salvaging operation. It is this wrestling bout with existence that first bleached and then scorched the hair on his scalp. (NCBU)[1]

Further recorded reflections on "the common man" in yet another essay on this topic provide more valuable backdrop for a host of Narayan's characters; in a piece he titles "Rare to Meet: The Common Man," Narayan suggests that most of us consider ourselves "uncommon," yet surely there is a great field of shared experience, feeling, and response:

> a certain general all-round inadequacy is a chronic condition with him. Starting with his home—if there had been just one more room [...]. There must be something always lacking somewhere [...] if there had not been so many dependents at home, if his wife could understand a little more of the financial implications of her proposals, if the landlord could be a little more humane... if... if... if... there are far too many ifs in his life [...] the word "if" is like a key-hole through which he gains a peep at an expansive world full of sunshine and comfort. (NCBU)

Combined, these passages develop a general "type" of character that Narayan was indisputably drawn again and again to introduce, develop, explore, and follow within the "common" milieu of Malgudi—which, as critics of Narayan so frequently remind us, is often universal in its particulars. Some—or many—of these traits are present in Chandran in *The Bachelor of Arts*, in both Savitri and Ramani in *The Dark Room*, in Krishna in *The English Teacher*, in Srinivas (and Ravi) in *Mr. Sampath*, in Margayya in *The Financial Expert*, in Jagan in *The Vendor of Sweets*, in Raju in *The Guide*—in virtually *all* of Narayan's novels. People with expectations—not great expectations, but modest and hopeful expectations—who are frequently denied (by various agencies) and then must "wrestle with existence" in a "grand salvaging operation." This salvaging operation, however, becomes the adventure and the wrestling bout defines and reveals the nature of self.

Some of these details are reminiscent of the elements of Narayan's own personal experience, which he describes in *My Days* (1974). He resisted his family's efforts to secure him a good job following receipt of his B.A. in 1930 and returned instead to live with his grandmother, where he dedicated himself to writing. Working on his first novels, working also as a Mysore reporter for *The Justice*, a Madras newspaper (an anti-Brahmin newspaper, interestingly, Narayan himself being Brahmin), Narayan seemed to be enjoying the life he envisioned for himself as a young man, but then his father died (1937) and he became responsible for paying rent on the family home. Compounding the financial pressures came the tragic death of his young wife, Rajam, from typhoid in 1939 (he never remarried). As Narayan speaks of the "common man" and his encounter with forces greater than himself, he reflects not only the experience of those familiar to him, but his own experience, as well. Three of his first four novels are either partly or largely (as is the case with *The English Teacher*) autobiographical.

Narayan's early immersion as a reader in the works of Shakespeare, Scott, and Dickens clearly left their mark on him, and it is apparent that Shakespeare's ability (as Samuel Johnson has famously established in his *Preface to Shakespeare*) to create unique, individual characters who nonetheless strike a chord within us as universal types is likely a primary source of inspiration for Narayan in creating his central ("common man") characters. Most often, this key feature of Narayan's art is lauded by critics, but Kirpal Singh has centred on this as one of the author's shortcomings. In his essay "The Ordinary and Average as Satiric Traps,"[2] professor Singh asks why, "in spite of their wit, vision, and charm," Narayan's novels have proved (to him) to be less engaging, less satisfying, than the novels of Raja Rao and Mulk Raj Anand ("with whom Narayan shares the crown of Indo-English fiction" [79]). Singh credits Narayan's craftsmanship, his versatility, his control of tone, his ability to tell an interesting story, his gift of characterization. Singh concludes that it is the *combination* of Narayan's insistence on "the ordinary" and the pervasive tone of satire in the fiction. "Ultimately," he writes, "satire [...] alienates" (81). The average and ordinary become "the butts of relentless ridicule" (82). Beneath the "comic vision" Narayan is noted for runs a sense of the author's *distance* from the ordinary characters he creates. In the end, Singh suggests, Narayan's work lacks the "immensity" of Rao's and the sincere commitment of Anand's.

On the contrary, in her book *Narayan: A Study in Transcendence*, Mary Beatina Rayen has focused on Narayan's ability to expose us to the transcendent in life via his treatment of the commonplace, or mundane. Specifically, she focuses on paths to the transcendent via immersion in the mundane, considering at length what she labels "naïve transcendence" as it is revealed in *Swami and Friends* and *The Bachelor of Arts*, then looking at Narayan's fuller development of this approach in *The English Teacher* ("mature transcendence") and *The Guide* (a still more "mature transcendence"). She concludes that "Narayan encourages the idea that the highest life is only to be found by seeking or accepting experiences that carry us into a strange and often bewildering realm. [...] But that 'other realm' must be [...] accessible to ordinary people, prepared by ordinary experience."[3] This reading of Narayan is consistent with that offered years earlier by K.R.S. Iyengar, who argues that through the recurrent Narayan narrative pattern of disrupted life followed by a return to order we find that

> the soul of Narayan's fiction is not in this delicately self-adjusted mechanism of ironic comedy, but rather the miracle of transcendence and the renewal of life, love, beauty, peace.[4]

While there is certainly something to be said for both of these poles of interpretation—and while it is certainly true that Narayan worked for a time as a journalist (to which Singh attributes, perhaps, Narayan's "profile" as a voyeur rather than a participant) and that Narayan was steeped in the religious epics from a very young age (thanks mostly to his uncle who, along with his grandmother, helped to raise him) and had a decidedly mystic strain in his personality—there is little or nothing offered in the personal writings of Narayan himself to overtly support either view, the flatly descriptive/ironic or the mundane as suggestive/transcendent. That he was acutely conscious of the "common" or "average" is evident; what the average is seen or intended to reveal—other than itself—is less obvious.

Another of Narayan's hallmark traits has been the clarity and simplicity of his style, joined with the brevity of his novels. Indeed, there is nothing like *The Serpent and the Rope* in the Narayan catalogue, the novels typically running in the immediate range of two hundred pages (*Talkative Man* being the [ironic] exception at approximately 120 pages). And yet, like the seeming transparency of Narayan's insistent focus on the common or ordinary, the notion of "simplicity" is also somewhat problematic. Despite the fact that Narayan writes for an international, often Western audience (made evident also by his habit of providing brief explanations or definitions after introducing some terms, concepts, or events that his Indian readers would immediately understand without the annotation), Western readers of Narayan may at times feel that they are "missing something," that behind the simple tale may lie a source in the great epics or in regional lore, or that the themes are suggested by principles of Hinduism to which they have not been exposed. In other words, Narayan has sometimes been regarded with respectful suspicion, as though behind the quiet and simple façade lie layers of suggestiveness.

To some extent this is true, particularly in the later novels, but it would be unwise to suspect Narayan of symbolist intentions or of routinely offering ancient tales or characters in modern dress and situations. Nonetheless, V.S. Naipaul, for one, has found himself—once he actually visited India—puzzled by Narayan's representation of reality, a reality he that he had found so immediate and accessible in the fiction:

> The small town [Narayan] had staked out as his fictional territory was, I knew, a creation of art and therefore to some extent artificial, a simplification of reality. But the reality was cruel and overwhelming. In the books his India had seemed so accessible;

> in India it remained hidden [...] I did not lose my admiration for Narayan; but I felt his comedy and irony were part of a Hindu response to the world, a response I could no longer share. And it has [...] become clear to me [...] that for all their delight in human oddity, Narayan's novels are less the purely social comedies I had once taken them to be than religious books, at times religious fables, and intensely Hindu.[5]

One does ultimately gain from Narayan a sense of acceptance, what M.M. Mahood has said is, to Narayan's cult-followers, "the source of that luminous quality [...] a serene fatalism" which to other readers may be regarded as "social unawareness,"[6] a sense of acceptance behind the narratives tracing his characters' struggles, a feeling that things will carry on regardless, that the rhythms of life are larger than the conflicts and traumas they involve. Narayan lends support to this view in, again, "Rare to Meet: The Common Man." After detailing the common man's struggle with his difficult circumstances, Narayan goes on to say that

> far too many of us go on wasting our energies in tilting against impossible windmills, kicking against some unpleasant set of facts [...] [the common man] endures a great deal with perfect resignation. (NCBU)

In the novels and short stories, we are frequently reminded that beyond the fringes of Malgudi are the Mempi Hills, the jungle, an expanse of life extending into the unknown, a primal existence that has carried on and will carry on for eons, whatever the nature or result of the latest human tragedy or travesty.

Many times during his career Narayan has insisted on the straightforward character of his work, asking us to simply read and enjoy what he writes and fearing, as Wordsworth had feared, that as critics (via "our meddling intellect") we will "murder to dissect." For example, in a letter to a group of academic conferees gathered in Mysore on the occasion of his eighty-fifth birthday (1992), Narayan wrote:

> I feel that no one should read too much meaning or significance into my writing. I write because I have no other business in life and I also enjoy the sense of relief after finishing a book [...]. I appeal to you as a reader to read the book as a story normally, enjoy or suffer it, but don't dissect or analyse it to extract a significance which I never intended [...]. I am convinced that when a composition leaves my desk and assumes the printed *avatar*, it acquires an unsuspected vitality and lives a life of its own, revealing significance and meaning to a reader in which I have no part. I can only watch such results with surprise—and sometimes dismay.[7]

As he suggests here, Narayan has always been suspicious of the academic/critical community—although that community has played a prominent role in perpetuating his work. A very clear articulation of his view is contained in a brief, undated personal essay titled "My Educational Outlook":

> If a classification is called for I may be labelled "anti-educational." I am not averse to enlightenment, but I feel that the entire organization, system, outlook and aims of education are hopelessly wrong from beginning to end [...]. Educational theories have become progressively high-sounding, sophisticated, and jargon-ridden. (NCBU)

Narayan, then, may best be taken at his word. He is primarily an observer of men. He sees significance in the details of everyday, "common" life and individuals. He is a teller of tales. He values simplicity, clarity, brevity. He is not interested in opaque theory; he feels that meaning is revealed through experience.

Narayan's first novel, *Swami and Friends* (1935), was published through the intervention of a friend and neighbour (Purna) who was studying at Oxford. Through him, Graham Greene came into contact with the young author's work, became especially interested in it, and took it upon himself to place the book with a reputable English publisher (Hamish Hamilton). Greene was responsible for the title *Swami and Friends*, changing it from Narayan's *Swami, the Tate*, suggesting that it would then have the advantage of "having some resemblance to Kipling's *Stalky and Company*, to which I am comparing the book on the dust cover."[8] Greene arranged the details of the contract and remained closely involved until the novel was published. Narayan's indebtedness to Greene is inscribed on the inside cover of a copy of *Swami and Friends* Narayan presented to Greene[9]: "But for you, 'Swami' should be in the bottom of Thames now." Overwhelmed by Greene's generosity, Narayan developed a friendship with him that extended over nearly six decades. Although the two authors did not meet until the 1950s, they corresponded regularly and Greene continued to champion Narayan's work over the years, and continued to consistently encourage him as a writer and to offer much valued critiques. In the way that he accepted responsibility for seeing to the publication of *Swami and Friends*, Greene likewise worked intensively on Narayan's behalf for the publication of his next novels, *The Bachelor of Arts* (a title that Greene changed from Narayan's *Chandran*) and *The Dark Room*; Narayan's debt to Greene can hardly be overemphasized.[10]

With the publication of *Swami and Friends*, Narayan establishes the locale and some of the traits that have distinguished his narrative style and approach from the beginning. In this first novel we are introduced to Malgudi, with its citizens' pride the river Sarayu, "glistening like a silver belt across the north" in the moonlight (11); we first encounter the Albert Mission School (which Swaminathan and his friends attend),

Lawley Extension, Nallappa's Grove, the Mempi Hills, Market Road, Kabir Street—all names and features that return in novel after novel as Narayan confirms and then reconfirms his fidelity to the microcosm of Malgudi. Aside from the pleasure one may experience as a reader by simply taking up the first of the author's many novels, it becomes particularly interesting to read *Swami and Friends* in light of the relatively frequent criticism of Narayan that he manages so persistently to avoid directly representing the social and political trauma occupying center stage in India during his time. The novel's first pages introduce us to "the scripture master, Mr. Ebenezar [...] a fanatic" teaching in the Albert Mission School. Swami ordinarily finds the scripture hour "not such a dull hour after all" because of the vivid stories. But Ebenezar's Christian tirades finally move Swami to anger:

> "Oh, wretched idiots!" the teacher said, clenching his fists. "Why do you worship dirty, lifeless, wooden idols and stone images? Can they talk? No. Can they see? No. Can they bless you? No. Can they take you to heaven? No." [...] Next minute his face became purple with rage as he thought of Sri Krishna: "Did our Jesus go gadding about with dancing girls like your Krishna? Did our Jesus go about stealing butter like that arch-scoundrel Krishna? Did our Jesus practice dark tricks on those around him?" He paused for breath. The teacher was intolerable today. Swaminathan's blood boiled. He got up and asked, "If he did not, why was he crucified? [...] If he was a god, why did he eat flesh and drink wine?" As a brahmin boy it was inconceivable to him that a god should be a non-vegetarian. In answer to this, Ebenezar left his seat, advance slowly toward Swaminathan, and tried to wrench his left ear off. (3-4)

This altercation leads Swami's father to address a letter of complaint to the headmaster, closing with a threat to remove his son from the school "if you do not want non-Christian boys in your school" (5).

The chapter titled "Broken Panes" also counters the stereotype of Narayan the novelist who ducks political narrative. Swami's troubles in the school become exacerbated when he finds himself inadvertently drawn into an anti-British demonstration. As he approaches the right bank of the Sarayu one evening in August of 1930, he encounters more than two thousand citizens gathered in defiance of British rule. Foreign-made jackets and caps are being tossed on to a heap and burned. Swami is pressured to toss his own cap into the flames, although he is unsure whether it is British or Indian made. Swami is moved by the lectures—although, young as he is, he finds some of the political rhetoric absolutely befuddling ("'We are slaves of slaves' [...] to Swami [...] this part of the speech was incomprehensible" [95]). The following day Swami finds a swarm of students gathered outside the front gates of the Albert Mission School, boycotting classes, and he becomes absorbed into the mob. After breaking most of the windows in the front of the school, they march to the nearby Board High School, which has not closed for the day, and begin smashing windows there in the name of Indian independence. Swami becomes intoxicated by the energy of the mob and thrills at the shattering of glass:

> With tremendous joy he discovered that there were many glass panes untouched yet. His craving to break them could not be fully satisfied in his own school. He ran around collecting ink bottles and flung them one by one at every pane that caught his eye. (100)

These incidents are as far as Narayan goes in evincing British-Indian tensions during the colonial period (while Swami does not have any truly anti-British sentiment in him), with some further reverberations to be found also in his second novel, *The Bachelor of Arts,* and in fact he manages quite effectively in *Swami and Friends* to show us to what extent British influences have been absorbed into the rhythms of daily life. Aside from the names and places themselves—Albert Mission School, Lawley Extension, etc.—there is the central component of the novel (which certainly is *not* Christian zealousness or anti-British demonstrations), the hub that unifies Swami's group of friends, the focal point of the boys' true passion: the game of cricket. Everything else—school, politics, parents—is peripheral to cricket. Any contradiction between—on the same day—burning British cloth, then playing cricket with his friends does not occur to Swami (nor to his friends), and Narayan wryly leaves the entangled loyalties without comment, focusing instead on the depth of the boys' feelings for each other and for the game at the heart of their "club." In this sense, Narayan establishes immediately in his first novel his ability to obliquely suggest the depth and complexity of the characters' experience within the framework of a rather fast-paced, often humorous, simple but engaging, rather "bare bones" style of narrative.

Narayan's second novel, *The Bachelor of Arts* (1937), lacks the effective humor and genuine warmheartedness of *Swami and Friends* and also lacks the pathos and poignancy of his third novel, *The Dark Room.* Nonetheless, it is a rather enjoyable piece in its own right and is noteworthy chiefly because of some of the trends and characteristics it continues from the first novel, as well as because of what it anticipates in several of the later, more significant works. The novel continues the semi-autobiographical track begun with *Swami*, with Chandran's lack of motivation or direction immediately following his graduation, coupled with the career advice (and prodding) proffered him by family members, relatives, and well-wishers being similar to Narayan's own experience as he describes it in his autobiography *My Days*. Chandran's later involvement in the newspaper business is also suggestive of the author's, but the autobiographical elements seem to end here. *The Bachelor of Arts* follows chronologically, in a sense, on the heels of *Swami*, in that *Swami* involves us with the school-aged boy and *The Bachelor of Arts* then takes us into and beyond the college years (though with a different character), ending with Chandran's marriage. *The Dark Room* then investigates the experience of marriage, as does the fourth novel, *The English Teacher*. Once Narayan emerges from his personal tragedy and the publication of *The English Teacher*, however, the line of narrative development represented by the first four novels shifts and the author moves out of what might be regarded as his "early phase." Aside from the return to Malgudi in the second novel with a number of the place names within the town reintroduced (which suggests the author's commitment by this time), and aside from its following chronologically on the material in *Swami*, one of the elements in the novel reminiscent of its predecessor is the rumbling of anti-British sentiment. Chandran is certainly not a political radical himself, but is not without some resentment. As he sits in the college auditorium,

> his eyes wandered about the hall. [...] He kept gazing at Professor Brown's pink face. Here he is, Chandran thought, pretending to press the bell and listen to the speeches, but really his thoughts are at the tennis court and the card-table in the English Club. He is here not out of love for us, but merely to keep up appearances. All Europeans are like this. They will take their thousand or more a month, but won't do the slightest service to Indians with a sincere heart. (19)

Chandran's sentiments are mild when contrasted with those of his classmate Veeraswami who volunteers to read a paper before the Historical Association on the topic of "The Aids of British Expansion in India":

> On a fateful day, to an audience of thirty-five, Veeraswami read his paper. It was the most violent paper ever read before an association. It pilloried great Britain before the Association, and ended by hoping that the British would be ousted from India by force. (79)

Veeraswami later disappears from the narrative (and Chandran's life) as he takes up a crusade to move about the country organizing a movement he calls the Resurrection Brigade, designed to foment violent revolution (his missionary zeal anticipates, in some ways, the fanaticism of Daisy in her family planning efforts in *The Painter of Signs*, written nearly forty years later).

These anti-colonial reflections remind us that Narayan's work has not been entirely without them, and yet they are merely peripheral to the main thrust of the novel, which is clearly the tension between youthful individualism, naivete, and "new thinking," on one hand, and the power of tradition, on the other. This becomes a major theme of Narayan's, one that he never tires of exploring.

In Narayan's third novel, *The Dark Room* (1938), he delves into a more serious and somber theme, turning aside from the semi-autobiographical reflections on childhood and late adolescent/young adult life that he offers in the first two novels. While Narayan is often noted for his recognition of the potency and centrality of tradition, in his treatment of Savitri he demonstrates his sympathy for a strong, intelligent, and faithful woman who finds herself incapable of escaping from a marriage turned sour. Her will and passion are clearly present as she storms out of the house after confronting her blatantly unfaithful husband, but her imagination and skills fail her as she attempts to remove herself from the confines of her existence. Within hours she throws herself into the River Sarayu, hoping to drown. Even after she is saved and taken to a nearby village and there meets the incorrigible, almost tyrannical (and extremely capable) village woman Ponni, and even though Ponni attempts to set her on a new "career path" by getting her to work as a temple caretaker for the local priest, she discovers that she is incapable of living outside of her customary environment. She finds herself too intimidated to survive when disconnected from what she has been bred to know and what she has come to know, and so returns home, resigned to what she has so recently and passionately renounced. The contrast between the two women is significant, and the contrast between Savitri and Daisy, whom Narayan takes up in *The Painter of Signs* (1976) is sharp. Graham Greene, commenting on *The Dark Room* in his introduction to a reissue of *The Bachelor of Arts*, sees the novel as the most tragic of Narayan's works, even more so than *The English Teacher*, noting that the earlier novel evokes a more bitter experience, that "the killing of love [is] more tragic than the death of love" (ix).

Following publication of *The Dark Room*, Narayan writes to Greene that he is planning a "mighty long book next" set in an ancient period. He indicates that he is drawn to the ancient setting primarily because he is "slightly tired of middle-class life."[11]

This novel was never written, and the departure from middle class life was not realized. Because of the great disruptions caused by the war and by his wife's death in 1939, Narayan did not publish a novel again until *The English Teacher* in 1945. The 1940s were fertile years for the short story, however, with three volumes published in India through Narayan's Indian Thought Publications: *Dodu and Other Stories* (1943), *Cyclone and Other Stories* (1945), and *An Astrologer's Day and Other Stories* (1947). The short stories further solidified Narayan's growing reputation as a skilled craftsman of the incident, capable of a considerable range of theme. "An Astrologer's Day" stands out as probably still his most popular short story, a piece that showcases his trademark irony and his ability to deliver a delightful O'Henryesque surprise ending. The later short stories, included in *A Horse and Two Goats* (1970) and *Under the Banyan Tree* (1987) continue in the same vein, displaying Narayan's range from humor to compassion, and clarifying the author's principle that situation—the story—is paramount.

The English Teacher (1945, also titled *Grateful to Life and Death*), the most autobiographical of his novels, is divided into two distinct narrative halves, the "domestic" half which follows Krishna's life as a young and rather bored teacher of English in a small school—and then his marriage to Susila; and the "mystic" half which centers on Susila's death and Krishna's subsequent efforts to establish contact with his wife's spirit, and his experiences of her presence. All of this follows quite closely from Narayan's own circumstances, and writing the novel, he has often indicated, served as a purgative or (semi-)healing exercise for him. The mystic elements are out of keeping with the rest of Narayan's work, yet they are as described as matter-of-factly as one would expect from him.

After publication of *The English Teacher* the novels turn outward, away from the autobiographical, sequential narratives, and center repeatedly on a cross-section of Malgudi citizens. For the most part, the novels published after *The English Teacher* establish several of the themes which we tend to identify with Narayan's work, one being the mildly (and sometimes sadly) comic bravado or heroic impulse of the common man—that is, a sense of self that exceeds the limits of reality but that allows or encourages the "small man" to act in response to difficult circumstances (what V.S. Naipaul has described as "small men, small schemes, big talk, limited means"). Another recurrent theme becomes the arrival or intrusion of the stranger (often a stranger with an unusual name and typically someone with a mysterious or implausible background), someone whose arrival creates a crisis—at least in the lives of a small set of characters—and whose actions and eventual departure accelerate the process of self-discovery for the novel's protagonist. An additional, and dominant, theme (or perhaps device) in Narayan's middle and later novels would have to be what may be called "the fateful moment," a particular point in a character's experience which, upon the character's reflection, appeared as a sort of crossroads and choosing which became a fateful or determining situation. Narayan often manages to present these moments as typical, mundane sorts of instances common to us all, but which also become imbued with a sort of uncanny magnetism. Finally, the power of tradition in relation to the individual remains a theme running consistently through the Narayan corpus from the early works through to the most recent.

Mr. Sampath, The Printer of Malgudi (1949) is notable for its embodiment of these themes or methods that inform the later works while also standing as a transitional work in that it carries over some of the themes or techniques of the earlier narratives. Autobiographical elements again appear via the central character, Srinivas, who is pushed by domestic and financial pressures to become professionally committed as a writer, initiating *The Banner* (somewhat reminiscent of Narayan's short-lived *Indian Thought*, which appeared during 1941) after a period of occupational trial and error ("He thought of all those years when he had tried to fit in with one thing or another as others did, married like the rest, tried to balance the family budget and build up a bank balance. Agriculture, apprenticeship, in a bank, teaching, law" [*Sampath*, 11]). The printer of the paper, Sampath, also issues from Narayan's own experience, as Ram and Ram point out (332-37),[12] and this printer figure (working with his staff hidden from view behind a large curtain, through which one hears voices and the sounds of the presses) reenters in *The Man-eater of Malgudi*.

More significant, though, are Narayan's use in *Mr. Sampath* of the hauntingly coincidental occurrence and fateful choices we see often in subsequent novels, as well as the inclusion of details that take us briefly into the absurd—or into a sort of caricature of reality—and eventually lead to some vital insight and the end of an experiential cycle, a return after what becomes an odd adventure. Taken together, *Mr. Sampath* and *The Financial Expert* (1952), Narayan's next novel, fit together closely as a textual pair.

Srinivas's first insight/compulsion leads him to Malgudi, clear—for a change—about what he must do ("the solution appeared to him in a flash" [13]). In need of a printer, he is introduced to Sampath, a man with a commanding air who quickly agrees to take on *The Banner* and Srinivas finds himself connected with the printer almost as though he has little choice in the matter. Events in *Sampath* follow a mundane (or "common") track until Sampath's staff go out on strike and Srinivas (as screenwriter) follows Sampath into a film-making venture. Within this context, the bizarre surfaces, and Narayan's satire comes to the fore. Anticipating painful difficulties Narayan would find himself confronting in the early 1960s, he writes in *Sampath* of Srinivas's frustration over the film studio's gross manipulation of what he had written: "He saw without much flutter, the mangling that was going on with his story [...] [but] he very soon accommodated himself to the notion that they were doing a picture of their own entirely unconnected with the theme he had written" (178). Sampath, as one of the producers, asks Srinivas, "you are not annoyed about these changes, are you?" He answers, "Not at all; why should I worry about it?" Sampath continues, "We are taking liberty only with the details, you know, but we are keeping to your original in the main treatment." "Oh yes, yes," Srinivas said, feeling that this was the familiar eyewash every film-maker applied to every writer" (179).

Narayan relies on coincidence as a narrative device when the long lost object of young love-sick artist Ravi's passion seems miraculously found again in the form of Shanti, the co-star of Sampath's film. Sampath's own lust for Shanti nearly destroys him and his family, and Ravi truly loses his mind over her, as he crashes the film set, carries Shanti off with others chasing after in a scene straight out of slapstick comedy. The unearthly strangeness of this—together with Ravi's subsequent insanity—finds parallels in elements of *The Financial Expert*, *The Man-eater of Malgudi*, and *Talkative Man*, certainly, but it marks the first occurrence of its type in Narayan's novels.

In the midst of this violent chaos—chaos brought about by exaggerated passion or obsession—Srinivas experiences a profound vision, an epiphany, quietly steps aside upon gaining a glimpse of his place in the vast scheme of things, and returns to his life/work as writer and editor of *The Banner*, caring for Ravi and more involved with his own family. This sense of return to the fundamental after a strange flight into the surreal anticipates the narrative structure of his ensuing novel, *The Financial Expert*.

The Financial Expert is a particularly significant novel because in it Narayan establishes a set of themes and devices that become consistently central to his work thereafter. The narrative traces the dramatic financial rise and fall of his central character, Margayya who, although he has very little money at the beginning of the novel, is convinced all along of the almost mystical power and significance of money; as he explains it to his wife, "Money alone is important in this world. Everything else will come to us naturally if we have money in our purse" (21). The great puzzle, of course, is how wealth could possibly come to him, since he has little means to begin with and confines his business dealings to "blanket-wrapped rustics" and, as Suresh Raval has indicated in his assessment of the novel, its "central and dramatic irony is that the financial expert is in fact not an expert in anything in any honest way" (89). Nonetheless, even prior to his financial successes,

> He viewed himself as a saviour of mankind. "If I hadn't secured three hundred rupees for so-and-so, he would be rotting in the street." His mind began to catalogue all the good things money had done as far as he could remember. He shuddered to think how people could ever do without it. If money was absent men came near being beasts. (27)

This inflated sense of self-importance, a common theme in Narayan's novels after the publication of *The English Teacher*, always provides a source of some humor simply through the irony realized by the distance between what the reader clearly perceives of the character and the character's own perception of self, or at least the possibility of self.

Margayya's bloated self-estimation is further supported when, after visiting a temple priest out of desperation over his meager income, the priest listens to Margayya's tale of longing for wealth, power, influence, and respect, and decides that Margayya must propitiate the goddess Lakshmi—and that, so far as the priest can discern, Margayya is fortunate in that the goddesses Lakshmi and Saraswathi appear to be battling over him. Margayya "felt immensely powerful and important. He had never known that anybody cared for him [...] and now to think that two Goddesses were fighting to confer their favours on him!" (50).

Margayya's forty day *puja*, prescribed by the priest as the means by which to win the favour of Lakshmi, becomes humorous because we easily see how shallow his religious sense is; the length to which he will go to earn his dreamed of fortune only highlights the limits of his skill *and* his imagination. If Dr. Pal were not to appear—literally out of the blue—and virtually drop the manuscript of his *Bed Life* directly into Margayya's hands, Margayya's fortunes would almost certainly not have changed. The change seems clearly fortuitous—and yet, in classic Narayan fashion, events are also arranged so that Margayya's assumptions of personal value and divine favour are (at least for a time) validated. Shortly after the *puja* ends, Margayya is on the road to becoming a rich man.

The sudden and highly influential appearance of Dr. Pal exemplifies the Narayan device of introducing the mysterious stranger, a character who not only changes the course of the central character's experience, but who also has a personal magnetism that draws the protagonist into events that redefine his life. This theme often occurs together with the equally common theme or device employed by Narayan, that of the fateful event, or the critical or pregnant moment. In *The Financial Expert*, this moment occurs when Pal offers Margayya the opportunity to buy *Bed Life* from him and make a fortune publishing it; he is willing to part with it for whatever Margayya has in his purse—whether two rupees or two thousand. Margayya cannot decide for several minutes, anguishing over the proper course to follow. As Pal informs him, and as could be said for a significant number of Narayan's novels which contain the same critical moment as a pivotal narrative device, "Every man must make his choice in life. This is a cross-roads at which you are standing" (89). Of course, Margayya finally (perspiring) turns over his purse, which contains his last twenty-five rupees.

The fateful moment in *The Financial Expert*—with Pal appearing almost magically, then forcing the bargain with Margayya, holding out the "treasure" of his book for whatever Margayya might have in his purse—carries overtones of the folk tale or the fairytale about it and is representative of similar situations in some of Narayan's other later fiction. Much of Narayan is straightforward realism, comically tinged and marked by a modest recording of domestic detail, but then there are the moments when the ordinary reality is transformed to the unreal. Another example of this from the same novel occurs after Margayya has sold his rights to the book to his partner, the publisher, and then enters into another private banking scheme. Margayya soon begins to earn fantastic amounts of money—cash is coming in by the bagful. Soon the house is filling with it, and Margayya must move his wife to another room—and then another—as the entire house threatens to become filled to the rafters with money. "You will have to clear out of the upstairs room, too [...]. Only till I build a vault somewhere" (201). And as the cartoon-like vision of unimaginable wealth grows, we see Margayya's subsequent grotesque physical transformation—he stops eating, begins coughing, rarely sleeps, and wastes away.

Also in classic Narayan fashion, Dr. Pal serves simultaneously as both saviour and destroyer. If not for Pal, Margayya would not have amassed such staggering wealth, but as his wealth increases, so does his obsession, and as his obsession grows, his family life and his health fail. And as Margayya reaches what turns out to be the peak of his fortunes, Pal is whispering into Balu's ear that he must press his father for half of all he has, which he convinces him is his by right (and no doubt also Pal's, by extension, particularly as Margayya has steadily increased the amounts he has conferred upon Balu, who in turn, together with Pal, is lavishly spending it on wine, women, and gaming). The ambiguity and irony effected through the character of Pal become stock in trade for Narayan, especially in some of his better known novels such as *The Guide* and *The Painter of Signs*.

Another of the intriguing aspects of *The Financial Expert* is that, as a result of his tumultuous experiences, Margayya does not appear to have gained any significant insight; he does indeed appear to have been abandoned by Saraswathi. Because he is not terribly embittered by his financial catastrophe and because Balu and family (are forced to) move back into Margayya's home, and because Margayya is seen doting on his grandson in the end (in the way he doted on Balu when he was very young) one might conclude that Narayan offers us another literary representation of a character arriving painfully at a realization of what is of greater and lesser value, *and yet* we also witness Margayya at novel's end encouraging his son, first, to take up his father's old trunk and return to the banyan tree across from the Cooperative Bank and again set up the money lending business; when Balu refuses, Margayya himself decides that he will do it, as soon as he is well enough, thus choosing to reenter the same experiential pathway.

Similar ambiguities and ironies epitomize *The Guide* (1958), although Narayan adheres more closely to his earlier mode of more straightforward realism in *Waiting for the Mahatma* (1955). Michel Pousse has characterized Narayan as a "Gandhian novelist" because his "heroes are ordinary people whose lives take on a religious dimension [and who] revolutionize their inner selves" (85). The non-violence, questing for truth, reorientation of self, etc. that Pousse cites does indeed apply to Narayan's work (more overtly in some pieces than in others), yet *Waiting for the Mahatma* is the only work to directly center on Gandhi and the *swaraj* movement. Less successful and not so highly acclaimed as some of the previous novels, it is interesting precisely *because* of its historical specificity while it also includes thematic and character elements that mark its being clearly consistent with the Narayan corpus. While Narayan has on occasion been criticized for ignoring in his novels most of the political issues of his time, Graham Greene, in a letter dated July 19, 1954, expressed to Narayan his disappointment on finding politics filtering into Malgudi since until that time he had experienced in Malgudi a more universal quality.[13]

Narayan's most highly acclaimed and widely read (and translated) novel has been *The Guide.* Surely it represents the peak of the author's ability to manage ambiguity and irony, while it introduces a more daring narrative technique and allows for some contemporary satire, as well. Like *Mr. Sampath* and *The Financial Expert,* it illustrates the dangers of obsessiveness—but it also, like *Waiting for the Mahatma,* suggests an ironic turn on this theme by following the character's movement toward self-realization (or, at the very least, marked self-improvement) as a result of *following* this passion. The passion/obsession becomes a gateway to a more spiritual experience. This is true for Sriram in *Mahatma,* via his pursuit of Bharati, a disciple of Gandhi, and it is certainly true of Raju in *The Guide.*[14]

In *The Guide* Narayan also once again pursues the theme of coincidence, developing it more extensively than in any other novel.[15] Raju is opportunistic, to be sure, but opportunities seem to recurrently drop into his lap, and Raju reminds us several times of his fatalistic response to events—that he *has* to "play the role assigned" to him, first as tour guide, then as Rosie's manager, then as sanyasi. Raju is compelled by his own nature and by circumstances to make choices. He became a guide because, as he admits, "I never said, 'I don't know.' Not in my nature, I suppose. If I had the inclination to say 'I don't know what you are talking about,' my life would have taken a different turn" (*Guide* 47). Raju becomes obsessed with Rosie not by choice, but because it just happens. He becomes bound up in Rosie's success because he cannot bear to be away from her, and her skill as a dancer is allowed to finally shine. He becomes a "holy man" not because he wishes to mislead Velan and the other villagers, but because he can see no other option but to seek shelter in the small temple after leaving prison—and because food comes to him without having to work for it.

Also, in his new role as "spiritual guide," Raju feels compelled to answer the questions put to him, just as he had as a fledgling tour guide. In the end this chain of events forces Raju into difficulties from which he cannot remove himself—he faces drought with the villagers, is forced into a fast and in doing so is forced toward self-recognition and true insight. The tension between inevitability ("what must happen must happen" [18]) and chance is a persistent theme of Narayan's, but nowhere is it so fully and effectively managed as in *The Guide*.

The relationship between Raju and the peasant Velan becomes more interesting and more significant, ultimately, than the Raju-Rosie relationship since Narayan explores so skilfully the concept of control. In the end, Raju is controlled by the humble Velan (although this is not Velan's intention) and Raju is forced to confront his personal shortcomings and to adopt some responsibility. William Walsh has reminded us of the novel's place among other tales of transformation in India, in which "the source of change is outside the psyche in some mysterious law of life" (132); and in *The Guide*, in the Eastern tradition of accepting contradiction, remarking on the interchangeable rather than on the contradictory, "the con man and the martyr are hardly to be distinguished and are finally identical" (133).

The success of *The Guide* marked Narayan's true "arrival" as an international literary figure; the novel was translated into various languages, and within a few years of its publication came offers to present versions of the work on stage and screen. No doubt these were exciting prospects for Narayan, suggesting great possibilities for the future. The film and stage experiences during the early 1960s proved in the end, however, to be disappointing and even bitter experiences for Narayan. Narayan found himself during the later 1950s and into the 1960s increasingly engaged in the business aspects of authorship, responding personally to numerous requests (most of them from within India) for reprint rights of various short stories, for permission to translate particular novels, etc.—Narayan occasionally opened the door to some of these possibilities, while specifying fees that, typically, were regarded by his petitioners as too high (NCBU). He did agree to a stage version of *The Guide*, with script written by Harvey Breit and Patricia Rinehard, first performed in 1961 (with Laurence Olivier having invested in the first English production) at Oxford and Cambridge; delays in realizing a West End production in London led producer William Darrid to turn instead to Broadway. At that point, Narayan stepped in with questions regarding the play's script, arguing that the play violated the spirit of the novel, and also arguing that Breit's stage rights to the play had expired; lengthy legal wrangling ensued.[16]

Narayan also became disillusioned with the film adaptation of *The Guide*, even though the film was selected by the Film Federation of

India as India's best picture to compete for the Foreign Language Oscar of 1966. Indian actor and producer Dev Anand entered into a production arrangement with a film company owned and operated by Pearl Buck and Ted Danielewski. Narayan was alienated and ultimately very disappointed by the film producers' insistence on creating an epic travelogue sort of production out of his work which, as always, he considered necessarily local, simple, and very much tied to South India.[17] As if these experiences were not enough, Narayan also became embroiled during this period in legal hassles over the filming of *Lawley Road*[18] by a company centered in Puerto Rico.

Since no other films or stage adaptations of his work ensued, it is safe to assume that Narayan emerged from these troubles determined to stick to the business of writing and to protect the rights to his own material. As the first novel to appear after *The Guide, The Man-eater of Malgudi* (1961) continues to stand as among the favourites of Narayan's readers. *Man-eater* shares a good deal with *The Guide* stylistically, but especially in the characters of Raju (*Guide*) and Nataraj *(Man-eater)*, a small-business printer in Malgudi. Nataraj is not the manipulator that Raju is, but he has some of the same resourcefulness and comic sense of his own self-importance. Since Nataraj's small shop adjoins that of a much larger print shop (with its twin cylinder "original Heidelberg" chugging noisily away), customers are not often aware of the limited scope of Nataraj's own business, which appears more extensive than it is—an impression which he certainly does nothing to discourage.

Some lines from *Man-eater* are also very close to those from *The Guide*, especially concerning the theme of compulsion or inevitability. For example, in *Man-eater* we read:

> a new set of circumstances seemed to be approaching me in an enveloping movement. This was the first time I had heard of an animal hospital. I could have just said, 'I don't know anything about it,' and ended the matter there, but my nature would not permit it. I always had to get into complications. So I said, 'All right, let us see what we can do for poor Kumar [the temple elephant]. What is the matter with him?' (85)

One can easily envision *The Guide's* Raju as having spoken these words, compelled as he repeatedly is to "play the role assigned" him by circumstance. The overextended and impulsive self becomes critical to *Man-eater*, as it is to so many of Narayan's novels.

Similarly, the transition from mock-heroic to the truly or potentially heroic takes center stage in *Man-eater*, as it does to some degree in *The Guide*. Nataraj's awareness that the monstrous hunter and taxidermist Vasu plans to kill the temple elephant and use his legs as umbrella stands—and Nataraj's desperate desire to prevent this—supplies the novel with its effective suspense, and the novel moves skilfully toward climax with these two forces arrayed against one another; *Man-eater* builds suspense perhaps more successfully than any of Narayan's other novels.

And yet one may feel a sense of anticlimax as Nataraj's desperate attempts to thwart the slaughter of the sacred elephant—for the smaller, weaker, though better man, Nataraj, commits himself to stopping the enormous, powerful, and gruesome Vasu—become unnecessary in the end. Vasu's accidental death by his own hand, by slapping a mosquito on his forehead, defuses the buildup of tension (focused on impending confrontation), yet clearly places the novel in the arena of myth as Narayan displays its solid reflection of *rakshasa* tales, which suggest that demons will swell with their own sense of power but will ultimately bring about their own doom.[19] As Sastri suggests to Nataraj at one point in the narrative, "The universe has survived all the *rakshasas* that were ever born. Every demon carries within him, unknown to himself, a tiny seed of self-destruction" (173).

The tale—with its grossly implausible elements such as the blustering, coarse taxidermist pushing his way into the home of a decent and life-preserving Hindu, and then filling his flat with animal hides in stinking vats, spilled blood, etc., not to mention a steady train of prostitutes[20]—such a tale gains its strength (despite its otherwise weak conclusion) by fitting into a longstanding genre and participating in perpetuating the themes centering on the tension between preservation and destruction, piety and blasphemy, moral strength and physical strength, etc. That it manages to do so and retain the hallmark comic Narayan touch helps to explain its wide appeal. As a *New Yorker* reviewer aptly puts it,

> It is a situation that belongs in a farce [...] yet [...] history always adjusts the balance, so that those who have used the power they had often die with puzzled expressions on their faces. [...] [Narayan's] sweet-tempered determination to think well of his fellow men gives a golden tone of sanity and happiness to an enchanting comedy that is also a very serious statement of fundamental Indian ideas.[21]

Narayan continues his moral explorations in *The Vendor of Sweets* (1967). Jagan, the sweet vendor, who considers himself a disciple of Gandhi—fond of repeating pithy quotations from the Mahatma and of focusing on how to continue weaving Gandhian principles ever more deeply into his own lifestyle (while also being a shrewd shopkeeper)—displays some of the same discontent as an individual and some of the same bitterness over his ruptured relationship with his son (Mali) that we see in Margayya of *The Financial Expert.* As Jagan decides to retire from the world, thus entering into the final stage of life in traditional fashion, Narayan manages to depict his decision in neatly ambiguous terms: on the one hand, Jagan recognizes that the time is right and is committed to his Hindu principles and the practice of a worthy tradition; on the other hand, he sees the very limited success of his business, the void of life without his wife, the impossible frustration of his struggles with his westernized son (and his Korean-American girlfriend), the decay of his house, etc. The tensions between commitment/retreat, tradition/modernity, pre- and post-independence values, East/West, ability/inability, value/imperfection, loneliness/community pervade the novel from start to finish. *The Vendor of Sweets* is slower-paced and more pensive than either *The Guide* or *The Man-eater of Malgudi*, but it is of a piece with them in its greater attention to moral issues, and it anticipates *The Painter of Signs* in its evident attention to social trends.

The Painter of Signs (1976), written during the Emergency established by Mrs. Gandhi, utilizes the population control campaign for its narrative foundation. Daisy, the zealous government agent serving the cause of family planning, emerges as the central and strongest character, with Raman, the sign painter, struggling throughout the novel to first control his own emotions, then to "catch" and gain some control over Daisy as his lover. Daisy is surely Narayan's most potent female character, though not his most sympathetic or endearing. Both she and Raman are obsessive—she with her family planning crusade, and he with Daisy. Of how Raman might warm up to such a zealous militant, despite her physical charms, Narayan never convinces the reader. Instead he opts again for a narrative making use of his devices of the intrusive and ultimately disruptive stranger (as with Dr. Pal, Rosie, Vasu and, later, Dr. Rann in *Talkative Man*) and of a character immediately drawn into a web of events seemingly beyond his control. Raman becomes entranced by Daisy immediately—much like Raju with Rosie (*The Guide*), Sriram with Bharati (*Waiting for the Mahatma*), and Ravi with Shanti (*Mr. Sampath*). In his review of *The Painter of Signs*, in fact, Carlo Coppola emphasizes what he sees by this time as anticipated patterns in Narayan:

> Those familiar with his fiction know in advance some of the elements which will constitute the story: the novel will be set in Malgudi [...]; the hero will be ambitious and made to cope with conservative societal elements which keep him from realizing his desires; an older female relative—a mother or aunt—will represent the "traditional" point of view and thus attempt to restrain the hero; the love interest is provided by a young lady whom the hero fancies but eventually loses; and throughout there will be the gentle Narayan humor derived from irony, which springs from the character's self-deception, foibles, and misunderstanding.[22]

Coppola is right that by the time *The Painter of Signs* appears certain patterns in Narayan's fiction had become apparent—this *may* explain the difficulty Narayan had in placing the work with an English publisher despite his strong international reputation. Graham Greene's intercession—which had certainly become far less necessary after the publication of *The Guide*, helped Narayan to secure a reputable publisher.[23]

Similar to *The Guide* and *The Man-eater of Malgudi*, Narayan builds suspense beautifully in *The Painter of Signs*, focusing on Raman's pursuit of Daisy and then, once he apparently has her, his struggle with feelings of guilt about his departing aunt and about Daisy's cavalier disregard of religious and social tradition. The mounting suspense surrounding an anticipated resolution of conflict via compromise or confrontation does not materialize, however, and the reader may feel the same sense of disappointment over an escapist conclusion (similar, perhaps, to *The Man-eater of Malgudi* despite its mythic reverberations, and to *Talkative Man*, a later novel—and perhaps similar even to *The Guide*, whose ambiguous conclusion some readers admit to feeling "cheated" by). Daisy suddenly turns cold—without any identifiable, immediate provocation—says the marriage will not work, and heads out for what will likely be years of service in remote areas. Such an abrupt reversal seems implausible, though it brings the novel quickly to a decisive close.

A Tiger for Malgudi (1983) stands as an interesting departure in some ways for Narayan. It surely takes him away from his focus on the lives of everyday common citizens of Malgudi and centers instead on the tiger Raja. As we enter into the mind of the tiger and experience his transformation from man-eater to vegetarian, it is clear that we are dealing with moral fable, placing the work thematically closer to *Waiting for the Mahatma* than any of the other novels. The theme of inner transformation becomes more pronounced in Narayan's works after *Mr. Sampath*, and Gandhian ideals such as *swaraj*, *satyagraha*, and *ahimsa* figure significantly in *Waiting for the Mahatma*, *The Guide*, *The Man-eater of Malgudi*, and *The Vendor of Sweets*, so *A Tiger for Malgudi* certainly "fits" with many of the later works in this sense, although it stands apart because of its nature as a beast fable.

Raja's transcendence of appetite, his eventual movement away from violence and his ability to control and ultimately suppress his "beastly' impulses are effected through the agency of the Master, a somewhat mysterious spiritual figure who suddenly appears at a critical moment in the text—when Raja is loose in the town and people have therefore panicked and gone into hiding. His surprising, sudden arrival and immediate impact remind one of the oddly sudden appearance of Dr. Pal in *The Financial Expert*, or of Sampath in *The Printer of Malgudi*. One learns that the Master's triumph over his own appetite has been a struggle, as his wife tracks him down in the Mempi Hills and begs him to return (suggestive of a similar device used in *Talkative Man*); she recalls his "inordinate demands for food and my perpetual anxiety to see you satisfied, and my total surrender to you night and day when the passion seized you" (170). Rather than compromising the Master's legitimacy or sincerity, however, her account (while it does introduce some comic ambiguity into the narrative) underscores the path he has travelled parallel to Raja's, and his ability to identify with the tiger's struggle for self-control. When Master decides to commit Raja to a zoo so that the tiger may bring pleasure to others, however, and then disappears from the narrative as abruptly as he entered, bringing the novel to a close, one may be inclined to agree with David Atkinson that "the closure of the novel might seem weak and contrived" (12), and thus be led to concede that the later novels consistently offer contrived, abrupt conclusions, despite the various merits they exhibit.

The truncated tale and abrupt ending are nowhere more evident than in *Talkative Man* (1986), and Narayan directly addresses this issue in a postscript to the novel. He maintains that the narrative

> would not grow beyond 116 typewritten sheets, where it just suddenly came to a halt, like a motor car run out of petrol. Talkative Man, the narrator, had nothing more to say. He seemed to feel, What more do you expect? (120)

While one may or may not be swayed by Narayan's rationale for the brevity and rapid denouement of his narrative (it is easily his shortest novel at 119 pages), he certainly offers in *Talkative Man* an entertaining and engaging work. He problematizes the tale somewhat by having Talkative Man (*TM*) explain that this is the narrative of a narrative: he tells us the story of his having told the story to "that enchanted Varma, [...] a born listener" (2); complicating matters nicely is *TM*'s admission that he is a compulsive story teller, and his presence as narrator is never lost sight of. The engrossing story that he relates centers on Dr. Rann, a man who appears in Malgudi unexpectedly one day, claiming to be a United Nations worker just back from Timbuctoo, and who immediately entrenches himself as a resident in the waiting room of Malgudi Station, despite the anxious concern of the station master, who is unable to encourage him to leave—until *TM* intervenes and makes Rann a guest in his own home, only to find him ultimately impossible to remove from there also. Narayan thus returns to the motif of the mysterious stranger which he successfully introduces in *The Guide* (Rosie), *The Man-eater of Malgudi* (Vasu), and *The Painter of Signs* (Daisy), as well as the motif of the intractable guest (most notably Vasu in *Man-eater*).

The secretive and subversive nature of Rann's activities, and the anxiety they engender in *TM*, his host, are reminiscent, again, of *The Man-eater of Malgudi*, but when Rann enters into his public lecture on the Cannibal Herb, a weed that will cover half the globe by A.D. 2500 and will lead to human extinction by A.D. 3000, both the theme of his lecture and his method of delivery evolve into the absurd, and we realize that we are on fairly new footing with Narayan—although one may be reminded of the love-crazed Ravi's destruction of the film set in *Sampath*, on the one hand, and certainly of the sense of impending conflict between Nataraj and Vasu in *Man-eater*, particularly as *TM* comes to learn that Rann has shaped mad plans to run off with a teen-aged girl whom *TM* has lovingly watched grow up. The critical moment of intervention never comes for *TM*, however (just as it does not for Nataraj), because in *deus ex machina* fashion Rann's wife arrives from Delhi and literally stuffs him into a car and drives him right out of the narrative.

Perhaps still brooding over the aborted narrative of *Talkative Man*, Narayan launched his final novel, *The World of Nagaraj*, in 1990, and resurrects *TM* as a minor though somewhat influential character in the novel. In fact, it seems apparent that Narayan realized this would be his final novel since he makes an obvious effort to include the names of most of the recognizable streets and other places around Malgudi (and even a couple of the characters, for example Raman the sign painter, as well as *TM*) encountered in his previous works, in almost curtain-call fashion. *Nagaraj* is in some ways a typical Narayan piece, yet it is more loosely structured and ambling, and while certainly it stands as a testimony to the author's declining powers (which, at 84 years of age, is certainly forgivable),[24] it also presents itself in a relaxed, devil-may-care style and contains a number of brief humorous passages and spots of witty dialogue. Generally, however, the novel sputters, tries to arise to a sense of climax, never quite makes it, and ends nearly as aimlessly as it begins—or as aimless as Nagaraj himself is described to be. Nagaraj, the financially comfortable, retired, fifty-something congenial drifter about Malgudi, remains obsessed from the novel's beginning to its end with his grand ambition to write a great work on the sage Narada—and the plans go virtually nowhere. He thinks about the project a great deal, draws himself up to get started, makes a couple of focused efforts to gain information and help from others, but ultimately realizes only frustration. No one around him understands why he should trouble himself with such an effort since he does not need to do it, and they wonder what compels him to such a labour that is clearly resulting in his despondency and anxiety. Quite likely, Narayan reflects here something of his own condition at this stage in his life—comfortable, well regarded, modest, easy-going and generous, yet driven to write—perhaps the "one great work" that he feels (perhaps) he has never delivered, and finding his efforts to launch the project either perpetually interrupted (as Nagaraj's are by the disruptive appearance of his nephew Tim) or, perhaps more likely, that the well has simply dried up. In any case, *Nagaraj* never manages to involve the reader via intriguing conflict—though it attempts to do so as we follow the struggle between Nagaraj and his more practical but mean-spirited brother Gopu over the irresponsible behaviour of Tim (will Tim straighten out? return with Gopu to the village? turn his back on both families?). Ultimately, the resolution of this conflict (brought on by Narayan's recurrently utilized motif of an outsider's sudden and surprising, intrusive arrival) proves anticlimactic, as Tim and his wife suddenly reappear at Nagaraj's home—and only extend (apparently forever) Nagaraj's disappointment over his inability to regain the peace and quiet he needs to engage fruitfully in writing his magnum opus. Just as Nagaraj's great work never really gets started, the novel itself similarly becomes repetitious and without a strong or clear sense of direction.

* * *

R.K. Narayan was so prolific for so long that to accurately characterize his work with a small set of generalities is no simple task. That he has been committed to writing would be a comic understatement worthy of the author himself; aside from the many novels coming at fairly regular intervals over nearly sixty years, the volumes of short stories, the translations of the epics, the retelling of other traditional myths and tales, the autobiography, and the personal and travel essays, the number of letters that Narayan wrote—along with the notebooks filled with scribblings on various topics—reveal a mind that betrays its sheer restlessness despite the tone of quiet and calm simplicity, and its tenacity, despite the apparent resignation often ascribed to him. In his novels Narayan has remained focused, for the most part, on the lives of common people, and he has persisted from beginning to end in his efforts (or natural inclination) to walk the fine line between the comic and the tragic (or at least the sad). His playful sense of humor and his penchant for irony are prevalent throughout his work, and of course his fidelity to Malgudi became part of his signature. There is a marked movement toward more overt moralism as he passes into the 1960s and beyond, a trajectory anticipated by *Waiting for the Mahatma* and *The Guide*. While it may be tempting to list what we do *not* find in Narayan's work—the anguish of people caught in the press of harsh social and political realities, etc.—to appreciate Narayan is to see him for what he has been over his lengthy career: a storyteller with one foot firmly in the folk tradition and the other foot solidly in the comic realist-satirist tradition, gifted in engaging readers in sometimes unbearably light narratives while supplying wry insight into our universal hopes and struggles.[25]

Notes

1. NCBU shall be used to designate Narayan Collection, Boston University—the R.K. Narayan collection held in the Department of Special Collections, Boston University.
2. Kirpal Singh, "The Ordinary and Average as Satiric Traps: The Case of R.K. Narayan," *R.K. Narayan: Contemporary Critical Essays*, ed. Geoffrey Kain (East Lansing: Michigan State UP, 1993) 79-87.
3. Mary Beatina Rayen, *Narayan: A Study in Transcendence* (New York: Peter Lang, 1993) 136.
4. K.R.S. Iyengar, *Indian Writing in English* (New York: Asia Publishing House, 1973) 385.
5. V.S. Naipaul, *India: A Wounded Civilization* (New York: Vintage Books, 1977) 12-13.
6. M.M. Mahood, "The Marriage of Krishna: Narayan's *The Man-Eater of Malgudi*," *The Colonial Encounter: A Reading of Six Novels* (London: Collings, 1977) 94.
7. R.K. Narayan, *R.K. Narayan: Critical Essays*, ed. A.L. McLeod (New Delhi: Sterling Publications, 1994) vii.
8. Letter dated August 10, 1935, Narayan collection, Boston University.
9. This volume is held in the Graham Greene collection, Burns Library, Boston College.
10. Even as late as May 4, 1974, Narayan writes to Greene that "with every book [...] I am full of misgivings and doubts until you read and tell me your opinion of it" (BLBC).
11. Letter dated April 3, presumably 1939, Greene collection, Burns Library, Boston College.
12. According to Ram and Ram, Sampath is modelled on M.S. Cheluviengar, proprietor of City Power Press in Mysore (as well as being an amateur actor), and actually known as "Sampath." Narayan became involved with Sampath the printer, and he remembers this also in *My Days*.
13. Greene collection, Burns Library, Boston College.
14. I have argued this view at length in an earlier essay, "Eternal, Insatiable Appetite: The Irony of the Baited Hero in R.K. Narayan's Fiction," *R.K. Narayan: Contemporary Critical Essays* (East Lansing, Michigan: Michigan State UP, 1993) 101-14.
15. The short stories—in the way of classic short stories—also often turn on surprising coincidences or fortuitous but ultimately very significant occurrences, most notably perhaps in "An Astrologer's Day," which Graham Greene valued most highly among Narayan's short stories.
16. The legal correspondence surrounding this issue is contained in the R.K. Narayan Collection, Department of Special Collections, Boston University.
17. Narayan details his experience with the film production in an essay held in the Narayan Collection, Special Collections Department, Boston University.
18. "Lawley Road" is the title of one of Narayan's short stories, the center piece of his volume of short stories *Lawley Road and Other Stories* (1956).
19. Narayan also discusses this explicitly, with reference to *The Man-eater of Malgudi*, in his introduction to *Gods, Demons, and Others* (1972), his collection of retold myths.
20. The exaggerated character of Vasu leads me also to consider the early influence

of Dickens on Narayan, since Vasu as caricature seems suggestive of characters such as Scrooge, Gradgrind, or Uriah Heep.

21. Mary Beatina Rayen, *Narayan: A Study in Transcendence* (New York: Peter Lang, 1993) 123.
22. Carlo Coppola, rev. of *The Painter of Signs*, by R.K. Narayan, *World Literature Today* 51 (Spring 1977) 333.
23. Greene expresses his disbelief and aggravation over this state of affairs in a letter to V.S. Naipaul, dated May 17, 1976 (Burns Library, Boston College).
24. *Nagaraj* is not the end of the road for Narayan, however; he published *The Grandmother's Tale and Selected Stories* in 1994. The "selected stories" are reprinted from earlier works, while "The Grandmother's Tale" is new (first published by Indian Thought in 1992). It is at least as effective as *Nagaraj*, yet it offers a return to one of the author's established themes—the estranged or abandoned wife going out to retrieve her wayward husband.
25. I am grateful for funding received through the professional development fund, Embry-Riddle University, which supported my research in the R.K. Narayan collection, Special Collections, Boston University, as well as in the Graham Greene collection housed in the Burns Library, Boston College. I am also especially grateful to Dr. Howard Gotlieb for granting me access to the Narayan materials at Boston University, and to Sean Noel, Special Collections librarian at Boston University, for his generous assistance. Thanks goes also to John Atteberry, special collections librarian at Burns Library, Boston College, for his help in allowing me access to the many Narayan-Greene letters held in the Graham Greene collection. I am also grateful for permission received from the Graham Greene estate, via David Higham Associates, London, to quote from the letters of Narayan and Greene held among Greene's personal documents in the Greene collection. Likewise, I am grateful to Dr. Howard Gotlieb for permission to quote from the materials in the R.K. Narayan collection at Boston University.

AN R.K. NARAYAN BIBLIOGRAPHY

Primary Sources

Novels

Swami and Friends. 1935. Chicago: U of Chicago P, 1980.

The Bachelor of Arts. 1937. Introduction by Graham Greene, 1978. Chicago: U of Chicago P, 1980.

The Dark Room. 1938. Chicago: U of Chicago P, 1981.

The English Teacher. 1945. Chicago: U of Chicago P, 1980.

Mr. Sampath, Printer of Malgudi. 1949. Chicago: U of Chicago P, 1981.

The Financial Expert. 1952. Chicago: U of Chicago P, 1981.

Waiting for the Mahatma. 1955. Chicago: U of Chicago P, 1981.

The Guide. 1958. New York: Viking Penguin, 1992.

The Man-eater of Malgudi. 1961. London and New York: Penguin Books, 1983.

The Vendor of Sweets. London and New York: Penguin Books, 1967.

The Painter of Signs. 1976. New York: Viking Penguin, 1993.

A Tiger for Malgudi. 1983. New York: Viking Penguin, 1994.

Talkative Man. 1986. London and New York: Penguin Books, 1986.

The World of Nagaraj. New York: Viking Press, 1990.

Collections of Short Stories

Malgudi Days. 1972. New York: Viking Penguin, 1995.

Dodu and other Stories. Mysore: Indian Thought Publications, 1943.

Cyclone and Other Stories. Mysore: Indian Thought Publications, 1944.

An Astrologer's Day and Other Stories. Mysore: Indian Thought Publications, 1947.

Lawley Road. Mysore: Indian Thought Publications, 1956.

A Horse and Two Goats. 1970. New York: Viking Press, 1986.

Old and New. Mysore: Indian Thought Publications, 1981.

Under the Banyan Tree. 1985. London and New York: Penguin, 1987.

A Story-Teller's World. New Delhi: Penguin Books India, 1989.

The Grandmother's Tale and Selected Stories. Hopewell, New Jersey: Ecco Press, 1994.

Other Works

Mysore. (Travel). Mysore: The Government Press, 1939.

Next Sunday. (Essays). Mysore: Indian Thought Publications, 1956.

My Dateless Diary. (Travel). Mysore: Indian Thought Publications, 1960.

Gods, Demons and Others. (Indian Mythological Stories retold). 1964. Chicago: U of Chicago P, 1993.

The Ramayana. 1972. New York: Viking Penguin, 1993.

Reluctant Guru. (Essays). Delhi: Hind Pocket Books, 1973.

My Days. (Autobiography). 1974. New York: Harper Collins, 1999.

The Emerald Route. (Travel). Bangalore: The Government of Karnataka, 1977.

The Mahabharata (condensed prose version). 1978. Chicago: U of Chicago P, 2000.

A Writer's Nightmare, Selected Essays 1958-1988. New Delhi: Penguin Books India, 1988.

Secondary Sources

Books on R.K. Narayan

Badal, R.K. *R.K. Narayan: A Study*. Bareilly: Prakash Book Depot, 1976.

Biswal, Jayant K.A. *A Critical Study of the Novels of R.K. Narayan: the Malgudi Comedy*. New Delhi: Nimal Publishers & Distributors, 1987.

Dnyate, Ramesh. *The Novels of R.K. Narayan: A Typological Study of Characters*. New Delhi: Prestige, 1996.

Goyal, Bhagwat S. *R.K. Narayan: A Critical Spectrum*. India: Shalabh Book House, 1982.

Harrex, S.C. *Fire and the Offering: The English Language Novel of India 1935-1970.* Calcutta: Writers Workshop, 1978.

Holmstrom, Lakshmi. *The Novels of R.K. Narayan.* Calcutta: Writers Workshop, 1973.

Kain, Geoffrey, (ed.). *R.K. Narayan: Contemporary Critical Essays.* East Lansing: Michigan State UP, 1993.

McLeod. A.L., (ed.). *R.K. Narayan: Critical Essays.* New Delhi: Sterling Publishers, 1994.

Naik, M.K. *The Ironic Vision: A Study of the Fiction of R.K. Narayan.* New Delhi: Sterling Publishers, 1983.

Pontes, Hilda and Ezekiel Nissim. *R.K. Narayan.* Atlantic Highlands, New Jersey: Humanities, 1983.

Raizada, Harish. *R.K. Narayan: A Critical Study of His Works.* New Delhi: Young Asia Publications, 1969.

Ram, Susan and N. Ram. *R.K. Narayan: The Early Years, 1906-1945.* New Delhi: Viking Books India, 1996.

Rama, Atma. *Perspectives on R.K. Narayan.* India: Vimal Prakashan, 1981.

Ramana, P.S. *Message in Design: A Study of R.K. Narayan's Fiction.* New Delhi: Harman, 1993.

Rayen, Mary Beatina. *Narayan: A Study in Transcendence.* New York: Peter Lang, 1994.

Sales-Pontes, A. Hilda. *R.K. Narayan.* New Delhi: Concept, 1983.

Sharan, Nagendra Nath. *A Critical Study of the Novels of R.K. Narayan.* New Delhi: Classical Publishing Company, 1993.

Singh, P.K. *The Novels of R.K. Narayan: A Critical Evaluation.* New Delhi: Atlantic Publishers, 1999.

Singh, R.A. *The Malgudi Novels: A Study.* Bareilly: Prakash Book Depot, 1991.

Sinha, U.P. *Patterns of Myth and Reality: A Study in R.K. Narayan's Novels.* Delhi: Sanbarbh Publishers, 1988.

Sundaram, P.S. *R.K. Narayan.* New Delhi: Arnold-Heinemann India, 1973.

——. *R.K. Narayan as a Novelist.* Delhi: D.K. Publishers Distributors, 1988.

Vanden Driesen, Cynthia. *The Novels of R.K. Narayan.* Nedlands, Australia: Centre for South and Southeast Asian Studies, U of Western Australia, 1986.

Varma, R.M. *Major Themes in the Novels of R.K. Narayan.* New Delhi: Jainsons Publications, 1993.

——. *Some Aspects of Indo-English Fiction.* New Delhi: Jainsons Publications, 1985.

Walsh, William. *R.K. Narayan: A Critical Appreciation.* Chicago: U of Chicago P, 1982.

A Selection of Critical Articles Written on R.K. Narayan

Afzal-Khan, Fawzia. "Genre and Ideology in the Novels of Four contemporary Indo-Anglian Novelists: R.K. Narayan, Anita Desai, Kamala Markandaya and Salman Rushdie." *Dissertation Abstracts International* 47.4 (1986): 1328 A.

Asnani, Shyam M. "The Use of Myth in R.K. Narayan's Novels." *The Literary Endeavor: A Quarterly Journal devoted to English Studies* 3.3-4 (1982): 19-31.

Chauhan, P.S. "The Commonwealth of the Imagination: Narayan and Naipaul." *Language and Literature in Multicultural Contexts.* Suva, Fiji: U of South Pacific, 1983: 89-96.

Chellappan, K. "The Apocalypse of the Ordinary: The Comic Myths of R.K. Narayan." *The Literary Endeavor* 3.3-4 (1982): 52-59.

Cronin, Richard. "Quiet Quiet India: The Despair of R.K. Narayan." *Encounter* 64.3 (1985): 52-59.

Desai, Anita. "Malgudi." *London Review of Books* 8.21 (4 Dec. 1986): 23-24.

Greene, Graham. Introduction, *The Bachelor of Arts.* London: Heinemann, 1978.

Langran, Phillip. "R.K. Narayan and V.S. Naipaul: A Comparative Study of Some Hindu Aspects of Their Work." *Dissertation Abstracts International* 49.11 (1989): 3356A.

Mishra, Pankaj. "The Great Narayan." *New York Review of Books* 48.3 (22 February, 2001): 44-47.

Murti, K.V.S. "Bacchus and Buddha: Salman Rushdie and R.K. Narayan. *The Commonwealth Review* 1.2 (1990): 157-68.

Naik, M.K. "Malgudi Minor: The Short Stories of R.K. Narayan." *The Laurel Bough: Essays Presented in Honour of Professor M.V. Rama Sarma.* Bombay: Blackie & Son, 1983. 193-202.

Olinder, Britta. "Aspects of R.K. Narayan's Narrative Technique." *Actes du Congres d'Amiens.* Paris: Didier, 1987. 463-72.

——. "R.K. Narayan's Short Stories: Some Introductory Remarks." *Commonwealth Essays and Studies* 8.1 (1985): 24-29.

——. "Reality and a Myth in R.K. Narayan's Novels." *The Literary Criterion* 20.2 (1985): 8-22.

Pandit, Manorma. "Detachment and Liberation in the Novels of R.K. Narayan. *Dissertation Abstracts International* 46.22 (1986): 3355 A.

Philip, David Scott. *Perceiving India Through the Works of Nirad C. Chauduri, R.K. Narayan, and Ved Mehta.* New Delhi: Sterling Publishers, 1986.

Piciucco, Pier Paolo. "Femininity in the Fiction of R.K. Narayan: a Study." *Indian Writings in English*. Vol. 7. Manmohan K. Bhatnagar and M. Rajeshwar (Eds.). New Delhi: Atlantic Books, 2000. 34-47.

Pousse, Michel. "The West in R.K. Narayan's Novels." *Commonwealth Essays and Studies* 9.2 (1987): 99-108.

——. "R.K. Narayan as Gandhian Novelist." *The Literary Criterion* 25.4 (1990): 77-90.

Rani, K. Nirupa. "Autobiographical Element in R.K. Narayan's Early Novels." *Journal of Indian Renaissance* 45.3 (1976): 44-48.

Sharrad, Paul. "Tradition and Tragedy: Anita Desai and R.K. Narayan." *The Commonwealth Review* 2.1-2 (1990-1991): 181-82.

Singh, Satyanarain. "A Note on the World View of R.K. Narayan." *Indian Literature* 24.1 (1981): 104-9.

Walsh, William. "R.K. Narayan: The Unobtrusive Novelist." *Review of National Literatures* 10 (1979): 59-69.

Westbrook, Perry D. "The Short Stories of R.K. Narayan." *Journal of Commonwealth Literature* 5 (1968): 41-51.

Woodcock, George. "Two Great Commonwealth Novelists: R.K. Narayan and V.S. Naipaul." *Sewanee Review* 87 (Winter 1979): 1-28.

____. "The Maker of Malgudi: Notes on R.K. Narayan." *Tamarack Review* 73 (1978): 82-95.

Studies of Narayan in Books not Exclusively Focused on the Author

Agnihotri, G.N. *Indian Life and Problems in the Novels of Mulk Raj Anand, Raja Rao, and R.K. Narayan*. Meerut: Shalabh Prakashan, 1993.

Iyengar, K.R.S. "R.K. Narayan." *Indian Writing in English*. New York: Asian Publishing House, 1973: 358-85.

Mahood, M.M. "The Marriage of Krishna: Narayan's *The Man-eater of Malgudi*." *The Colonial Encounter: A Reading of Six Novels*. London: Rex Collings, 1977. 92-114.

Mehta, Ved. *John is Easy to Please*. Harmondsworth: Penguin, 1971.

Mukherjee, Meenakshi. *The Twice Born Fiction: Themes and Techniques of the Indian Novel in English*. New Delhi: Heinemann, 1971.

Narasimhaiah, C.D., ed. *Fiction and the Reading Public in India*. Mysore: U of Mysore, 1967.

——. *The Swan and the Eagle*. Delhi: I.I.A.S., 1987.

Nasimi, Reza Ahmad. *The Language of Mulk Raj Anand, Raja Rao, and R.K. Narayan*. Delhi: Capital Publishing House, 1989.

Saxena, O.P. *Glimpses of Indo-English Fiction*. New Delhi: Jainsons, 1985.

Walsh, William. *Indian Literature in English*. London: Longman, 1990.

2

Mulk Raj Anand

BASAVARAJ NAIKAR

Mulk Raj Anand was born on 12th December 1905 in Peshawar in the North West Frontrier Province of pre-Partition India, Lal Chand Anand and Ishwar Kaur happened to be his mother and father respectively. He was educated at Khalsa College, Amritsar and at the University of London. In London he earned his Ph.D. in Philosophy in 1929 under the supervision of Professor G. Dawes Hicks, an eminent Kantian scholar. In England he came in close contact with famous writers like Lawrence Binyon, D.H. Lawrence, F.R. Leavis, Middleton Murry, Herbert Read, Aldous Huxley, F.C. Bartlet, C.D. Broad, Bonamee Dobre'ee, Eric Gill, A.K. Coomaraswamy and others. Anand read voraciously in world philosophy and travelled widely in Europe. He began his literary career in 1932, when he wrote his first novel *Untouchable*. In 1935, he wrote his second novel *Coolie*. In 1938, he organized the Progressive Writers' Movement and fought against Fascism and imperialism. At the end of the World War-II, he returned to Punjab, India. In 1948 he visited Russia. In 1955 he organized the first Asian Writers' Conference in New Delhi. He represented Indian Writers at the first conference of Afro-Asian Writers held in Tashkent in 1958, and also the second conference held in Cairo. In 1961 he visited Australia on a tentative tour and attended Australian Peace Conference in Melbourne. In 1962 he was appointed as Tagore Professor of Arts and Literature in Punjab University but he resigned from the post in 1965 because of his very progressive views. In 1963 he visited Cuba. Writing is only part of his life. An art critic of international reputation, he edited an art-journal, *Marg* devoted to the rediscovery of Indian culture including painting, architecture, sculpture, dance, drama, music, arts and crafts. The range of Anand's interests is astonishingly wide which includes literature, philosophy, dance, art criticism and cookery etc. In 1966 he was appointed as the Chairman of the Lalit Kala Academy, New Delhi. He was honoured with Padma Bhushan award in 1967. Anand is known for his humanism, which includes the best and most vital elements in western as well as Asian philosophies. Denying the existence of God and the supernatural he affirms the centrality of human life and enhancement of human happiness.

Untouchable (1935) happens to be the first novel written by Mulk Raj Anand under the deep influence of Mahatma Gandhi. It is an archetypal novel dealing with the worst evil of Indian society *i.e.*, untouchability perpetrated by the *varna* system propounded by *The Laws of Manu*. Bakha the protagonist of the novel is an untouchable coming from the lowest strata of Indian Society. The selection of a character like Bakha testifies to Mulk Raj Anand's belief in the dignity of labour. Bakha has to clean the latrines more than twice a day—a job disliked by the upper caste people. The novel depicts the events that happen in one day of Bakha's life. A sensitive boy, Bakha suffers a great deal of humiliation at the hands of caste-Hindus. The hypocrisy of the brahmin priest who curses him for polluting the temple by his standing outside the door and who does not mind molesting his sister Sohni irritate him. When he touches Lallaji in the market inadvertently, the latter slaps him. When he finally encounters Colonel Hutchinson, Mahatma Gandhi and Iqbal Nath Sarshar, he begins to dream of becoming an honourable man. The novel is a powerful indictment on the caste discrimination and hypocrisy of the Hindus, especially brahmins.

His second novel *Coolie* (1936) is conceived and executed on an epic scale. The protagonist of the novel is a hill boy called Munoo who is an orphan and who is forced out of his village in search of a livelihood. First he works as a servant-boy at the house of a middle-class Babu, and then in a pickle factory in another town. Then he reaches Bombay and works in a cotton mill from where he escapes when the Hindu-Muslim riot is sparked off. The car of an Anglo-Indian woman knocks him down. He works for her as her page-cum-rikshawallah and eventually dies of consumption. At all stages of his life, Munoo is ill treated, insulted and disdained. Anand again upholds the dignity of man by making a labourer of the lowest strata of Indian society the protagonist of his novel. It also shows Anand's attack on the class system, capitalism, and communalism and Karma.

In *Two Leaves and a Bud* (1937) Anand denounces the evil of poverty and cruelty and rejects the theory of Karma. Gangu, the protagonist of the novel is a middle-aged peasant, who is goaded by the loss of his land and hut to greedy money-lenders, goes to Assam and joins service in Macpherson Tea Estate, where he is exploited by the merchants. His wife Sajani dies of malaria. Gangu has no money even to conduct her last rites. The British planters are not sympathetic to the Indian workers. An Englishman Reggie chases Leila, daughter of Gangu and shoots the father when the latter intervenes. The court declares that Reggie is not guilty. The novel is an attack on the evil effects of imperialism, capitalist economy and exploitation of helpless labourers. The novel happens to be inferior to *Coolie* as propaganda overrides art in it.

Lament on the Death of a Master of Arts (1938), the shortest of Anand's novels deals with the problem of education. Nur, the protagonist, suffers months of physical agony caused by tuberculosis, crushing poverty, loss of mother, and ill luck. Thrashed by teachers in school, he is forced to get an MA degree, which proves to be an insufficient passport into officialdom. Burdened with a wife and a daughter, constantly pestered by his father, he is compelled to take up the job of a clerk in a post office. Finally under the burden of heavy and mechanical work, he succumbs to death. The novel iterates Anand's belief that modern education in India is a failure as it cannot guarantee a job to a man equal to his qualifications. An educated man like Nur is torn between two worlds—old and new. He can neither go back to his father's profession of menial job nor can he become an officer. He becomes a misfit. Nur represents millions of the educated youth of India. The novel is so gruesome and macabre that it easily reminds us of Poe's short stories. The tone of the novel is pathetic rather than tragic

The Village (1939) trilogy deals with the turbulent career of a Punjabi peasant. *The Village* is symbolic of the tragedy and hope of India simultaneously. It stands for a village in transition from orthodoxy to modernity. Lal Singh, the protagonist rebels against orthodoxy and pities his father Nihal Singh who represents orthodoxy. Lal Singh gets into trouble and runs away from his village to join the army. Anand's disapproval of the theories of Karma and God are evident in the novel.

Across The Black Waters (1940), the second volume of the trilogy, is an elaborate running commentary on the four years' war. Lal Singh joins the Indian army which joins the French and English armies at Marseilles. He moves from Marseilles to Orleans, to Calais and to Festubert and so on. He trains himself as a soldier right on the battlefield and fights the enemy but ends up as a prisoner of war in German hands. The novel illustrates Anand's denunciation of war, the attendant cruelty and violence and the ultimate meaninglessness of it all.

The Sword and the Sickle (1942), the third volume of the trilogy is a continuation of Lal Singh's life history. Lal Singh returns to his village after five years of stay in Germany as a war prisoner and is shocked to learn that his family is broken up and his property lost. Having lost his glamour as a soldier, he joins an association with a Count in Uttar Pradesh and fights the evil of landlordism. But they meet with failure because of lack of unity and leadership. Finally Lal Singh is arrested and put behind bars. The novel expresses Anand's attack on the meaninglessness of war, the evil of landlords and the exploitation of the poor peasants. It is blatantly a political novel in which propaganda overshadows artistic element.

The Big Heart (1945) a little powerful novel expresses Anand's plea for the mastery of machine for the human prosperity. It is an effective dramatization of the efforts of industrialization on the traditional rural communities of India. Ananta, the protagonist returns from Bombay to Billimaran village in Amritsar and organizes all the jobless coppersmiths into a union and decides to fight against the factory newly opened there when Ralia, Satyapal and his group try to break the machines in the factory. Ananta tries to reason with them, but is ironically killed by them. Ananta becomes a martyr. Anand teaches the lesson that the machine is a gift from the west which needs to be assimilated into the Indian life for the well-being of all the sections of society, and that human happiness can be achieved through the elimination of pain and cruelty.

Seven Summers (1951), the first part of a seven volume of autobiographical novel *Seven Ages of Man*, depicts the first seven years of Krishnan's childhood. Krishnan is an autobiographical projection of Anand himself. Insatiable curiosity, questioning, frolicking, wonders and fear and so on characterize Krishnan's childhood, which is symbolic of an Indian childhood. Krishnan mischievous and curious by nature pesters his mother for eatables and answers to his questions. He has the first glimpse of the incomprehensible phenomenon of death when his younger brother Prithvi dies. He notices that both his parents are victims of superstitions, like belief in god-men, magic, horoscopes and stellar influences. He observes that both his father and mother believe in God, karma and previous life. The novel offers a deep insight into child psychology as well as Indian sociology.

The Private Life of an Indian Prince (1953) is an expression of Anand's attack on feudalism and the attendant cruelty, callousness and megalomania and plea for liberty and democratic socialism. Victor, the protagonist, is an eccentric and a tyrannous King of Sham Pur who indulges in womanising and ill-treats his subjects by burdening them with heavy taxes and confiscation of their property. Under the intoxicating influence of the guiles and wiles of Ganga Dasi, he gradually loses control over his mind. The oppressed masses form a Praja Mandal and demand justice from the prince, who is finally compelled by Sardar Vallabbhai Patel to sign the Instrument of Accession. Prince Victor goes to London where he is haunted by the memories of his mistresses. After being summoned back to India, he is found implicated in a murder. Finally he turns insane and ends up in a lunatic asylum. Anand treats the tyrannical prince and his fall with due humanistic sympathy, in spite of denouncing the negative aspects of feudalism.

The Old Woman and the Cow or *Gauri* (1960) demonstrates Anand's plea for woman's emancipation and equality with man. It is the story of Gauri's growth from docility and innocence to defiance and self-confidence. Gauri who is initially gentle like a cow marries Panchi and suffers a great deal at the hands of her mother, mother-in-law and husband Panchi till she meets an enlightened city doctor, Colonel Mahindra under whose influence she grows conscious of her worth and identity and decides to lead an independent life, when her chastity is suspected by her husband. Colonel Mahindra happens to be the mouthpiece of Anand in articulating his humanism and plea for woman's equality, identity and self-reliance. Anand's choice of a female protagonist for the novel in 1960s when Indians had not yet heard of feminism is indeed as admirable as prophetic. Whereas gods save Sita in the Ramayana, Gauri in modern India saves herself by the sheer strength of her soul.

The Road (1961) is a sequel to *Untouchable* in that it castigates caste hypocrisy, belief in God and Karma and affirms and upholds the dignity of labour and progress of man. In spite of Thakur Singh's stubbornness, caste superiority and obstacles and threats, Bikhu and Dhooli Singh, the two untouchables successfully construct the road with the help of a road-engine. Though *Road* is informed by Anand's humanism, it is less successful than *Untouchable* as a work of art as Bikhu is not as fully realized as Bakha is.

Death of a Hero (1961) is inspired by Anand's belief in liberty and secularism and his attack on religious fanaticism, fatalism and narrow nationalism. Maqbool Sherwani, the protagonist, who is a young poet of the National Conference rushes back from Srinagar to his hometown Baramula to help the people to escape from the terrorism of Pakistani aggression. But ironically enough, his own friends join the aggressors. He is captured and imprisoned by the invaders and ultimately shot dead in cold blood after a ridiculous trial. Anand's plea for pity and compassion and attack on war, violence and barbarity are manifest in the novel.

Morning Face (1968) the second in the series of *Seven Ages of Man*, is a continuation of *Seven Summers* and describes the growth of Krishnan from childhood to boyhood. Krishnan moves with his family to his hometown Amritsar that proves to be the "City of Dreadful Nights." Here also Krishnan is unhappy to know that people are superstitious. He is also angry at the British oppression. He seriously begins to question the existence of God and caste consciousness of Indians, and the inferior status of women. Krishnan's boyhood is characterized by a rationalistic interrogation of all traditional values and evils. He receives much love from Devaki, Shakuntala, and Mumtaz (his brother's mistress). To resolve his mental conflict, he tries writing verse, reading Dickens, Thackeray, Tolstoy and *Gorky* and writing fiction.

Anand's third autobiographical novel, *Confessions of a Lover* (1976) commutes history and autobiography and deals with Krishnan's adolescence and his endeavours to seek solutions in the seemingly nightmarish world of the changing political scenario. In this novel there is almost a teeming alliance between his life and the environmental pulls, a steady poise and equidistance he tries to maintain. He takes delight in reading poetry, comes under the influence of Dr. Mohammad Iqbal, a poet-philosopher and is initiated into the evanescent world of poetry. At the end of the novel Krishnan finds himself in self-imposed exile in London, leaving the comforts of home and the affection of his Indian friends. The novel, in the fashion of a cinematic montage, focuses its attention of Krishnan's translation to intense role-playing as a poet and as a lover. Deeply imbued in his narcissistic self-absorption, he finds it difficult to come out of his solipsistic circle.

The Bubble (1984) is an autobiographical novel written by Mulk Raj Anand's hero-anti-hero Krishnan Chander Azad. After a brief spell in the Gandhi movement, when his pro-British father beats his mother for Krishnan's going to jail, the hero goes to the West on a philosophical quest. The naive poet from the 'Ocean of Nectar' faces many torments of loneliness in self-exile. An unexpected meeting with the adolescent beauty Irene, step-daughter of a scientific genius, Professor Rhys, compels Krishnan to become a novelist, to celebrate 'love at first sight,' to experience Laila-Majnu like sexual-spiritual passion and emotional tension. When Irene goes back to her native Ireland, away from her orthodox mother, to work with Maud Gonne in the liberation movement, Krishnan appeases his longing for her in the euphoria of conversation in Bloomsbury with eminent writers and thinkers like E.M. Forster, Leonard and Virginia Wolf, Palms Dutt, J. Krishamurthy, Bertrand Russell and others. In this brilliant novel Anand breaks out from the orbit of the hackneyed novel about who should go to bed with whom to make novel what it was when it was first invented in India by Dandi and Somadeva and in the puranas, to what it became in novelists from Goethe to Thomas Mann and Andre Gide—the *Bildungsroman*, mingling imperceptible feeling with passionate ideas, in the highly charged conscience of his hero-anti-hero. The narrative combining ten novellas is as much a recreation of several near contemporary legends, as it is transformation, through the fiery poetic imagination of a naïve poet, who had been led to forget his own human condition and that of the many silent ones, into the belief in 'live in action.'

In *Pilpali Saheb* (1985), the autobiography of his childhood under the Raj, Mulk Raj Anand has written an honest account of his infantile feelings, dimly glimpsed stirrings into the life of the Imperial

British-Indian army in whose midst he grew up. Unlike most autobiographers who say little about the important first years of childhood, Anand has reminisced in this first part of his narrative, about the parental 'donts,' narrated his own ridiculous ambition to wear a sola hat and shown the slaves of the empire always saluting the ghostly apparitions of the White Sahibs.

Nine Moods of Bharata (1998) is very relevant commentary on contemporary Indian life. In it, Anand's alter ego, Krishnan Chandra Azad, embarks on a pilgrimage in search of meanings and resolutions of the contradictions, which had plagued him throughout his childhood and adolescence. His Talisman is Mahatma's injunction always to remember the suffering of those who are the most in need. The contradictions are skilfully described as we accompany Krishnan, the sensitive, brooding twenty two-year-old seeker/poet only recently returned from England. He accompanies the former World War I German internee—a seeker of a different kind—of art-treasures and photographs for future sale, who is inclined to thievery when the opportunity arises. It is a time of desperation and cruel human behaviour, the result of drought, exploitation and ignorance.

All of the nine *rasas* (aesthetic sentiments) which will be evoked in the paintings of Ajanta caves are intuited on the journey. These events are the background to prepare Krishnan for his encounter with the Buddhist tales. With the help of a guide who happens to be an outcaste, the young Krishnan enters the painted universe of the caves. There he finds reflections of everything he has been observing throughout his life. The second half of the book is his confrontation with the Jataka Stories, those age-old folk tales in which the Buddha, as *bodhisattva* in previous lives, reveals his compassionate nature in many different forms, the tales which had already sustained the people for centuries. Like the troupe of Krishnan's new friends upon approaching the caves, the ancient artists felt the Buddha's compassionate nature at the heart of their being.

The novel is no sentimental moralizing retreat into obscurantism or veiling of today's societal realities by parading a Buddhist panacea. His emphasis on *Karuna* (*compassion*) as a healing path is as profound as relevant to the modern man suffering from loneliness and anxiety.

Anand has published several short story collections, like *The Lost Child and Other Stories* (1934), *The Barber's Trade Union and Other Stories* (1944), *The Tractor and the Corn Goddess and Other Stories* (1947), *Reflections on the Golden Bed and Other Stories* (1954), *Selected Stories* (1954), *The Power of Darkness and Other Stories* (1959), *Lajwanti and Other Stories* (1968), and *Between Tears and Laughter* (1973). Most of these stories deal with humanistic themes like the plight of the poor and the downtrodden, evils of caste-system, poverty, ill-treatment of women, miserly businessmen, priestly exploitation, greed, vanity, selfishness, callous bureaucracy, feudalism, the Machine and so on. Most of these themes are expanded in his novels. The stories are generally written in realistic style, but some of them attain lyrical heights and the quality of fables.

Anand's love for children has inspired him to write many books for children. In *Indian Fairy Tales* (1946), *Aesop's Fables* (1960), *More Indian Fairy Tales* (1961) and *Folk Tales of Punjab* (1974) he has retold the famous Indian stories for the benefit of children. These stories are written in a gripping style.

Anand is not merely a creative writer with a strong social commitment, but also a thinker with a wide range of interests bordering on the encyclopaedic. He has written many treatises and delivered many lectures on the theory and practice of literature, and use of English Language in India. His autobiography like *Apology for Heroism* (1946) and monographs like *Roots and Flowers* (1972), *Author to Critic* (1973), *Conversations in Bloomsbury* (1981) and articles like "Towards a New Indian Literature" (1936), "A Writer's Confession of his Faith" (1952), "Creative Writing in the Present Crisis" (1963), "How I Became a Writer" (1965), "What Shakespeare Means to Me" (1965), "The Story of My Experiments with a White Lie" (1968), and others testify to his critical awareness based on his creative practice. He believes that all great literature is propagandistic though there may be a difference of degree in it.

As a literary critic, Anand is an art-critic, too. His prestigious journal *Marg* is exclusively devoted to art-criticism based on Indian art like painting, sculpture, dance and drama. His books like *Persian Paintings* (1930), *The Hindu View of Art* (1933), *The Bride's Book of Beauty* (1947), *The Indian Theatre* (1950), *The Dancing Foot* (1957), *Homage to Khajuraho* (1962) illustrate his live and varied interest in Indian art.

Anand is also a cultural critic of India. His interests range from cookery to sexology to civilization. His *Curries and Other Indian Dishes* (1932), *Marks and Engels on India* (1939), *On Education* (1947), *Kama Kala* (1958), *Is There a Contemporary Indian Civilization*? (1963) and several other articles amply testify to his live interest in the cultural issues of India.

A MULK RAJ ANAND BIBLIOGRAPHY

Primary Sources

Fiction

Untouchable. London: Lawrence & Wishart, 1935.

Coolie. London: Lawrence & Wishart, 1936.

Two Leaves and a Bud. London: Lawrence & Wishart, 1937.

Lament on the Death of Master of Arts. Lucknow: Naya Sansar, 1938.

The Village. London: Jonathan Cape, 1939.

Across the Black Water. London: Jonathan Cape, 1940.

The Sword and the Sickle. London: Jonathan Cape, 1942.

The Big Heart. London: Hutchinson International Authors, 1945.

Seven Summers. London: Hutchinson International Authors, 1945.

Private Life of an Indian Prince. London: Hutchinson International Authors, 1953.

The Old Woman and the Cow. Bombay: Kutub-Popular, 1960.

The Road. Bombay: Kutub-Popular, 1961.

Death of a Hero. Bombay: Kutub-Popular, 1963.

Morning Face. Bombay: Kutub-Popular, 1968.

Confessions of a Lover. New Delhi: Arnold-Heinemann, 1976.

The Bubble. New Delhi: Arnold-Heinemann, 1984.

Autobiography-Part I, Pilpali Saheb. New Delhi: Arnold-Heinemann, 1981.

Collections of Short Stories

The Barber's Trade Union and Other Stories. London: Jonathan Cape, 1944.

Indian Fairy Tales (Retold by Mulk Raj Anand). Bombay: Kutub Popular, 1946.

The Tractor and the Corn Goddess and Other Stories. Bombay: Thacker & Company, 1947.

Reflections on the Golden Bed and Other Stories. Bombay: Cuiren Book House, 1954.

Selected Stories. Moscow: Foreign Language Publishing House, 1954.

The Power of Darkness and Other Stories. Bombay: Jaico Publishing House, 1959.

Aesop's Fables (Retold by Mulk Raj Anand). Bombay: Dhawal Popular, 1960.

Lajwanti and Other Stories. Bombay: Jaico Publishing House, 1966.

Between Tears and Laughter. New Delhi: Sterling Publishers, 1973.

Folk Tales of Punjab. New Delhi: Sterling Publishers, 1974.

Non-Fiction

Persian Paintings. London: Faber & Faber, 1930.

Curries and Other Indian Dishes. London: Desmond Harmondsworth, 1932.

The Hindu View of Art. London: George Allen & Unwin, 1933.

The Golden Breath. Studies in Five Poets of the New India. London: John Murrey, 1933.

Marx and Engels on India. Allahabad: Socialist Book Club, 1939.

Letters on India. London: George Routledge & Sons, 1942.

Apology for Heroism. London: Lindsay Drummond, 1946.

Homage to Tagore. Lahore: Sangam Publishers, 1946.

The Bride's Book of Beauty (in collaboration with Krishna Hutheesing). Bombay: Kutub-Popular, 1947.

On Education. Bombay: Hind Kitabs, 1947.

The King-Emperor's English. Bombay: Hind Kitabs, 1948.

The Story of India. Bombay: Kutub Popular, 1948.

Lines Written to an Indian Air. Bombay: Nalanda Publication, 1949.

The Indian Theatre. London: Dennis Dobson, 1950.

The Dancing Foot. New Delhi: Ministry of Information & Broadcasting, 1957.

The India in Colour. New York: McGraw-Hill, 1958.

Kama Kala. Geneva and New York: Nagel Company, 1958.

Homage to Khajuraho (in collaboration with Stella Kramrisch). Bombay: Marg Publications, 1962.

Is There a Contemporary Indian Civilization? Bombay: Asia Publishing House, 1963.

The Volcano (some comments on the Development Rabindranath Tagore's Aesthetic Theories and Art Practice). Baroda: M.S. University, 1967.

Roots and Flowers. Dharwar: Karnatak University, 1972.

Author to Critic. The Letters of Mulk Raj Anand and Saros Cowasjee. Ed. Saros Cowasjee. Calcutta: Writers Workshop, 1973.

Conversation in Bloomsbury. New Delhi: Arnold-Heinemann, 1981.

Articles

"Towards a New Indian Literature." *Left Review* 2.12 (Sept. 1936).

"Anglo-Indian Literature." *Life and Letters To-Day* 15.5 (Autumn 1936).

"The Censorship in India." *Bombay Chronicle* 27 December 1936.

"Homage to Spain." *Congress Socialist* 2 (1 May 1937, 15 May 1937, 29 May 1937, 11 September 1937).

"English Novels of the Twentieth Century on India." *Asiatic Review* 39 (July 1941): 244-51.

"National Freedom in the U.S.S.R." *Labour Monthly* 24 (Nov. 1942).

"Rabindranath Tagore." *New Spirit.* Ed. J.W.L. Martin. London: Dennis Dobson, 1946.

"Introduction" to *Rice and Other Stories* by K.A. Abbas, Bombay: Bombay International Book House, 1947.

"A Writer's Confession of His Faith." *Bharat Jyoti* 27 April 1952.

"New Bearings in Indian Literature." *Literary Review* (Summer 1961).

"Is Indian Literature Sufficiently Indian?" *United Asia* 13.6 (Nov./Dec. 1961).

"Trends in the Novel." *Cultural Forum* (Tagore Number) 1961.

"The Place of a Gifted Individual in Indian Society." *The Year Book of Education: London,* 1961.

"The Writer's Role in National Integration: A Discussion." *Indian Literature* 1 (1962): 50-58.

"A Letter." *A Souvenir Volume of Appreciations* (The Radhakrishan Number), Madras-Hyderabad, 1962.

"Creative Writing in the Present Crisis." *Indian Literature* 1 (1963): 70-77.

"The Place of Art in University Education." *Journal of University Education,* II.I (Sept. 1963).

"The Concept of an Asian Mind." *Contemporary Indian Literature* IV (Oct.-Nov. 1964): 6-7 and 8-9.

"Jawaharlal Nehru." *Cultural Forum* (Special Number on Jawaharlal Nehru) VI. 4 (Nov. 1964).

"How I Became a Writer." *Contemporary Indian Literature* V.11-12 (Nov.-Dec. 1965): 13-15.

"Is Universal Criticism Possible?" *The Literary Criterion* VII (Winter 1965): 68-75.

"Kipling and Forster." *Quest* 47 (1965): 41-55.

"A Note on Modem Indian Fiction." *Indian Literature* VIII.1 (1965), 44-57.

"What Shakespeare Means to Me." *Contemporary Indian Literature* (May-July 1965).

"The One and the Many: Some Changing Social Patterns of New India." *United Asia* XVIII.I (Jan.-Feb. 1966).

"The Role of Creative Writers and Artists in the Developing Countries of Afro-Asia." *Afro-Asia and World Affairs* III.I (Spring 1966): 18-21.

"The Sources of Creative Writing." *Indian Literature* VII (Sept. 1967).

"Whither India?" *Gandhi Marg.* 44.XI (October 1967).

"Speech." *Soviet Review* 21 (March 26, 1968).

"The Question of Modernity." *Modernity and Contemporary Indian Literature.* Simla: Institute of Advanced Study, 1968. 43-49.

"The Story of My Experiments with a White Lie." *Critical Essays on Indian Writing in English.* (Eds.) M.K. Naik, S.K. Desai and G.S. Amur. Dharwar, 1968.

"When Our Hearts Were Young and Gay." *Times of India*. Bombay, 22 Dec. 1968.

"What Good is Literature For?" *The Banasthali Patrika* 5.14 (Jan. 1970).

"The Spirit of Man in Indian and South-East Asian Culture Since the End of Western Domination." *Afro-Asian Writings* 2.6 (Oct. 1970).

"Burning Conscience." *Afro-Asian Writings* (July 1971).

"Pigeon-Indian: Some Notes on Indian-English Writing." *Studies in Australian and Indian Literature*. Eds. C.D. Narasimhaiah and S. Nagarajan. Indian Council for Cultural Relations, 1971.

"Anglo-Saxon Attitudes: Twentieth Century English Fiction about India." *The Image of India in Western Creative Writing*. Ed. M.K. Naik, S.K. Desai and Kallapur. Dharwar, 1971.

"Tradition and Innovation." *Lotus* (January 1972). [Formerly *Afro Asian Writings*]

"What Price Red Book, Comrade?" Open Letter to Mao. *Blitz* 12 Feb. 1972.

"The Vision of Bhai Vir Singh." *The Tribune* 13 Feb. 1972.

"The Changelink—An Indo-Anglian Novelist's Credo." *Indian and Foreign Review* 9.23 (15 Sept. 1972).

"Trends in the Modern Indian Novel," *Journal of Indian Writing in English* (Jan. 1973).

"Macaulay's Vociferous Logic." *Indian and Foreign Review* 10.24 (1 Oct. 1973).

Secondary Sources

Books on Mulk Raj Anand

Berry, Margeret. *Mulk Raj Anand: The Man and the Novelist*. Amsterdam: Oriental Press, 1971.

Cowasjee, Saros. *So Many Freedoms. A Study of Major Fiction of M.R. Anand*. New Delhi: Oxford UP, 1977.

Fisher, Marlene. *The Wisdom of the Heart. A Study of M.R. Anand*. New Delhi: Sterling Publishers, 1985.

Gupta, G.S. Balarama. *Mulk Raj Anand, A Study of his Fiction in Human Perspective*. Bareilly: Prakash Book Depot, 1974.

Lindsay, Jack. *The Elephant and the Lotus. A Study of the Novels of Mulk Raj Anand*. Bombay: Kutub-Popular, 1965.

Murthi, K.V.S. *The Sword and the Sickle—A Study of M.R. Anand's Novels*. *Mysore*: Geeta Book House, 1983.

Naik, M.K. *Mulk Raj Anand*. New Delhi: Arnold-Heinemann, 1973.

Niven, Alastair. *Yoke of Pity*. New Delhi: Arnold-Heinemann, 1978.

Paul, P.S. *The Novels of Mulk Raj Anand. A Thematic Study*. New Delhi: Sterling Publishers, 1983.

Rajan, P.K. *Studies in Mulk Raj Anand.* New Delhi: Abhinav Publications, 1986.

Riemenschneider, Dieter. *An Ideal of Man in Anand's Novels.* Bombay: Kutub Popular, 1967.

Sinha, K.N. *Mulk Raj Anand.* New York: Twayne Publishers, 1972.

Sharma, K.D. (ed.). *Perspectives on Mulk Raj Anand.* Ghaziabad: Vimal Prakashan, 1984.

Bhatnagar M.K. and Rajeshwar Mittapalli, eds. *The Novels of Mulk Raj Anand.* New Delhi: Atlantic Publishers, 2000.

Individual Chapters in Books

Amur, G.S. et al. *Essays on Comparative Literature and Linguistics.* New Delhi: Sterling Pub., 1984.

____. *Indian Reading in Commonwealth Literature.* New Delhi: Sterling, 1984.

Bald, S.R. "Novelists and Political Consciousness." *Literary Expression of Indian Nationalism 1917-1947,* 1982.

Baker, Denys Val, ed. *Writers Today.* London: Sidgwick & Jackson, 1948.

Cowasjee, Saros. *Author to Critics. The Letters of M.R. Anand to Saros Cowasjee.* Calcutta: Writers Workshop, 1973.

Deirett, M.E. *The Modern Indian Novel in English. A Comparative Approach.* University Libre de Bruxelles, 1966.

Dhawan, R.K. *Explorations in Modern Indo-English Fiction.* New Delhi: Bahri, 1982.

Hemenway, Stephen. *The Novel of India* (I–II). Calcutta: Writers Workshop, 1975.

Harrex, S.C. *The Fire & The Offering. The English-Language Novel of India, 1935-1970.* Calcutta: Writers Workshop, 1977.

Iyengar, K.R. Srinivasa. *Indian Writing in English,* Bombay: Asia Publishing House: 1962.

Kachru, B.B. *The Indianization of English.* Delhi: Oxford UP, 1983.

Kalinnikova, Elena. *Indian English Literature: A Perspective.* Ghaziabad: Vimal Prakashan, 1982.

Mukherjee, Meenakshi. *The Twice Born Fiction.* New Delhi: Heinemann, 1971.

Melwani Murlidas. *Themes in Indo-Anglian Literature.* Bareilly: Prakash Book Depot, 1977.

Mc Cutchion, David. *Indian Writing in English.* Calcutta: Writers Workshop, 1973.

Mokashi-Punekar, S. *The Indo-Anglian Creed.* Dharwar: Prasaranga, Karnatak University, 1979.

Naik, M.K. et al., eds. *Critical Essays on Indian Writing in English.* Dharwar: Karnatak University, 1968.

Narasimhaiah, C.D. *The Writer's Gandhi.* Patiala: Punjabi University, 1967.

____. *The Swan and the Eagle.* Simla: Indian Institute of Advance Study, 1969.

Nicholson, Kai. *A Presentation of Social Problems in the Indo-Anglian and the Anglo-Indian Novel.* Bombay: Jaico Publishing House, 1972.

Prasad, H.M., ed. *Response: Recent Revaluations of Indian Fiction in English.* Bareilly: Prakash Book Depot, 1985.

____. *Studies in Indian Fiction in English.* Dharwad: Prasaranga, Karnatak University, 1983.

Sharma, K.K. *Indo-English Literature.* Ghaziabad: Vimal Prakashan, 1962.

Verghese, C.P. *Essays on Indian Writing in English.* New Delhi: N.V. Publications, 1975.

Walsh, William. *A Human Idiom: Literature and Humanity.* London: Chatto & Windus, 1964.

____. *A Manifold Voice.* London: Chatto & Windus, 1964.

____. *Commonwealth Literatures.* London: Oxford UP, 1973.

Williams, Haydn Moore. *Studies in Modern Fiction in English* (1). Calcutta: Writers Workshop, 1973.

Critical Articles, Reviews, Chapter in Books

Abidi, S.Z.H. *"Mulk Raj Anand's 'Coolie': A Critical Study."* Bareilly: Prakash Book Depot, 1976.

____. *Mulk Raj Anand's "Untouchable": A Critical Study.* Bareilly: Prakash Books Depot, 1976.

Asnani, Shyam M. "The Indian Princes: Their Portrayal in the Indo-English Novel." Commonwealth Quarterly 3.11 (June 1979).

____. "Form and Technique in Mulk Raj Anand's Novels." *Indian Scholar* 2.2 (July 1980).

____. "Socio-Political Concerns in the Novel of Dr. Mulk Raj Anand." *Triveni* (April-June 1976).

____. "The Theme of East-West Encounter in the Novels of Mulk Raj Anand." *Littcrit* 4.2 (Dec. 1978).

____. "Untouchability and Mulk Raj Anand's Untouchables." *The Banasthali Patrika* 6.16 (Jan. 1971).

Badal, R.K. *Indo-Anglian Literature: An Outline.* Bareilly: Prakash Book Depot, 1975.

Bhattacharya, Bhabani. *"Indo-Anglian." The Novel in Modern India.* Ed. Iqbal Bakhtiyar. Bombay: The P.E.N. All-India Centre, 1964.

Bose, Amalendu. "Indian Writing in English." *Indian Writing in English.* Ed. K.N. Sinha. Delhi: Heritage Publishers, 1973.

Bald, S.R. "Politics of a Revolutionary Elite: A Study of Mulk Raj Anand's Novels." *Modern Asia Studies* 8.4 (1974).

Brown, F.J. "Review of *The Big Heart.*" *Life and Letter To-day* 47.99 (Nov. 1945).

____. "Prophet of Revolution." *Bharat Jyoti* 15 Dec. 1946.

Bhattacharya, R.K. "*Two Leaves and a Bud:* Truth and Fiction." *Kakatiya Journal of English Studies* 2.1 (Spring 1977). ["Mulk Raj Anand Special Number," Department of English, Kakatiya University, Warangal].

Catter, D. "Probing Identities: *Untouchable, Things Fall Apart* and *This Earth, My Brother...*" *The Literary Criterion* 19.3 (1979).

Dutt, Prabhati Kumar. "Mulk Raj Anand in Relation to Tagore, Prem Chand and Sarat Chatterji." *Contemporary Indian Literature.* 5.11-12 (Dec. 1965): 19-20.

Gowda, Anniah H.H. "Mulk Raj Anand." *Literary Half-Yearly* 4 (July 1965): 51-60.

Gupta, G.S. Balarama. "The Humanism of Mulk Raj Anand." *Contemporary Indian Literature.* Aug. 1967.

_____. "*Coolie*—A Prose Epic of Modern India." *Karnatak University Journal* 12 (1968).

_____. "Anand's *Big Heart*: A Study." *The Banasthali Patrika.* 5.13 (July 1969).

_____. "Woman in Anand's Shorter Fiction." *Karnatak University Journal* 13 (1969).

_____. "Anand's *Old Woman and the Cow* in Human Perspective." *Karnatak University Journal* 14 (1970).

Kurmanadham, K. "Women Characters in Dr. Anand's Novels." *Contemporary Indian Literature* 6 (June-July 1966).

_____. "The Novels of Dr. Mulk Raj Anand." *Triveni* (Oct. 1967).

Pant, M.C. "Mulk Raj Anand the Man." *Contemporary Indian Literature* 5.11-12 (Nov.-Dec. 1965).

Ratan, Jai. "Meeting with Mulk Raj Anand." *Writers Workshop Miscellany* 8 (Sept-Oct. 1961).

Zaheer, Sajjad. "Mulk Raj Anand." *Contemporary Indian Literature* 5.11-12 (Nov.-Dec. 1965).

3

Raja Rao

RAGINI RAMACHANDRA

"The longest journey begins with a single step," said Lao Tse, the Chinese philosopher and the entire corpus of India's most distinguished novelist Raja Rao seems to be a poetic testament of this truth. His metaphysical odyssey which encompasses all three worlds in his later novels (thanks to his penchant for an exploration of the Self) nevertheless, displays disarmingly simple and innocuous beginnings reflected in the very choice of themes in his earlier works. The locale itself that the young artist chooses for his stories gives them a "local habitation and a name." It is not France or England that provides the backdrop but a humble village with its mud-walled houses and thatched roofs; these earlier writings smell in fact of the soil and of regional flavours. It may be the dusty roads of Malakad or the sparkling waters of the Hemavathy or the overhanging Harihara hills. What with the young author's unerring eye for detail, the familiar landmarks of a village like the elephant-headed rock; the neem-tree by the pipal; the pipal platform; the temple; the valleys and gardens of mango and coconut, rice and sugar-cane, apart from a myriad other things, spring to life at once.

Having left India for France at the early age of 19 to pursue his studies in history and philosophy in Sorbonne University it is significant that Raja Rao should have still felt an inner compulsion to write about the Indian scene. The result of such a creative effort is his first Collection of Short Stories, *The Cow of the Barricades and Other Stories* (1947). Most of the pieces included here figure in his subsequent Collection as well, *The Policeman and the Rose* (1978).[1] Such for instance are "Javni," "Akkayya," "The Little Gram Shop," "The True Story of Kanakapala," "In Khandesh" and "Companions," not to speak of the title story itself of the earlier volume, "The Cow of the Barricades."

It is understandable that *social* concerns and preoccupations should be central to Raja Rao's writing during this phase of his career when he is just settling down to his vocation. Hence does one encounter stories like "Javni," "Akkayya" and "The Little Gram Shop" where the young artist tries to grapple with mundane life and all its "stony hardships." "The Little Gram Shop" itself becomes a sort of metaphor for "the little world of man" where ignorant man plays his role ignominiously and life's sordidness has a full play. The author delves into the dark recesses of this world to depict human greed and brutality not occasioned so much by *want* as by *ignorance* (*avidya-kama-karma*). Pettiness and cruelty defile life's sanctity and it is evident that some of the characters in these three stories are hardly convinced of the "holiness of the heart's affections." The resultant callousness and coarsening of life are as much the focus of attention as poverty and misery. "The Little Gram Shop" captures the full pathos arising out of such a predicament.

Though still "an apprentice to his craft"[2] the "promise of a master is manifest everywhere" (3) as C.D. Narasimhaiah incisively observes in his monograph on Raja Rao, manifest in the handling of plot, character, situation, language and sensibility. Characterization is indeed Raja Rao's forte here evident in the way each one of his major characters is vividly etched in our minds. Irony here is dark and sombre and humour is present only occasionally.

As for language and style one can catch glimpses of the later Raja Rao so early as in this story. Here are the beginnings of a master who is committed to evolving an idiom of his own that was soon destined to develop into what is today known as Indian English. Expressions like "corner-house," "red-man," "village-kid," "hell-moving cries," "a mouthful of curses"; swear-words like "you witch, you donkey's kid, you bloody [...]"; exclamations like "Ayyo... ayyo" or "Ha... Haa..." "He! he"! even the gurgling sound of the hookah as in "gud... gud"; songs, prayers, superstitions, pictures of gods in the kitchen—all testify to Raja Rao's brand of creative writing. It is trite to add how the native idiom is employed here to convey a sensibility that is distinctly Indian.

Raja Rao's powers of description are best sampled in his graphic presentation of the "pomp and generosity" (74) of Chota's marriage procession through sensuous details featuring the garlanded bridegroom with a "gold-laced turban, a filigree-worked achkan," (74) a "bridal Rolls-Royce car" (74) amidst illumination and fireworks, followed by hundreds and hundreds of people which brought tears to Beti's eyes not to mention Beti herself in her "300 Re Benares sari" (74) or Motilal in a "Calcutta dhoti" (74).

This anticipates the later Raja Rao of *The Serpent and the Rope* whose splendid enactment of Saroja's wedding takes us back to the immemorial past of India and helps us re-discover the value of tradition.

That Raja Rao's concerns at this stage are more social than spiritual in nature are evidenced by yet another story belonging to this phase, namely, "Akkayya," meaning "elder sister," which is a poignant portrayal of a child-widow and her countless woes in an orthodox society plagued by outmoded rituals and social taboos. And when she died, "everybody looked annoyed and uneasy" (59). Her death was a "nuisance," and "none of them wanted to take the responsibility of performing Akkayya's obsequies" (60).

This story, concludes the narrator, was perhaps "her only funeral ceremony" (60). The final act of betrayal comes when after having received the news with "irritation" and "disgust," Akkayya's relations bathe, have their dinner and go to a cinema. A certain stench pervades the air and one feels nauseated not so much by the stink of disease as by the aberration in human nature.

However, the much anthologised story continues to be "Javni" and rightly so, avers C.D. Narasimhaiah, for Javni, the low-caste servant "finds her way to fiction in a central way" (4). Attention has justly been drawn to all the significant landmarks of village life evoked so faithfully even within the compass of a short story, like the pipal tree, the dusty roads, the rumbling carts, the cawing crows, the creaking door, sunbeams stealing through the tiles, sacks of rice in the byre, the calf nibbling wisps of hay if not throwing a "heapful of dung" splashing across the cobbled floor, etc, etc.

Very soon we see Javni herself face to face, a woman past 40, with strange, rapturous eyes, grey hair and slightly wrinkled skin, speaking peasant Kannada and drawling her vowels interminably while addressing her mistress or her brother Ramappa. But her "bare, broad forehead" (83) said everything—it communicated pain and widowhood. Notwithstanding a special bond she has established with her mistress, her place is the byre where she sits in the dark, "swallowing mouthfuls of rice that sounded like a cow chewing the cud" (88). This is something revolting to Ramappa but any argument with his sister on this score is futile, for it is her strong conviction that eating with a woman of low caste is "irreligious" and one's "affection" need not cloud one's judgment. All that a shocked Ramappa could say out of a sense of shame and guilt is: "Javni sat and ate. The mechanical mastication of the rice seemed to represent her life, her cycle of existence" (89).

Like Akkayya, Javni too is a victim of misfortune, her husband having died of snakebite and the women in her husband's household making her life "miserable." However, it is the character of Javni that is the high point of the story. If for the people in the town, "she is good like a cow" (86), for Ramappa "she is a sweet thing" (87), a "most wonderful soul" (96) and for Sita she is "her friend, her only friend" (96), in fact, "almost a mother" (87). So much so anyone who comes in contact with a heart like hers will "bloom into a god" (96), believes the narrator.

The tale ends with the family's departure from the village and the inevitable sobs and tears and farewells. But what saves the conclusion from slushy sentimentality is the admirable twist the author lends it in looking upon Javni, seated upon a rock with a huge pipal tree behind her and vast sky above her, as "so small, just a spot in space" (97). So imperceptibly does she merge with nature she presents an enigma to the baffled narrator who asks himself in humility; "who was she?" (97).

This sense of mystery pervades the title story "The Cow of the Barricades" and also a few others like "India—A Fable" and "The Policeman and the Rose" in the second volume of stories.

What unites these pieces is the author's predilection for the metaphysical. The tone, the language, the imagery, the symbolism all make their own demands on the reader who has to summon all his resources to pluck the heart of the mystery. The cow Gauri is at once a fact and a symbol. We see her standing, kneeling, ambling, nibbling, shaking her head and bending her legs if not drawing her tongue and walking like "a holy wife" (37). Her mysterious appearances and disappearances prompt the query; "Master, can you tell us who this cow may be?" (36). And the Master (whose identity is shrouded in mystery) initially responds light-heartedly saying she may be his "baton-armed mother-in-law" (36) if not the mother of one of them. Later adds more seriously that she is perhaps the "great mother's vehicle" (36); "a fervent soul who had sought the paths of this world to be born a sage in the next, for she was so compassionate and true" (37). The merchants said: "May be she's Lakshmi, the Goddess" (37). "Young and old fall at the feet of this "strange visitor" (37) with "a very human look" (41).

Since the story is replete with allusions to the Mahatma's men fighting in the country against the red-man's government it becomes evident before long that the cow is symbolic of the country in chains and the Mahatma is Gandhiji himself trying to surmount the "barricades." In the process Gauri falls to the Red-man's bullet, "a vehicle of god among lowly men" (41), but she lives in the hearts of people. Statues and images are made and worshipped. But the mystery persists: "where is she, Gauri?" (41) the people ask but believe only the Master knows where she is, for he says: "Gauri is waiting in the Middle Heavens to be born. She will be reborn when India sorrows again before she is free" (41).

"The Policeman and the Rose" also has a similar teasing quality about it what with its highly metaphorical language and complex symbolism. The simple and innocuous sentence at the start of the story: "All men are arrested the moment they are born" (113) might be the author's way of hinting at the great truth that all mankind is overpowered by destiny at the very start of its career. "There's a divinity that shapes our ends." Hence the dominance of the policeman who stands at the "cross-road" reckoning with life and death; past and present; time and timelessness. To be "discharged" when "the time came" is our "business." To realize this "Knowledge," the narrator "opened a shop of Hindu eyes" (119) and "gave eyes to many" (119). The profundity of these statements cannot be missed. The narrator's overmastering obsession with the idea that one is under *arrest,* one is "arrested immediately" (115) by the policeman and that one wants to be "free" leaves us in no doubt about his profound involvement with the *human condition.* Hence his allusions to sleeping, dreaming and wakeful states; to knower and the Known; to death of deaths and to the kingdom of Travancore where there are no "prisons" according to the Travancore code which is the "Truth," the "beautiful Truth" (126).

It need not be laboured how Raja Rao is attempting something most unconventional in this story—in the choice of both subject and symbolism. There are moments when the material turns abstruse and the reader has to grope. But if one has an intuitive understanding of the central principal that governs this story it is because its importance communicates itself even before it is understood through hints and guesses.

The short story "Nimka" is perhaps "the best of its kind by an Indian writer at least in English"[3] that can stand comparison with the work of the great European masters. Between this and the earlier stories lies a gap of more than two decades and one encounters a maturer Raja Rao who can operate on multiple planes of reality with consummate ease and artistry. The social, the intellectual and the philosophic elements are woven into one another to form a fine tapestry. Critics like C.D. Narasimhaiah have justly conferred praise upon its "unsuspected range of material" (133) that goes on expanding like "concentric circles" (133). This, the critic believes, was clearly beyond the reach of the author of "Javni" or for that matter even *Kanthapura* and belongs decisively to the phase of *The Serpent and the Rope* when Raja Rao had learnt to range through whole continents and cultures and more importantly to infuse into his writings a sensibility that is distinctly Indian.

Thus these two *Collections* not merely establish Rao as an important writer of Short Stories but also serve as companions to his future seminal writings, beginning with *Kanthapura* (1938),[4] his very first novel which made a sensation in the early 60's for not merely its authentic portrayal of village life but also its bold experimentation with language unlike anything the readers of English fiction had encountered before.

This is not to say that it won instant approval. In fact, it is one of the ironies of Indian English literature that despite its singular achievement in matters of language and style as well as in its remarkably faithful presentation of peasant life and sensibility it was neglected for well over two decades and when it caught the attention of the academics and intelligentsia at home its unconventional use of language raised the eyebrows of "purists" who frowned upon its glaring departure from what they called "chaste" English—in other words "standard British English." Conformity to the latter was the norm and this novel which did not represent either King's or Queen's English was an aberration. Consequent to its unorthodoxy it soon found itself in the eye of a storm and its many detractors came down heavily upon its "obscenity" as well. But thanks to the concerted and sustained efforts of discerning scholars and critics like C.D. Narasimhaiah, M.K. Naik and others to win attention to its merits, this "controversial" novel became less offensive and in course of time even those who had earlier ridiculed its style, syntax, diction and idiom grew more moderate in their criticism. The novel was now not so unpalatable after all! It is interesting that when Raja Rao was awarded the Sahitya Akademi Prize for his *Serpent and the Rope*, it was as the author of *Kanthapura* that he was referred to in the citation! It is superfluous to comment how this brand of Indian English has today become not merely acceptable but respectable, thus bringing the wheel to a full circle and fulfilling the author's prophetic words: "Time alone will justify it" (Foreword to *Kanthapura*).

The *Foreword* to the novel which makes manifest the author's intentions and objectives is itself a daring piece of writing. It is amazing that the young author, barely 26 should have had the courage to declare: "We cannot write like the English. We should not [...]. Our method of expression therefore has to be a dialect which will some day prove to be as distinctive and colourful as the Irish or the American" (Foreword). And perceptive readers of Raja Rao know that it is no empty rhetoric either, for this is precisely what he set out to do and what he has succeeded in achieving.

Turning his attention to style next, he realizes the need to infuse the tempo of Indian life into English expression. Hence this breathless tale, true to the tradition of Indian story telling, the sad tale of his village as a grandmother might have told a newcomer of an evening. Of course, the telling has not been easy, he admits, for "one has to convey in a language that is not one's own the spirit that is one's own" (*Foreword*). And, to repeat, *this* is just where the novel's unique success lies, in conveying the various shades and nuances of a certain thought movement without making them look "maltreated" in English, the language of our intellectual, if not emotional make-up.

Kanthapura is a novel of village life, a village that lies in the valleys of Himavathy, "curled up like a child on its mother's lap." The village like any other in India has a rich *sthala-purana*, a legendary history of its own that gives meaning to the life of the people. Goddess Kenchamma who came down from the heavens thanks to Sage Tripura's penances to kill a demon that was troubling them ages and ages ago not merely waged a battle and slayed the monster but also fortunately settled down to protect the village folk through famine and disease, death and despair. Which explains why the Kenchamma Hill is all red even today. Such is their implicit faith in the goddess that she becomes the centre of their lives. All life, in fact, revolves around Her-birth, marriage, death.

The village presents a complex caste structure with its Brahmin quarter, Pariah quarter, Weavers' quarter and a Sudra quarter. The village at once comes to life even in the early pages of the novel through intimate, first hand descriptions of the people and their houses. To cite a few notable examples: Post-master Suryanarayana with his "double-storeyed house" (4), Patwari Nanjundiah who had "even put glass-panes to the windows" (5), Patel Range Gowda "lean as an areca-nut tree" but a veritable "Tiger" (8) amongst the villagers and his "nine-beamed house" (8), pock-marked Sidda who owned a "*thothi* house" (7) with a big verandah, large roof and a granary and so on and so forth.

Raja Rao's powers of observation, description and characterization are seen at their best in the way he can invest a character with a distinct identity through a mere prefix to the name that sheds light on either the personality or the profession of the individual in question. In a small village in India people are identified either by their vocations or by their possessions and so the entire novel abounds in such tell-tale names that lend colour as well as authenticity to the narrative. At other times people are identified through their physical abnormalities if not their virtues. The degree of intimacy a character enjoys with others is convincingly brought out in expressions like "our Moorthy" or "our Sastri." Such is the novelist's fidelity to village lingo that he sometimes attempts a literal translation of words and phrases from Kannada, his own native language as in: "Tell us, Kenchamma, why do you seek to make our stomachs burn?" (2-3), where "stomachs burn" is a variation of the stereotyped "heart-burn"! On other occasions one might catch the very inflexion of the speaker's voice as in: "Take it Bhattare' only one cup more, just one" (31). What one must also note here is the little suffix attached to Bhatta's name, for Bhatta is the First Brahmin of the village and also a rich and influential Zamindar. So it won't do to address him merely by his name. Hence the honorific suffix, literally lifted out of the Kannada language which is indeed a stroke of genius. He does the same again when "Moorthy" becomes "Moorthappa." One might also note the coaxing and the cajoling that forms an inevitable part of the ritual of food-serving in an Indian household especially at a marriage or a festival. To make it even more authentic, the writer freely infuses words like *payasam, khir* and *pheni* into the English language, perhaps for the first time and preserves the rhythms of native Kannada.

If expressions like "Red-Man's Government" and "Kitchen queen" strike us with their originality, exclamations like "Rama-Rama"; "Siva-Siva"; "he-ho," "Ayyo...Ayyoo" invoke a sensibility that is distinctly South-Indian. Customs, rituals, social practices, proverbs, superstitions, all have their part to play in invoking rural atmosphere with uncanny precision. One solitary example might be cited to illustrate the point: "When a lizard clucked we said, 'Krishna, Krishna!' And with dawn came sleep" (209).

Such is Rao's understanding of village life and such his linguistic competence to render the same even in English that nothing looks "alien." A simple phrase like "lay leaves" for dinner, as against "set the table" proper to a western set-up should substantiate the claim. Another important ingredient of style that Rao uses to capture the tempo of Indian life is the repeated use of the conjunction "and" which makes the narration truly "interminable." Even complicated relationships that are an integral part of Indian family life get adequately expressed as in: "He is my wife's elder brother's wife's brother-in-law" (39).

The description of the *Harikatha* itself by Jayaramachar is a masterpiece of enactment, wherein a traditional mode of story-telling is ingeniously adopted to introduce a contemporary theme, namely the birth of Gandhi so as to liberate his country from the invaders, which brings us to the crux of the novel, that is the Freedom Movement and the impact of Gandhi on the masses notwithstanding strong opposition from some quarters initially. The struggle for Freedom and the advent of Gandhi into this obscure, almost anonymous village and the countless touching sacrifices these humble folk make forms a substantial part of the novel, without, it is significant to note, letting the narrative become overtly *political*, for nationalism is interwoven with yet another strand, namely religion, which in a sense is the warp and woof of this book.

The seamy side of the struggle is not lost sight of either. Life on the Skeffington Coffee Estate, exploitation of the coolies, atrocities on women and police brutalities are all rendered in excruciating detail. The entire village is turned upside down and in the end it is pathetic that there should be "neither man nor mosquito" (259) in Kanthapura. Yet such is the novelist's affirmation of life that he still lets his narrator admit magnanimously knowing that nothing can be the same:

> there is something that has entered our hearts, an abundance like the Himavathy on Gauri's night, when lights come floating down. (256)

This is the poignant tale that we hear from one who knows his village from the inside.

If *Kanthapura* is about a back-of-beyond village, *The Serpent and the Rope* (1960)[5] with its spiritual concerns and metaphysical preoccupations marks a leap into the infinite. Here is a truly *Indian* novel, which gives us a breath of the *real* India that seems to have eluded so many other writers either before or after Raja Rao. In the words of C.D. Narasimhaiah, here is a novel, which makes India *real* not only to Europeans but to Indians as well.[6] And yet its distinction lies in incorporating at the same time an *international* perspective prompting the same critic to call it a "truly international novel"[7] and Edwin Thumboo to describe it is as a "universal"[8] work.

It is significant that nearly a quarter of a century should separate *The Serpent and the Rope* from *Kanthapura.* It is possible that Raja Rao, the *sadhaka,* the serious and committed writer that he is chose to spend this long period of "silence" in meditation and self-discovery. The protagonist Ramaswamy's own quest for the Absolute and his understanding of Illusion and Reality makes this metaphysical novel largely autobiographical.

The very title of the novel (rather unusual for a fictional work) takes us back to Sankara who used the metaphor of the "serpent" and the "rope" to suggest *sathya* and *mithya,* substance and shadow and in the process highlight the role of the *Guru,* the spiritual teacher in initiating the ignorant into ways of wisdom and helping them cross the flux of life.

The novel is about the "sad and uneven chronicle" of its hero for whom "life is a pilgrimage" (28) and he himself "a holy vagabond" (11). This highly sensitive and introspective young man with a reflective cast of mind engages himself in a voyage of self-discovery and we follow him through the twists and turns of his spiritual quest. The opening page of the novel itself offers a poignant portrayal of man's orphaned existence on earth reflected in the hero's predicament: "I was born an orphan, and have remained one" (7).

What begins as *personal* gathers metaphysical overtones as the novel proceeds. Hence, the theme of homelessness finds a tragic culmination in Ramaswamy's agonized outburst: "There is nobody to go to now: no home, no temple, no city, no climate, no age" (407).

In this moment of crisis—driven to it, the readers are well aware, by his failed marriage—it is not god that he needs, but a guru whom he implores, even in the middle of a dreadful winter night, as the trees of Luxembourg are crying, to come, give him his touch and vouchsafe to him "the vision of Truth" (408). This is the young man who on an earlier occasion had movingly ruminated on a possible release from it all: "There must be a way out Lord; a way out of this circle of life" (236).

Notwithstanding his intellectual attainments and grounding in Vedanta, Rama can still feel the word *dukkha* with almost his entrails dropping out into his hands. For him "*dukkha* is the very tragedy of creation, the sorrow of the sorrow that sorrow is" (82) whereas for Madeleine, his French wife, it is "mere sorrow" and this, ironically from one who turned increasingly to Buddhism, but then it was the "intellectual brilliance" of Buddhism that attracted her to it. Despite these differences Rama "accepts" Madeleine thanks to his wise recognition that difference is "self-created." He even kneels down before her gods in the faith that to wed a woman is to wed her gods (86) and participates in all her superstitions though she herself does not do in his. The marriage breaks down as most others in the novel do except perhaps the symbolic ritual marriage between Rama and Savithri, because

The real marriage is like 00, not like 010.

When the ego is dead is marriage true. (296)

One realizes that marriage is central to this novel but no marriage has been ideal. Hence the novelist's invocation of the Upanishadic ideal inherent in the truth Yajnyavalkya imparts to Maithreyi: verily the wife is dear not for the wife's sake but for the Self's sake (26). Hence the collapse of all marriages and hence the novelist's recourse to myths, legends, folklore to point to the illusoriness of human relationships anchored as they are in ego. The moving tale of Radha and Krishna in particular where Radha foolishly wants to "possess" Krishna is an eloquent commentary on the unreality of the world. Raja Rao summons this mythic past of India to uphold its validity for the present when man is trapped in a prison of his own making.

So the whole novel is an enactment of the idea that "India is not a country like France [...] or like England" (380) but "an idea, a metaphysic" (380) that Rama carries in his pocket wheresoever he goes. That India represents an idea, an idea of the Absolute is the whole point of the story. It is therefore understandable that Ramaswamy should be interested in seeing this India, "the India of my inner being" (248) "the India of Brahma and Prajapathi; of Varuna, Mithra [...] of Harischandra and Yajnyavalkya" (248). It is like seeing his *Antara Ganga,* inner Benares, wheresoever he may be. Hence he is *not* a stranger anywhere. "Man must wed to belong to this earth," he says and belong he does whether it is France or England as borne out by his splendid evocation of London, Cambridge, Paris and South of France not to speak of his many poetic utterances suggestive of a rare degree of emotional involvement.

If the foregoing passages speak eloquently of Ramaswamy's sense of inclusiveness and catholicity of outlook that makes him wonderfully receptive to outside influences, his response to his own Benares is no less revealing. The entire section devoted to this "eternal," "surrealist" city is evocative, highly surcharged with emotion as it is. One can feel Mother Ganga flowing in one's veins as her presence is invoked through the resonance and majesty of Sanskrit language. Such the authenticity of narration that one can almost visualize Tulsidas writing the *Ramayana* "just there" (13) next to Rewa Palace or farther down *see* the Buddha himself walking down the steps to wash his alms bowl if not imagine the Upanishadic Sages discussing "on these very banks" (25) some four or five or six thousand years ago, "the roots of human understanding" (25-26). The ethos of this timeless, holy city is captured admirably through both the profound and the profane.

No assessment of the novel would be complete without a reference to the theme of East-West encounter or its celebration of the Feminine Principle. While there are scores of novels in Indian English Fiction treating East-West encounter *The Serpent and the Rope* is unsurpassed in its mature handling of this complex issue inducing C.D. Narasimhaiah to comment that *The Serpent and the Rope* begins where E.M. Forster's *A Passage to India* ends,[9] for Forster lacked the necessary credentials to probe deeper. It required Raja Rao's kind of vision and equipment to treat the theme adequately and satisfactorily. The answer to this problem as to many others lies in a transcendence of ego rather than any other. Hence the inevitable conclusion of the novel with the hero's longing for Travancore where with the help of his Lord, his Master, he will reach a point from where there is no returning.

It is against this background that the celebration of the Feminine Principle acquires an additional significance. Savithri is both a fact and a symbol, symbol of Knowledge that her namesake carries in the *Vedas* and in Sri Aurobindo. Hence the presence of several passages given to the glorification of Savithri in particular and Woman in general.

All this is not to mean that the novel deals with material that is exclusively abstruse. Though there are occasions when it does tend to be overtly discursive giving the impression of being rather unassimilated into the texture of the novel, the work does demonstrate how Raja Rao *has* a deep understanding of the social and he can revel in descriptions that are concrete and sensuous when he wants to. Saroja's wedding in the novel for instance is a masterpiece of enactment bringing into play several aspects of Indian life simultaneously.

Thus is it rightly observed that here is a novel of "social transactions" as well as "celestial concerns" both transmuted into an art form that would earn it exalted praise from a discerning scholar and critic like C.D. Narasimhaiah who calls it a "fictional marvel."[10]

The Cat and Shakespeare (1971)[11] is in many ways a logical sequel to *The Serpent and the Rope* in that while the former ends with the hero's longing to go to Travancore to seek the vision of Truth, the latter begins with the narrator-hero already there receiving lessons of wisdom from his friend and neighbour Govindan Nair, in a sense, the real hero of the novel, besides continuing the novelist's life-long preoccupation with the Feminine Principle. Raja Rao himself calls this "tale of modern India" a "metaphysical comedy." While the intriguing title has invited endless interpretations, the highly complex symbolism of the novel has left many exasperated! But thanks to pioneering efforts of perceptive critics this highly compact but baffling work with its exceptionally original use of language, style, imagery and symbolism has yielded many of its secrets rendering its central core more intelligible today.

The novel opens with an allusion to house building, which, the discriminating reader perceives before long, acquires a symbolic meaning. Ramakrishna Pai's overmastering desire to build "a house of three stories" (21) reflected in his repeated and persistent references to it scattered all over this slender volume assumes the form of an obsession. A remark like: "A house of three stories these days is a safe investment" (22) might at first appear quite a commonplace, even banal to the casual, unsuspecting reader, but its repeated use leaves one in no doubt that this disarmingly simple and innocuous statement embodies a profound, metaphysical concept, in the same way as the ration card with its three colours, green, red and blue (note the deliberate choice of colours) corresponds to the three *gunas* of Hindu philosophy, *tamas, rajas* and *satva*. It is the third state that poses the greatest challenge. Hence the narrator's supreme urge to build the "third story."

Similarly if the ration shop represents the world, the Ration Office with the "big boss" stands for God's governance of the world. Hence the validity of: "can you imagine a state without a government?" (63). Obviously the ration shop is Raja Rao's equivalent for Shakespeare's "stage." It might be seen how such an interpretation can help in explicating the underlying symbolism of a statement like: "Shakespeare knew every mystery of the ration shop" (83). Shakespeare's pervasive presence in the title not to speak of several echoes from his plays must suggest how he is integrated into the text and through it into the Indian psyche itself. For Raja Rao Life is *leela* (play). Indeed "where play begins, reality begins" (98). His men and women like Shakespeare's must work out their *karma* though in different ways governed as they are by a different value system. If the western critic by and large contends with "evil," we in India do so with "illusion" (*Maya*) and hence the symbolism of the "wall" in the novel suggesting the barrier that hinders man's perception of Reality. Similarly one can read meaning into other things associated with the ration shop like "scales" and "accounts." It is amazing how even simple objects of daily life are put to an unsuspected use and how even great truths are expressed through a language that is at once playful, casual, witty and ironic. Indeed, the talking voice of the novelist is one of the novel's greatest achievements. If the novel has an edge over even *The Serpent and the Rope* it is largely because of the concrete equivalent the author has succeeded in finding for his most abstract ideas that now get transmuted into a felt experience.

One of the dominant motifs of the novel is the glorification of the Feminine Principle. That the Cat should represent this Mother Principle is astounding, for it redounds to Raja Rao's credit that he should have had the courage to make what is popularly believed to be an "unclean" and "unholy" animal a symbol. The cat alone knows. It alone loves. It carries the kitten by the scruff of its neck and carries it to the loft. That is why Govindan Nair is always talking of the mother cat and that is why he is "so carefree" (74). "Have you ever seen a kitten fall"? (68) he asks in his wisdom. But deeply distressed over human predicament which he sums up with uncanny precision and insight as in "A kitten sans cat, that is the question" (82) he urges man to "Learn the way of the kitten. Then you're saved. Allow the mother cat, sir, to carry you" (74).

Of course for the brahmin Bhoothalinga Iyer who can no more understand truth than the buffalo can see a straight line (42) the cat is a "pariah animal" (74). Which god ever rode a cat, he asks. So it was "improper," "unholy" (75). Only rats exist for him, not cats. But "destiny chooses the exact fact for your redemption" (71). And so the cat comes to the ration shop like a "god" (88). All the office is "one noumenal silence" (88). It proves to be an agent of death for Bhoothalinga Iyer but also an agent of liberation, for even as he dies he is released from bondage. That is the reason why Nair makes John "kneel" before the Mother Cat. He who had earlier insulted it by stuffing it into a rat's cage in his ignorance now surrenders to the Absolute in reverence.

It is interesting that it should be the non-brahmin Govindan Nair who recovers such spiritual truths (the *Astavakra Samhita* was his constant companion) and in fact even explain Brahman to the brahmin. He also knew more Sanskrit than the latter. Thanks to his "big heart" (36), he can be a "half-brother" (36) to mankind. His many acts of compassion should justify the claim. A superb portrayal of his character with his eccentricities as well as endearing qualities forms one of the fascinating aspects of this novel, as we follow him through his "fearful twists and trysts and imponderables, to some majesty" (14). Lastly just one or two examples to suggest how Raja Rao manipulates language to achieve the intended effect: Saroja is "busy inspecting the rope-making" (31), meaning she is lost in a world of illusion. "I go and come" (36) is essentially Indian in sentiment and sensibility. "How can you say with what is not what is?" (89) captures the chasm between the real and the unreal, as does this line: "you do not see the cat, you see the cage" (73). A simple, banal statement like, "In fact he himself is—running" (10) is the novelist's ingenious way of capturing, even while expressing the obvious, a state of *being*, when the agent and the action are *One*! With what little effort can all duality be resolved in the hands of a master! Brief, epigrammatic sentences, short and direct questions, axiomatic sayings, philosophic reflections, adaptations of Shakespearian English if not that of Goldsmith—all have their part to play in enhancing the novel's appeal.

As for its profound vision of life, one can't do better than quote C.D. Narasimhaiah who thinks that it has a "validity not only for the contemporary Indian situation, but for our entire fragmentary civilization."[12]

The next novel *Comrade Kirillov* (1976)[13] is not one of Raja Rao's much discussed works, yet merits greater attention than it has done so far. Not merely is it slender in size but imbued with philosophy and metaphysics like its predecessor *The Cat*. In fact, it is even described as a "spiritual autobiography."[14] Writing on the novel A.N. Gupta calls it a "classic" which will assure its author a permanent place in Indian Writing in English even if he does not write anything more. Though he fears that its intellectual tone may not ensure it a wide audience he believes it certainly deserves "more serious recognition" (133). For that matter he even suggests the subtitle of "a metaphysical novel" (131) to this unusual work about a communist hero, a South Indian brahmin, Padmanabha Iyer introduced to us as Kirillov. Like other novels before, this one also is a first-person narrative, with the narrator telling us how he first met his Communism in Kirillov, who sets his foot first on American, later on English soil, learns German to read Marx and Engels; French to read Fourier and Saint Simon and slowly "the holy Russian tongue" (14) to absorb Lenin. After this initial introduction it is the novelist's insights into his character that in turn bring to the fore many complex issues, that absorb the reader's attention. Kirillov swears by Communism and proudly declares that Logic is his religion and Communism his motherland. His fierce loyalty to this political ideal finds expression in unequivocal language when he asserts that the only God he knows is the common man; the only worship the Party meeting and the only morality a classless society. He is confident that this revolution which has already made a heroic beginning in China will come to India also. Truth for him is achieved in the communist world and "he who ignores it, ignores a metaphysical certainty" (44), for "Communism had a metaphysic" (48). What with "new humanism," he is optimistic of finding a panacea for the hungry and houseless millions of the country and with this hope he waits for the "beatific vision of Indian Liberty" (38), he a thirsty soul, pines for a "vision of the messiah" (9) who would make it a reality. Interestingly he himself has a great part to play in winning attention and respect for the Indian struggle, "little by little Kirillov became an authority on India's place in the war effort" (62) and his manuscript on Indian struggle, bought by a progressive publisher is described as "a great document for international understanding" (62).

Yet there is more to his character than meets the eye, "a strange mixture" of patriot and iconoclast that he is. With this paradoxical element built into his nature the reader encounters a man of idiosyncrasies, to whose intellect anything that is Indian, Hindu, to be more precise, is anathema! Harshly critical of theosophy and metaphysics, God and Heaven, Indian politics and the Mahatma, he calls "all this God-God business" (83) "rank humbug" (83) which the narrator calls "Communist perversity" and his wife Irene "Marxist baggage" (101). But Kirillov's own vehement protest is only a facade, for deep down he is intensely Indian and speaks of India "as though he were talking of a venerable old lady in a fairy tale who had nothing but goodness in her heart" (58). In fact, "his Indianhood would break through every communist chain" (91) or "Occidental veneer" (113) as Irene would put it in her Diary whenever anyone spoke against Gandhi or the Congress. Though he himself was "virulent" in his attack on Gandhi he would not let anyone say a word against him. Irene knew that at heart Gandhi was his God and she once saw even a tear, "one long tear" (101) when he spoke of Gandhi. She knew too that she would become his enemy if India was "not described as all virtue" (102). He might ridicule "metaphysical yearnings and God-ward beckonings" (40) but would himself close his eyes and go into "profound meditation" at times and Irene records how in his own day he had even studied the *Mantra-Sastra*, that is the science of the holy-word-of the creative syllable, the four stages of the word principle and there were times when the whole afternoon he spent copying texts on the *sphota* for the benefit of Irene who would wonder if "a European husband would ever have thought of such gifts" (95).

Such is the story of this "Sadhu of Communism" (72) presented engrossingly by the novelist. A long silence yet again and then emerges what many consider to be his *magnum opus, The Chessmaster and His Moves* (1988)[15] with its theme of zero vs. infinity; horizontal vs. vertical; the personal vs. the impersonal; the dualistic vs. the monistic and its insistence on complete dissolution of all contradictions. In its sheer sweep, breadth, range of concerns and preoccupation with the Feminine Principle, it is an extension of *The Serpent and the Rope*, and even more ambitious in scope.

The question of man's orphaned existence on earth is central to this novel as well what with the protagonist having lost his mother and the whole world being reduced to "nothingness" as it were. Sivarama Sastri not merely feels "alone" but is like "someone lost in the ruins of a labyrinth" (47). Dogged by a sense of "non-belonging" (47) he loses "sight of things" (6). He who had felt a "certain reality" (47) when his mother was alive suddenly realizes that "something bewildering" (6) was happening to the "cosmos" as well. "The earth and sky were no more immediate" (6). Hence the quest for the Mother Principle that forms the crux of the novel. The whole work might be seen as an act of salutation to this Principle, accounting for glowing references to Woman scattered all over the novel.

It should not come as a surprise therefore if Sivarama should affirm: "Without woman, there is no kingdom, no world" (83). She is "the total kingdom" (338). In a sense it is the women characters of the novel who not only give "bone and blood" to Sivarama's abstractions but also provide for a "sense of the real." "Magic is woman" (158), "woman is magic" (159) seems to sum up in a nutshell Raja Rao's philosophy of life.

Sivarama Sastri is seen predominantly in relation to four major women characters, namely Suzanne, Mireille, Jaya and his sister Uma. It is mainly through his dealings with them that his personality unfolds itself before the reader. While Suzanne recalls to the reader's mind Madeleine of *The Serpent and the Rope*, Jaya is a replica of Savithri and Uma of Saroja. Like Ramaswamy himself Sivarama also goes to France on a French Government scholarship to pursue his research where he falls in love with a young French woman he meets. He subsequent relationships with Mireille and Jaya on different planes should justify the observation that these two novels have much in common with each other. The Feminine Principle finds its supreme expression in Jaya as in Savithri of the earlier novel. The superlative language that Raja Rao uses to describe Jaya leaves us in no doubt that the character *is* idealized as Savithri also *was* before. More than half the novel is devoted to her. But Sivarama is not destined to make his life with any of them as Jaya and Mireille are married women and Suzanne to whom he is almost betrothed drifts away from him and so Sivarama is rendered "homeless."

If the character of Uma is pervasive and the brother-sister relationship is idealized it is in keeping with Raja Rao's total design—to establish the centrality of Woman, whether as wife, lover, beloved, mother, daughter or sister. She has time and again demonstrated in her various roles how powerfully she can impinge upon the novelist's consciousness.

It is significant that Sivarama who asks himself at the beginning of the novel: "we are all born outsiders, and where find a home, lord where?" (242) should comment towards the end, resting his head on Uma's bosom, "I was home, was I?" (708). Critics might of course point to an element of scepticism in the question tag "was I?" But it would perhaps be more appropriate to interpret the interrogation as the novelist's attempt to keep the question open, avoiding giving the impression of having arrived at a destination, for the quest of the Mother Principle is an endless, unceasing, on going process.

In bare outline as well as the hero's intellectual and spiritual pursuits the novel's affinity with *The Serpent and the Rope* is indeed striking. Since there is an overlapping of themes it is sometimes questioned in critical circles whether *The Chessmaster* can be viewed as an advance over *The Serpent*. The novel might also have attracted criticism for its formlessness, lack of plot, structure, action and concreteness no less than its obtrusive metaphysical musings but then it has also earned high praise from writers like R. Parthasarathy and Edwin Thumboo. While the former describes *The Chessmaster* as "the most authentic and eloquent account of 'spiritual fermentation' (Arthur Koestler's phrase) in modern fiction,"[16] the latter believes this "truly universal"[17] work goes beyond *The Serpent and the Rope* and offers "the broadest, deepest internationalism we have in fiction."[18] If despite its cosmic sweep and illuminating vision of life questions are still asked about its successful handling of all this material in artistic terms, it must be confessed that the work needs to be re-read and re-valued which might bring its own rewards in the end. Not for nothing did our ancient rhetoricians emphasize the value of *akhandacharvana* (infinite chewing).

Rao's subsequent work, *On the Ganga Ghat* (1989)[19] happens to be a Collection of short stories which interestingly are not assigned separate titles but are simply numbered as though to signify the eternal flow of Life like that of Mother Ganga herself, for characters, events, situations follow in quick succession like the unnameable waves of the ocean lending support to the novelist's observations of life as "procession" caravan, "oboe song," etc, etc.

In a brief Prefatory Note to the book, Raja Rao himself remarks that "these stories are so structured that the whole book should be read as one single novel." If that *is* made possible it is because of the Ganga herself who flows through the pages of the novel as it were, forming its chief life-line which gives these different stories not merely a continuity but unity as well. Yet the first and the last pieces cannot be categorized as "stories," for truly speaking they are more in the nature of reflections or meditations on cause and effect, action and reaction and life's many incomprehensible mysteries that induce the author to ask in awe and wonder some fundamental questions like:

Was Benares a city or a Sanskritic statement? (16)

Or

Who made this rope [...]
What destiny brought the rope and the string together [...]. (18)

Such philosophical musings notwithstanding, one encounters on the whole an admirable blending of the human and the philosophical, which saves the general tone of the work from deteriorating into the didactic. That the author should present life's "multiple riches" (91) in less than a hundred—odd pages should serve as a tribute to the artist in Raja Rao. His sensuous descriptions of the everyday things of life and concrete particularities in memorable, native idiom should silence even his bitterest critics who accuse him of revelling in the abstract at the cost of palpable, tangible life. Indeed, one is treated as much to "celestial visions" (56) as to the pulsating rhythms of ordinary life. At one level all Benares might look like a city "seen in a dream" (110) but at another even its chill can be made chillingly real as in: "Benares chill is like a carpenter's winch, it spins on itself, and pierces straight to the white of bone" (95).

Raja Rao the wordsmith can let the reader experience the magic of words at such moments when he describes the world moving "on its hinges, circular and clear" (43) or the earth becoming a "turning top" (15) on Shiva's palm, or when silence "sparkles" and "whirls"; sound "flies" when one sings and loveliness "dances." Truly this book which catches the various nuances of multiple languages, shapes and colours of the pilgrims, "from the guttural Tamil speakers to the nasal Bengalis" (12) provides the necessary human touch. Even while some of his characters are spiritually inclined, the others are intensely human thus striking a fine balance between the two worlds.

It doesn't take long for the reader to realize that the real protagonist of this novel is Benares. All is Benares (93), "Happiness is on the Ganga Ghat" (83), "Once you come to Benares how can you ever leave it?" (52). Statements such as these reinforce the hypnotic appeal the holy city has for everyone who figures in the story, be he rich or poor, high or low, prince or pauper, sick or healthy, man or woman, bird or beast. Judging by the way they are all drawn irresistibly to this "most sacred city" to work out their salvation it is apparent that Benares in Raja Rao's hands becomes a symbol, a metaphor for transcendence as Byzantium is to Yeats. His men and women and their ancestors have come to this Benares "life after life" (12) and established "a pilgrim link between man and man" (12). Indeed, the whole novel is an artistic enactment of the truth, "Home is Ganga Ghat" (83). This is the nucleus around which all life revolves and this is the final resting place on earth for all those souls who come aspiring to have "intimations of immortality." "All ends at the Ganga Ghat" (126).

The novelist's powers of observation, gifts for characterization, innovative use of language, imaginative use of myths, faith in the Feminine Principle, all this, surpassed only by his luminous insights, place the book in the mainstream of his works. However, the most notable feature of this novel is his treatment of the sacred river itself right from the first chapter when we see her "turning, bending in her legendary crescent form" (16) to the final chapter when we see her assume the stature of *Jnana-ganga*. When knowledge, as Ganga, flows, "death is dissolved into truth" (127). She is *nija bodha rupa,* "the form of consciousness pure" (123). With the consciousness that the "holiest of all holy places of pilgrimage, the Manikarnika" (123) is within oneself the novel comes to an end. Thus the mighty city of Shiva and the primeval river Ganga are both an aid to man's perception of the highest Reality and it is characteristic of Raja Rao that transcendence should be achieved *through* and *not* outside of, the concrete, material plane of reality, in *artistic* terms.

The whole book is a hymn to the river goddess as it were, in modern idiom, which however like the Sanskrit hymns of earlier times, embodies within its each syllable a deep adoration of the Mother, the Mother of Compassion.

Raja Rao's search for truth, which began several decades ago, continues in *The Meaning of India* (1996)[20] as well, his non-fictional work where the accent is on "abolition of contradiction, of duality" (*Introduction*) which for him constitutes the "meaning of India" (*Introduction*). In this brief but lucid introduction to the work he expresses his love of playing with ideas which is comparable to playing a game of chess. The mood here is indeed playful, language buoyant and the tone seemingly light-hearted. So much so one *does* get the feeling that the great writer is playing a fascinating game with concepts knowing *he* is the game. His invitation to the reader too to join him is a fitting finale to a *Foreword*, which offers all the "delight" (*rasa*), of the "game!"

This Collection of 17 essays spanning two sections (1) "The Meaning of India" and (2) "The Meaning—in Meaning" initially explores in particular "the geographyless homeland" that India is which Rao calls "Perspective" (*darsana*). Consequently "It is not a country (*desa*), nor a climate but a mood (*rasa*) in the play of the Absolute" for "truth has no geography" (17). Significantly does one find a juxtaposition of this timeless, eternal India with the foreign observers' vision of the "splendour that is India" (16) to arrive at the truth that in either case "this light and splendour has been the celebration and the history of India" (15).

To sum up, the book with its allusions, characteristic of Rao, to the Vedas, the Upanishads, the philosophy of Buddha and Nagarjuna, the teachings of Sankara, the writings of Bhartrhari, the poetry of Mallarme and Valery promises to provide "a window on eternity," or to be more exact, a window on the eternal meaning of India.

His biography of Mahatma Gandhi titled *The Great Indian Way* (1998)[21] is a moving exploration of the Indian conception of God, Truth and "soul force" involving a sacrifice of the self as a prelude to self-realization.

This profoundly engaging biography of the Mahatma makes one thing abundantly clear at the very outset. It is *not* just "another life of Gandhi," (*Preface*) by a run-of-the-mill biographer who may, at his best, be true to facts but does not know how to make facts "melt into life" (*Preface*). This is where one feels the magic wand of Raja Rao's creativity, the *breath* of his pen that can make facts "flow into event" (*Preface*) and what is more, infuse the event with *rasa*, flavour. If facts do not remain as facts in his hands, it is because he knows more than anyone that facts in themselves are "shrill" and that what is important is the "essence" of fact that must "shine."

Small wonder if Rao, steeped in the great Indian past should represent an "area of promise" and make an indelible impression upon the minds of his countless admirers. Notwithstanding the current euphoria generated by a whole new crop of younger writers, often revelling in surface brilliance, it must be acknowledged that Rao alongwith Anand and Narayan has put India firmly on the map of the world in Fiction.

Notes

1. Raja Rao, *The Policeman and the Rose* (New Delhi: Oxford UP, 1978). All subsequent references are to this edition only and will be made in the body of the text itself.
2. C.D. Narasimhaiah, *Raja Rao* (New Delhi: Arnold Heinemann, 1973) 3. All subsequent references are to this edition only and will be made in the body of the text itself.
3. C.D. Narasimhaiah, *Afterword, The Policeman and the Rose* 132.
4. Raja Rao, *Kanthapura* (Madras: Oxford UP, 1947). All subsequent references are to this edition only and will be made in the body of the text itself.
5. Raja Rao, *The Serpent and the Rope* (London: John Murray, 1960). All subsequent references are to this edition only and will be made in the body of the text itself.
6. Narasimhaiah, *Raja Rao* 126, 127.
7. C.D. Narasimhaiah, "Raja Rao: Novel as Magic Casement of Celestial Concerns and Social Transactions," *The Literary Criterion* 33.3 (1998) 44.
8. Edwin Thumboo, "Raja Rao: *The Chessmaster and His Moves.*" *World Literature Today* (Autumn 1988).
9. Narasimhaiah, *Raja Rao* 127.
10. Narasimhaiah, *Novel as Magic Casement* 39.
11. Raja Rao, *The Cat and Shakespeare: A Tale of Modern India* (Delhi: Hind Pocket Books, 1971). All subsequent references are to this edition only and will be made in the body of the text itself.
12. Narasimhaiah, *Raja Rao* 168.
13. Raja Rao, *Comrade Kirillov* (New Delhi: Orient Paperbacks, 1976). All subsequent references are to this edition only and will be made in the body of the text itself.
14. A.N. Gupta, "*Comrade Kirillov*: An Appraisal," *Perspectives on Raja Rao*, ed. K.K. Sharma (Vimal, 1980) 128.

15. Raja Rao, *The Chessmaster and His Moves* (New Delhi: Vision Books, 1988). All subsequent references are to this edition only and will be made in the body of the text itself.
16. R. Parthasarathy, "*The Chessmaster and His Moves*; The Novel as Metaphysics," *World Literature Today* (Autumn 1988) 562.
17. Edwin Thumboo, *The Chessmaster* 572.
18. Edwin Thumboo, *The Chessmaster* 567.
19. Raja Rao, *On the Ganga Ghat* (New Delhi: Vision Books, 1989). All subsequent references are to this edition only and will be made in the body of the text itself.
20. Raja Rao, *The Meaning of India* (New Delhi: Vision Books, 1996). All subsequent references are to this edition only and will be made in the body of the text itself.
21. Raja Rao, *The Great Indian Way: A Life of Mahatma Gandhi* (Delhi: Vision Books, 1998). All subsequent references are to this edition and will be made in the body of the text itself.

A RAJA RAO BIBLIOGRAPHY

Primary Sources

Fictional works by Raja Rao

Kanthapura. London: George Allen & Unwin Ltd. (1938); reprinted in the Champak Library, Bombay: Oxford UP, 1947.

The Cow of the Barricades & Other Stories. Bombay: Oxford UP, 1947.

The Serpent and the Rope. London: John Murray, 1960.

The Cat and Shakespeare: A Tale of Modern India. New York: Macmillan, 1965. (Indian ed.). Delhi: Hind Pocket Books, 1971).

Comrade Kirillov. New Delhi: Orient Paperbacks, 1976.

The Policeman and the Rose. Delhi: Oxford UP, 1978.

The Chessmaster and His Moves. New Delhi: Vision Books, 1988.

On the Ganga Ghat. New Delhi: Vision Books, 1989.

Non-fictional works

The Meaning of India. New Delhi: Vision Books, 1996.

The Great Indian Way: A Life of Mahatma Gandhi. New Delhi: Vision Books, 1998.

Secondary Sources

Books on Raja Rao

Bhattacharya, P.C. *Indo-Anglian Literature and the Works of Raja Rao*. Delhi: Atma Ram, 1983.

Dey, Esha. *The Novels of Raja Rao (The Theme of Quest)*. New Delhi: Prestige, 1992.

Hardgrave, Robert L., ed. *Word as Mantra, The Art of Raja Rao*. New Delhi: Katha, 1998.

Naik, M.K. *Raja Rao*. New York: Twayne Publishers Inc., 1972.

Narasimhaiah, C.D. *Raja Rao*. New Delhi: Arnold-Heinemann, 1973.

Narayan, Shymala, A. *Raja Rao: Man and His Works.* New Delhi: Sterling Publishers Private Limited, 1988.

Niranjan, Shiva. *Raja Rao: Novelist as Sadhaka.* Ghaziabad: India Vimal, 1985.

Niven, Alastair. *Truth Within Fiction: A Study of Raja Rao's* The Serpent and the Rope. Calcutta: Writers Workshop, 1987.

Paranjape, Makarand, ed. *The Best of Raja Rao.* New Delhi: Katha, 1998.

Rajeshwar, Mittapalli and Pier Paolo Piciucco, eds. *The Fiction of Raja Rao: Critical Studies.* Delhi: Atlantic Books, 2001.

Ramachandra, Ragini, ed. *Raja Rao: An Anthology of Recent Criticism.* Delhi: Pencraft International, 2000.

Rao, K.R. *The Fiction of Raja Rao.* Aurangabad: Parimal, 1980.

Sharma, K.K. ed. *Perspectives on Raja Rao: An Anthology of Critical Essays.* Ghaziabad: Vimal, 1980.

Sharrad, Paul. *Raja Rao and Cultural Tradition.* New Delhi: Sterling, 1987.

Singh, R.S. *Raja Rao's Kanthapura: An Analysis.* Delhi: Doaba House, 1973.

Srivastava, Narasingh. *The Mind and the Art of Raja Rao.* Bareilly: Prakash Book Depot, 1980.

World Literature Today, Special issue on Raja Rao, U of Oklahoma, (Autumn 1988).

Articles from books and journals

Ahmed, Ali. "Illusion and Reality: The Art and Philosophy of Raja Rao." *The Journal of Commonwealth Literature* 5 (1968): 16-28.

Bhalla, Brij M. "Quest for Identity in Raja Rao's *The Serpent and the Rope.*" *Ariel* 4.4 (1973): 95-105.

Davies, M. Bryn. "Raja Rao's *The Serpent and the Rope*: A New Literary Genre ?" *The Commonwealth Writer Overseas: Themes of Exile and Expatriation.* Ed. Alastair Niven. Brussels: Didier, 1976. 265-69.

Dayal, P. "The Image of Woman in the Novels of Raja Rao." *Punjab University Research Bulletin (Arts)* 16.1 (April 1985): 45-53.

Desai, S.K. "Transplantation of English: Raja Rao's Experimentation with English in His Works of Fiction." *Indian Writing in English* (Fiction). Ed. S.K. Desai. Kolhapur: Shivaji University Department of English, 1974. 1-32.

Gemill, Janet Powers. "Elements of the Folktale in Raja Rao's *The Cow of the Barricades.*" *World Literature Written in English* 20.1 (Spring 1981): 149-61.

Harris, Wilson. "Raja Rao's Inimitable Style and Art of Fiction." *World Literature Today* (Autumn 1988): 587-90.

Kantak, V.Y. "The Language of *Kanthapura.*" *Indian Literary Review* 3 (April 1985): 15-24.

____. "Raja Rao's *Kanthapura.*" *Perspectives on Indian Literary Culture.* New Delhi: Pencraft International, 1996.

Kaul, R.K. "*The Serpent and the Rope* as a Philosophical Novel." *The Literary Criterion* 15.2 (1980): 32-43.

Mani, Laxmi. "Voice and Vision in Raja Rao's Fiction." *South Asian Review* 4 (1980): 1-11.

Mathur, O.P. "The East-West Theme in *Comrade Kirillov.*" *New Literature Review* 4 (1978): 25-29.

Mukherjee, Meenakshi. "Raja Rao's Shorter Fiction." *Indian Literature* 10.3 (1967): 66-76.

Nagarajan, S. "A Note on Myth and Ritual in *The Serpent and the Rope.*" *The Journal of Commonwealth Literature* 7.1 (1972): 45-48.

Naik, M.K. "*The Cow of the Barricades and Other Stories*: Raja Rao as a Short Story Writer." *Books Abroad* (Autumn 1966): 392-96.

____. "*The Cat and Shakespeare*: A Study." *Indian Literature of the Past Fifty Years (1917-1967).* Ed. C.D. Narasimhaiah. Mysore: Prasaranga, 1970. 147-76.

Narasimhaiah, C.D. "Raja Rao's *Kanthapura:* An Analysis." *Fiction and the Reading Public in India.* Ed. C.D. Narasimhaiah. Mysore: Prasaranga, 1967. 60-83.

____. "Raja Rao: Novel as Magic Casement of Celestial Concerns and Social Transactions." *The Literary Criterion* 33.3 (1998): 37-47.

Paniker, K. Ayyappa. "A Conversation with Raja Rao on *The Cat and Shakespeare.*" *Chandrabhaga* 2 (1979): 14-18.

Parameshwaran, Uma. "Karma at Work: the Allegory in Raja Rao's *The Cat and Shakespeare.*" *The Journal of Commonwealth Literature* 7 July 1969: 107-15.

Parthasarathy, R. "*The Chessmaster and His Moves:* The Novel as Metaphysics." *World Literature Today* Autumn 1988.

Powers, Janet, M. "Initiate Meets Guru: *The Cat and Shakespeare* and *Comrade Kirillov.*" *World Literature Today* (Autumn 1988): 611-17.

Sharma, Som P. "Raja Rao's Search for the Feminine." *Journal of South Asian Literature* 12.3 (1977): 95-101.

Thumboo, Edwin. "Raja Rao: *The Chessmaster and His Moves.*" *World Literature Today* (Autumn 1988): 567-73.

Westbrook, Perry D. "*Comrade Kirillov*: Marxism and Vedanta." *World Literature Today* (Autumn 1988): 617-20.

Studies of Rao in Books not Exclusively Focused on the Author

Iyengar Srinivasa, K.R. "Raja Rao." *Indian Writing in English.* Bombay: Asia Publishing House, 1962. 302-20.

Krishna Rao, A.V. *The Indo-Anglian Novel and the Changing Tradition: A Study of the Novels of Mulk Raj Anand, Kamala Markandaya, R.K. Narayan and Raja Rao, 1930-64.* Mysore: Rao & Raghavan, 1972. 107-33.

Larson, Charles R. "Revolt and Rebirth, Cultural Renewal: Raja Rao's *Kanthapura* [and] Kamala Markandaya's *Two Virgins." The Novel and the Third World.* Washington, D.C.: Inscape, 1976. 131-51.

Maini, D.S. "Raja Rao's Vision, Values and Aesthetic." *Commonwealth Literature: Problems of Response.* Ed. C.D. Narasimhaiah. Madras: Macmillan, 1981. 64-89.

Mukherjee, Meenakshi. *The Twice Born Fiction: Themes and Techniques of the Indian Novel in English.* New Delhi: Arnold-Heinemann, 1971. 89-94, 139-45.

Narasimhaiah, C.D. "National Identity in Literature and Language: Its Range and Depth in the Novels of Raja Rao." *National Identity.* Ed. K.L. Goodwin. London/Melbourne: Heinemann Educational Books, 1970. 153-68.

Parthasarathy, R. "Tradition and Creativity: Stylistic Innovations in Raja Rao." *Discourse across Cultures: Strategies in World Englishes.* Ed. Larry E. Smith. London: Prentice-Hall, 1987. 157-65.

Ramachandra, Ragini. *"The Serpent and the Rope*: An Indian Novel." *Confederate Gestures: Search for Method in Indian Literature Studies.* Ed. Charu Sheel Singh. New Delhi: Associated Publishing House, 1993. 154-63.

____. "Raja Rao: The Chessmaster of Indian English." *Makers of Indian English Literature.* Ed. C.D. Narasimhaiah. Delhi: Pencraft International, 2000. 132-40.

Unnikrishnan, K. "Guru-Disciple: A Paradigm for Indianness in Raja Rao's Fiction." *Makers of Indian English Literature.* Ed. C.D. Narasimhaiah. Delhi: Pencraft International, 2000. 141-48.

4

Khushwant Singh

P. BALASWAMY

During the post-Independence scenario the Indian literary field was so full of possibilities and waiting for entrepreneurs, however ill-equipped they could be, since a new kind of market awaited their products with a rather increasing hunger. Novices and amateurs did not have to face the possibility of a gruelling test before their work could be included as part of the main cannon, as it was happening in the West. A book could be written with the simple and straightforward title *Indian Writing in English* and become such a sought-after volume of history and criticism that many Western and Indian scholars had no other reference work of its type for some decades at least. In the Indian academic circles and university departments, the question with a satirical and wry tone was often asked: "What and where is Indian Writing in English?" Efforts were frantically made to make the new body of writing visible and viable.

When the best-seller lists included a new novel, immediately the book and its author were conscientiously promoted and made larger than life. It was rather a short step for other professionals like teachers, administrators, journalists *et al* to become writers and get more recognition as such. If someone could get noticed by a Western reviewer/critic, his/her work received more serious attention than its quota from the Indian reading public and the critical establishment, irrespective of the merits/demerits of the published work; if the writer and the Indian critic belonged to the same region/linguistic group, the assessment of his work was often uncritically adulatory. Quite ironically, yet understandably, such creative works were simply absorbed in the canon without a serious attempt to evaluate and classify them. Journals and magazines which started to cater to the small group of students and teachers of this new area did not often exercise their editorial rights to select, reject, revise etc, as their counterparts in the West were wont to do.

The novels and short stories produced by Khushwant Singh and his place/worth as a creative writer have to be evaluated against this background. He had gained international recognition as a journalist, editor of some prestigious national magazines like the *Illustrated Weekly of India*. His accomplishment in his job as the editor must have made him confident of his success as a creative writer, too. The result is four novels, one omnibus collection of short stories, about twenty non-fiction authored books, ten edited works, and eleven translations. Singh has a natural flair for narration and can keep the reader engrossed in his tale, provided he does not allow his satirical and cynical tendencies to overwhelm the artist in him. He has an eye for the details and in some of his short stories and in his first novel, *Train to Pakistan* his employment of social realism as a technique and his penchant for satire are truly impressive. However, objectively speaking, his *weltanschauung*, his apparent rejection of cultural values, his phallocentric narratives and his inherent incapacity to turn the "felt emotion" into "art emotion" deprive him of a permanent place among the great Indian writers in English. It should be stressed in no uncertain terms that international reputation as a columnist/journalist and social commitment can never be substitutes for an artistic vision or creative imagination.

Khushwant Singh's first novel *Train to Pakistan* (1956), a microcosmic novel that created such a deep understanding of the complex issues involved in the communal flare-up after the Indian independence, was so contemporary and so daringly expository that it was acclaimed as a significant and valuable contribution to the Partition literature. As the events portrayed in that novel had been witnessed in flesh and blood just nine years ago, the work created a sense of solid reality and a feeling of danger, desperation and violence of an unprecedented scale. The work has also been interpreted in the postcolonial context as a protest novel against imperialistic designs, communal violence and the indifference of the Indian bureaucracy. Set in a village called Mano Majra, on the border of Punjab in India with a rail track leading to Lahore in Pakistan, the events and characters portrayed in this novel could be taken to be replicas of those that happened in many parts of north India at the time of partition.

The novel captures the mindlessness of the communal violence with great objectivity and also in a chilling fashion through the portrayal of the situation before and after the carnages. Mano Majra is a sleepy and obsolete community where, its citizens, lacking in civilized amenities, mark their time according to the arrival of trains at the railway station. Sikhs form the majority and the Muslims lead a dependent life, but the symbiosis between the groups had ensured that life has gone on peacefully for all. The pastoral charm, the idyllic beauty of the village and the seemingly-eternal peace of the locale create a sense of the unchanging nature of Mano Majra. The impact of such opening descriptions of the novel is to create an impression of an Indian rural utopia, especially when the other parts of India are engulfed in the fires of the communal carnage. There may be a stray incident such as the killing of a Hindu moneylender Ram Lal by the dacoits. The village *budmash* (bad man) Jugga Singh's complicity in a few earlier criminal cases make him the prime suspect in the Ram Lal murder. Otherwise the scenario is quite peaceful and simple. However, the peace and co-existence are in a sense deceptive and contain the seeds of disruption and destruction. Rather suddenly, the atmosphere changes dramatically when a 'ghost train' arrives from across the border with a full load of corpses. The horror of the ghost train's cargo is accentuated through indirect references rather than direct descriptions. The contrast between the rural ambience portrayed in the background and the frenzied violence caused by the arrival of the 'ghost' train in the foreground seems to be intentional, yet quite effective as a novelistic technique.

The train, which is a symbol of modern technology introduced by the British Government in India, has quite effortlessly been assimilated into the fabric of the rural India. The villagers are still awestruck by the power displayed by the train, but they have accepted it as an integral part of their lives, more so due to its ability to transport them to newer civilizations and power centres. The mobility provided by the train is a wonderful facility—a way to freedom, an avenue of escape and a path to new adventures. Khushwant Singh's utilization of this symbol of modernity seems to have yielded rich dividends, though one cannot be certain whether he, as a greenhorn to the art of fiction, was conscious of all the artistic complexities and effects of that symbol. Yet, "trusting the tale and not the teller," the reader can certainly realize the following subtleties. The train, the bridge and the rail track perform multiple functions in the novel—firstly, their accumulated symbolism accentuates the rural ambience, its peace and harmony and the creditable achievement of harmonious coexistence among the followers of different religions—Hindus, Muslims, Sikhs; secondly, the train, by transporting a train load of corpses from across the border, is the harbinger of death and the destroyer of the idyllic communal harmony that prevailed so far; thirdly, the train and the bridge also present some kind of solution to the communal discord, as they provide a platform for the sacrifice rendered by Jugga—the "forget-and-forgive" ideology presented through his willingness to indulge in meaningful action, after an attitudinal and ideological change. This novel certainly celebrates and valorises bridges as symbols of reconstruction and reconciliation.

The events of the novel move rather effortlessly as Khushwant Singh has managed to create a clever balance between the fictional characters and the real incidents. Jugga Singh, who used to have his way everywhere, be it in love-making with Nooran, his Muslim love, or in handling the arrogant and cunning policemen, serves as a dramatic foil for the educated and socially-committed Iqbal Singh. That Jugga is in the class of Malli, the dacoit, is made clear in the beginning of the tale. Yet, Jugga grows in the course of the novel and shows certain inherent traits, which surprise the reader. To be sure, the novelist's attitude to life as well as his espousal of certain cynical/satirical ideology makes him use Jugga as an exemplary figure who can rise to heroic heights overcoming all narrow considerations and even be ready to give up his life for the sake of the larger good.

Even as the novel's major themes are the mindless communal violence, the impact of partition on innocent lives, and the deep chasm that was created among the people of the same place on religious lines, Khushwant Singh is also keen on exposing the weak-kneed intellectuals and armchair socialists, their inability to rise up to a challenge. He juxtaposes the rough and unsophisticated Jugga, "the son of the soil," against the cowardly and indecisive city-bred Iqbal and projects the low-down 'budmash' as one capable of rising to heroism, while the 'intellectual' fails to initiate any meaningful action. It is this part of the novel that has a spontaneity and relevance, bringing out the irony and complexity of modern Indian life in a convincing manner, which elevates the novel from a documentary status to fiction worth reading.

Khushwant Singh's cynical and satirical view of the Indian officials, including the police force, comes out quite overtly in his portrayal of the Magistrate/Divisional Commissioner Hukum Chand and the Sub-Inspector of Police. Both exercise their authority in a cavalier fashion, on the basis of opinions formed due to their prejudices. Hukum Chand is impervious to the gathering communal storm, handling the events in an inept and rather irresponsible manner. The fate overtaking the villages and small towns of the partition era seems to be so inexorable that the larger schemata makes the characters, with the exception of Jugga, appear like puppets on a string. Their roles are so defined by the social situation that the human element is missing, contributing to the dissatisfaction in the reader with the overall effect of the novel. A perceptive Indian critic observes on this aspect of Khushwant Singh's art:

> There is another suspicion that comes to the mind when one reads Khushwant Singh. It is that he does not care, does not believe in the existence of the human beings he creates in his fiction. This is natural because [...] the novelist in Khushwant Singh is always actuated by the strings that are manipulated from somewhere backstage by the sociologist in him. As a result, human beings become just data to the novelist, creating an attitude that is poisonous to the life of the art.[1]

The two-dimensional nature of some of his characters, including the major ones, and the predictability of their behaviour, the way events in the novel seem to take on a pattern on the expected lines—these inartistic features of the novel disappoint the expectant reader who has been prepared by the ambiguities and imbedded design of the first part of the novel. The almost wooden nature of the police force, its hideous face alone revealed and no matching and convincing rendering of their stereotyped words and actions, the cruelty of their methods exposed but the provocations not reasonably dealt with—above all the cynicism with which the whole portrait of the police raj is done—all add up to the dissatisfaction one feels as one reads through the middle part of the novel.

Khushwant Singh trips in yet another aspect—in making certain equations and relationships rather ostentatious and manipulated. When Jugga has Nooran, the daughter of a Muslim weaver, as his sweetheart, it looks plausible; but, when Hukum Chand wants to have a teenage girl to pander to his sexual urges, they arrange to bring Haseena, yet another Muslim teenager. The reason that could be cited that there were no Hindu families in Mano Majra could be faulted by the argument that there were many other villages in the area from where a Hindu/Sikh prostitute could have been procured for the 'Sircar.' It does appear to be rather contrived when one takes note of the compelling circumstances for the final drama and sacrifice—that Jugga wants to save his sweetheart Nooran and Hukum Chand is eager to evacuate the Muslims from Mano Majra due to Haseena's presence in the refugee camp; both men happen to be Hindus and the victims, Muslims! There is something pat and evitable in that.

Despite such lapses, *Train to Pakistan* has undoubted merits as a social novel with indelible images of the catastrophe that overtook the Indian subcontinent at the time of its independence. It served a definite purpose with a remarkable effect—to rouse the conscience of all the people at all levels.

Khushwant Singh was not, however, highly satisfied with his own achievement in his first attempt at full-length fiction, describing it as more a documentary than a novel, despite its huge commercial success—it was translated into thirteen European languages and was running into many editions both in the west and in India. In his Introduction to the Penguin edition of the Collected Novels, he rather simplistically states that his second novel *I Shall Not Hear the Nightingale* "is a better novel than *Train to Pakistan*." He further observes: "Not many people agree with me" (*Introduction* ix). True, one cannot agree with him on this point. Authorial statements are not supposed to have critical validity in view of the theory of "intentional fallacy." Therefore, without assigning any importance to Singh's opinions, one can weigh the worth of the novels under consideration and conclude that the first novel of Khushwant Singh is easily his best work of fiction, after all analysis is done. That it was his only novel to win an International award—the Grove Press Award for the Best work of fiction from India in 1954 when it was first published under the title *Mano Majra*—may be taken as conclusive proof.

Writing a novel under an ideological compulsion and finding that it was a lucrative profession, Khushwant Singh next decided to satisfy his own instincts on what should constitute material for fiction and turned to his own community and his own family for such material. Even though practising the Sikh religion in an orthodox manner or following its tenets in a blind fashion was never his cup of tea, Singh had always taken pride in his Sikh origins, by growing unshorn hair and beard according to that tradition and wearing a turban. It should have occurred to him that an intense disagreement in a Sikh family between a father and his young son due to their political allegiance would provide the basis for a dramatic conflict and that the clash of attitudes and values would afford him a fine opportunity to deal with contemporaneous issues of India. As he briefly mentions in the Introduction, his own family had offered the stuff for his fictional treatment of Sikh family values and issues.

I Shall Not Hear the Nightingale was published in 1959 when Singh was flush with the success of *Train to Pakistan*. The new novel was set in the year 1942-43 when the famous Quit India Movement had put the whole nation in turmoil. The nationalist feelings ran high throughout the country, but in Punjab, rather strangely, the response was rather muted. The factor that a sizable number of Sikhs served the Indian Armed Forces under the British regime may have something to do with that phenomenon. Many spirited Sikhs felt keenly that their patriotism was suspect and wanted to make amends, but were not wise enough to know the technique or smart to achieve the desired results. Khushwant Singh takes such a young man as his protagonist and sets him against his own father who happens to be a chip of the old block. The ideological conflict between the father and son is, however, domesticated through the interface between the highly-religious mother and the recalcitrant family members.

The equations within the family are, however, rather stale and hackneyed. Sardar Buta Singh is the proverbial civil servant whose loyalty to the Crown is unshakable and who is equally convinced about the necessity of the British continuing to rule India. His father and grandfather had served in the army, so he continued that distinguished line and like them had mentioned the English king or queen in his evening prayer to the Guru. The Gandhi phenomenon has, however, brought home certain aspects of the reality around him, yet it is perplexing to him why any Englishman would like to see the end of British rule in India. An intrusive author narrates the rest:

> But many besides Taylor had begun to say so. And most of the Indians were actively agitating for its end. In this state of flux Buta Singh had decided on a muddle-headed and somewhat dishonest compromise. When he was with Englishmen he protested his loyalty to the Raj. 'At my age, I cannot change,' he would say. When he was amongst his own countrymen he would be a little critical of English ways. He let his own son cast his lot with the Nationalists and did not object to his organizing students and making political speeches. (*Nightingale* 182)

A neat portrait of the stereotype of the loyal servant, this description is one of many recurrent passages of the same kind. Khushwant Singh is content to toe the familiar line and does not toil much to make his chief character exceptional.

No less unexceptional is the character of Sher Singh, his only son, the ambitious Nationalist student-leader. In his eagerness to prove the mettle of Sikh youth, Sher makes brave speeches without matching them with suitable action, for the simple reason that he does not possess the wherewithal, either in will power, character or intelligence. Carried away by superficialities, he lives in a dream world of heroic action and cheering adulatory crowds. At the most, he can shoot a harmless and useless crane only, or in a desperate moment attack with his friends' help an unwary Jhimma Singh, the headman who serves as a police spy. Spineless coward that he is, Sher Singh sheds open tears when the Anglo-Indian sergeants beat him up mercilessly in his own house in their attempt to get the truth from him about his accomplices. Rather inexplicably, Sher Singh is not normal in his sexual drives and finds his young wife Champak's eagerness for sexual fulfilment an aberration. Understandably, however, his terrible weakness/cowardice is exposed when he is under duress. But for his mother's advice to him in the prison not to turn traitor on his friends, he would have capitulated and revealed all, to the disgrace of his family and community. His father expectedly refuses to visit him in custody, adding to the agony. Their conflicting attitudes and actions would have headed towards a stalemate but for the bold and faith-based action initiated by Sabhrai, his mother. Her tragic death due to the pneumonia caught by her in the *gurudwara* where she goes to pray for her son and for the honour of her family somehow brings about a compromise between the poles-apart father and son.

I Shall Not Hear the Nightingale purports to focus on this domestic conflict against the backdrop of national politics, but straggles with its short and not-so-short diversions on the salacious escapades of young cricketer Madan with his friend Sher Singh's wife and sister in Simla, along with dissertations on the lack of privacy for Indians and the consequent prohibitions/inhibitions on sexual behaviour in public and private, which include titillating accounts of the middle aged, fat and ugly widow, Shunno enjoying forbidden pleasures with an ascetic and virile Muslim priest. Such diversions may serve a limited purpose of social criticism or moral inquisitions, but the reader is unable to perceive how such spicy and sensational parts of the novel could be integrated with the organic development of the plot. Considering the fact that the author shows an increasing tendency, in his subsequent fictional works, to indulge in the use of such sexually explicit narrations as part of the demonstration of his uninhibited attitude to sex, one is forced to conclude that they serve no artistic purpose or design.

The characters of the novel speak and act on predictable lines, with the exception of Sabhrai, the matriarch with a stern code of conduct. Her world is filled with religious devotion, rituals, familial gatherings and observance of fasts. As long as the events move on a placid note, the father and the son, and the two young women, Champak and Beena, appear to keep their roles intact. But when there is a crisis, such as the arrest and torture of Sher by the police or Beena's discovery of Champak's liaison with Madan, their vulnerability is exposed and they act in a confused and pointless manner. The character delineation suffers in such phases of the novel due to the fact that they are so unreal and the novelist could not present all the psychological complexities authentically. The only figure who possesses some individuality is Sabhrai with her adherence to traditional values and practices. The Taylor couple is so much impressed by her courage and steadfast observance of her principles that Mrs. Taylor persuades her husband to release the boy quite unilaterally. That Sabhrai can find peace ultimately without any inputs from her husband and son speaks for the authenticity of her character. Unfortunately, all the other characters seem so unconvincing that the author himself is unable to end the story on a decisive note, putting an end to its meandering course. The lack of artistic vision that would have held the characters and events together makes it a banal and restless story. A critic makes this highly insightful observation on the final effect of the novel:

> The novel lacks integrality and organic development: the clash of personalities and political commitments, and the resulting strains on personal relationships, play their own part in the thematic progression of the novel, but what is lacking, in spite of the pervasive emphasis on irony and realism, is a quality of cohesion and feeling which is responsible in good art for the transformation of the raw and the random into the related and the meaningful. The end is hurried through, justified by Buta Singh's complacent recall of a pat quote from Shakespeare—"All's well that ends well." (Kulshrestha 127)

If Khushwant Singh's objective is to expose the delinquent heroes of the revolutionary movement, their adolescently boastful attitude and their indulgence in deceit, depravity and selfishness (as shown in Madan's case), his satire and irony are only partially successful as there is a lack of depth and psychological realism in these portraits. For instance, Sher is presented as lacking in standard sexual drive, unable to satisfy his young wife's normal desires, driving her into absurd acts of provocation with the innocent servant boy and, more seriously, to commit adultery with Madan in Simla. This is rather strange and not convincingly presented, leading the reader to suspect that Champak's plight is used by the novelist as a ruse to indulge in passages of explicit descriptions for, perhaps, titillation of the superficial readers. Some critics are forced to call Champak a nymphomaniac,[2] when there is no justification for it, nor supported by authentic events/situations. In fact, one is convinced that the depiction of Sher as uninterested in normal sexual activities is again a ruse to introduce subtle Freudian elements in the narrative to link his obsession with a gun as his attempt to compensate for his alleged impotence, but the result is not so subtle after all!

The style employed by the author in this novel can be said to be simple, direct and ironical. In his descriptions of men and events Singh is economical and concrete, but when it comes to tracing the thoughts of his main characters, he employs the omniscient narrative technique. However, the shifts in point of view occur too frequently and have a confused effect on the reader. There are some attempts to capture the spirit of the Indian speech rhythms, as in the scene of Beena's encounter with a native woman in Simla, but they are not quite effective. The long descriptive passages on the Indian seasons, the social/domestic crisis of lack of privacy and the quotation-filled accounts of Sikh religious ceremonies create an impression of documentary being offered in the garb of fiction. The problem, once again, is the failure of the artist to integrate his materials with a vision specially chosen for the novel. *I Shall Not Hear the Nightingale* is a flawed work that rode to limited success on the back of its famous predecessor.

An objective analysis of the novelist's worth in terms of artistic merits, without being influenced by extraneous factors like popularity and success of the writer in a related field, thus shows up the inadequacies of Khushwant Singh as a creative artist. That he had obviously ran out of material and techniques to produce another creditable work comparable to his first novel is revealed as one looks at the following facts:

After completing his second novel in 1959, it took him more than twenty-five years to write another work of fiction, viz. *Delhi*, which was published only in 1989. The label 'novel' is rather loosely employed in describing this saga, both by the author and the publisher, for it is a collection of accounts, fictional mostly, of the rulers of the city of

Delhi. (In fact, the author frankly admits in his Introduction to the Penguin edition that the loose episodes could not be linked effectively to make them an artistic whole—"The daunting task was to string these episodes together and make them read like one continuous story. Over twenty years I tried many methods of linkage and admitted failure to find a satisfactory one," he writes ruefully [ix].)

All the material for this work had been culled out of history texts, memoirs, and public narratives and none of it came out of his imagination.

This elaborate explication is necessary to show that his talents as a novelist (whatever he displayed in his first work) were declining over the years and completely dried up by 1999 when his latest fiction appeared. Containing more than 370 pages in 21 chapters, *Delhi* is undoubtedly a big book, claimed by the publisher in the blurb as "a vast, erotic, irreverent magnum opus." To be sure, there is no contesting of these claims, which reveals, incidentally, a commercial objective and practice to induce more readers into buying it. That *Delhi* became a big commercial success, a phenomenon which took its author by total surprise, can in no way add up to its merits as a work of fiction. Structure, theme, narrative technique and point of view, character-delineation and style—in all these aspects this book is woefully deficient. Notwithstanding the fact that the author has been candid enough to admit his failure to make it a novel, an objective analysis should be attempted to establish the credentials of one's initial response to this work.

Yugoslavia's Ivo Andric had constructed the story of Yugoslavia through events that occurred on a bridge in his Nobel-prize winning book *The Bridge on the Drina.* Taking inspiration from this creation, Khushwant Singh has narrated the story of Delhi, the city where he spent most of his life. Methodically he has browsed through ancient, medieval and modern historical narratives written by Indian, Mughal, British and contemporary historians that give a first-hand account of the experiences of the Kings, Emperors and other kinds of rulers who had control of the big metropolis at various points of history and made use of them extensively.

The narrative is, however, discontinuous, probably resulting from the bulk of the material to be covered and also due to the avowed intent of the author to deal with the history of the city over seven hundred years. The first of the episodes narrates the experiences of a Hindu accountant working at a Muslim *kotwal* (a kind of market) in the 14th century; the next episodes deal with subsequent centuries and the happenings therein till the current events of this century are also covered. The author tries to make some kind of connection of the historical account with the previous inter chapter (Bhagmati) by taking the reader to the historical site in its present condition. But the Bhagmati chapters soon run out of ideas of connectivity and in stead become narcissist, with the lurid accounts of the narrator's sexual encounters with other women who cross his life. Unfortunately, the effect of such inter chapters is negative, leaving a feeling of insipidity and ineffectuality. The structure of the book thus lacks any kind of unifying pattern or cohesion, highly essential for any novel.

Since there is no unity in its form, it goes without saying that there is no corresponding focus on a single theme in *Delhi*. Though the primary objective is the explication of the paradox of the author's fascination with Delhi in spite it being ugly, repulsive and unhealthy, the narration is mostly descriptive and hardly discursive. Lacking in a thematic focus, the narration cannot be anything but amorphous, straggling and disruptive. The narrative techniques employed in *Delhi* also vary, again without any thematic necessity dictating their type. Just for the sake of variety, the author makes it first person narrative in some episodes, but they lack any pattern/scheme. Point of view has been one of the weakest aspects of Khushwant Singh's fiction from the beginning; there is no point in denigrating its improper use in this book alone. In the episode titled "1857," one of the longest episodes in the book, running to more than 70 pages, the alternative voices heard—those of Alice Aldwell, Bahadur Shah Zafar, and Nihal Singh—apparently shift the locale and perspective, in order to give an integrated perception of the events connected with the First War of Independence. But, any reader unfamiliar with the history of India at this stage is confused and even bewildered, more due to the shifting points of view.

As for the characters, Khushwant Singh's idiosyncratic and even coloured perception of persons of different communities and religions imposes some kind of unreality and vagueness on the characters. There is some attempt to present the other side of some of the historical personages, like Aurangzeb and Bahadur Shah Zafar, but they sound stale and stereotypical with very little space available for developing them. It would be an arduous task for any writer of historical fiction to make the historical figures sound and look authentic, since the images of such figures may be quite diverse in the public perception. Khushwant Singh has neither the proper equipment nor training to deal with such difficult delineations. The overall effect of the woodenness of the characters, the stilted dialogue mouthed by them and the predictability of their actions make the reading dismal.

Possibly aware of the weaknesses of his narrative, Khushwant Singh makes all efforts to enliven the tales. Characteristically, he resorts to the technique of using titillating material; the Mughal preponderance with the sensuous life, with exceptions like Aurangzeb, comes in handy in many episodes. He exercises some restraint in the earlier episodes as if to show his serious preoccupation with history, but in the later episode *1857* he allows all his fantasies full play. The narrator's sexual relationship with the hermaphrodite Bhagmati often turns into lewdness and perversity. Ironically, his fascination with the transvestite remains a mystery, rather a stale one!

The author notes with amusement in the Introduction to the Penguin collected edition that the book *Delhi* was an instant best-seller and wonders at the taste of the readers. Perhaps one reason why many Delhi citizens bought this book had to do with their urge to learn all about the Mughal rulers in the context of the increasing support—in the late eighties and early nineties—to the political party that swore by a Hindu ideology. One of his lady characters makes the observation that the narrator must dislike the Muslims intensely as he reels out facts and figures about the atrocities committed by Mughal rulers on the Hindu population. The episodes on the Mongolian King Timur and Nadir Shah of Iran reveal the chillingly devastating killings of Hindus in millions by those alien kings as they invaded Delhi and plundered it of all its gold. Cruelty and inhumanity of a magnitude unknown to the people of our times was casually practised upon the Delhi population by their troops. Even more shockingly, the precept that kingship knows no kinship was widely and scandalously demonstrated by the Mughal rulers. When Khushwant Singh presented an account of all such atrocities from the past, the present-day populace probably tilting toward a Hindu ideology seems to have lapped it up, lock, stock and barrel. Echoing the amused remark of the author, one has to wonder how a book devoid of any artistic merit could have sold in such large numbers, but for such extra-literary reasons.

In between the writing of fiction, Khushwant Singh has produced a considerable number of non-fiction—histories of Sikhs, books and articles on politics and current affairs, and translations of Punjabi works. His journalistic writings had gained wide recognition as they often treated current subjects with candour, vivacity and common sense. Future readers will in all probability remember Singh as the author of standard work of histories of Sikhs. Probably reminded of his early fictional success, he ventured to write yet another novel after a gap of ten years and it has resulted in *The Company of Women* (1999). The blurb of the Viking edition claims that it is "an uninhibited, erotic and endlessly entertaining celebration of love, sex and passion." One tends to agree with this description, except that the word "love" should have been replaced by "lust." Further, in his 'Author's Note' Khushwant Singh states:

> As a man gets older, his sex instincts travel from his middle to his head. What he wanted to do in his younger days but did not

because of nervousness, lack of response or opportunity, he does in his mind.

I started writing this novel when I was eighty-three. I finished it at eighty-five. An equally apt title for it could be: "The Fantasies of an Octogenarian."[3]

After this kind of confession, any critical reading of this novel with an objective of looking for artistic merits in it would be equal to flogging a dead horse.

The Company of Women, due to its endlessly erotic descriptions, can only be named hard core pornography, going by the parameters of Indian English fiction. Khushwant Singh, as confessed to in his Note, has indulged in all kinds of fantasies in the garb of telling the secret life of Mohan Kumar, a divorcee. Getting divorced from his nagging, ill-tempered wife, Sonu, the millionaire Mohan invites sophisticated society ladies to spend some time with him as his drawing-cum-bed room companion, with suitable monetary compensation. A procession of women, educated or illiterate, invades his bed and climb out of it after highly erotic and almost superhuman copulations are performed. Yet, Mohan's sexuality is insatiable for many, many years, compelling him to take any available woman, regardless of consequences.

There is no pretension to making such a story in anyway relevant—social, political, historical or artistic. Requirements of aesthetic plot construction norms have been gleefully ignored and there are no claims about its thematic focus, either. The character-delineation techniques are merrily dispensed with, since there are no demands made on complexities/ambiguities in the characters. Some kind of social realism is reflected in the character of Mohan Kumar, a prototype of phallus-obsessed males of modern times, who flaunt an amoral attitude to sex and extra-marital relationships. But, most of the other characters are cardboard figures; there is a sense of unreality and hollowness about the character of Sonu, in her assumed antagonism to Mohan and conjugal life with him. Undoubtedly there are a number of Sonus in the higher classes of modern India, but there are no convincing reasons offered for her quarrels with Mohan, notwithstanding the coddling encouragement she gets from her parents serving as an impetus. One has to conclude that but for Sonu's intransigent decision to break with Mohan there would not be any credible reason for his launching on a lustful adventure with assorted women, which the novelist uses as a plausible alibi for his 'fantasies.'

Even to the adolescent readers, these lustful adventures of Mohan will soon lose their novelty/fascination, since this kind of titillation cannot be sustained for long. The meandering course of the novel, in which the narrative is shared by Mohan and his novelist-friend who happens to know everything that has occurred to Mohan, cannot end in a meaningful manner, since the objective of the work is itself dubious and double-faced. A man who had not bothered about morality and marital fidelity strangely starts reading religious literature, the *Bhagavad Gita*, and reciting the *Gayatri mantra*, a verse homage to the Sun God offered by every devout *Brahmin*. The question whether the novelist is trying to convey any moral message through the actions performed by his protagonist during his last days of his life is natural to raise its head; it is certainly not a part of the pattern of the narrative set from the beginning, as the "unending celebration of sex" concludes on a pathetic note of Aids virus infecting him and driving him to suicide. In the final count, the novel degenerates into inane pornography.

Khushwant Singh's contribution to the genre of short stories, however, might claim him a small, but sure niche in its history. *The Collected Short Stories of Khushwant Singh* (1989) is an omnibus edition containing all the stories published earlier under different titles. The stories deal with different aspects of Indian life, on the inevitable theme of 'East meets West' and on some whites' uncommon experiences in India. They are marked by irony and satire, based on Singh's ability to assimilate closely-observed facts of the Indian way of life. Many of them are quite absorbing, neatly entertaining, and often very witty and bitingly satirical. All the stories are not to be rated high, but a few certainly merit to be equated with the best of their kind in India. One may include "Karma," "Kusum," "The Riot," "The Memsahib of Mandla," "When Death comes to Daulat Ram," "Man, How the Govt of India Run!" "The Bottom-Pincher" and "India is a Strange Country." The choice may vary, depending on individual tastes, but these mentioned show a variety, some kind of spontaneity, and above all that feeling of authenticity and a fidelity to the basic tenets of life. Their ability to surprise the reader with a revelation of some interesting facet of life elevates them from the rest. The often-anthologised "Karma" is a good instance of brevity, subdued satire and ironic ending laced with poetic justice. The underplay in the portrait of Sir Mohanlal, the anglophile, the dry yet authentic description of Lady Lal and her betel-chewing *bonhomie* with the porter, the inebriated British soldiers and their characteristically callous treatment of the 'niggar' in their first-class compartment—all add up to the fine effect of the compact story. In the story on Kusum, the sudden insight provided at the end of the story about a teenage girl's libidinous instincts and the change in her perspective of the male world, all caused by a petty and saucy trader, show that Singh is capable of connecting facts of life with a vision. But, the satirical tendency in him often mars the effect of some other stories, otherwise good in their conception and execution.

Some of his other well-known stories such as "The Mark of Vishnu," "Mr. Kanjoos and the Great Miracle," "A Bride for the Sahib," fail to provide total satisfaction as they display certain predetermined notions about people and events on the part of the author, though the tales are better in technique and structure. The unreality of the characters and the prejudicial view of the cultures by the author, along with a too severe view of personal predicaments, make them defective as stories. These stories suffer from some limitation arising from his total dependence on the socio-materialistic interpretation of life.

The final assessment of Khushwant Singh as a fiction writer is that he dons the sociologist garb too often to the discomfort of readers who expect him to perform well on the basis of his abilities as a creative writer. His first novel *Train to Pakistan* promised so much, but our hopes have been belied by his subsequent novels, some of which can hardly merit that label. As Kulshrestha succinctly puts it,

> In his exclusive concern with things as they are, the artist in him fails to capture the subtleties and surrounding nuances which light up facts, and tends to describe and explain, rather than vivify and dramatise, write about rather than create. (131)

It looks certain, since the creative period is over for Khushwant Singh, that he will go down in the history of Indian English fiction as a one-novel author, with *Train to Pakistan* serving a historical necessity.

Notes

1. Chirantan Kulshrestha, "Khushwant Singh's Fiction," *Indian Writing Today* 11 (1970) 125.
2. Haydon Moore Williams, "Khushwant Singh and the Sikhs," *Studies in Modern Indian Fiction in English*, vol. II (Calcutta: Writers' Workshop, 1973) 143.
3. Khushwant Singh, Foreword, *The Company of Women* (New Delhi and New York: Viking, 1999).

A KHUSHWANT SINGH BIBLIOGRAPHY

Primary Sources

Novels

Train to Pakistan. London: Chatto and Windus, 1956; New York: Grove Press, 1961; as *Mano Majra*, Grove Press, 1956.

I Shall Not Hear the Nightingale. New York: Grove Press, 1959.

Delhi: A Novel. New Delhi and New York: Viking, 1989.

The Company of Women. New Delhi and New York: Viking, 1999.

The Collected Novels: Train to Pakistan, I Shall Not Hear the Nightingale, Delhi. New Delhi: Penguin Books, 1999.

The Collected Short Stories of Khushwant Singh. New Delhi: Ravi Dayal, 1989.

Non-fiction

The Sikhs. London: Allen and Unwin, 1953.

The Unending Trail. New Delhi: Rajkamal, 1957.

The Sikhs Today: Their Religion, History, Culture, Customs, and Way of Life. Bombay: Orient Longman, 1959.

Fall of the Kingdom of the Punjab. Bombay: Orient Longman, 1962.

A History of the Sikhs 1469-1964. Princeton, New Jersey: Princeton UP; London: Oxford UP, 2 vols. 1963-66.

Ranjit Singh: Maharajah of Punjab 1780-1839. London: Allen and Unwin, 1963.

Khushwant Singh's India: A Mirrors for its Monsters and Monstrosities. Bombay: India Book House, 1969.

Indira Gandhi Returns. New Delhi: Vision Books, 1979.

We Indians. New Delhi: Orient Longman, 1982.

Delhi; A Portrait. New Delhi and Oxford: Oxford UP, 1983.

Many Moods Many Faces. Ed. Rohini Singh. New Delhi: Rupa & Co, 1989.

My Bleeding Punjab. New Delhi and London: UBSPD, 1992.

How the Sikhs Lost Their Kingdom. New Delhi: UBSPD, 1996.

Secondary Sources

Books on Khushwant Singh

Dubey, S.K. *Khushwant Singh: A Critical Study of His Novels.* New Delhi: B.R. Publishing Corporation, 1999.

Sahane, V.A. *Khushwant Singh.* New York: Twayne Publishers, 1972.

Singh, Rohini, ed. *A Man Called Khushwant Singh.* New Delhi: UBSPD, 1996.

Articles and chapters on Khushwant Singh

Belliappa, K.C. "The Elusive Classic: Khushwant Singh's *Train to Pakistan* and Chaman Nahal's *Azadi.*" *The Literary Criterion* 15.2 (1980): 62-73.

Harrex, S.C. "Partitioned Hearts: The Fiction of Khushwant Singh." *The Fire and the Offering* (I). Calcutta: The Writers' Workshop, 1977.

Kulshrestha, Chirantan. "Khushwant Singh's Fiction." *Indian Writing Today* 11 (1970): 122-31.

Morey, Peter. "Post-Colonial DestiNations: Spatial Re(con)figurings in Khushwant Singh's *Train to Pakistan* and Rohinton Mistry's *A Fine Balance.*" *Fictions of India: Narrative and Power.* Edinburgh: Edinburgh UP, 2000.

Mukherji, Meenakshi. *The Twice Born Fiction: Themes and Techniques of Indian Novel in English.* London and New Delhi: Heinemann, 1971.

Patil, Mallikarjun. "Khushwant Singh." *Encyclopedia of Literature in English.* Ed. M.K. Bhatnagar. New Delhi: Atlantic Publishers, 2001.

Prasad, Madhusudan. "Some Post-independence Indian English Novelists: An Overview." *Perspectives on Indian Fiction in English.* Ed. M.K. Naik. Delhi: Abhinav Publishers, 1985.

Prempati, D. "*Train to Pakistan*: Some Reflections." *Three Contemporary Novelists.* Ed. R.K. Dhawan. New Delhi: Classical Publishing Company, 1985.

Ramaiah, D. "Khushwant Singh—*Train to Pakistan*: The Novel and the Film." *Encyclopedia of Literature in English.* New Delhi: Atlantic Publishers, 2001.

Ravindranathan, S. & R.K. Jacob. "Khushwant Singh Writes at Home: A Post-Colonial Reading of *Train to Pakistan.*" *Journal of Indian Writing in English* 27.1 (1999): 24-28.

Shahane, V.A. "The Novel as Realistic Epic: *Train to Pakistan.*" *Three Contemporary Novelists.* Ed. R.K. Dhawan. New Delhi: Classical Publishing Company, 1985.

Srinath, C.N. "The Writer as Historical Witness: Khushwant Singh's *Train to Pakistan* and Chaman Nahal's *Azadi.*" *The Literary Criterion* 25.2 (1990): 58-66.

Williams, Haydon Moore. "Khushwant Singh and the Sikhs." *Studies in Modern Indian Fiction in English.* Vol. II. Calcutta: Writers' Workshop, 1973.

____. "The Doomed Hero." *Three Contemporary Novelists.* Ed. R.K. Dhawan. New Delhi: Classical Publishing Company, 1985.

5

Kamala Markandaya

USHA BANDE

Kamala Markandaya (born 1924) is one of the major first generation Indian woman novelists writing in English. Her writing career spans almost four decades from the 1950s to the 1980s, during which she wrote ten novels; and in almost all these works she is preoccupied with the social realities and the emergent national consciousness. Kamala Markandaya is, however, neither a committed writer nor a propagandist; all she does is to project the image of the changing society by weaving it into a variety of themes and situations. With the publication of her first novel *Nectar in the Sieve* in 1954, she came into limelight as a social realist who could convey her thematic concerns with economy of expression and artistic integrity, without being didactic. This first successful novel was hailed as an "epic" of Indian village life and was followed in quick succession by: *Some Inner Fury* (1957), *A Silence of Desire* (1961), *Possession* (1963), *A Handful of Rice* (1966), *The Coffer Dams* (1969), *The Nowhere Man* (1973), *Two Virgins* (1974), *The Golden Honeycomb* (1978), and *Pleasure City* (1982). Her works have received critical acclaim for their themes, crisp style and rich texture; and with each successive novel she seems to have achieved distinction as an important Indian novelist. R.S. Singh extols her "sense of involvement in the social life of India, her keen observation combined with critical acumen, and the feminine sensibility,"[1] which brought her international fame; while Stephen Hemenway, calling her a "productive, popular and skilled" writer observes that with her "calm, reflective and economical style" she is the superb representative of the emerging Indian women writers.[2] Looking back today from our vantage point in time we can claim that though in the matter of form and technique Markandaya is not very innovative; and that the influence of the Western genre of the novel is much too implicit on her works, she shows an extraordinary richness of subject matter and wide range of themes.

Some of the prominent thematic concerns of her works revolve round the East-West encounter, confrontation between tradition and modernity and the clash of values. Within this pattern, she weaves a richly variegated picture of life, arranging her ideas and philosophy with deft touches of feminine sensibility. The resultant picture of human suffering and endurance becomes a vehicle of her moral vision without letting the works be framed within an ideological construct. Like Ernest Hemingway she seems to wonder at the human capacity to endure, and proclaim that man/woman was not made for defeat, and that man/woman may be destroyed but not defeated. Here is a whole gallery of personages who stand up with remarkable courage in the face of difficulties. Rival forces are clearly at work but the author seems to have chosen to channel her impressive understanding of the Indian society, the nature of change within it, and the effect of that change on the individual, into a sort of mythology. Each of her works shows intense and disquieting perceptions of the way of life going through a nightmarish transformation and the inability to stop that change.

Some critics complain that Markandaya returns to the theme of East-West encounter too often to lend it credibility. Justifying her tendency to repeat the theme of the conflict between the East-West "codes and convictions," Madhusudan Prasad says that it could be because she herself has been a living example of a person posited in that situation. Prasad, however, regrets that in dealing with the theme she lacks the epic dimension of Raja Rao and the sharp sociological concerns of Anand.[3] But as Markandaya asserts in one of her letters, since art imitates life, her aim has been to present an image of the society artistically, holds the mirror to the flow of life, and creates art without succumbing to propaganda. William Walsh appreciates Markandaya's strength "in the delicately analysing" relationships and feels that she is at her best, "an impressive best, in dealing with the problems of the educated and middle class, and she has a gift for delineating the self-imposed laceration of the dissatisfied."[4]

Markandaya's frequent return to some of the themes can be understood if we throw a glance at the historical and political background of the time when she was writing. In fairness to the author it could be argued that the country was passing through the social and political ferment during the thirties and the forties of the 20th century when Kamala was growing up. With the freedom struggle at its intensity, rapid changes were in the offing in the society. At the personal level, young Kamala Markandaya worked as a journalist and was also involved in social work in the villages. Like Roshan Merchant of her novel *Some Inner Fury*, she experienced the social turmoil at first hand, and as a social worker, she saw the life of farmers and the weaker sections of the society at close quarters. With her detached imagination, and acute observation, she wrought up the raw material of experience and realized from it perceptions which were to yield rich plots when she started handling her themes.

Kamala Markandaya's experiences of life have been varied and deep-set. As the daughter of a staunch but well-to-do Tamil Brahmin family, she was steeped in tradition; as a Western-educated young woman, she questioned the efficacy of those values. This generated a kind of questioning consciousness, a confusion and a protest. Surveying the prominent themes that the Indian-English novelists writing between the 1930s to 1970s chose from, S.C. Harrex summarizes the topics under six headings and a number of sub-headings: themes of protest and reforms, India's modern destiny, social and cultural transformation, the questions of regional and communal identities, East-West encounter and questioning affirmation of tradition.[5] Markandaya's themes fall within this graph. Harrex discusses Markandaya in another context elsewhere and mentions the sense of identity as a significant motif running parallel to her main themes in her novels. Rochelle Almeida's recent study assesses comprehensively the autobiographical elements in her novels, the Western influence in her choice of themes and the sociological veracity in her novels. The critic feels that Markandaya distorts reality when she depends upon her imagination to flesh out the plots, she appears authentic and enlightening when her personal observations and experiences are at play.[6] The novelist's own confrontation with the western culture and her sense of dislocation following her marriage to an Englishman and her expatriate status have probably found artistic expression in her works. But, it should be granted that there is no evidence of cultural schizophrenia born out of alienation. She is at ease as much with her Indian characters as with the Western, though in portraying Indian women like Mira, Rukmani, Sarojini and others her Indian sensibilities are at their masterly best. It is then that the "insider" seems to be at work but this could not be affirmed of her English characters where she suddenly seems to assume an "outsider's" posture. Her Western characters are convincing but still they are understood with a lopsided view. That she continued to write about India and Indian life from England speaks for the "race-culture-contact,"[7] which is the fountainhead of her creativity. The two different sets of social and cultural values: one imbued by birth and the other acquired consciously after marriage give her two distinct experiences. The two are antithetical but she strives to delve below the surface idiosyncrasies to work out a synthesis and understand the natural human being within. In fact, Markandaya is a conscious artist; she does not let the experiences of life and the actual lived realities enter directly into her fiction, but she uses them as raw material to give authenticity to her art. Commenting on the interplay of tradition and change in her art Shiv K. Kumar points out that what distinguishes her most intensively from other Indian novelists is her acute awareness of a gradual shift in values that has been taking place in this subcontinent during the past two decades or so.[8]

Kamala Markandaya's strength as an artist lies in the seriousness and authenticity she lends to her handling of the themes of tradition and modernity, the abiding cultural values, and the cross-cultural interaction in their various dimensions. She is not unduly biased in favour of any particular culture; on the contrary, she assesses the strong and weak points of both the East and the West and demonstrates them through her characters or her themes. Indian mysticism and spiritualism may be appreciable, but so is the Western rationalism and scientific temper. Though she has a soft corner for her poor Indian brethren, she is critical of illiteracy, poverty, economic backwardness, and population growth. For example, in *Nectar in a Sieve*, she does not narrate the reasons for Nathan's troubles but as an expert novelist she shows us that it could partly be due to his half-a-dozen children. In the same novel she lets Dr. Kenny be her mouthpiece to condemn poverty and superstitions, and the villagers insensitivity to these because of religious-cultural factors. She covertly appreciates Dandekar's modern rational approach in *The Silence of Desire*, but she does not repudiate the need for faith and spirituality. Thus, while criticizing ignorance, poverty, superstitions, she upholds the abiding values of the culture. She assails Western materialism (as of Caroline in *Possession*) although she does not underestimate the contribution of the West to Indian thought. Each of her protagonists displays sufficient mental agility to protest against the existing suffocations and yet to maintain a balance. Changes are inevitable, she seems to say, but the dynamics of change are powerful and may not be adhered to blindly. Thus, the kaleidoscopic picture of life she presents becomes a real vignette of life. There are troubles, disappointments, failures, but these can be surmounted with courage and will power. Hers is an optimistic though tragic vision of life. She does not delve deep, like Anita Desai, into the psyche of her characters to probe their imaginary troubles, nor is she concerned like Arun Joshi with their existential *angst.* What she portrays is the drama of life played within the cultural milieu of modern India, the joys and pains of the rapidly changing society and the relief born out of the cultural continuity.

Markandaya is not very innovative in her narrative technique. Usually, she changes her strategy as per the requirement of her plot. In *Nectar in a Sieve*, for example, Rukmani, an illiterate peasant woman narrates her story. The mood of the novel is placid and as a critic terms it, one of "gentle nostalgia."[9] The narrational technique is effective in so far as it conveys the tragic sense of life, but it lacks authenticity as the author puts too much philosophy in the mouth of her semi-literate protagonist to become palatable. *Some Inner Fury* and *Possession* also have first person narrators, though Anasuya, the narrator of *Possession* recounts the story of Caroline and Val. In the rest of her novels third person omniscient narrators are used. In most of her works, the central consciousness is female. Markandaya tells her stories in a direct manner and chronological order. She uses flashbacks or dramatic digressions very rarely and that too only as per the requirement of the plot. Her novels are open-ended and the plots are often subservient to the themes. Sometimes, she is so preoccupied with the leitmotif that she allows it to dominate her style with the result that the entire structure of the novel weakens. This is particularly so with *Two Virgins* and *Possession* where the novelist's attention is focused on the clash between tradition and modernity, and the East-West divide, respectively.

Markandaya's characters, both major and minor, are convincingly drawn. They are ordinary men and women we encounter in everyday life, with scant claim to heroism or superhuman courage, but they have indomitable will power to survive all predicaments. For example, Shoshana M. Landow assesses the value of suffering in *Nectar in a Sieve* as a cultural construct and extols Rukmani and Ira for their uncanny ability "find [...] sureness and inner peace" in suffering.[10] The same could be said of other Indian women who bear their lot stoically. Markandaya is equally at ease with her Westerners, but she tends to view them, particularly the women characters, from her own cultural angle, as she does in the case of Caroline in *Possession* or Helen in *The Coffer Dams*. By and large, Markandaya is a fine artist, and after placing her characters in particular situations she tries to find ways and means to help them get over the difficulties or reconcile with their fate with dignity. The torn loyalties of her characters speak of the effect of the changing times on their psyche but she employs the art and craft of her writing to see them through. Her success as an artist lies in the fact that no two characters are alike, even their social backgrounds are not identical yet her tragic vision successfully weaves them together.

Nectar in a Sieve (1956), Kamala Markandaya's first novel, brought her immediate recognition. It is designed to capture the tragedy of Indian village life affected by poverty, hunger and the influx of modernization. The rural folk, particularly the farmers, are the helpless victims of natural, social and economic forces that are beyond their grasp. Hailing it as a fictional epic of Indian rural life, critics have compared the novel with Pearl S. Buck's *The Good Earth*, Bhabani Bhattacharya's *So Many Hungers* and Alan Paton's *Cry, Beloved Country*, for the treatment of the theme of poverty and for painting a realistic picture of the life of the farmers. It is through this story of Rukmani that Markandaya gives voice to the subaltern. What makes the tiny novel so powerful is the stark depiction of the Indian reality—economic backwardness, the scourge of large families, illiteracy and the helpless/ hapless complacency with which the farmers endure the assault of existence. That they emerge out of the suffering with dogged will power is appreciable, but the author appears to be uncertain to call suffering really grand. Her mouthpiece Dr. Kenny voices typical Western sentiments when he chides Rukmani and says, "There is no grandeur in want—or in endurance" (105). Rukmani, however, knows better and she stoically asserts that if one were not able to endure, one would be shattered; there is, in fact, no choice. She broods on Dr. Kenny's exhortations thus: "O, well, and what if we gave in to our troubles at every step! We would be pitiable creatures indeed to be so weak, for is not a man's spirit given to him to rise above his misfortunes" (105). With this spirit, Rukmani and her ilk face life, and the novel becomes a saga of courage in its most seminal form.

Thematically, the novel revolves round the questions of poverty, economic deprivation, social taboos and traditional outlook. Underneath this broad pattern run the tiny currents of allied problems. There is a muffled indictment of some of the social norms—the craving for sons, the disregard of the girl child, illiteracy and the government's apathy towards the condition of the villages and the poor. Nathan and Rukmani's poverty is as much due to natural causes as to their inordinately large family. The sons they have craved for desert them one by one and they are left with only Selvam, compounder to Dr. Kenny. The desire for children drives Ira's husband to abandon her as a barren woman. Ira gives birth to an illegitimate child but the author does not indict her. Instead, she is shown as a self-sacrificing woman who by sacrificing her most precious being to provide food to her brother dying of hunger transforms her act as her strength not her lust; and second, the birth of the child washes off the stigma of barrenness. So great an emphasis is laid on fertility that Kamala Markandaya lets Nathan's moral voice, upbraiding his daughter drown in Ira's self-sacrificing goodness.

Technically, the novel has received both scathing criticism and mild approval. A first person narration, *Nectar in a Sieve* gives a long rope to Rukmani to record her life. She recollects the events of her life with Nathan with due warmth and clarity. However, the semi-literate protagonist donning the mantle of lofty ideas, philosophical thoughts and psychological probing appears unconvincing. The story is "somewhat tampered" says a critic, asserting that "action is subordinated [...] to an individual's thoughts and feelings."[11] Referring to the novel as "melodramatic," R.S. Singh feels that the author has exaggerated the circumstantial pressure on the narrator and that the ordeals of Nathan and Rukmani appear "enigmatic, contrived a little too cleverly, rather than developed on chance events alone."[12]

Markandaya has had the experience of living and working in villages when she was involved in social work. She understood the problems of the peasant class; saw their suffering, their resentment to industrialization and their distrust of industrial and economic change. In making Rukmani the authorial voice of the novel, she has fulfilled a significant purpose that of giving a first hand picture of a typical farmer woman—strong, hard working, uncomplaining, tolerant and able. Rukmani has often been compared to the 'mother earth' and to *shakti*. She is resolute and once she takes a step, she sticks to it as is revealed in the first few paragraphs of the novel when she upholds her decision to bring the leper boy, Puli with her from the city, "what is done is done, there can be no repining" (1), she says. The novel takes off from this point and a reflective, benevolent, affectionate but strong Rukmani recounts her life and through her the village community is revealed to us.

From the peasant community and the village life, Markandaya shifts her attention to the higher middle-class and the city in her second novel *Some Inner Fury* (1955). It has as its major theme the East-West encounter born out of the clash of interests and values between the British masters and their Indian subjects. Significantly, the conflict is also between the Anglicized Indians like Kitsamy and the upholders of Indian values like Govind and Premala. Dramatized against the Quit India movement, the novel reveals the predicament of Mirabai, torn between her love for Richard and her patriotic pride. That the latter should overpower her in the end, giving her strength to sacrifice her love, speaks of the author's leanings. The novel also tracks the violence building up inside the nationalist Indians until it spurts out claiming valuable lives. The title is suggestive of the inner turmoil at two levels: Mira's emotional inner fury and the country's political rage.

Between the themes of the East-West encounter and the ferment of the freedom movement, Kamala Markandaya has deftly woven the love story of Mira and Richard to lend a deeper dimension to the main framework. Individual love appears puny and defenceless as against the enormity of the hatred for the British, spread far and wide. In this vitiated atmosphere, love is substituted by violence and death, and none is spared from the engulfing fire—neither the British symbolized by Richard, nor the Anglicized Indians represented by Kitsamy, and not even the nationalist Indians like Premala. Focusing on the theme of love and death in the novel, R.K. Srivastava observes that Richard senses the pervading danger and "measures the smallness of Mira's love against the enormity of general hatred for the British."[13] Richard feels insecure in the pervading atmosphere of hatred, "It is a terrible thing, to feel unwanted. To be hated" (120). "This feeling isn't for you" (218), Mira tells Richard but her assessment appears rather juvenile, which does not take into consideration the gravity of the situation.

Richard's reaction is far more mature and realistic, "Do you think people can be singled out like that? One by one each as an individual? At a time like this? After today?" Earlier, judging from Mira's pejoratives, Richard had remarked quietly, "Has it infected you too—all this 'your people,' and 'my people?'" (218). In fact, Mira is "lost in the political confusion" as Harrex points out, to gauge the intensity of the outside situation and her inner demands.[14] Mira is certainly raw and naïve to believe that she and Richard are inseparable, that her antagonism for the British would not affect Richard as an individual, that their love would withstand all outward political storms, and that even the nationalists would not target Richard.

Mira's decision to part ways with Richard is neither sudden nor unaccountable. The novelist gives sufficient hints all through the narrative to clarify Mira's inclination. In Madras, she works for Roshan Merchant's nationalist paper; her relationship with her adopted brother Govind, a staunch nationalist and with Premala based on deep faith and understanding; later, she resents Hickey's false verdict and reacts sharply to the British flawed sense of justice and resolves to join the procession,

> Soon, I would go too. When the tail of that procession went through the door, I would join it, and Richard would stay behind. This was not a time for decision, for he knew he could not come with me, and I knew I could not stay: it was simply the time for parting. (285)

By thus infusing in Mira the clarity of thought and the courage to make a hard choice without any vacillation, Kamala Markandaya has taken a decision for herself and solved the major dilemma of bringing the novel to a convincing finale.

The ending of the novel has raised critical debate regarding Richard—is he alive or dead at the close of the novel? Critics are divided on the issue. Those who assert that the mob fury killed Richard, take their clue from the reference to "the little silver box" in Mira's cupboard that contains "the scrap of material torn from Richard's sleeve" which she had "picked from the dust when it was all over" (5); Mira opens the box at the beginning of the novel and feels a searing pain to look back on life. Srinivas Iyengar, R.K. Srivastava, H.M. Williams and Meenakshi Mukherjee believe that Richard is dead, killed by the furious mob, while S. Krishna Sarma and some others contend that there is nothing in the novel to suggest "physical injury caused to Richard, not to speak of death."[15] Whether Richard is dead or alive, the fact is, he is no more a part of Mira's life; the ending of the novel is grim and the sense of loss is complete. Between the past and the present of Mira there lies a whole range of memories, bitter and sweet.

Some Inner Fury is a woman-centred novel and focuses on the part played by women in India's freedom struggle. It would not be wrong to contend that Mira, though not a feminist in the sense of being a rebel, shows sufficient traits of resistance to both male hegemony and the colonial subjugation. The first person narrative technique is circular in motion as Mira recasts her past and in doing so she links it with her present. The novel ends where it began.

In *A Silence of Desire* (1963), her third novel, Markandaya's focus shifts from the Westernized rich class to the middle class perceptions. The East-West conflict gives way to the clash between the male rational approach in facing life's realities to the female view based on faith and sentiments. The author subtly finds a via media to deal with this ticklish questions of rationality and faith and without indicting or appreciating any one outlook. The novel is also a pointer towards the dichotomy in male psyche: there is a vast difference between what Dandekar expects from his wife and what he himself does. Kamala Markandaya, though not a feminist writer, has astutely tried to probe her male character's psyche to reveal male hegemony and patriarchal dominance in the domestic sphere.

The author is as much interested in the situation created by Sarojini's frequent and stealthy trips to the Swami as in the authoritative attitude of Dandekar. In the earlier two novels Markandaya dwelt primarily on her women protagonists. Here, the Indian male seems to interest her, and it is through him that we understand Sarojini. A clerk in a Government office, Dandekar is a traditional husband who has one set of rules for himself and the other for the females. For him, a wife means a constant prop to *his* household, with no personal demands. Sarojini is an ideal wife

> good with the children, an excellent cook, an efficient manager of his household, a woman who still gave him pleasure after fifteen years of marriage [...] she did most things placidly [...] and from this calm proceeded the routine and regularity that met the neat and orderly needs of his nature. (7)

For Dandekar, life is smooth. He gets the best of everything: good food punctually served, a cot to sleep on (while the others slept spreading their mattresses on the floor), a neat home and a complete family:

> Three children, no debts, a steady job, a fair pile of savings that his wife methodically converted into gold bangles, a necklace, ear-rings and brooches less for ornamentation than the security it represented. (6)

Dandekar had never visualized any change in this set-up. When the change comes because of Sarojini's ill health and her secret visits to the Swami, he is distraught. He becomes frantic, jealous, prying and unscrupulous.

For Sarojini, going to the Swami is a question of simple faith. She has a growth in her womb and instead of getting medical help she prefers faith cure. She does not take her husband in confidence because she knows that he with his Western notions of rationality he would not accept the Swami and his faith healing. For Sarojini, the Swami is an epitome of power, it is silent power of faith, and as a critic observes, "His is the silence—not of desire, fear or anger, but of a powerful personality, capable of inspiring thought in others without having recourse to speech."[16] In contrast, Sarojini's silence is the silence of the weak; she keeps her motives a secret because she cannot face her husband. It is the Swami who empowers her. A critic calls Sarojini as searching for autonomy and concludes:

> She is an independent enough figure to emerge and confront male reality, quietly but insistently, as wife and mother [...]. Whatever form the male control may take in her life, she would be free in those matters which are vital to the core of her being.[17]

Dandekar's silence is the silence of anger and fear; he is afraid of the Swami's power over his wife. He realizes that he will not be able to wrench her faith away. In desperation he turns to prostitutes, neglects his children and home, nags Sarojini and in turn suffers isolation. These methods prove damaging and detrimental to the peace of his family. Markandaya shows how the subaltern and self-effacing person can also be empowered with faith. Sarojini agrees to go in for the operation not because she is convinced of its efficacy but because the Swami assures her that she would be cured if she gets operated. The Swami gives her faith in life and in God; he succeeds where Dandekar's rationality fails. Sarojini faces the operation with composure and is healed. The Swami gives her a personality, a vision to look in "to turn the eye inward and find there the core of being" (199). She faces Dandekar boldly when she tells him

> I do not expect you to understand—you with your Western notions, your superior talk of ignorance and superstition when all it means is that you don't know what lies beyond reason and you prefer not to find out." (87)

In the end, Sarojini appears strong while Dandekar, dangling between faith and reason, the Eastern notions and the Western pragmatism looks uncertain. Kamala Markandaya achieves what she began with her first novel: the strength of the Indian woman.

The conflict between the Western and the Eastern values takes on socio-cultural economic colour in *Possession* (1963). While a number of scholars dwell on the novel's symbolic and allegorical meaning, and study it as "a parable of colonialism,"[18] recent trends in feminist criticism identify "anti-patriarchal rage"[19] in Caroline and Anasuya's approaches. Scholars and critics, both Indian and Western, have also spotted other themes in the novel, such as a quest for identity, for spirituality, as against the mundane.

Going by the rhetoric, the picture is simply thus: Caroline is unscrupulous, possessive and a victimizer; Val is helpless, lonely and a victim; Anasuya is the only "sane" voice who sees through Caroline's greed and tries to rescue Valmiki. Anasuya is, in fact, the author's alter ego that vacillates between the Eastern and the Western values. Ultimately, she upholds the ingrained Indian ethos. Lady Caroline Bell rich, beautiful, vivacious dominates over all those who come into her contact: Val, Jumbo, Ellie, Annabel and Anasuya, except the Swamy. And, she possesses them all: Val, by her money power; Jumbo, by her British superiority, Ellie and Annabel because of her elevated social position; and Anasuya, through Valmiki, for whom Anasuya feels responsible. These people around her serve the same purpose and fulfil the same needs as does Minou, Valmiki's pet monkey. The little monkey "is bought for show" and is possessed for personal and social amusement; likewise, Caroline retains these person's around her for personal satisfaction and social glorification. But, whereas Val repents for having used the animal for "ends of my own," Caroline glories in having owned a human being. She tells the Swamy at the end of the novel, "Valmiki is yours now, but he has been mine. I shall take care to make him want me again; and on that day I shall come back to claim him" (233), thus asserting her ownership rights over Val.

The assertion of proprietarily relationship with Val is important for Caroline, because ownership is the basis of her identity. True, Caroline has everything by way of possession: power, prestige, wealth, and looks. She is "really rich, in the English way, with landed estates and money in sterling; really well-born, descended from a long line of men who ruled India [...] and she is reputed to be beautiful" (3). But, to wear Val as a "diamond [...] on the necklace round her throat for her friends to admire" (55) is far more satisfying. In order to keep this "nugget [...] shining brightly" (124) in her coffers she uses all means fair and foul; cajoling, forgery, tricks, lies and finally sex. Critics of Kamala Markandaya condemn Caroline for exploiting a helpless boy; they call it almost an incestuous relationship considering Val's age, but what we censure as morally and ethically wrong can be psychologically understood, though not justified if we take into account her "the terrible overpowering craving for possession" (111). To be fair to Caroline, let us grant that she is not monstrous nor is she "bizarre" as the headman of the village calls her, she has grace and elegance and as Anasuya agrees, she has something about her that is "spiritually appealing" (152).

Anasuya is a Westernised Indian, dangling between Indian value-system and the British way of life. H.M. Williams is rather hard on her when he calls her "an embittered and confused person."[20] To my mind, Anasuya is basically a kind, helpful and companionable person, "the gentle Hindu lamb" (107), as Caroline often teases her. As an Indian she is intrinsically drawn to those values that uphold the will to give and to share; on the other hand, Western influence makes her individualistic and acquisitive. Intellectually, her acceptance of the West is complete; emotionally, it is flawed. Consequently, we find her fluctuating, unable to take a stand.

Valmiki is a psychologically rich character, introduced to the readers as a "simpleton," a good for nothing goatherd. Caroline gives him a taste of life, worldly pleasures and the power of money. But that Val should come back to his penury after having seen the best of the mundane world—money, glamour, fame, sex and love—shows his unconscious inclination towards the basic values of life. His return is what Iyengar calls "atmasamarpam."[21] *Possession* is a pointer towards the universality of Markandaya's art and craft. She seems to suggest subtly the necessity to cultivate an inner vision in which man develops a sense of security and identity by inculcating faith in what one is and not in what one possesses. Possession is "slavery" as Iyengar points out because we are possessed by what we possess.

Once again Kamala Markandaya shifts her attention, in *A Handful of Rice* (1966) to the exodus to the cities by the rural poor and the socio-cultural economic problems the uncertainties of urban life. It is the story of a peasant boy who comes to the city, undergoes a crisis of character, as he is lost in its labyrinthine mode of life, but is saved from further degradation by his basic value-system. We see life through the eyes of a male protagonist and the female characters are not much active or effective though Ravi's mother-in-law has been depicted as a formidable woman. It is India of the early decade after the Independence when the villagers "lived between bouts of genteel and acute poverty—the kind in which the weakest went to the wall, the old ones and the babies dying of tuberculosis, dysentery, the 'falling fever,' 'recurrent fever' and any other name for what was basically, simply nothing but starvation" (12). The city, however, had no jobs for the poor and the unqualified. The likes of Ravi drifted into the world of crime and underground activities increasing the law and order problem.

Ravi, coming to the city with golden dreams realizes pretty soon that life is difficult here. For a while he joins Damodar who initiates him into the world of unlawful activities. It appears adventurous initially but Ravi's conscience does not allow him to do something unethical. He accepts Apu's offer of a job and decides to lead a gentleman's life. Ravi, she tells us, does not accept the unexciting work of being an apprentice to the tailor merely on ideological basis; in fact, he has an ulterior motive. He wants to be friends with Nalini, Apu's young, bright-eyed daughter. Ravi's dream of marrying Nalini materializes soon but life as a householder brings its responsibilities. Ravi sees the social and economic disparities in city life and feels depressed. He loses faith in Apu's ways of dealing with the rich, finding it ridiculous that Apu should treat his clients as little gods; he is repulsed to see him bribing the watchman at the gate of a rich Memsahib so as to get an audience with his prospective moneyed client; he resents when the shopkeeper of the ready-made garments sells the clothes at higher price than was paid to the poor tailor. He tries to fling aside Apu's code of conduct and mode of dealings but with disastrous results. He loses some of his valued clients and suffers losses. As a victim of circumstances, Ravi acts recklessly, he is not only unfair to Nalini but is also callous towards the other members of the family. His act of raping his mother-in-law is an unimaginable act of violence born out of frustration.

Ravi is not callous by nature, though. His trouble springs from his inability to better his lot, to provide timely medical help to his ailing son who dies for want of proper care, and from a silent rage at the world in which dishonesty is rewarded. He is appalled to find Damodar thrive by corrupt means while he, with his hard work and honest dealings is not in a position to buy even the basic necessities for his family. This sickening order of things and his shattered dreams turn him to revolt but at the end of the novel we see Ravi unable to take to throwing brickbats to harm others. One can appreciate Ravi's final act of moral goodness but it does not redeem him, nor do things change on the domestic front. Nalini is drained of all pleasures of life; she is denied even the simple joys of togetherness. Ravi, an anti-hero, though good-hearted, appears immature, callous towards his wife and impatient to better his lot. His parents are more practical and though illiterate they know "that things would never be any better." Young as he is, Ravi could see only light and no darkness. His parents' attitude and acceptance of fate sickens him and he leaves the village in the belief that the city would be a heaven for him with a good job and a bright future. Here is loss of innocence of a male; the typical problem faced by a female would be the subject of her *Two Virgins*, to be discussed later in this easy.

The Coffer Dams (1967), according to Uma Parmeswaran, is "a turning point in her [Kamala Markandaya's] literary career and has deeper implications in the context of expatriation."[22] In *The Coffer Dams* she focuses on the question of industrialization, an issue she only touched upon in *Nectar in a Sieve* (that is, about the tannery and the villagers' reactions to it). India, after the Independence, was passing through a ferment of change and Markandaya saw the need for the country to go in for industrialization and scientific development to overcome economic backwardness. In the novel under consideration she writes a full-fledged story of the construction of the Dam in which the English and the Indian participate with zest. As in *Possession* an English woman develops close ties with an Indian (this time a tribal) and seeks fulfilment of her desires through him till she passes through self-berating and returns to her English husband. The novel, though called a tragedy ends on a conciliatory note.

The story moves between two realities: the construction of the Dam and the residue of the colonial past that the English engineers tend not to forget. The conflict accentuates as the Indians, now no longer British subjects, resent their erstwhile masters' dismissive attitude. The superiority-inferiority syndrome plays fully on the psyche of both the Indians and the English and produces a clash of race and culture. The English Engineers and other officials segregate themselves from the Indians and take precautions to keep their distance from the inferior natives. "We like keeping ourselves to ourselves," says Jackson and Clinton's rigid superiority corroborates it. For them the Indians are primitive who "worshipped birds and beasts and probably snakes, decking the forest with scruffy hutches which they knocked up out of driftwood and crammed with leaves and flowers for their deities" (76). The English, therefore, make their own England with "the trim square plots of emerging garden, the gravelled paths, the white washed boulders that demarcate and uphold private property rights" (11). It is interesting to see how Helen escapes this tight British order and gets involved with the Indians.

While the plot and the sub-plot advance on the given lines, the characters emerge with sharp racial and cultural contours. Howard Clinton, Rawlings, Millie, Mackendrick represent the English attitude to life; Krishnan and Bashiam stand for the Indian outlook. Clinton is devoted to his work and has a dogged determination. He is resolute to complete the work on the Dam before the monsoons set in and he removes all obstacles from his path with impunity: he neglects Helen, curbs the initial resistance of the Indian workers with dexterity and takes hard decisions without thinking of the consequences. His pugnacious behaviour alienates him not only from his wife but also from the Indian workers. It is Mackendrick who becomes a bridge between the Indians workers and the English officials by his more sensible and sensitive approach.

Unable to bear her loneliness, Helen eventually turns to the Indians for company and realizes that Bashiam and the tribals are far more human and humane, warm and responsive to affection than her English countrymen; and she drifts towards Bashiam. Initially, her attraction for him is tinged with curiosity, which soon blossoms to friendship and love. With Bashiam, Helen relishes a kind of fullness of life, with "a deep quiet pleasure" (42) adding "colour" to her existence. Helen is positioned between Clinton and Bashiam and she represents both the English values and an inclination towards Indian ethos. While she reaches out to the warmth of the Indian character, she cannot forsake her Western pragmatism. Humane and compassionate though she is, her relationship with Bashiam is only at the physical level and as soon as Bashiam is incapacitated, she withdraws from him. But credit goes to Helen for not acting on impulse; she does not walk out of her marriage, as does the heroine of Ruth Jabvala's *Heat and Dust.* Markandaya saves Clinton-Helen marriage by dexterously allowing Helen a change of perception.

Bashiam is a lovable character. The tribals hold him in respect and the English engineers recognize his power over the workers. Before him even Clinton, otherwise resolute and ruthless Clinton appears helpless. Clinton learns to like Bashiam for his devotion to duty and honest hard work though he hates his guts in being friendly with his wife. Bashiam relinquishes his hold on Helen after the accident and shows his determination and mental resolve. However, Bashiam brooding philosophically in the end appears unconvincing and gives a feeling that the plot has been manufactured to suit the requirement of the theme. The novel uses the stream-of-consciousness technique whenever the author tries to probe the psyche of her character. The language is powerful and is marked by long descriptive passages.

Kamala Markandaya shifts her attention in *The Nowhere Man* (1972) to the problem of an expatriate who suffers all his life due to dislocation. Despite living in England for decades, the central character Srinivas, remains a marginal man, alienated and isolated in a country where he has a host of good friends but where he is unable to belong. Unlike her earlier works, which are set in India, this novel is situated in England and affords us an opportunity to view the clash of cultures from a different angle. Adjustment and acceptance of a country has to be on both the sides, Markandaya seems to suggest, otherwise there is rejection and the consequent rootlessness. If Srinivas fails to adjust to the country, the country too disowns him. His children manage to be a part of the scenario they are born into but they remain unaware of the magnitude of their loss: they have lost the link with India, the country of their ancestors. Thus, the loss to both the generations is massive and irretrievable. The novel gains psychological dimension as the writer weaves the themes of displacement and East-west conflict with the question of human relations; it becomes the study of a dislocated man and can compare well, to an extent, with Anita Desai's Baumgartner, the German Jew who fails to assimilate in India and remains at the periphery all his life. However, while the Englishmen like Fred are hostile to the aliens, the Indians in Desai's novel just let the Jew be, never bothered by his presence; this is the basic difference between the attitude of the two races.

Two significant psychological as well as external causes generate and accentuate Srinivas's problem of alienation: first, since his migration to England was not by choice but by force Srinivas never feels at home in the alien surroundings; second, Srinivas is an idealist and a self-effacing man whose values hold no significance at a time when the overall atmosphere of one of uncertainties during the War years. One cannot appreciate his idealism when he fails to guard the honour of his newly wed wife. During a raid on Srinivas's home in India, the English police sergeant lifts up Vasantha's skirt, but Srinivas does not react because he was too busy guarding the trunk in which the body of the youth was placed. This indifference towards the honour of his wife create a kind of apathy in their relations and though Vasantha remains his wife and companion till her death, she seems to have developed a cold attitude towards her marriage. The Gandhian ideals he professes to follow all his life endear him to a couple of friends but by and large these do not help him earn the goodwill of others. His sons, who are more English than Indians, could not identify with him, and Fred does not recognize his good gesture that saved him (Fred) from the clutches of the law.

Through Srinivas, Kamala Markandaya portrays the character of a man who is an amalgam of both the Indian and the Western values and who is unable to solve the conflict produced by the two contradictory systems. On the one hand, he is an Indian in his disregard for materialism: he does not want to possess property in England lest he be tied down to the soil; on the other hand, he follows a bohemian way of life and accepts the Western mode. His disease that Dr. Radcliff diagnoses as leprosy begins with his typical reaction to stepping on excreta. In good faith he gives notice to his tenants to vacate the house and antagonizes the English community further. As a helpful neighbour and a reliable friend he is respected and liked; but he is too idealistic to understand the current of hatred running around him. His wife Vasantha is a practical woman with foresight and it is because of her that the family could settle down respectably in their own house in England. They name it *Chandraprasad* after their ancestral home in India, but unfortunately it could never be a substitute for the ancestral house.

After Vasantha's death, he is lonely and forsaken he becomes friendly with Mrs. Pickering and admits her to his house but her presence creates more troubles socially. Mrs. Pickering, however, remains a prop to him. She helps him in his financial troubles; she even cares for him till the final moment. After his death when Dr. Radcliff mourns and thinks that the English community was the root cause of his death, "and we have all had a hand in it" (298), Mrs. Pickering sees no reason to blame herself and says, " 'blame myself,' said Mrs. Pickering. 'Why should I? I cared for him.' And indeed, that seemed to her to be the core of it" (299). Srinivas dies a distraught man in the end, never able to resolve the problem of his identity.

The central consciousness of the novel is Srinivas. The story opens with Srinivas visiting Dr. Radcliff to have his disease diagnosed. From this incident, his mind moves back to trace the circumstances that have been the cause of the disease, and takes the reader back to his home in India and the reasons for his migration. It is through Srinivas's memory shuttling back and forth that the story of his life is revealed to us. The mode of narration is realistic. Markandaya has entered the field of the psychological novel to expose the deep recesses of the psyche of her character.

Two Virgins (1975) has often come under scathing criticism for its weak plot and artistic flaws. K.S. Ramamurti, for example, calling it "a problem novel" draws our attention to the lack of a well-defined thematic pattern to it but feels that the work is redeemed because as

> "the story of a young girl who ruins herself and brings disrepute on the family by yielding to the temptation of a glamorous career [...] *Two Virgins* has, at least by implication, some of the themes"[23]

that Kamala Markandaya has handled in her earlier works. Niroj Banerji terms it a "disappointing" (Banerji 100) work in which the novelist seems to have lost touch with the real India. Probably, the changes brought in by the impact of modernity in a traditional society and the hazards of the lure of city life continued to grip the author's imagination even after her migration to England. She looks at India standing at a distance in time and space and weaves the story of the two sisters who are drawn by their newly awakened adulthood into the voluptuous world of sexuality. In her earlier works *Nectar in a Sieve* and *A Handful of Rice* young men leave the protected, simple village life for greener pastures and suffer; in *Two Virgins* a young woman Lalitha spells disaster for herself and her family by plunging into the unknown zone. Reading the novel from a woman's angle, Santha Krishnaswamy extols the author's "balanced examination of human nature," and remarks that Kamala Markandaya does not ascribe Lalitha's tragedy only to the newer influences but also to her conventional upbringing.[24]

The conflict between the traditional and the modern outlook, the rural and the urban ethos, the depth of wisdom of the older generation as against the shallow vanity of the new, has been clearly brought out through Lalitha and Saroja. The sisters grow up in the conventional rural environment of their traditional home but they are also exposed to education and the new ideas brought in by people like Miss Mendoza. The older generation is critical of Miss Mendoza's school with its Western notions of Maypole dance, free mixing up of men and women and the individualistic approach to life. Aunt Alamelu chides her brother for the disaster brought in by the English education devoid of tradition, "Brother, she said, it is not for us, puny denizens of this immoral age, to question the wisdom of our ancient mentors [...]. You have given your children rights, Brother, and they have come to roost" (177-78). Whatever the views of the older generation, it cannot be denied that the atmosphere in the girls' home is not insulated. The racy stories of sexual adventures and exploits told by the woman folk with sufficient humour and relish and oblique references give a foretaste of sexual knowledge to the budding girls. They also witness the most vulgar form of sex around them: their Amma's unabashed advances towards the Sikh trader, Amma and Appa's sexual life, Jayamma's experiences recounted with unconcealed details and the sly sexual hints given by men and boys. The girls cannot be termed as innocent, though they are not physically corrupted. They become aware of the body and its demands that remain under check because of the traditional social codes.

Lalitha and Saroja, though brought up in the same atmosphere, react to their realities differently. Saroja is docile, obedient and timid; Lalitha is bold, outgoing and manipulative. She comes under the impact of Miss Mendoza more readily than does Saroja. Saroja's dream is limited to being a good wife and a mother of "lots of lovely, cuddly babies." To Lalitha it is a "peasant's ambition" not worth much (57-58). For her, life means glamour, money and status and flying high above the clouds. She sees an opportunity to fulfil her dreams through Gupta, without realizing that the man is not reliable. She becomes a victim of her own vanity as well as ignorance. Though both the sisters are feminine in their own way, it is Lalitha who is conscious of her beauty and its spell on the people around her. She manipulates her looks, her "feminine desirability and sexual power" but lands in a dreadful mess.

The novel has a number of flaws, no doubt: there is not plot, the thematic structure is lose, the characters are subservient to the events and as Nissim Ezekiel points out, the characters are "puppets manufactured for those who know nothing about India,"[25] the style and technique of narration make the work a weak link to her other works. Notwithstanding the faults, it could be argued in defence of the author that she gives us an early version of feminism in Indian fiction—men like Gupta have always exploited girls and women in their innocence. While the male can get out of the trouble by simply shifting the blame on the girl and her femininity, as Gupta does, "Lalitha is a woman with the natural desires of a woman," it is the female who suffers. Woman should, therefore, develop the ability to define her freedom for herself. The modern ideas are not all vile but then the traditional wisdom not all good. Markandaya makes a valid point on which much feminist thought has revolved of late: that a female who crosses the threshold is bound to be punished by the patriarchal hegemony. The character of Lalitha, despite the fire and zeal she displays remains shallow while Saroja who appears timid in the beginning emerges as a warm, passionate and bold young woman who knows how to protect herself.

The Golden Honeycomb (1977) is one of the earliest Indian English novels dealing with the Princely States and can well be compared to works such as Manohar Malgonkar's *The Princes*, Mulk Raj Anand's *The Private Life of an Indian Prince*, and Gita Mehta's *Raj*. Unlike the others, Markandaya traces almost one hundred years of the history of the Royal family till India achieves Independence. In the corpus of Kamala Markandaya's fiction, *The Golden Honeycomb* holds a significant place because it focuses on the Indian history during the British regime and shows how the historical events affected the fate of the native princes. The novel is a chronological account of the Devapur State and the cunning with which the British rendered the rulers helpless. The novelist also depicts the relations between the English and the Indian princely states, on the one hand and the native princes and their subjects on the other. In both these situations the relations are tenuous and tension ridden. The English wanted to hold on to the country that they called "a gem in the British Crown" and as the Prologue to the novel records, they adopted all means fair or foul to tighten the noose around the native kingdoms. Consequently, the rulers of the States all over India remained weak and almost the mouthpieces of the British regime whereby they alienated their own subjects.

After stating the facts in her Prologue, Markandaya handles the early history of the Bawajiraj family of Devapur. Bawajiraj I is deposed for his nationalist inclinations and a Kshtriya young man is chosen to ascend the throne as Bawajiraj II. The choice is deliberate with a view to have a puppet king who would safeguard the interest of the English masters and Bawajiraj II turns out to be exactly that. After the second Bawaji's death in a hunting expedition, his young son is made Bawajiraj III under the Dowager Maharani's supervision. Due care is taken to give him the required English education so that he too voices the English men's sentiments and safeguards their interest.

The main plot revolves round the rule of Bawajiraj III, his son Rabindranath's nationalistic leanings, the intrigues in the palace and India's Independence. With these strands interwoven with the main theme, the novelist takes care to etch out each character with his or her specific traits. Here is Rabi, who grows up to become a boy of independent temperament and we soon gather that he has been duly influenced by his mother and grandmother who instill him with patriotic fervour. Rabi refuses to toe his father's line and declines to join the Chief's College and the Military Academy because these churn out Brown Sahibs with loyalties to the British. As a contrast to his father, Rabi loves his country, understands its ills and has affection for the commoners. Rabi does not appreciate his father's loyalties to the British masters; he is particularly irked by its abject reality when he sees his father, Bawajiraj III, bowing before the alien Emperor during the Delhi Darbar.

He is pained and ashamed at the dismal servility to which the ruler of an independent kingdom is reduced. The Bawajiraj family goes to Bombay to get their consignment of cars, and it is in Bombay that Rabi is hurt in a mill-workers' strike and is tended with care by Jaya in her hut. This incident not only gives him a chance to feel one with the commoners but also provides him an opportunity to experience a woman's nearness. After World War II, a wind of change blow and Rabi is quick to accept the altered realities.

The novel is a fine mixture of historical realities and fictional setting. It shows Markandaya's subtle art in handling the characters and situations and reveals her deep insight into human relationships. Despite his weakness and servile attitude as a ruler, Bawajiraj is a lovable character. He is a loving father, a ruler with a clear conscience and a man of family. His conversations with Mohini reveal some of his endearing traits: he respects his mother, the Dawager Rani, Manjula, he is loyal towards Mohini, his mistress and he is duly attached to his wife and their four daughters. He gets upset at Rabi's wild habits and does not appreciate his links with the common riff-raff but that can be understood if we take into consideration his upbringing and his position as a king. Bawajiraj is a keen observer and sees through the various individuals that are a part of his kingdom—the Dewan, the English resident and the others.

There are many women who influence the course of Rabi's life and by implication the course of the action of the novel—Manjula (Rabi's grandmother), Mohini (Bawaji's mistress and Rabi's mother), Usha (the Dewan's daughter), Sophiee (the resident's daughter), and Jaya and Janaki (women from the labour class). Each of these women shows strength of character according to her role in the entire drama of the Devapur State. Mohini and Manjula influence Rabi and give him a set of values that stand him in good stead later in life. As Santha Krishnaswamy puts it "the woman who is aware of the silent and invisible barriers against her and who overcomes them, retaining her own sense of integrity is the one who is able to nurture people, men and women in need," and in portraying her strong and able women characters in *The Golden Honeycomb*, Kamala Markandaya "opens up newer, mature frontiers by stressing the importance of filial and conjugal life."[26]

Pleasure City (1982) adds a new dimension to Kamala Markandaya's art and craft of writing. It takes her a long way away from the British India or the recently free India struggling to stand on her feet. Now, it is the India marching ahead in time and developing fast. No longer is there resentment to industrialization as it was to the tannery or to the dam. The coming up of a tourist complex in the vicinity of the quiet coastal village may affect the life of the villagers, mostly the fisher folk but that is inevitable. A mutual understanding and respect for each other's point of view replaces the East-West conflict. The third person narrative shows maturity though the novel does not claim to have much of a theme. The structure is dense, forward moving and neat but episodic in character. The thin theme apparently revolving round the construction of the holiday resort named 'Shalimar' soon acquires a different colour as the author gets engaged in building up on Tully-Rikki relationship on a higher, human plain. The Indo-British relations in the post-colonial era do not seem to have the residue of the earlier/obvious superiority-inferiority syndrome but the astute author does not let us forget the gap prevailing in the status of the two most unlikely friends—Tully and Rikki.

AIDCORP, a multinational organization has accepted the assignment of building a holiday resort in a coastal village in South India. As is Markandaya's wont, she lets the village be unnamed and the location unspecified. She starts with a graphic description of the poverty and hardships faced by the fisher community to introduce Rikki, an orphaned fisher boy, who is to be the mainstay of the novel. He has lost all the members of his family at the sea but has learnt to accept the blows of fate stoically. A fisher family adopts the boy and Mrs. Bridie's school chisels him into shape. Intelligent and artistically oriented, Rikki learns from Mr. and Mrs. Bridie various arts like making tiny models of cathedrals and ships, and also pebble mosaics. These arts, coupled with his natural aesthetic sense bring him closer to Mr. Tully later in the novel when the English gentleman arrives as the Director of the AIDCORP. Soon, Tully and Rikki forge a friendship that sees them through the building of Shalimar and the renovation of Avalon. When the time comes for Mr. Tully to depart after the completion of the project, both feel the pinch of separation.

Tully-Rikki friendship forms the basis of *Pleasure City*. If Rikki is attached to the able Britisher for his "riches of imagination," Tully is equally fond of Rikki for his honesty and perceptions of beauty. The author lets them form close ties without letting the reader forget that there is still a wide gap between their social status: Tully is the Director of the AIDCORP and the descendant of the family of consuls who ruled over India; Rikki is an impoverished, orphan boy for whom life is a struggle. Notwithstanding the difference, the two learn to appreciate and accept each other. They need each other, too. The narrative recounts some of the activities that the two enjoyed together:

> And Tully, aiming for a late sail, would come upon him in the evening, after pool duty, standing in the prow, singing. Not film hits, which he favoured, but one of those ditties, haunting, slightly tinny, that, early on, one heard the women singing when the fishing boats rode on. (328)

Rikki enjoys the picnics, the work on Shalimar and the renovation of Avalon. If Rikki were possessive about his trinkets, Tully would gladly let him be: "Rikki had always had the power. The boat belonged to him. Tully would bequeath it to its proper owner, a proper resolution of at least one equation" (328). As surfers both are at par with each other, "Tully, trained in Cornish waters, a surfer since so high; Rikki sea-bred, with his inherited, internal gyro; both fully capable of appreciating the finer points" (296).

Apart from Shalimar, another house that is central to the novel is the old castle named Avalon, built by Tully's grandfather long back when he was the proconsul of the area. The castle is in ruins and Tully decides to renovate it. Here for once, Kamala Markandaya's imagination moves in the vicinity of the gothic as she describes the ruined castle, with crumbling walls, a dilapidated garden and the weird look of its fortifications. But, Markandaya stops at that and does not plunge into the usual female Gothic in which the uncanny and the eerie play a major role in dealing with the psyche. The renovation of the castle becomes a significant event to cement the bond of friendship. Rikki shows his art and craft in decorating the pool with stone mosaic and giving a sleek look to the garden. Avalon soon throbs with life and gives back to its owner the rhythms life as "a natural return" (341).

The novel has its artistic flaws as well as strength: its clipped sentences and crisp language helps in evoking the required effect and rhythm of life of the area, falling in cadence with the sea, the symbol of eternity and the Shalimar, the sign of modernity. As a contrast to the glittering new resort stands Avalon, the old castle, exuding the old world charm, reminiscent of the colonial past. The colonial and the post-colonial stand side by side as witness to human relationship forged on a common bond of human need for good will, affection and understanding. The plot, however, is weak and the theme vacillates between the construction of Shalimar and the repair of Avalon. Were it not for the higher aspects of the human spirit, the thematic structure would have crumbled down. The novel has a few minor female characters, none of them memorable except perhaps Mrs. Bridie. Of the other characters, mention may be made of Sandhu, the wrestler, Miss Carmen Alvarz, the Spanish dancer, Valli, Rikki's adopted sister, Apu, the village headman and Rikki's foster-father and Amma Rikki's foster-mother. These characters add depth to the story and save it from being mere episodic.

Notes

1. R.S. Singh, *Indian Novel in English* (New Delhi: Arnold-Heinemann, 1977) 136.
2. Stephan Ignatius Hemenway, *The Novel in India*, vol. 2 (Calcutta: Writers Workshop, 1975) 52.
3. Madhusudan Prasad, *Perspectives on Kamala Markandaya* (Ghaziabad: Vimal Prakashan, 1984) ii.

4. William Walsh, *Commonwealth Literature* (London: Oxford UP, 1973) 19.
5. S.C. Harrex, *The Fire and the Offering*, vol. I (Calcutta: Writers Workshop, 1977) 15-16.
6. Rochelle Almeida, *Originality and Imitation: Indianness in the Novels of Kamala Markandaya* (New Delhi: Rawat, 2002).
7. Niroj Banerji, *Kamala Markandaya: Critical Study* (Allahabad: Kitab Mahal, 1977) vii.
8. Shiv K. Kumar, "Tradition and Change in the Novels of Kamala Markandaya," *Osmania Journal of English Studies* 6.1 (1969): 1.
9. S.Z.H. Abidi, "Kamala Markandaya's Narrative Technique," *Perspectives*, ed. Madhusudan Prasad 241.
10. Shohana M. Landow, "The Value of Suffering in Kamala Markandaya's *Nectar in a Sieve*," *South Asian Women Writers: Another Approach to Feminism*, ed. Ranjani Obesekere (Princeton: Princeton UP, 1989).
11. Niroj Banerji, *Markandaya* 123.
12. R.S. Singh, *Novel* 138.
13. R.K. Srivastava, *The Novels of Kamala Markandaya: A Critical Study* (Amritsar: Guru Nanak Dev University, 1998) 64.
14. S.C. Harrex, "A Sense of Identity: The Novels of Kamala Markandaya," *The Journal of Commonwealth Literature* (June 1971) 65.
15. S. Krishna Sarma, "*Some Inner Fury*: A Critical Perspective," *Perspectives*, ed. Madhusudan Prasad 111.
16. Margaret P. Joseph, *Kamala Markandaya* (New Delhi: Arnold-Heinemann, 1980) 37.
17. Shantha Krishnaswamy, *The Woman in Indian Fiction in English: 1950-80* (New Delhi: Ashish Publishing House, 1984) 199-200.
18. K.R. Srinivas Iyengar, *Indian Writing in English* (New Delhi: Sterling, 1962) 445.
19. R.K. Srivastava, "Woman as Possessor: A Reflection of Kamala Markandaya's Anti-Patriarchal Rage and Divided Consciousness in *Possession*," *Punjab Journal of English Studies* 4 (1989): 41-54.
20. H.M. Williams, "Victims and Virgins: Some Characters in Kamala Markandaya's Novels," *Perspectives*, ed. Madhusudan Prasad 30.
21. Iyengar, *Indian* 443.
22. Uma Parameswaran, *A Study of Representative Indo-English Novels* (New Delhi: Vikas Publishing House, 1976) 85.
23. K.S. Ramamurti, "*Two Virgins*: a Problem Novel," *Perspectives*, ed. Madhusudan Prasad 198-99.
24. Krishnaswami, *Woman* 229.
25. Nissim Ezekiel, rev. of *Two Virgins*, by Kamala Markanadaya, *The Illustrated Weekly of India* (15 June 1979).
26. Krishnaswami, *Woman* 229.

A KAMALA MARKANDAYA BIBLIOGRAPHY

Primary Sources

Novels:

Nectar in a Sieve. New York: The John Day Company, 1954; Bombay: Jaico Publishing House, 1956.

Some Inner Fury. London: Putman & Co., 1955.

A Silence of Desire. London: Putman & Co., 1963.

Possession. Bombay: Jaico Publishing House, 1963.

A Handful of Rice. London: Hamish Hamilton, 1966; New Delhi: Orient Paperbacks, 1966.

The Coffer Dams. London: Hamish Hamilton, 1967; Delhi: Hind Pocket Books, n.d.

The Nowhere Man. London: Allen Lane, 1972; Bombay: Orient Longman, 1975.

Two Virgins. 1973; New Delhi: Vikas Publishing House, 1975.

The Golden Honeycomb. London: Chatto & Windus, 1977; New Delhi: B.I. Publications, 1977.

Pleasure City. London: Chatto & Windus, 1982.

Article

"Why Do I Write in English?" *Adam International Review* 36 (1971) 42-43.

Secondary Sources

Books and Anthologies

Almeida, Rochelle. *Originality and Imitation: Indianness in the Novels of Kamala Markandaya*. New Delhi: Rawat, 2000.

Badal, R.K. *Kamala Markandaya*. Bareilly: Prakash Book Depot, 1973.

Banerji, Niroj. *Kamala Markandaya: A Critical Study*. Allahabad: Kitab Mahal, 1990.

Jha, Rekha. *The Novels of Kamala Markandaya and Ruth Jhabvala*. New Delhi: Prestige Books, 1990.

Joseph, Margaret P. *Kamala Markandaya*. New Delhi: Arnold Heinemann, 1980.

Misra, Pravati. *Class Consciousness in the Novels of Kamala Markandaya*. New Delhi: Atlantic, 2001.

Prasad, Madhusudan, ed. *Perspectives on Kamala Markandaya*. Ghaziabad: Vimal Prakashan, 1984.

Srivastava, R.K. *The Novels of Kamala Markandaya: A Critical Study*. Amritsar: Guru Nanak Dev University, 1998.

Papers and Articles on Kamala Markandaya

Appasamy, S.P. "*The Golden Honeycomb*: A Saga of Princely India by Kamala Markandaya." *The Journal of Indian Writing in English* 6.2 (July 1978).

Argyle, Berry. "Kamala Markandaya's *Nectar in a Sieve*." *Ariel* 14.1 (1973): 35-45.

Bande, Usha. "Beyond Culture: A Study of Kamala Markandaya's *Possession.*" *Manascarya: An International Journal of Cultural Studies* 4-5.3 (1998): 24-33.

Barche, G.D. *"Inside the Haveli* and *The Nowhere Man:* A Study in Upanishadic Principle." *Psychic Knot: Search for Tolerance in Indian English Fiction.* New Delhi: Bahri Publications, 1998. 139-50.

Chandrashekharan, K.R. "East and West in the Novels of Kamala Markandaya." *Critical Essays on Indian Writing in English.* Eds. M.K. Naik et al. Dharwar: Karnatak UP, 1968. 62-85.

Chauhan, P.S. "Kamala Markandaya: Sense and Sensibility." *The Literary Criterion* 6.2-3 (1976): 134-47.

Dunn, T.A. "Intensity and Crispness." *The Journal of Commonwealth Literature* 5 (July 1968).

Fracht, S. "A Study of Kamala Markandaya's *A Handful of Rice.*" *English Journal* 57 (Nov. 1968): 1143-46.

Geetha, P. "Kamala Markandaya—An Interpretation." *Commonwealth Quarterly* 3.9 (Dec. 1978).

Harrex, S.C. "A Sense of Identity: The Novels of Kamala Markandaya." *The Journal of Commonwealth Literature* 6.1 (June 1971): 65-78.

Horst, Mary Hooper. "Kamala Markandaya." *New Circle* 18.7 (March 1973): 41.

Iyer, Sudha R. "The Need for Tolerance: A Study of Kamala Markandaya." *Psychic Knot: Search for Tolerance in Indian English Fiction.* New Delhi: Bahri Publications, 1998. 69-76.

Jain, Jasbir. "The Novels of Kamala Markandaya." *Indian Literature* 18.2 (April-June 1975): 36-43.

Kumar, Shiv K. "Tradition and Change in the Novels of Kamala Markandaya." *Osmania Journal of English Studies* 7.1 (1969): 1-9.

Landow, Shoshana M. "The Value of Suffering in Kamala Markandaya's *Nectar in a Sieve.*" *South Asian Women Writers: Another Approach to Feminism.* Ed. Ranjini Obeysekere. Princeton: Princeton UP, 1989.

Montgomery, Ruth. "Kamala Markandaya's *Nectar in a Sieve.*" *Wilson Library Bulletin* 28 (Nov. 1963).

Parameswaran, Uma. "India for the Western Readers: A Study of Kamala Markandaya's Novels." *Texas Quarterly* 10.2 (Summer 1968).

Prasad, Hari Mohan. "The Quintessence of Kamala Markandaya's Art." *Commonwealth Quarterly* 3.9 (Dec. 1978).

Rao, A.V. Krishna. "The Novels of Kamala Markandaya: A Study." *Studies in Contemporary Indian Fiction in English.* Ed. A.N. Dwivedi. Allahabad: Kitab Mahal, 1987. 213-51.

Rao, K.S. Narayan. "Kamala Markandaya as a Craftsman." *Indian Writing Today* 8 (April-June 1969).

____. "Some Notes on the Plots of Kamala Markandaya's Novels." *Indian Literature* 7.1 (March 1970).

Rao, Vimala. "Indian Expatriates." *The Journal of Commonwealth Literature* 10.3 (April 1976).

Srivastava, Ramesh K. "Clinton-Helen-Bashiam Relationship in Markandaya's *The Coffer Dams*." *Panjab Journal of English Studies* 8 (1993): 17-28.

Thakur, Guruprasad. "And Never the Twain Shall Meet—Kamala Markandaya's *Nowhere Man*." *Explorations in Modern Indo-English Fiction*. Ed. R.K. Dhawan. New Delhi: Bahri Publications, 1982. 199-207.

Venkateshwaran, Shyamala. "The Language of Kamala Markandaya's Novels." *The Literary Criterion* 9.3 (Winter 1970).

Studies of Markandaya in Books not Exclusively Focused on the Author

Afzal-Khan, Fawzia. *Cultural Imperialism and Indo-English Novel: Genre and Ideology in R.K. Narayan, Anita Desai, Kamala Markandaya and Salman Rushdie*. University Park, P.A.: Pennsylvania State UP, 1993.

Harrex, S.C. *The Fire and The Offering*. 2 Vols. Calcutta: Writers Workshop, 1977.

Hemenway, Stephen Ignatius. *The Novel in India*. 2 Vols. Calcutta: Writers Workshop, 1975.

Iyengar, K.R. Srinivasa. *Indian Writing in English*. Bombay: Asia Publishing House, 1973. 438-50.

Kalinnikova, Elena J. *Indo-English Literature: A Perspective*. Ghaziabad: Vimal Prakashan, 1982. 149-63.

Krishnaswamy, Shantha. "Kamala Markandaya: Autonomy, Nurturance and the Sisterhood of Man." *The Woman in Indian Fiction in English*. New Delhi: Ashish Publishing House, 1984. 160-235.

Mukherjee, Meenakshi. *The Twice-Born Fiction: Themes and Techniques of the Indian Novel in English*. New Delhi: Sahitya Akademi, 1982. 80-84, 109-12.

Naik, M.K. *A History of Indian English Literature*. New Delhi: Sahitya Akademi, 1982. 236-39.

Parameswaran, Uma. *A Study of Representative Indo-English Novelists*. New Delhi: Vikas Publishing House, 1976. 85-140.

Rajeshwar, M. "The Unconscious Desire and its Fulfilment: Kamala Markandaya's *A Silence of Desire*." *Indian Women Novelists and Psychoanalysis*. New Delhi: Atlantic Publishers, 1998. 45-52.

Seshadri, Vijayalakshmi. *The New Woman in Indian-English Women Writers Since the 1970s*. New Delhi: B.R. Publishing Co., 1995.

Williams, Haydn Moore. *Studies in Modern Indian Fiction in English*, vol. II. Calcutta: Writers Workshop, 1973. 166-69.

6

Nayantara Sahgal

JASBIR JAIN

Nayantara Sahgal's literary work spans nearly five decades with her first work *Prison and Chocolate Cake* appearing in 1954 and her first novel *A Time To Be Happy* in 1958. She has gone on to write three autobiographies covering a period from 1943 to 1965, but often moving backwards to capture memories of her childhood, her parents, her grandparents and the early years of Gandhian India. These volumes are *Prison and Chocolate Cake* (1954), *From Fear Set Free* (1962) and *Relationship: Extracts from a Correspondence* (1994).

The first two have a sense of immediacy as they are a sorting out of her own experiences soon after they had happened, while the letters in the third volume record her emotional self struggling with conventional social impositions and breaking free as she moves towards redefinitions of freedom and morality.

Three of her early novels, *This Time of Morning* (1965), *Storm in Chandigarh* (1969) and *The Day in Shadow* (1971), are autobiographical as far as they build on her own emotional experiences and conflicts. But they are also political as they capture the political happenings and environment of the newly independent India, the changing face of bureaucracy, the shifting value structures and loyalties. Her fifth novel, *A Situation in New Delhi* (1977), marks a break with autobiography and concerns itself with the nature of power and political governance. The new leadership is obsessed with the idea of progress and development and has abandoned all concern for the human being. The novel captures the unrest prevalent in the country during the 60s and 70s because of economic disparities, social inequalities and the non-involvement of the upper classes in nation-building activities.

The later three novels published between 1985 and 1988 are markedly different from her earlier work as they move away from immediate political events to the early decades of the twentieth century. Of these *Rich Like Us* begins with the national Emergency declared by Indira Gandhi in 1975 and moves back through the personal histories of Rose and Sonali to the nineteenth century, while the other two locate themselves in the early decades of the twentieth century. *Plans For Departure* is concerned with the years 1912 to 1918 and *Mistaken Identity* with 1929-1932 and the novels focus on interpreting the complex cultural formations of these periods within a historical framework.

Sahgal belongs to a generation of writers who, even if their creative career is post-1947, their childhood experiences fall within the colonial period. Like a majority of her other contemporaries she went through the western system of education—governesses at home, an English medium school (Woodstock, Mussourie), and four years at Wellesley in America. The last because her parents were unwilling to give any guarantee to the British government regarding non-participation in politics, a guarantee which was required to enable her to study in India.

The education system, a gift of Macaulay's Minute of 1835, was designed at alienating the student from his/her background, a sense of alienation which Sahgal in a Plenary Address she delivered in 1989 (ACLALS Conference), defined as the "schizophrenic" imagination,[1] divided as one was between an alien language and system of thought which represented power and the claims of the political and cultural reality prevalent at home.

Sahgal's work needs to be placed simultaneously in several different traditions for it has an inbuilt multiplicity. There is first the tradition of the national political discourse; second, that of Indian Writing in English; third, of women's writing in India, and fourth of the fictional tradition as developed in the West. It also need to be placed amongst the category of work which is part of a decolonising process and generically it projects a new kind of biographical history of the nation which has its own structures.

In 1978, I had written a monograph on Nayantara Sahgal, the first full-length study published on her and taken up during the years of the Emergency when Sahgal was anathema (because of her anti-Establishment views). Later in 1994, this was revised in order to include her later works. Over the years and through this long association with her work, I have analysed it in different contexts and perspectives at various times looking at it both through realistic and metaphorical frameworks. It is increasingly clear that in its totality, it presents a history of the processes of decolonization, beset with the crisis in humanistic values which stood discredited once they came to be placed outside power structures.

Humanism had developed as an ideology within the imperialistic discourse. The "white man's burden" had all along carried within it the civilizational mission and the assurance of human values. But in practice it simply could not do so, rooted as it was in the belief in cultural superiority and guided by racial and cultural discrimination.

The Second World War dismantled a whole lot of myths and belief-structures and humanism was the first casualty. At such a time to undertake to separate humanistic values from this association, as well as to free them from traditional religious structures and to firmly place them within codes of behaviour relevant to everyday life and functional within marriage, business relationships and political struggles was an act of courage on Sahgal's part. And this centrality which she gave humanistic values demanded that the self be defined anew. The problem was how to free humanism from a passive goodness and infuse it with the fiery energy and dynamism of the doers in order to make it meaningful.

There is another seam in her work which has not been sufficiently tapped. Seen primarily as a feminist, it remains to define her feminism as rooted in the larger framework of human rights, of personal freedom and right to the body. Placed within domesticity her early heroines gradually move on to wider spaces, areas of competition and face problems of survival and this movement blurs the boundaries between the home and the world, rather than submit to the separation between them. The self is always in question as the individual struggles with the imposition of roles which tradition and convention thrust on him.

There is a tension in all her work between two oppositional discourses—one of humanism which calls for consideration, compassion and reaching out to others and the other of power which is spurred on by an aggressive ruthlessness in pursuit of its goals. This tension functions also at the level of cultural encounters, which are placed within hegemonic (and thus unequal) structures. There is no clear-cut demarcation between 'them' and 'us' but an on-going critiquing of all freedom-denying institutions, roles or codes of behaviours. Resistance and acceptance constantly nudge each other as primeval instincts of aggression and possession impersonate as progress and development because a great deal which is of value also happens to be primeval.

Religion is another category which is problematic. All religions share a basic faith in human values and the primacy of moral life directed towards goodness. But in practice the stress on religious identity creates barriers, leads to intolerance, hatred and division and the closing-in of the mind. It becomes a major agent of aggression as different religions confront each other in the national space.

The human being is a political being but the forces which mould human character are categories like religion, culture, upbringing, power (or the absence of it), and experience. Those who have to fight for their survival acquire a fighting instinct, as for instance the orphans and refugees and even when they pursue positive policies they tend to sideline human concerns, men like Kalyan Sinha (*This Time of Morning*) Gyan Singh and even Inder (*Storm in Chandigarh*). But this is not universally applicable. Aggression can also born out of plenty and gentleness out of dispossession. One of the problems, Sahgal addresses in her novels, is the need to cross the boundaries between goodness and passivity on the one hand and ruthlessness and efficiency on the other. There is a felt need to make goodness effective.

Sahgal's work has been critiqued and evaluated from different perspectives—as a feminist, as a political writer, as a writer of social documentaries, and as an advocate of Gandhian ideologies. But none of these frames are entirely adequate or sufficient unto themselves. There is a need to place these issues within the larger contexts of history and the processes of decolonization. Though she resists being placed in categories like colonial or postcolonial, it is not possible to avoid the use of such terms as she has lived through these stages and has captured the political scene from the 40s to the 70s with an uncanny understanding of the undercurrents, of the processes at work and of the men and women who have been at the helm of affairs.

The political novel engages itself with contemporary moves and policies and explores the human elements in political decisions. But the moment there is a search for continuity, it acquires a historical dimension. And any retrospective analysis is more dispassionate, even if more anguished than a contemporary one. Nations and people remain rooted in their past. From this point of view her three novels of the 80s are most significant as each one of them traverses the past in order to trace the origins of the present situation and though it is easy to blame other, and perhaps not too difficult to dismantle myths, it is difficult to accept one's failures. But if one is honest, there is no escape from facing the reality.

Plans for Departure is the only one of her novels to work through a European consciousness. Anna Hansen is the main observer-eye. As she is from Denmark she falls outside the direct imperial-colonial relationship but is not entirely free from memories of an imperial past now enclosed within the folds of a nine-hundred-year old history. As she goes for long walks in Himapur, she tries to visualize the onslaught of the early Indo-Aryan invasion, the people in the valley "must have been paralysed in their tracks as the attacker from the north-west bore on them" (20). This visual image simultaneously attacks both—the notion of the Hindus as the indigenous people and the imaging of the Muslim as the 'other.' Anna has been in India for several months and has spent time at the Theosophical Society established by Countess Blavatsky and headed by Annie Besant during the period of the novel who "was up to her English ears in Hinduism and national politics" (29). Anna is suspect because of this association with subversive activities. Thus the lines are drawn across not race or religion but on the basis of political loyalty to the British Crown.

Annie Besant's interest in Hinduism and Anna's interest in the theosophical society also place the effort of men like Croft, the American missionary, within this power relationship. When Christians stay away from church as Anna does, or move to other religions like Annie Besant, they subvert the civilizing mission of the white races.

Both Henry Brewster and Croft, each in his own way, are non-believers in the code of the white man. Brewster is conscious of the racial distancing. The uprising of 1857 brought the company rule to an end but also along with it the free mixing of races. The rule of the Crown created a deliberate distance and led to an unconscious growth of resentment on part of the Indians. Brewster is sensitive to this and realises that the Empire sooner or later will have to prepare for its own dismantling. Croft's obsession with saving the souls of men, places him outside racial considerations. He is concerned with social justice rather than with imperial authority.

The narrative is framed at one level by Tilak's speech which is termed seditious, and traces through his obsession with patriotism, other events of a similar nature, going back to the legend of Tulsidas's rejection by his wife. At another level Tilak's imprisonment, the serving of the sentence at Mandalay prison, the subsequent release, the First World War, these supply an external time frame. The beginning, through memory, causality and recollection keeps shifting to other beginnings—her relationship with Nicholas, involvement with the suffragette movement, her home in Denmark. And the ending, similarly keeps on shifting—1917, then 1920, and then 1961. But within the years 1908 to 1917 several events conglomerate in the little hill town of Himapur which reflect upon the imperial project and the colonial response. Anna, both emotionally and physically, lives within a universalist framework. The hills remind her of Alps, she can sense a kinship with people from different racial and religious backgrounds.

Anna's approach to the past is not necessarily focused on historical events. She realises that the past is a mixture of legend and myth as well. The past fascinates her but when she discusses it with Sir Nitin he finds the legends surrounding Tulsidas "most unscientific" (45). In the character of Sir Nitin we have the man of science who is indifferent to all else, he is in fact a British "stooge." Through his character, both the British pursuit of science and the Indian homage to their cultural superiority, are ridiculed. The Brahmo Samajis who are referred to as second class Christians are also critiqued.

Just as no country has been totally free from the imperial-colonial framework, no relationship is free of oppression. Oppression exists between castes and communities and between men and women. The suffragette movement is used as a reference point for Anna's journey to India, but it also serves another purpose. It carries oppression to foreign shores. The movement has thrown up its own martyrs like the freedom struggle in India has thrown up martyrs like Khudiram Ghose. History does not consist solely of events. It is made by men and the traits they have imbibed, the cultures they have grown up in, the traditions they have inherited. There is an affinity between Tulsidas and Tilak. Both men are carried toward their goal by their obsessions.

Rich Like Us also takes up the issue of human character and colonialism in the context of 'sati.' Courage, honesty and integrity are the qualities which build a nation. The same impulse for power which characterises the ruthlessness of the Emergency also characterises social relationships. And the same passivity which accepts that atrocity is also responsible for the submission to imperial control. Surprised by her own removal from her post, Sonali feels humiliated and turns to her father's memory who has recently died, for emotional sustenance. As she goes through his papers, she finds a manuscript written by her grandfather in 1915 and some newspaper cuttings of 1829 related to the sati law, and another cutting of an 1823 letter 'to the editor.' These materials lead her not only to trace her family history but also the history of a people. The manuscript provides an account of Sonali's great grandmother's forced performance of 'sati.' And the remaining papers provide evidence of the resistance to the sati practice by sections of society. Sonali's great grandfather was a man of liberal views and he had consistently resisted this practice. But ironically enough it is his widow who is forced into the act as part of a bargain for her son's future.

This atrocity is re-enacted when Dev, Rose's stepson, subjects her to a twentieth century version of sati by getting her out of the way by having her killed. Civilization, it appears, has either not progressed or has progressed only in matters of brutality. The implication is also that we need to shoulder greater responsibility for our own debased values rather than blame them all on colonialism. It is the unquestioning support for arbitrary power which leads to the misuse of power. Other revolutions, in other lands and times, speak of a similar ruthlessness and aggression—the Russian revolution, the Partition, the bombs at Hiroshima and Nagasaki—all of them are movements and happenings which have bypassed the human being for dreams of power or of fight against oppression. Even a legitimate fight for freedom can deteriorate into brutality if it violates the ethical code of human life. Sahgal restates the Gandhian dilemma in *Rich Like Us.*

The historical framework of *Mistaken Identity* actually covers three years 1929 to 1932, but it uses this period, which was full of political agitations and upheaval for analysing the various ideological strands contesting with each other in the struggle for freedom.

Sahgal's historical novels employ a slightly different strategy than her political novels. Both *Plans for Departure* and *Mistaken Identity* work through enclosed spaces. Himapur in the first novel is isolated from other power centres and brings together people of different kinds who represent different interests—administrators, both committed as well as disinterested through the figures of Brewster and Pryor, missionaries, British stooges, neutral observers, and people like the photographer who are transmitters of the patriotic impulse. It is an enclosure where other influences are distanced and can work only indirectly.

Similarly in *Mistaken Identity* a cross-section of Indian society in terms of religion, economic status and political interest is herded together and through a constant interaction with each other, the people move from disinterest and confrontation towards an understanding of each other's point of view and respect and sympathy. Her other novels work through plural narratives, juxtapositions and parallelisms, but in these two novels other narratives are like tributaries, confessions or sub-narratives. They move towards the past through memory and towards the future through time. Space is defined to allow the flow of time to be arrested temporarily before it stretches itself in different directions. History represents continuities and discontinuities. In *Plans for Departure* the Gandhian movement is placed in the direct line of descent emanating from Tilak's speeches, programme of non-cooperation and imprisonment. Towards the end of the novel Jason (Anna's grand-son-in-law) tells his wife, "nothing would have turned out as it did afterwards if these particular things hadn't happened before." (*Plans for Departure* 144)

In *Mistaken Identity*, the trope of identity defies all artificial limits, it refuses to be contained by any definitions of singularity and slips through to trace continuities, inheritances and underlying impulses. The novel is also not limited by history, it is concerned with the larger debate of nationhood and self, both of which work through plural configurations.

Sahgal has a tendency to trace continuities, to look for causes and roots. For her the past has a direct relationship with the present and memory is thus a necessary route to self-knowledge. Gandhi and Gandhian ideas are a consistent concern with her even as she subjects them to a close scrutiny and at times mockery and ridicule. She is a child of Gandhi's India and her childhood home was steeped in Gandhian thought with both her parents involved with the freedom struggle, her uncle, Jawaharlal Nehru, and grandfather, Motilal Nehru, also engaged in it and Gandhi a frequent visitor to the house. For Gandhi the most important concern was the individual, not power, not merely freedom, but the more valuable freedom of the individual enabling him to be human. *Satyagraha* as a method involved a whole process of introspection and growth and was non-violent in its relationship not only with the 'self' but also with the 'other.' It fostered the qualities of integrity and courage, qualities essential for any kind of civilizational discourse and the task of nation-building. But retrospectively, it takes on the form of an intervention which was not allowed its full fruition and abandoned half-way to make space for the all absorbing pursuit of power.

In her very first novel, *A Time To Be Happy* (1958), the Gandhian legacy is still dominant as the indigenisation of the British companies and of political culture is taking place. Gandhian idealism inspires men like Sanad, and even the British who stay on in India fall under its spell. But in her very next novel, *This Time of Morning* (1965), the idealism of the freedom movement is being shelved in favour of the notion of progress and efficiency. In *Storm in Chandigarh* (1969) the politics of ruthlessness and compromise are in full control bypassing all else, while in *The Day in Shadow* (1971), the full impact of these power structures on personal relationships is in evidence. The questions of individual space and of a living morality which takes cognisance of the human need to relate are taken up. Marital relationships, the writer points out, also reflect power structures.

There is a strong feminist thrust in all her writing. Placed within the context of the writing of the fifties and sixties, she displays a highly developed consciousness of the gendered nature of morality and social structures. This is another kind of discrimination which needs to be addressed. It is a patriarchal society, a 'husband-centred' world where women have no independent identities and where to get away from a husband is like running an obstacle race. The relationship takes on the form of a prey and predator if it is a loveless one or does not base itself on respect for the other. This kind of a situation is evident in novel after novel irrespective of race and religion—Rashmi and Dalip, Neil and Marta (*Morning*), Saroj and Inder (*Storm*), Simrit and Som (*Shadow*) and Lucille and Croft (*Plans*). Examples can be multiplied, but I think the point is made.

All marriages however, do not necessarily fall into the same pattern. There are good men who value the human aspect of marriage. But the men who fall into this category, reflect the traits fostered by the Gandhian attitude towards power. Kailas Vrind in *This Time of Morning*, Sonali's father in *Rich Like Us* as well as Kishorilal in the same novel, Bhaiji in *Mistaken Identity* and in some measure Vishal Dubey and Harpal Singh in *Storm in Chandigarh*, all these men are not necessarily placed within love relationships, but their code of ethics reflects a concern for the individual. Yet somehow though these men have the necessary moral strength, they allow themselves to be brushed aside. Why? They don't fight hard enough? Raj Garg in *The Day in Shadow* is more assertive. And of the women, though the characters in the earlier novels allow themselves to be bypassed, withdrawing into silent suffering, Simrit decides to walk out of her marriage (*Shadow*), Sonali takes up cudgels for Rose in *Rich Like Us*, and the Rani, Bhushan's mother in *Mistaken Identity* is the bravest of them all.

Gandhian ideology in its advocacy of a non-violent struggle also rules out expediency and compromise. Through continued self-introspection it insists upon an open dialogue with the self. Repeatedly the question arises whether it can be used as an effective method within (a) personal relationships and (b) in international relations in order to counter aggression. How far can individual morality fight naked aggression? How does one deal with men like Som and Inder who are motivated by the impulse to power and treat women as possessions, or men like Kalyan Sinha who use them, and who confess that they have no patience for prison terms or for the nurturing of relationships conducive to communication? Not for them the long-term process of creating a strong individual. They are men who function without a conscience.

All along, in her novels, while there is a great deal of admiration for the strength and dignity of the Gandhian process and a realisation of the heavy price we are paying by bypassing it, there is also the awareness that the political method rides roughshod over it and the average man is ill-equipped to understand the Gandhian strategies. Bhaiji, in *Mistaken Identity*, is an example of one such person who has absorbed the practice and its outward symbols—the observing of fasts, the daily spinning of khadi and the rest, but he has not been able to rise to the level of intellectual interrogation and remains till his death a toothless, passive wisp of a man. Kailas Vrind in *This Time of Morning* begins to have doubts whether non-violent resistance can be effective against external aggression; Kalyan Sinha rejects the very basis of its ideology while Hari Mohan uses it as an access to power. And Somnath in the same novel, is of the view that governance calls for a different set of qualities than a freedom struggle.

A striking fact is that men who are ruthless are either orphans, refugees or unhappily married. Kalyan Sinha was adopted during a famine (*Morning*), and Gyan Singh (*Storm*) also has no family to speak of. These are people who have never learnt to love or be loved, survival has engaged their total attention.

Sahgal's middle novels reflect India's retreat from Gandhian thought and if the spirit of the Mahatma survives anywhere "it is certainly not India."[2] The late sixties mark a post-Nehruvian era and Indira Gandhi's rise to power. During these years Sahgal wrote a weekly column for the *Indian Express* group of papers (the Sunday edition went by the name of the *Sunday Standard*) and was clearly anti-Establishment in her criticism of the suppression of democratic rights, and the indifference to the human being *vis-à-vis* the notion of progress so evident in politics.

Gandhian ideology seeks the self's maturity to the level of self-transcendence. There is no place in it for any sense of personal ego. Kailas Vrind (*Morning*) and Sardar Sahib (*Shadow*) are willing to sacrifice even their personal reputation for the nation. They posit a different idea of leadership. Usman and Devi (*Situation in New Delhi*) also display similar concerns. But all along there is an erosion in these values and a rapid taking over of all moral space by ideas of development, with the result that the task of nation-building is neglected. The pattern of governance in free India begins to duplicate colonial power structures.

Religion is also a major concern in Sahgal's work. The revivalist aspect is briefly touched upon in *Plans for Departure*; its cultural hold is taken up in *Storm in Chandigarh*. Vishal Dubey and Trivedi both are Brahmins; Trivedi wonders how can they fulfil the traditional tasks of Brahminism—of priest, law-giver, adviser to sovereigns, custodian of the intellectual and spiritual heritage of the race (*Storm* 76). What use with this heritage to ordinary men? In some measure Gandhi also drew his inspiration from Hinduism and its ethical text *The Bhagawad Gita* and *satyagraha* drew its strength from the concept of *karma* which has an inbuilt duality. It could encourage fatalism as well as inspire action.

Debates on religious issues are embedded in every novel. In *A Time To Be Happy*, the narrator explains the concept of *karma* to McIvor. Similarly in *The Day in Shadow* the passivity and casteism of Hinduism is critiqued and doubts are raised whether it can meet the challenges of modernity. Several of her characters refer to the hold of religion in derogatory terms. The Hindus, Kalyan Sinha feels, are stagnating in turgid waters. Dubey in *Storm in Chandigarh* is of the opinion that they need a tearing up from their roots.

This was a period when cow slaughter became a public issue and Sahgal wrote several journalistic features on Hinduism, the more significant among them being "Fresh Air on Hinduism" (*Sunday Standard*, 1 December, 1968), "Conscience and the Hindu" (14 December, 1973), "Religion and Its Travesty" (*Sunday Standard*, 27 April, 1969). Other writers like Mulk Raj Anand in *Is there an Indian Civilization* (1963), and Nirad Chaudhuri in *The Continent of Circe* (1965), also voiced their discontentment with Hinduism. It was at this time—1962—that V.S. Naipaul published his first book on India, *An Area of Darkness* which puts the blame for India's backwardness on its dominant faith which happens to be Hinduism.

Religion is of significance because it spills over into cultural attitudes, governs our actions and marks our identity. Men act in accordance with their beliefs. And Hinduism because it is characterised more by practices than by tenets, is far more pervasive than other religions. Sahgal's concern, however, is not limited to Hinduism alone. In *The Day in Shadow*, Christianity comes in for a close examination. Raj Garg is a Christian and Ram Krishan debates in his mind the strengths of Christianity *vis-à-vis* Hinduism. Christianity spent itself in the search for good. The Hindu stresses "existence and acceptance" (1971) while the Christian concerns himself with improvement and treats life like a hands-on job. Gandhi had inducted a degree of vitality into Hinduism, but it had now (in the 60s) lapsed into tolerance and passivity. Christianity, on the other hand, has in the main focused on the present and has applied itself to the pursuit of progress.

There are several other Christian characters in Sahgal's novels and the two which make a positive impact are Anna Hansen in *Plans for Departure* and Michael Calvert in *A Situation in New Delhi*. Anna is everywhere, curious, determined, positive, and Michael invests heavily in friendship. Their concern with the individual is in terms of freedom, relationships and equality, not with fasting, or simple observances of purity, or with narrow concerns of personal salvation. One needs to get one's hands soiled if one wants to clean up a mess.

Christianity is identified with western culture and most foreign characters are Christians, but they are not all of kind. While there are the compassionate ones like Neil (*Morning*), Henry Brewster (*Plans*) and Rose (*Rich Like Us*), there are also the ruthless specimens amongst them like Pryor (*Plans*) and the Sam's German friend Vetter (*Day in Shadow*), and the missionaries with their obsessions with Christ's Kingdom like Croft in *Plans for Departure*.

Islam first surfaces in *A Situation in New Delhi* when the multi-religious nature of the political scene is recognised along with its failed ideals of secularism. Usman, the Delhi University Vice-Chancellor and Devi's close friend, is not merely an idealist, but a thinker fired with imagination. He has formulated an educational plan which he wants to implement, a plan aimed at bringing about structural changes. He tells Devi that "You can't make a revolution in thin air," it has to come from the ground under your feet (115). And in *Mistaken Identity*, Bhushan's lifelong pursuit of Razia functions at the level of a national allegory, expressing a wish to cross boundaries, to merge with the other.

There are, in fact, no defined religious categories—religions can, and should evolve and establish a living relationship between individual values of integrity and social values of compassion and sharing. And these values are required in both personal and public worlds. The close connection between the personal and the public world is manifested time and again. It is impossible to keep the two apart. There can be no clinical approach to the reality which surrounds us. Cultural and religious attitudes overflow into development policies and implementation of ideas. If there is a disjunction between the two, then it calls for an in-depth analysis of the social structures and the impediments which thwart it. One of the impediments happens to be the naked pursuit of power.

Sahgal's work on Indira Gandhi's rise to power is an analysis of this impulse to power, while her own book *Voice of Freedom* (a collection of lectures she delivered in American universities during the Emergency), is about the need for an open society which provides space for individual developments. Dissent is a strong requirement in a democracy for it acts both as a corrective and a warning. It allows space for the perspective of the other. The Emergency is resented primarily on this count, that it put down dissent, it wished to project the state as the only authority—and a monolithic one at that.

Hidden behind this need for dissent is the critiquing of the Indian democracy, which is different from western democracies because of its colonial experience, low level of economic development and high level of illiteracy. The intellectual—and the political leader in such a situation have an additional responsibility and need to have a highly developed sense of conscience. Mere symbols just were not enough. Nation-building required a spirit of dedication higher than the self. This issue is taken up at great length in *Rich Like Us* where the dictatorial approach of the new generation of leaders is criticised.

There is another collection of essays *Point of View: A Personal Response to Life, Literature and Politics* which contains several comments on her own novels including *The Day in Shadow* and *Mistaken Identity*; on Indian writing in English "The Testament of an Indo-Anglian Writer," an essay which discusses the relationship between Indianness and the English language; on cultural encounters "Some Thoughts on the Puzzle of Identity" and several essays on the political situation criticising a one-leader, one-party approach and advocating a fresh look on the other political options available. She firmly believes in the process of a dialogue, which is necessary for reaching out to the other and for individual creativity to surface.

It is this idea of communication which is also very central to the man-woman relationship, which is, in its essence a power relationship. Women have been subjugated both by traditional culture and social attitudes. Feminine virtue is defined through adherence to norms, suppression of female sexuality, and at times separation between the body and the mind. Childbearing may continue even in a loveless marriage. And women who are perceived merely as possessions, are denied their selfhood, freedom of will and mind, in fact their humanity.

Almost all Sahgal's novels are women-centred. *Mistaken Identity* is the only novel to work through a male consciousness. Sahgal describes it as a novel with two heroines ("and that too in purdah") but without a hero (*Point of View* 51). And these women placed in different situations, facing different kinds of oppression, realise that there is no social recognition for the kind of oppression they face, for tradition grants it legitimacy. In the early novels, marital conflict arises out of the division of the couple along ideological lines—with one partner being westernised and the other engaged in the freedom struggle but in the later novels it is a more marked difference of attitude.

Sahgal's work, surprising for a feminist writer, also has cases of bigamous marriages. One such marriage is in *A Time To Be Happy* and another, which also happens to be inter-racial in *Rich Like Us*. A third instance is in *This Time of Morning* Prabha who is Harilal Mathur's first wife is uneducated and simple, while the second wife is modern and educated. He, however, has a living relationship with both of them. But Ram who marries Rose while he already has a wife in India (*Rich Like Us*), does not maintain a living relationship with Mona. Houses are shared in both the novels but territories are divided and it is the women who suffer.

Women as they ask for space or try to work out their relationship find that they have to contest primitive attitudes. Men want to possess not only their (the women's) present but also their past and future, thus feeding the ancient myths of the virgin bride and the virtuous wife. Thus pre-marital relationships are viewed as acts of infidelity. Inder punishes Saroj for having cared for a man at some time before their marriage. The whole attempt is to make her feel guilty for a spontaneous attraction, a guilt which would require her to do penance for the rest of her life through subordination. Guilt renders a relationship unequal. Men do not feel guilty, they just feel betrayed. Men are free to go into multiple relationships, women are expected to be monogamous not only within marriage but also before and after—in childhood and widowhood—which moulds their whole existence to the requirements of the male principle.

Adulterous relationships question the institution of marriage and the supremacy it gives a man over the person of a woman, specially when it is treated as a sacrament rather than as a contract. When this relationship is placed on an unequal footing right at the beginning by subordinating the woman to a man's desire and control, it places a great deal of trust in the ability of the two people to handle their relationship, which very often they are not able to do. In fact, sexual morality is gender-based. Sahgal by centre-staging the body in the man-woman relationship draws attention to the fact of how the body is used for controlling all kinds of freedoms—freedom of action, of thought, of belonging, responding, of choice, of social interaction, and of historical time. By basing definitions of morality on one-sided chastity and fidelity, the woman is placed within an inner circle of life which excludes her from the free flow of life around her. This cripples her mind and body and also affects her character. The relationship between sex, love and values is emphasized over and over again to show their interconnectedness for the fullness of a human being.

A large number of relationships are portrayed in novel after novel of marriages of people from different generations and describe how the compromises are worked out to sustain them. In the two earlier novels there are fairly full portrayals of the parents' generation and the incongruities which have crept in—the second marriages, the total obedience, the rich sexuality and male indulgence, and also the possibility of love for a man other than the husband as it happens in the case of Maya and the narrator in *A Time to be Happy*, but at the same time the impossibility of running away from the social codes. *This Time of Morning* goes further ahead with men shown as oppressed as in the relationship of Uma and Arjun, but the present state of affairs can perhaps be traced to some earlier incompatibility. It also refers to (though it does not work out the causes) Rashmi's unhappy relationship with Dalip, and her subsequent short-lived affair with Neil Berensen whose own marriage with Marta is on the rocks. The issues of adultery and divorce, not necessarily linked in the writer's mind but working simultaneously, are introduced in this novel as she moves away from the traditional definitions of morality. The figure of the lover whose love goes unrequited and unexpressed is symbolised by Rakesh, a lonely male figure, a recurring figure in her novels and enabling her to use the singleness of this man for the projection of an ideal non-physical love. But unmarried men are not necessarily always the compassionate figures one would want them to be, they are often ruthless, unscrupulous and exploitative, represented by such figures as Kalyan Sinha who is obsessed by national concerns but bypasses the human, thus creating a dichotomy within himself; they are also represented by men from the business world who make light of their women secretaries.

Storm in Chandigarh shifts from the generational portrayals to peer group marriages and we have four of them—Saroj and Inder, Jit and Mara, Vishal Dubey and Leela, Gauri and Nikhil. These relationship have their own tensions. Inder is unfair to Saroj trying to punish her for something that was part of growing up while he himself indulges in an adulterous relationship with Mara. Vishal's relationship with Leela is over, he has never been able to reach her despite the love he has felt for her all along. His character contrasts sharply with Inder's who lives in the world of divided morality. Inder feels at rest with himself with Mara, for he satisfies a need in her. And Mara turns to Inder because the gentleness of Jit does not mean anything to her. Sex is recognized as an important part of marriage, and when adultery takes place it places sex in a sphere outside the recognized moral code, thus freeing the relationship from permanence.

This is further highlighted in *A Situation in New Delhi* where Devi has a fulfilling relationship with both Michael and Usman. She needs this physical expression to sustain her emotional being. Both these relationships comment on the physical deprivation placed on widowhood by traditional norms. They also recognize the body.

The novel which falls between *Storm in Chandigarh* and *A Situation in New Delhi, The Day in Shadow* problematises this. This novel, unlike the earlier novels, works through a single relationship of Simrit and Som which has failed despite children, despite wealth and all the other external trappings of a successful marriage primarily because of the incompatibly of their world-views. Simrit wants to nurture, to build, to cherish. The flowers on the creeper at the window mean something to her. Not so Som. He is interested in accumulating wealth, in making money, in his male heir and his ammunition deals. Means do not matter to him, only the ends. His sensitivity to others is as if dormant. People do not mean anything to him. Thus when Simrit asks for a divorce, he vindictively places her under a financial arrangement which cripples her by the tax problem but nobody recognizes it as an exploitation. Simrit came to represent for the writer the average, acquiescent woman who allows herself to be exploited because she "is not part of the creating, active world."[3] She is symbolic of the Hindu race; she is not an individual, she is "a culture, a tradition, a patient, enduring passivity" (*Point of View* 18).

In *Rich Like Us*, the woman question is again presented through multiplicities ranging over nearly a century—the great grandmother who commits Sati, the Kashmiri mother who is aggressively expressive *vis-à-vis* the Maharashtrian father who is gentle and receding, Rose who knowingly walks into a second marriage but does not betray her ideals, Mona who endures but not passively, instead through a lot of noise, Nishi who submits to Dev because she comes from a many-daughtered family. None of these women is a professional or career conscious. Marriage is a life-long career for almost all of them, except for Sonali who is an IAS officer. Sonali remains unmarried till the end though she unhesitatingly gives herself to Ravi Kachru when they are at Oxford. Their relationship is placed outside marriage but is free of guilt.

Another dimension of marriage is explored through the Anna-Nicholas relationship, when Anna is hesitant to commit herself to a life long burial of the self within the roles of wife and mother. And she decides to travel to India to explore her own self. All the three marriages which are foregrounded are of foreigners—Henry-Stella, Croft-Lulu,

Anna-Nicholas—though there are three others in the background, that of Nitin's elder sister, of Anna's grand-daughter Gayatri with Jason, and Pryor's marriage to Stella. By doing this Sahgal takes marriage into a larger sphere and avoids cultural stereotypes. Man-woman relationships, however cultural specific they may be, reveal similar power structures. Lulu is no longer relevant to her husband's mission in life, Henry and his wife split over faith and absence. Faith in an Empire, and Pryor is involved in empire-building not in relation-building. The positive relationships which emerge are those of Anna-Nicholas and Gayatri-Jason because they cater for the needs of the individual self. Nicholas decides to stay back for the funeral of the suffragette and waits for Anna to come back from her travels. The embedded narrative of Tulsidas's obsessed love for his wife which is transferred to a similar obsession with God, is another example of the extremes of relationship and the metamorphosis of this obsession into sublimation.

The striking fact is that though love, marriage and sex are projected and discussed; motherhood is not really problematized or valorised. It remains incidental expect in some measure in *The Day of Shadow* where Simrit has a houseful of children and an alienated son who takes after his father.

Compared to her contemporaries Sahgal's stand on women and female sexuality and the concern with woman's right to her body is both unconventional and subversive. From amongst her early contemporaries of the fifties—Kamala Markandaya, Santha Rama Ram and Attia Hosain—she can be singled out for her boldness in relating the issue of sex, to individual freedom and the desire to free a woman from being treated as a possession. This falls within a larger humanistic concern. Other writers explore sexuality but explore it either within marriage or as an act of aberration akin to prostitution. Women writers in Indian languages had however, even touched upon lesbianism in the 40s, but still worked within the trope of marriage where the wife turns to another woman on account of her husband's neglect.

Sahgal has a remarkable sense of irony, which she expresses through wit and comedy. Fun is made of customs and practices, adjectives render character depictions very graphic and render them human—Bhushan's whole affair with Razia and the storytelling sessions in the prison cell in *Mistaken Identity* open out reality in different ways, but the end result is comic. Similarly in *Rich Like Us* the seriousness of the Emergency is balanced by the lightness and frivolity of Dev's parties and Nishi's submissive character. The comic stance gives her an upper hand as a narrator and helps frame her plots within an objective perspective.

Sahgal's plots function through juxtapositions, polarities, crossing-overs and subversion. The search for meaning in life and politics works itself through subversion of static social structures and their deathlike stranglehold. This subversion is worked through a play with reality, the use of fantasy as a dream of the impossible specifically in *Mistaken Identity*, through the creation of a mystery framework and the incorporation of myth in *Plans for Departure* and the symbolical in *Rich Like Us*. The pursuit of impossible dreams is as important to her as the practical need to cope with the harsh realities of life.

The structural experimentation in Sahgal's work often goes unnoticed as she populates her world with a host of characters, specially in the early novels, and absorbs a great deal of political environment in the narration. But under this seemingly sprawling structure there is an intricate pattern, specially in her later novels where the motifs are interlinked. The earlier juxtaposition of opposites has given way in them to the form of a mystery novel. Both *Plans for Departure* and *Mistaken Identity* work through dropped clues which are picked up later, create a curiosity as to the events and the motives.

In *Plans for Departure* Stella's portrait and the role of the photographer in projecting it in its ornate setting recurs again and again. Brewster reads Anna's letters and thus has access to her thought processes but not so Anna who lives with her suspicions. The dead body of the spaniel creates another mystery as does Lucille's death—is it murder, suicide or accident? All evidence points towards Croft as the murderer for it is not in Lucille's nature to kill herself while Croft, who is capable of being ruthless, no longer needs her. Again the manner in which both Lucille and Anna feel as if they were held in captivity, projects the invisible strength of the patriarchal structure and the imperial authority. Getting away from Himapur is not a matter of choice or will but of planning, disguising of intentions, pleading for freedom and subterfuge. The forces work in opposition. Anna's own character and background are revealed bit by bit and for Sir Nitin she remains a mystery right till the very end.

All the above incidents work in collusion to create a complex flow of events. Even Henry Brewster's confessional letter which reaches Anna after his death is not fully revelatory. The surprise comes when Pryor's wife happens to be Stella, the woman who is imagined to have been murdered by Henry Brewster. It is like the rising of a ghost.

The Manor House where Nicholas and Anna decide to set up their home is again a place of expanding spaces and historical memories. It is a conjunction of the past and the present. It has a castle's twin-towered entrance, arched doorways, a dungeon and winding turret staircase. In fact, a sprawling house, the right kind of setting for Anna who is obsessed by mysteries and connections.

Working somewhat on similar lines, *Mistaken Identity* also employs the pattern of a jigsaw puzzle, the different pieces of which need to be put together by the reader. The title itself suggests a mystery. Bhushan's being taken prisoner while on his journey homewards carries within it not only echoes of totalitarian structures but also has an element of mystery. There is no apparent cause. The subsequent Kafkaesque trial unwinds illogical patterns which do not make any connections. But gradually as layer upon layer of the past is stripped off its surface meaning, reality begins to alter. What is the truth and is truth ever accessible? Why are the riots caused? Where has Razia disappeared? Why did Bhushan attend the function celebrating the Russian poet? Who is he?

Events which had not appeared to be at all significant suddenly begin to acquire sinister dimensions. It is difficult to believe that the lawyer's version as presented in court is about the same happenings. The narrative of the trial is matched by Bhushan's storytelling sessions in the cell. He is a male Sheherazade. The sessions are never continuous, and Bhushan narrates it only in fragments, he does not follow any linear pattern. Both the contents and the style of narration create a third world which with its comic understatement incorporates the element of fantasy. And the lawyer's interpretation, the awe and curiosity of his fellow prisoners, and the public trial, all these replay the events of the past in different ways, adding objective comments to experiences of a very personal nature.

Stella's appearance as Mrs. Pryor in *Plans for Departure* puts an end to the highly imaginative construction of Anna's fears. In the same manner Razia's appearance as the Turkish gentleman's wife in *Mistaken Identity* brings to an end Bhushan's search for his childhood beloved. But there is one striking difference. While Stella appears almost at the end, Razia appears fairly early in the novel and is thus able to trigger off a new set of events forcing both Bhushan and the reader to go over the past.

The hidden strength of Sahgal's plots lies in their denotative quality. If all the political references are explored, the novel opens up in different directions both spatially and temporally. Every little reference, every little clue is waiting to be explored like the references to Turkey, the Khilafat Movement, the Rani's fascination with Russia, the attempt to grow a garden in the desert, the American connections. Is the prince a failed poet or is the medium of his dreams different? Also, beneath the imperial thrust of the white races lies a larger India which defies the colours on the map. It is made up of a 'hybrid' culture, a hybridity which goes back by several centuries.

Sahgal's narrative consciousnesses also goes on shifting as she uses interior monologue, documents, diaries and letters in different novels. In *Rich Like Us* she works alternately through Rose and Sonali, presenting two narratives side by side.

Despite these well-defined characters who work their way towards self definition and questioning her novels are decentred. They present a larger reality than a confined narrative can contain for the number of issues she raises embrace a living society. Her work offers a critical biography of the country and records changes in the political culture and scenario right from the idealism and the hybridity present in the India of the freedom struggle through to the dictatorial stance of Indira Gandhi, the shift in the goals of the national leadership and the loyalties of the bureaucratic culture. From that point onwards she turns backwards and through this unfolds several contradictions in the imperial attitude towards India, their double morality, their "crude white arrogance," and exposes the several myths propagated by them. But at the same time she does not turn away from India's pluralistic culture towards any narrow fundamentalism. Instead she shifts the whole debate to a redefining of universal parameters by extending the meaning of freedom to all human relationships as they work across race and gender and applying the same code of morality to all—men and women, rulers and ruled, by questioning social injustice across class, race and gender. Sahgal frames all cultures by their inherent hybridities and pluralisms.

But this "universalism" does not imply an imposition of the white codes and knowledge systems on the coloured people, on the other hand it subverts them compelling them to incorporate the values of the coloured world. The Rose-Ram (*Rich Like Us*) and the Gayatri-Jason (*Plans for Departure*) relationships provide this kind of a continuity. There is a very incisive essay "Some Thoughts on the Puzzle of Identity" (Ravenscroft Commonwealth Literature Lecture, 1993) where she talks about identities, cultures, ideologies, relationships, diasporas and argues for a more egalitarian climate to construct a truly common identity (92). Her non-fictional work supports her fiction. Together they present an innovative and courageous writer of our times.

Notes

1. Other writers like Attia Hosain (b. 1913) and Shashi Desphpande (b. 1938) have also referred to this sense of alienation. Meenakshi Mukherjee calls it the "exile of the mind".
2. Nayantara Sahgal, *The Sunday Standard* 23 Nov. 1969.
3. Nayantara Sahgal, "My New Novel," *Hindustan Times* 18 Dec. 1971.

A NAYANTARA SAHGAL BIBLIOGRAPHY

Primary Works

Novels

A Time To Be Happy. New York: Alfred Knopf, 1958; in England by Victor Gollancz and in India by Orient Paperbacks (n.d.).

The Time of Morning. New York: W.W. Norton, 1965; in England by Victor Gollancz and in India by Orient Paperbacks.

Storm in Chandigarh. New York: W.W. Norton, 1969; in England by Chatto and Windus and in India by Orient Paperbacks.

The Day in Shadow. New York: W.W. Norton, 1973; in India by Vikas Publishing House, New Delhi, 1973; Bell Books, 1975.

A Situation in New Delhi. London: London Magazine Editions, 1977.

Rich Like Us. London: Heinemann Ltd., 1985.

Plans For Departure. London: W.W. Norton and Co., 1985.

Mistaken Identity. London: Heinemann Ltd., 1988.

Non-fiction

Prison and Chocolate Cake. New York: Alfred Knopf, 1954; in England by Victor Gollancz and in India by Jaico, 1964.

Freedom Movement in India. New Delhi: National Council of Educational Research and Training, 1970.

A Voice for Freedom. New Delhi: Hind Pocket Books, 1977.

Indira Gandhi's Emergence and Style. New Delhi: Vikas Publishing House, 1978.

Relationships: Extracts from a Correspondence. New Delhi: Kali for Women, 1994 (with E.N. Mangatrai).

Point of View: A Personal Response to Life, Literature and Politics. New Delhi: Prestige, 1997.

Articles

"Creativity and Constraint." *Publishing in India* May 1989.

"Promising Young Women" (short story). *The Illustrated Weekly of India* January 1959.

"Testament of an Indo-Anglian Writer." *Indian and Foreign Review* 10.4. 17-19.

"The Schizophrenic Imagination." *Unbecoming Daughters of the Empire.* Eds. Shirley Chew and Anna Rutherford West Yorkshire. Sydney: Dangaroo Press, 1993.

Secondary Sources

Books on Nayantara Sahgal

Bhatnagar, Manmohan. *The Fiction of Nayantara Sahgal.* New Delhi: Creative, 1996.

Jain, Jasbir. *Nayantara Sahgal.* Jaipur: Printwell, 1978. Revised and enlarged edition, 1994.

Rao, A.V. Krishna. *Nayantara Sahgal—A Study of Her Fiction and Non-Fiction.* Madras: M. Seshachalam and Co., 1976.

Articles on Nayantara Sahgal

Anklesaria, Zerin. "Narrative Technique in Nayantara Sahgal's Plans for Departure." *The New Indian Novel in English: A Study of the 1980s.* Ed. Viney Kirpal. New Delhi: Allied, 1990.

Jain, Jasbir. "The Emperor's New Clothes: The Emergency and Sahgal's *Rich Like Us.*" *The New Indian Novel in English: A Study of the 1980s.* Ed. Viney Kirpal. New Delhi: Allied, 1990.

____. "Sahgal: The Novel as Political Biography." *Recent Commonwealth Literature.* Eds. R.K. Dhawan et al. New Delhi: Prestige, 1989.

____. "Sahgal's Political Journey: Stepping Outside The Frame." *Colonial Consciousness: Black American, African and Indian Fiction in English.* Ed. Ramesh K. Srivastava. Jalandhar: ABS Publication, 1991.

Jussawala, Feroza. "Of Cabbages and Kings: *This Time of Morning and Storm in Chandigarh.*" *The Journal of Indian Writing in English* 5.1: 43-50.

Lal, Malashree. "The Shift From Female Centred to Male-Centred Narrative in the Novels of the 1980s: A Study of Anita Desai and Nayantara Sahgal." *The New Indian Novel in English.* Ed. Viney Kirpal. New Delhi: Allied, 1990.

Patnaik, Bibudhendhra Narayan. "Nayantara Sahgal's Novels" *Sambalpur University Journal* 4 (Dec. 1971): 38-43.

Rao, A.V. Krishna. "Historical Consciousness the Novels of Nayantara Sahgal." *The Journal of Indian Writing in English* (July 1990): 24-43.

Thomas, T.K. "The Hindu Ethos—A Novelist's Perspectives." *Religion and Society* 20.4 (Dec. 1973): 54-71.

Interview

Jain, Jasbir. "Establishing Connections: An Interview." *Nayantara Sahgal.* Jaipur: Printwell, 1994.

7

Anita Desai

D. MAYA

Anita Desai's works mark a new and mature phase in Indian English fiction. Mulk Raj Anand, R.K. Narayan and Raja Rao had already enriched the Indian novel in English by their phenomenal contribution when Anita Desai started writing in the sixties. The fifties had witnessed the emergence of eminent women writers like Kamala Markandaya, Nayantara Sahgal and Ruth Prawer Jhabvala who merged into the main stream with their male contemporaries—Manohar Malgonkar, Bhabani Bhattacharya, Khushwant Singh and K.A. Abbas. The legacy of colonialism hang heavily on these writers whose themes centred on the socio-political and cultural issues resulting from colonisation. Along with colonial and post-colonial issues, Nayantara Sahgal's novels foregrounded the emotional incompatibility between partners in arranged marriages and voiced the woman's need for space in a patriarchal society.

Anita Desai cannot therefore be called a pioneer in fictionalising the Indian woman's cause. But she can claim the unique distinction of giving a new dimension to Indian English fiction through her very first novel—*Cry, the Peacock* (1963)—which shifted the focus to the unexplored realm of the female psyche. Her early novels concentrate on the feminine sensibility at war with the hostility and callousness of a male-centred universe. (*Cry, the Peacock, Voices in the City, Where Shall We Go This Summer?*). Later novels—*Fire on the Mountain, In Custody, Baumgartner's Bombay* and *Clear Light of Day*—reveal her sensitive apprehension of the existentialist angst of the modern man trapped in islands of loneliness, equally alienated from family and society. With more than ten novels and two short story collections to her credit, Anita Desai is today the most well-known among Indian women novelists in English. Twice she was short-listed for the prestigious Booker prize. The range and sweep of her fictional oeuvre is remarkable. In the poetic and extremely sensitive use of English, in the evocation of images that transcribe the human condition and in the poignant fictionalisation of the human predicament, Anita Desai's skill is incomparable.

Anita Desai is unusually reticent about her personal life. She was born in Mussorie in 1937, of a Bengali father and a German mother. The mixed parentage might be a reason for the choice of English as the medium for self-expression. She says:

> According to the rules laid down by critics, I ought to be writing half my work in Bengali, the other half in German. As it happens, I have never written a word in either language. Possibly I found English to be a suitable link language, a compromise. But I can state definitely that I did not choose English in a deliberate and conscious act. If it did not sound like a piece of arrogance, I'd say perhaps it was the language that chose me.[1]

Anita Desai completed her education at Queen Mary's College, Delhi and at Miranda College, University of Delhi. She is a graduate in English literature and is at present a member of the Faculty of Mount Holyoke College, Massachusetts, USA. Her parentage, her upbringing and expatriate experience has given her a cosmopolitan outlook and a sympathetic understanding of the painful aspects of the human predicament—loneliness, rootlessness and alienation of the sensitive and the tender-hearted. Endowed with remarkable sensitivity, she can apprehend the emotional problems of her fellow beings. This delicate sensitivity speaks for itself when she remarks:

> I confess I am afraid of speaking out about the art of writing, the mechanics of my craft. I have an intuitive and deep fear that by speaking of something subterranean and subconscious, I will destroy it—it is something so very frail. (Desai 47)

The words reveal a withdrawn self that turns inward. It is this tendency to turn her focus on to the unexplored inner regions of the human self—the female self in the earlier novels—that won her a space for herself among Indian English novelists. Her novels span an extensive range of issues. They map the evolution of a writer from obsession with the unrevealed inner world of her female characters to themes of perennial interest to all. The preoccupation with the female psyche gives way to issues of larger human interest imaging the author's own growth to maturity. *Bye-Bye Blackbird* has been said to be the novel closest to her personal experience as immigrant. A prominent theme running through her novels is the aloneness of the human being stranded in this isolated island of human destiny. It is poignantly depicted in novels like *Fire on the Mountain, In Custody, Baumgartner's Bombay* etc. *In Custody* and *Baumgartner's Bombay* have males as the central voices. Baumgartner is the only character reminding us of Desai's German parentage. The burden of existence hangs heavy on most of her characters. Neurosis or death is the way out for some of them; Maya in *Cry, the Peacock*, and Monisha in *Voices in the City* are examples. But there is a more positive approach in later novels like *Village by the Sea, Clear Light of Day* and *In Custody. Journey to Ithaca* thematises deeper spiritual urges that transcend national and religious barriers. *Fasting, Feasting*—the book recommended for Booker Prize in 2000—voices the culture schism between India and America and the way life side-steps certain individuals leaving them to fast. The vignettes from Indian life centring on a middles class family are juxtaposed with glimpses of American family life and the cultural incompatibility of the Indian youth in America.

The modern sensibility that seeks expression through Anita Desai's novels is that of the average middleclass Indian—a product of the multicultural, multilingual, multireligious Indian society. Her own mixed parentage, her early education in a Christian missionary school in Delhi—itself an amalgam of Muslim, British and Hindu cultures—must have made the author particularly sensitive to the conglomeration of cultures woven into the very texture of Indian life. Her later status as a non-resident Indian must have sharpened her sensibility towards the emotional and cultural instability of the modern Indian. Desai's protagonists, mostly centred in the cities, turn out to be drifting, alienated products of a mixed heritage.

Dislocation or uncentredness—geographic, emotional or cultural—can be seen to be the root malady underlying the sense of alienation and rootlessness setting in on Anita Desai's characters. With women it often results from an incompatible partnership with an insensitive, practical and successful male. The voids in understanding lead to partners drifting apart resulting in death, neurosis, murder, etc. The choice of an urban locale as fictional background validates the emotional insecurity of her protagonists. The sensitive individual—male or female—is poised against hostile or indifferent forces of the family or the society leading to suffering and unmitigated loneliness. Desai should not be called a social realist because "her forte" as K.R. Sreenivasa Iyengar puts it, "is the exploration of sensibility—the particular kind of modern sensibility that is ill at ease."[2] Her canvas is the mindscape of her characters and it is the inner reality she explores. The conflict between self and society or forces beyond the self and the search for solutions or answers on the part of the self assumes the pattern of a quest within the framework of the narrative. The quest seldom leads to success. Arya Ghosh comments about her novels: "They are torn [...] her novels chart a peculiar path of circularity where texts only begin and rebegin, and 'end' by coming back to the point of beginning once more."[3]

The epigraph to her novel *Journey to Ithaca* reminds us that the goal Ithaca—is unattainable. What really matters is the journey and the search.

Desai's debut novel *Cry, the Peacock* (1963) is a woman-centred narrative in the first person. It gives voice to the fears, anxieties and sorrows of a hypersensitive woman—Maya—verging on neurosis. Her practical, worldly-wise husband Gautama has a philosophical approach to life but is emotionally distanced from Maya's demented sensibility fluttering in every wind of imagined disaster. The opening incident of the death of the pet dog Totto is employed to show the emotional incompatibility between husband and wife. To Maya the event takes on the proportions of an unbearable tragedy, but to Gautama, it is an everyday event to be managed efficiently and dismissed. Anita Desai succeeds in bringing out through trivial incidents of everyday life, like their response to flowers, late-evening scents of the garden, and the stars in the sky, the widening emotional gulf between partners. Maya's exaggerated reactions make her high-strung. She creates her own island of loneliness and grieves of Gautama's inability to fulfil her expectations. A pampered and motherless childhood spent in the care of her wealthy father has left her unfit to surmount the tensions and anxieties of normal existence. The fear of a prophecy of the death of one of them on the fourth year of their married life intensifies Maya's neurotic fears. Gautama's reaction to Maya's hysterics is normal and his absorption in work to escape her nervous tantrums is the typical reaction of a spouse trapped in an unenviable alliance with a neurotic woman. Gautama is exasperated with Maya's growing agitation which is beyond his comprehension.

The emotional locale for the narrative of a shattered female psyche is carefully constructed in the opening section (Part I) with the description of the pet dog lying rotting in the sun. The reek of dead flesh spreads in the house and the waiting ravenous crows and the flies swarming around increase Maya's horror and dismay. This is in sharp contrast to the sensuous world outside to which Maya is highly receptive; she rejoices in the "vivid, explosive, mobile life"—"the world of sounds, senses, movements, odours, colours, tunes" (92). The truth of living is to her the ability to perceive, appreciate and enjoy the beauty in the little things around—"sun-silkened trees and milk-mild rivers," "the curved arc of a bird's wing, the steam rising from a pot of tea" or "the caress of a familiar hand." She is a child jubilant in this world of senses and the mature world of matter-of-fact people frightens and disgusts her.

Maya's degenerate, neurotic brain leads to the ghastly revelation that she is reluctant not to leave Gautama, but this pulsating world. The gradual disintegration of Maya's world is narrated through her own words. The narrative gains in authenticity as Desai records the instances of fever, headaches, mounting fears of death, thoughts of murder, and violent outbreaks of temper with even a warning to the reader that what she is writing now may not be the truth, but only hallucinations. By the time she deliberately schemes the death of Gautama, her withdrawal from normalcy is complete. An unsuspecting Gautama is easily led to the terrace and pushed down by a single stretch of her hand to certain death below. The peak of Maya's madness is seen in the climactic scene where she narrates the incident to Gautama's mother and sister, offering them tea and biscuits as on any other visit, justifying the act and seeking their support and approval. In the last chapter the author takes over the narration and reports the tragic end of the distraught Maya in her father's house as she jumps down from the balcony.

Cry, the Peacock is the poignant presentation of neurosis resulting from fissures generated by emotional and intellectual alienation between partners. Anita Desai evokes the right atmosphere through the rich imagery characteristic of her style and the apt use of symbols. The psychological issue in Maya's life attains the dimensions of existential agony because it is rooted in the essential loneliness that corrodes her being and makes it impossible for her to find meaning in an arid existence. Marital discord contributes to the existential agony of an essentially lonely being.

Aloneness of the individual is a persistent theme in Anita Desai's novels. The sensitive human being suffers from a sense of alienation which could reach the intensity of an existential malaise. Reasons that provoke dislocation in the individual self could be the oppressive/ hostile nature of the society, the emotional distancing of a partner in a marital alliance or the state of exile as immigrant. It can lead to frustration, a longing for escape or even suicide.

Voices in the City (1965), the second novel of Anita Desai is a brilliant exposition of the alienation suffered by certain dislocated individuals trapped in the claustrophobic life of the metropolis. As the highly evocative title signifies, the voices in the city are oppressive, jarring on the fine sensibility of the sensitive individuals who have been forced into this large and open arena of competition, rivalry and the mad race for success. Nirode, Monisha and Anila re-enact the emotional trauma of the sensitive souls caught in the lonely islands of their selves. The callousness of the metropolis is evoked through a spirit of the place that pervades the novel. As Meena Beliappa remarks, Anita Desai "seeks to relate the subjective world of the individual to the spirit of the place."[4] The oppressive forces of the city seem to operate within the consciousness of the characters. As an artist and an alien, Nirode is oppressed by the "monster city" (150). The city is to him a symbol of disintegration, pressing in on him and forcing him into mechanical jobs alien to his creative, artistic temperament. Nirode is possessed by an intense desire to escape, but only to the anonymity of the artist's existence. Highly emotional, he evades the practical aspects of life like the quality of the paper, the print and cover-design of his magazine 'Voices,' payments to the press and to the contributors, leading to the failure of the magazine.

Nirode's sister Monisha who comes to Calcutta when her husband Jiban is transferred there, identifies Calcutta with "the city of Kali, Goddess of death" (138). It intensifies the claustrophobia experienced by her in the joint family of her in-laws. "Marital life is to her, devoid of love, privacy and children." Monisha can be grouped with the hypersensitive females in Anita Desai's novels who are distraught with a sense of the futility and emptiness of life being reduced to petty jobs, pensions, price of vegetables and the cooking of food. "In this what is then my life? Only a conundrum that I shall brood over forever with passion and pain, never to arrive at a solution? Only a conundrum—is that, then, life?" (124-25). Monisha's tragedy is that she, like Nirode, sought meaning in an existence that is reduced to practical trivialities by others. She is doomed to suffer total emotional alienation which finally seeks expression in suicide. R.S. Sharma remarks that the novel "communicates most powerfully the tragedy of human existence in a dehumanized society."[5]

Monisha can be listed among the unfortunate victims of incompatible marriage alliances; but her tragedy attains the dimensions of the existential anguish of a sensitive and lonely human soul. Anita Desai's extraordinary power to create an intense sense of locale that envelops and consumes the characters is most pronounced here.

The other artists—Dharma and David—introduced in the novel remind us of the artist-fugitives in Tennessee Williams' plays. They linger on the margins of life, refusing to become involved, as though afraid of the noise, confusion and competition of metropolitan life.

Cry, the Peacock gains in intensity because the entire story is contained by Maya's neurotic sensibility. In *Voices in the City* the oppressive cityscape that envelops and destroys the sensitive beings trapped in it is equated with their mother as well as Kali. Monisha's death leaves Nirode with the certainty of his own impending death. Images of failure, destruction and futility are replete, evoking an atmosphere of loss, death and pain.

Alienation at different levels forms the theme of Anita Desai's third novel *Bye-Bye Blackbird* (1971). The plight of the Indian immigrant domiciled in England is depicted with all its attendant emotional problems. The nostalgic longing of the colonized for his 'second home' gives way to disillusionment and frustration at the racial prejudice, indifference, contempt and outright hostility of the British for the Asian immigrants. The Indian is reduced to the clan of 'wogs' and English doors and windows are tightly closed against him.

A pet theme with post-colonial writers, Anita Desai examines the issue from different angles by making her protagonist Adit marry an English lady Sarah. The Adit–Sarah relationship is subject to tension generated by the umpteen little everyday events that bring out the culture schism between the orient and the occident. Desai represents through Adit Sen and Dev different stages of the immigrant experience. Adit's admiration for everything English and his infatuation for British ways of life and dress mark the initial stage of the immigrant experience. Dev's contempt for Anglophiles is unlike usual immigrant behaviour; but in the second stage it is he who shows the typical attitude by getting acclimatised to the land and its culture and feeling reluctant to leave. Disillusioned with the land and its people, Adit the blackbird decides to leave. The unfriendly silence and the reserved formality of the English have a chilling effect on Adit and his friends. Their loud, boisterous talk and laughter, their uninhibited incursions into other people's privacy strike Sarah as crude and unrefined. Adit's Bengali music jars on her English sensibility. The unwashed dishes of the previous night left in the sink and the cat cosily resting on the teacosy administer culture shocks to Adit. He is often possessed by nostalgic longing for home, for an Indian sunset and Indian food. Cultural incompatibility surfaces sharply in Adit's encounters with his in-laws. "The placidity, munificence and the ease of England" (210) experienced through his in-laws disgust him beyond endurance. He feels he could not bear to see "one more pale, expressionless British face. If one were to approach him, he wd hit it, hit it" (119). Exposure to English literature and music develops a sense of identification with the English in the colonized; hence the rude shock caused by their cold rejection. As Parthasarathy puts it,

> "Coloureds" is what they call us
> Over there.[6]

In the Adit–Sarah relationship Sarah does not side with the British. She belongs to the Desai clan of alienated beings suffering from "an anguish of loneliness" (35) and torn by uncertainty about her own identity. She wonders:

> Who was she—Mrs. Sen who had been married in a red and gold Benares brocade sari one burning, bronzed day in September, or Mrs. Sen, the Head's Secretary. (38)

Anita Desai has made Sarah's predicament more pitiable than Adit's because she has no assurance about acceptance from her own people. She is reluctant to meet even her parents, being uncertain about their attitude. Adit, on the other hand, is sure of his roots. He is confident of his place within the cultural fold of India because he has never severed his ties. Marriage to Adit has made Sarah a fractured personality ashamed of her Indian husband, still totally devoted to him. The social ostracisation she suffers in her native society compels her to submit to Adit as though to transcend the separateness of her individual identity.

Desai's narration of Sarah's predicament—her struggle to adjust and her efforts to cope with the loneliness that envelops her being—does not attain the poignancy of the portrayal of Maya in *Cry, the Peacock* because of the omniscient narrative technique adopted. Sarah's sensibility does not enfold us as Maya's, leaving us mere observers of her miserable plight. When Adit decides to leave for India Sarah feels that she is bidding goodbye to her English self rather than to England.

There are three threads in the narrative—Adit's story, Dev's story ad Sarah's story. The process of being and becoming enacted in the characters is represented through the journey pattern. The subtext narrates the untold story of racial antagonism voiced by Mrs. James, Mrs. Miller, a snobbish bus conductor or a cheeky schoolboy. However, Anita Desai does not allow the issue to steal centre stage as in Kamala Markandaya's *The Nowhereman* (1974). Nor does she adopt a feminist perspective and project male chauvinism as the reason for Sarah's suppressed identity. The highly symbolic title gains in significance when at the end of the novel Dev repeats the words "goodbye, blackbird" as Adit and Sarah leave for India. It can be interpreted as Dev's farewell to Adit the blackbird or his farewell to his own Indian self. Desai's poetic style and highly evocative imagery attribute a lyrical quality to her prose.

Variation in the central theme hardly affects the undercurrent of loneliness and alienation running through her novels. The alienation of woman caught in a self-destructive alliance surfaces as a related issue to the existential theme. To apply the term "feminist" to Anita Desai will be to limit the scope and range of her thematic concerns. But woman's search for space remains *one* of her primary concerns. A novel that has lent itself to feminist readings is Desai's *Where Shall We Go This Summer?* (1975). It traces the journey of a woman to her parental home—a journey that could be interpreted in feminist terms as the refusal of the temporal order and the search for a landscape that would accommodate her and enable her to combat the hostile forces of the patriarchal world of men. Her reluctance to let her fifth child be born on this earth is a bold expression of her protest against a society that stifles sensitivity and destroys the innocent and the sincere. The central characters bearing the archetypal names—Sita and Rama—are far from a reincarnation of the mythical figures. The rough, masculine approach of Raman jars on Sita's hypersensitive nature frightening her out of her wits and driving her to the mad decision to retain the child in her womb. Her frenzied mind takes refuge in the delusion that the magic aura of her late father still pervading his home in the island of

Manori would help preserve her baby. She goes to Manori with her children in an act of defiance bringing to a climax the conflict with her husband.

The void between reality and imagination comes heavily down upon Sita as she reaches Manori. The enchanted island had the charisma of a Utopia in her imagination. The actual visit to Manori sheds it of its glamour, its aura of magic, thus forming an equally unpalatable substitute for the insensitivity and hostility of an unhappy married life in urban sophistication.

Unlike *Cry, the Peacock* and *Voices in the City* where the protagonists succumb to their neurosis and kill themselves, Sita accepts the need to face life with all its grossness and ugliness. This positive avowal of life manifests in her readiness to go back to the fold of marital life and the responsibilities of motherhood when Raman comes. She even shares Raman's thoughts and anxieties about the children and the need to continue the routine that life has settled into: "Life must be continued and all its business—Menaka's admission to medical college gained, wife led to hospital, new child safely brought forth, the children reared, the factory seen to, a salary earned, a salary spent" (101).

Sita's change in attitude marks a positive acceptance of life and of the man–woman relationship in the traditional way. The experience in Manori leads Sita to a reassessment and perfect understanding of her situation out of which must have arisen her decision to return to the fold of the family. The major concern for Indian women novelists writing in English has been the delineation of woman's growth into self-awareness. Desai's stance in *Where Shall We Go This Summer?* is a clear indication that she does not advocate a gyno-centric struggle leading to woman's liberation in western feminist terms. The familial bond of which woman is the crux, has to survive. The bonds of Indian tradition have to be preserved.

The theme of aloneness reaches its most poignant fictional representation in *Fire on the Mountain* (1975). The three females caught in the web of loneliness belong to the category of the oppressed and victimised women inhabiting Anita Desai's fictional scenario. Nanda Kaul, the central consciousness has deliberately opted for loneliness and has chosen as her residence the isolated house on the ridge of a mountain at Carignano in Kasauli. The barren mountains and the starkness of the landscape with its hard rocks and tall pines become metaphors for the loneliness of the human soul. The busy schedule of a Vice Chancellor's wife and the innumerable demands it made on her as neglected and unloved wife, busy mother and the pleasing hostess at the Vice Chancellor's dinner table have made her exasperated with life. Carignano offered her the anonymity and escape she longed for.

Raka, the great grand-daughter of Nanda Kaul is sent to Carignano by her mother and is most unwelcome in the bastion of the recluse. Raka comes as silently and unobtrusively as an insect and so totally ignores Nanda Kaul that the old lady discovers with a sense of shock that if she was a recluse by choice, Raka was one by instinct. Nanda Kaul found that she was "the finished, perfect model of what Nanda Kaul herself was merely a brave, flawed experiment" (47).

She realised that Raka had not "arrived at this condition by a long route of rejection and sacrifice—she was born to it, simply" (48). The indifference and total neglect of her by Raka breeds in her a desire for communication—for some link with this unusual child. What Raka is, is mainly the result of the unhappy married life of her parents and her mother's frequent bouts of illness.

The third woman in the story is Ila Das, a spinster and a much-hated social worker in the backward village. Her anti-dowry campaigns and family planning propaganda have provoked the anger and despise of the ignorant but rude country folk. The author has pictured her as an ugly and clumsy woman, extremely poor, always badly dressed and half starved and ashamed of herself. Ila's voice was her tragedy. She cackled and screamed causing agony to the ears of the listeners. The visit of Ila Das is used by the author to give the reader an insight into Nanda Kaul's childhood and her regal life as Viceroy's wife presiding over a full house. In Kasauli the village priest was her adversary. He prevented the villagers from using medicines and encouraged child marriage, undoing whatever Ila Das as a social worker tried to teach them. Existence had become a severe struggle for her.

> Her rackety existence looked so precarious, she felt that one stone thrown, one stick tripped would be enough to end it. (133)

Nanda Kaul's fears come true as Preet Singh, whose seven-year old daughter's marriage to an old man Ila Das had tried to prevent, strangles her on her way back home and rapes her brutally. The news of Ila's murder brings home with brute force the truth of her own unhappy life. Her husband had never loved her and had carried on a lifelong affair with Miss David, the mathematics mistress, whom he had not married because she was a Christian but whom he had loved all his life. And her children were all alien to her nature and she neither understood nor loved them. She lived alone in Carignano because that was what she was forced to do, reduced to doing.

In the midst of fullness Nanda Kaul's life had been barren and empty. Ila, with her genteel upbringing was a misfit in the village and the laughing stock of the villagers. The horrible end of her miserable existence completes the circle. The novel ends as Raka comes back to the house after a long period of unnoticed absence and declares that she has set fire to the forest.

Anita Desai probes the psyche of these three lonely creatures and portrays them with remarkable sympathy and understanding. Life has dealt with them harshly. The attempt of the three women to encounter life bravely appears almost pathetic. The three narratives are deftly interconnected by the barest possible links so as not to destroy the isolated nature of their existence. The novel is a remarkable fictional achievement in which through minimum dialogue and action Anita Desai inscribes the stories of three alienated beings. A Sahitya Akademi award winner, *Fire on the Mountain* grips us by its intense power of narration and is beyond doubt one of the best novels by Anita Desai.

The theme of *Clear Light of Day* (1980), according to the author, is "about time as a destroyer, as a preserver and about what the bondage of time does to people."[7] The theme of time in relation to eternity inspired by T.S. Eliot's *Four Quartets* only adds a new dimension to the novel which again tells the story of the alienation of Bim whom life has slipped by. Tara's visit with her diplomat husband Bakul to the old and shabby house in Old Delhi where Bim lives with their retarded brother Baba provides an excellent opportunity to the author to view the action from a dual perspective—of the past and the present—, every incident in the present triggering off memories from the past. The faded and shabby house where time has been standing still, and the city of old Delhi reduced to a historic remnant of the past, become metaphors for the stagnation in the lives of Baba and Bim. Anita Desai contrasts the luxurious life of Tara and her diplomat husband Bakul with the sparse existence of the prematurely greying Bimla and her retarded brother.

One of the powerful devices used by Anita Desai is the evocation of a sense of time as a continuum where incidents from the past have their repercussion on the present and extend to the future. Tara's presence brings to Bim the shocking awareness that Time which has had a rejuvenating effect on Tara has destroyed her, crushing her within its soggy mass. The burden of the consumptive Raja, the retarded Baba and the alcoholic Mira masi has stripped Bim of her ambitions and her youthfulness. She describes herself and Baba as figures in a "faded old picture in its petrified frame" (5). Time had stood still for them. Bim's students describe old Delhi, discarded by the British for New Delhi, as a great cemetery where every house was a tomb. Memories of the communal riots that tore the city linger in the air.

Past guilts, fears, ambitions and frustrations surface as the sisters confront memories of shared experiences in the past. The rancour and bitterness against Raja pour out as Bim shows the condescending letter Raja wrote to the sister who had nursed him through consumption back to health and new life.

The consciousness of the paradox of time as Eternity and Time as flux is inextricably linked with Bim's inward journey of self-exploration which is also a journey into the past leading onto a re-evaluation of human relationships, of unfulfilled ambitions and frustrations. The realisation Bim arrives at, is one of the most positive insights afforded by Anita Desai. The knowledge of their togetherness fills her inner self like the radiance of the day and she is moved by love and forgiveness for Tara and Raja. This new insight into life and its meaning, into love and togetherness floods her being.

Desai shows history impinging itself on the personal life of the characters. The freedom movement, the communal riots of 1947, and the death of Gandhiji have their indirect impact on the Das family. The partition of India is enacted within their personal lives too as Raja leaves for Hyderabad.

The structure of the novel is an index to the maturity of the novelist's craftsmanship. The narrative falls into four parts, the second part forming the time-pivot of the book and is therefore the lengthier. The shifting pattern of Time conveys a strong sense of the eternal intersecting with the transient. The stream of consciousness style adopted for narration builds a sense of the flux of time and of time as a continuous flow even though narration never assumes a chronological or linear pattern. Time here is an emotional sequence of events. The summer of 1947 is apprehended by the sisters as a period flooded by momentous events.

Literature, poetry and music add to the texture of the life of the characters. What Bim could not forgive about Raja is his total neglect of his poetic talents after his marriage to Benazir. Tara is jealous of the infatuation for poetry that links Raja and Bim. She wonders at their ability to recite long passages of poetry from memory. The words from the *Life of Aurangazeb* bring home to Bim a sudden awareness of the aloneness of the human self in its last journey throwing into insignificance all the trivialities that disturb personal relationships in our everyday existence. Quotations from Eliot's *Four Quartets* deepen the concept of time which is central to the novel. Discussions on music and actual musical performances also blend into the texture of the novel. Even the narrative pattern of the novel lends itself to a comparison with the sonata form in music, the different sections of the novel corresponding to the five movements of the sonata. The music concert that Bim and Baba listen to at the end of the novel is a fitting finale to the novel structured in the pattern of a musical sonata. The remarkable maturity of style is matched by maturity in the choice of the theme and the perspective of life afforded by the positive ending. The theme transcends the temporal and the transient and discusses the eternal and the existentialist—the issue of human loneliness, of Time in its transience and eternity—and enduring human values.

The novel, *Village by the Sea* (1982) set in the valley of Thul expresses the author's anxiety regarding the social, economic and cultural transformation in the wake of industrialisation. Anita Desai shows remarkable insight into the far-fetched consequences of industrialisation in an agrarian village—the confiscation of cultivable land for the building of factories, the weaning away of people from the traditional occupation of farming, and the dumping of industrial waste into the sea killing its natural wealth, the fish, are grim possibilities envisaged by the author. Desai highlights at the same time the need for progress. Through young Hari's consciousness is depicted the villagers' perception and awareness of the changes setting in. The far-reaching effects of the establishment of a major factory in the village are beyond their imagination and comprehension; but Hari's exposure to the city makes him conscious of the need to adapt to the changes. The change in Hari's perspective becomes symbolic of the awakening of a sleepy little village to the winds of change sweeping over the rest of the world.

Hari's exposure to the claustrophobic sense of oppression in the congested city serves to make him aware of the blessings of the village—some land and a house of his own, the access to sea-breeze, and fresh air. The period spent in Bombay is also an apprenticeship to Hari to enter the arena of life. When he returns to the village with his earnings, he has definite plans about the future, unlike the villagers who endure their hardships and live in eternal poverty without seeking any other means of escaping their plight. Hari proposes to set up a poultry farm in the tiny bit of land that can never grow enough food for the family and as the factory comes up, he would perhaps be the owner of the first watch-repair shop in the village. Anita Desai's vision is infused with an idealistic fervour, making almost an idyll of village life. In spite of the hardships and sufferings portrayed in the first part of the novel, the predominant tone is one of hope and optimism. Even Hari's alcoholic father is shown as cured of his drinking habit and looking after his wife with absolute devotion. The kindness of the de Silvas and their new tenant—Sayyid Ali Sahib—is almost too good to be real. The romantic idealisation here comes in sharp contrast with the bleak picture of an Indian village under the shattering impact of industrialisation depicted in Kamala Markandaya's *Nectar in a Sieve*. In *A Handful of Rice* Kamala Markandaya draws a terrifying picture of the wild competition and struggle for existence in an industrialised society which has moved away from the values of village life. Desai seems to advocate an attitude of acceptance and adaptability keeping pace with the inexorable turning of the wheels of progress.

The existential dilemma of Deven, a middleclass man with mediocre talents working as college lecturer in the little town of Mirpore forms the theme of *In Custody*. As in *Village by the Sea* a male forms the central consciousness. The effort here is to see man in his relationship with family and society and an investigation and evaluation of the individual's role in the scheme of things. It is significant that with a male as protagonist, the author adopts a different technique of presentation. Desai might have felt more at home with the feminine sensibility.

Deven's anxiety is about his unfulfilled ambitions and dreams. He is despondent that success has never come his way; life has never offered him an occasion to come into the limelight and he is doomed to continue the dreary drudgery of a monotonous life. Desai here posits her male protagonist in a "socially secure" context with a salaried job and a family but makes him a symbol of the drifting, discontented modern Indian lured by western notions of success, but too incompetent and aimless to achieve them and hence frustrated and despondent. Deven's dissatisfaction with life shows in his career as a college lecturer, and in his role as husband. He is a 'boring' teacher; he is a grumbling husband; he is an unrecognised poet. The crushed dreams of Deven are rejuvenated when a friend Murad entrusts him with the task of interviewing the famous Urdu poet Nur Shahjehanabadi for a special issue of his journal. The novel is unique in its faithful portrayal of Deven's predicament till he receives the invitation and the disillusionment that sets in when he actually enters the illustrious poet's domain. The gulf between dream and reality is so wide that the much anticipated interview with Nur, who is always surrounded by 'friends,' relatives and admirers, turns out to be a fiasco. Deven realises that even the famous poet whom he had imagined to be presiding over his ethereal kingdom is trapped in the mundane reality with its innumerable cares and worries. Deven had always thought of art and reality as two distinct entities and the region of art as pure, and high above reality untouched by its corruption. Now he finds his 'hero presiding over "a derelict court full of the louts and lafangas of the bazar world who enjoyed nightly gazal, biriyani and kababs at the poet's cost" (50). The poet's privacy is so rudely invaded that Deven realises with a shock that life has to be lived in the midst of all its ugliness. Deven had attributed his failure as a poet to restrictions on his free will and the responsibilities that burdened him, taken him into custody. In spite of his genius and his achievements, Nur is found to be equally entrapped with a sick wife and a young school-going child to care for, and weighed down by poverty and several dependents, "he was as trapped as Deven even if his cage was more prominent and attracted more attention" (131).

For the first time Deven is able to relate poetry and life and he feels that perhaps poetry could provide the answers for life's problems. But after the encounter with Nur, Deven realises that genius blooms even within the trappings of sordid reality. The realisation of this truth enables Deven to face reality. A transformed Deven takes stock of his empirical existence and decides to commit himself to his responsibilities. Commitments in life cannot be evaded, according to the Bhagavad Gita and the philosophical wisdom of the Gita offers the incentive to Deven to return to his duties and responsibilities. The transformation in Deven is effected by a need to face life, even in custody. Escape is only for cowards. As in *Clear Light of Day* here too the novel closes on a positive note.

The protagonist in *In Custody* symbolises the dilemma and anxiety of many a modern young Indian. Education, career and the fancy for art are factors that alienate the modern youth from the society and family. Deven's wife Sarala is an equally frustrated being, but he is incapable of understanding her and the misery they share never unites them. Deven hardly realises that his solipsism has created his cage. The interview is visualised as the door to liberation and an opening into the world of art and achievement. Ironically enough, Deven hopes to gain the recognition he has failed to get in the little town of Mirpore, in the busy impersonal city of Delhi, where the individual is reduced to a nonentity in a whirling mass of humanity.

Deven's drama of escape and retrieval is enacted against the background of a society fast moving towards westernised notions of progress through science and technology. Discussions among the lecturers in the college throw up issues like brain drain, and the desire to escape to the glamour of the west. Deven with all his artistic aspirations is not free from the inferiority complex suffered by teachers of art subjects in a world where science alone has prominence. His own creative efforts have come to naught and he is afraid to confront his mediocrity because success is not for the mediocre.

Deven's desperate efforts to tape Nur's poems in the midst of the confusion and noise and frequent interruptions of Nur's crowded household could be turned into a ridiculously comic situation by a slight ironic twist. The inimitable ironic touch of R.K. Narayan might have made the situation amusing. But Desai extends to Deven the sympathy and understanding she has lavished on her neurotic, hypersensitive, female protagonists. As all Deven's efforts to put Nur's poetry into safe custody miscarry, and students threaten to beat him up and college authorities demand an explanation for misspent money, Desai makes the reader view it all as unfortunate events in Deven's desperate struggle to make life meaningful.

> He had imagined he was taking Nur's poetry into safe custody, and not realised that if he was to be custodian of Nur's genius, then Nur would become his custodian and place him in custody too. This alliance could be considered an unendurable burden—

or else a shining honour. Both demanded an equal strength. (*In Custody* 203)

This idea of the interdependence of the poet and the critic or the creator and the receptor of poetry is at the core of the novel. More than that the novel is a positive affirmation of the individual's place in society and his need to accept it with all its burdens and responsibilities.

Village by the Sea, Clear Light of Day and *In Custody* mark Anita Desai's venture into male domains and male sensibility, extending the range and scope of her fiction. Anita Sinha comments on *In Custody* as "the most remarkable novel in Desai's repertory." The cinematic adaptation of the novel too has been successful.

Baumgartner's Bombay (1988) is an interesting landmark in the novelist's career. Themes which have been dwelt on in novel after novel—alienation, aloneness of the individual, the self-society dichotomy—find their resonance in this novel as well. But the resourcefulness of the author becomes manifest in the remarkable variation effected in the fictionalisation of the theme. In the choice of the protagonist—a male, a German and a Jew—, in the use of the metanarrative technique in the telling of the German's tale, in the extension of the dimensions of her fictional art, Anita Desai establishes her indisputable right to distinction. The theme of aloneness seems to be a perpetual fascination with Desai that she deals with it in different individuals, in different social contexts and situations, with a remarkable sensitivity that makes her perceptive to every subtle shade and colour of it. In *Fire on the Mountain* she seemed to have scaled the highest peaks of aloneness; but *Baumgartner's Bombay* with its unique choice of the central character transcends even *Fire on the Mountain* in its poignancy. Hugo Baumgartner is the very symbol of loneliness; a German and a Jew he is doubly alienated; a poor foreigner domiciled in the drab areas of the city of Bombay, he is totally distanced from the society around. His yearning belong to India finds expression in the novel: "It seemed desperately important to belong and make a place for himself" (93).

Family forms a recurrent ideological framework in the novel, providing a sharp contrast to Baumgartner's present situation. Baumgartner's religion, his status as a foreigner, his poverty and the absence of an immediate family are cited as the dominant factors responsible for his alienation. The ideal of the family is a recurrent dream to Baumgartner, which he treasures as his private safeguard against the animosity of society, and the disruptive, political forces that had conspired to destroy it in Germany. We are made to realise that as a German, he is totally alienated from the history and politics of his land, and the rise of Nazism. Facts closely associated with Baumgartner's present status are deliberately thrust to the margins of the narrative.

The inability to find a space for himself either in Germany or in India makes Baumgartner a recluse. "Germany there, India here—India there, Germany here. Impossible to capture, to hold, to read them, to make sense of them. They all fell away from him, into an abyss" (216).

Memories of Baumgartner's childhood and his nostalgic recollections of family signify a culture, a way of life where literature, music and arts have their place and life consists of interesting moments when ideas are exchanged and art is enjoyed. Goethe, Schiller and Heine adorned the bookshelves. Songs, poetry and flowers made life meaningful. The memory of the idyllic past remains with Baumgartner as a throbbing pain, and a longing for the impossible. Baumgartner's life is the story of dislocation, displacement and loss. The saga of deprival begins with the first displacement of the Baumgartners from their own house in Germany. It was in the internment camp as a prisoner of war that he had a taste of communal life. Through all the adverse circumstances a sustaining force has been the cherished dream of a family.

> When he saw the pale blonde young woman in the adjoining enclosure bending to lift wet laundry out of a basket, then unbending to pin it to a washing line, he realised that it was for this form of living that he pined: simple, routine, repetitive, calm. (126)

The small, filthy, nondescript flat in Bombay with the maimed, homeless cats that he shelters, stands in sharp contrast to the ideal. Lotte, his only friend, also lived amidst violence and abuse. The gulf between reality and dream is felt with added intensity through the picture of a family who have made the pavement their home. His own yearning for home might have persuaded Baumgartner to give shelter to Kurt, the German boy. The contrast between them is brought out in different ways. Baumgartner's exile from his country is the consequence of his reaction to the horror of Nazism; his sensitivity to the finer things in life like literature, music and art compels him to thrust the memories of war and the brutalities of Nazism to the peripheries of the mind. Kurt, on the other hand, is a wild product of the anarchy of contemporary history.

Baumgartner's story is that of the suffering, persecuted Jew—one who is running away or withdrawing from life. But unlike other Jews the spirit of resistance is foreign to him. His identity as a Jew alienates Baumgartner from Germans, Indians and from himself. He looks at the Jew's body as something alien to him. He talks of it as 'other.' The body with the colour of his skin, hair and eyes becomes symbolic of his Jewishness and his alienation from himself. We are reminded of his foreignness by the words 'firanghi' and 'unwanted' reverberating through the text. The inertia and fatigue he experiences make him shy away from all activities, withdrawing into his shell like "an old turtle" (11) or like "a mournful turtle" (109). Baumgartner-Kurt opposition is a re-enactment of the self-society conflict worked out in the other novels. The difference is that here the characters remain as symbols and the conflict does not become active. Baumgartner's moral superiority and refinement—qualities that endear him to the reader—make him an alien to the society. The point of contact with the society is established in that moment of violence, when Kurt stabs him.

Baumgartner's story does not end with his death. It continues through the letters he has left. The author lends voice to Baumgartner, who has been silent in the last phase of his life, through his letters. They are his mother's letters written in long, spidery flourishes. Significantly enough, the narrative opens with Lotte, the only friend Baumgartner had in India, looking through the letters that she had brought from Baumgartner's flat where he lay murdered for the few silver trophies he treasured. From the silence of his life and death, Baumgartner is resurrected as it were, through the letters. There is the suggestion of mysterious meanings that the letters might unlock. Writing becomes self-reflexive here and the novel takes on the tone of a metanarrative with Lotte feeling the impact of the written word, of the letters drowning her in their sweetness.

Lotte, the reader, is overpowered by the written word which objectifies and makes tangible the memories of Baumgartner. The power of the written word as that which can lend form and substance and actuality to the abstract and the unreal, is emphasised. Within the narrative framework it is also an act of bringing the dead Baumgartner back to visibility. Immediately after the scene where Lotte is shown reading the letters, the narrative shifts to the past with Baumgartner opening the door and appearing on the landing.

The novel ends with Lotte reading the letters, the scene with which it opened. The letters preserve a world of sweetness and love and tenderness between the son and mother in this chaotic world of betrayal, violence and hostility. They function almost as a text within the text—representing the ideal against the actual. The author invests immortality on the ideal since it is preserved by the written word and is therefore imperishable. There is also the implication that it is more valuable. The epigraph of the novel quoted from T.S. Eliot, alludes to the cyclic nature of life: "In my beginning is my end: In succession/ Houses rise and fall" (*East Coker*).

The eternity that Eliot advocates in *Four Quartets* is hinted at in the text through the positing of the immortal word in its dichotomy with the actual and the real. Eliot's words could also apply to the narrative which ends where it begins. This circularity of the text is a phenomenon we notice in Desai's other novels also.

Baumgartner unmistakably belongs to the group of sensitive

romantics inhabiting Anita Desai's world. The romantic streak in him manifests in his longing for the unfulfilled ideal of domestic happiness, his aversion and horror for the rude actualities of history, and his occasional retreat into the dream world of love and sweetness symbolised by his mother's letters. Exiledom is another factor that establishes him as a romantic.

The narrative's self-reflexiveness about its locale makes it distinct from other novels of Anita Desai which though imbued with a heavy sense of locale hardly stands apart and discusses India. In *Baumgartner's Bombay* the change in perspective is warranted by the choice of a German as protagonist who comes to India with the fascination for the exotic east, only to be totally disillusioned. The gulf between the exotic India of his imagination and the real, crowded, impersonal Bombay which became his India, is too startling for Baumgartner. "India has two worlds or ten. She stood before him, hands on her hips, laughing that blood-stained laugh: Choose! Choose!" (85-86)

The exotic India alluring the foreigners has been a pet theme with post-colonial writers. Desai had taken the position of an insider in her earlier novels, taking for granted the locale against which the drama of her novels was played out. With *Baumgartner's Bombay,* a marked difference in perspective is noticeable which could be attributed to her own status as an immigrant in USA and her semi-German parentage. The much explored journey patterns find its resonance here as well as in *Journey to Ithaca.* The quest does not lead to any positive findings in Baumgartner's case; but India does not frustrate him; rather it puzzles him by its enigmatic quality. In *Journey to Ithaca* the spiritual dimensions of the quest leads to the awareness that the journey, the quest, is more important than the goal. The epigraph to *Journey to Ithaca* offers the key to the novels of Anita Desai, everyone of which maps the journey of the self towards self-realisation and fulfilment. The journey seldom reaches its destination; the quest often ends in frustration and disillusionment.

Though the protagonists in Anita Desai's novels hardly reach Ithaca, they realise the validity and significance of the quest. The quest is a process of self–exploration. The inward journey leads to positive affirmations in *Where Shall We Go This Summer, Bye-Bye Blackbird, Clear Light of Day* and *In Custody.* Central to the narrative of *Journey to Ithaca* is Matteo's spiritual quest that brings him to India. The void in communication and understanding between the partners Matteo and Sophie widen because of the divergent goals they seek—the one spiritual and the other physical and emotional. The timid hesitant nature of Matteo the Italian is in sharp contrast with the arrogant demanding temperament of Sophie. They could be considered as representatives of hippies who journeyed to the east in search of meaning, enlightenment, love and marijuana. Most of them, like Matteo were inspired by Hesse's *Journey to the East*. Sophie is disgusted by the dirt, heat and squalor of India, as Matteo's journeys prolong and the search continues. She falls a victim to drugs, becomes ill and frustrated. He goes from one place to the other in search of a guru and a spiritual abode till he reaches the Mother's ashram—a veritable heaven. To Matteo it marks the end of all journeys. He dedicates himself to the worship of God at the feet of the Mother, goes through every trial, takes up all kinds of hard work. The response to the Mother's ashram reflects the temporal difference and emotional rift between Matteo and Sophie. The beautiful surroundings and the infinite peace of the ashram fills Matteo with a sense of contentment, but Sophie sulks and groans and keeps away from all contact with the Mother and the other inmates of the ashram. With the birth of the second child she feels an acute sense of betrayal because of the indifference of Matteo and she leaves for home with the children. The novel opens with Sophie's return to a sick and emaciated Matteo suffering from hepatitis. She nurses him and suggests that they should leave home together to their children when he is fully recovered. Matteo refuses and Sophie sets out to prove to Matteo that the Mother he worships is just an ordinary lady who was a dancer and a married woman. Sophie's journey down the Mother's past—from India to Alexandria and back to India—becomes a journey of self-realisation and enlightenment for her. The story of the Mother's spiritual quest forms a narrative embedded within the narration of Sophie's journey. The restless schoolgirl Laila from Alexandria (Egypt) goes to Paris and USA and then to India along with a dance troupe led by Krishna. Much later when she loses her prominent position in the dance troupe and is substituted by a younger girl, she joins a group of pilgrims going to the Himalayas and discovers there in a temple on a mountain top, the Guru she has been seeking all her life.

The story of Laila's search—with all its rebuffs and anxieties and the final experience of overwhelming joy—is revealed to Sophie through her personal entries in a diary that Krishna shows her. The restless spiritual yearnings that possessed Laila from childhood and the story of her transformation to the Mother so moves Sophie that she returns at once to the ashram. Sophie's transformation, we realise, has been effected by the power of Laila's narrative. The narrative within the text transforms Sophie's story. But Sophie's journey does not end at the ashram. She finds the Mother dead and a desolate Matteo, gone to the Himalayas. Matteo can be presumed to be on the last lap of his journey. Journeys are only beginning for Sophie. Her decision to go where Matteo has gone, is an affirmation of the enlightenment she has attained. We, the readers too, realise by now, that what is important is not the destination, but the journey. Sophie who had triumphantly returned to the ashram with the weapon of her new knowledge, feels defeated and crushed to find that her chief adversary had gone on her last journey.

The three different strands of the story are linked by Sophie. Time shifts between past and present and the story moves from one locale to the other. The first scene is in the hospital where Sophie reaches to look after Matteo and the next is back in Italy where the children—Giacomo and Isabel—are left with their grandparents. Giacomo is modelled after his father as a sensitive, emotionally insecure person, in need of comfort and solace from his younger sister taking the place of his absent mother. The anxiety and insecurity of the deserted children of Matteo and Sophie is conveyed touchingly through a few scenes. Chapter 11 hurtles us back to Laila's restless childhood and then to Sophie's search. The end of Sophie's search with the hard-won knowledge about the Mother is symbolic of what awaits man at the end of every search. We are also made to realise that journeys never end and every journey leads only to another.

As Cavafy's lines indicate, Ithaca is a symbol for unfulfilled human longings expressed in quests that yield lessons more valuable than Ithaca itself. This novel provides the key to all the other novels of Anita Desai, which can be described together as narratives of disillusionment.

The novel leaves the reader disillusioned for it lacks the depth the theme demands. The fact that Desai has chosen to present the story from Sophie's point of view raises the question whether Desai wanted to present the Mother, who undoubtedly is modelled on the Mother of Sri Aurobindo Ashram, in an unfavourable light? The Mother's portrait in the novel cannot be said to be totally prejudiced. Though the novel invests the Mother with the power, spirituality and mystery of a deified personality, the fictional character hardly attains the spiritual aura of the real Mother. The author's limited vision curbs the perspective of the reader and reduces the scope and immensity of the subject chosen. Sophie becomes almost the mouthpiece of the author with the reductionist, demythifying attitude she adopts. Here Anita Desai remains almost at the level of Sophie. Within the fictional framework the enlightenment afforded to Sophie is about the futility of all journeys and paradoxically enough, their worth. *Journey to Ithaca* leaves the feeling that the author has wandered out of her terrain into domains beyond her understanding. The novel would have gained in sublimity if it has been written by one who has passed through the torment of a spiritual quest.

Fasting, Feasting (1999), the latest novel of Anita Desai, evokes the same frustrating sense of non-arrival. The novel contested neck-to-neck till the last round for Booker Prize. The two sections of the novel focus on two different parts of the globe—the one centring on an upper middle class Indian family and the other on an ill-adjusted Indian immigrant temporarily housed in an American family. The two sections read like two disconnected pictures juxtaposed to convey the glaring culture contrast between India and America.

The fasting/feasting syndrome operates at different levels in the narrative. Life sidesteps certain unfortunate individuals whereas the bounties are showered on the chosen few. The denied and the gifted, the emotionally starved and the saturated—the binary runs through the novel. Arun, the young Indian immigrant in America is presented from a very different perspective than the one in currency. Pampered in food and over-protected at home, he is totally incapable of adjusting to the changed cultural milieu and floats adrift like a Nietzchean hero. The much-dreamt of America romanticized as the ultimate goal for the young Indian professional is stripped of the aura of the promised land and presented as an emotional desert.

Several issues surface in the novel. The Indian marriage market and its treacherous bargains trapping girls into misalliances, victimising them for dowry and impoverishing families, is exposed in all its ugliness through Uma's story. The resentment of children oppressed by the anxiety and possessiveness of over-ambitious parents is enacted through Arun's longing for total anonymity. Emotional starvation and the need for spiritual sustenance among the members of the American family where father, mother and children exist like isolated islands of loneliness, and culture shocks encountered by young Indian immigrants in America are other concerns in the novel.

Anita Desai chooses to tell the story from the perspective of Uma—the discontented, intellectually backward, emotionally starved woman in a middle class family—whose parents think and act for her, leaving no room for difference of opinion or for her own longings. Through Uma's admiring and slightly jealous eyes we are made to see her sister Aruna who has beauty, intelligence, smartness and the good fortune to get the most eligible husband she wanted. At every stage of her life, denial and starvation are Uma's lot while Aruna enjoys the best things in life. With the birth of Arun, Uma's education is stopped. Arun, a late product of the aged parents and the much longed-for son, is petted and watched over so assiduously that his plight is as miserable as that of a caged bird. Uma's occasional escapes into the loving world of the nuns, to an evening out with her cousin Ramu or a trip to holy places with Mira masi always end in some mishap or other. The long-awaited marriage turns out to be a trap for dowry by an already married man whose family is elsewhere. The bewildered Uma, left untouched by her husband, toils clumsily in the joint family of the in-laws and comes to know the truth only when her fuming father comes to take her away. With that all hopes of a life of her own are crushed for Uma. The frustrated parents wreak vengeance by making Uma work from morning to night, never letting her out of sight, denying her even the occasional moments of innocent enjoyment with her book of poems or her collection of cards and bangles. Uma's naivety and her limited vision are conveyed with remarkable authenticity. Uma's frustrations are touching, for they have the innocence of an uncorrupted child's thwarted desires. Desai comes down to her intellectual level to tell the story of 'fasting.'

Juxtaposed to Uma's story of denial is Arun's starved existence in America. Cultural dislocation added to geographic displacement has reduced Arun's life to a non-committal, non-belonging existence where every word has to be carefully uttered so that hostilities do not surge. The family his father arranged for him to spend the vacation as paying guest, is very different from his own. The father, mother, son and daughter have hardly any understanding of each other. During the first semester of his education in America Arun had tried to keep away from everyone, "every cell of his body being filled with a resistance to being included" (171). When his father arranged for him Mrs. Patton's house, he was overcome by the sensation of

> his family laying hands upon him, pushing him down into a chair at his desk, shoving a textbook under his nose, catching that nose and making him swallow cod-liver oil, spooning food into him, telling him: Arun this, Arun that, Arun nothing but [...]. (171)

Arun's efforts to remain totally uninvolved at the Pattons is swept away by the overpowering hospitality of Mrs. Patton who compels him to eat his dinner with her, and to accompany her on her shopping expeditions. When she forces him to go with her for swimming and sunbathing, Arun is shocked and embarrassed. Though he is genuinely concerned about Melanie whom he finds vomiting twice at home and later at the beach, he refrains from opening the subject to Mrs. Patton for fear of being mistaken to take an interest in Melanie. He is disturbed to find the indifference with which she is treated by the family and even Rod, her brother, dismisses her illness as resulting from eating too much candy. Without involving himself in any attachments or emotional ties, Arun manages to leave the place, bestowing on Mrs. Patton the packet of tea and the brown woollen shawl his mother had sent.

Arun fits into the large group of alienated beings who constitute Anita Desai's fictional world. Arun's life in India was an endless preparation for one examination after another. He never knew joy in his childhood or adolescence. The life in America only prolongs the stretch of greyness his life had been. Desai shows how the domineering parents suffocate Uma and Arun by their over-anxiety and solicitousness. The image of fasting would apply well to these emotionally starved beings, whose list stretches to include, apart from Arun and Uma, Mira masi and Anamika.

This is one novel in which the author confronts social issues like dowry and arranged marriage which she has evaded so long. Uma's plight is that of the girl who does not have a marriage "to show" and is shelved as shameful, unwanted property. The narrative of Anamika's tragic life and death is the retelling of many an unfortunate young girl's marriage in India today. The poignancy of her tragedy is intensified by repeated references to her extraordinary beauty and talents. The fact that even an exceptional girl like Anamika cannot escape the constrictions imposed by marriage is quite frustrating. Mira masi, on the other hand, is almost liberated in the freedom sanctioned by her spiritual allegiance. She tries to offer such a release to Uma too, by suggesting to her parents that she is blessed by God and is the beloved, the chosen, of Lord Shiva. Uma however, is too immature and unenlightened to seize spirituality as an escape. The way offered by Mrs. Dutta is more appealing to her and she feels depressed when denied permission to go and work outside.

The narrative ends abruptly with Arun leaving for the hostel. Like vignettes drawn from real life, the two sections are left incomplete, without any rounding off, suggesting the continuity of their starved lives. The novel can be read as the fictionalisation of possession and dispossession, one of the issues repeatedly dealt with by Anita Desai. The possessiveness of the parents denies space to Arun and Uma, making Arun hostile to all human company and Uma a recluse from life. Desire for possession and resistance to possession form one of the basic sources of conflict and tension in human life and the theme is central to Anita Desai's novels.

Desai has published two collections of short stories—*Games at Twilight and Other Stories* (1978) and *Star Dust and Other Stories* (2001). The stories in the first collection deal with the local and the familiar, choosing everyday moments of significance to build her narratives. The author seems to be closer to everyday actualities in these short stories. The later collection spans a number of geographic places and the stories reveal depths of meaning unrevealed at the first reading.

Most of Anita Desai's novels evoke a strong sense of place. In *Cry, the Peacock* it is the colours and forms and the sensuous beauty of the locale that are carefully built up, suggesting Maya's sensitivity to nature and Gautama's blindness to it. Through images and symbols, Desai builds in *Voices in the City* the oppressive sense of the city closing in on the human being, denying space to the individual. *Cry, the Peacock* and *Voices in the City* can almost be described as lyrical novels. In *Bye-Bye Blackbird*, as the image of the blackbird itself suggests, racial antagonism is made felt experience through apt images. In *Where Shall We Go This Summer?* and *Village by the Sea* the oppressive images of the city are contrasted with the sense of open space, fresh air and sea breeze. One almost feels that the city is the major villain in the novels, in the oppressive role it adopts against sensitive individuals dashing their heads and crushing themselves against its artificial brilliance. A sense of place pervades *Fire on the Mountain*. The dryness of the deserted landscape of Carignano powerfully brings out the emotionally starved existence of Nanda Kaul, Ila Das and Raka. The novel is a unique instance of image and theme blending perfectly. In *Clear Light of Day* old Delhi chosen as the chief locale of the action is repeatedly compared to a cemetery, where life has ceased to be, where nothing takes place and the people left in the dull, drab house are like figures petrified within a frame. The garden, the house and even the smells and sounds of the place evoke only memories of a dead past and have no spark of life left in them. Desai's capacity to create the mood and build the right atmosphere for the action is incomparable. Arya Ghosh remarks about *Baumgartner's Bombay*:

> Anita Desai's novels are known for their visual grittiness. But when it comes to the description of Bombay, the power of the 'eye' fails. Bombay stands like a stolid, impenetrable wall of noise, glare and heat, an undistinguishable mass of a swirling, heaving crowd. This is Baumgartner's Bombay—the Bombay that he has "marked out" for himself. (Ghosh 257)

In *Journey to Ithaca* the contrast between the exotic India that can grant answers to every spiritual question is contrasted with the frustrating images of real India with all its squalor, dirt and disease. India appears differently to different people; the nature of the vision is shaped by the eye of the beholder. It is not the landscape as such but the contrasting atmosphere of the family in India and America that is evoked in *Fasting, Feasting*. The author remarks:

> I prefer the word 'pattern' to 'plot' as it stands more natural, and even better, if I dare use it is Hopkins's word 'inscape'—while plot sounds arbitrary, heavy-headed and artificial, all that I wish to avoid.[8]

The word 'inscape' is appropriate to describe the technique of Desai's novels which are interior monologues or probing into the human psyche. Her concerns are basically existential. Socio-political issues of the contemporary world are thematised as problems of secondary importance leaving the centre stage to perennial concerns like alienation, loneliness and the individual's quest for identity and self-realisation. Though her early novels are woman-centred, we are made to realise that she does not advocate women's liberation of the western feminist mode. Her women return to the fold of the family or kill themselves. She does not advocate breaking of the familial bonds. Desai's perspective is shaped by Indian philosophy and Indian ways of thinking, refuting any criticism questioning her national loyalties or her Indianness.

A controlled form of stream of consciousness is employed in most of the novels. The psychological nature of the theme more than justifies the form. Speaking of her mode of narration she remarks:

> Writing is not an act of deliberation, reason and choice. It is a matter of instinct, silence and waiting. It is the movement of the wing one tries to capture not the bird. That is, it is the image that matters, the symbol, the myth, the feat of associating them, of relating them, of constructing with them.[9]

A succession of images that externalise the internal conflict is the mode adopted in most of the novels. Manipulation of time is another characteristic feature. Time constantly shifts between past and present and the present is always subject to the inevitable influence of the past.

There is a merging of the first person, second person and third person narration in Anita Desai's novels. Mostly the Jamesian method of the "indirect and oblique view" of narration is employed.[10] Narrative voices shift and alternate, lending themselves to multivalent readings. The text becomes the site of proliferate meanings and multiple readings making writing meaningful.

Notes

1. Anita Desai, "Indian Writing in a Foreign Language," *The Literary Criterion* 36.3 (2001) 46.
2. K.R.S. Iyengar, "A Note on Anita Desai's Novels," *The Banasthali Pathrika* (Jan. 1969) 64.
3. Arya Ghosh, "*Baumgartner's Bombay* and the Irony of Possession," *The Postmodern Indian Novel in English,* ed. Viney Kirpal (Bombay: Allied, 1996) 256.
4. Meena Beliappa, *Anita Desai: A Study of Her Fiction* (Calcutta: Writer's Workshop, 1971) 26.
5. R.S. Sharma, *Anita Desai* (New Delhi: Arnold Heinemann, 1981) 66-67.
6. Parthasarathy, *Rough Passage* (Delhi: Three Campus Books, 1977) 17-18.
7. Interview with Sunil Seth quoted in R.S. Pathak: "The Alienated Self in the Novels of Anita Desai," *The Fiction of Anita Desi,* ed. R.K. Dhawan (New Delhi: Bahri Publications, 1989) 44.
8. Atma Ram, "An Interview with Anita Desai," *World Literature Written in English* 16.1 (April 1977) 101.
9. Ramesh K. Srivastava, *Perspectives on Anita Desai* (Ghaziabad: Vimal Prakashan, 1984) 3-4.
10. Miriam Allott, *Novelists on the Novel* (London: Routledge and Kegan Paul, 1959) 188.

AN ANITA DESAI BIBLIOGRAPHY

Primary Sources

Novels

Cry, the Peacock. Delhi: Vision Books, 1963 (repr. in 1983).

Voices in the City. Delhi: Orient Paperbacks, 1965.

Bye-Bye Blackbird. Delhi: Hind Pocket Books, 1971.

Where Shall We Go This Summer? Delhi: Vikas, 1975.

Fire on the Mountain. New Delhi: Allied, 1977.

Clear Light of Day. New Delhi: Allied, 1980.

In Custody. London: Heinemann, 1984.

Baumgartner's Bombay. London: Penguin, 1989.

Journey to Ithaca. New Delhi: Ravi Dayal Pub., 1996.

Fasting, Feasting. London: Chatto and Windus, 1999.

Short Stories

Games at Twilight and Other Stories. London: William Heinemann, 1978.

Village by the Sea. New Delhi: Allied, 1982.

Diamond Dust. London: Vintage, 2001.

Secondary Sources

Books on Anita Desai

Allott, Miriam. *Novelists on the Novel*. London: Routledge and Kegan Paul, 1959.

Asnani, Shyam M. *New Dimensions of Indian English Novel*. Delhi: Doaba House, 1987.

Beliappa, Meena. *Anita Desai: A Study of Her Fiction*. Calcutta: Writer's Workshop, 1971.

Choudhury, Bidulatha. *Women and Society in the Novels of Anita Desai*. New Delhi: Creative Books, 1995.

Dass, Veena Noble, ed. *Feminism and Literature*. New Delhi: Prestige, 1995.

Dhawan, R.K., ed. *Explorations in Modern Indo-English Fiction*. New Delhi: Bahri Publishers, 1982.

____., ed. *The Fiction of Anita Desai*. New Delhi: Bahri Publications, 1989.

____., ed. *Indian Women Novelists*. Set I. New Delhi: Prestige Books, 1991.

Driesen, Cynthia Vanden. *Centering the Margins: Perspectives on Literatures in English from India, Africa, Australia*. New Delhi: Prestige Books, 1995.

Gupta, G.S. Balarama, ed. *Studies in Indian Fiction in English*. Gulbarga: JIWE, 1987.

Iyengar, K.R. Srinivasa. *Indian Writing in English*. New Delhi: Sterling, 1962.

Jain, Jasbir. *Stairs to the Attic: The Novels of Anita Desai*. Jaipur: Printwell Publishers, 1987.

Jena, Seema. *Voice and Vision of Anita Desai.* New Delhi: Ashish Publishing House, 1989.

Kamini, Dinesh, ed. *Between Spaces of Silence: Women Creative Writers.* New Delhi: Sterling, 1994.

Kirpal, Viney, ed. *The New Indian Novel in English: A Study of the 1980s.* New Delhi: Allied, 1990.

____., ed. *The Postmodern Indian English Novel.* New Delhi: Allied, 1996.

Perspectives on Indian Fiction in English. Ed. M.K. Naik. New Delhi: Abhinav Publications, 1985.

Narasimhan, Raji. *Sensibility Under Stress: Aspects of Indo-English Fiction.* New Delhi: Ashajanak Publications, 1976.

Pathak, R.S., ed. *Indian Fiction in English: Problems and Promises.* New Delhi: Northern Book Centre, 1990.

Prasad, Madhusudan, ed. *Indian English Novelists.* New Delhi: Sterling, 1982.

Sharma, Kajali. *Symbolism in Anita Desai's Novels.* New Delhi: Abhinav Publications, 1991.

Sharma, R.S. *Anita Desai.* New Delhi: Arnold Heinemann, 1981.

Sinha, Anita. *Feminist Visions: Indian English Women Novelists.* New Delhi: Creative Books, 2000.

Srivastava, Ramesh K., ed. *Perspectives on Anita Desai.* Ghaziabad: Vimal Prakashan, 1984.

Articles

Acharya, Shanta. "Problems of Self in the Novels of Anita Desai." *Indian Women Novelists* (1.1). Ed. R.K. Dhawan. New Delhi: Prestige Books, 1991.

Aithal, S. Krishnamoorthy. "The Ballad of East and West Updated: Anita Desai's *Bye-Bye Blackbird.*" *Perspectives on Anita Desai.* Ed. Ramesh K. Srivastava. Ghaziabad: Vimal Prakashan, 1984.

Amanuddin, Syed. "Anita Desai's Technique." *The Fiction of Anita Desai.* Ed. R.K. Dhawan. New Delhi: Bahri Publications, 1989.

Ambekar, K.P. "Symbolism in *Where Shall We Go This Summer?*" *The Fiction of Anita Desai.* Ed. R.K. Dhawan. New Delhi: Bahri Publications, 1989.

Asnani, Shyam M. "Anita Desai's Fiction: A New Dimension." *New Dimensions of Indian English Novel.* Delhi: Doaba House, 1987.

____. "The Indian English Novel with a Unique Vision: A Study of *Clear Light of Day.*" *New Dimensions of Indian English Novel.* Delhi: Doaba House, 1987.

Banerjee, Uma. "An Existential Approach to Maladjustment of Marital Relations in Anita Desai's Novels." *Indian Women Novelists* (1.2). Ed. R.K. Dhawan. New Delhi: Prestige Books, 1991.

Barche, G.D. "Facets of Feminism in Indian English Fiction." *Indian Women Novelists* (3.1). Ed. R.K. Dhawan. New Delhi: Prestige Books, 1995.

Bhatnagar, P. "The Theme of Man-Woman Relationship in the Novels of Anita Desai." *Indian Women Novelists* (1.2). Ed. R.K. Dhawan. New Delhi: Prestige Books, 1991.

Chellappan, K. "Being and Becoming in Anita Desai's *Where Shall We Go This Summer*?" *Subjects Worthy Fame: Essays on Commonwealth Literature in Honour of H.H. Anniah Gowda.* Ed. A.L. Mc Leod. New Delhi: Sterling Publishers Pvt. Ltd., 1989.

Cronin, Richard. "The Quiet and the Loud: Anita Desai's India." *Imagining India.* Richard Cronin. London: The Macmillan Press, 1989.

Desai, Anita. "The Indian Writer's Problems." *Indian Women Novelists* (1.2). Ed. R.K. Dhawan. New Delhi: Prestige Books, 1991.

____. "Indian Writing in a Foreign Language." *The Literary Criterion* 35 (2001): 3.

Driesen, Cynthia Vanden. "Resisting/Sighting Caliban's Sisters: Voice and Agency for Third–World Women." *Centering the Margins: Perspectives on Literatures in English from India, Africa, Australia.* New Delhi: Prestige Books, 1995.

Ghosh, Arya. "*Baumgartner's Bombay* and the Irony of Possession." *The Post-modern Indian Novel in English.* Ed. Viney Kirpal. Bombay: Allied, 1996.

Hashmi, Alamgir. "*Clear Light of Day*: Between India and Pakistan." *The New Indian Novel in English: A Study of the 1980s.* Ed. Viney Kirpal. New Delhi: Allied, 1990.

Iyengar, K.R. Srinivasa. "A Note on Anita Desai's Novels." *The Banasthali Pathrika* (Jan. 1969).

____. "The Women Novelists." *Indian Writing in English.* K.R. Srinivasa Iyengar. New Delhi, Sterling, 1962.

Jain, Jasbir. "The Use of Fantasy in the Novels of Anita Desai." *Indian Women Novelists* (1.2). Ed. R.K. Dhawan. New Delhi: Prestige Books, 1991.

Kumar, Shiv K. "Desai's *Games at Twilight*: A View." *Perspectives on Anita Desai.* Ed. Ramesh K. Srivastava. Ghaziabad: Vimal Prakashan, 1984.

Lal, Malashri. "The Shift from Female-Centred to Male-Centred Narrative in the Novels of the 1980s: A Study of Anita Desai and Nayantara Sahgal." *The New Indian Novel in English: A Study of the 1980s.* Ed. Viney Kirpal. New Delhi: Allied, 1990.

Mathur, O.P. "The Indian Protagonist and the Western Experience." *Commonwealth Fiction* (1). Ed. R.K. Dhawan. New Delhi: Classical Publishing Company, 1988.

Nabar, Vrinda. "Image of India in *Clear Light of Day.*" *Indian Women Novelists* (1.4). Ed. R.K. Dhawan. New Delhi: Prestige Books, 1991.

Nandakumar, Prema. "Sombre the Shadows and Sudden the Lights: A Study of Anita Desai's Novels." *Perspectives on Indian Fiction in English.* Ed. M.K. Naik. New Delhi: Abhinav Publications, 1985.

Panigrahi, Bipin B. "Self-Apprehension and Self-Identity in *Clear Light of Day.*" *The New Indian Novel in English: A Study of the 1980s.* New Delhi: Allied, 1990.

Paranjape, Makarand. "*Journey to Ithaca*: A Letter on Recent Indian English Fiction." Ed. Viney Kirpal. *The Postmodern Indian Novel in English.* New Delhi: Allied, 1996.

Pathak, R.S. "The Alienated Self in the Novels of Anita Desai." *Indian Women Novelists* (1.2). Ed. R.K. Dhawan. New Delhi: Prestige Books, 1991.

Piciucco, Pier Paolo. "'An Artist is an Outsider to Society': Discussing a Decades Long Literary Career with Anita Desai." *Englishes* 9.3 (1999).

Ram, Atma. "An Interview with Anita Desai." *World Literature Written in English* 16.I. (April 1977).

Sharrad, Paul. "Tradition and Tragedy: Anita Desai and R.K. Narayan." *Indian Women Novelists* (1.3). Ed. R.K. Dhawan. New Delhi: Prestige Books, 1991.

Swain, S.P. "Alienation and Adjustment: A Study of Anita Desai's *Village by the Sea.*" *Indian Women Novelists* (3.2). Ed. R.K. Dhawan. New Delhi: Prestige Books, 1995.

Wandrekar, Kalpana S. "The Ailing Aliens: *Bye-bye Blackbird*: A Symptomatic Study in Schizophrenia." *Indian Women Novelists* (1.3). Ed. R.K. Dhawan. New Delhi: Prestige Books, 1991.

8

Arun Joshi

PIER PAOLO PICIUCCO

The strange case of Arun Joshi clearly illustrates that literature not only is an articulated art form and a cultural vehicle, but a business as well. An introspective and inward-looking man, who did not feel at ease with the literary world, Joshi did not impersonate the stereotype of the writer actively involved in the promotion and circulation of his own writing. What made the difference, though, was that his fiction can be largely associated with the seventies, a period when Indian fiction in English was still an undiscovered literary phenomenon, waiting for a Salman Rushdie to make it palatable to Western tastes. His publishers, although promoting many among the foremost Indian novelists of that time, despite their efforts, had a limited range and were not supported by an efficient distribution network: in addition, their books rapidly went out-of-print and had to be looked for in libraries or cultural institutions. They obviously remained cut off from international circuits. What is more, postcolonial criticism probably still found Indian fiction a bit too difficult to approach and sought material to theorise in other areas of the world. The result is that even though there has been a general consensus among (Indian) critics in seeing Joshi among the most important writers of that period, his name has remained utterly unknown to those who were outside this geographically restricted circle.

Son of a famous botanist and eminent academician, Arun Joshi was born in 1939 in Varanasi where he lived until he was 7. Afterwards his family spent the next few years in Lahore, then, with Partition, went back to Indian Punjab. After secondary school, he got a scholarship to the U.S. where he went and got a degree from the University of Kansas in Engineering and Industrial Management. Later he did his Master from M.I.T. While in the U.S. he worked in a mental hospital, where his uncle was a psychiatrist, and dealt with chronic schizophrenics, an experience which left a deep impression on his mind and which is partially revived in Billy Biswas, possibly his most famous fictional character. Back in India, where he had always felt he belonged, he got a job on the management staff of an Indian company, before trying the adventure of founding small companies of his own, producing diesel engines, machine-tools, foundry products and automative parts. Incidentally, we may add that many of the elements encountered so far compose the background of his first novel. At the same time he became the administrator of a philanthropic institution, coordinating research and training regarding the human side of industry, from labour to upper-echelon staff. It may sound odd, but the curriculum of this dynamic industrialist is the same as that of an outstanding novelist who turned to creative writing as a hobby; it should come as no surprise therefore that his ability to switch from one world to another diametrically opposed one returns in many of his fictional works, until reaching the status of leitmotif in Som Bhaskar's predicament. In the 1993 dry season before the advent of the monsoons, all of a sudden Arun Joshi died of the complications following an asthmatic crisis, asthma being an affliction he shared with two of his main characters—Sindi Oberoi and Ratan Rathor.

The Foreigner, his debut novel, dates back to 1968. At a time when Indian fiction in English had still not encountered the favour of the market, Joshi was fortunate enough to find on his way critical esteem and encouragement from the influential Khushwant Singh who, after reading the manuscript, had a crucial role in promoting the fortunes of this emergent author to the publisher. Critics generally agree in recognizing in this fictional work the novel that is most overtly autobiographical in tone, although, one should add, the other works are also rich in elements drawn from the author's experience. *The Foreigner* is a novel which anticipates the interests postcolonial criticism would develop toward the hybrids' predicament, the sociological and psychological facets that lead the diasporic individual towards cultural alienation. The protagonist, Sindi Oberoi, is a young man whose rootlessness is only partially due to his personality: born in Kenya of an Indian father and an English mother, at the age of 4 he remains an orphan and is left under the care of an uncle. Moved by an instinctual thrust towards self-accomplishment, and free of any emotional link towards country or family, in order to achieve a superior education, Sindi goes to England first and to the U.S. later. Scarred by his sad childhood, though he proudly wears a mask showing indifference to his fate, he makes use of a good dose of cynicism to avoid being trapped in any kind of emotional bond. In this sense Sindi already provides a prototype for many of Joshi's future heroes: mostly males, revealing the relevance autobiographical elements had in his narration, these characters find themselves caught between the interstices of two faraway worlds, persuaded that their duty is to find a compromise between the opposites. Generally introverted, somewhat self-centred, they are prey to an acute sense of loneliness although they actively and fully take part in the mechanisms of society, of which they sooner or later become outstanding exponents. Their accentuated feeling of unease, clearly set in a well-defined social texture, is deeply analysed in psychological terms, often displays a philosophical side and is mostly resolved through recourse to Indian mysticism. It is this apparently incurable malaise that prompts their instinctual response which, suppressed at the beginning, explodes in its total disruptive force at a later stage and leads them towards liberation, obviously after having exacted a high price for this. What distinguishes Sindi from all Joshi's other characters, however, is his possible likeness to Camus's Mersault, declaredly one of Joshi's models. Sindi, a foreigner wherever he goes, is therefore an outsider in existential terms.

If Sindi provides a model for many of Joshi's heroes to come, so does June for his heroines. June Blyght is Sindi's sweetheart at the time of his stay in the U.S. A pretty young woman, she is the first example of that ideal femininity which important female characters in Joshi's fiction represent. A particular alchemy makes male and female characters embody the archetypal essence of male and female principles, with possible links with the Samkhya philosophy as well as with Jungian theories. In short, where man is thought, woman is action, or, as best exemplified in *The Last Labyrinth*, men are the wanters of this world, women the givers: neither of the two acquires primacy over the other but it is the complementarity of their roles which leads them toward release and completeness. What is interesting to note is that, although female characters—and June's death is the first significant example—are prone to sacrifice all for their men, they are always portrayed as being independent, endowed with a charmingly positive energy and the capacity of giving, so that they have often won the sympathies of gender criticism.

June Blyght is a lively and cheerful woman who always has a positive view of life and whose main goal seems to be that of being of use to other people. Unconditionally generous and idealistic in her disposition, she feels trapped when she understands too late that she has given all of herself without expecting to receive anything in return. The mechanisms leading to her (and Babu's) tragedy are bitterly set forth as for the first time she asks for love, instead of giving it.

Her death is closely linked to Babu's case which is instrumental in ushering in the delicate theme of the heavy influence an important (and inflexible) father may exert on his son, again dictating the timing of the calamity in *The Strange Case of Billy Biswas* and still full significant in *The Last Labyrinth*. In the triangle Sindi-June-Babu, it is the latter's immaturity, the consequence of the all-pervading presence of his father, which determines and posits the bases for the tragic events which occur. Babu, on the other hand, is also instrumental in providing a very detailed picture of the difficulties an Indian immigrant finds on his arrival in the Western dreamland and how his naive ideas need to be measured against a number of problems he had previously underestimated. His figure, along with that of Sindi's, of course, makes it clear that the gap is too wide and that bonds between East and West can only lead to catastrophic epilogues, making efforts to the contrary desperately vain. In the end of the novel, Sindi's likely affair with Babu's sister Sheila, a relationship which is not the fruit of an instinctual reciprocal interest like the one with June but has gradually taken shape through harmonious sympathy and understanding, is further proof of this interrelational breakdown.

As a debut novel, *The Foreigner* was a considerable achievement also in terms of narratorial ability. Events are not always narrated in chronological order but follow a route creating great suspense, although the recurrent use of anticipation prepares the reader for all the major turning points. The incipit, describing Sindi identifying Babu at the morgue, for instance, already anticipates a crucial episode happening halfway through the novel.

In 1971, three years after *The Foreigner*, Joshi published his second novel, *The Strange Case of Billy Biswas*, possibly his most famous work. While in his literary debut Joshi analysed in psychological and existential terms the impossibility of a merge between the East and the West of the world, and thereby dealt with a topic other Indian English novelists were also concerned with, in this second novel he enormously amplified his focus on this particular divide, bringing to the fore the concept that India can be looked at as a universe apart, with her own East and West within. The gap is in fact not so much the distance that exists between New York and Delhi, but rather between the so-called "civilised" and the "primitive" world. As a sense of imminent and unavoidable tragedy hangs over the novel from the very beginning, the world of *The Strange Case of Billy Biswas* has sometimes been paralleled to a Thomas Hardy's view of the cosmos, while other critics have underscored that Billy's irresistible call to the primeval is reminiscent of D.H. Lawrence atmospheres. However, the author of English literature with whose work *The Strange Case of Billy Biswas* has most parallels is undoubtedly Conrad. To begin with, the tale related by a witness narrator, intrigued by a number of odd circumstances, as well as by an alluring, never predictable protagonist, make call to mind Marlowe's days and the strategies he adopted. In addition, Billy's adventure and the uncompromising challenge with his soul call to mind Lord Jim's predicament, although one should add that Joshi seems to be, if possible, even more at ease and fascinating in the treating the ethical problems involved; thirdly, the general topic of a journey to the interior, both in geographical and psychological terms, makes the unexplored *saal* forests of the Maikala Hills a new Indian interpretation of the

Congo river. *The Strange Case of Billy Biswas* cannot however be said to be a postcolonial context *tout court*, in that this novel hardly writes back to the canon; what it does instead, is to take inspiration from these literary sources and re-elaborate them to present a gripping tale, entirely collocated in a modern Indian context.

Billy Biswas, Joshi's least tamed hero, is introduced early on as an anarchist at the time of his university years in the U.S. and Romi, the witness narrator of the story, does not fail to spot an extraordinary person in him: while in New York, Romi has to look for a place to live and Billy does not think twice about sharing his place with his newly-met friend. Although a genuine sympathy between these two immigrants readily develops, Billy is far from being a nostalgic youth suffering from homesickness: he soon impresses Romi with his extreme spontaneity towards Americans and America and by showing total indifference to the East-West divide, despite the fact that he remains Indian to the core. What amazes Romi in particular is the way Billy seems to make a home wherever he goes: Billy's choice of an apartment is in the most degraded area of Harlem, in the cheerful company of some ex-convicts (one of whom will be assassinated later on), but he finds himself equally at ease in the extremely elegant and sophisticatedly-furnished Manhattan flat of his friend Tuula Lindgren, a young Swedish psychiatrist working in the U.S., with whom Billy has vibrant and brilliant discussions linking his interest in anthropology with hers in psychiatry. It is her analysis of the powers working inside him that finds confirmation in the course of the plot: in her words, he is exceptionally sensitive to a kind of primeval force, called *urkraft*, common to all human beings, that however seems to exert a commanding influence on him, and to which Billy, according to her prevision, is likely to give in at a certain stage in his life. This he does, but the capitulation will emerge as a period of tremendous crisis for him because the turn towards his real self seems to drive him in the least fitting direction.

Billy's decision to radically invert the course of his life, contrary to what the reader expects, is in no way a long-pondered resolution. It turns out as events develop that Billy, a professor of anthropology at the University of Delhi, was about to be annihilated by his forced surrender to a routine life in a society and a family which he did not feel his. Continuous quarrels with his wife over trivial matters and pervading emotive instability threatening all his relationships, included that with Romi, are signs of impending calamity. His frenetic and impulsive escape to another life and another world, with all the contours of a romantic deed, allows no compromise: all searches to trace him prove vain because he, in his own characteristic way, has already fully assumed the responsibilities for this dramatic change. A woman not as pretty as his wife Meena, but expressing an irresistible primeval eroticism, temptingly attracts the Professor of Anthropology fascinated by tribal cultures and acts as the first step in his total transformation. Billy's liberation, which again presents existential overtones, is triggered by an extremely intense sensual urge whose contours Joshi skilfully blurs with those of a mystical drive. Therefore, it is in a highly dramatic way that Billy unexpectedly finds out that what he needs is a kind of life in contact with nature and its rhythms, uncontaminated by the stiff rules of a phoney society. When ten years later Billy suddenly pops up from the forest to approach his surprised friend Romi, he is again the spontaneous and fascinating talker of the times of their stay in the States.

That Billy the university student and Billy the tribal are to be seen as a continuum, interrupted by his return to India and marriage to Meena, is hardly a surprise. The influence of an authoritative father with major expectations of him does not allow Billy to freely choose his way, unless he keeps his father out of his life. Having gone to the U.S. to get a degree in engineering to please his father, Billy pursues his own interests instead and, unknown to his parents, takes up anthropology. It is not coincidental, then, that when Billy's secret becomes public, it is his father who leads the fatal manhunt through the Saikala forest.

On the other hand, Billy's revolt is blatantly against the rules and the modes of a society which does not grasp the full potentialities of the individual and which mercilessly suppresses all minorities. Joshi continues his criticism of India's upper social strata already begun in *The Foreigner*, but this time he does not need to personify the ruling (and corrupted) class as he had previously with Mr. Khemka: Mr. Biswas Sr., although representing an entire generation and a well-circumscribed social group, is not a negative character after all, and this, in a sense, makes the tones of an announced tragedy still more poignant. Billy's being introduced as an anarchist, then, is not an investigation of his ideological bias but it rather qualifies his rebellion against his society and its rules.

The Apprentice, published in 1974, makes condemnation to society the central topic of the novel. As the previous work had already done, this novel also pivots around the possibility of presenting a two-faced character: Ratan the narrator, in fact, is not the Ratan protagonist of the plot. From the beginning, the reader, similarly to what happens in Ford Madox Ford's *The Good Soldier* (to which this novel has been sometimes compared), conjectures that something is underway because the narrator suspiciously detaches himself from his own fate but one needs to go through the whole of the novel to clear away this halo of mystery.

The fictional technique adopted by Arun Joshi surely contributes to the uniqueness of *The Apprentice*, so that the novel has sometimes been tagged as a fictional experiment. In a very ingenious way, Ratan narrates the facts of his own life to a listener, whose name we never learn; what is relevant is that of the imaginary dialogue between the two, the novel only records the voice of the narrator and not that of his interlocutor, leaving the reader the illusion of a monologue. The listener/interlocutor/implied reader of the whole story is nevertheless actively participating in it, affecting the mechanisms of the tale in ways not so different from those Padma will adopt a few years later in Rushdie's *Midnight's Children*. He is young, well-mannered, sensitive, generous, idealistic, proud of being a National Cadet. He always pays great attention to every detail of the story he is being told, so that if Ratan gets confused while digressing and forgets what he was relating, he helps him to find the thread of his thoughts again. His questions are wise and sharp so that he at times impersonates the role of the inquisitor and at the times that of the confessor; even if he has to go to study for his exams, he patiently waits for Ratan to conclude the episode he is relating. In short, he is the ideal listener.

On the other hand, Ratan is the ideal orator, who needs a public to fully achieve his goal. We know very little of his present situation until nearly the end of the novel, when his predicament is fully exposed: in the meanwhile, however, he grips the reader's attention thanks to his brilliant use of various rhetorical devices and his spicy use of spoken Indian English. He is a little past middle-age, talks with the self-confidence of an experienced man, is educated and endowed with an uncommon intelligence. The relationship he establishes with his listener may on the one hand seem that found in the ancient Indian epics, with an old sage teaching a lesson to a talented disciple, but on the other it presents the ideal father-son dialogue, as accidental hints variously scattered in the narration seem repeatedly to suggest. The story he recounts, the reader gradually understands, is meant as an expiation of past wrongs on his part, while it is a sort of advice for the uncontaminated youth intended to prevent him from committing similar misdeeds. This is why while Ratan remains detached from his previous experience, he is carried away by the importance of his tale, continuously digressing, losing the thread of his thoughts, abandoning himself to sentimentalism and in turn relating events according to their immediate emotional impact rather than to their chronological order.

If the young cadet has a role similar to Padma's, Ratan can be easily compared to Saleem not only for his oratorical skill but also for his association with India, which, in any case, is not so evident as in Rushdie's novel. Ratan, whose family name displays a strong link with Indian history, takes about three months to relate the whole of his tale to the young cadet and the background to their plot appears to be the rehearsals for the processions for the celebration of Republic Day. The tale is therefore set in an atmosphere infused with euphoric postcolonial nationalism fully incarnated by the protagonist; on the other hand, it is interesting to note that the narrator distances himself from this elated perspective as the plot develops. Ratan's story narrates the feverish pursuit of a career by an intelligent Punjabi boy who arrives in Delhi determined to make a life of his own. At the beginning this is hard and, despite his value, Ratan is forced to endure a number of humiliations, which the narrator still finds it embarrassing to share with his young interlocutor. At any rate, the protagonist's blinding determination to make a career, like Billy's uncontainable primordial drive, wins in the end and it is significant to note that his personal success is linked to the national achievement of freedom from the colonial past. Ratan becomes an officer in a department for war purchases at the Ministry of Defence and soon changes his life-style, abandoning the humble companions he had lived with (and who had tried to help him), thereby personifying the amnesia of the colonial aftermath, rhetorically expounded as a celebrated moment of arrival, both on a personal and a national level.

During the years of the Indo-Chinese conflict, a sad chapter in recent Indian history generally avoided by Indian English novelists, the nationalist Ratan makes public speeches in favour of nationalist sentiment but he accepts a bribe to clear a defective stock of weapons. His betrayal of his country is then poignantly exemplified by the suicide of the Brigadier, Ratan's childhood friend, who, having received the malfunctioning war materials on the front, had deserted his post. Ratan's confession would have saved the Brigadier from court-martial, but the protagonist's hesitation proves fatal. It is in this context that Ratan is forced to undergo a deep crisis of conscience, adopt a humble way of life, and review his past life in a new light. The reader understands the title only in the last pages: in order to redeem his past Ratan has become an apprentice of God and every morning, before going to his office, he goes outside the temple and cleans the shoes of the congregation. This open ending divided critics between those who approved of the drastic change in Ratan's character and those who passed judgment on him for his self-centred avoidance of a public confession of his transgression, making it evident that Billy's anarchism surfaced again in Ratan's instinctual neglect of an earthly justice in favour of his own.

Characteristically suspended between two worlds, in 1975 Joshi dedicated himself to a non-fiction work illustrating the business story of the philanthropic institution he worked for, *Lala Shri Ram: a Study in Entrepeneurship in Industrial Management*, but he also found time to get *The Survivor, a Selection of Stories*, his only collection of short stories, published. This is a small paperback volume with ten short stories, which revisit the themes of Joshi's fiction. The conscious degenerate fall of Kewal Kapur, the protagonist of the title story, is illustrated with irreverent detachment as the only alternative to the stifling canon of a degenerate society, to some extent similar to Billy's decision. The opening story, *The Gherao*, is another which deserves attention, creating a dichotomised world, without the possibility of communication between the two extremes.

The Last Labyrinth (1981) won Joshi the prestigious Sahitya Academy Award. In it the novelist focussed with meticulous care on the schizophrenic predicament of his heroes and wrote a novel, notable for its remarkable peaks of imaginative power. The background to the story is a weird, aged *haveli* (construction) in old Benares, the result of the multi-style experiments by eccentric architects who added various parts to it over the years. The effect is a strangely mesmerizing sort of house, apparently built without logic, which is at the same time a real habitation and fitting metaphor for the desperately frenetic and unconscious search engaged in by the typical Joshi's seeker, from Billy's primeval drive to Ratan's pursuit of a career. Inside this world, everything is constantly on the verge of folly, schizophrenia, hallucination.

As already happened with his predecessors, Som Bhaskar, the narrator-protagonist of this novel, is highly influenced in his choices by his parents, and in this case their control is exercised on him indirectly because they are already dead. Som's father was a scientist who relentlessly investigated the First Cause and at his death, along with a fortune, Som inherits his father's passion for existential enquiry. Som's mother incarnates the quintessential feminine model in Joshi's fiction: a pious woman, she is endowed with an unshakeable faith around which all her system gravitates. Although seeming to take distance from both of them, Som is deeply affected by them, to the point of describing their deaths with cynicism. His father, who had died of a heart attack, is said to have died of "melancholia" for his unresolved search, while his mother, who had cancer, actually died because she had refused to take the pills the doctor had ordered for her, confident that her faith would cure her instead; hence, Som's diagnosis is "cancer and Krishna." Obsessed with giving a sense to his existence, Som, a young businessman, engages in a feverish search for meaning in his life and remains caught midway between his father's and his mother's predicaments, which cause an illness which strangely affects his sleep routine. Som, therefore, is the man between two worlds *par excellence*, fighting his way between reason and faith; the existentialist Western philosophers and the *Bhagvad Gita*; his wife Geeta (who unsurprisingly bears the same name as a sacred text) and his lover Anuradha; love and hate; Bombay and Benares; life and death; sacrifice and whim. He personifies in his own name these dualisms, Som meaning sun and Bhaskar moon.

It is this man who accidentally approaches the Benares haveli, inhabited by a strange couple: Aftab, an impractical businessman, and his woman Anuradha, who soon magnetically attracts Som. In the effort to win her, the protagonist wildly hunts her, a resolution which totally plunges him into the labyrinthine and obscure building she inhabits and which fatally deprives him of any certainty and steady reference point. From this moment on a deep aura of mystery surrounds the events of his life making this novel a mystic thriller: he cannot make out Anuradha's real role, the nature of her relationship with Aftab, the ways of the strangely fascinating female guru Gargi, the conduct of his specialist, doctor K. (whose real name Kashyap, bizarrely mentioned only once, recalls the old name of Benares): he is even driven to suspect a puzzling deal between his wife and his lover Anuradha.

Matters become complicated as Som has a heart attack: although he miraculously survives it, he is depressed by Anuradha's decision to dump him. The spellbound attraction she exerts on him seems to leave him no alternatives. Mostly, in fact, all the choices and doubts of Som's predicament seem to lead him inevitably towards her, portrayed as a strangely fascinating woman, defying all definitions, seen at times as a cruel, indifferent *femme fatale*, at others as an ethereal spiritual guide, and even as a woman ready to immolate herself for her lover. Because of this, his hunt of her acquires the two-fold dimension of an uncontrollable urge and a whimsical obsession driving him to take revenge on Aftab, by purchasing the shares of his nearly bankrupt company. Through these two channels, Anuradha successfully steers him to a temple on the mountains, where Som finds the solution to many of his puzzles: at the time of his attack, she made a vow to renounce her love for Som if he lived. Som's choice not to surrender to this deal is partly due to his agnosticism and partly to his being kept apart from a decision concerned with his own destiny, so he proceeds to Benares to take Anuradha with him. In the open ending Anuradha disappears, leaving critics with a number of possible different interpretations of the final mystery.

Following the publication of *The Last Labyrinth*, Joshi took a break before returning to his second activity as a novelist: while his first four works were published in a period of time of thirteen years, readers had to wait for almost ten years to find him again on the scene, this time with *The City and the River* (1990). Quite unexpectedly, the last fictional work by Joshi marks a turn in a new direction. Possibly conditioned by the exceptional decade dominated by Rushdie, who had turned the parodic mode into a highly successful formula, in this work Joshi approaches a new literary canon akin to a modern fable, a parable of contemporary times, whose significance is almost entirely to be interpreted through recurrence to a symbolic code.

The writing style soon displays the effects of a revolution. The narratorial voice, that had been so characteristically distinguished with a hurrying mood, at times with a feverish urge, to relate events whose weight made the slightest delay seem like unbearable suffering, acquires the faraway detached tone of epic tales, in which the omnipresent narrator reports all kinds of episodes, whether trivial or catastrophic, without the least emotional concern. Joshi therefore does without a number of his recognised literary fortes: the deep analysis of his heroes' soul, the elaboration of the emotional feedback resulting in his typical aphorisms, are therefore put aside in favour of his experiments with a new formula.

Although taking an entirely new path, however, *The City and the River* also re-elaborates a number of the "old" topics. Joshi re-exhumes Ratan Rathor and the young cadet, dresses them in somewhat epic robes and obtains the Great Yogeshwara and his disciple, the Nameless One, to whom the tale is being told. As happened in *The Apprentice*, there is an old sage occupying almost the whole of the stage alone, and the message conveyed is again a clear social denunciation of the wrongs of the world. The city and the river of the title, in fact, can also be seen as the all-pervading dichotomy of Joshi's vision, the Bombay and the Benares of *The Last Labyrinth*, the Delhi and the Maikala Hills of *The Strange Case of Billy Biswas*, along with other instances which have already been touched upon.

The novelist skilfully constructs the two opposing entities so as to discourage easy parallels with known referents. The city and the river, to begin with, have no other names which allow them to be identified: the city, in particular, is surrounded by the Seven Hills as Rome is; is crossed by a sacred river reminding one of the Ganges; has some nearby pyramids like Cairo; finally, it has dungeons in the Gold Mines, possibly evoking South African scenery. Similarly, the temporal setting seems deliberately confused, with laser weapons, satellites and helicopters existing side by side with mountain hermits, astrologers, *yajnas* and primitive civilizations.

The Great Master who soon becomes the dictator of the city, and whose ambition is then to dominate the river, also has multiple symbolic referents. He is quite clearly modelled on Shakespeare's Julius Caesar, delineating him from the start as the quintessential tyrant. Many Indian critics, then, have not failed to see in his deliberations, and especially in the bulldozing of the poor quarters of the city, a reminder of Indira Gandhi's Emergency, while others have interpreted the same scene as alluding to South Africa's apartheid. Of course, creating two different peoples who speak languages that cannot be understood without translators, and in particular having the characters of the City generally bear English names as opposed to the allies of the River who mostly have Sanskrit-derived names, also makes it possible to read the domination described in the story in terms of colonial history.

Despite moments of particular interest in the narration, critics, however, for the first time found it difficult to emphasize the positive aspects of the novel as a whole, which, with its 260 pages, remains the longest book written by Joshi. Yet, the possibly excessive length is not the only reason for its partial failure: the reader already acquainted with his previous works cannot fail to note that the detachment in the narration seems to be that of the novelist toward his tale, as well as that of the narrator. The sense one had in the previous works that behind the narration level there existed a deep-felt urge never arises from the pages of *The City and the River* which, symptomatically, met sympathetic reviewers among those who had not read Joshi's earlier novels.

About three years later, on 19 April 1993, alone as many of his absorbing questers had been, Arun Joshi was found dead in the bedroom of his Delhi house, following a fatal cardiac arrest.

AN ARUN JOSHI BIBLIOGRAPHY

Primary Sources

Fictional Works

The Foreigner. New Delhi: Hind Pocket Books, 1968.

The Strange Case of Billy Biswas. New Delhi: Hind Pocket Books, 1971.

The Apprentice. New Delhi: Orient Paperbacks, 1974.

The Survivor: a Selection of Stories. New Delhi: Sterling, 1976.

The Last Labyrinth. New Delhi: Vision Books, 1981.

The City and the River. New Delhi: Vision Books, 1990.

Secondary Sources

Books on Arun Joshi

Prasad, Hari Moham. *Arun Joshi.* New Delhi: Arnold Heinemann, 1985.

Dhawan, R.K., ed. *The Fictional World of Arun Joshi.* New Delhi: Classical Publishing Company, 1986.

——., ed. *The Novels of Arun Joshi.* New Delhi: Prestige, 1992.

Ghosh, Tapan Kumar. *Arun Joshi's Fiction: the Labyrinth of Life.* New Delhi: Prestige, 1996.

Bhatnagar, M.K., ed. *The Novels of Arun Joshi. A Critical Study.* New Delhi: Atlantic, 2001.

Bhatt, Indira and Alexander, Suja. *Arun Joshi's Fiction. A Critique.* New Delhi: Creative, 2001.

Articles and Essays

Asnani, Shyam. "A Study of Arun Joshi's Fiction." *Literary Half-Yearly* 19.2 (1978).

Bhatnagar, O.P. "Arun Joshi's The Foreigner." *The Journal of Indian Writing in English* 1.2 (1973).

Chingre, C.D. "Contrast and Technique in Arun Joshi's *The Strange Case of Billy Biswas.*" *Indian Journal of English Studies* 30 (1991-92).

Damodar, G. "The Outsiderist Tradition in Joshi and Desai." *Kakatya Journal of English Studies* 13 (1993).

Das, R.J. "Moral Dilemma in Arun Joshi's *The Apprentice.*" *Journal of Literature and Aesthetics* 1.2 (1981).

Devi, P. Janiki. "Search of Identity in the Novels of Arun Joshi." *Journal of English Studies* 10.1 (1978).

Dutta, Padma. "Problems of Individuation: A Critique on Arun Joshi's Use of Symbols and Archetypes in *The Last Labyrinth.*" *The Journal of Indian Writing in English* 18.1 (1990).

Hedge, M.G. "Distance and Discovery as Techniques: A Study of the Narrative Strategy of *The Strange Case of Billy Biswas.*" *Osmania Journal of English Studies* 25 (1989).

Jain, Jasbir. "Foreigners and Strangers: Arun Joshi's Heroes." *The Journal of Indian Writing in English* 5.1 (1977).

Jeevan, Parvathi. "Image of Woman in the Novels of Arun Joshi." *Commonwealth Quarterly* 16.4 (1980).

Kher, Inder Nath. "The Archetypes of Love and Death in Arun Joshi's *The Last Labyrinth.*" *Journal of Indian Writing in English* 20.1-2 (1992).

Mathur, O.P. "Survival and Affirmation in Arun Joshi's Novels." *Worlds Literature Today* 63.3 (1989).

Meitei, M. Mani. "Indian Ethos in Arun Joshi's *The Last Labyrinth.*" *Language Forum* 19.1-2 (1992).

Mohan, Devinder. "The Language of the Splintered Mirror: the Fiction of Arun Joshi." *Ariel* 14.4 (1983).

Piciucco, Pier Paolo. "Fictional Technique and Rhetorical Devices in Arun Joshi's *The Apprentice.*" *Indian Writings in English.* Eds. Manmohan K. Bhatnagar and M. Rajeshwar. New Delhi: Atlantic, 2000.

Prasad, Madhusan. "Cornering Arun Joshi: A Critical Perspective on *The Last Labyrinth.*" *Scholar Critic* 4.6 (1984).

Radhakrishnan, N. "The Women Characters of Arun Joshi." *Scholar Critic* 4.6 (1984).

Rao, Ramakrishna A. "Arun Joshi's Voids and Labyrinths." *Literary Endeavour* 2.4 (1981).

Reddy, V. Gopal. "*The Apprentice: An Existential Study.*" *Kakatya Journal of English Studies* 5 (1983).

Ross, Robert. "The Clash of Opposites in Arun Joshi's *The Last Labyrinth.*" *Literary Criterion* 25.2 (1990).

Srinath, C.N. "The Fiction of Arun Joshi: the Novel of Interior Landscape." *The Literary Landscape: Essays on Indian Fiction and Poetry in English.* New Delhi: Mittal, 1986.

Srivastava, K. Ramesh. "Intricate Alleys in Arun Joshi's *The Last Labyrinth.*" *Indian Journal of English Studies* 28 (1989).

Swain, S.P. "Sindi Oberoi: Arun Joshi's Alienated Hero in *The Foreigner.*" *Indian Literature Today.* Vol. 1. Ed. R.K. Dhawan. New Delhi: Prestige, 1994.

Verma, K.D. "Alienation, Identity and Structure in Arun Joshi's *The Apprentice.*" *Ariel* 22.1 (1991).

Walter, Inna. "Arun Joshi's Vision of Life, Love, God and Death in *The Last Labyrinth.*" *Studies in Indian Fiction in English.* Ed. G.S. Balarama Gupta. Gulbarga: JIWE, 1987.

Interviews

Bannerjee, Purabi. "A Winner's Secret." *Sunday Statesman* 27 Feb. 1983.

Mathai, Sujata. "I'm a Stranger to My Books." *Times of India* 7 July 1983.

Piciucco, Pier Paolo. "An Interview with Arun Joshi." *The Journal of Indian Writing in English* 25.1-2 (1997).

9

Bharati Mukherjee

FLORENCE D'SOUZA

Bharati Mukherjee,[1] was born in Calcutta on 27th July 1940. Her Brahmin father, Sudhir Lal Mukherjee, owned a pharmaceutical drug manufacturing plant and her mother was Bina Bannerjee. Bharati Mukherjee has two sisters. At the age of eight, she spent two and a half years in Europe with her family, in London and then in Switzerland. On her return to India, she attended the Loreto Convent in Calcutta. In 1959, she passed her B.A. (Hons.) in English Literature from Calcutta University. In 1961, she obtained an M.A. in English and Ancient Indian Civilisation from Baroda University. She left India at the age of twenty-one, with an International Peace Scholarship, to attend the Writers' Workshop at the University of Iowa. In 1963, she passed her Master of Fine Arts and a degree in creative writing from the University of Iowa. On 19th September that same year (1963), she married Clark Blaise, a Canadian American whom she had met at the Iowa Writers' Workshop. In 1964, their first son, Bart Blaise, was born in Iowa City. From 1966 to 1978, Clark Blaise and Bharati Mukherjee lived in Montréal in Canada, where Mukherjee lectured in English at the McGill University. In December 1967, their second son, Bernard Blaise, named after the Jewish-American writer Bernard Malamud, was born in Montréal. In 1969, the University of Iowa awarded Bharati Mukherjee a Ph.D. on "The Use of Indian Mythology in E.M. Forster's *A Passage to India* and Hermann Hesse's *Siddhartha.*" In 1972, Mukherjee obtained Canadian nationality. In 1973-1974, having won the Canada Arts Council Award, she spent a year in Calcutta. In 1976-1977, having won the Shastri Indo-Canadian Award, she directed the Indo-Canadian Shastri Institute in New Delhi. In 1978, she and Clark Blaise moved from Montréal to Toronto. In 1980, they moved from Toronto to the USA where Mukherjee taught at Skidmore College, Saratoga Springs, having found the racial discrimination prevalent in Canada unbearable. She then moved through a series of teaching appointments in the USA, at Queen's College, NY, Columbia University, NY, and the City University of New York. In 1988, she obtained American nationality. Since 1988, she has been living in

San Francisco, and holds the post of Professor at the University of California at Berkeley.

Bharati Mukherjee's writings include six novels, two collections of short stories, two non-fiction essays written in collaboration with Clark Blaise (*Days and Nights in Calcutta*, 1977, being travel memoirs of their one-year stay in Calcutta in 1973-74; and *The Sorrow and the Terror: the Haunting legacy of the Air India Tragedy*, 1987, with portraits of the 329 victims who died in the Air India plane crash in Ireland in June 1985, caused by Sikh terrorists), as well as several journalistic articles and interviews.

A thread that runs through all Mukherjee's eight works of fiction, is difference—cultural, religious, racial, sexual and economic class difference. In the contemporary world in which her fiction is set, various upheavals—crippling legacies of colonialism, migration, instances of discrimination and violence, encounters with cultural otherness—can cause what Stuart Hall terms "inner expropriation of cultural identity."[2] If this debilitating silencing is to be overcome, a thorough understanding of Alterity is necessary. However, in order to understand the other side of Difference, a fixed sense of self has to be foregone and a negation of one's initial values, culture and very Being are imperative, in order to enable a chameleon-like slipping into new identity positionings. Only then, according to Abdul R. Jan Mohamed, does "syncretic cultural possiblity" emerge, opening up the never-ending historical process of Becoming once more, despite experiences of disruption and difference.[3] It is at the cost of this confident stepping out of self, that difference can become something positive, a celebration of variety and a pleasure, instead of functioning as an instrument of hierarchisation, stereotyping, fear and oppression.[4] This paper will attempt to analyse the ways in which Mukherjee portrays this partial Othering of Self in her fiction, where the textual strategies seem to coincide with the adventures of her protagonists in an open-ended demystification of Difference.

In Mukherjee's first novel *The Tiger's Daughter* (1971), several instances of inversion of the Insider/Outsider opposition mark the exploration of the Other side of Difference. The textual device of letters is used to reinforce the adoption of the view from the outside. When in the USA, the protagonist Tara received various letters from her parents in Calcutta, in particular, proposing meetings with eligible Bengali bachelors (*TD* 15-16). Despite these parental injunctions, she however married an American of her own choice. From Calcutta, she exchanges letters with her husband David in America, and discovers an unfamiliar "David of aerogrammes" (*TD* 77). She also finds herself defending the callousness and apparent passivity of India's affluent classes towards India's poor against David's outrage at their omission to fight against injustice (*TD* 157), when in fact she herself had felt a distance from their "aristocratic oneness" (*TD* 54).

Visions and nightmares also convey an insight into the Other side of things. At Vassar, Poughkeepsie, in the US, Tara would pray to the goddess Kali when she felt the stress of her own difference from "these polite Americans." At such moments, a smiling vision of the simultaneously serene and furious Kali would appear to reassure her (*TD* 14). This contradictory image of Kali can be seen as an emblem of the polyvalence which includes certain characteristics as well as their opposites at the core of each Being, illustrating the fluid complexity of identity and reality. Also at Poughkeepsie, a greater awareness of other Indiannesses appears in Tara's vision of terror where she sees herself sleeping on a sidewalk, like the homeless poor of Calcutta, while "headless monsters" wink at her from "eyes embedded in pudgy shoulders" (*TD* 17). Tara's unconscious identification with Calcutta's poor produces an unsettling effect.

Certain motifs depict otherness in *The Tiger's Daughter*. Tara's grand-aunt Arupa embodies the otherness of excessive despair and madness in her family's legends (*TD* 11). While Tara attends a Chamber of Commerce Charity Fair, she has a feeling of an approaching apocalypse as she poses for a photograph with the pushy Marwari merchant Tuntunwala. For no particular reason, we learn that on this occasion she was "nervously jingling" her unfortunate aunt Arupa's wedding bangle (*TD* 96). This deliberate lack of connection between Tara's intuition of impending disaster and her abandoned aunt's bangle can be read as an inner weakness in Tara or as an omen of future mishaps in the text. It is as if irrationality were rearing its head in the fabric of the text itself. Motifs like "dry holes" and "dry fields" convey Tara's desolation upon rediscovering the Indian countryside, perceived as "alien and hostile" (*TD* 26, 31). Joyonto Roy Chowdhury's compassion for the plight of the affluent, young men and women of Calcutta is captured in the image of "trapped gazelles." They are at the same time so different from his older, less naive self and so similar to what he had been in his twenties, that the thought "frightened" him (*TD* 9). The otherness of the non-Bengali, non-Brahmin, Marwari merchant, P.K. Tuntunwala, is expressed through the motif of a Spider: "impassive and calculating," "a selfish energy." He evolves into "the National Personage," a possible political saviour and even "a prophet," but is forced to helplessly witness mob violence in the final scene (*TD* 27, 29, 32, 160, 241).

Textual Otherness in *The Tiger's Daughter* appears through references to English poetry—Tennyson, Keats, Sassoon, Rupert Brooke and even a deliberate parodying of W.H. Davies' "Leisure" ("What is this life if, full of care,/ We have no time to stand and stare"). Thus English poetry plays the ambivalent role of a means of displaying literary erudition and of making fun of pedantry (*TD* 84, 102, 120). Joyonto Roy Chowdhury's disjointed word games introduce an incongruous eeriness. While sitting in the terrace café of the Catelli-Continental, Joyonto makes "short-sighted visionary small talk" with himself. For example, "Truth is a head on a stake" or "On the skeletons of cows skyscrapers will rise." In the final scene of street violence, before being ultimately rescued by the police man Popo, Joyonto seizes a microphone to address Tara with word clusters. Some striking instances are "Bats with baby faces" and "I shored against my ruins." Despite their apparent incoherence, against the backdrop of the rioting crowd, they take on a prophetic tone (*TD* 51, 246). The fact that they appear in italics underlines their disturbing quality. Social Otherness features in Tara's frightening encounter with a Tantric with matted hair at the funeral pyres by the river bank (*TD* 101), in her confrontation with a hysterical little girl with leprosy in a squatters' shanty settlement (*TD* 141), and in the Washington Mc Dowell episode. The latter brings comic relief amidst the mounting tension in the novel. His Scottish sounding surname seems in disjunction with his Black American appearance and "Afro" hairdo. Since his Bengali hosts had only a series of stereotypes as points of reference about Blacks (Masai Africans, Tarzan, Conrad's *The Nigger of the 'Narcissus'*), Washington Mc Dowell turns out to be a far cry from their expectations about an emblematic representative of the U.S. of A.

By approaching Otherness from a multitude of angles, *The Tiger's Daughter* dedramatises its frightening aspects without reducing alterity to an all-encompassing sameness. It thus seems to open the door to deeper cultural dialogue.

The exploration of Difference takes a dystopic turn in Mukherjee's second novel *Wife* (1975). The apparently straightforward narrative structure turns out to be splintered by a series of nightmarish images that mark the protagonist Dimple Dasgupta-Basu's growing alienation from her sense of self. Thus, despite her conventional upbringing in Calcutta, her naive dreams of becoming "Sita, the ideal wife of Hindu legend" (*W* 6) and her arranged marriage to the mechanical engineer Amit Basu, her early married life in Calcutta is scarred by thoughts of a dead baby lizard in her pillowcase (*W* 23), a violent confrontation with a pregnant mouse that she leaves "horribly misshapen, bloody from the blows" (*W* 36) and unexplainable impulses to flush a gifted pet goldfish down the toilet bowl (*W* 40)! Her bizarre daydreams of neurosurgeons, sinister abortionists and men with broken teeth and dirty fingers "who dug into her body in a dark, suburban garage" (*W* 34), and eerie visions of her unborn baby with "wrinkled skin like a very old man's and a large head filled with water" (*W* 43), culminate in her deliberately skipping her way to abortion with a skipping rope in order to be rid of the "tyrannical" fetus she was carrying (*W* 34, 43). Already a yawning gulf between Dimple's fantasies and the realities of her married life is perceptible.

In the second part of *Wife*, difference appears as the strangeness of being in a foreign land. As she tries to adapt to the very different lifestyle of New York, Dimple becomes addicted to daytime TV shows with inspiring names like "The Guiding Light" where everything "was about love" (*W* 73). This exotic TV universe is in sharp contrast with "the scary, ugly kind of death" constantly mentioned in the American newspapers and in her friends' conversations where "muggings, rape, murder" were frequent features (*W* 73, 85). Dimple's feelings of helplessness, caused by the gap between life's promises and day-to-day reality, find expression in "waking nightmares" during her hours of insomnia in which men with "baby faces and hooded eyes," move alongside of "roaches scuttling in the closet" (*W* 97) and in an upsetting dream where Dimple sees a very Americanized Indian friend, Ina Mullick, washed up on an American beach as a dead body draped in Dimple's own sari (*W* 103). Worrying tendencies to violence appear in Dimple's wondering if "she could make Amit die in his sleep" (*W* 98) and in her feeling of hatred for the furniture and plastic flowers in the home of their Indian hosts in Queens. When she deliberately breaks off three plastic petals while supposedly dusting the plastic flowers and perceives them to be "like detached ear lobes" or "parts of her own body," this can be read as an indication of her descent into a form of schizophrenia (*W* 105).

Dimple's inner obsessions and mental wanderings based on images imbibed from TV series tend to dominate her consciousness in the third part, undoing her contact with reality completely. When Amit appears to be indifferent to news of the suicide in India of a woman friend of a friend, Dimple seeks revenge in a bout of "postnightmare lucidity" and discovers a thrill in the idea of piercing Amit's body (*W* 117). Later in the "unnerving silence" of their sublet apartment in Manhattan at 4 o'clock in the afternoon, Dimple observes her own panic and suicidal desires in a mirror-image, where she sees herself as "a small, stiff lump, hair arranged like black bat wings against the sky blue pillow" (*W* 128). However, far from permitting an acceptance of her human condition, this encounter with her reflection in the mirror is only a further step in Dimple's slow unhinging from reality. In a showdown between Ina Mullick and Ina's hunchbacked, toothless and dentured woman lover Leni Anspach, in the Basu's sublet apartment, Dimple's china rhinoceros ashtray, a wedding gift that she had carried from India, gets broken, and Dimple ends up pouring tea nonstop, like an ill-programmed robot, inundating cup and tray (*W* 147, 153). Dimple considers this as "the end of an era in her own life" and discovers that protest can be "enjoyable" (*W* 149, 153). The grotesqueness of this scene only accentuates the atmosphere of mental instability and violence. Difference is portrayed here as a growing sense of isolation in Dimple, in relation to her husband and circle of friends. Dimple becomes aware that TV "was becoming the voice of madness" (*W* 176) and then conceives of an extravagant scheme where she would kill Amit and hide his body in the freezer, thereby feeling "very American somehow, almost like a character in a TV series" (*W* 195). In the final climax of the novel Dimple feels "something had torn loose and was hanging in space" (*W* 208). This can be understood as a part of herself, leaving her shattered within. She is thus able to assess her own actions calmly, comparing her role always to that of the wives in soap operas (*W* 211). The last scene depicts Dimple in the kitchen of their rented home feeling "she was falling apart like a very old toy" (*W* 212) and stabbing Amit from behind in the neck, near the mole just under the hairline, using a kitchen knife to make seven stabs in a row. The TV screen and Dimple's private screen merge in the novel's final sentence: "Women on television got away with murder" (*W* 213). The unrealisable projections of American TV films and talk shows are portrayed as catalysts in Dimple's slide over the edge of reality, making her experience of difference a tragic journey down a path of no return.

In her introduction to her collection of twelve short stories entitled *Darkness* (1985), Mukherjee makes a declaration about her aesthetic aims as an immigrant writer—while identifying with the immigrant outcasts in Canada and the United States of America, she is determined "to hear America singing even in the seams of the dominant culture" (*D* xv). Her momentum is thus resolutely turned towards integration with the new community. Difference can therefore be read in this collection as "a metaphor," "a particular way of partially comprehending the world" in an overall "exuberance" and celebration of "fluid identities" (*D* xv), as opposed to a nostalgic looking backwards to lost origins in a mindframe of exile. In the first story "Angela" for example, the first-person narrator is a mutilated refugee from Bangla Desh, adopted by an American family named Brandon in Iowa. Despite her "bony, scarred body," in fact Angela is a healthy adolescent, since the story opens with an unmarried Brandon sister named Delia in a coma after a car accident. Delia's adopted brother Kim from Korea and her adopted sister Angela from Bangla Desh (the narrator) who were with her during the accident, escaped with minor injuries (*D* 7, 8, 14). This is underlined twice by Nurse Grimlund who declares fatalistically: "There's no telling who'll be taken and who'll be saved" (*D* 7, 14). This reference to the Christian concept of Grace which chooses but cannot be chosen reminds Angela of the Christian orphanage in Dhaka, where she was nursed back to life after having been tortured by soldiers in the Bangla Desh forests (*D* 4) and from where she was adopted by her American family. This leaves Angela with the impression that Grace is "a black, tropical bat cutting through dusk on blunt, ugly wings" (*D* 5). Hardly an exalting image. The ambivalences of her situation are highlighted by the offers of intimacy and domesticity that Angela receives from the Indian Dr. Vinny Menezes (*D* 14). They reveal Angela to be caught between traumatic memories of her ordeals in the tropics amidst mud and leeches (*D* 15), an awareness of the physical scars she bears (*D* 14) and her eagerness to assimilate and not waste her life (*D* 12, 14). Through the vicissitudes of Angela's experiences which are mirrored in the digressions and time hops included to introduce the numerous characters involved, a tremendous energy and optimistic enjoyment of life give the text buoyancy.

In "A Father," the Bhowmick family, originally from Ranchi in Bihar, having settled in Detroit, go through the upheavals of adapting to the American way of life. The story is remarkable for its images and reversals. The image of "the goddess of wrath and vengeance," Kali-Mata, appears several times. First, she is the patron goddess that Mr. Bhowmick invokes for protection (*D* 50). Then, she takes on an "admonitory" aspect, while Mr. Bhowmick notices that the tongue the goddess stuck out at the world suddenly seemed "scarlet and saucy" (*D* 52). Then, as his neighbour's sneeze in his Detroit neighbourhood seems to augur bad luck for Mr. Bhowmick at the start of his journey to work one morning, he feels "the goddess's scarlet little tongue tip wagging at him" (*D* 54). When he is overcome with guilt at his failure to love his 26-year old daughter Babli, he has the impression the goddess was "sticking out her tongue at him" (*D* 57). On learning that the unmarried Babli is pregnant, he begins to pray to Kali-Mata at nights (*D* 62). As the story ends with the revelation that Babli's pregnancy is through artificial insemination, her shocked father perceives in her a living incarnation of the goddess Kali herself, especially when she screams at him and he sees her tongue "thick and red, squirming behind her row of perfect teeth" (*D* 63). The reference to Kali underlines the otherness of the Bhowmick family in their Detroit setting, while also revealing the potential of familiar family members to change into frightening Others. The reversal of roles between Mr. Bhowmick and his wife during the scene of confrontation with Babli, as Mrs. Bhowmick, the progressive, driving force in the couple throughout, seems to go to pieces at the horror of the idea of a syringe replacing a human father, does not last long. Mr. Bhowmick who had been trying to separate his wife and daughter as they fought, ends up attacking Babli with the rolling pin himself, and it is once again his dynamic wife who stops the violence by calling the police (*D* 64). "A Father" can be read then as a feminist exploration of feminine otherness, in addition to its theme of immigration and cultural adaptation.

The last story in the collection *Darkness*, entitled "Courtly Vision" can be interpreted as an example of textual and aesthetic Otherness. First of all, it is a textual presentation of an (imaginary) artistic work from another medium, namely painting. The charm of the story lies in its functioning as an artistic creation in its own rights, while adopting certain technical characteristics of the Mughal miniature genre of painting. In an interview, Bharati Mukherjee has stated her interest in Moghul miniature painting as an art form:

> My image of artistic structure and artistic excellence is the Mughal miniature painting with its crazy foreshortening of vanishing point, its insistence that everything happens simultaneously, bound only by shape and colour. In the miniature paintings of India, there are a dozen foci, the most complicated stories can be rendered on a grain of rice, the corners are as elaborated as the centres. There is a sense of interpenetration of all things.[5]

The multiplication of points of focus makes possible the juxtaposition of several scenes, while the absence of perspective reduces distance in space (and time) to an all-encompassing foreground (in an eternal present), and the dehierarchized treatment of the centres and the peripheries enables the artist to explore the Other side of normatized representations, endowing the work with a subversive liberty.

In the story "Courtly Vision," this dehierarchized representation is apparent in the choice of characters and the supposed indications of the painting's provenance, which give it a contemporary museographical slant, registration number and estimated price complete. The date also turns out to be suspect since the Mughal Emperor in 1584 was Akbar (who reigned from 1556 to 1605) and was indeed known to receive European adventurers and Portuguese priests in a spirit of humanist curiosity and syncretism. However, the Jahanara Begum, with whom the text opens, was in fact a daughter of Shah Jahan (three generations after Akbar!) and lived from 1614 to 1680, whereas Akbar's capital of Fatehpur Sikri had been abandoned for lack of an adequate water supply in 1610, soon after Akbar died, and several years before the birth of Jahanara Begum! Also, the court painter mentioned twice, Basawan, was indeed a well-known painter of Mughal miniatures who lived around Akbar's and perhaps Jahangir's (1605-1627) time. But the fact is that Basawan was reputed for making excellent copies and imitations of European engravings and paintings, much sought after at that period. This makes the Moghul courtier's bored, indifferent reactions to the religious paintings spread out by the Portuguese priests particularly ironical. It shows clearcut oppositions between eastern and western aesthetics in pictorial art to be arbitrary and exaggerated, since they were in full osmosis in fact in the 16th and 17th centuries. There is also a contradiction in the double mention of Basawan in the text and the fact that the technical label at the end declares "Painter unknown." The Emperor's injunctions to his artist, in italics in the text, underline the ambiguities of the relationship between an official art patron with despotic, capricious demands and the necessary liberty required by a creative artist. And these are only a few of the possible readings of Mukherjee's extremely rich text. It comes as an appropriate closure to a collection that is conceived around the theme of postcolonial Indian immigrants in North America, since it is set in India at a period when Europeans were making migrant journeys from West to East.

Bharati Mukherjee's next collection of eleven short stories published under the title *The Middleman & Other Stories* (1988) incorporates migrant characters from various corners of the globe, mainly Asian. This collection can also be read as an exploration of the Other side of Difference since the author uses certain motifs, situations and narrative procedures to illustrate the complexities of difference in the lives of her characters. For example, in the story "Loose Ends," the first-person narrator, the Vietnam veteran Jeb Marshall, presents the image of a reticulated python that he had had occasion to contemplate at the age of seventeen. A parallel is established between the "brown and passionless" eyes of the python, the patient intelligence of all of Vietnam and the middlemen who like locusts, sharks and pythons have taken over all the major cities in the world, including in Jeb Marshall's native Florida, with their pimping of illicit goods and services against "a payoff, a delivery, a contact" (*M&OS* 49, 50). The image is developed with the repulsive detail of python turds or snakeshit to convey the idea of "coiled power" and of a disgusting kind of "cash crop" (*M&OS* 49). Another trope in "Loose Ends" is that of Alice in Wonderland and her disappearance down the rabbit hole into a mysterious, unknown world. It is used in this story, in an inverted form, to present the othering of America—by the Vietnam war, by mercenary middlemen and by well-organised immigrants—as if Alice had taken the familiar America with her down the hole, leaving behind an unrecognisable, uncomfortable place (*M&OS* 48, 54). This is underlined by the image of a family homestead with a front door and a back door. On two occasions, the Vietnam veteran-narrator feels that while he was at the war front "barricading" the front door, strange changes and newcomers had entered his native America and Florida through the back door (*M&OS* 48-53). That he is doing his best to adapt to the changed circumstances is evident from the final image of the story where Jeb Marshall, as a mercenary on the run, feels he has himself become a python (*M&OS* 54): "This is what I've become. I want to squeeze this state dry and swallow it whole."

In "Danny's Girls," the narrative covers some two years in the life of its adolescent narrator, the son of expatriate Gujaratis who, after being expelled from Uganda, settled in Flushing, New York. In this story, the narrator's experience of otherness is within himself, mirrored in his relationship with Danny Sahib, the hustler, seven years his senior, as well as in his relationships with persons of the female sex: his Aunt Lini, a business minded widow; one of Danny's catalogue-brides, the good looking Rosie from Nepal; and the Hindu-American princess, Pammy Patel. The Otherness the narrator experiences is his need for self-affirmation and his desire for "a real woman like Rosie" (*M&OS* 147). He goes through a crisis when "the grown-up orphan in Danny, the Survivor" asserts his position of authority over the narrator. This makes the narrator realize that he was doing "a strange, pimpish thing" in distributing Danny's catalogue-bride flyers and posters and that he wanted to be more than an "errand boy" and a "hijra, eunuch," deprived of any rights to express his own male desires. He also wished to step out of the guilt and demands for academic excellence imposed on him by his mother and Aunt Lini (*M&OS* 148). The crisis is resolved as if by magic when Rosie acknowledges him as a person by accepting him in her bed. The last sentence of the short story affirms the narrator's self-confident stepping into his own life, having tamed the Otherness of his doubts and inner conflicts: "And for the first time I felt my life was going to be A-Okay" (*M&OS* 149).

Throughout this collection, *The Middleman & Other Stories*, the experience of Difference is portrayed as a step which, through self-questionings and gropings for solutions, enables survival and onward progress.

Bharati Mukherjee published a novel entitled *Jasmine* in 1989. The eponymous first-person narrator has a life of constant migration from one situation to another, embodying different selves in each situation. These mutations of identity are accompanied by a series of name changes that can be seen as experiences of Difference within the Self. The young girl Jyoti of Hasnapur, becomes Mrs. Jasmine Vijh in Jullundhar, then she moves to Florida and is called Jazzy by an American benefactress Lillian Gordon, she reverts to her initial name Jyoti in the Punjabi ghetto in Flushing, is renamed Jase or Jassy by her employers in New York, Taylor and Wylie Hayes and their adopted daughter Duff, is transformed into Jane Ripplemeyer as Bud Ripplemeyer's partner in Baden, Iowa, before becoming Jase again to Taylor and Duff Hayes at the end of the novel. These dizzying identity and role changes enable her to explore ever new facets of herself as she adapts to the changes in her life. They are emphasized by the image of a hurtling stone: "I feel at times like a stone hurtling through diaphonous mist, unable to grab hold, unable to slow myself, yet unwilling to abandon the ride I'm on" (*J* 138). Another striking image that underlines difference in the novel is borrowed from a Punjabi proverb: "The villagers say when a clay pitcher breaks, you see that the air inside it is the same as outside" (*J* 15). It is as if the entire novel is an attempt to illustrate the permeability of the boundary between Self and Other, Inside and Outside. The pitcher image occurs again to contrast the outlook of Jyoti's peasant father who had never got over the upheaval of having to flee from Lahore to Hasnapur during the Partition in 1947 and lived in nostalgia for the past, as opposed to her own forward-looking determination: "Fact is, there was a difference. [Between the poetic Punjabi of Lahore and "the crow-talk Punjabi" of the Jullundhar district.] My father was right to notice it and to let it set a standard. But that pitcher is broken. It is the same air this side as that. He'll never see Lahore again and I never have. Only a fool would let it rule his life" (*J* 43). Difference cannot be ignored but should not be allowed to become an obstacle to happiness and survival. The broken pitcher image also marks the end of an epoch and an opening onto newness, when Jasmine accomplishes the ceremony of *anoomarana* or burning with an object belonging to the deceased person as a last rite of homage to her dead husband Prakash Vijh (*J* 79, 114).[6] This can be read as a feminist re-writing of the patriarchal rite of Sati where the widow was supposed to accept immolation on the funeral pyre of her dead husband, since in *Jasmine* it marks a choice to plunge forward despite the presence of death, with a convenient desertion by Lord Yama, the god of death, and the beginning of Jasmine's journey in America:

> I said my prayers for the dead, clutching my Ganpati. I thought, the pitcher is broken. Lord Yama, who had wanted me, who had courted me, and whom I'd flirted with on the long trip over, had now deserted me. (*J* 120)

Thus, the broken pitcher and the desertion of Lord Yama liberate Jasmine from the constraints of the past permitting her to launch into new discoveries in a new continent.

A series of irruptions of violence are also markers of Difference throughout Jasmine's trajectory. Right at her birth her mother, in whose eyes daughters were curses, had tried to end Jyoti's life. Jyoti's elder sisters' first view of Jyoti was of a baby with "a ruby-red choker of bruise" around her throat. However, Jyoti survived her mother's disillusioned though well-intentioned sniping (*J* 40). Then, while accompanying the neighbourhood women to the fields during the morning latrine hour in Hasnapur, Jyoti encountered a mad dog and courageously killed it with a wooden staff she had collected by chance. The description of the dog is repulsive: "Its eyes glowed red, its slack jaws foamed" (*J* 56). Jyoti's act of self-defence is unflinching: "I let it crouch and growl its low, terrible, gullety growl. I took aim and waited for it to leap on me. The staff crushed the dog's snout while it was still in mid-leap" (*J* 56). Thus violence surfaces without warning in the most familiar surroundings.

Jyoti's father died prematurely in a horrible accident. He was gored by a maddened bull that attacked him from behind as he was going through a field on the way to a friend's hut (*J* 58). This unexpected instance of violence in the life of Jyoti's family can be read as an illustration of James Gleick's book on Chaos Theory, a quotation from which forms the epigraph to the novel, highlighting "the twisted, tangled and intertwined" geometry of the universe.[7]

In a series of further violent incidents, Jyoti's beloved schoolteacher, Masterji, was brutally shot with thirty bullets by fanatic youths of the separatist Sikh movement, despite Masterji having been a pious Sikh himself (*J* 85-86); her husband, Prakash Vijh, was killed by a bomb planted by Sikh Khalsa Lions in the central bazaar of Jullundhar, Jyoti's own escape on the occasion having been miraculous (*J* 92-94); and Jasmine was raped in the Flamingo Court motel in Florida, by Half Face Bubba, the white Vietnam veteran who ran a shrimper boat between the Caribbean and the Gulf Coast of Florida (*J* 115-17).

Then, in a dramatic turning of the tables, the rape victim transforms herself into an incarnation of the bloodthirsty goddess Kali, by slitting her own tongue. With a vision of "ribbons of bright blood" before her eyes, this transformed Jasmine stabs her aggressor Half Face to death:

> What a monstrous thing, what an infinitesimal thing, is the taking of a human life; for the second time in three months, I was in a room with a slain man, my body bloodied. I was walking death. Death incarnate. (*J* 119)

In the course of her adventures in America, Jasmine has three more encounters with violence. On a Sunday outing in a New York park, with Taylor Hayes and Duff, Jasmine spots her husband's Sikh murderer, Sukhwinder, in the guise of a hot-dog vendor. Feeling vulnerable and exposed as an illegal immigrant without papers, despite her strong attachment to Duff and Taylor Hayes, Jasmine takes the radical decision that she will leave New York and move to the state of Iowa, in order to keep out of Sukhwinder's reach (*J* 188-89). Again, the threat of violence brings change and otherness into Jasmine's life.

Out of the blue, one of Bud Ripplemeyer's bank clients named Harlan Kroener dropped by at Bud's house two days before Christmas and shot Bud with his rifle, making Bud a paraplegic for life (*J* 193, 198). Jane's and Bud's and their adopted Vietnamian son Du Thien's lives were irrevocably changed after that unexpected encounter with violence.

The last violent upheaval in the novel is the suicide of Darrel Lutz, a young farmer neighbour of the Ripplemeyers, who reared hogs and was in love with Jasmine. Darrel appears already lost because of "failed amibitious design" and association with white survivalists. Jasmine reads "blown circuitry" behind Darrel's eyes while he tries to seduce her (*J* 218). Soon after, in a nightmare-like scene, Jasmine, accompanied by the crippled Bud, discovers Darrel's body suspended from his roof by an extension cord, with his feet chewed off by his "crazed, carnivorous hogs" (*J* 234). The trope of an astronaut's unsuccessful lift-off is used to describe the human failure in Darrel's suicide.

And yet, through all these traumatic confrontations with wild Otherness, Jasmine's courage and determination to go on never flounder. Her reckless departure for a new beginning in the far West with Taylor Hayes and Duff at the end of the novel can be seen as a measure of her optimistic belief in the unexplored possibility that life offers with each new day.

Another interesting chain of images that introduces Otherness in *Jasmine* is linked to the Hasnapur astrologer, an old man with a cackling voice who dispensed his predictions cross-legged under a banyan tree. Not only does the novel open and almost close with him (*J* 3, 240), but his gloomy foretellings of widowhood and exile for Jyoti constitute one of the main springboards of Jasmine's efforts throughout. Indeed the novel can be read as an unflagging attempt to "re-position the stars," however many mishaps and setbacks they may portend. The image of "the old man under the banyan tree" is present as Jasmine makes plans to migrate to the USA with her husband Prakash: "We'd start with new fates, new stars. We could say or be anything we wanted" (*J* 85). Even in an Iowa relief fund Charity fair, an image of the old astrologer cackles his predictions to Jasmine amidst buffet breakfasts and pony rides, confirming her status of exile among aliens (*J* 203). The old astrologer then appears as a vestige from an ancient past (*J* 229). And the last scene of the novel is a triumphant gesture of defiance to preordained life paths that impose obedience and conformism—the liberating force of the fluid frontier pushing indoors proves stronger than all inhibiting influences:

> Adventure, risk, transformation: the frontier is pushing indoors through uncaulked windows. Watch me re-position the stars, I whisper to the astrologer who floats cross-legged above my kitchen stove. (*J* 240)

Otherness and Difference are no longer bugbears requiring protective cocoons of security. They are, instead, challenges to be confronted squarely with fortitude, and play the role of positive stimuli of change and innovation.

Mukherjee's next novel *The Holder of the World* came out in 1993. Amidst the exuberant richness of its construction, we will select only one aspect[8] as a means of studying the way in which this novel explores the Other side of Difference: the epigraphs to each of the four parts, taken from John Keats's "Ode on a Grecian Urn." Keats's meditation on a piece of pottery from classical Antiquity with its famous aphorism

"Beauty is Truth, Truth Beauty" is taken in small extracts of two lines at the beginning of each part of Mukherjee's novel. There is a deliberate asymmetry here, since Keats's poem has five stanzas and the novel has only four parts—Keats's third stanza therefore is deliberately left out in the sequence of quotations used by Mukherjee. This asymmetry is further reflected in the series of (fictitious) Salem Bibi paintings which serve as landmarks and indicators to the 20th century narrator Beigh Masters in her search for details on the life and adventures of her distant relative from the 17th century, Hannah Easton. Indeed, we learn that they formed a series of "five crudely framed miniatures" (*HoW* 14), again in asymmetry with the four parts of the novel. A further disequilibrium lies between the opening line of Keats's poem "Thou still unravish'd Bride of quietness/ Thou foster-child of silence and slow time," which also forms the epigraph to the first part of Mukerjee's novel, depicting Hannah Easton's childhood and youth in New England as well as in old England as the wife of the sea adventurer Gabriel Legge, and the fact that the narrator chooses to rename the last painting in the Salem Bibi series initially known as "The Apocalypse," precisely with the title "The Unravish'd Bride" (*HoW* 17-18; 277). We learn that this painting incorporates many scenes with the eyes of the three main characters forming a triangle—the Salem Bibi's eyes, the eyes of her Hindu lover, Raja Jadav Singh of Devgad, and the eyes of the Mughal conqueror Aurangzeb. The question of an unravished bride stands contradicted, especially since the Salem Bibi was pregnant at the time. The action represented covers the final battle between Aurangzeb and Jadav Singh in 1700, in which Jadav Singh was vanquished and killed. This constitutes the climax of the novel's unfolding but is however embedded at the beginning as well as at the end of the text. The use of the title "The Unravish'd Bride" can be understood, then, as a subversive deviation from logical sequence. In addition, the first two lines of the "Ode on a Grecian Urn" carry allusions to 'quietness,' 'silence,' and 'slow time.' These can be read as a self-conscious underlining of Mukherjee's narrator's persevering efforts over eleven years to piece together scraps of information about Hannah Easton's life, mainly from 1670 to 1701 (*HoW* 138, 279). Since all the data collected leaves gaps and dead-ends that Beigh Masters has to supplement through her imagination, in order to make her narrative come alive before her reader's mind's eye, they can be linked to the enigmatic 'quietness' and 'silence' of Keats's 'unravish'd bride,' which are followed by a series of quizzical questions in the poem. Also, the messy blending between the reconstitution of Hannah Easton's life and the reports of Beigh Masters's research in the text can be perceived as a debunking of Keats's admiration before the ideal perfection of the created art object ("She cannot fade, though thou hast not thy bliss,/ For ever wilt thou love, and she be fair!").

The second part opens with the first two lines of Keats's second stanza in the "Ode on a Grecian Urn": "Heard melodies are sweet, But those unheard/ Are sweeter; therefore, ye soft pipes, play on." These lines seem to acknowledge the value and the autonomy of visual and verbal art as separate from the reality they represent, since they function mainly through associations in the imagination of the beholder/ reader. Indeed, the entire second part is made up of a fictitious reconstitution of the activities of the English factory of Fort St. Sebastian on the Coromandel Coast in the years 1695 to 1700. However, Mukherjee introduces notes of discordance in the polyphonic manner in which her narrator renders the events by exposing the incoherences in the available versions of history. Although Higginbottham, the English Chief Factor of Fort St. Sebastian at the time is reported to have been commended by the Fort St. George Council for restoring "stabilitie and respecte to the English nation" after some trade mishaps, we learn that the stone sloop etched on Higginbottham's tombstone in the English cemetery in Fort St. Sebastian was, in fact, an acknowledgment of his inimical destruction of the sloop of a rebellious local merchant. When Beigh Masters visited his tomb in the 1990's, she found the famous stone etching of the sloop trampled by goats and encrusted with marine salt, a pathetic parody of Rupert Brooke's poem "The Soldier," since she sees this outpost "corner of England forever"[9] more as a "commemoration of impotence" than anything else (*HoW* 188).

In this second part, we also come across another of the five miniatures of the Salem Bibi paintings. This one, entitled "The Foreign Traveler" is dated c. 1700 and shows "an emaciated firangi in a Muslim ascetic's garb." This provides a suggestion that Gabriel Legge, contrary to what was believed and circulated at the time, did not die in "the drownings and butcheries of December 1700" (*HoW* 207) but lived on in India in the company of a black Bibi ("a seductive, veiled, dark-skinned woman" in the miniature). In addition, the narrator Beigh Masters chooses to rename this painting as "Entry into the Garden" in a deliberate reversal of the Biblical Fall of Adam and Eve from the Garden of Eden. Far from affirming the perfect, ideal otherness of art and literature, Mukherjee's novel emphasizes its own artificial piecing together, and the disharmonious divergences from which it has been fashioned.

Part Three opens with Keats's lines "Who are these coming to the sacrifice?/ To what green altar, o mysterious priest." Here again, there is an ironic distance between the initial context of Keats's lines and Mukherjee's appropriation of them, highlighting her intention to explore difference. While Keats's lines evoke a temple sacrifice in Ancient Greece and a whole town emptied of its inhabitants as they congregate at the altar for the ritual on "this pious morn," Mukherjee's text underlines the despotic fanaticism of Emperor Aurangzeb and the ruthless wars fought between Hindu camps and Muslim camps at the time. The narrator subtly shows the fanaticism practised by both parties, without taking sides. Fanaticism on the Hindu side is shown in Jadav Singh's visceral commitment to cruelty and vengeance against Aurangzeb (*HoW* 233) and in the old Queen Mother of Devgad's ruthlessness, expressed in popular ballads of the region in which she took the role of "a multi-armed goddess riding a lion and hurling thunderbolts against the armies of the grand Mughal" (*HoW* 232). In a chilling interview with Aurangzeb, Hannah Easton encounters his cold-blooded fanaticism under the protection of the all-merciful Allah who requires of his faithful as a "duty" that they "bring the infidel before the throne of judgment" (*HoW* 269). This absolute view is symbolized in the diamond of the Emperor's Tear representing the tear the Emperor sheds as he discharges his often painful duty. This diamond tear was contained in an intriguing mobile exhibit where a golden replica of Aurangzeb's hands held a golden orb representing the world, on one side of which a lion nuzzled a lamb. The Emperor's Tear was embedded between the top of the golden world and the upper tip of the golden fingers (*HoW* 263). The irony, in relation to Keats's "Ode on a Grecian Urn," resides in the exquisite beauty of this ornamental piece of craftsmanship which paradoxically stands for Aurangzeb's tyranny, belying Keats's aphorism "Beauty is Truth, Truth Beauty." The title of the novel *The Holder of the World* also denounces this despotic pretension to control over all the empires in the universe, since it reveals the violence and bloodshed that this entails.

The brief, final section of the novel opens with two lines from the middle of Keats's final stanza in "Ode on a Grecian Urn": "Thou, silent form, dost tease us out of thought/ As doth Eternity. Cold Pastoral!" Their selection as the epigraph of the fourth and last part perhaps hinges on the tension between the bafflement provoked by the "silent form" of the art object and its cold distance from the warmth and disorder of real experience. It could be a self-conscious jibe at the multiple meanings contained in any work of art, leaving truth entirely in the eye of the beholder, with the risk of ending in an impasse, in case of incomprehension by the same beholder! This is consolidated in the narrator's ambivalent reaction to her computer-wizard companion's synthesisation of given moments of reality through very complex technical processes [his programme X-2989 (*HoW* 5, 278)]; his dream of a "Crystal Garden" of perfect computerized interactivity (*HoW* 279); his Data Plasma, (*HoW* 259, 279). On the one hand, we have her disappointment at the application of what sounded like an exciting principle in theory, since there was also the possibility of simply producing "an endless parade of faucets" in the complex attempt at computerized Time Retrieval (*HoW* 278-79). Yet, she agrees to "jump into" a given picture by means of an individual "mind search" through that same interactive computer programme in order to find a solution to her lengthy hunt for the exact location of the diamond, the Emperor's Tear (*HoW* 281-83). The novel's preoccupation with Time is corroborated in Keats's phrase "As doth Eternity." It is no coincidence that the novel closes with an invocation to Time, underlining the vital necessity of the Time factor in all textual attempts to stretch "out and back to the uttermost shores" (*HoW* 286). As illustrated by the use of extracts from Keats's "Ode on a Grecian Urn" then, *The Holder of the World* can be perceived as an inventive appropriation of the aesthetic principles contained in Keats's poem through a subversive exploration of Difference—in artistic mediums, in logical sequence, in art as a form, in the disharmonious multiplicity of meanings, in religion, in the moral value of Beauty, in technology and along the axis of Time.

Bharati Mukherjee's next novel *Leave it to Me* was published in 1997. In this novel, disjointed snatches of memory (*LiM* 9) and an experimental attempt at introspection through poetry-writing serve as triggers for the protagonist-narrator's exploration of her own, personal Otherness (*LiM* 15, 17, 202), since she had been adopted from India by American parents at the age of two (*LiM* 87). The fragmented nature of the narrator's memories before her adoption is a stimulus for her to find out more about her progenitors and the circumstances of her birth and early childhood (*LiM* 49, 94). However, these steps often lead to dead ends or irretrievable blanks (*LiM* 61, 164). Having discarded her identity as adopted child Debby of the American Di Martino family (*LiM* 10, 62), this abandoned daughter of unidentified parents births herself into a new identity as "Devi Dee," choosing to claim as her mother, the daughter of the Cosmic Spirit, "Earth Mother and Warrior Goddess," endowed with the contradictory powers to save and to kill (*LiM* 5-6, 9). The terrifying aspects of the Mother Goddess are popularly symbolized in India in her protruding tongue. The association of the goddess's tongue with fear and violence appears in a sudden prolepsis of the final scene of catastrophe at the very beginning of the novel: the narrator sits with the head of a lover on her lap and "the ferrous taste of fear" in her mouth "as though my whole body were tongue" (*LiM* 10). Here, the character Debby seems to merge with the image of the goddess Devi. With an ironical twist, the goddess's tongue lends itself to a double interpretation through a deliberate textual ambivalence when Ham Cohan introduces Devi to her Bio-Mum for the first time, before the mother-daughter relationship is clarified between them. The scene takes place in a designer clothes store near Sacramento, where Devi has been trying different ways of draping a layered "Seven Veils" dress on herself. Jess Du Pree suddenly emerges from behind a rack of caftans and lays a possessive claim on Ham which Ham honours with a "long and hard" kiss. Devi reasserts her presence by announcing who she is without stopping to "check for tongue positions." The "tongue positions" could apply to the middle-aged lovers or also to Devi herself, who enters the fray, tongue first, in the typical style of the goddess Devi (*LiM* 113). This voluntary stepping into Otherness by the narrator is a means of coming to terms with an erased self.

Certain striking images are used to underline this ontological Otherness. For example, the abandoned dog image is interpreted by the adolescent Debby's acquaintance, Wyatt, as "a chance" to be taken, not blown, since his philosophy of life encompassed "the Ultimates" (Love and Death, Kindness and Killing) as sitting side by side (*LiM* 12-13). From then on, Debby tended to unthinkingly identify with "the freakish dog in the pound" (*LiM* 52). In a later flashback, Devi recollects a small-town courthouse scene where the Gray Nuns in India had brought the infant Devi to her mother, but the woman had denied any blood connection whatsoever with the child, before the Judge and the court of law (*LiM* 125; 223-24). The poignancy of this rejection is underlined by the image of pariah puppies suckling "on the saggy tits of a scarred, bony bitch" in the courthouse yard (*LiM* 223). Destiny's "bizarre loops" (*LiM* 233) are further depicted through "the pattern of veins on the inside of my eyelids" (*LiM* 9), which reappears as "familiar veins like snakes squirm across my eyelids" (*LiM* 172). The unpredictability of human trajectories is further referred to by an Indian burger-muncher at McDonald's. For him: "The concept of Karma is that fate is very dynamic [...] when on a dead-end street, jump into alternate paths" (*LiM* 80). Ham Cohan uses earthquakes and fault creep theory to help Devi come to terms with the complexity of identity: "[Ham explained] about creeping and gliding and sliding movements along fault lines, pleasant pressure [...] and then wham, bang, whoa! the Big One breaks the body in two" (*LiM* 223). All these images can be seen as developments of the basic theme of Otherness within the self in *Leave it to Me.*

A voluntary resorting to borrowed Otherness to make sense of human lives is expressed in *Leave it to Me* through a series of allusions to literary and cinematographic texts.[10] For example, Debby experiences satisfaction upon setting fire to her employer-lover Frankie Fong's house in Saratoga Springs. It is a righting of the balance in a cinematographic sense, since the "simple Saratoga secretary" (*LiM* 44) thus achieved an "accomplishment" on the same scale as Frankie Fong's Flash Video series: "A spectacular extravaganza of light, sound, heat. I was an auteur, too" (*LiM* 53). The film producer Ham Cohan, whom Devi meets in San Francisco while he was doing an on-location shooting of an episode for his film series "The Father of his Country," turns out to be an admirer of Frankie Fong's films on Flash (*LiM* 78-79). Ham also mentions Quentin Tarantino as being part of the

Flash Fan Club. Since Tarantino is known for his 1994 film "Pulp Fiction," a thriller about gangsters and violence,[11] this sets the entire novel in the kickboxing extravaganza-blockbuster-Pulp Fiction register, with plenty of special effects.

Devi Dee herself uses a Flash ploy when a thriller writer she escorts for the Media Escort Agency takes her to the Snow White bar run by a former buddy of his from his marine days. Since the barman's "ghost check" of Devi is a little too physically probing, Devi gives him a Flash-style karate chop, inspired from the Flash film "The Sadist from San Diego." But far from producing any conclusive results on the barman, Devi only hurts her palm (*LiM* 193). However, when things really come to the crunch on Ham's house boat in Sausalito, Devi is able to draw on her genes with "violent propensities" and to apply all the Flash series tactics, in order to successfully tumble her serial-killer Bio-Dad by kneeing him, while fusing the meat cleaver he was wielding to her own arm and making it soar and plunge several times into her Bio-Dad's anatomy. The Pulp Fiction-type action of this scene of parricide is highlighted by video-film indications like "FREEZE TAPE" and "TAPE ROLLING" (*LiM* 235). This adds to the melodramatic effect created.

Another striking example of violent action inspired from pulp adventure films is the episode of the Vietnam veteran Loco Larry's sudden shoot-out in a peaceful suburban home garden. On an impulse, Loco Larry decides to play post-apocalypse Robinson Crusoe by burying an arsenal in "a good garden site," intended as a stowing place for "weatherproof storage underground" (*LiM* 170). This reference to Defoe's emblematic, lone survivor tale is like a warning of catastrophes to come. It is not by chance that Francis Ford Coppola's *Apocalypse Now* (1979)[12] features a mad martinet Colonel who withdraws to the hills and fights his own war against the background of the Vietnam war. The film was criticised for being hollow and intellectually empty with scenes of gratuitous violence. This scene in *Leave it to Me*, where an unhinged Vietnam veteran shoots two women in a quiet, suburban setting has a parodic ring in its exaggerated details. The face of the owner of the suburban home after the shooting is described as "a pulpy mess, exploding in record tropical heat like overripe fruit" (*LiM* 172). Parallels with cinema are established through comparisons between "real time" and reel time, in scenes of mayhem (*LiM* 172), and Larry's impression that he was playing a scene "with network cameras rolling" (*LiM* 173).

In a further lowbrow literary allusion, the narrator makes new associations between what had been isolated facts. While attending a public reading by the author of a syrupy romance novel as part of her Media Escort agency job, Devi realizes that the version Jess Du Pree had given Devi of her ultra-erotic experience "with an alien god" in an exotic, tropical desert, linking it to the highbrow poetry of Emily Dickinson, as part of a profound and liberating feeling of physical, spiritual and emotional "wantonness" (*LiM* 155), was, in fact, nothing but a cliché-ridden romance fantasy: "Bio-Mum had scripted her life—and mine—on a romance novel off a rack" (*LiM* 162). Here, the reference is textual and literary, but the effect is the same as with the filmic references: a debunking of solemnity and snobbish exclusiveness with a simultaneous dashing of lofty illusions. On the whole, *Leave it to Me*, with its two major themes of ontological Otherness or identity quest, and Media scripting or borrowed Otherness, together with its final apocalyptic scene of "the sparks flying down like fiery rain, sky hissing into sea" (*LiM* 240) as the Big Quake hits the San Francisco Bay, expresses the difficulties and vicissitudes of achieving Selfness, since the battle has to be waged non-stop until the ultimate moment of annihilation.

In Bharati Mukherjee's most recent novel, *Desirable Daughters* (2002), she explores the Other side of Difference in a paradoxical, irrational way. Gilles Deleuze has defined such illogical trajectories of becoming as "zig-zag lines of flight," since they appear to slalom beyond the constricting poles of selfness and otherness:

> There are lines, which cannot be reduced to the trajectory of a point, and which escape from the structure, lines of flight, becomings, without a future or a past, which resist the binary machine, a becoming-woman which is neither man nor woman, a becoming-animal which is neither beast nor man. Non-parallel evolutions, which do not proceed by differentiation, but which jump from one line to another, between completely heterogeneous beings; cracks, imperceptible breaches which break the ordered lines, even if only to continue elsewhere, leaping across the significant separations [...].
> Not that the two terms [of binary opposition] exchange places, they do not exchange anything at all, but the one can only become Other, if the Other becomes yet again something else, and if the two terms are erased."[13]

We will follow three instances of such zig-zag lines of Becoming beyond Otherness in Mukherjee's rich and complex text, in order to understand its functioning—the patriarchal male characters who embody tradition, certain intertexts, and some of the important female figures. There are three important patriarchal male characters,—the narrator's great-great grandfather Jai Krishna Gangooly (*DD* 6); the narrator's father, Motilal Bhattacharjee (*DD* 32); and Bishwapriya Chatterjee, the man the narrator married in 1983 (*DD* 23). These three male characters can be seen as the structuring elements of the narrator's identity and life, coming as she does from a conservative, patriarchal Bengali

Brahmin background. However, breaches appear in their excercise of patriarchal authority as the text unfolds. For example, Jai Krishna Gangooly failed to father a son until the age of seventy, when in 1909, his ninth wife finally gave birth to a boy (*DD* 19). The paradox is developed further in his link with the narrator: it is not through direct father to son lineage that Jai Krishna Gangooly plays the role of founding pater familias in the novel—his son's daughter was the narrator's maternal grandmother Didima (*DD* 284). So, it is more through daughters and women that Jai Krishna Gangooly stands as the narrator Tara's ancestor. Motilal Bhattacharjee, the narrator's father, plays an ambivalent role. Although an embodiment of conservative tradition, his patriarchal authority is seriously compromised in his failure to beget a son and further in the frustration of his attempts to find an appropriately "suitable boy"[14] for each of his three desirable daughters. In all three cases, Motilal Bhattacharjee's daughters did not correctly honour the age-old Brahminical endogamic tradition. Further, Motilal Bhattacharjee's own decision to withdraw to the mountains for greater spiritual seclusion, after having completed his paternal householder's duties, in due conformity with the Brahminical norms and prescriptions, is ridiculed and criticized. First of all, irony can be perceived in the discrepancy between the ascetic claims and aspirations of Motilal Bhattacharjee [his refusal of a phone connection in his mountain abode (*DD* 292)] and the large number of servants and other material comforts he arranges for in that remote region (*DD* 296). In addition, Motilal's wife is under no illusions about the so-called spiritual benefits of "giving up life's good things" (*DD* 297). She is convinced that looking at the hills and making pilgrimages are not indispensible to experience God (*DD* 302). Her down-to-earth attitude constrasts strongly with Motilal's attempts at other-worldliness. And yet, Tara moves beyond anger in the face of her father's authoritarian behaviour throughout, unlike her eldest sister who bore him a lifelong grudge (*DD* 179, 182, 230). After her harrowing experience of seeing her house in San Francisco go up in flames and her ex-husband severely injured, Tara visited India and stopped in Rishikesh, together with her 15-year old son, Rabi, simply in order to be with her parents for a while (*DD* 293). That she bears no bitterness against her father is evident in her accepting to go through his family book collection with him in the company of Rabi (*DD* 305), and in her savouring of the complicity between her father and her son (*DD* 303).

In the case of Bishwapriya Chatterjee, also, a zig-zag trajectory can be traced, endowing him with individual depth, beyond manichean positionings. Astonishingly, Bishwapriya remains firmly attached to the Brahminical normative ideal of Dharma or duty, a cut and dried blueprint for material and spiritual felicity, despite his Americanization and acquisition of vast wealth. Based on a "hoard of inherited confidence," preserved among Bengali Brahmins from Calcutta, he acts on the unshakeable conviction that "everything Bish Chatterjee did was best" (*DD* 44). However, so much undiluted male brilliance and wealth, with ultra-traditional demands on her as the dutiful wife and mother, led Tara to seek a divorce from him (*DD* 82). His sole feeling of failure, then, stems from his lack of success in his "fundamental duty" to "support and sustain his marriage" (*DD* 265). His overdetermined commitment to Dharma and duty only rings in Tara's ears as "the Hindu version of some born-again cult" (*DD* 267). The paradoxical turn comes in his self-sacrificing saving of Tara, when her house explodes in a burst of flame. Tara emerges from the crisis relatively unscathed, while her conservative, high-flyer, ex-husband comes out of it with a lifelong hobble, permanent breathlessness and damaged vocal cords. He bears these enormous personal set backs as merely "distressing, but somehow, divinely ordained" (*DD* 278-79). This exceptional fortitude can be understood as a Deleuzian line of flight reinterpretation of the age-old, optimistic belief of non-Brahminical and Brahminical Hinduism in the inevitable rebuilding of the cosmos, after wrecking (*DD* 279). This re-reading of orthodox Hindu precepts seems to lie somewhere in-between hard-line Brahminical traditionalism and eclectic Westernized progressivism, while including popular, non-Brahminical Hindu beliefs as well.

The use of a series of intertexts in *Desirable Daughters* can be seen as a deliberate attempt by the narrator to incorporate myths and symbols from varied horizons in order to make sense of contemporary, diasporic experience. The exploration of Difference can be observed in the inclusion of motifs and poetical images from strange cultural backgrounds. The most striking example is that of the sea-monster known as the Kraken, slumbering in the ocean's depths, only to suddenly awaken without warning, provoked by a fire: "Then once by man and angels to be seen,/ In roaring he shall rise and on the surface die." These lines from Tennyson's poem entitled "The Kraken" are quoted by Ronald Dey in a letter to the narrator, Tara. They play the role of "gloomy auguries" in the text (*DD* 132). Indeed, the legend of this awesome monster is borrowed from Nordic mythology where it was used by sailors to warn against dangerous currents that could engulf unsuspecting ships, such hazardous spots being taken to indicate the likely presence of the terrifying Kraken below the surface of the ocean.[15] In Mukherjee's novel the Kraken can be associated with the spectre of international terrorism that rears its ugly head in the person of the false Christopher Dey. In an interesting extension, the narrator uses Tennyson's line "from many a wondrous grot and secret cell" to denounce the smugness of Brahminical privilege, which she likens to "the darkest cave," thereby associating the discriminating feeling of superiority that comes of birth and breeding, with the latent destructive power of the Kraken. The monster appears again in the text when Tara hears of Ron Dey's sudden death in a car crash in Bombay, linking the idea of the Kraken irrevocably to terror and tragedy (*DD* 248).

A desire to overcome the fear of catastrophe is discernible in an implicit association between an apparently random reference to W.B. Yeats's poem "The Lake Isle of Innisfree" and the "hideous ball of orange and purple fire" that consumed Tara's home and maimed her ex-husband (*DD* 205, 271). However, in "The Lake Isle of Innisfree," the image of "There midnight's all a glimmer, and noon a purple glow" is situated in an idyllic, peaceful setting ("small cabin," "bee-loud glade," "lake water lapping with low sounds by the shore"), whereas the "orange and purple fire" in the novel is the instrument of destruction, unfurled in all likelihood by terrorists targeting the too-successful Bishwapriya Chatterjee. The incongruous connection between the two images remains a bare, unexplained suggestion, and leaves the door open to multiple interpretations.

A similar link can be established with a passing mention of Yeats's poem "Among School Children," in which the line "How can we know the dancer from the dance?" appears.[16] Indeed, an echo of this line can be traced in Tara's father's statement: "God pulls our strings, we dance the dance" (*DD* 205, 304). However, the contexts of the two lines seem to have nothing in common. In Yeats's poem, the reference can be understood to be to the composite wholeness of natural beauty and wisdom, embodied in the chestnut tree, a body dancing and the "brightening glance" of a poet or artist. These seem to defy analysis or any rational attempt to separate "the dancer from the dance." The source of the beauty, wisdom or artistic inspiration remains an unexplainable mystery, and does not appear to necessarily spring from any external, transcendental source. In contrast to this, Motilal Bhattacharjee's sententious pronouncement seems to harbour no doubt as to the teleology of God's influence on human lives and appears as a reproachful reminder to Tara of the need for humility and submission, as opposed to her too great liking for independence. It reads then as an instance of difference between the father and the daughter, the former clinging to tradition and religious orthodoxy, while the latter seems to be exploring the avenues of change and new ways of thinking, present in Yeats's poem. The strong contrast between the two approaches can be perceived as subversive or deliberately ironical.

Another chain of intertexts coalesces around the character Andras Karolyi, Tara's Hungarian lover. He plays the role of alter-ego to the conquering, Brahminical hero, Bishwapriya Chatterjee (*DD* 77). Andy's profession is retrofitting which entails detecting earthquake faults and reinforcing houses to make them as earthquake-proof as possible. Andy's earthquake fault theory functions as a trope for identifiable and unidentifiable dangers, expressed in the acronyms PIFL and PUFL (*DD* 92, 127).[17] In addition, he is a Zen Buddhist and practises massage and Oriental meditation. This gives Andy a world-view that is different from the more frequently encountered world-views of Christianity and Hinduism (*DD* 148-50). He also adopts the Buddhist manner of formulating fables and parables to deal with problems, great and small (*DD* 149-50). This makes his interventions function like a contrapuntal intertext in relation to the main narrative. He conceptualizes conflicts (as, for example, the threat posed to Tara by the false Christopher Dey) as simply part of the ongoing existence of the universe and therefore to be ignored. An image Andy uses to understand a sudden crisis is a rubbing against each other of tectonic plates with the possibility of either of the sides, in friction, suddenly gaining the upper hand in an unpredictable burst of violence (*DD* 127). He attaches importance to what is not visible (*DD* 47, 49). The overall result is that thanks to his adherence to Zen wisdom, Andy moves in a "different groove" distinct from the other characters and he is proud of his out-of-step difference: "He was always a few beats behind everyone else, and that was the way he liked it" (*DD* 168). However, Tara cannot always follow the advice he gives her (for example, "Step away from it," or "Let it go," (*DD* 91, 279), not being a Zen Buddhist herself, and being more implicated in the events than Andy.

Thus, intertexts weave difference into the text by introducing images and symbols from varied fields and cultures.

This brings us to certain female figures who also incorporate a note of difference into the text, embodying a counter-current to the mainstream of its layout. Among the female figures in *Desirable Daughters*, there are several Hindu goddesses. They seem to represent the supernatural realm that exceeds human rationality. Apart from Adya Ma, the primeval fertility goddess revered in Bengal (*DD* 69), Shitala Devi, the goddess associated with small pox and malaria, most often by non-Brahmin castes, (*DD* 13, 57), and the goddess Shakti or the female energy of the Hindu Godhead (*DD* 295), three virtuous wives of Hindu myths are mentioned together: Sita, Savitri and Behula (*DD* 134).

The most intriguing Hindu goddess in the novel is undoubtedly the goddess Manasha. Her association with venomous snakebites is corroborated by epithets like "Cobra Deity" (*DD* 29) and "Queen of Snakes" (*DD* 304). Paradoxically, this goddess in her familiar cobra-form seems to be an ingenious way of rendering mishaps and set backs into echoes of some far greater terror, thereby making them less terrifying and more acceptable (*DD* 149-50). Thus, it need not seem bizarre that she should be considered responsible for the death of the Tree Bride's adolescent husband in 1879 (*DD* 11-13). The terrorist

Abbas Sattar Hai, who posed as the narrator's nephew and finally blew up her house with explosives is understood by Tara's father to have been "a form of goddess Manasha, perhaps, the ever-opportunistic snake goddess, who can slither into any space, over or under any barrier" (*DD* 304). This makes possible the acceptance of all experience, pleasant and unpleasant, as part of "some larger destiny" (*DD* 304). The mention in the novel of an apparently contradictory popular aphorism "Bishey Bish Khai" or "the only antidote for poison is poison," supposed to contain an irrefutable nugget of ancient wisdom, can be perceived in several ways: for example, as a means of making "connections on the cosmic level" or as an ironical denunciation of a too-convenient evacuation through myth of all that is difficult to explain or accept ("a cosmic pun waiting for a punch line") (*DD* 304). However, the very existence of popular, non-Brahminical folklore about such "an insecure and therefore demanding goddess," half-mortal and half-goddess or half-sage (since her human mother is reputed to have been sired by either the god Shiva or the sage Kashyapa) which attempts to rationally explain the irrational entry of any venom or unexpected pain into human lives, has to be acknowledged as a fascinating invention (*DD* 304).

The retrieval of the little known "history" of the freedom fighting activities of the narrator's great grand-aunt, the Tree Bride or child widow, Tara Lata Gangooly (1874-1944), instates her as an emblematic female figure of the novel, especially since the first and last chapters are about her. They can be read as homage to the resilience of Indian women despite or perhaps because of constant oppression and marginalization by the male-dominated, patriarchal system of all of Indian society, since time immemorial. Here again, simplistic binary opposition is circumvented through a Deleuzian zig-zag line of flight. Difference and even misfortune become an opportunity for the summoning of "new energy" thanks to discipline and self-knowledge (*DD* 280). The narrative of the Tree-Bride's anti-Raj political action despite her never having left her father's house in all her seventy years of existence, until the British "dragged her off to jail" where she "had been killed" (*DD* 289), seems to be an illustration of the narrator Tara's realization that "ordinary lives enclose an extraordinary kernel" (*DD* 279). Paradoxically, it is through her political martyrdom and death that this unacknowledged woman in Mishtigunj, "the poorest place on earth" (*DD* 17) achieved an unbelievable feat: she "gradually changed the world." A commemorative plaque erected in Mishtingunj, by the Government of what became in 1947 East Pakistan, "in the name of all its citizens, whatever God they may worship" (*DD* 20), acknowledges the services of this defenceless Hindu widow on the same level as such renowned Freedom Fighters as the "hated Mahatma Gandhi" and the "martyred Subhas Bose" (*DD* 289). An amazing reversal of what at first sight could appear as simply a tragic destiny. Not only was she able to rise above her family and her community, but she also left an inspiring mark among people of religions other than her own, in a nation that became partitioned from what had been her nation. It is in this reaching out across boundaries that she can be understood to have "changed the world" (*DD* 17).

The narrator Tara's own trajectory can also be read as a journey through the other side of Difference. The entire novel comes over as an attempt by Tara to explore her own individuality and acknowledge her difference from her two sisters, her family and her community. This is underlined by the repetition in varying versions of a nursery rhyme: "We are sisters three/ as alike as three blossoms on one flowering tree" (*DD* 16, 21, 23, 266). The greatly differing choices and outlooks of the three sisters illustrate that a sameness of desh or place of origin and of family genes does not in any way guarantee similar experiences through life. In Tara's case it is after many ups and down, including a divorce, a roots search and a fire that nearly caused her death, that she arrives at a realization of what her true vocation might be—to tell stories in order to bear "witness to dying traditions," to mark "the value of a passing moment," to acknowledge "groups marked for extinction," simply because of their beauty (*DD* 280). And thus, the reader is made a witness to the birth of a writer in the very unfolding of the text. A significant motif seals this very personal choice—the unmarked trail, or "shanko" in Bengali, which appears on the first and last pages (*DD* 3, 310). Beyond the permanent structures and paved roads lies "the muddy shanko between rice paddies and flooded ponds," which "finally disappears into a distant wall of impenetrable jungle" (*DD* 3). The courageous decision to pick a way through such uncharted territory seems to be indicated in the epigraph of the novel: "No one behind, no one ahead./ The path the ancients cleared has closed./ And the other path, everyone's path,/ Easy and wide, goes nowhere./ I am alone and find my way." It is perhaps telling that this epigraph was initially a Sanskrit verse, which was adapted by Octavio Paz, and translated (into English) by Eliot Weinberger. In this third-hand version, this bold choice can be interpreted as a stepping out of rigid, sclerosed tradition, through the very means used by tradition to perpetrate itself, in a voluntary zig-zag line of flight.

To conclude, this study of Bharati Mukherjee's six novels and two collections of short stories can only bring us to an open-ended conclusion since all her fictional creations seem to be centred around Otherness and Difference. They all appear to illustrate what Emmanuel Lévinas calls "dialogic thought" where the questioning is more important than the answer, since it opens on to an awakening to the Other within the Self, and an awareness of the plural infinity of meaning, that always did, does and always will exceed rational understanding.[18] This results in a new kind of subjectivity that refuses the contented satisfaction of Being and self-awareness, since it involves a paradoxical, ongoing process of self-renewal through an ever-deepening relationship with the unknowable difference of Otherness.[19] Mukherjee's literary writings thus tend towards stepping beyond "the stifling monologues of Self and Other" and "the orderly discourses" of the bourgeois subject and traditional societies,[20] in a dynamic impulse of the imagination that suggests the simultaneous evolution of different realities and selves.

Notes

1. I would like to acknowledge here the support I have received from Christine Lorre of the University of Paris 3 in the preparation of this paper.
2. Stuart Hall, "Cultural Identity and Diaspora," *Colonial Discourse and Post-Colonial Theory—A Reader*, eds. Patrick Williams and Laura Chrisman (New York: Columbia UP, 1994) 395.
3. Abdul R. Jan Mohamed, "The Economy of Manichean Allegory: the Function of Racial Difference in Colonialist Literature," *Critical Inquiry* 12.1 (Autumn 1985): 58-87. See pp. 65, 69, 78.
4. See Ania Loomba, *Colonialism/Postcolonialism* (London: Routledge, 1998) 104-23.
5. Bharati Mukherjee, "A Four-Hundred Year-Old Woman," *The Writer on her Work-II*, ed. Janet Sternburg (New York: Norton, 1992) 33-38, esp. 38.
6. See Judie Newman, "The Madwoman in the Motel," *The Ballistic Bard-Postcolonial Fictions* (London: Arnold, 1995) 144-72, esp. 160.
7. See Judie Newman, "madwoman," for a detailed and illuminating analysis of the incidence of chaos theory in Bharati Mukherjee's novel *Jasmine*, esp. 150-69.
8. See my article "The Paradoxical Position of an Immigrant Writer: Bharati Mukherjee, neither Global nor Particular?" *The Global and the Particular in the English-speaking World*, ed. Jean-Pierre Durix (Dijon: Editions Universitaires de Dijon, 2002) 67-77, for a study of other intertextual aspects of *The Holder of the World*.
9. Rupert Brooke, "The Soldier," *The Poetical Works of Rupert Brooke*, ed. Geoffrey Keynes (London: Faber & Faber, 1946) 23. "If I should die, think only this of me:/ That there's some corner of a foreign field/ That is forever England. There shall be/ In that rich earth a richer dust concealed;/ A dust whom England bore, shaped, made aware,/ Gave, once, her flowers to love, her ways to roam,/ A body of England's, breathing English air,/ Washed by the rivers, blest by suns of home.... Etc.
10. See my article "Immigrant writer" esp. 75, for other intertextual aspects of *Leave it to Me*.
11. John Walker, ed. *Halliwell's Film & Video Guide* (London: Harper Collins, 1997) 604.
12. John Walker, ed. *Film & Video* 33.
13. Gilles Deleuze, Claire Parnet, *Dialogues* (Paris: Champs Flammarion, 1996) 34, 88. (Translation into English, mine.)
14. An allusion is made, here, to Vikram Seth's bestseller novel *A Suitable Boy* (London: Phoenix, 1993), which, among other things, features the arranged marriage system in India.

15. See *Chambers's Encyclopaedia*, vol. 6 (London: Georges Newnes, 1955) 255. The Kraken is reported to have been first described in a published text, by the Norwegian Bishop Pontoppidan, in 1750.
16. W.B. Yeats, *The Poems*, Collection: Everyman's Library, ed. Daniel Albright (London: David Campbell Publishers, 1992) 261-63. AMONG SCHOOL CHILDREN, Stanza VIII: "Labour is blossoming or dancing where/ The body is not bruised to pleasure soul,/ Nor beauty born out of its own despair,/ Nor blear-eyed wisdom out of midnight oil./ O chestnut tree, great-rooted blossomer,/ Are you the leaf, the blossom or the bole?/ O body swayed to music, O brightening glance,/ How can we know the dancer from the dance?" (1927).
17. *Desirable Daughters* 92: "A PIFL is a Previously Identified Fault Line." [...] "A PUFL, a Previously Unidentified Fault Line, is a killer."
18. Emmanuel Lévinas, *Dieu, la Mort et le Temps* (Paris: Grasset, Collection: Le livre de Poche, Biblio Essais, 1993) "Le Même et l'Autre": 160-65.
19. Emmanuel Lévinas, *De Dieu qui Vient à l'Idée*, (Paris: J. Vrin, 1982) "La Pensée et l'Etre et la Question de l'Autre": 173-88.
20. See Kumkum Sangari, "The Politics of the Possible," *Cultural Critique* (Minneapolis: U of Minnesota P, 1987) 157-86, esp. 186.

A BHARATHI MUKHERJEE BIBLIOGRAPHY

Primary Sources

Novels

The Tiger's Daughter. Boston: Houghton Mifflin, 1971; New York: Fawcett Crest (Ballantine), 1992.

Wife. Boston: Houghton Mifflin, 1975; New York: Fawcett Crest (Ballantine), 1992.

Jasmine. New York: Grove Weidenfield, 1989; London: Virago Press, 1991.

The Holder of the World. New York: Alfred A. Knopf, 1993.

Leave it to Me. New York: Alfred A. Knopf, 1997; London: Chatto & Windus, 1997.

Desirable Daughters. New York: Hyperion, 2002.

Short Stories

Darkness. Markham Ont.: Penguin Books Canada, 1985; New York: Fawcett Crest (Ballantine), 1992.

The Middleman & Other Stories. New York: Grove Press, 1988; London: Virago Press, 1992.

Non-fictional Works

(a) In collaboration with Clark Blaise

Blaise, Clark & Bharati Mukherjee. *Days & Nights in Calcutta*. New York: Doubleday, 1977.

____. *The Sorrow & the Terror: the Haunting Legacy of the Air India Tragedy*. Markham Ont.: Penguin Books, Canada, 1987.

____. "After the Fatwa; Publish & Perish." *Mother Jones* 15:3 (April-May 1990). 28-31; 61-65.

(b) Other Non-fictional Writings

"An Invisible Woman." *Saturday Night* March 1981: 36-40.

"Mimicry & Reinvention." *Proceedings of the 2nd Triennial Conference of the Canadian Association of Commonwealth Literature,* held at the University of Winnipeg in October 1981. Ed. Uma Parmeswaran. Calcutta: Lal, 1983: 147-57.

Boyers, Robert and Bharati Mukherjee. "A Conversation with V.S. Naipaul." *Salmagundi* 54 (Fall 1981): 4-22.

"Writers of the Indian Commonwealth." *Literary Review* 29-4 (Summer 1986): 400-01.

"Immigrant Writing: Give us your maximalists!" *New York Times Book Review* 28 Aug. 1988: 1, 28-29.

"Talking Cures." *The Nation* 247-17 (5 Dec. 1988): 620-22.

"Prophet & Loss: Salman Rushdie's Migration of Souls." *Village Voice Literary Supplement* 72 (March 1989): 9-12.

"A Four-Hundred year-old Woman." *The Writer on Her Work-II: New Essays in New Territory.* Ed. Janet Sternburg. New York & London: Norton, 1919: 33-38.

"Love Me or Leave Me." *Visions of America: Personal Narratives from the Promised Land, A Multicultural Anthology of Autobiography & Essay.* Eds. Wesley Brown & Amy Ling. New York: Persea Books, 1993. 187-94.

"Beyond Multiculturism [sic]: Surviving the Nineties." Iowa City: Iowa Humanities Board, 1994.

"Two Ways to Belong in America." *The New York Times* 22 Sept. 1996.

Secondary Sources

Books of Criticism on Bharati Mukherjee

Alam, Fakrul. *Bharati Mukherjee,* New York: Twayne, 1996.

Dhawan, R.K., ed. *The Fiction of Bharati Mukherjee: A Critical Symposium.* New Delhi: Prestige, 1996.

Nelson, Emmanuel S., ed. *Bharati Mukherjee: Critical Perspectives.* New York: Garland, 1993.

Critical Works in which Bharati Mukherjee is discussed

Bardolphe, Jacqueline, ed. *Short Fiction in the New Literatures in English.* Nice: Faculté des Lettres & Sciences Humaines, 1989. 189-96.

Bharucha, Nilufer & Vilas Sarang, eds. *Indian-English Fiction: 1980-1990, an Assessment.* New World Literatures Series: 77. New Delhi: B.R. Publishing Corporation, 1994. 105-14 : 139-50.

Nelson, Emmanuel S., ed. *Reworlding: The Literature of the Indian Diaspora.* Westport, Connecticut: Greenwood Press, 1992. 35-49; 51-61.

Newman, Judie. *The Ballistic Bard: Postcolonial Fictions.* London & New York: Arnold, 1995. 144-72.

Prasad, Madhusudan, ed. *Indian English Novelists.* New Delhi: Sterling, 1982. 71-86.

Ross, Robert, ed. *International Literatures in English: Essays on the Major Writers.* New York: Garland Press, 1991. 487-500.

Articles on Bharati Mukherjee

Carb, Alison B. "An Interview with Bharati Mukherjee." *The Massachussetts Review* 29-4 (1988): 645-54.

Chanda, Tirthankar. "Talking to Bharati Mukherjee." *Commonwealth Essays & Studies* 18-2 (Spring 1996) Dijon: Editions Universitaires de Dijon: 56-62.

Connell, Michael, Jessie Grearson and Tom Grimes. "An Interview with Bharati Mukherjee." *Iowa Review* 20-3 (1990): 18-29.

D'souza, Florence. "The Perception of the Self in Bharati Mukherjee's *Jasmine.*" *Commonwealth Studies & Essays* 17-1 (Autumn 1994): 10-17.

____. "Crossing Borders in Bharati Mukherjee's *The Middleman & Other Stories.*" *Journal of the Short Story in English* 27 (Autumn 1996): 68-82.

____. "The Paradoxical Position of an Immigrant Writer: Bharati Mukherjee, neither Global nor Particular?" *The Global and the Particular in the English-Speaking World.* Ed. Jean-Pierre Durix. Dijon: Editions Universitaires de Dijon, 2002. 67-77.

____. "The Americanization of an Immigrant Writer: Bharati Mukherjee." *Journal of Literature & Aesthetics.* Ed. S. Sreenivasan. (July-Dec. 2002) (to be published).

Jain, Jasbir. "Foreignness of the Spirit: the World of Bharati Mukherjee's Novels." *The Journal of Indian Writing in English* 13-2 (1985): 12-19.

Jussawalla, Feroza. "Chiffon Saris: the Plight of South Asian Immigrants in the New World." *The Massachussetts Review* 29-4 (1988): 583-95.

Levin, Martin et al. "Bharati Mukherjee." *Contemporary Literary Criticism.* Volume 53. Detroit: Gale, 1989. 261-72.

Mandel, Ann. "Bharati Mukherjee." *Dictionary of Literary Biography.* Volume 60. Detroit: Gale, 1986. 266-69.

Nazareth, Peter. "Total Vision." *Canadian Literature* 110 (Fall 1986): 184-91.

Nelson, Emmanuel S. "Kamala Markandaya, Bharati Mukherjee and the Indian Immigrant Experience." *The Toronto South Asian Review* 9-2 (Winter 1991): 1-9.

Rajan, Gita. "Bharati Mukherjee (1940-)." *Writers of the Indian Diaspora: a Bio-Bibliographical Critical Sourcebook*. Ed. Emmanuel S. Nelson. Westport, Connecticut: Greenwood Press, 1993. 235-42.

Sant-Wade, Arvindra & Karen Marguerite Radell. "Refashioning the Self: Immigrant Women in Bharati Mukherjee's New World." *Studies in Short Fiction* 29-1 (Winter 1992): 11-17.

Wickramagamage, Carmen. "Relocation as a Positive Act: the Immigrant Experience in Bharati Mukherjee's Novels." *Diaspora* 2-2 (1992): 171-200.

10

Shashi Deshpande

JASBIR JAIN

Shashi Deshpande (born 1938) is one of those writers whose work reflects the whole gamut of Indian cultural issues. Deshpande began writing late and moved to fiction after an apprenticeship in journalism and short story writing. Besides five collections of short stories—*The Legacy*, 1971, *It Was Dark* and *It Was the Nightingale* both in 1986, *The Miracle* and *Intrusion and Other Stories* in 1993 and *The Stone Women* in 2000, she has published eight novels, two of which are suspense novels. She has also written four novels for children.

Her first novel to be published was *The Dark Holds No Terrors* in 1980. This was followed by *If I Die Today* in 1982, a short novella dealing with death and *Roots and Shadows* in 1983 which is the story of Indu's inheritance. *That Long Silence* followed in 1988 and two novels, *The Binding Vine* and *Come Up and Be Dead* both appeared in 1993. Her two recent novels are *A Matter of Time* (1996) and *Small Remedies* (2000). The dates of publication of the middle novels are not necessarily the dates of their composition. I have a feeling that *If I Die*, *Come Up and Be Dead* and *Roots and Shadows* were written earlier than what the publication dates indicate, and form a phase of transition from short stories and detective fiction to her later novels. She has gone on record saying that *Roots and Shadows* was completed in 1978 while *The Dark Holds No Terrors* in 1979.

Deshpande's work can easily be singled out from amongst other writers writing in English on several counts. The thickly populated world of her novels, the joint families, the working out of relationships within families and marriages, the fine insight into human character, her boldness in the treatment of sex and sexuality and crossing of caste and class barriers. Her work is not restricted to the urban middle class, instead she explores the lives of people who barely manage to survive within the norms of respectability and households which lack modern facilities and sophistication. The urban lower classes are projected as human beings and not merely as servants to be accommodated in their roles.

All her novels to date work through a feminine consciousness, Saru in *The Dark Holds No Terrors*, Indu in *Roots and Shadows*, Jaya in *The Long Silence*, Urmi in *The Binding Vine*, Sumi in *A Matter of Time* and Madhu in *Small Remedies*. The two detective novels also have women narrators, Manju in *If I Die Today* and Devi is the dominant voice in *Come Up and Be Dead*. There is no attempt at selecting a male protagonist but equally there is no attempt at focusing only on the feminine perspective. Women narrators transcend their gender in order to explore the male psyche and avoid stereotypical projections of patriarchal structures. Their inbuilt compulsions are presented with compassion and understanding.

Loss through death, bereavement, awareness of mortality—these form one main strand in her novels. Another trope is that of guilt—guilt at role-deviation, the guilt of loss and of failure. Between these two tropes of guilt and bereavement the author works out her sensitive analysis of the institution of family and marriage, the prioritising of the male child, gender constraints, the psychology of unfulfilled dreams and the historicity of the present.

The Dark Holds No Terrors opens with Saru coming home after nearly fifteen years. The news of her mother's death has brought her home. Saru is a doctor, married and with two children but she has not been able to shake off the fears of the past or the guilt which has been thrust upon her ever since the death of her young sibling, Dhruva.

There is the guilt for not being the male child her mother so much loved, and also the guilt that she failed to respond immediately to Dhruva's call for help. Things are never the same after that. Saru feels neglected and estranged, and also rebellious. Her marriage to Manu is one such act of rebellion and the mother's attitude has been unyielding and unforgiving. This homecoming is significant from many aspects. There is a need to belong, to pay homage to her dead mother, to reach out to her living father. And in this there is a desire to build relationships in order to forget the fears of the past. Also it is an act of choice. When she comes home, an adult woman, she has come back not merely to bridge the differences, but also to claim her rightful place within her parental home.

Saru, whose marriage is under stress at this particular time because of a successful career which evokes her husband's jealousy, has come back partly also in order to work her way toward recovery and rehabilitation.

Her mother had died of cancer and had been ill for more than a couple of years. During this period she had time enough to summon her daughter, forgive her and claim her as her own. But she did none of these things. She even forbade her husband from informing Saru. Thus Saru's return home is also a test of her father's loyalty to her mother's memory. How and in what manner will he relate to her becomes an important issue in itself.

The silences between the two are rendered bearable by several things. Her father recedes quietly into the background, accepts her as she is; Madhav, a student whom they had taken on as a tenant, is another softening factor. The presence of a third person introduces justification for the routine activity in the house.

Saru's father is also a foil to the character of Manu. He is gentle and soothing. And Saru finds that he has adopted the role of the housekeeper with remarkable ease, in order to meet the exigencies of his life. The relationship with Madhav is any easy one.

The 'dark' of the title is her own past, her memories of childhood, the fifteen-year estrangement, the sense of having been abandoned and the fears of her subconscious mind. As she relives these years in the fragmented family on her return, she is exorcising the ghosts of the past.

The novel works around three main strands of thought the first of which is problematising of the institution of family, the second of the syndrome of the male child and the third of Saru's coming to terms with her own self. As the narrative opens out both time and reflection play an equal role in helping her sort out her fears, apprehensions, aversions and uncertainties. In this both her father and Madhav play an important role. The man whom she has always considered feeble is in fact gentle and tolerant. As she goes over the past she realises that he had always supported her unobtrusively, silently and unconditionally. He had been the one who had supported her desire for higher studies and sent her to the medical college. And yet it had seemed to her that his silence accused her as much as her mother's open hostility.

Motherhood is not valorised in Deshpande's novels. In fact mother–daughter relationships are perpetually under question. In this novel as well as in *A Matter of Time*, the *Binding Vine* and *Small Remedies* the conventional idea of motherhood is subjected to scrutiny. Part of the problem arises with a mother's love for a male child as in *The Dark Holds No Terrors*, and part in the conflict between the need to be independent and free *vis-à-vis* the totalising claims of motherhood. Also in some measure it comes to rest on the mother–daughter relationship where domineering mothers destroy their daughters.

Through this mother–daughter relationship the woman to woman relationship is problematised across generations. It is a complex, protective, empathising relationship. All women are not at loggerheads, all of them are not obsessed by the need for a male child nor is the relationship with a girl child constrained by gender relationships. Families are built on marriages which are heterosexual. And the equation between the husband–wife becomes crucial in determining the mother–

child relationship. Indu in *Roots and Shadows* is the only one of her heroines who is motherless and has no memories of her mother. All other women have a love–hate relationship with their mothers whether it be Saru (*The Dark Holds No Terrors*) or Sumi's relationship with her mother on one hand and her daughters on the other (*A Matter of Time*), or Urmi's with her mother in *The Binding Vine* or Savitri bai's with her daughter in *Small Remedies.*

There are very few same sex siblings except in *A Matter of Time* but there are friendships between sisters and sisters-in-laws as in *The Binding Vine.* Thus the contextualising of a woman within a male world is central to Deshpande's concern. Men, as they represent different kinds of masculinity, are indispensable to her world. In *The Dark Holds No Terror* three different kinds are projected. Saru's father who is gentle and withdrawn, Madhav who is caught between personal and family loyalties and Manohar, a failed romantic whose failure takes a violent form.

He reflects the quiet, meditative man who does not necessarily consider that masculinity needs to be demonstrated through aggression. He is the equivalent of a sage, a non-worldly man who deviates from the accepted behaviour patterns in his own way. He does not interfere with the mother–daughter relationship, his routine is set, his interest in his grandchildren is non-worldly and controlled. He does not frame his wife's photograph and hang a garland around it as is done in most Indian houses with the portraits of the dead. His taking up the household chores in this two-man household is absolutely natural for this ascetic man. He is not obsessed with womanly duties but only with the bare minimum necessary for survival. And he becomes the confidant for his grown up daughter, something which his wife could never become.

Madhav temporarily becomes the younger brother Saru had lost. When Madhav is called back home to help trace his lost brother, Saru begins to realise how the individual's right to personhood is thwarted at every point. Saru herself has had to fight for everything for her right to her parents' attention, her individuality, her job, even her beauty and has had to constantly struggle with her feelings of inadequacy. This struggle has made her both bitter and angry. It is during this period which she spends with her father that she is able to get rid of the resentment she has felt against her grieving mother. She learns to grows into the role of a housekeeper and carries her medical knowledge lightly as she attends to the claims of her neighbours.

It is, when Madhav is summoned home, that the father and daughter find themselves without any buffer between them. The two of them are left alone to sort out the past, to apportion blame, to sit on judgment, to confess and to discuss her marriage. It is for the first time that the father and daughter really learn to talk or to listen to each other. The resentment and the withdrawal are partially done with, and replaced by a new sense of self-awareness. Yet there is no miraculous restoration. It is a slow, painful process of self-realisation.

Roots and Shadows is, in many ways, a different kind of novel. Indu, the rebel who has married of her own choice, has a job and lives in the city, is suddenly summoned to her great-aunt's deathbed. Indu suddenly finds herself the heiress of her great-aunt and the centre of the various family claimants. The joint household has an assortment of relatives and dependents. Several of its members have moved out for personal reasons. Indu's own father makes only an occasional appearance and one of her uncles stays in the city. But those who stay at home have to bear all the burden. They are like permanent features and are expected to offer refuge and hospitality to the rest of the nomadic population.

Indu's great aunt Akka is a childless widow who has earned her wealth through fidelity to her old husband in an unequal marriage. She has survived through the relationship as if through a punishment, but in the end has gained her strength from it.

Thus both family and marriage are problematised. But this house bustling with life, and four generations of family members throws up other issues—issues related to kinship patterns, individual freedom, familial support and the dictates of tradition. Indu's cousin Mini has no other choice available to her except to get married according to her parents' wishes. And in this new relationship, more than the man it is the status of a married woman which has become important to her. Indu finds that her sympathies for her are mislaid.

This is one novel where death does not leave that lingering sense of bereavement which inhabits her other novels. And when in a brief moment of sympathy Indu slips into a relationship with Naren, she doesn't brood over it. There is no feeling of guilt despite this adulterous lapse. Instead Indu learns to take a rational stand where her marriage with Jayant is concerned. She realises that the romance which inhabits the minds of women enslaves them and that as an individual, she has a right to her own body.

Indu has inherited both Akka's indomitable courage and shrewd judgment. The only one of her heroines to be an heiress, Indu reinforces the feminine inheritance in more way than one. She handles the family's affairs firmly, decides to ignore the many pressures being exerted upon her and decides to sell the house. This dislocation rather than be an uprooting experience becomes a liberating one as the sprawling family is forced to come to terms with its feuds, jealousies and exploitations of each other.

It is also a liberating experience for Indu as she decides to get out of the romantic submission to Jayant and to make space for herself within her marriage, to do what she really wants to do rather than constantly bow to the necessities of the household.

There is a kind of intense human quality about the family. The ordinary people acquire depth as their lives are unfolded in the various communications, dialogues and confessions shared with Indu. Old Uncle, a distant cousin of the family, lives with them and has readily been accepted by the family. But his grandson Naren continues to be an outsider. Later in the novel, Naren dies a death by drowning, unloved and uncared for except by old Uncle and Indu. Naren symbolises all that is rebellious, free and deviant. His personality attracts Indu in several ways and his death leaves them uncertain as to whether it was an accident or a suicide.

Indu's ambition for developing a career in writing is shared by Jaya, the narrator of *That Long Silence.* The four part novel is about Jaya's questioning of herself and her relationship with her husband Mohan, who in order to escape from the restrictive life of poverty moves from modest aspirations to still higher ones and in this process of social climbing gets involved in some shady deals. In order to become unavailable for sometime Mohan and Jaya move into an old flat which Jaya had inherited. This forced retreat into the past, into the chawl-like flat lets loose all past ghosts, memories, and claims of relationships; it places them simultaneously amidst helping hands as well as inquisitive eyes, forcing them to take measure of themselves.

The past as it unfolds itself carries images of large families, endless pregnancies and endless deprivation, the constant and brutal use of a woman's body and death in waiting as both the fertile and the barren women die. Male insensitivity and brutality, with men showering all their frustration on the women, also become evident. Within this chaotic existence, the one stable factor is a woman's wifehood which is considered a necessary sanctuary and a blessing camouflaging within it all its hidden miseries, conflicts and the uncomplaining burden which women carry.

The novel begins at a point of crisis, mid-way between the nominal attainment of middle class successes and a return to the earlier life style and travels through the past. As Jaya goes over the past, she realises in how many different ways Mohan has pushed her and appropriated her space and her relationships, and also in how many different ways he has limited her, inhibiting even the free expression of her natural generosity and fellow-feeling. It is a detailed analysis of a married relationship where the male bulldozes over all personal claims and sensitivities. This is a shared history of most women. They begin to relate to the outside world through the minds of their men, but all the while also build up a hidden, and often silent, communication with other women, with aunts and mothers, sisters and mothers-in-law and neighbours. Thus while there is a vertical relationship through tne male, their is the horizontal one through other women, the undercurrent of the conspiracy of silence.

That Long Silence reinforces the physical exploitation which takes place in a loveless marriage which is an ongoing concern with Deshpande. Akka's thirty-year old husband who forces himself on the thirteen-year old girl (*Roots and Shadows*) and Saru's sadistic husband (*The Dark Holds No Terrors*) both these relationships are reflected in the relationship between Mohan's parents. Yet, mothers, generation after generation lead their daughters to the slaughter and sons, generation after generation, unthinkingly follow in the footsteps of their fathers, even if they have earlier stood aside in disapproval and hatred. These patterns of behaviour are reproduced irrespective of class. And Deshpande opens out many such experiences in order to demonstrate both the centrality of marriage with its inbuilt clamouring for a male heir and its exploitativeness. Women cease to be angry, they give in to passive acceptance, and continue to pray for the "kumkum" on their forehead.

Places are often left vague in Deshpande's novels. They are cities and townships, they have a name, but not necessarily a presence. This is in direct contrast to the work of Anita Desai where cities like Calcutta, Delhi and Bombay create an ambience and pressure of their own. Deshpande on the other hand concentrates more intensely on families and relationships, on the collapse of communication as the male ego becomes more and more self-absorbed and focuses on worldly successes. But in this novel Bombay comes alive as Jaya delves into the memories of the past, the lives of Nayana, Jeeja and Tara, the acting aspiration of Makarand mama, and as it is contrasted with the life in Lohanagar (where Mohan was first posted) and Saptagiri where Jaya had grown up, the urban environment throws up a different set of problems.

Bombay also becomes a focal point in *The Binding Vine* which followed *That Long Silence.* In this novel, the Bombay chawls, the hospital, and the workday routine strongly affect relationships. *The Binding Vine* continues the exploration of many of the concerns which are so central to *That Long Silence* and develops them further.

In *That Long Silence* as the narrative develops, Jaya begins to look at her own role in the making of her marriage a little more closely. She has been too unquestioning, too docile, concerned with the ends rather than the means. Can she totally absolve herself of her share in Mohan's moral lapse?

A woman's whole life—her childhood and adulthood both—are totally geared towards a male centre in which the central male, above father and above son, is the husband. Unending fasts are observed by the Hindu woman, a continuous self-mortification disguised as piety motivated by the sole desire of avoiding widowhood. It is not human goodness which is privileged, nor is it the functional aspect of a relationship, but the physical presence of the man and his right of ownership.

Amidst this surrounding awareness, suddenly her earlier insulation is punctured and the fortnightly 'Seeta' story, she is committed to write, never gets written. The strangeness of her diary pages stares her in the face. She falls back as her own resources unsullied by status and uncontrolled by sanity and finds that the world she had so carefully built had collapsed. She felt totally dislocated. Bit by bit, through fragmentary revelations of the past, the success story is unravelled to reveal the conscious efforts both—Jaya and Mohan—have made at forgetting the past. Memory is selective and one learns to falsify emotions and hide one's true feelings not only from others but also from oneself. Mohan has worked hard at acquiring an education and a middle class status, forgetting that his mother was a cook and that an old man paid for his education as an act of charity. Jaya has suppressed her anger and modelled both her prosaic recordings in the diary and the 'Seeta' stories on the culturally governed images of womanhood.

The two central parts of the novel are devoted to the unravelling of the past through various encounters, surfacing of memories, physical surroundings and a self-questioning while the first and fourth are more directly concerned with the present, with the Mohan–Jaya relationship and the inquiry being conducted against Mohan. In the fourth part, Jaya goes home to look for the mail as well for her son who has been temporarily lost and Mohan makes a trip to Delhi to sort out his affairs. The novel which is more a woman's novel than any other novel of Deshpande's, and which is full of minute details of everyday life, the hopes and dreams and the insignificant happenings, ends on a positive note. The crisis has forced a whole lot of rethinking. And there is hope for a new beginning. Jaya has recovered her lost self and along with that her capacity to dream. She has decided to get rid of the silence which women have lived with for ages.

The Binding Vine carries forward three narrative strands introduced in her earlier novels. Akka's marriage of terror and unhappiness from *Roots and Shadows* is projected in Urmi's dead mother-in-law Mira's experience. Mira, who did not love the man so obsessively in love with her, was given no freedom to opt out of the relationship. Love and passion are viewed as a male right, women are supposed to fall in love and oblige. Mira's relationship with her husband is one long nightmare. It is rape within marriage. And Mira who writes poetry and keeps a diary, dies while delivering her child. With echoes of the Rukhmabai case of the late nineteenth century where the husband insisted on the restoration of his conjugal rights, Mira's life illustrates the traumatic aspects of a loveless marriage, and of one-sided love. The male impulse to possess the woman and override female resistance marks an aggression which is backed by social approval through marriage.

Urmi's questioning of the mother-daughter relationship is a continued exploration of Saru's relationship with her mother in *The Dark Holds No Terrors*. Urmi resents her mother, resents having been sent to her grandparents during her childhood, but it is only now that she learns that she had been sent away at her father's behest, because he had wanted to protect her from any possible assault.

This novel also shares the theme of bereavement so central to *The Dark Holds No Terrors*, only Urmi is grieving over her dead daughter and not a male child. As Urmi learns to cope with it, she gets involved in other people's lives, finds the young doctor attracted towards her and begins to think about the nature of sexuality.

Published in 1993, *The Binding Vine* takes up for its theme a real life case of sexual assault resulting in the victim's going into coma. This happened to a nurse in a Bombay hospital, a woman who is still alive and still in coma. In the novel this brutal rape is conducted upon a young girl Kalpana and by her own uncle—her mother's sister's husband. This uncle of hers is a lecherous man and keen to take her for a second wife. But Kalpana is in love with a young man closer to her own age and unwilling to be sacrificed for the security of her childless aunt. But male desire claims her as its own and Kalpana is raped, clawed into, brutally bitten.

The foregrounding of the social networking which seeks to exploit a woman even while seeking to protect her, places the female body at the centre of the social discourse. The narrative conflict is born out of the women's attempts to free themselves from this centrality of the body but menstruation, marriage, rape, motherhood, breast feeding, fasting and the use of ornaments—all function as traps, and each one of them is either a symbol of status, or falls in line with the social definition of a good woman, or is practised in order to avoid widowhood. Only when the woman's perspective is foregrounded do the categories of rape and resistance surface.

The woman–to–woman friendship is also highlighted here as it even cuts across class and role boundaries. Urmi has a very good relationship with her husband's half-sister and she develops an empathy with Shakutai, Kalpana's mother. But somehow it is her own mother she resents. In developing relationships between mothers-in-law and daughters-in-law and other women within the kinship network, Deshpande is simultaneously reflecting a deep reality of Indian family patterns and reversing the popular image of animosity between relationships established through marriage. Further she traces the matrilineal aspects of tradition as property is handed over by Akka to her grandniece (*Roots and Shadows*) and Urmi reconstructs her mother-in-law's female experience from her diary and poems. It is significant that the limited space the woman gets is only the pages of a diary and the little tin box in which her belongings are stored.

Urmi's grieving over her daughter is also indicative of her sense of loss, at the double disruption in this feminine tradition. She has failed to relate to her mother. And now this failure is duplicated in the next generation by the death of her daughter.

While her two early novels are inhabited by men, specially *Roots and Shadows* which has a long line of uncles and nephews, in *The Dark Holds No Terrors* Saru is alone in a house inhabited by her father, Madhav and Dhruva's memory an all male world, Jaya in *That Long Silence* relates to the various women in the chawl—neighbours, tenants, servants children—and digs up her memories of female relatives and dependents, and Urmi in *The Binding Vine* works through female relationships. Friendships with women are strengthening. They provide space for confidence and sharing but they also reflect the unwritten restrictions imposed by society. The segregation between the sexes is enforced through social structures and sanctioned relationships. Her friendship with Bhaskar is commented upon both by her mother and her sister-in-law and both advise her to consider the social implications, leading Urmi to think about reworking her space within her marriage.

By introducing the concept of marital rape, Deshpande not only anticipates the surfacing of this issue in feminist discourse in India, but also reflects upon feminist history in the Indian context and the rights of a wife *vis-à-vis* the husband. The notion of romantic love as an obsessive imposition on the woman is also put forth as representing an anti-romantic stance, a deconstruction of the idea of love necessarily being a fulfilment.

The marginalisation of women takes place in several contexts. In novel after novel women are given new names at the time of marriage. This happens to be a common Indian practice very much in force at least till the though early decades of the present century, there are bound to be some differences from region to region, class to class and in accordance with levels of education. Urmi's mother-in-law is rechristened Nirmala. The naming ceremony is very important. It asks for an emotional severance from an earlier self, a shedding of the native skin and symbolises a change of role, a new birth, a new self as well as a new house. Is this surgical separation really possible? The uprootedness which is inscribed in a woman's life is underscored by this naming ceremony which automatically announces transfer of the woman from one role to another.

Women learn to live for others and through others and in the process erase themselves. Mira's diary refers to an incident when an astrologer had read all their horoscopes except their mother's because the mother felt that she really had no life apart from her family. And Vanaa, her sister-in-law, lives a life fully anchored to the needs of her family. It seems her husband Harish, even when he is away, has some remote control over her.

Shakutai's narrative, like Akka's in *Roots and Shadows*, opens out the negative aspects of passion. Poverty makes it worse. The newly married bride follows her husband to Bombay, afraid of being a burden on her parents and finds herself living in a room full of men, where her husband wishes to sleep with her indifferent to both her feelings and the presence of others.

Urmi, however, recognises the nature of female passion which society is at such great pains to deny. She misses her husband when he is away for such long spells. When he is away at sea, she is conscious of her bodily hungers, and longs for the touch of intimacy. She loves Kishore deeply and intensely, but she is also aware that physical desire can be aroused even in the abstract. Bhaskar's presence can also arouse it. Chastity and virtue are self-imposed restrictions, not necessarily the absence of desire.

The novel ends with Kalpana's aunt committing suicide. The shock of her husband's destructive desire, the sense of betrayal she experiences and the guilt she lives with, make it impossible for her to continue with the act of living. Love can be very demanding, very cruel, destructive and ugly. Yet it is needed for surviving, for the act of living. The various relationships do not only reveal the complexity of human needs, but also the irrelevance of social models if they have become meaningless. Shakutai and her sister both are victims of the normative structures which surround them else Kalpana need not have been sacrificed. Vanaa and Urmi have a slight advantage because of their education and class background and are in a better position to negotiate their social reality.

Bereavement is the subject of yet another novel, *A Matter of Time* published in 1996. It is the loss of a male child during a journey which brings about a rift between Kalyani and her husband leading to a total division of the house. The house 'Vishwas' is a symbol of stability, but for this family it has become one of instability. This house has always been in search of an heir. Kalyani is the only daughter of her parents, and in order to keep the property in the family. Manorama, her mother, got her brother to marry her daughter. The only male child of this union, a mentally retarded boy, strayed away from his mother causing a permanent division of the house with the husband and wife living on different floors.

Sumi is the other child of this couple and the novel opens with her husband Gopal walking out of their marriage. Nothing has happened. And there is no other woman. It is simply a question of withdrawal. Gopal wants to recede into himself and seeks his freedom from the marriage bond. While others try to him bring back, Sumi does not even attempt to do so.

The first one to go to Gopal is Sumi's mother, Kalyani, who sees in this a replay of her own life. The next is his daughter who does not plead but threatens a legal action. Gopal finds himself helpless because his withdrawal is beyond his control. Others step in to act as substitute supporters, his father-in-law who takes his daughter and grandchildren to 'Vishwas,' and his nephew, Romesh, who places some money in Sumi's bank. And as the house is once again peopled, and relatives find their way there with offers of advice and expressions of concern, each one of the family members tries in her own way to rehabilitate herself.

Aru forms a friendship with a woman lawyer whose help she has sought to take action against her father; Sumi who is house-hunting finds a strange understanding emanating from a prosaic house-agent, Charu acquires a boy friend. Family connections come alive. Doda and Premi descend upon them. And this house full of women has several moments of laughter when through narration, recollection, queries and responses the past comes alive. But that is only on the surface. Their lives are still rudderless. Gopal continues living over his pupil's printing press in his ascetic, self-contained manner and Sumi refrains from making any claims on him. There is a strange passive acceptance on her part of the separation thrust upon her and she progresses in another direction. First a job, then involvement in the job and then the writing of a play for a class performance. She is just beginning to discover herself when the end comes. On the eve of her departure to take up new responsibilities (and residence) in a school, she and her father die in an accident as they ride a borrowed scooter.

The novel makes several comments on relationships of all kinds—within marriage, with siblings, family relationships, generational slipovers, and relationships with one's self. Sumi's father and her husband, both have withdrawn suddenly from their families. There is a retreat from involvement. In both cases there is the absence of a male child and in Gopal's case an overwhelming presence of women. Why is the male presence so essential? And women, is it possible for them to look beyond marriage and beyond the body to discover other hidden selves? Strangely enough Sumi's father begins to develop a relationship with her once she is back in the house with her daughters. It is if he has once again picked up the threads of life with the presence of his grandchildren.

Again Kalyani's life has been spent in sexual deprivation, but there is also the suspicion that the loss of the mentally retarded child may have been a subconscious need to be free of him. There is in this a rejection of the role of a subjugated motherhood. The loss of a male child also comments upon the ability of the women to sustain themselves on the strength of their children irrespective of their sex. The male child symbolises a continuity primarily for the father. The incident has a long-term affect on the husband–wife relationship and calls into question all family relationships. Its social and familial ramifications are innumerable.

Families have a wonderful way of coming together at times of crisis and of dispersing once things are settling down. The house with its divisions and space renders this possible. Deshpande's critiquing is never satirical or cynical, but the institutions are seen not as monolithic structures but as ones with hidden nooks and corners, surfaces and hidden depths and with a wide range of relationship patterns. Families and marriages are made up of individuals, who act both as cohering agents and as disruptive factors.

A Matter of Time has several subnarratives woven into it, many of them which move into the past—Kalyani's life, Gopal's childhood; Romesh, Gopal's nephew's, relationship with Gopal whom he calls Guru; Romesh's parents, and their relationship with Gopal; Manorama, Kalyani's mother's marriage to Vithal—and the whole range of conspiratorial management behind the scenes. These subnarratives act as decentralizing factors with no individual protagonist being the sole concern of the story. Lives are interlinked and interdependent. The narrative may be projected through a dominant consciousness, but it is not a centralized, single voice.

Space is yet another dominant concern in this novel as also in her other novels. Only in this it is foregrounded because the novel opens with the description and the history of the house 'Vishwas'. It is the house which governs inheritance, marriage and family relationships. Later Sumi's search for a house, the detailed description of the room in which Gopal lives, Sumi's dream about a house of her own in her new job, all reinforce the need for space and roots. Her earlier novels also prioritise space. Indu inherits Akka's house and has to take the painful decision to dispose of it, a decision which marks a dispersal of the family and a final freedom for Indu in *Roots and Shadows*.

Other houses also have a formidable presence and hold memories. Saru when she comes back home to her parents' house (*The Dark Holds No Terrors*), Jaya as she takes a look at her life in the Dadar flat (*That Long Silence*), and Madhu as she begins to feel at home in the house at Bhavanipur (*Small Remedies*). Deshpande in her interview with Lakshmi Holmström has commented upon her need to have the image clear, "For me it is essential—almost as essential as it is for a movie director—to have the shape of the house clear."[1]

It is amazing as to how many facets human relationships can have. And it is also surprising how deviation from the expected behaviour can set free a long chain of events. Deshpande works out the tangle of relationships through a double narrative in *Small Remedies* which also takes up for its theme the subject of bereavement. Madhu is a journalist, a part-time writer like Jaya and Indu in her previous novels, and has recently lost her son Adit in a bomb blast. This has affected her relationship with her husband. In an attempt to help her cope with her depression, her friends ask her to do a biography of Savitribai Indorekar, a famous singer who was at one time a next door neighbour, and with whose daughter Munni, Madhu had struck up a friendship.

On the face of it there are these two main narratives running parallel to each other—one of Savitribai's life and the other of Madhu's—but in fact there are several more. Munni has always denied her parentage and has consistently attempted to run away from the shadow of her famous mother. Munni's life is spent in pursuit of normalcy which her mother has destroyed by taking to music as a profession, by acquiring a Muslim lover and giving birth to Munni out of that union. The mother and daughter work in opposite directions and while the mother is almost ruthless in the pursuit of her talent, the daughter is equally determined to seek anonymity in the folds of a family. Both of them deny each other.

Savitribai never mentions her. And in her the conventional image of a sacrificing and a caring mother is dismantled. She is also not obsessed by the need for love and discards her love just as she had walked out of her family. In large measure it is the either/or choice which again is the accepted code reflecting the belief that women cannot have a full life if they pursue a career.

There is also another subnarrative of Madhu's marriage and her husband's jealousy. The guilt she feels is not actually at the death of her son but at the breakdown of communication between her and her husband. Their estranged relationship affected also their relationship with their son Adit, who had begun to avoid them. Her husband Som, almost a carry over from Nayantara Sahgal's *The Day in Shadow*, looks upon her with suspicion regarding her pre-marital friendship with a man. The distrust arising out of this suspicion destroys their relationship.

There are yet several other narratives, those of Madhu's childhood, of her father's mistress, her aunt Leela's unusual marriage and her stepchildren and Madhu's mother's family. And finally the connection with her hosts at Bhavanipur. It is during this time spent at Bhavanipur that Madhu begins to resume life and starts a renegotiation with herself with the help of her hosts, the mirror reflection of Savitribai's life, the memories of the past, Joe's brotherly protection, and the crisis caused by Savitribai's illness. Music and religion, both are placed in a situation of conflict with religion claiming purity and music offering devotion. Religion, like family and marriage, is seen to be a patriarchal structure and music as one which encourages deviation, spontaneity, transgression. With Savitribai's Muslim protégé taking her place in the religious performance, a reconciliation takes place, one which is a harbinger of Madhu's return to Som for the first death anniversary of their son. The past has to be allowed to go, and finally one needs to realise that one cannot possess one's dead.

The endings of several of her novels are a working out of reconciliatory patterns, except for *A Matter of Time.* People return to heir homes, families, husbands and wives, but the return is always marked by a change of perspective. The message is always of an in-between condition. Life has to go on and as we cannot live through passive acceptance space has to be won or yielded or made. Death, bereavement, guilt, expiation—these are some of the familiar tropes of her novels but the complex pattern of relationships, the thickly populated novels with sprawling extended families of several generations are markedly different from the work of many of her contemporaries. She writes about women, but not necessarily always about the female psyche. Instead it is the interstitial spaces, the multitude of relationships which come between the making of a self and the recovery of a self.

Her two detective novels also project a similar worldview except for the fact that the events move at a faster pace and people die not through accidents or illness but they are killed, got rid of because of fear or aggression, in short murdered. The first of these, *If I Die Today,* is a short novella with Guru, a philosophical person placed amidst a group to doctors. He is terminally ill and is staying with one of the doctors for his treatment. But he is also the observer eye with death staring him in the face, and disinterested in his own existence, he is keen to confront truth and compel others to do the same. This habit of his leads to an uneasy situation when ghosts from the past are brought out into the open. A series of murders is triggered of and Guru is the first victim. As other murders follow, everybody begins to suspect everyone else. Children are sent away. There are silent accusations, hidden fears and a state of general panic. The next to die is Tony, a death by drowning. There are other deaths which are narrated—Prabhakar Tambe the union leader and also Sumant's first wife. Finally, it is discovered that it is the intense, and probably the incestuous love of Vidya, the Dean's sister, which has led to Guru's and Tony's deaths. The destructiveness of possessive love is the evil which has disrupted the life of the closely-knit hospital community. The novel does not merely read as a suspense mystery. It raises several other questions and makes a very good use of the setting—the hospital, its staff, the terminally ill patient and the professional secrets which prick the conscience of the doctors as they move between the personal and the professional.

Come Up and Be Dead is set in a girls' school and many well be taken as an adolescent mystery, where young girls are being lured into a call girl racket and the racketeers systematically begin to get rid of those they feel are likely to expose them. Kshama Rao who is the new Headmistress of the school is an ambitious woman. Her cousin Devi is invited to come and keep house for her and help in looking after her dependent brother who is not "all" there. The rest of the story is actually a contrast between these two character types—Kshama and Devi—and the different ways in which they organise life, relate to people, cope with emergencies and the like—one independent, hard and ambitious, the other homely, gentle and caring. It is Devi who plays the amateur detective and is thus instrumental in Kshama's final rehabilitation.

Shashi Deshpande has also written several short stories. Of these a whole series relate to the interpretation of the characters of the *Mahabharata*. Several of these are included in *The Stone Women*. Her stories, like her novels, deal with relationships, with one difference. They are, at times, more radical, even sexy in their themes and statements. The stories capture little moments of nostalgia, of perversion and terror, of the disruptive events of life. They weave an atmosphere. But their length forbids any long term dwelling on the issues, hence they are crisp and brief. Myth is interwoven into almost all her narratives, into her language, images and references.

In contrast to her novels, several of her short stories have a male protagonist and work through a male consciousness and perspective. She herself questions this choice in one of her essays, *The Dilemma of a Woman Writer*. Why this unconscious or unconscious choice? To attain objectivity and a certain distancing, or to prove to herself her versatility, or to pare down emotions, or more seriously an attempt to be taken more seriously, "to get out of my woman's skin?"[2]

Deshpande has very consciously and analytically commented upon her own writing and the stance she has adopted. Anger at being taken non-seriously, at being relegated to a women's world, and being evaluated and judged primarily as a woman writer, Deshpande feels, is an emotion which needs to be lived through. The final test is the quality of writing—its "sincerity, integrity and professionalism" (*Dilemma* 231).

The craftsmanship of her stories is worked out in detail and there is a quality both of subtlety and directness about them. The cultures, specifically of the Maharashtra-Karnataka region, can be clearly discerned in her descriptions and her language. This characteristic is a strength. As she does not use too many glosses, except for clarifying the relationships, the nuances of language, the turn of a phrase, the description of a practice, all bring out the specificity of her background, imparting it a high degree of authenticity and bringing out the diversity of Indian culture. In one of her interviews, she described herself as a regional writer, a term which is coming into vogue, but perhaps with a different meaning. It represents a category of writers who are moving away from urban centres even while writing in English. In itself it is not a new development, for the tradition exists. We can trace it through R.K. Narayan, Ruskin Bond, and now Neelum Saran Gour. It also indicates a refusal to be limited by the use of English language to writing about the anglicised urban people, or to be uniformly clubbed together under the label of 'Indian Writing in English.' Thus the acknowledgment of differences and diversities within it, is also in a way an evidence of the confidence and maturity which these writers possess and now display.

It is difficult to pin down Deshpande's work to any one description. Despite the detailed descriptions of relationships, surroundings, feelings and emotions, her work slips through the fingers eluding any single framework or a defining norm. If compelled to do so, a critic may best describe her as a writer of multiplicities.

The individual consciousness despite its psychological moorings is never totally isolated. The feminist perspective does not work entirely in opposition to the patriarchal structures, but also perceives men themselves as the victims of patriarchy—men who withdraw, who fail to communicate, who in fact reject the patriarchal model of masculinity. As these men and women analyse their failures and problems in order to work their way out of the state of crisis, they accept an erosion of the stereotypical projections, and work their way to reinterpreted morality, sexuality or individuality, as the case may be. They bring out the vulnerability of human beings rather than the strength. No one begins by being strong. The strong, heroic images are culturally imposed, not personally or individually worked out. And 'strength' often becomes a barrier both where self-knowledge and the relationship with others are concerned.

Notes

1. Lakshmi Holmström, "Interviews Shashi Deshpande," *The Fiction of Shashi Deshpande*, ed. R.S. Pathak (New Delhi: Creative Books, 1998) 243.
2. Shashi Deshpande, "The Dilemma of the Woman Writer," *The Fiction of Shashi Deshpande*, ed. R.S. Pathak (New Delhi: Creative Books, 1998) 230.

A SHASHI DESHPANDE BIBLIOGRAPHY

Primary Sources

Fictional Works

The Legacy. Calcutta: Writers' Workshop, 1971.

The Dark Holds No Terrors. Delhi: Vikas Publishing House, 1980; New Delhi: Penguin 1990.

If I Die Today. New Delhi: Tarang Paperbacks, 1982.

Roots and Shadows. Hyderabad: Sangam Books, 1983.

It Was Dark. Calcutta: Writers' Workshop, 1986.

That Long Silence. London: Virago Press, 1988; New Delhi: Penguin 1989.

Come Up and Be Dead. New Delhi: Vikas Publishing House, 1993.

The Binding Vine. London: Virago Press, 1993; New Delhi: Penguin 1993.

It Was the Nightingale. Calcutta: Writers' Workshop, 1993.

Intrusion and Other Stories. New Delhi: Penguin, 1993.

A Matter of Time. New Delhi: Penguin, 1996.

Small Remedies. New Delhi: Viking, Penguin Books India, 2000.

The Stone Women. Calcutta: Writers' Workshop, 2000.

Articles

"The Dilemma of the Woman Writer." *The Fiction of Shashi Deshpande.* Ed. R.S. Pathak. New Delhi: Creative Books, 1998.

"Them and Us." *Unbecoming Daughters of the Empire.* Eds. Shirley Chew and Anna Rutherford. Sydney: Dangaroo Press, 1993.

"Afterword." *The Stone Women.* Calcutta: Writers' Workshop, 2000.

"On the Writing of a Novel." *Indian Women Novelists.* Vol. 5. Ed. R.K. Dhawan. New Delhi: Prestige, 1991.

Secondary Sources

Books on Shashi Deshpande

Atrey, Mukta and Viney Kirpal. *Shashi Deshpande: A Feminist Study of Her Fiction.* Delhi: B.R. Publishing Corporation, 1998.

Bala, Suman, ed. *Women in the Novels of Shashi Deshpande.* New Delhi: Khosla Publishing Home, 2001.

Pathak, R.S., ed. *The Fiction of Shashi Deshpande.* New Delhi: Creative Books, 1998.

Sebastian, Mrinalini. *The Novels of Shashi Deshpande in Postcolonial Arguments.* New Delhi: Prestige, 2000.

Articles on Shashi Deshpande

Dickman, Sue. "Interview with Shanti Deshpande." *Ariel* 29.1 (Jan. 1998).

Dinesh, Kamini. "Moving out of the Cloistered Self: Shashi Deshpande's Protagonists." *Margins of Erasure: Purdah in the Subcontinentel Novel in English.* Eds. Jasbir Jain and Amina Amin. New Delhi: Sterling Publishers, 1995.

Dwivedi, A.N. "The Shorter Fiction of Shashi Deshpande: Search for Self." *The Fiction of Shashi Deshpande.* Ed. R.S. Pathak. New Delhi: Creative Books, 1998.

Dwivedi, Amarnath. "Recurring Metaphors in Shashi Deshpande." *The Fiction of Shashi Deshpande.* Ed. R.S. Pathak. New Delhi: Creative Books, 1998.

Gangadharan, Geetha. "Denying the Otherness" (Interview). *The Fiction of Shashi Deshpande.* Ed. R.S. Pathak. New Delhi: Creative Books, 1998.

Gopinath, Suman. "Breaking that Long Silence." *Sunday Herald* 25 Sept. 1994.

Gupta, Santosh. "Feminine Identity, Myth and Society in the Novels of Shashi Deshpande." *Memories of the Second Sex: Gender and Sexuality in Women's Writing.* Eds. Dominique S. Verma and T.V. Kunhi Krishnan. Mumbai: Somaiya Publications, 2000.

____. "*The Binding Vine* of Relationship in Shashi Deshpande's Novels." *Critical Practice* 6.2 (June 1998).

Havely, Cicley Palser. "Dancing with an Old Flame: The Postcolonial Legacy in Sahgal, Deshpande and Markandaya." *Mapping Cultural Space: Postcolonial Indian Literature in English.* Eds. Nilufer Bharucha and Vrinda Nabar. New Delhi: Vision Books, 1998.

Holmström, Lakshmi. "Interviews Shashi Deshpande." *The Fiction of Shashi Deshpande.* Ed. R.S. Pathak. New Delhi: Creative Books, 1998.

Khan, A.G. "Shashi Deshpande's Heroines: Prisoners by Choice." *The Fiction of Shashi Deshpande.* Ed. R.S. Pathak. New Delhi: Creative Books, 1998.

King, Adele. "Shashi Deshpande: Portraits of an Indian Woman." *The New Indian Novel in English: A Study of the 1980s.* Ed. Viney Kirpal. New Delhi: Allied Publishers Ltd., 1990.

Meitei, M. Mani. "Subversing Phallogocentrism; Feminine Discourse in *Roots and Shadows.*" *The Fiction of Shashi Deshpande.* Ed. R.S. Pathak. New Delhi: Creative Books, 1998.

Palkar, Sarla. "Of Mothers and Daughters, of the Great Divide: Shashi Deshpande's *The Binding Vine.*" *The Postmodern Indian English Novel.* Ed. Viney Kirpal. Delhi: Allied Publishers Ltd., 1996.

Pandey, K.M. "Tearing the Veil: *The Dark Holds No Terrors.*" *The Fiction of Shashi Deshpande.* Ed. R.S. Pathak. New Delhi: Creative Books, 1998.

Piciucco, Pier Paolo. "Houses and Homecoming in the Fiction of Shashi Deshpande." *The Journal of Indian Writing in English* 29.2 (July 2001).

Rama Rao, Vimala. "In Conversation with Shashi Deshpande." *The Fiction of Shashi Deshpande.* Ed. R.S. Pathak. New Delhi: Creative Books, 1998.

____. "Myth and Folkore in Shashi Deshpande." *The Fiction of Shashi Deshpande*. Ed. R.S. Pathak. New Delhi: Creative Books, 1998.

Ramamoorthi, P. "'My Life my Own': A Study of Shashi Deshpande's Women." *Feminism and Recent Indian Fiction*. Ed. Sushila Singh. New Delhi: Prestige, 1991.

Riti, M.D. "There's No Looking Back." (Interviews Shashi Deshpande) *The Fiction of Shashi Deshpande*. Ed. R.S. Pathak. New Delhi: Creative Books, 1998.

Sengupta, S. "*That Long Silence*: Imagery of Death, Decay and Desolation." *The Fiction of Shashi Deshpande*. Ed. R.S. Pathak. New Delhi: Creative Books, 1998.

Tripathi, J.P. "*The Binding Vine* and Indian Ethos." *The Fiction of Shashi Deshpande*. Ed. R.S. Pathak. New Delhi: Creative Books, 1998

Tripathi, Malinabh. "Gender Identity and Inner Space in *The Dark Holds No Terrors*." *The Fiction of Shashi Deshpande*. Ed. R.S. Pathak. New Delhi: Creative Books, 1998.

Viswanatha, Vanmala. "Interview with Shashi Deshpande." *Literature Alive* 1.3 (Dec. 1987).

11

SALMAN RUSHDIE

NEIL TEN KORTENAAR

It is fitting that Ashcroft, Griffiths, and Tiffin borrowed the title of their influential work of postcolonial theory, *The Empire Writes Back,* from an essay of Salman Rushdie's. More often than Walcott, Coetzee, Achebe, Soyinka, or any other candidate for the honour, Rushdie is hailed as the epitome of the literary postcolonial, and his 1981 novel, *Midnight's Children,* as the quintessential postcolonial text. *The Satanic Verses* (1988) is celebrated as the defining novel of migration in the era of globalization. Rushdie's canonization derives in part from his status as an immigrant in the metropole and in part from his notoriety outside academic literary circles, but is primarily attributable to his condensation of many of the anxieties and concerns identified as postcolonial: how to imagine the nation-state; how to write the history of those denied history; how to locate oneself in a world of intersecting languages and communities; how to be postmodern and write from the periphery; how to imagine hybridity and migration. Rushdie's books feel as though they belong in the company of Homi Bhabha and Gayatri Spivak rather than with Mulk Raj Anand or R.K. Narayan.

From the moment it appeared, *Midnight's Children* has seemed to readers at once like the culmination of Indian writing in English and like a break in the tradition, utterly changing how India would be perceived and written about. Anita Desai remembers hearing the then unknown author reading from the newly published *Midnight's Children* with "a voice that everyone present recognized instantly as being the voice of a new age: strong, original, and demanding of attention." Although, in retrospect, it is possible to find an Indian ancestor for Saleem Sinai, Rushdie's narrator, in G.V. Desani's *All About H. Hatterr,* Rushdie's postmodernist magic realism was clearly inspired by Laurence Sterne, Günter Grass, and Gabriel García Márquez. At the same time, in a notorious paradox, its combination of fantasy, volubility, and narcissism made *Midnight's Children* feel Indian in a way that no previous novel had. The novel's exuberant excess (its long, breathless, non-periodic sentences, compound words, and exhaustive catalogues);

its simulation of urgency (the incomplete sentences and compulsive repetition); its heteroglossia (the presence of Hindi-Urdu words, translations from Urdu into English, and modern Hobson-Jobson Indian English); and its borrowing of cinematographic technique (the trailer, the close-up, and the flashback) all purport to reflect not just the way Indians speak but the way Indians are. The novel appropriates Orientalist notions of India as exotic and magical in order to suggest potential, difference, and excess, and it becomes impossible to determine where India ends and Orientalism begins. This break in the tradition successfully redefined the tradition. Many are the subsequent writers inside and outside India, like M.G. Vassanji, Shashi Tharoor, and Arundhati Roy, who have measured themselves against *Midnight's Children.*

It is tempting to say *Midnight's Children* was the novel Rushdie was born to write. Like Saleem Sinai, Rushdie was born in Bombay in 1947. He is therefore, in all probability, the first writer in English from the postcolonial world to write without personal experience of colonialism. A family joke had it that, after Rushdie was born on June 19, the British hurried to pack their bags and leave. Many of Saleem Sinai's experiences growing up are versions of Rushdie's own life, fictionalized and much exaggerated. Rushdie's parents, Anis Ahmed Rushdie, a Muslim businessman, and his wife, Negin Rushdie, née Butt, like the parents of Saleem Sinai, had both been previously divorced. Methwold's Estate, where Saleem grows up, is based on Westfield Estate. Windsor Villa, where the Rushdies lived, becomes the novel's Buckingham Villa, which Ahmed Sinai buys from the retreating colonial William Methwold, and where he and his family live among the Englishman's furniture and appurtenances. The view from Saleem's bedroom window, across Warden Road to Breach Candy Swimming Pool and, beyond that, to the Arabian Sea, was the view from Rushdie's own window. Saleem goes to John Connon and Cathedral Boys' School just as Rushdie did. And Rushdie's parents, like the Sinais, ran into legal trouble with the government after Partition. They eventually moved to Karachi, where Anis Rushdie, like Ahmed Sinai, set up a towel factory.

There is, of course, a major difference between Saleem's life and Rushdie's. At the age of fourteen his father sent Rushdie to study at Rugby in England. Rushdie went on to read history at Cambridge, where his father had studied before him, and has lived in England ever since until his recent move to New York. Saleem Sinai, on the other hand, as befits an allegorical figure of India, lives all his life in the subcontinent. Born at the exact moment that India achieved independence, Saleem suffers whatever happens to the nation-state. As Richard Cronin has pointed out, Saleem's Indianness is actually a function of Rushdie's Britishness. It is in England that the non-resident Indian must ask what his relation to India is, and in England that India will be identified with the map, with the narrative of history books, and with the newsmaking activities of its politicians. Prior to Rushdie, even explicitly political novels like *Kanthapura* by Raja Rao or *Waiting for the Mahatma* by R.K. Narayan focused on the village or the town rather than the nation. Tagore or Rao or Narayan did not write sweeping accounts of Indian history because they were immersed in India; India was their world. Rushdie's masterpiece, however, is directly concerned with the state and political history.

The totalizing perspective of *Midnight's Children* presumes a cosmopolitan English-language reader. The novel provides all the background that an interested Western reader unfamiliar with Indian history would need to know. Saleem embeds in his narrative English translations of the Hindi-Urdu words he uses and explains his many references to religion and history. He even tells us when he has made an error. As a result, many a Western reader has relied on *Midnight's Children*, as on the film *Gandhi*, for a pocket overview of twentieth-century Indian history. This doubled perspective, at once national and cosmopolitan, accounts for Rushdie's mixed reputation in India. Harish Trivedi has been the most vocal of those who resent that Western critics and academics treat Rushdie as if he invented India or gave the continent a voice.

Midnight's Children may be the novel he was born to write, but it was not Rushdie's first published novel. While working as an advertising copy writer after coming down from Cambridge, he submitted a novel to a competition for science fiction held by Victor Gollancz. *Grimus* (1975) did not win the prize but was published nonetheless. In that novel, a native American (the other kind of Indian) pursues a spiritual journey across the ocean to the island of Qaf and up the mountain at the island's centre. That first novel is now inevitably read for what it reveals of the author of *Midnight's Children*, but if we read it as its first readers must have done, without knowledge of the author's South Asian origins, all its echoes of postcoloniality disappear. The placeless and timeless fantasy setting suggests the cosmopolitan writer who takes for granted the universality of his subject matter. While it is true that the text is primarily informed by Muslim sources that many of Rushdie's readers would be unfamiliar with—the novel's cosmology is based on *The Conference of the Birds* by the twelfth-century Sufi poet Farid ud-Din Attar—the novel does not highlight cultural difference but assumes somehow an ability to transcend all cultures.

In retrospect, *Grimus* reads as if Rushdie were deliberately avoiding the role that would later be his, of Indian author and spokesman for the new minorities in Britain. What would become Rushdie's great theme—the one world that contains both India and England, a world created in the first instance by empire but which now must also include the mass migrations that have transformed the face of London and England—that theme seems originally to have appeared to him as a problem to be avoided by leaving the earth behind. Rushdie has shown a propensity for other, parallel universes throughout his career, but only in *Grimus* does the parallel dimension of the novel not intersect at all with the universe of history.

The author of *Grimus* is a reader of Joseph Campbell and Mircea Eliade who believes that all cosmologies can be united by a clever twenty-seven-year-old punster with enough ambition. The young Flapping Eagle pursues the transcendent which, according to the Sufi paradigm that underwrites the novel, is also the immanent: in *The Conference of the Birds* thirty birds on a spiritual quest come to realize that they themselves are the Simurg (meaning "thirty birds") that they seek. Unity is found in the many, as Saleem Sinai also finds when he learns that India is the sum of all Indians. At the same time the one person who imagines that he himself is divine, the Grimus of the title (an anagram of Simurg), proves thereby that he is but a demonic parody of the divine and must be defeated. This bears no small resemblance to the role played by Indira Gandhi in Rushdie's next novel.

Midnight's Children is in some senses the converse of *Grimus*: it is about a particular history and a particular nation, and it recovers the place Rushdie knows most intimately, the house where he grew up. But it, too, obscures what the author finds difficult to deal with: his status between nations and between cultures. Rushdie's narrator, Saleem, occupies an ambivalent location, at once inside and outside, the observer and the observed. His is at once a partial perspective close to Rushdie's, based on limited personal experience and distorted by memory, and a totalizing vision inspired by the map and national history. The novel's mixture of allegory and autobiography proves very volatile. The emphasis on phenomenological truth and on the vagaries of perception and memory make the novel seem modernist, while the play with intertexts, the grotesque fantasy elements, and the metafictional commentary by the narrator advertise its postmodernism. All Rushdie's novels seek to combine the incompatible and to yoke the incongruous. In most of them, that wild ambition is also their weakness. In *Midnight's Children*, Rushdie's greatest book, the constellation of incompatibles—allegory, *bildungsroman*, self-conscious metafiction—all ultimately pull in the same direction and avoid the absurdity they risk. The different narrative strands complement each other because self, nation, and text are intimately related: the modern nation and the self of the modern citizen are imagined in the same way, and both are textual in the sense that they rely on words, narrative, and metaphor.

Perhaps Rushdie was more in control of his art in *Midnight's*

Children because he was paradoxically *less* in control of his narrative than he would be in his later novels. In an interview in *Kunapipi* he has described how a first draft of the novel, which was narrated in the third person, was taken over by the voice of Saleem: "It was like a coup: he just simply took a deep breath and started talking, and 500 pages later he stopped." Rushdie's allegorical creation, a puppet embodying the author's ideas about India's progress since independence, somehow acquired the divine spark of self-consciousness, and became a rival voice taking over the narration of his life. All the later novels are narrated by voices that share Rushdie's opinions and sensibility. Even where, as in *The Moor's Last Sigh* and *The Ground Beneath Her Feet*, the narration is by a character in the story, there is no distinction between what that character tells us and how we are intended to read. Rushdie's most recent novel, *Fury*, departs from his previous work in its extended use of free indirect discourse to give readers access to Malik Solanka's thoughts. Once again, however, although Solanka sounds almost exactly like a Saul Bellow character, it is impossible to distinguish his sensibility from Rushdie's own. We feel that Rushdie has put into each of these works all that he knows. Only in *Midnight's Children*, has he risked a significant distance between himself and the narrative voice. Saleem Sinai is an absurd figure, a mimic man and a madman, who often thinks differently than Rushdie does or than he wants his readers to. We can conclude, however, from the great lengths to which Rushdie has gone, both in the novel itself and after its publication, to ensure that he not be mistaken for his creation that much of the ironic distance between author and narrator is filled with panic. Saleem Sinai, the narrator furthest from Rushdie, also comes too close to him for comfort. The result of this uncomfortable and uncertain distance is that only in *Midnight's Children* has Rushdie been able to include more than he himself knows that he knows.

From Tagore's *Gora* through Prem Chand's *Gift of a Cow* and Raja Rao's *The Serpent and the Rope* to Anita Desai's *Clear Light of Day*, the main line of Indian fiction has been characterized by dialogism, the pitting of ideologies and personalities against each other in debate. *Midnight's Children*, on the other hand, presents the eerie combination of a single story-teller who can do many voices, whose narcissism feels like polyglossia. Saleem Sinai declares that he has patterned his narration on the oral story-telling of his Goan ayah, Mary Pereira, and of the old Kashmiri boatman, Tai, as well as on the *Arabian Nights*. As soon as he finishes each chapter of his memoirs, Saleem Sinai reads it aloud to Padma, an illiterate female worker in the Braganza pickle factory where he is holed up in an office, and their relation echoes that of oral story-teller and listener. At the same time, Saleem's isolated circumstances, cut off from the world in a tiny space lit by a single Angle-poised lamp, remind us that he is not an oral story-teller but a writer who imitates oral story-telling. His narration is addressed in the first instance to educated non-Indian readers above Padma's head as it were.

The mixing of scales in *Midnight's Children*—Saleem is at once an unprepossessing young man of no particular competence, a hero with secret superpowers, and an allegorical figure for the nation—is inevitably comic, and the result is often darkly satirical: whatever hopes Saleem had as a young man are dashed in 1975 when Indira Gandhi (referred to throughout as the Widow) declared a State of Emergency. The satire suggests that the nation and the liberal democracy that it stands for are threatened from below as well as from above, by an unreasoning violence bred by poverty and represented by Shiva, Saleem's agemate with whom he has been changed at birth, and by the furies of communalism. Indira Gandhi, Shiva, and Saleem all have a legitimate claim to represent India, and they are related to each other as superego, id, and ego. The ego (Saleem) must preserve itself against the threat of castration by the superego (the Widow) and resist being overwhelmed by the violent energy of the id (Shiva).

Midnight's Children won immediate acclaim, and Rushdie would return to it throughout his career. In 1987 he made a BBC documentary, *The Riddle of Midnight*, about Indians like himself and Saleem who had been born in the year of independence. In the late 1990s he wrote a screenplay (published in 1999) for a film version of the novel, that was to have been shot in Sri Lanka until the government withdrew its approval for the project. Rushdie, however, seems also to have resented or, at least, mistrusted the way he was identified with his Booker-Prize-winning novel, for he immediately set out to write a novel as different as he could.

Shame (1983) is also recognizably postmodernist in its self-reflexivity and its combination of history and fantasy, and, like its predecessor, it concerns itself with the politics of the subcontinent. However, it is deliberately more claustrophobic and drier in feel than the vastness and lushness of *Midnight's Children*. The narrative is an allegory of contemporary Pakistani politics, rather than, as in the previous novel, the story of someone who reads the world allegorically. Politicians do not make a direct appearance, as Indira Gandhi did in *Midnight's Children*, but are represented by pseudonymous caricatures: Pakistani prime minister Murtaza Ali Bhutto and president Zia ul-Haq are satirized under the names Iskander Harappa and Raza Hyder. As in satirical allegory, the characters are flat, the structure is very polarized, and the end feels predetermined.

We can perhaps account for the novel's claustrophobia by saying *Shame* is about Pakistan rather than India. Rushdie had visited his parents in Karachi from England, but never felt at home there. He tells of trying to produce and act in a performance of Edward Albee's *The Zoo Story* for Karachi TV but being stymied by censors. Rushdie always contrasts Pakistan unfavourably with India. Whereas India is the world's largest democracy, Pakistan has been for many years a military dictatorship at risk of becoming a fundamentalist theocracy. Where the land of Nehru, the secular India favoured by Rushdie, defines itself in pluralist terms as having room for many religions, Pakistan is defined as the Land of the Pure.

The claustrophobia of the setting of *Shame* is reflected in narrative events: Omar Khayyam Shakil, ostensibly the novel's anti-hero, spends the first twelve years of his life locked in a labyrinthine mansion. While Saleem Sinai expands to the size of the world of *Midnight's Children* and there is no getting away from his voice, Rushdie deliberately set out to make the hero of *Shame* a hollow at the centre of the novel. He succeeded perhaps too well. We learn of Shakil's birth of at the beginning of the novel and the novel ends with his gruesome dismemberment at the hands of his wife, but otherwise he figures too little in the novel to hold it together.

The omniscient narrator of *Shame* speaks as the author of the book. Within the narrative he justifies his right as an outsider to comment on affairs at "home." In other words, he cannot be separated from Rushdie. *Midnight's Children* is a Bombay novel, and Saleem Sinai's authority depends on the fact that he is in Bombay while he writes. The setting of *Shame*, a fictional country playfully nicknamed Peccavistan, resembles Pakistan as seen from a great distance and the novel does not pretend to be there.

Rushdie's voice interrupts the narration to discuss how the novel was originally inspired by actual incidents in London. The first such incident was an immigrant father's murder of his daughter whose love for a white boy had brought shame to the family. Rushdie is fascinated with Muslim notions of honour and its corollary, shame. He makes Sufiya, Raza Hyder's daughter and Omar's wife, mentally retarded (a cruel echo of Zia's own daughter's handicap) so that she can stand for innocence and purity. She is not allowed to know about sex and is kept locked up in the attic like Jane Eyre's madwoman. She suffers a disease of the immune system, symbolic of the self-loathing instilled in her by a mother who does not love her but cares only for the honour she might besmirch. Rushdie links sexual repression with political repression: together they breed a bizarre collective unconscious seething with anger. Sufiya's sexual repression leaves her open to possession by a force called the Beast. The theme of irrational and motiveless anger, already explored in the figure of Shiva in *Midnight's Children*, will return in all of Rushdie's work, taking the form of race riots in *The Satanic Verses*, domestic murders in *The Moor's Last Sigh*, and serial killings in *The Ground Beneath Her Feet* and *Fury*. As always in Rushdie, there is a distinct ambivalence about violence, which is feared and abhorred but also imagined as inevitable and apocalyptic in the sense of revealing the hidden truth of the world. Another incident that inspired the author of *Shame* was something that happened to his sister: when set upon by racist youths in the London underground, she paradoxically felt not anger but shame. The narrator indulges a fantasy of what would have happened if the victim had instead rounded upon her attackers with superhuman strength. Sufiya Hyder feels all the shame that others *should* feel for their corrupt and evil actions but that, paradoxically, the dwellers in the land of the pure feel only for female sexuality.

If *Midnight's Children* was the book Rushdie was born to write, *The Satanic Verses* (1988) is the one in which he found his great theme: how to put England and India in the same novel and imagine the world that contains them both. In *The Satanic Verses* he has put the most of himself, including his early experience of humiliation at Rugby (the kippered herring incident suffered by Saladin Chamcha), the research that he did at Cambridge into the seventh-century world of Mohammed, the Kensington neighbourhood where his family lived from 1962 to 1964, his early ambitions as an actor, his marriage to an Englishwoman (his first wife, Clarissa Lugard, becomes, with apologies to Samuel Richardson, Pamela Lovelace), his troubled relationship to his father (Saladin is reconciled with his dying father at the end of the novel), and his affair with Robyn Davidson in Australia (the inspiration for the mountain-climber Alleluia Cone in the novel). *The Satanic Verses* combines the personal with the political and the newsmaking. The bomb that destroyed an Air India 747 over the Atlantic on June 23, 1985 is the inspiration for the novel's opening scene, in which two Indian Muslims fall into the English Channel from an Air India plane exploded by Sikh terrorists. The race riots that ravaged Brixton and Southhall in the 1980s become the Brickhall riots in the novel. The Ayatollah Khomeini figures prominently as the Imam, in exile in the West which he abhors. The liberal political sympathies that Rushdie developed as executive member of the Camden Committee for Community Relations and that he has regularly displayed in his journalism and in his public comments also receive fictional expression in *The Satanic Verses*, which memorably depicts the demonization of racial others and police brutality in Thatcher's England.

Midnight's Children felt encyclopaedic, as if Saleem Sinai had swallowed a world, but it also explained the Indian background to an audience that might be unfamiliar with it. By including all that had gone into his own making and by minimizing explanation, Rushdie has made *The Satanic Verses* more resistant to the reader. Relatively few of the readers who can catch the intertextual play with *Othello* and *Our*

Mutual Friend will also know about the episode of the Satanic Verses in the history of the Koran. How many people who know the history of Islam's founding also know Rolling Stones lyrics? By including elements from so many disparate sources on the grounds that all of them have gone onto his own making, Rushdie has divided his readers into camps, those who know some things and those who know others, and has effectively written about a culture of one.

As always in Rushdie, the one splits to become two. Saleem Sinai in *Midnight's Children* is shadowed by Shiva, his dark alter ego with whom he was changed at birth and who has as much claim as he does to represent India. *Shame* explicitly alludes to *Dr Jekyll and Mr Hyde* in its two characters Shakil and Hyder, and in the pairing of Harappa and Hyder. In *The Satanic Verses* we again have doubled characters: Saladin Chamcha (whose name, literally "spoon," means "toadie" or "sycophant") and Gibreel Farishta, whose name means the Angel Gabriel. Saladin (originally Salahuddin Chamchawalla) is an Indian Muslim who wants to reinvent himself as English. His name associates him with the Muslim leader at the time of the Crusades, but he sees himself as a latter-day William the Conqueror out to conquer England by becoming English. Gibreel, on the other hand, is an Indian Muslim who wants to reinvent England so that it will have room for him, a process he calls "tropicalization." Although Gibreel is the character with whose atheism and hybridity Rushdie is most comfortable, and Saladin is largely an object of satire as the quintessential mimic man, it is Saladin whose life borrows most from Rushdie's own.

Saladin Chamcha, whose name recalls Kafka's Gregor Samsa, suffers a metamorphosis: the man who had sought redemption as an Englishman grows horns, hair, and a tail, and his demonic appearance attracts the hostile attention of the police. This experience teaches him the true, racist nature of England, which sees him as a devil and thereby makes him into one. While recovering from his beating in a clinic, he meets others who have been transformed into strange mutants, among them a manticore and a woman with glass skin. The manticore tells him that the transformation is effected by the power of description. When people are told they are less than human, they and others start to believe it. This is the magic of words, and in particular of stereotypes and ideology.

London in the novel becomes a magical, surreal place variously called Ellowendeeowen, Mahagonny, Babylon, and Alphaville, and there are plenty of allusions to Wonderland, the Looking Glass, Oz, and Peristan. There is, however, another source of magic: religious belief and the possibility of other worlds. In *Midnight's Children*, religion was the source of poetic imagery and playful allusion but was not central to the novelist's concerns. The magic realism in *The Satanic Verses* is closer to *Grimus*, which also tackled questions of faith and transcendence, than to *Midnight's Children* and *Shame*. The modern-day immigrant Gibreel, who has played gods in Hindu "theologicals" but has lost his own faith, goes slowly mad and has terrible dreams in which he finds himself an angel reciting scripture to a seventh-century prophet called Mahound near a town called Jahilia very much like Mecca. He dreams as well of a modern prophetess called Ayesha who inspires faith in Indian peasants and leads them on a pilgrimage to the sea in order to cross the water to Mecca.

Central to the novel is the historical matter of the Satanic Verses. The Koran was dictated to Mohammed by the angel Gibreel and then in turn dictated by Mohammed to a scribe. However, apocryphal legend has it that certain passages dictated by the Prophet, in particular, lines in Surah 53, "The Star," making room for the worship of the pagan goddesses Al-Lat, Al-Uzza, and Manat, were excised when political circumstances altered and were replaced by the current lines that scoff at the possibility of deities existing alongside Allah. While orthodoxy dismisses the verses as later forgeries designed to discredit the Revelation, legend attributes the excised verses to the devil who tricked Mohammed. Rushdie is fascinated by the dilemma suggested by the scandal: how can one ever be sure that one's revelation comes from God and not the devil? Gibreel in his role as angel is amazed to discover that, instead of passively receiving the revelation, Mahound is able to control the messenger: the prophet commands Gibreel's recitation of both the verses recognizing the goddesses and the later verses denouncing them. The words are Mahound's rather than Gibreel's, and the prophet's willingness to be God's mouthpiece is inseparable from his claim to speak for God. The scribe Salman, who takes down Mahound's dictation, has his own faith in the infallibility of revelation shaken when the prophet fails to notice that he has deliberately changed a few words.

Rushdie relates the founding of a world religion in the seventh century to the condition of twentieth-century immigrants in London by asking the same question of both: "How does something new come into the world?" The novel starts with a big bang on "New Year's Day or thereabouts": the explosion of Air India flight 420 over the English Channel from which Chamcha and Farishta fall to earth. Rushdie rejects the notion of creation *ex nihilo*, out of thin air. Instead immigration, and by implication, all creation, is re-creation: the past is fragmented into a debris of broken memories and broken tongues which must be recombined. Immigration is a fall from paradise (the plane is called "Bostan," the name of one of the gardens of paradise), and a death and rebirth: the immigrant, like the convert, must die to the old self and be born again.

Newness is never absolute. No matter how strangely altered, the other can only be imagined in terms of the already familiar. A pessimistic answer to the question of how newness enters the world is that there is only ever imitation. Both Saladin and Gibreel earn their living as mimics. Chamcha is the Man of a Thousand Voices and One Voice, whose ventriloquism makes possible his career on radio. Gibreel is an actor who lipsynchs to playback singers. The impossibility of newness and the inevitability of imitation do not, however, doom people to inauthenticity. If newness as such is impossible, original combinations (putting things together in the hope that their juxtaposition will emit sparks) are always possible. Indeed the novel's implication is that everything original was once imitation. Rushdie's own style, rich as ever with puns and allusions, is based on the migrant tropes of translation and metaphor, both of whose etymologies mean "carrying across."

Some forms of imitation are creative and others are derivative and debilitating. Mimicry, or bad imitation, obeys the commands of others. It is filled with self-loathing, the desire to be who you are not, and therefore confirms the power of others. The opposite is not a return to authenticity. Authenticity, as represented by the black Briton Uhuru Simba's pretend-African name, is also always mimicry. The self is never whole but is made of cracks and absences and mirrors. There never was a core self, so there can be no return to roots and consequently no betrayal. The self is no more than the roles it plays. What Rushdie suggests is that, once we give up searching for authenticity, we can appreciate that everything is performance. Imitation becomes creative and liberating when it becomes conscious of itself as imitation. To avoid becoming the prisoner of a role one must remember that it is but a role. Englishness itself, Saladin's preferred role, is always just a role, even when played by the English. It is a role Pamela, his upper-class English wife, seeks to escape.

The possibility of reinventing the self is, of course, both the promise and the temptation of the immigrant condition. Upon realizing he is as featureless as a jelly, Saladin puts on a haughty demeanour that becomes a second self. There are, however, limits to the potential for self-invention, as Saladin finds out. Once you construct a particular voice and face, they become you and change becomes painful. Accents are particularly hard to shed. Yet the face and voice that Saladin has constructed with such effort begin to let him down: a Bombay lilt returns to his voice. He feels he is not himself, but what does that mean? It would seem old selves do not disappear but continue as ghosts or shadows haunting the present self. Moreover, as his own unhappy experience as a devil proves, the freedom of self-invention has limits imposed by the world of others.

Although descriptions bring into being what they describe, the world remains larger than any description. That is why it is always possible to rewrite the debilitating descriptions by others. The poet Jumpy Joshi writes a poem based on Enoch Powell's terrible image of "rivers of blood," in which he turns the metaphor on its head and makes it something the immigrants themselves can use. Saladin's own incarnation of the devil, the result of racist projection, receives a new valence when he is adopted by immigrant youth as a figure of heroic black resistance filling their dreams. Rushdie argues, rather tenuously, that he himself is doing something similar when he takes the name Mahound, a derogatory term from the Middle Ages, to refer to a figure like the Prophet.

How then does newness come into the world? First it must be dreamed. Artistic creation requires the courage to dream a thought, speak it, and thereby make it true. That is, however, only the first step. The dreamer must get another to share the dream: "A man who believes in himself needs someone to believe in him to prove he's managed it." At its crudest, this second step is a problem of marketing. Hal Valance the advertising magnate see ethnicity as just another image to be exploited or avoided. The novel prefers to think of inventing a world as a problem of faith. Gibreel is divine as long as Indian moviegoers think he is, and he ceases to be when they cease to believe. The loss of faith is the death of God. The converse is also true: the successful artist, like a prophet, brings a world into being by inspiring others with faith. The Prophet himself, Rushdie suggests, dreamt a world into existence which others wanted to share. Rushdie seems to have thought, somewhat naively, that in making the Prophet an artist like himself, he was redeeming Mohammed for a secular age.

The Satanic Verses, as big and as risky as *Midnight's Children*, fails, however, to cohere. Its contradictions sabotage its important ideas. In particular, the novel cannot decide what its attitude to the devil should be. Saladin is given his horns by the racist police who see immigrants as demonic others. But Saladin is also given his horns by Rushdie for precisely the opposite reason: not because he is foreign but because he is a snob and a mimic man who wants to deny India and be British. Moreover, the man who has been made a devil as a result of racial demonizing is later possessed by a demon of jealousy and resentment resembling the Beast that possesses Sufiya Zinobia in *Shame*. Having internalized the devil that others see or unleashed the devil that always lurks within, Saladin looks for someone to blame for his blasted hopes and takes his revenge on Gibreel. Newly aware of the power of words, he acts like Iago in *Othello* to manipulate Gibreel and plant the seeds of a soul-destroying suspicion and jealousy. Is the devil an invention used to rob others of their humanity or a force of darkness deep in the human heart? The question is complicated because the narrator introduces himself as the devil, a Romantic Promethean figure and rival creator who has "all the best songs." It is hard to imagine that the devil who narrates the novel is also the source of all evil. Rushdie, it seems, does not care that these forms of the devil are incompatible. The confusion between social construction and innate evil as explanations of events mean that the great race riot that is the climax of the book is insufficiently imagined. It is not given the usual political or sociological explanations, but is presented as a matter of individual choices: Saladin chooses left and so damns himself, but forgiveness and redemption are always possible. Such Dickensian sentimentality accords poorly with the novel's postmodern emphasis on language as the source of all meaning.

Rushdie has always run into difficulty steering between words and the world. Indira Gandhi successfully sued him for libel over *Midnight's Children*, and later editions have removed an offending sentence that described her indifference to her dying husband. *The Satanic Verses*, of course, caused a much greater furor. The novel was first banned in India, where it was feared it would cause offence to Muslims. Muslims in Britain burned the book in angry demonstrations, and on Valentine's Day, February 14, 1989, the Ayatollah Khomeini pronounced a fatwa calling for the Rushdie's death as a blasphemer. The author and his then wife, Marianne Wiggins, went into hiding, protected by the British secret service.

What offended Rushdie's attackers was less the blasphemy that the Prophet had invented the Quran than the use of the name Mahound and the presence in Jahilia of a whorehouse where the prostitutes took the names of Mohammed's twelve wives. Rushdie was forced to defend a novel that preaches that descriptions can remake the world by arguing that it was only fiction after all. The postmodern author who came of age listening to rock and roll in London in the sixties seems to have been genuinely surprised that heresy, profanity, and blasphemy do not carry positive connotations everywhere. For a brief moment Rushdie announced that he had been converted to Islam, but he quickly resumed the more congenial role of symbol of artistic freedom and human rights. The controversy that erupted over *The Satanic Verses*, pitting the right to free speech against the need to show respect for cultural others, exposed contradictions at the heart of Western liberalism. The majority of Rushdie's fellow writers and of postcolonial critics have came out in support of the right of the artist to say whatever he liked, as did Rushdie's political enemies like Margaret Thatcher. Most also celebrate his blasphemy and his irreverence as necessary weapons in the struggle against fundamentalism. Nevertheless a few, like Germaine Greer and John LeCarré, have criticized him for attacking a vulnerable minority.

Rushdie's literary output since the fatwa has been marked by a refusal to be silenced. In 1990 he published *Haroun and the Sea of*

Stories, a children's book written for his son, in which young Haroun must rescue his story-telling father from the evil forces that want to silence all stories. Khattam-Shud fears stories because they cannot be controlled and are by nature subversive. Rushdie also released a collection of essays and reviews entitled *Imaginary Homelands* (1991), which reminded his readers of how fine a critic he could be and how persuasive a cultural analyst. For the most part, these essays were published before the fatwa, but the volume includes the important essays written in his own defence: "'In God We Trust,'" "In Good Faith," "Is Nothing Sacred?," and "Why I Have Embraced Islam."

Rushdie was determined that his writing not be affected by his circumstances. *The Moor's Last Sigh* (1995), his first novel since the fatwa, shows no abatement of literary ambition, but marks a reinvention of Rushdie's art, stripping it of allegory and adding passion. Although it returns to the Bombay of *Midnight's Children, The Moor's Last Sigh* is more concerned with love and art than with the nation. That does not make the novel less political. The novel is a pessimistic updating of Indian political history, chronicling the rise of corruption and Hindu fundamentalism, phenomena not foreseen by the author of *Midnight's Children*. For its satirical caricature of Bal Thackeray, the Hindu fundamentalist demagogue whose Shiv Sena wields power in Bombay, the novel was banned in India. *The Moor's Last Sigh* locates Rushdie's politics in a larger frame. The novel's narrator, Moraes Zogoiby, writing, like Rushdie himself, under a death warrant, is the descendant of Catholics and Jews born in Bombay. The "Moor" can trace his ancestry back to Boabdil, the Moorish leader who surrendered the Alhambra to Ferdinand and Isabella in 1492, the year that saw both the Reconquista from the Moors and the expulsion of the Jews from Spain. 1492 marks the end of a Muslim civilization based on the tolerance of minorities, and the beginning of a peculiarly modern form of intolerance that has spread across the globe in the form of ethnic nationalism and religious fundamentalism.

Rushdie the novelist attributes to the example of Günter Grass his own desire never to be satisfied but with each novel to "start all over again and do it better." Constant renewal is, however, perhaps a better description of the career of García Márquez than of either Grass or Rushdie. The new direction in Rushdie's magic realism marked by *The Moor's Last Sigh* resembles the change in the career of Gabriel García Márquez represented by *Love in the Time of Cholera* (1984), also a story of obsessional love in a violent world. In retrospect, Rushdie seems almost to be consciously mapping his career against that of the Columbian novelist. *Midnight's Children*, an epic that reads history in terms of genealogy, feels like an Indian version of *One Hundred Years of Solitude*. *Shame* is best understood as an Asian rewriting of the Latin American dictator novel and, in particular, of *The Autumn of the*

Patriarch. The long luxurious sentences describing the eighteen shawls that Rani Harappa embroiders and in which she records the shamelessness of her husband Iskander, sound like direct allusions to the chapter-long sentences in García Márquez's novel. In their depiction of political tyranny, both novels blend satire and fantasy, horror and absurdity, and both take a perverse delight in what they abhor. An affinity to the Marxist Columbian novelist, conscious or not, may also have motivated Rushdie's decision to accept the invitation of the Sandinistas to travel to Nicaragua in 1986 and to write a journal of that trip, *The Jaguar Smile* (1987).

In spite of Rushdie's efforts, however, it is hard not to feel that there has been a creative falling off since the fatwa. *The Moor's Last Sigh* is not *Love in the Time of Cholera,* and *The Ground Beneath Her Feet* (1999) and *Fury* (2001) have disappointed most critics. The Booker Prize is, of course, not the final word on literary merit, but in retrospect it is hard to quarrel with the judges. *Midnight's Children* won not just the Booker but also the title of Booker of Bookers in 1993, as the best novel to have won the prize in its twenty-five-year history. *Shame, The Satanic Verses,* and *The Moor's Last Sigh* were all nominated for the prize in the years they were published but did not win, and the later novels have not even been nominated.

As if to emphasize the break that occurred in his career, Rushdie's later novels frequently allude to his earlier novels and, in particular, to *Midnight's Children.* The author of *Midnight's Children* was accused of pessimism for ending that novel with a vision of apocalyptic disintegration, a charge that Rushdie countered by claiming that the exuberant style was a celebration of India. In *The Moor's Last Sigh* we learn what happened to Saleem Sinai's son Aadam, who carried so many of the hopes in that earlier novel and for whom Saleem is writing his memoirs. Eighteen years after his birth, Aadam Sinai has become a corrupt businessman dealing in drugs, arms, money-laundering, and procuring. In a disavowal of what in retrospect appears as the naive optimism of *Midnight's Children,* Rushdie describes him thus:

> It seems he was originally the illegitimate child of a Bombay hooligan and an itinerant magician from Shadipur U.P., and had been unofficially adopted, for a time, by a Bombay man who was missing-believed-dead, having mysteriously disappeared fourteen years ago, not long after his allegedly brutal treatment by government agents during the 1974-77 Emergency.[1]

This is the same ironic gesture made by James Joyce when he undermines Stephen Dedalus, the hero of *A Portrait of the Artist as a Young Man,* in the later novel *Ulysses. The Ground Beneath Her Feet* even partially redeems William Methwold, the representative colonizer who returns to England in *Midnight's Children*: we learn that he is actually a scholar of Indian mythologies, and far from being a racist, he marries a Parsi widow, the mother of the novel's hero, Ormus Cama. In *Fury* we learn that Malik Solanka's inner demons stem from his abuse as a child by his stepfather in Noor Ville in Methwold's Estate (Noor Ville is where the American girl, Evie Burns, Saleem's first love, lived).

Rushdie's monograph for the British Film Institute on the film *The Wizard of Oz* (1992) faults that movie for betraying its own most important truth: the lesson of the film should not be that there is no place like home, but that it is necessary to leave home to find better things. Rushdie himself has repeatedly bidden farewell to the East, first in *Shame*, then in *The Ground Beneath Her Feet*, and most recently in the introduction to his screenplay of *Midnight's Children*. As the constant return to *Midnight's Children* suggests, however, Rushdie has not been able to shake the East so easily. A collection of stories entitled *East, West* appeared in 1994. The nine stories are divided into three sections: the first, set in India, called "East"; the second, set in Europe, called "West"; and the third, involving Indians in England, called "East-West." In 1997 Rushdie won a lawsuit to reclaim ancestral property at Solan in Himachal Pradesh, and he has returned to tour India with his son Zafar. Even as he renounced the East, Rushdie co-edited *The Vintage Book of Indian Writing, 1947-1997* (1997) with his new wife, Elizabeth West.

In retrospect, the tension in his work between home and the world may always have been Rushdie's greatest strength. If so, it has also proved his greatest artistic hurdle. The aesthetic failure of *The Satanic Verses*, perhaps the boldest literary attempt to represent the migrant self since Henry Roth's *Call It Sleep* in 1934, bears witness to the difficulty of imagining the single world implied by globalization and the transnational movement of populations. In that novel Rushdie thought he was genuinely engaging with religion and with questions of racism, but arguably he can be seen to have been reducing difference to postmodern sameness.

Since the fatwa it has sometimes seemed that Rushdie has left not just home, but the world altogether. The strange flatness of the Bombay that is the primary setting of *The Moor's Last Sigh*—everything happens indoors—is perhaps attributable to Rushdie's inability to visit. *The Ground Beneath Her Feet* is about an international popular culture best exemplified by rock music. We are asked to imagine a world in which world music got its start in the seventies when an Indian rock band called VTO, led by the lovers Ormus Cama and Vina Apsara, was all the rage in England and America: the Indian invasion. The thinness of this large novel is not just attributable to its lack of political purchase—there is no discussion, as in *The Satanic Verses*, of cultural difference or racism; migration and translation pose no serious problems—the thinness results from the nature of the global stage inhabited by the characters. Everyone listens to the same music and participates in the same circuits of celebrity. In *Fury*, the latest novel, set in New York, where Rushdie has moved to be closer to the centre of the art and literary world, the global stage and the cast of international characters appear curiously indebted to CNN. The rich allusiveness that so characterized the early novels has been replaced by references to brand names and the news stories of the year 2000, as if the author had spent far too much time in front of his television. Where *Midnight's Children* and *The Satanic Verses* had been filled with references from around the world, most of which had to be explained for a Western reader, *Fury* is filled with references to ephemera: the names of stars and local scandals. The novel very deliberately dates itself. The centre of this world is New York; the margins resemble a risible Pacific island the size of Fiji called Lilliput-Blefescu. Swift's Lilliput was a satire of England; Rushdie's Lilliput is a satire of small faraway islands. The modern world of New York in *Fury* is perhaps closest to the cultural no-place of *Grimus*. Indeed the science-fiction fantasies that Malik Solanka invents for television and the internet sound very close in spirit to Rushdie's own first novel.

A recurring figure in Rushdie's novels is the man who, because of the existence of parallel dimensions, is able to tap into the spirit of the times in a more direct way than others can. Saleem Sinai uses his telepathic powers, located in his nose, to become All-India Radio. Aurora Zogoiby's Moor paintings are allegories of Indian history and prophecies of the fate of her son. Ormus Cama relies on his dead twin brother to hear the classics of pop music before they have even been recorded. And Malik Solanka is filled with a murderous rage against his wife, a form of the same fury that results in serial killings in New York and in civil wars around the world. Rushdie's notion of the spirit of the times has clearly changed in the course of his career: where once it had been identified with radio and a national consciousness, and later it found expression in rock music and a global consciousness, most recently it has shifted to television and the internet. Rushdie has himself always been remarkable as a prophet. Scenes in *The Satanic Verses* foreshadow the author's own fate. This prophetic quality itself becomes the subject of the later novels: Malik Solanka finds himself in the midst of a revolution in Lilliput-Blefescu where all the participants wear masks representing characters he himself has invented.

In *The Ground Beneath Her Feet* and *Fury*, the tremendous imaginative resources that generated the energy of *Midnight's Children* go into producing male fantasies of ideal women. In *Fury* all that is left of Rushdie's magic realism is the beautiful Neela's capacity to make heads turn whenever she walks past. The protagonist, who closely resembles Rushdie in his life circumstances—Malik Solanka is famous as a creator, has difficulties with his three ex-wives, and has recently moved to America—wins her simply by falling in love with her. In a negative review of V.S. Naipaul's *The Enigma of Arrival*, Rushdie cites Borges who said that, in a riddle to which the answer is *knife*, the only word that must never be used is *knife*. Rushdie then points out that the word *love* does not figure anywhere in Naipaul's narrative, from which he adduces that the author is a loveless man. What if one turned Borges's dictum around: would it follow that a novel that spoke only of love could not be about love at all? Rushdie's last two novels are about love for a woman so ideal that every male in the world desires her. We cannot help but feel that the male protagonist's desire requires the desire of all other males for its validation. The author of *The Satanic Verses*, who once laid such store by self-consciousness, is haunted by romance.

In all his work before the fatwa, Rushdie's treatment of desire was always comic and allegorical. There was something infinitely suggestive, yet comic, in the scene in which Aadam Aziz, Saleem Sinai's grandfather, falls in love through a perforated bedsheet with a woman he can only see in parts, or in Amina Sinai's unconsummated love for Nadir Khan. The doubling and splitting by which Rushdie generates character inevitably filled his fiction with love triangles and made jealousy and rivalry important themes. There was, however, something not fully serious about Colonel Sabarmati's shooting of his wife and her lover in *Midnight's Children*, or about Saladin's doggerel verses which aroused Gibreel's sexual jealousy in *The Satanic Verses*. In *The Moor's Last Sigh*, *The Ground Beneath Her Feet*, and *Fury*, although the characters continue to be generated by doubling and splitting and are therefore as thin as cartoons, readers are somehow expected to share their overblown passions. That we do not fall in love with Evie Burns or Jamila Singer, as Saleem does, is part of the satiric and comic success of *Midnight's Children*. That we cannot join Gibreel Farishta, Vasco Miranda, Rai Merchant, or Malik Solanka in their adoration of Alleluia Cone, Aurora Zogoiby, Vina Apsara, or Neela is a weakness in the later novels.

Perhaps the closest Rushdie comes to depicting convincing love is in his protagonists' relations to their sons. Saleem Sinai writes his memoirs for his son, and *Midnight's Children* is dedicated to Rushdie's own son Zafar. *Haroun and the Sea of Stories* was also written for Zafar and is about a son who seeks his missing father. *Fury* ends with Malik Solanka returning to claim his son who has been raised by his estranged wife. The claim on a son at the end of a novel by a man who remains bitter towards his own father and has done nothing to earn his son's love feels, however, suspect.

Another symptom of the thinness of Rushdie's output since *The*

Satanic Verses is that his most important theme after romantic passion has become celebrity. Just as we know that the protagonists of Rushdie's later novels are great lovers because they win the love of the most desirable woman in the world, so, too, although we cannot see their paintings, hear their songs, or see the television shows they write, we know they are artistic geniuses because they are world-famous. Celebrity, of course, is a brittle theme, usually more suitable for satire than for winning the reader's sympathy. It is hard not to read the later books in terms of what has happened to Rushdie himself. If celebrity has become his major theme, it is surely because Rushdie himself has become such a public persona. The rock band U2 set to music and recorded some of the lyrics from *The Ground Beneath Her Feet*. Rushdie has appeared as himself, the famous author, in the British film *Bridget Jones's Diary*. And he regularly pontificates in the *New York Times*.

Roger Clark attributes the relative failure of Rushdie's later novels to his refusal to engage any longer with religion. Rushdie the atheist and secularist had long been fascinated by religious cosmology, by images of ideal wholeness threatened by demonic chaos, by the search for transcendence, by prophecy and apocalypse. Ever suspicious of organized religion, he nevertheless thought of himself as engaged with religious questions, even if always from a point of view closer to heresy than to orthodoxy. Although less interested in allegory and ostensibly more concerned with character, the later novels read more like polemics than do the early novels. Certainly they admit of less doubt. The later novels engage with mythology (*The Ground Beneath Her Feet* is based on the myth of Orpheus and *Fury* on the Eumenides), but the mythology is Greek and literary and has no relation to religion.

Note

1. Salman Rushdie, *The Moor's Last Sigh* (Toronto: Knopf, 1995) 342.

A SALMAN RUSHDIE BIBLIOGRAPHY

Primary Sources

Novels

Grimus: a Novel. London: Gollancz, 1975.

Midnight's Children. New York: Knopf, 1981.

Shame. London: Cape, 1983.

The Jaguar Smile: A Nicaraguan Journey. London: Picador, 1989.

The Satanic Verses. New York: Viking, 1989.

Haroun and the Sea of Stories. New York: Granta Books in association with Viking, 1991.

The Wizard of Oz: A Short Text About Magic. London: BFI, 1992.

East, West. London: Jonathan Cape, 1994. New York: Pantheon Books, 1994.

The Moor's Last Sigh. Toronto: Alfred A. Knopf Canada, 1995.

The Ground Beneath Her Feet. New York: Henry Holt & Co., 1999.

Fury. London: Jonathan Cape, 2001.

Secondary Sources

Selected Books and Essays on Salman Rushdie

Aravamudan, Srinivas. "Being God's Postman is No Fun, Yaar: Salman Rushdie's The Satanic Verses." *Diacritics* 19.2 (1989): 3-20.

Reder, Michael, ed. *Conversations with Salman Rushdie*. Jackson: U of Mississippi P, 2000.

Baucom, Ian. *Out of Place: Englishness, Empire, and the Locations of Identity*. Princeton: Princeton UP, 1999.

Bhabha, Homi. *The Location of Culture*. London: Routledge, 1994.

Birch, David. "Postmodernist Chutneys." *Textual Practice* 5.1 (1991): 1-7.

Booker, M. Keith, ed. *Critical Essays on Salman Rushdie*. New York: G.K. Hall, 1999.

Brennan, Timothy. *Salman Rushdie and the Third World: Myths of the Nation*. London: Macmillan, 1989.

Clark, Roger Y. *Stranger Gods: Salman Rushdie's Other Worlds*. Montreal: McGill-Queen's UP, 2001.

Cronin, Richard. "The Indian English Novel: *Kim* and *Midnight's Children*." *Rushdie's Midnight's Children: A Book of Readings*. Ed. Meenakshi Mukherjee. Delhi: Pencraft International, 1999. 134-48.

Dell'Aversano, Carmen. "Worlds, Things, Words: Rushdie's Style from *Grimus* to *Midnight's Children*." *Coterminous Worlds: Magical Realism and Contemporary Post-colonial Literature in English*. Ed. Elsa Linguanti et al. Amsterdam: Rodopi, 1999. 61-70.

Desai, Anita. "Introduction." *Midnight's Children*. Salman Rushdie. New York: Everyman, 1995. vii-xxi.

English, James F. *Comic Transactions: Literature, Humor, and the Politics of Community in Twentieth-Century Britain*. Ithaca: Cornell UP, 1994.

Gorra, Michael. *After Empire: Scott, Naipaul, Rushdie*. Chicago: U of Chicago P, 1997.

Hamilton, Ian. "The First Life of Salman Rushdie." *The New Yorker* (Dec. 25, 1995—Jan. 1, 1996): 90-113.

Harrison, James. *Salman Rushdie*. New York: Twayne, 1992.

Islam, Syed Manzurul. "Writing the Postcolonial Event: Salman Rushdie's August 15th, 1947." *Textual Practice* 13.1 (1999): 119-35.

Kane, Jean M. "The Migrant Intellectual and the Body of History: Salman Rushdie's *Midnight's Children*." *Contemporary Literature* 37.1 (1996): 94-118.

Kortenaar, Neil ten. "Postcolonial Ekphrasis: Salman Rushdie Gives the Finger Back to the Empire." *Contemporary Literature* 38.2 (1997): 232-59.

Lipscomb, David. "Caught in a Strange Middle Ground: Contesting History in Salman Rushdie's *Midnight's Children.*" *Diaspora* 1.2 (1991): 163-89.

Lopez, Alfred J. *Posts and Pasts: A Theory of Postcolonialism.* Albany: SUNY Press, 2001.

Mukherjee, Meenakshi, ed. *Rushdie's Midnight's Children: A Book of Readings.* Delhi: Pencraft International, 1999.

Parameswaram, Uma. *The Perforated Sheet: Essays on Salman Rushdie's Art.* Delhi: Affiliated East-West Press, 1988.

Rushdie, Salman. "*Midnight's Children* and *Shame.*" *Kunapipi* 7.1 (1985): 1-19.

Spivak, Gayatri Chakravorty. *Outside in the Teaching Machine.* New York: Routledge, 1993.

Suleri, Sara. *The Rhetoric of English India.* Chicago: U of Chicago P, 1992.

Uprety, Sanjeev Kumor. "Disability and Postcoloniality in Salman Rushdie's *Midnight's Children* and Third-World Novels." *The Disability Studies Reader.* Ed. Lennard J. Davis. New York: Routledge, 1997. 366-81.

12

Amitav Ghosh

JOHN THIEME

There is a moment in Amitav Ghosh's ethnographic "history in the guise of a traveller's tale,"[1] *In An Antique Land* (1992), when the narrator-persona, a figure who bears an obvious resemblance to Ghosh himself, is struck by an untypical remark made by one of the Egyptian villagers, among whom he is living. He comments, "it was the first time that anyone in Lataifa or Nashawy had attempted an enterprise similar to mine—to enter my imagination and look at my situation as it might appear to me" (*IAL* 152). Such an attempt at imaginative empathy characterizes all Ghosh's writing to date and seems to be the product of a humanist concern to transcend culturally constructed differences.

Nevertheless there are commonalities between several of his major interests and the concerns of postcolonial theorists who take a constructivist view of culture. Like Edward Said, Ghosh draws attention to the artificiality of the East-West binaries of Orientalism.[2] Like Homi Bhabha, he demonstrates the hybrid, interstitial nature of cultures, as articulated through language. Like Ranajit Guha and the Subaltern Studies scholars, he endeavours to recuperate the silenced voices of those occluded from the historical record. In interview he distances himself from such theorizing,[3] though he does admit to a commonality of interest with those engaged in the Subaltern Studies project, several of whom are "old friends," with whom he went to school and college (Silva and Tickell 173); and, while he scrupulously acknowledges all his debts, his writing tends to conceal rather than foreground any interests he may have in postcolonial debates. Discussing his endeavours to give voice to subalternity, Robert Dixon says:

> Ghosh develops a style of writing that is sufficiently nuanced and elusive to sustain the "theoretical fiction" of a recovery of presence without actually falling back into essentialism. This is achieved by a fluid and at times confusing deployment of the lexicons of both liberal humanism and post-structuralism, though without allowing his writing to be affiliated with either—in the hundreds of endnotes

to *In An Antique Land*, there is not one that refers to a European theorist.[4]

Whether primarily fictional or factual—he blurs the divisions—all Ghosh's work is researched with a meticulous attention to detail and he has spoken of the pleasure he derives from "dealing with documents."[5] However, the research that informs his writing mainly confines itself to specifics—the minutiae of such subjects as weaving and phrenology in *The Circle of Reason* (1986), medieval mercantile culture and etymologies in *In An Antique Land* and medical historiography and cyber technology in *The Calcutta Chromosome* (1996)—and when it occasionally allows itself to erupt into generalization, it avoids contemporary theoretical jargon.

So, while all Ghosh's impressive and remarkably varied body of work to date, an oeuvre which is unsurpassed among his Indian-English contemporaries of the post-Rushdie generation, appears to demonstrate a sure-footed sense of contemporary cultural debates, it denies them any significant explicit presence in his writing. The explanation could be seen to lie in his apparent commitment to metonymic rather than metaphoric expression. Though he repeatedly unpicks the assumptions engrained in European mercantile capitalism and elitist discursive hegemonies, both Western and non-Western, his concern with the recuperation and rendering of individual experiences operates against the kind of totalizing theory that habitually consigns subalternity to oblivion. Paradoxically, though, while metonymy appears to take precedence over metaphor in his writing, the more one reads his work, the more its emphasis on particularities appears to speak to larger issues. Like a latter-day V.S. Naipaul, albeit one who demonstrates the capacity to empathize with rather than stand aloof from his subjects,[6] Ghosh seems, though his carefully realized representation of specifics—past, present and, in the case of *The Calcutta Chromosome* future—to address many of the central concerns that are troubling contemporary consciences, among them the construction of cultural difference, the interaction of traditional and modern technologies and discourses, the tensions between Eastern and Western value-systems and the merits and demerits of globalization, in its various avatars.

While undertaking doctoral research in Egypt, Ghosh developed an interest in the routes of cultural exchange through which the pre-colonial Indian Ocean cloth trade operated and, as Robert Dixon has pointed out, weaving is a dominant trope in his early work. It functions in two ways: as an organizational device, in which disparate strands are juxtaposed to create unexpected linkages and analogies; and as a central motif, with Ghosh repeatedly interrogating the binaries of Western rationalist thought by demonstrating that received historiography has constructed dichotomized models of cultural interaction, as surely as Western colonialism introduced political policies of "divide and rule." The minutiae of Ghosh's practice put flesh on Said's contention that Orientalism operated both textually and through direct military intervention, as in the case of Napoleon's invasion of Egypt.[7] Thus, while the inner narrative of *In An Antique Land* begins as an archival detective-story, in which the Ghosh narrator tries to unearth the identity of the "slave" of a twelfth-century Jewish merchant, this investigation gradually expands into a quietly stated polemic against the European violence that destroyed the centuries-old "peaceful traditions" of the Indian Ocean trade, built upon "the rich confusions that accompany a culture of accommodation and compromise" (*IAL* 287-88).

Ghosh was born in Calcutta in 1956 and, asked about the personal experiences that had been most influential on his writing, has spoken of the city as "a kind of constant that runs through all my books [...] the centre of my imaginative world."[8] His father was a Lieutenant-Colonel in the army and his assignments meant that during his youth Ghosh spent time in Sri Lanka, Iran and East Pakistan (later Bangladesh), while being based at boarding school in India. Much of his writing focuses on families and one branch of his own family lived in Burma (Myanmar), a connection which he has traced, in fictional form, in *The Glass Palace* (2000), particularly drawing on the experience of his uncle, the timber-merchant Jagat Chandra Dutta.

Ghosh attended Doon School in Dehra Dun and one of New Delhi's most illustrious educational institutions, St. Stephen's College, during a period when, in his own words, "India was in the high noon of nationalist self-confidence" (Piciucco 69) of a kind that was to vanish just a few years later. Several of his fellow-students later achieved prominence as novelists or as figures in the Subaltern Studies movement. After leaving St. Stephen's with a B.A. in History in 1976, he obtained an M.A. in Sociology from the University of Delhi in 1978. He went to St. Edmund Hall, Oxford to do postgraduate work and in 1979 obtained a diploma in social anthropology, while also spending time in Tunis learning Arabic. In 1980 he went to Egypt to do fieldwork for his doctoral research under the auspices of the Faculty of Arts, University of Alexandria. He was awarded his Oxford D.Phil. in Social Anthropology for his thesis on "Kinship in Relation to the Economic and Social Organization of an Egyptian Village Community" in 1981. His later ethnographical work, *In an Antique Land*, in which the central figure is a researcher who has obvious affinities with Ghosh, can be read as a companion-piece to the thesis.[9]

Ghosh has lived in Delhi, done fieldwork in Cambodia and Burma and written for a wide range of publications. He has held academic positions at a number of universities, including Delhi University,

Columbia University and Queens College of the City University of New York, where he is Distinguished Professor. His writing has received numerous awards. These include a Prix Medicis Etranger for *The Circle of Reason*, the Sahitya Akademi Award for *The Shadow Lines* (1988), the Arthur C. Clarke Prize for science fiction for *The Calcutta Chromosome*, the Pushcart Prize (an award given for stories, poems and essays published in a literary magazine in the U.S.) for his essay, "The March of the Novel through History: My Father's Bookcase" and the Grand Prize for Fiction at the Frankfurt International e-Book Awards for *The Glass Palace*. Controversially, he declined the best book award for the Eurasian region of the Commonwealth Writers Prize for *The Glass Palace*, on the grounds that he was unaware that his publishers had entered the book for this Prize and objected to the classification of "Commonwealth Literature."

Ghosh lives in New York with his wife, Deborah Baker, author of *In Extremis: The Life of Laura Riding* (1993) and a senior editor at Little Brown and Co., and his children Leela and Nayan.

Ghosh's first novel, *The Circle of Reason*, follows the fortunes a young weaver, Alu, who is brought up in a Bengal village and, after a false accusation that he is a member of a terrorist group, subsequently flees westwards, first to a fictional Gulf state and later to Algeria. The novel suggests that weaving is a diasporic activity which transcends national origins and unites worlds that have habitually been viewed as separate; and in so doing, it anticipates Ghosh's later contention in *In An Antique Land* that the medieval trade-routes functioned as a mobile inter-continental network that was largely unaware of Western Oriental/ Occidental bifurcations.

Alu is indisputably the main protagonist, the glue that holds a nomadic novel together, but for much of the action he is the silent centre around which an abundance of other stories are told. Many of these include fabulist elements and, although Ghosh never departs from the bounds of what is strictly possible, the use of fantasy suggest a world-view that has affinities with both contemporary magic realism[10] and a range of South Asian narrative traditions. Indian influences include the Sanskrit classics and twentieth-century Bengali literature and these two strands come together towards the end of the novel, when a character attempts to stage a production of Tagore's *Chitrangada*, a dance drama based on an episode in the *Mahabharata*.

Magic realist elements are particularly prominent in the second of the novel's three parts, set in Ghosh's Middle Eastern oil state, al-Ghazira. Here extraordinary events that reflect the collision of traditional and modern value-systems are sometimes reminiscent of happenings in Gabriel García Márquez's Macondo. When Alu is buried in the collapsed debris of a newly built commercial complex, he is saved by two antique sewing machines on which a huge slab of falling concrete comes to rest "just a hair away from his nose" (*CR* 240). A cross-eyed egg-seller is said to be able to see Cairo and Bombay simultaneously (245-46). A seventy-five-year-old woman, renowned "for her astonishing ugliness," is "much loved of the pearl divers and boatmen because she could scare sharks into tearing out their own entrails simply by grinning into the water" (255). And just as Márquez's *One Hundred Years of Solitude* begins *in medias res* with a cryptic phrase that anticipates a subsequent action ("Many years later, as he faced the firing squad, Colonel Aureliano Buendía was to remember that distant afternoon when his father took him to discover ice"[11]), *The Circle of Reason* employs a complex series of analeptic and proleptic references, partly to engineer suspense, but also to suggest the convergence of the ordinary and the extraordinary and to eliminate the possibility of reading the narrative passively, as a causal, linear chain of "real" occurrences. On the opening page, the narrative voice relates:

> Years later—thirteen to be exact—when people talked about all that had happened [...] it was generally reckoned that the boy's arrival was the real beginning. Some said they knew the moment they set eyes on that head. That was a little difficult to believe [...].
>
> Someone said: It's like a rock covered with fungus. But Bolai-da [...] wouldn't have that. He said at once: No, it's not like a rock at all. It's an *alu*, a potato, a huge, freshly dug, lumpy potato. (3)

Throughout the novel events are recounted in this manner, as so much rumour and gossip—"people talked," "it was generally reckoned," "Some said they knew," "That was a little difficult to believe," "Someone said"—a mode of narration which enables Ghosh to bridge the divide between the readily believable and the fantastic. The "magic realism" of the novel is a product of the oral folk imagination, a certain way of narrativizing experience, rather than an incursion into what is genuinely supernatural. In the Bengali first section, a plane is said to have conceived a child (98), but subsequent revelations make it clear that this conception is far from immaculate, when it transpires that human intercourse has been responsible. Nothing in the novel is finally supernatural: when one of the novel's iconic objects, a copy of René Vallery-Radot's *Life of Pasteur* turns up in Algeria thousands of miles away from the place where it was last seen, this may be extraordinary, but it is a coincidence of the kind that one finds in many picaresque novels.

As the title suggests, Reason is a paramount theme of the novel. In Part 1, Alu's uncle and foster father, Balaram, is a passionate advocate of a supranational vision of scientific reason, inspired by the work of Louis Pasteur, which leads him to undertake a campaign against germs and brahminical superstition in the local village. In Part 2, the generally silent Alu becomes his heir, when after his brush with death in the collapse of the commercial complex, he waxes lyrical on Pasteur's achievements and finds himself the founder of an anti-capitalist community, devoted to the eradication of both germs and the personal ownership of money. The theme continues into Part 3, where Balaram's original inspiration, the copy of the *Life of Pasteur*, is finally cremated, along with the body of one of the novel's central figures, in a scene which stresses the necessity of accommodations that enable ancient traditions to have valency in the contemporary world. Reason, as the title suggests, is circular and the view that the novel propounds is antipathetic to linear historiography. In the first part, Balaram's main rival is his "doppelganger," Bhudeb Roy, who opposes his vision of circularity with a belief in the "straight lines" (99), on which the technological progress of Europe, America and Japan has been founded. Though Balaram's world is destroyed at the end of this section, the primacy of reason in the novel remains unchallenged, as Alu migrates to new climes and ensures the continuation of Balaram's cyclic vision through his weaving and his continuation of the campaign against germs.

Ghosh's remarkably assured first novel lacks the structural tightness of his later fiction. Its brilliance lies in its *Panchatantra* or *Thousand and One Nights*-like[12] capacity for juggling a range of stories. At one point a character says, "You know whenever anything happens people think of a thousand stories" (215) and this aptly describes the method of the novel itself. Its proliferating tales lack authority in the sense that they are the product of individual imaginations and tellings. Yet each takes on a life of its own, as the novel moves between narrative strands as easily as it navigates the trade-routes that link supposedly separate countries and cultures; and such fluidity challenges notions of discrete nationhood and other forms of identity in a manner that anticipates the dominant impulse in Ghosh's later work.

The Circle of Reason concludes on an affirmative note that has not entirely been prepared for, with Alu, now no longer a fugitive, about to return "home" and an assertion that "Hope is the beginning" (423). Yet, in one sense, such optimism *has* been anticipated throughout by the text's emphasis on the circularity of Reason, which has been particularly associated with the trope of Alu's loom and the activity of weaving. Earlier Ghosh has concluded a passage on the romance of "cloth" with a panegyric on the unifying, transcultural benefits of the weaver's loom:

> Man at the loom is the finest example of Mechanical man; a creature who makes his own world as no other can, with his mind. The machine is man's curse and his salvation, and no

machine has created man as much as the loom. It has created not separate worlds but one, for it has never permitted the division of the world. (55)

Although the novel dramatizes a range of cultural conflicts, ultimately it expresses a humanist creed, which unsettles a range of binaries, such as those between tradition and modernity, nature and technology and East and West.

Ghosh's second novel, *The Shadow Lines* focuses on a very particular personal history—the experience of a single family—as a microcosm for a broader national and international experience. The lives of the narrator's family have been irrevocably changed as a consequence of Bengal's Partition between India and Pakistan at the time of Independence and the subsequent experience of the East Pakistan Civil War of 1971, which led to the creation of Bangladesh. The "shadow lines" of the title are the borders that divide people and, as in all Ghosh's work, one of the main emphases is on the arbitrariness of cartographical demarcations. Towards the end, when members of the family are about to undertake a journey from Calcutta to their former home in Dhaka, the narrator's grandmother wants to know whether she will "be able to see the border between India and East Pakistan from the plane" (*SL* 154), an ingenuous response which nevertheless foregrounds the absurdity of the revisionist map-making of the politicians responsible for Partition.

The family journey to Dhaka to rescue an aged relative and in the climax of this episode the narrator ponders the deadly effects of borders, when his second cousin, Tridib, a figure who has always exercised a particularly potent hold on his imagination, is killed amid the communal violence. Although he concedes that the political map-makers were well-intentioned, he is struck by the fact that the bonds that link Dhaka and Calcutta are closer than ever: "each city was the inverted image of the other, locked into an irreversible symmetry by the line that was to set us free—our looking-glass border" (234). Shadow-lines are, however, more than just the frontiers constructed by politicians. They have other resonances in the text and, as I have put it elsewhere, "They are the lines of demarcation that separate colonizer and colonized, present and past, self and image. Ultimately they are the signifying acts that construct notions of discrete identity."[13] As always, Ghosh is not only at pains to demonstrate the porousness of geographical borders, but also the artificiality of a range of binary categorizations of culture and areas of the human psyche.

The notion of the "looking-glass border" extends far beyond divided Bengal and when the narrator comes to see himself as the mirror-image of an English character he has never met, it bears a marked relationship to forms of colonial discourse that define non-European subjectivity as the inferior partner in a two-way power relationship:

> Nick Price, whom I have never seen, and would, as far as I knew never see, became a spectral presence beside me in my looking glass, growing with me, but always bigger and better and in some ways more desirable. (55)

The narrator's twinning with this larger "spectral presence" suggests both complicity in the hierarchized binaries constructed by such discourse, and also, in a manner typical of Ghosh's recurrent erosion of culturally constructed borders in favour of a broader humanism, affinities which transcend such divisions. And, despite ostensible acquiescence in the role of inferior partner in the colonial equation, the narrator emerges as epistemologically superior. As a colonial, his knowledge of the colonizer's culture far exceeds his English counterpart's familiarity with his world and with such knowledge comes a surer understanding of how the relationship operates. When he eventually travels to London, he knows the way to the Price family's house (thanks to his familiarity with the A-Z street atlas of the city) and astonishes its occupants by his detailed familiarity with its interior, though he has never been there before. Again it is a metonym for the colonized subject's familiarity with the colonizer's world, which remains unreciprocated. In this case, it is knowledge that has been relayed to him years before, when Tridib's niece, Ila, has drawn the house's floor-plan for him in the dust of a basement room in Calcutta. Colonial knowledge, it is suggested, is written in dust, a Gothic trace of Victorian Empire. The table in the room has been brought from the Crystal Palace and since it has been shipped to India in pieces and consigned to subterranean neglect ever since, the shadow-lines in question provide a vivid expression of the gap between the supposedly ideal world of the colonizer and the flickering Platonic shadows the colonial subject glimpses on the wall of the cave.

The Shadow Lines is similarly concerned with the linguistic implications of this predicament, locating the gap between signifier and signified in a postcolonial context. At one point the narrator foregrounds this issue very explicitly, commenting that "between that state [love] and its metaphors there is no more connection than there is between a word such as mat, and the thing itself" (99) and throughout the text there is an emphasis on ways in which subjectivity is constructed through linguistic shadow lines. The particular Indian dimension of this emerges most clearly when the narrator expresses the view that life on the subcontinent is different from elsewhere because it is lived "without analogy" and there is an acute sense of "the special quality of loneliness that grows out of the fear of the war between oneself and one's image in the mirror" (205). In such a reading of Indian culture—

and needless to say it is a reading that is not shared by many observers[14]—metonymy not metaphor is the characteristic mode of Indian discourse, and certainly the novel, like all Ghosh's writing, appears to turn on a metonymic rather than a metaphorical axis and so, according to its narrator's view, could be seen as typically Indian. However, such a view runs the risk of essentializing "India" and, given the novel's subtle representation of the interpenetration of cultures, this seems antithetical to its tone. Arguably a way out of the dilemma is to question the structuralist binary that sees "metaphor" and "metonymy" as opposing modes. Just as a classic Western allegory such as *Pilgrim's Progress* achieves its effects through vividly realized circumstantial detail and a supposedly realistic work such as *Robinson Crusoe* moves in the opposite direction to provoke allegorical readings,[15] Ghosh's method in *The Shadow Lines* sanction readings which see it as a brilliant allegory of the deleterious effects of political partitioning and colonial power hegemonies.

Finally, though, it is a novel that insists on transcending political imperatives in favour of a broader-based humanism. The narrator's fascination with Tridib seems to arise from his seeing him as representing the possibility of entry into "a place where there was no border between oneself and one's image in the mirror" (35). With the benefit of hindsight, this passage, which comes comparatively early on in the novel, appears to serve as a coda to the later "mirror" passages. Collapsing the distance between self and mirror-image provides a highly personal alternative to the articulation of difference, which the novel associates with political action; it offers escape from the artificial shadow lines that divide contemporary Bengal's two mirrored communities and from the sense of difference expressed in the narrator's sense of being twinned with his English *doppelgänger*, Nick Price. Such humanism has been unfashionable in leftist Western discourses, such as poststructuralism and postcolonialism, in recent decades. It is, however, a creed that has affinities with a range of sub-continental value-systems, and in Ghosh's case its more obvious departure-point is the humanism of such Bengali artists as Rabindranath Tagore, whom Ghosh acknowledges as an influence,[16] and Satyajit Ray, whom he has referred to having profoundly affected "his way of looking at things" (Silva and Tickell 172).

At first sight *In An Antique Land* appears to be both generically and thematically a departure from *The Circle of Reason* and *The Shadow Lines*. An apparently factual "history in the guise of a traveller's tale," it moves between two narratives. The more extensive is ostensibly a travel-book, in which a Ghosh persona, engaged in anthropological research in Egypt, describes his experiences living in a fellaheen village. In the shorter, which has also been published as "The Slave of

MS. H. 6," the persona pursues the fugitive traces of the "slave" of a twelfth-century Jewish merchant—in Egypt, the Malabar coast of India, the U.K. and finally the U.S—and in so doing pieces together a narrative of the life, not only of the subaltern slave, "Bomma," but also of his master, Abraham Ben Yiju. In fact, the distance between *In An Antique Land* and the two earlier novels is much less than initially appears to be the case. The text transgresses generic categories by drawing on the conventions of travel-book, novel, ethnography and academic history in a subtly subversive way. It also demonstrates the connections between Egypt and India in much the same manner as *The Circle of Reason* weaves connections between the sub-continent, the Middle East and North Africa and *The Shadow Lines* exemplifies both the artificiality of national frontiers and the interconnectedness of supposedly separate places and experiences.

The account of the quest for the slave draws readers into an anthropological detective-story, which serves as a metonym for the difficulty of the task of excavating subaltern identity. At the same time, in piecing together a skeletal biography of Ben Yiju, the text also engages with the equally fascinating historiographical project of narrativizing the life of a liminal merchant, who is the personification of Indian Ocean trade-routes that confound the East-West bifurcations of Orientalist cartographies. Ghosh represents Ben Yiju as a cultural broker who moves unself-consciously between supposedly discrete worlds, just as the writer himself points up analogous Indian-Egyptian connections in the contemporary Egyptian narrative. Ghosh has spoken in an interview of the pleasure he derives from combining apparently unconnected narratives to see what connections may emerge (Piciucco 70-71) and the parallels that issue from the juxtaposition of the two narratives of *In An Antique Land* afford a particularly striking example of this method in action.

Ghosh's technique blends archival research and fiction. Speculating on Ben Yiju's marriage to a non-Jewish woman, he says, "If I hesitate to call it love it is only because the documents offer *no certain proof*" (*IAL* 230; my italics). Commenting on how Bomma became Ben Yiju's slave, he writes, "From certain references in Ben Yiju's papers *it seems likely* that he took Bomma into his service as a business agent and helper soon after he had established himself in Mangalore [...] the terms [...] were probably entirely different from those suggested by the word 'slavery' today" (259; my italics). Starting with the comment that Bomma's first appearance on "the stage of modern history" is little more than "a prompter's whisper" (13), Ghosh opens up a "trapdoor into a vast network of foxholes where real life continues uninterrupted" (16) by "grand designs and historical destinies" (15). Similarly, his account of contemporary fellaheen village life focuses on micro-histories,[17] "tiny threads, woven into the borders of a gigantic tapestry" (95). Again, the emphasis on borders is as interesting as the use of the weaving trope. Ghosh's Egyptian characters, figures that would be relegated to the margins of more conventional histories, come alive as individuals in their own right. At the same time they become representatives of the subalterns emancipated by Nasser's Revolution, whose lives are now undergoing rapid change as a result of "the real and desperate seriousness of their engagement with modernism," their desire to escape from what they see as their "anachronistic" (200) situation, by ascending a ladder of technological development. The central tension of the contemporary narrative emerges from the Ghosh persona's accounts of his dialogues with villagers bent on learning about Indian customs, in order to make comparisons between the two cultures' success in engaging with modernity. Such conversations reach a climax, when, in an episode that Ghosh has published separately ("The Imam and the Indian"), the persona finds himself arguing with the local Imam as to which nation is technologically superior and is horrified to realise that he has competed by using the rhetoric of modern violence and in so doing has become "a conspirator in the betrayal of the history that had led me to Nashawy; a witness to the extermination of a world of accommodations that I had believed to be still alive and in some measure, still retrievable" (237).

When he returns in 1988, after an absence of seven years, he finds fellaheen village life has changed dramatically: two to three million Egyptians have migrated to Iraq, to provide a work-force to replace Iraqis fighting on the fronts in Iran and Kurdistan. Such a focus on the transnational movement of peoples, with its accompanying emphasis on the hybrid, unsettled aspects of cultures, is typical of Ghosh's writing, but his analysis remains rooted in material realities and a humanism that is a world away from the specular detachment of postmodernist and postcolonial commentators on the liminal, whose theorizing bypasses the actualities of lived lives. When these Egyptian workers' Iraqi lives are suddenly terminated by the outbreak of the Gulf War, this is no Baudrillardian hyperreal media event for them. It signals the end of a way of life. The text closes with the persona watching television in Egypt, along with a dozen villagers, all desperately hoping to catch a glimpse of one of their number, another subaltern who appears to "have vanished into the anonymity of History" (353).

In the historical narrative, Ghosh's emphasis on the mobility of the pre-Enlightenment trading networks of the eastern Mediterranean and the Indian Ocean might seem to suggest a similar pattern of migration, but again the analysis is culturally specific: he makes a sharp distinction between such movements and those of the post-colonization period and the contemporary globalized world. The demise of the centuries' old "culture of accommodation and compromise" of the Indian Ocean trade comes with the advent of Portuguese colonization, which take control of the trade "by aggression, pure and undistilled" (288), refusing any attempts at co-operation. "[T]he peaceful traditions of the oceanic trade" (287) have been the products of a travelling culture that is a world away from those of colonial mercantilism and contemporary global capitalism and the section of *In An Antique Land* that deals with their destruction evokes the earlier episode of the narrator's conversation with the Imam and its culmination in his regret that the older "world of accommodations" is a thing of the past. Again the two narratives converge. Contemporary Egyptian social realities dispel his elegiac view that a gentler dialogic network of exchange still exists; the historical sections locate the loss of this nexus in relation to the violence of European colonization. Such "violence" is perpetuated in the rhetoric that leaves him competing with the Imam to "establish a prior claim to the technology of modern violence" (236).

The text's investigation of lines of cultural transmission is also conducted through linguistic detective-work, which again repudiates the notion of hermetically sealed cultures. Ben Yiju's letters are written in a language, "Judaeo-Arabic [...] a colloquial dialect of medieval Arabic, written in the Hebrew script" (101), which challenges contemporary dichotomies and suggests linkages between two peoples with shared Aramaic heritages. Etymological excavation becomes a crucial part of the text's archaeological dig to solve the riddle of the slave's identity. Eventually the persona arrives at a conclusion on the provenance of his name, which enables him to suggest a very precise origin. This locates him as someone "who had been born into one of the several matrilineal communities which played a part in the Bhuta-cult of Tulunad"; and it is at this moment that he feels that the subaltern, Bomma is ready "to become a protagonist in his own story" (254).

Similar investigations of linguistic origins run right through *In An Antique Land*. An early passage debates the cultural encodings implicit in various languages' names for Cairo and Egypt (32-33). Towards the end the text records that English "sugar" comes from Arabic "sukkar," a word derived from a Sanskrit source, while, as it were "in commemoration of traders like Ben Yiju" (269), north India still uses "misri," a word derived from the Arabic Masr, which, the earlier passage has explained, is the Egyptian word for both Cairo and Egypt as a whole. The obvious ironies in such tangled genealogies are still, of course, dependent on tracing linear etymologies, but the movement of the *text* is circular, as the sugar passage takes readers back to the earlier Cairo/Masr passage. However, perhaps the most striking erosion of a linguistic shadow-line in *In An Antique Land* comes when the persona discovers that the "simple, rustic [Arabic] dialect" (103) he has acquired in the fellaheen village is of more use to him in reading Ben Yiju's Judaeo-Arabic than his knowledge of classical Arabic. Again there seems to be a convergence across the centuries, which, if it does not exactly suggest the underlying sameness of subaltern experience, nevertheless suggests certain congruences opening up in the liminal spaces between the records of elite historiography.

The Calcutta Chromosome is ostensibly more fictive than *In An Antique Land,* but it also interweaves a network of traces—from the history of malaria research, theological movements generally deemed to be heretical in the West and slightly futuristic computer technology *inter alia*—to provide the possibility of an alternative subaltern history, which exists in parallel with colonial history as an equally—or possibly more—potent epistemological system, albeit one which has traditionally operated through silence. The main narrative of the novel involves a re-examination of the history of late nineteenth-century malaria research by a possibly deranged Calcutta-born man named Murugan, who is convinced that Ronald Ross, the British scientist who was awarded the 1902 Nobel Prize for Medicine for his work on the life-cycle of the malaria parasite was not a "lone genius" (*CC* 57), a brilliant British dilettante who outstripped all of his contemporaries. Murugan believes there is a secret history that has been erased from the scribal records of the colonial society and from medical historiography more generally and has set out to uncover the hidden truth, a project which can be seen as a metonym for the attempt to recuperate subaltern agency more generally.

Murugan is first encountered through the mediation of a New York-based computer systems operator, Antar, who comes across a fragment of an ID card on the screen of his super-computer which sets him off on a quest to reconstruct the recent life-history of its missing owner. The owner in question is a man named Murugan, whom Antar has interviewed a few years before, on behalf of the company for whom he works, to try to dissuade him from a request to be transferred to Calcutta, so that he can pursue his "theory that some person or persons had systematically interfered with Ronald Ross's experiments to push malaria research in certain directions while leading it away from others" (36). Antar pursues Murugan through the resources of the World Wide Web. As early as *The Circle of Reason,* Ghosh had drawn attention to the relationship between the loom and the computer, in a passage which erodes East-West binaries and discloses the Asian origins of this supposedly European technology:

> And then weaving changed mechanical man again with the computer. In the mid-nineteenth century when Charles Babbage built his first calculating machine, using the principle of storing information on punched cards, he took his idea not from systems of writing nor from mathematics, but from the draw-loom. The Chinese have used punched cards to discriminate between warp

threads in the weaving of silk since 1000 BC. They gave it (unwillingly) to the Italians, and the Italians gave it to the rest of Europe, in the form of the draw-loom. (*CR* 57)

Now, in *The Calcutta Chromosome*, the Web actually takes over the role occupied by weaving in Ghosh's earlier work[18]: as well as being the virtual means through which Antar can cross continents in his quest for his fugitive subject, it also becomes a metonym for transnational communication more generally. Antar's search for Murugan leads the reader into a Russian doll-like assortment of other quests, which are gradually revealed to be interlocking narratives that erode both temporal and spatial shadow lines, in a manner similar to the seemingly very different narratives of *The Shadow Lines* and *In An Antique Land*.

Murugan's research has led him to the conclusion that Ross and other Western scientists working in the field of malaria research in India have been manipulated by their Indian helpers, led by a woman named Mangala, who appears to be both the high priestess of a secret medical cult, offering a cure for syphilis, and the brain behind the discoveries that eventually led to Ross's winning the Nobel Prize. So Ghosh's narrative discredits the Western scientist and instates an Indian female subaltern in his place.

The cult's discoveries are, however, concerned with far more than a malaria cure. They involve a counter-epistemology, which promises a form of immortality through the erosion of Western conceptions of discrete subjectivity. Mangala's discovery of the means by which malaria is transmitted has come about as a by-product of her real research interest. Working outside the strait-jacket of Western empirical methodologies, she has been attempting to evolve "a technology for interpersonal transference" (106), a means of transmitting knowledge "chromosomally from body to body" (107). In Murugan's view the relationship between Mangala's counter-science and that of conventional scientists such as Ross is analogous to the relationship between "matter and antimatter [...] rooms and ante-rooms [...] Christ and Antichrist and so on" (103). So, if one accepts Murugan's thesis, there is the possibility of a subaltern Manichean force which, though it operates through silence and secrecy, is at least as powerful as Western logocentrism.

The Calcutta Chromosome forces its readers to engage with is the possibility of an alternative historiography, in which traditionally disempowered subjects prove to be the real puppet-masters. The counter-science cult led by Mangala can only operate through silence, but the fictive reconstruction, in which Murugan, Antar and ultimately Ghosh engage, subverts the hegemonic dominance of Western logocentrism all the same. Ghosh links the cult with Gnostic theological sects and in so doing engages with Manicheism in an altogether more complex and historically grounded way than those post-colonial interpreters of Manichean allegory who use the term to suggest a Western discursive practice.[19] He only mentions Manicheism as such on one occasion in the novel (214). This is in a passage about the archaeological excavations of a woman who has been a devotee of a "Society of Spiritualists" that flourished in Madras at the same time as the Theosophical Society, which with its Gnostic beliefs was itself a late nineteenth-century challenge to Western monism. However, the Society is led by a woman who is seen as Madame Blavatsky's "arch-rival" (207) and her disciple, the Hungarian Countess Pongrácz, has become an advocate of the teachings of Valentinus (the Alexandrian-born Gnostic philosopher who took dualistic religious beliefs to Rome in the second century A.D.), as well as an excavator of archaeological traces of dualistic systems—Nestorian[20] as well as Manichean. Like the Countess Pongrácz, Ghosh discovers fragments of suppressed heterodox systems; and the novel's repeated emphasis on Silence provides a reading of the subaltern which suggests that a figure denied a voice by hegemonic cultures and deemed heretical in Christian thinking could exist as a viable power-player in his and, in this case even more, *her* own right.

The Calcutta chromosome and the possibility of effecting the "interpersonal transference" of knowledge occupies a central role in this investigation, since such transference would erode the barriers between elite and subaltern classes, between the purveyors and the recipients of knowledge. Everything about Ghosh's novel seems to be working towards this end. Structurally it moves between multiple stories and characters; and the near-repetition of variant forms of the same situation also works to dismantle the notion of discrete essentialist versions. Additionally, there is a final twist in the narrative, which takes the investigation of epistemological relationships into yet more subtle territory. Throughout the text readers are made aware that the borderline between discoverers and those who are discovered is an extremely porous one. Ross appears to be a discoverer who makes a revolutionary advance in the science of microscopy, but it seems he has been discovered and controlled by Mangala and her followers. Murugan investigates the secret history of malaria research and is in turn investigated by Antar. The last two chapters of the novel complicate and extend this pattern even further. Murugan follows the final stages of his trail with a magazine journalist, Urmila Roy, another quester who has been prominent throughout the novel. His thesis involves the belief that the counter-science cult is absorbed with "interpersonal transference" as part of a long-term strategy based on the notion that "to know something is to change it" (104). Towards the end the novel appears to be moving towards some kind of apocalyptic revelation and one wonders whether Murugan is about to become a victim or an initiate of the cult. Such ambivalence is, of course, central to *The Calcutta Chromosome's* procedure and its unsettling of the shadow lines between elite and subaltern subjects. Nevertheless there is a fresh surprise in the penultimate chapter when Murugan tells Urmila that *she* is the "chosen" (306) one of Mangala's contemporary incarnation, explaining:

> You see, for them the only way to escape the tyranny of knowledge is to turn it on itself. But for that to work they have to create a single perfect moment of discovery when the person who discovers is also that which is discovered. (306)

The final chapter provides an even more startling instance of a discoverer who is discovered. The text returns to Antar who, in his New York apartment with his super-computer, appears to be the ultimate discoverer of meaning within the novel. As the figure who frames the rest of the narrative, he alone seems to be immune from the possibility of complicity in conspiracy. But he too is a feverish investigator and the final chapter undermines the possibility of exempting him from the process of "interpersonal transference." He now begins to think that his computer's stumbling upon Murugan's ID card—the opening moment of the novel—has not, after all, been an accident; and the web of correspondences expands even further, as two of his New York friends, who have seemed to be no more than incidental extras in the frame-narrative, are absorbed into the visual images of Murugan's last day in Calcutta, which the computer is projecting for him. Another discoverer finds himself discovered. Nobody, the suggestion seems to be, is exempt from history or from playing an active role in the *historiographical* process. So perhaps the ultimate discoverer who is discovered by the novel is the reader. *The Calcutta Chromosome* has invited its readers to play the same kind of role as that undertaken by the persona in *In An Antique Land*, that of hermeneutic detective: to piece together its numerous clues in order to arrive, if not at a solution, at least at a possible version of meaning. The final insistence that all the investigators within the text are implicated in the material they are investigating leaves readers having to consider the possibility that they too are caught in the conspiracy of history. The positive aspect of this is, of course, that it offers liberation from the silence of the subaltern activity of reading.

While *The Circle of Reason* and *In An Antique Land* move westwards from India, Ghosh's most recent books, *Dancing in Cambodia, At Large in Burma* (1998) and *The Glass Palace* travel eastwards—to Burma (Myanmar), Cambodia, Malaysia and Singapore—again tracing genealogies that traverse national frontiers.

Dancing in Cambodia, At Large in Burma is made up of three parts: the two longish travel-essays of the book's title and a shorter Cambodian piece, "Stories in Stones." Ghosh's capacity to find patterns in apparently unconnected events is at its best in "Dancing in Cambodia," which links the 1906 visit of Cambodia's King Sisowath, his entourage and a troupe of Cambodian classical dancers to France with the recent history of the country decimated by the Khmer Rouge Revolution. Ghosh interviews a number of figures who provide living testimony to the interconnectedness of these two narratives. They include a famous dancer, Chea Samy, who has first-hand knowledge of King Sisowath and his daughter Princess Soumphady, by virtue of having been taken to the royal palace in 1925, at the age of six, to be trained in classical dance under the supervision of the Princess. She is also—and the matter-of-fact manner in which Ghosh records this makes the revelation all the more chilling—Pol Pot's sister-in-law (*DC* 5). Palace revolution and the French connection are motifs that run throughout the essay. Pol Pot has himself been taken into the palace at the age of six and appears to have been radicalized during his time as a student in Paris: his brother tells Ghosh that it was the "'knowledge he got in Paris that made him what he is'" (35). He has particularly admired Robespierre, basing the "ideological purity" (50) of his genocidal regime on the French revolutionary's belief in the virtue of Terror. Similarly, the grandson of King Sisowath's Palace Minister, Thiounn, becomes a central figure to a generation of Cambodian students in Paris and one of his protégés is Pol Pot. For the most part Ghosh documents these connections neutrally, but lest they be missed, he does point out:

> Few people in Cambodia think it particularly a matter of comment that Pol Pot and his ultra-radical clique share so many links with the palace. As a well-known political figure in Phnom Penh put it: "Revolutions and *coup d'état* always start in the courtyards of the palace." (25)

If one takes King Sisowath as the exemplar of Cambodian royalty—the text points out that his collaboration with the French has not been typical, but he remains its most fully described representative of the Cambodian monarchy—then perhaps this is not surprising. During his visit to France, the King wrote a Royal Proclamation for his subjects, in which he extolled the achievements of French technology, particularly in transport, and urged them to adopt mechanized methods of farming. In a passage that is evocative of Homi Bhabha, Ghosh points up the ambivalence of such colonial mimicry: "For all the apparent servility of its tone, [the Proclamation] makes no cultural or political concessions at all: the 'emulation' it calls for is entirely within the domain of technology and economics" (41-42). Again the attraction to the West is an attraction to technological modernity.

King Sisowath and Pol Pot may seem polar opposites, but with their common experience of palace life and their enthusiasm for certain, albeit different, aspects of French culture, they emerge as curiously twinned. In the period of reconstruction after Pol Pot's fall, the return to normality is associated with an art form that has palace associations: Cambodian classical dance. The text represents dancing as far more than a traditional Cambodian performance art; it becomes a trope for the indestructibility of the middle-class culture threatened with extinction during the Pol Pot era. The essay ends with an "epiphany" in Phnom Penh in 1988, "a moment when the grief of survival became indistinguishable from the joy of living" (51-52), as classical music and dance are performed once again for the first time. On this occasion, then, the humanist conclusion is not so much championing subaltern survival, but the resilience of an educated class threatened with extinction by a Western-inspired regime, which has declared war on the intelligentsia.

"Stories in Stones" considers the iconic significance of Angkor Wat, reputedly the largest religious edifice in the world, as a symbol of Cambodian identity, wryly reflecting that its omnipresence as a talismanic object pervades virtually every area of the nation's life—except religion. Ghosh's illustration of the proliferation of images of the Wat in a range of commercial contexts is not, however, simply evidence of the extent to which tradition and modernity overlap; it is another striking instance of a modern appropriation of an older tradition which erodes the humanist possibilities of earlier belief-systems.

"At Large in Burma" provides insights into an Asian country that has been particularly isolated from the outside world in recent years, again doing so through the medium of telling individual stories. Here the central figure is the leader of the country's democratic movement and winner of the 1991 Nobel Peace Prize, Aung San Suu Kyi, whom Ghosh first met while a student in Oxford in 1980 and whom he now interviews during two visits in 1995 and 1996. At one point he mentions having been "brought up to believe in the appropriateness of a strict separation between the public and the private, the political and the domestic" (83), with the corollary that it is wrong to reduce political movements to their leaders, but in Aung San Suu Kyi, he finds "the personification of Burma's democratic resistance to military rule" (74). So, in addition to providing a window on one of the world's more closed societies, the essay becomes another instance of Ghosh's characteristic historiographic method of illuminating national and communal issues by relating personal stories, though, as in "Dancing in Cambodia," it departs from his earlier focus on subaltern experience.

"At Large in Burma" also contains a section in which Ghosh travels to the Thai border in an attempt to understand the independence struggle of one of Burma's many minorities, the Kanenni. Naipaulian ironies emerge, when tourists visit refugee camps to see the Kanneni's long-necked "giraffe woman," oblivious of their history of oppression and displacement and unaware that they are "counterfeits of timeless rural simplicity" (94). Ghosh's own perspective is, of course, much more complicated and again centrally concerned with the impact of modernity. His main interest lies in trying to assess what "freedom" means to the Kanneni and whether the "putative nationalities" (100) around Burma's borders would be better off as separate states. His consideration of this issue culminates in a passage in which he revisits the central motif of *The Shadow Lines*:

> Burma's borders are undeniably arbitrary, the product of a capricious colonial history. But colonial officials cannot reasonably be blamed for the arbitrariness of the lines they drew. All boundaries are artificial: there is no such thing as a 'natural' nation. (100)

Consequently, his conclusion in the case of the Kanneni, and the sixteen or so other potential nation states around multi-ethnic Burma's borders, is that they would not benefit from being separate countries. So, like so much of Ghosh's work, this part of the essay presents a self-contained micro-history of a group, which can also be read as a metonym for a larger global debate. It holds a mirror up to late twentieth-century cultural theory on the nation state,[21] which both reflects and reverses commonly held assumptions, as it suggests that in the case of the Kanneni the "historical borders" (101) are probably best left unaltered.

The essay ends with an image which, as Ghosh flies out of Rangoon, suggests he is returning to the terrain of *The Calcutta Chromosome*: "the cabin filled with the whine of laptops logging on—the familiar buzzing sound, not unlike that of mosquitoes, feasting in mid-flight" (114).

Each of Ghosh's books to date has been different in form and point of departure and in *The Glass Palace* he employs the form of the family saga to tell an epic story that moves between Burma, India and the Malay archipelago and, beginning in the late nineteenth century, spreads across several generations. His prose style is at its simplest here, giving the illusion of a transparent neutral, historical record; and the novel is the least abstract work of a writer, whose whole oeuvre has preferred to make its cultural comments through concrete specifics rather than abstractions. Only occasionally does Ghosh allow himself to make analytical comments across the decades and such comments are usually placed in the mouths of his characters, as when the deposed Burmese Queen Supayalat, in exile in India, predicts that her family's fate foreshadows that of "golden Burma," saying that "A hundred years hence you will read the indictment of Europe's greed in the difference between the kingdom of Siam and the state of our own enslaved realm" (*GP* 88) and when a similar pessimistic view of the enduring consequences of imperialism is attributed to the reformist Uma and her New York Indian friends:

> They could see that it was not they themselves, nor even their children who would pay the true price of this Empire: that the conditions being created in their homeland were such as to ensure that their descendants would enter the new epoch as cripples, lacking the most fundamental means of survival [...]. (222)

Elsewhere the novel's depiction of the impact of social changes, especially the advent of modernity, is usually implicit. Numerous references to technological advances—particularly cars, cameras and communications—subtly sketch in the backcloth against which the characters' emotional lives are lived, though at times the cumulative weight of passages such as the following exemplifies what Ghosh refers to, in his concluding "Author's Notes," as a "near-obsessive urge to render the background of my characters' lives as closely as I could" (549):

> Mrs Khambatta's camera was an instrument of superb craftsmanship: a 1901 Graflex single-lens reflex, with a cube-like body, a bellows extension and a four-sided hood. It was fitted with a Globe wide-angle lens which proved perfect for the panorama deployed before the shutter [...]. (170)
>
> [...] This was a Duesenberg Model J. Tourster, Matthew explained. It had a hydraulic braking system and a 6.9 litre, straight-8 engine. It has chain-driven overhead camshafts and could do up to 90 m.p.h. in second gear. In top gear it could cruise at 116. (218)

Again, though, the method can be justified as a brilliant example of the novel genre reverting to its origins and constructing a quasi-realistic picture of actual life through the accretion of a welter of minutely realized details that have a metonymic force, in much the same way as Defoe's obsessive attention to the material circumstances of Robinson Crusoe's island or Moll Flanders' thefts creates its effect of verisimilitude.

The early parts of *The Glass Palace* are dominated by two characters whose separation becomes the pivot on which its first third turns, as the Bengali-born Rajkumar seeks to find Dolly, the girl he has only seen briefly as a ten-year-old attendant in the Royal Palace in Rangoon, at the time of the Burmese monarchy's deposition by the British. Such a plot, with its emphasis on love at first sight, separation and reunion is, of course, the stuff that romantic fiction is made of and at first the novel may appear to draw some of its narrative impetus from the conventions of such fiction. But it *is* only a third complete when Dolly and Rajkumar are reunited and after an initial refusal, she agrees to marry him. Subsequently, it travels onwards, snaking its way through the lives of later generations and not only showing the older couple ceasing to occupy centre-stage as they age, but depicting Dolly leaving Rajkumar and eventually entering a Buddhist nunnery. While this dénouement may appear to subvert the conventions of romantic fiction, it does so in an unsensational and protracted structure, which suggests that they never obtained in the first place. Of all Ghosh's works to date, *The Glass Palace* is the least concerned with overarching allegorical configurations. Its extended canvas spreads over a multitude of particular experiences and it tells the story of diverse individual lives, which intersect but frustrate attempts to shape them into neat patterns. If one looks for an impulse that links the various stories, it is perhaps to be found once again in a humanist approach that devotes itself to narrating the specifics of particular life-histories and refuses to reduce them to historiographical generalizations. This said, Ghosh's perennial interest in historiography is to be seen in revisionist perspectives on particular historical events. In the opening account of the British ousting of the Burmese royal family, as in *Dancing in Cambodia, At Large in Burma,* he deserts his interest in the retrieval of subaltern narratives for a focus on a more elite historiography, but his approach has a not dissimilar purpose, since it functions as a corrective to earlier histories, which he views as propaganda justifying British actions (Matthew). Similarly, he provides a minutely researched account of the lives of Indian soldiers in the British army in World War II, which deftly avoids anti-colonial simplism, by showing varying positions, but nevertheless succeeds in telling this history from an alternative point of view. And this finally has been the strength of all his writing to date. In the borderline territory between history and fiction, he has managed to develop a mode of writing, which, despite the generic variety of his works, repeatedly returns to individual lives in a manner that frustrates appropriation into the clichés of postcolonial theorizing and yet consistently addresses the issues that such theorizing has foregrounded as central to contemporary global experience in a sensitive and stimulating way.

Notes

1. Sub-title of the first American paperback edition (Random House, 1993).
2. See particularly his account of the Indian Ocean trade that flourished prior to Portuguese military intervention in *In An Antique Land*: discussed below.
3. On his view of the "postcolonial" and Bhabha in particular, see his comments in Silva and Tickell (171): "What is postcolonial? When I look at the work of critics, such as Homi Bhabha, I think they have somehow invented this world which is just a set of representations of representations. They've retreated into a world of magic mirrors [...]. Mind you, commentators such as Bhabha have done something very important, which is that they've somehow 'made' writers. When I began writing, it was very difficult if one were an Indian writing in English."
4. Robert Dixon, "'Travelling in the West': The Writing of Amitav Ghosh," *The Journal of Commonwealth Literature* 31.1 (1996): 16.

5. Pier Paolo Piciucco, "Pier Paolo Piciucco Interviews Amitav Ghosh," *Englishes* 12 (2000): 70.
6. In an essay on Naipaul's award of the 2001 Nobel Prize for literature, Ghosh acknowledges Naipaul's influence on his evolution as a writer: "It was Naipaul who first made it possible for me to think of myself as a writer, working in English," but he distances himself from Naipaul's views and opinions. ("Naipaul and the Nobel")
7. Edward W. Said, *Orientalism: Western Conceptions of the Orient.* (1978; Harmondsworth: Penguin, 1985) 42-43, 80 ff.
8. Neluka Silva and Alex Tickell, "Amitav Ghosh in Interview with Neluka Silva and Alex Tickell," *Kunapipi* 19.3 (1997): 171.
9. The relationship is explored in Srivastava.
10. The novel has received comparatively little critical attention, but has been seen in this way by a majority of those who have commented on it, *e.g.* James and Shepherd; Jacqueline Bardolph, "Les 'enfants' de Rushdie: quelle realisme, quelle magie," *Itinéraires et Contacts de Culture*, Vol. 25: *Le réalisme* merveilleux, Paris: L'Harmattan, 1998: 19-34; M.K. Naik and Shyamala A. Narayan, *Indian English Literature, 1980-2000: A Survey* (Delhi: Pencraft, 2001) 45-46.
11. *One Hundred Years of Solitude* (1967; trans. Gregory Rabassa, Harmondsworth: Penguin, 1972) 7.
12. Ghosh discusses the dissemination of the *Panchatantra* in "The March of the Novel through History: The Testimony of my Grandfather's Bookcase," pointing out that its "global diffusion" has been seen as "second only to the Bible" and mentioning that it engendered "some of the best known of Middle Eastern fables, including parts of *The Thousand and One Nights*" (7).
13. John Thieme, "Passages to England," *Liminal Postmodernisms: The Postmodern, the (Post-) Colonial, and the (Post-) Feminist.* Eds. Thoo D'haen and Hans Bertens (Amsterdam and Atlanta: Rodopi, 1994) 65-66.
14. Cp., *e.g.*, Rushdie's Saleem Sinai's view that a "lust for allegory" characterizes Indian thought, *Midnight's Children*, 1981 (London: Picador, 1982) 96.
15. Most notably as an economic success-story, in which Crusoe is an archetype of capitalist man [see Ian Watt, *The Rise of the Novel*, 1957; Harmondsworth: Penguin, 1963: 65ff; and Pat Rogers (ed.), *Defoe: The Critical Heritage*, London and Boston: Routledge & Kegan Paul, 1972: 166-68]; and as a Puritan spiritual autobiography of the same kind as Bunyan's *Grace Abounding to the Chief of Sinners* (see G.A. Starr, *Defoe and Spiritual Biography*, Princeton: Princeton UP, 1965).
16. See Amitav Ghosh, "The March of the Novel through History: The Testimony of my Grandfather's Bookcase," *Kunapipi* 19.3 (1997) 4, and Neluka Silva and Alex Tickell *Interview* 172.
17. Cf. Roy, who discusses Ghosh's use of this kind of historiographical method in *The Shadow Lines.*
18. For a more general discussion of ways in which the Internet can be seen to function in terms of weaving analogies, see my paper, "Patchwork Quilts, Trade Routes and Other (Inter-) Networks: Reflections on Literature and Globalization," literature keynote address at the 2001 SAUTE Conference, St. Gallen—to be published in *SPELL* (Swiss Papers in English Language and Literature).
19. See particularly Abdul R. Jan Mohamed, *Manichean Aesthetics: The Politics of Literature in Colonial Africa* (Amherst: U of Massachusetts P, 1983; also

Jan Mohamed, "The Economy of Manichean Allegory: The Function of Racial Difference in Colonial Literature," *Critical Inquiry* 12.1 (1985): 59-87.

20. Nestorian doctrine insists on the distinctiveness of the human and divine aspects of Christ.

21. *E.g.* Benedict Anderson's influential, *Imagined Communities: Reflections on the Origin and Spread of Nationalism* (London: Verso, 1983); and *Nation and Narration*, ed. Homi Bhabha (London and New York: Routledge, 1990).

AN AMITAV GHOSH BIBLIOGRAPHY

Primary Sources

Novels

The Circle of Reason. 1986. New York: Penguin, 1990.

The Shadow Lines. London: Bloomsbury, 1988; London: Black Swan, 1989.

The Calcutta Chromosome: A Novel of Fevers, Delirium and Discovery. London: Picador, 1996.

The Glass Palace, 2000. London: Harper Collins, 2001.

Non-Fiction

In An Antique Land. New Delhi: Ravi Dayal, 1992. London: Granta, 1994.

Dancing in Cambodia, At Large in Burma. New Delhi: Ravi Dayal, 1998.

Countdown. New Delhi: Ravi Dayal, 1999.

The Imam and the Indian: Prose Pieces. New Delhi: Ravi Dayal and Permanent Black, 2002.

Selected Articles and Essays

"The Imam and the Indian." *Granta* 20 (Winter 1986): 135-46.

"The Slave of MS. H. 6." *Subaltern Studies* 7: *Writings on South Asian History and Society.* Partha Chatterjee and Gyanendra Pandey (eds.). New Delhi: Oxford UP, 1992. 159-220.

"The March of the Novel through History: The Testimony of my Grandfather's Bookcase." *Kunapipi* 19.3 (1997): 2-13.

"Naipaul and the Nobel." Online. Amitav Ghosh's official website. http://www.amitavghosh.com/articles/naipaul2.html. Accessed 26 July 2002.

Secondary Sources

Books on Amitav Ghosh

Dhawan, R.K., ed. *The Novels of Amitav Ghosh.* New Delhi: Prestige Books, 1998.

Khair, Tabish, ed. *Shaping the World.* New Delhi: Permanent Black, 2003.

Articles and Essays

Bagchi, Nivedita. "The Process of Validation in Relation to Materiality and Historical Reconstruction in Amitav Ghosh's *The Shadow Lines*." *Modern Fiction Studies* 39.1 (1993): 187-202.

Belliappa, K.C. "Amitav Ghosh's *In an Antique Land*: An Excursion into Time Past and Time Present." *The Postmodern Indian Novel: Interrogating the 1980s and 1990s*. Ed. Viney Kirpal. Bombay: Allied Publishers, 1996. 59-66.

Bose, Brinda. "Footnoting History: The Diasporic Imagination of Amitav Ghosh." *In Diaspora: Theories, Histories, Texts*. Ed. Makarand Paranjape. New Delhi: Indialog Publishers, 2001. 235-45.

Chew, Shirley. "Texts and Worlds in Amitav Ghosh's *In an Antique Land*." *Re-Constructing the Book: Literary Texts in Transmission*. Eds. Maureen Bell, Shirley Chew, Simon Eliot, Lynette Hunter and James L.W. West III. Aldershot: Ashgate, 2001. 197-209.

Clifford, James. "The Transit Lounge of Culture." *Times Literary Supplement* 3 May 1991: 7-8.

Dixon, Robert. "'Travelling in the West': The Writing of Amitav Ghosh." *The Journal of Commonwealth Literature* 31.1 (1996): 3-24.

James, Louis and Jan Shepherd. "Shadow Lines: Cross-Cultural Perspectives in the Fiction of Amitav Ghosh." *Commonwealth Essays and Studies* 14.1 (1991): 28-32.

Kaul, Suvir. "Separation Anxiety, Growing-up Inter/National in Amitav Ghosh's *The Shadow Lines*." *Oxford Literary Review* 16.1-2 (1994): 125-45.

Khair, Tabish. "The Example of Amitav Ghosh: (Re)Establishing Connections." *Babu Fictions: Alienation in Contemporary Indian English Novels*. New Delhi: Oxford UP, 2001. 302-32.

Majeed, Jav, ed. "Amitav Ghosh's *In an Antique Land*: The Ethnographer-Historian and the Limits of Irony." *The Journal of Commonwealth Literature* 30.2 (1995): 45-55.

Mongia, Padmini. "Postcolonial Identity and Gender Boundaries in Amitav Ghosh's *The Shadow Lines*." *College Literature* 20.1 (1993): 225-28.

Mukherjee, Meenakshi. "Maps and Mirrors: Coordinates of Meaning in *The Shadow Lines*." *The Shadow Lines, with Four Critical Essays*. New Delhi: Oxford UP, 1995. 255-67.

Piciucco, Pier Paolo. "Deliberate Confusion of Time and Characters as a Leading Motif in Amitav Ghosh's *The Calcutta Chromosome*." *Englishes* 12 (2000): 51-65.

Roy, Anjali. "*Microstoria*: Indian Nationalism's 'Little Stories' in Amitav Ghosh's *The Shadow Lines*." *The Journal of Commonwealth Literature* 35.2 (2000): 35-49.

Srivastava, Neelam. "Amitav Ghosh's Ethnographic Fictions: Intertextual Links between *In An Antique Land* and His Doctoral Thesis." *The Journal of Commonwealth Literature* 36.2 (2001): 45-64.

Thieme, John. "Passages to England." *Liminal Postmodernisms: The Postmodern, the (Post-) Colonial, and the (Post-) Feminist.* Eds. Thoo D'haen and Hans Bertens. Amsterdam and Atlanta: Rodopi, 1994. 55-78.

___. "The Discoverer Discovered: Amitav Ghosh's *The Calcutta Chromosome*." *The Literature of Indian Diaspora: Essays in Criticism.* Ed. A.L. McLeod. New Delhi: Sterling Publishers, 2000. 274-90.

Viswanathan, Gauri. "Beyond Orientalism: Syncretism and the Politics of Knowledge." *Stanford Humanities Review* 5.1 (1995): 19-34. Also online: http://www.stanford.edu/group/SHR/5-1/text/toc.html

Interviews

Mathew, Lucose. "New Writers Are Caught in Media Circus." *The Week* 2 Sept. 2001. Online edition. http://the-week.com/21sep02/life9.html. Accessed 26 July 2002.

Piciucco, Pier Paolo. "Pier Paolo Piciucco Interviews Amitav Ghosh." *Englishes* 12 (2000): 65-72.

Silva, Neluka and Alex Tickell. "Amitav Ghosh in Interview with Neluka Silva and Alex Tickell." *Kunapipi* 19.3 (1997): 171-77.

13

Rohinton Mistry

SILVIA ALBERTAZZI

Rohinton Mistry, born in 1952 in Bombay, India, of Parsi descent, now lives in Canada, near Toronto. In 1975, after being awarded a B.A. in Mathematics and Economics at the University of Bombay, he emigrated. "In those days in Bombay, it was all engineering, medicine, law. I didn't want to do any of those things." He confessed in an interview. "Math and economics was a compromise between that and a plain degree in literature. (And) to be a success, you had to go abroad. There was more opportunity abroad." In Canada, where he received a B.A. in English and Philosophy at the University of Toronto, Mistry started writing short stories, winning two Hart House literary prizes and the Canadian Fiction Magazine's annual Contributor's Prize for 1985. Finally, in 1987 he published a collection of short stories called *Tales from Firozsha Baag* (which will become *Swimming Lessons and Other Stories from Firozsha Baag* in the US edition).

A born story teller, in his tales Mistry depicts middle class life among the Parsi community, as he recalls it from abroad. All his eleven intersecting stories are set in an apartment block in Bombay where a number of Parsi families live: all the people who live there are, in turn, the protagonists of one or more short stories. The author himself tells the last one, thus revealing that he comes from Firozsha Baag, too. In this way, Mistry can describe daily life among the Parsis of Bombay touching, at the same time, meaningful themes and significant issues of contemporary multicultural and migrant realities. To understand Mistry's work, one must never forget that Zoroastrian Parsis experienced mass migration to India from the very beginning of their history, in the 8th century, being persecuted in Iran after Islamic conquest. Then, they suffered again diaspora, this time to the West, after the independence of India, when, having being the favourite of the British rulers, they fell to disgrace at the end of the Raj. Mistry gives voice both to the feeling of malaise of his people, after decolonisation made their elitist position and Westernised attitudes very unpopular, and to his own sense of displacement in Canada. First of all, he tries to show the uniqueness of the Parsi community by focusing on their way of living and their cultural heritage. Then, he stresses the diasporic nature of Parsi social and historic experience, seeking the justification and the sense of his own story of migration in the perspective of the Parsi 'double displacement.'

Coming from people who today feel they are at the margins of Indian society, refusing nevertheless the dominating Hindu culture, in his stories Mistry tries to preserve the memory of his native environment and to testify the specificity of his being a Parsi, both in India and in Canada—especially in the short stories set in the Western world, or dealing with characters who tried their luck in North America. Mistry points to the problems of East-West relationships and to the difficulties of immigration. Even though only a few stories deal with immigration, the writer's attention to everyday Indian reality, together with the affectionate look he casts at the people of Firozsha Baag, show that typical urge "to reclaim" which, according to Salman Rushdie, is characteristic of migrant fiction. Moreover, the last story of the collection, "Swimming Lessons," while disclosing the autobiographical nature of the whole book, also acts as a commentary on it. In this small metafictional piece we are faced both with the Canadian world where the Indian writer has settled and his ancient Indian homeland, recreated through fiction, and with a new element: the reaction of the author's parents to the tales of Firozsha Baag. The different opinions of the two readers—Mother and Father—reflect the controversial impact of migrant fiction on the reading public. It can be read only as confessional narrative, full of nostalgia and regret (as Mother suggests) or it can be appreciated just as a literary work, as it is by Father, without confusing "what really happened with what the story says that happened."[1] In both cases, it is normative to appreciate migrant fiction as providing a different point of view. As Father says, "the only danger is that he [the author] changes and becomes so much like them that he will write like one of them and lose the important difference" (*Firozsha* 248). It is not by chance that in the USA Mistry's collection appeared with the title *Swimming Lessons and Other Stories from Firozsha Baag*. "Swimming Lessons" is very important in the economy of the whole collection: in the light of it, all the other tales appear like distant steps on the way to migration. The ideological potentialities of metafiction are thus exploited and applied by Mistry to the difficult medium of the short story. If it is true that Firozsha Baag is the place where all the stories but the last one are set, and where the book is read for the first time, one cannot forget that the stories were written in Canada. This gives this writing that particular sense of estrangement which constitutes the "important difference" not only between Indian and Western narratives, but also between tales told by native authors writing from inside and outside India. The metafictional dimension provided by the frame of Firozsha

Baag suggests the need for a revision of the traditional literary imagery available to the migrant writer and at the same time stands as a criticism of the book itself.

On the other hand, a story like "Squatter" translates into grotesque images a precise denounce of xenophobia, by epitomizing the problems related to immigration in the difficulties a young Indian man finds in coping with Canadian washrooms. With a sort of corrosive laugh, Mistry's hero, Sarosh, concludes his scatological tale declaring: "for some it was good and for some it was bad, but for me life in the land of milk and honey was just a pain in the posterior" (*Firozsha* 168). Sarosh's comic "immigration related" problem is told by an older lodger of the Baag, Nariman Hansotia, who delights in story-telling, in conformity with one of the oldest Indian traditions. In fact, the way Nariman tells his tales clearly derives from typical oral story telling, while reflecting Mistry's own poetics. "Nariman sometimes told a funny incident in a very serious way, and expressed a significant matter in a light and playful manner. And these were only two rough divisions, in between were lots of subtle gradations of tone and texture. Which, then, was the funny story and which the serious? [The] opinions were divided, but ultimately [...] it was up to the listener to decide" (*Firozsha* 147-48). So, by structuring his sentences carefully and choosing his words with extreme care, Nariman can turn a coarse joke into a "sad saga," while the reader can translate the pitiful story of young Sarosh—who can satisfy his physiological urges in the Western World only by simulating the squat of Indian latrines—into a metaphor both for the immigrant condition and for the act of story telling. Sarosh's failure in Canadian toilets ironically points to the necessity for the migrant writer to stick to the modes of his native tradition, without trying to adopt foreign standards. Pride of one's difference and rejection of demagogic attitudes towards foreigners are expressed by Nariman Hansotia with these words: "If you ask me mosaic and melting pot are both nonsense, and ethnic is a polite way of saying bloody foreigner" (*Firozsha* 160).

It has been noted that "Joyce's relatively gentle but penetrating irony appears to be Mistry's model in *Tales from Firozsha Baag*."[2] Actually, the young writer seems to have travelled far, at least from classical Indo-Anglian short fiction. Even though his tone apparently shifts from melancholy to irony, as for instance Narayan's usually does, in this latter a Chekhovian glance at reality brings to surface the vulnerability of human condition, while in Mistry the metafictional dimension provided by the frame of Firozsha Baag suggests the need for a revision of the traditional literary clichés available to the migrant writer. Reality is looked at from multiple points of view. The world is recreated in the spirit of multiplicity, and according to a sense of plurality which is typically Indian. Moreover, the careful construction of the collection allows the author to play at liberty with characters, time and plots. Since all the stories are enclosed in a single frame, past episodes and present memories mingle, dead characters are resurrected and mature people reappear as naughty children. In this sense, Mistry uses the setting of Firozsha Baag exactly as the French author Georges Perec did with his Parisian block of apartments in his novel *La vie: mode d'emploi*, "the last real event in the history of the novel," according to Italo Calvino. In fact, while the stories of both Mistry's and Perec's characters are interlocked, we learn about them through a series of suggestions, situations, memories which pass from chapter to chapter (or from story to story) like pieces of a puzzle. "Thus [Mistry] creates a vibrant image of a community caught in a cycle of restrictive traditions, economic needs, racial and religious tensions, as well as inner psychological conflicts" (Malak 190). This seems to be the most precise reproduction we can find in fiction of that "submerged population" which, according to Frank O' Connor, is at the centre of modern short stories. Mistry's Parsi families appear to be typical "groups of submerged populations," "as disturbing as Saroyan's Armenians, Willa Cather's spoiled artists, and Anderson's spoiled romantics," one might add with O' Connor.

In the light of these observations, it is particularly interesting to look at how Mistry deals with his women characters. Not by chance, the collection opens with "Auspicious Occasion," the story of a young beautiful girl married to an old man, who wears dentures and treats her like his servant. The story is both comic and sad, as is often the case with Mistry. We laugh when we see the old toothless protagonist craving lustfully for the naked body of a new servant; yet we cannot but feel ill at ease when, here as in almost all the other stories of the collection, Mistry exposes "gently, sensitively and truthfully a traditional community that still regards women as unclean, practices arranged marriages, and believes in magic, rituals and superstition" (Malak 195).

In 1991, Mistry published his first novel, *Such a Long Journey*, a story set in India in 1971, at the time of the war with Pakistan which ended with the independence of East Pakistan (Bangladesh). Dealing again with members of the Parsi community of Bombay, Mistry strikes the opposition between the values of family and tradition and the corruption of the outside world. Indian politics are the uncanny background of Gustad Noble's family life, as all the events of Indian history of the time mingle with Noble private life. A moral man, the head of a loving family, in his fifties Noble has to experience a complete upheaval of his life, owing to the sudden blowing up of politics in his smooth everyday routine. The adventures of this bank clerk, whose life is devastated by History are linked both to the situation of the Parsi community of Bombay in the seventies and to the larger horizon of Indian politics of the same time, characterised by a huge return of nationalism, by the corruption of Indira Gandhi and her Congress Party and the ascent of her inept son, Sanjay. In a vision which does not leave many hopes for the future, Mistry sees the India of 1971 as a country where public latrines can become temples while temples can turn into dust and ruins. During his long journey, Gustad Noble meets sorrow and death, and disillusion for his son's betrayal. He comes into contact with politic corruption, he gets involved in communal riots, and finally ends by appearing like an almost Kafkian creature. Like Kafka, Mistry not only worked in a bank before utterly devoting himself to creative writing; he is also equally aware of the uncanny hidden in the life of humble clerks and employees. Moreover, again in a Kafkian way, at the end of his journey Gustad realises that for him the *real* journey has just started or, better, that certain journeys never end and must go on in any case, even without hope, even without knowing their goal.

As it happens in his short stories, in *Such a Long Journey* Mistry mixes comic and tragic elements, while creating around Gustad a number of minor characters, all full of life and empathy. Among them, one cannot forget Gustad's wife Dilnavaz, with her fear of the evil eye and Miss Kuptitia's, the 'witch' whose help she seeks in order to remove it; Gustad's children Sohrab and Roshan; Major Bilimoria, the one who drives Gustad down into the abysses of politics; Mr. Dinshawji, Gustad's colleague at the bank, a teller of coarse jokes; and finally the retarded Tehmul, who talks at impossible speed. *Such A Long Journey* was shortlisted for the Booker Prize, won the Canada's Governor General Award, the W.H. Smith/Books in Canada First Novel Award, and the Commonwealth Writer's Prize for Best Book.

Mistry's second novel, *A Fine Balance*, published in 1995, was not only shortlisted for the Booker Prize, too, but it also won the Giller Prize, the Royal Society of Literature's Winfried Holtby Prize, the 1996 Los Angeles Times Award for fiction and was turned into a film by the same title in 1998. Moreover, shortly after its publication, the Faculty of Arts at Ottawa awarded Mistry an honorary doctorate. Set in India in 1975, during Indira Gandhi's state of Emergency, it is a neo-realist story of extreme poverty and true friendship among outcasts. In this novel, Mistry does not only deal with the misery of common people and the brutality of tyrannical politics: he also describes the horrors of a government work-camp, the tortures in state prisons, in short all the humiliation, the suffering and the wrong that poor people have to suffer under fascist governments. Actually, Mistry sees Indira Gandhi's politics as decidedly fascist, to the point that even the everyday life of ordinary people under her rule appears to be characterised by sheer brutality. Many critics talked of neo-realism when the book appeared, comparing this novel with the Italian fiction and especially cinema dealing with the lives of the underdog in the 40s and early 50s, or, nearer to Mistry's setting, to the works of the great Bengali film director Satyajit Ray. In fact, the Italian neo-realists as well as Ray try to depict the dramas of ordinary people objectively, leaving aside their own personal perspectives as far as possible, in order to catch the essence of otherness (the otherness of the poor and the poorest), and to come to terms with the ethical responsibility that this objective view demands. This is exactly what Mistry does in *A Fine Balance*, where poverty, misery and brutality are described and conveyed without sentimentality or easy—and sterile—pity.

Following the steps of other postcolonial writers who revised official history, re-writing it from the point of view of the victims and of the losers, Mistry tries to re-write the history of Indira Ganhdi's darkest years from the viewpoint of those who experienced the terrors of Emergency. Yet, instead of turning those saddest situations into a macabre horror tale, like Rushdie does for the more sombre days of Pakistani history in *Shame*, or instead of recurring to fable, fantasy and surrealism, like the same Rushdie does in *Midnight's Children*, Mistry prefers to stick to reality. Actually, one could talk of verism for this novel, using the label that was invented in the late XIX century to define that fiction which aspires towards a naked representation of reality, however disagreeable it may be, without any embellishments. Therefore, Indira Gandhi is not transmogrified into an horrible Widow with black and white hair, as happens in *Midnight's Children*: on the contrary, she is described with crude realism as a corrupted politician, who abused of her power, miscalculating the consequences of her deeds. No understatement is used in face of the despair, the violence and the absolute destitution which follow: like the Italian neo-realists, Mistry is interested in all aspects of humanity, and in the problems (even the most sordid ones) of the common man. Moreover, again like Italian Neo-realism, Mistry's verism is strongly revolutionary because, by showing the tragedies they led to in the lives of common people, it denounces wrongs which have been overlooked or neglected in the official versions of History.

Forced vasectomy, detention without trial, limitations of freedom of speech, media censorship, ambiguous family planning clinics are among the consequences of Emergency experienced by Mistry's protagonists. One of them, Ishvar, after seeing his dwelling been torn down to the ground by the City Embellishment programme, gets sterilised; then, as a result of a surgical operation in bad hygienic conditions has both his legs amputated and eventually loses his job as tailor, because without feet he cannot work at his sewing machine. But this is not enough: the disabling sterilisation of Ishvar and his friend Omprakash compels Dina, their lodger and employer, to give up her sewing shop, and to return as a servant to her brother's place. In the unnamed city by the sea where the novel is set, no one is exempt from the experience of cruelty: students are tortured and killed by the police; unmarried young women commit suicide to avoid being an economic burden for their families; young men die after forced vasectomy. Yet all this public violence leads to the discovery of compassion and human dignity, even though Mistry is very keen on avoiding the rhetoric of heroism acquired through extreme suffering. The lives of his four protagonists, who happen to share the same apartment, are mixed with the destiny of their country: in this way, public history and private stories go along together, influencing each other. This is the sense of the novel's title: one must find an ideal state of living, in between weakness and strength, misery and dignity, the private and the public.

The long novel, after dealing with the past lives of the four characters, concentrates on their painful experiences in 1975, and then follows Indira Gandhi who, performing "juggling acts with time past," gets out of power and in again, until her assassination in 1984. The final picture of New Delhi devastated by flames shows that, almost a decade after the Emergency, violence still dominates the Indian political scene, with Hindus massacring Sikhs to avenge their Mother Goddess. Quite interestingly, Mistry follows Indira's ascent to her Goddess status stressing all the grotesque motives hidden in her rise to power: her magniloquent speeches, which are contradicted by her actions; her will to appear as a popular icon, Indira who stands for India, or better for "Mother India," like the protagonist of a very popular 1957 Hindi film by Mehboob Khan; her nepotism; her demagogy, which is apparent in her habit of paying peasants to attend her open air speeches and feign interest in them (mainly to avoid being whipped by the police who thus punish those who don't appear interested enough). Opposed to Indira Gandhi's negative image of female power is Dina, the female protagonist of Mistry's novel, who survives among poverty, violence and abuse. A young widow, she refuses to go back to her brother's house after her husband's death and strives to keep her "fragile independence" by sewing garments and letting a room to a student in her apartment. Even though she is surrounded by examples of female weakness (her mother and her Aunt Bapsi, who both go out of their minds after the loss of their husbands) and, prevented from completing her studies by her brother, she is treated like a servant by him and his wife, Dina manages to educate herself in public libraries and to marry a man of her own choice, instead of the eligible bachelors proposed by her brother. Then, after the death in a car accident of her beloved husband, she struggles to go on without asking for her brother's charity.

A Fine Balance is not a political book nor a reportage about the conditions of the underdog. It is more of a fictional reflection about caste and privilege, in the light of the consequences of Indira Gandhi's political decisions on the unprivileged. Mistry is very keen on dealing with those people who are rarely represented in Indo-English fiction, which, being written by middle class and upper middle class authors, prefers to deal with the class they know better. A monumental answer to minimalism, *A Fine Balance* received enthusiastic acclaim and terrible criticisms. While reviewers like Pico Iyer compared it to Balzac's and Hardy's great epics of tragic realism, the Australian critic Germaine Greer accused Mistry of giving an untruly cruel portrait of India. Upset by the misery, the violence and the tragedy of the story, she disliked the book so much as to say she hated it during the BBC-TV panel discussion for the 1996 Booker Prize. In response, Mistry, usually a very reserved author, could not help calling her criticism "asinine."

Surely, *A Fine Balance* is a book completely out of tune with the times of minimalism, glamour, postmodernism and even magic realism. A tragic realistic epic, it seems to belong more to the XIX century season of realism and verism than to present day fiction. A book dealing with uncomfortable issues, it leaves us, in the end, with an even more uncomfortable question: where do we draw the line "between compassion and foolishness, kindness and weakness?"[3] After witnessing outcasts being forced to eat excrement, women's faces being ruined by acid, and slum people being forcibly sterilised, the reader gets the impression that Emergency with the capital E is but a metaphor for a society where "living each day is to face one emergency or another." It does not surprise, then, if middle-class educated readers like Germaine Greer found this book too strong for their palates. Yet, one could not find a better way to conclude a comment on Mistry's work than by quoting Iyer's words:

> [...] few have caught the real sorrow and inexplicable strength of India, the unaccountable crookedness and sweetness, as well as Mistry. And no reader who finishes his book will look at the poor—in any street—in quite the same way again. (Iyer)

It is not by chance that still in 2001, that is to say five years after its publication, *A Fine Balance* was chosen as Book of the Month by Oprah Winfrey on American TV: the discussion of the book on a very popular daytime talk show prompted Mistry's publisher to print an extra 700,000 copies, half a million of which sold. *A Fine Balance* was the second non-American book to be featured in Oprah Winfery's show and it was chosen to introduce American readers to Eastern reality, after September 11.

References to Greer's reaction to and criticism of *A Fine Balance* are to be found in Mistry's next novel, *Family Matters*, which was published in Spring 2002. "A while back, I read a novel about Emergency," one of the minor characters says,

> A big book, full of horrors, real as life. But also full of life, and the laughter and dignity of ordinary people. One hundred per cent honest—made me laugh and cry as I read it. But some reviewers said no, no, things were not that bad. Especially foreign critics. You know they come here for two weeks and become experts. One poor woman whose name I can't remember made such a hush of it, she had to be a bit pagal, defending Indira, defending the Sanjay sterilization scheme, defending the entire Emergency—you felt sorry for her even though she was a big professor at some big university in England. What to do? People are afraid to accept the truth. As T.S. Eliot wrote, "Human kind cannot bear very much reality."[4]

The reference to Greer, utterly unnecessary in the economy of this new novel, beside showing how much Mistry resented her criticism, is very important for understanding his poetics, that is to say his way of dealing with his favourite subject: the common life of ordinary people. As a matter of fact, in *Family Matters* as in *A Fine Balance* there is an attempt to depict the truth of real life honestly. Like Mistry's previous novel, this book can make readers "laugh and cry" as they read it and, even though in *Family Matters* there are no horrors, here, too, "the laughter and dignity of ordinary people" are present in every page. Moreover, the story, full of complicated religious and social conflicts, often related to the dynamics of the Parsi community, seems to be told on purpose to emphasise the impossibility of non Indian critics to understand the Indian situation. Yet, even if "India is not for beginners," as Mistry said at the launch of his new novel, the main plot of this work—concerning the problems related to the caring of a bedridden old man—is surely universal and understandable all over the world.

In this end-of-the-century India extended families where the old people are looked after and protected are no longer the rule. Like everywhere else in the world, the needs of a sick old father are at odds with low salaries, small flats, lack of public assistance, and the unaffordable costs of private nursing. Faithful to his promise to describe real life honestly, Mistry gives an almost naturalistic picture of a family whose harmony is threatened by the demands of a bedridden parent: bad smells, hygienic problems, all sorts of unpleasant situations are described in such a precise way that one cannot help thinking of French naturalism. Yet the general atmosphere is more relaxed: unlike in Zola's world (and unlike in Mistry's 'city by the sea') in this Bombay-Mumbai the greatest catastrophes are regularly avoided at the last minute. The only real tragedy seems to be everyday life, at least for this small world of clerks and teachers who are always denied higher opportunities. As a character says, "no matter where you go in the world, there is only one important story: of youth, and loss, and yearning for redemption. So we tell the same story, over and over. Just the details are different" (221).

Talking about his latest work, Mistry said that there is no pure good or pure evil in it, nor black or white, but "There is always a greyness in everything." Actually we could add that the whole book is immersed in a grey ambience, or better in an atmosphere full of nuances, where all the range of shades from black to white—all the possible shades of grey—are exploited. It is almost impossible to take side completely with one character—or against another. All the protagonists have equally good reasons for being loved or hated. While even Coomy, Nariman's stepdaughter, who appears to be scheming all the time against her stepfather, can be seen both as the villain of the story and as a victim of circumstance; Yezad, who starts as the man of goodwill and common sense in the tale, ends up by becoming a conservative Zoroastrian, dangerous for himself and his family. Moreover, even though, as far as the story goes on, we learn to appreciate Nariman's generosity and goodwill, we cannot help sympathising with Roxana's husband (and getting annoyed at the old man) when we see how his continuous demands threaten the harmony of her family. Mistry manages to explore all the ambiguities of family life very subtly by offering a picture of Indian lower middle class which reminds one of the small bourgeoisie you find in R.K. Narayan's 'comedies of sadness.' But while in Narayan's world politics are almost always in a remote background and do not affect everyday life in a consistent way, here on the contrary private problems mix with socio-political and religious conflicts so deeply that it is almost impossible to separate them.

As Mistry himself explains, religious, political and social issues are so complex and intermingled in the novel that there is even one character, Lucy, Nariman's Christian lover, who draws "onto herself so much of these conflicts that [she becomes] the essence of all the conflicts." Her story is told in a series of flash backs which are set apart in italics in the text, as they are meant to relate to Nariman's dreams and his almost unconscious musings over his unfortunate love story. In these italicised sections Nariman looks at his past through a veil of nostalgia, exactly like Mistry seems to do in all his novels. In fact, many critics reckon that Mistry's fiction must be mainly autobiographical, since in spite of being a Canadian resident for almost three decades now, he goes on writing only about the Parsi community of Bombay. Yet, the author himself points out that his novels are autobiographical only as far as "all fiction is autobiographical—imagination ground through the mill of memory." In this sense, the alter ego of Mistry in *Family Matters* is not Nariman with his remembrance of past things, but the young boy Jehangir, Roxana's younger son, through whose eyes we see much of the events happening in his family after Nariman's arrival. He writes the epilogue of the story in the first person. In the last scene, we see him turning eighteen and wondering what lies ahead for his family "in this world that is more confusing than ever" (487). The novel ends on this note of uncertainty. Nobody knows what the future reserves. Yet Jehangir's last word—which is also the last word of the book—is (ironically?) positive. Answering a question of his mother, he says: "Yes, I'm happy." Mistry comments: "Can he retain that way of looking at the world? If he can and he does turn into a writer, then he may become one of those people who helps us make sense of the world."

Notes

1. Rohinton Mistry, *Tales from Firozsha Baag* (London: Faber and Faber, 1987) 160.
2. Amin Malak, "Images of India," *Canadian Literature* 119 (Winter 1988) 189.
3. Pico Iyer, "Down and really out," *TIME Magazine* 147.17 (22 April 1996).
4. Rohinton Mistry, *Family Matters* (London: Faber and Faber, 2002) 202-03.

A ROHINTON MISTRY BIBLIOGRAPHY

Primary Sources

Fictional works

"The More Important Thing." *Canadian Fiction Magazine* 65 (1989).

Tales from Firozsha Baag. London: Faber and Faber, 1987.

Such a Long Journey. London: Faber and Faber, 1991.

A Fine Balance. London: Faber and Faber, 1995.

Family Matters. London: Faber and Faber, 2002.

Secondary Sources

Book of Criticism on Mistry

Jaydipsinh, Dodiya, ed. *The Fiction of Rohinton Mistry: Critical Studies.* London: Sangam, 1998.

Critical Works in which Mistry's Work is Discussed

Albertazzi, Silvia. *Translating India.* Bologna: Clueb, 1993.

Nelson, Emmanuel S., ed. *Writers of the Indian Diaspora.* London: Greenwood Press, 1993.

Articles about Mistry

Albertazzi, Silvia. "Passages: the 'Indian Connection' from Sara Jeannette Duncan to Rohinton Mistry." Maria Teresa Bindella and Geoffrey Davis (Eds.). *Imagination and the Creative Impulse in the New Literatures in English.* Amsterdam & Atlanta: Rodopi, 1993. 57-66.

____. "Migration in the Anglophone Fiction of the Eighties." *Commonwealth Literary Cultures: New Voices, New Approaches.* Eds. Giovanna Capone, Claudio Gorlier and Bernard Hickey. Lecce: Edizioni del Grifo, 1990. 409-18.

Barucha, N.E. "When Old Tracks Are Lost: Rohinton Mistry's Fiction as Diasporic Discourse." *The Journal of Commonwealth Literature* 30.2 (1995).

David, R.G. "Revisioning a Homeland in Michael Ondaatje's *Running in the Family* and Rohinton Mistry's *Tales from Firozsha Baag*." *Literary Half Yearly* 37.1 (1996).

Heble, A. "A Foreign Presence in the Stall. Towards a Poetics of Cultural Hybridity in Rohinton Mistry's Migration Stories." *Canadian Literature* 137 (Summer 1993).

Hancock, Geoff. "An Interview with Rohinton Mistry." *Canadian Fiction Magazine* 65 (1989): 143-50.

Iyer, Pico. "Down and really out." *TIME Magazine* 22 April 1996. 147.17.

Lambert, Angela. "The Guardian Profile: Rohinton Mistry." *The Guardian* 27 April 2002.

Malak, Amin. "Images of India." *Canadian Literature* 119 (Winter 1988): 101-03.

____. "Insider/Outsider Views on Belonging: the Short Stories of Bharati Mukherjee and Rohinton Mistry." Ed. Jacqueline Bardolph. *Short Fiction in The New Literatures in English.* Nice: Faculté des Lettres et Sciences Humaines, 1989. 189-96.

____. "The Shahrazadic Tradition: Rohinton Mistry's *Such a Long Journey* and the Art of Storytelling." *The Journal of Commonwealth Literature* 29.2 (1993).

Morey, Peter. "Post-Colonial DestiNations: Spatial Re(con)figurings in Khushwant Singh's *Train to Pakistan* and Rohinton Mistry's *A Fine Balance*." *Fictions of India: Narrative and Power*. Edinburgh: Edinburgh UP, 2000.

Myer, Emily. "Such a Long Journey—Rohinton Mistry." *The Bruswickan* Online. Netscape. 8 Nov. 2000.

Piciucco, Pier Paolo. "Bombay Under Canadian Eyes: Visions of the Indian Metropolis in the Fiction of Rohinton Mistry." Eds. Rajeshwar Mittapalli and Pier Paolo Piciucco. *Studies in Indian Writing in English*. Vol. 1. Delhi: Atlantic Publishers, 2000.

Ramachandra, R. "Rohinton Mistry's *Such a Long Journey*: Some First Impressions." *Literary Criterion* 19.4 (1994).

Ross, Robert. "Seeking and Maintaining Balance: Rohinton Mistry's Fiction." *World Literature Today* (Spring 1999).

Ruddy, Martin. "Rohinton Mistry, Writer from Elsewhere." *Canadian Literature and Culture in Postcolonial Literature and Culture Web.* Online. Netscape. 4 Nov. 2000.

Townsed, David. "Multiple Pleasures in Mistry's Journey." *Quilt & Quire* 57.3 (March 1991): 62.

Williams, D. "Cyberwriting and the Borders of Identity. What's in a Name in Kroetsch's *The Puppeteer* and Mistry's *Such a Long Journey.*" *Canadiana Literature* 149 (Summer 1996).

Whetter, D. "Telling Firozsha Baag: Space, Migration and Storyscape in Rohinton Mistry's *Tales from Firozsha Baag.*" *The Journal of Indian Writing in English* 27.1 (1999).

14

VIKRAM SETH

ALBERTA FABRIS GRUBE

Vikram Seth is a fairly young but extremely versatile writer who has had a variegated career—as a student of economics, translator, poet and novelist. Born in 1952, educated in India, he studied for two years at the University of Beijing and has lived in California and England. He is an anomalous individual who has often elicited negative reactions and unfavourable criticism for many reasons, including his unconventional development as a writer and possibly also because he has written books which were extremely successful and made him a rich man. Furthermore there is the problem of his national identity: should he be identified as an Indian writer, considering that he has lived mostly abroad and became well-known with *The Golden Gate*, which Gore Vidal called "the great Californian novel?" It is a very provocative question, which involves him as well as other writers of the so-called Indian diaspora, and is not easily answered. What is immediately apparent to his readers is that Seth is an artist at home with the world, absorbing influences from various cultural backgrounds. If the impact of English literature is immediately recognizable in his prose and poetic works, other traditions are also significant, starting with the Chinese, as shown in his translations of three poets from the Tang period. If it is a well recognized fact that in the 19th century Indian poets using English as their expressive means relied heavily on the Romantic poets of the period, Seth, our contemporary and a sophisticated writer, moves with great ease and nonchalance between different styles, handling modes and the conventions of different periods and different lands with extreme elegance and wit.

Travel books are particularly popular in Great Britain; in 1983 Seth published *From Heaven Lake: Travels through Sinkiang and Tibet*, a pleasant and entertaining account of his return home from Beijing, across Sinkiang and the Himalayan range. It was an eventful journey since Seth had decided not to use the most common means of transportation—trains and planes—preferring to try his luck hitchhiking, travelling in impervious, difficult regions, the relatively little known north-western provinces, still inhabited by a central Asian non-Han, Muslim population, the Uighurs, and finally seeing Tibet, a splendid, isolated country he had always ardently desired to visit. At the same time, such an unconventional journey gave him the opportunity of commenting on an intriguing period in the history of China which, after Mao's death, was experiencing the timid reforms of Deng Xioping, who was trying to improve the economic situation of the country. Travelling on his own, well-equipped with a critical mind, the writer can thus describe not only what he sees but can also try to make his readers aware of the problems and difficulties of the regime, drawing interesting parallels with the situation in India, a country which shared certain characteristics with China, although it differed in other ways. Apart from his often penetrating remarks on broad issues, the book is highly enjoyable for the lively portraits of people: fellow European students, police officers with whom he has to negotiate his travel permits, but above all people he meets and ends up knowing a little better, like Sui, the truck driver who takes him a long way towards Lhasa, "an alert-faced and vigorous chain smoker, compact in limb and confident in manner" (50), a friendly character who uncomplainingly accepts the hardships of his work and tries to make the best of it, going out of his way to strike a good bargain and to bring some delicacies to relatives or people he likes. Quite memorable is also Norbu, the young Tibetan who takes Seth to his humble but hospitable home, calmly talks about the persecution endured by his family at the hands of the Chinese occupants, impressing the author with his sober dignity. Human sympathy, a basic open attitude towards other human beings which seems to be a characteristic of writers like R.K. Narayan or Rohinton Mistry, is already evident in this text where Seth juxtaposes the stolid stupidity of the ubiquitous bureaucrats with the friendly relaxed attitude of most Chinese, ready to accept him, to help him when necessary, thus adding "to that reservoir of individual goodwill that may, generations from now, temper the cynical use of national power" (178). His concern for people and the quality of their lives does not prevent the writer from giving at least some impressions of both the natural and urban landscape he sees. He comments not only on the "stupefying architectural sameness, based on a stupefyingly ugly set of models" (37) which is typical of many Chinese cities and towns without the saving grace of the old quarters, but also writes about the stunning mountain views he comes across and less spectacular scenes like the sky above a ruined Buddhist temple in Dunhuang, described with the delicacy of a Chinese painting and the elegant perception of some of his early poems.

One cannot insist enough on the fact that Seth is a special writer, one who loves walking a tightrope, daring to be different, to discover or rediscover traditional paths, paying little attention to fashionable critical shibboleths. Thus in 1986, after having published an extremely sensitive book of poems *The Humble Administrator's Garden*, he wrote *The Golden Gate, a Novel in Verse*, daring to challenge his readers in a clever, original way. One can shock the reader writing outrageous things, using bizarre techniques, but one can also do it revamping an old-fashioned style, a much more challenging task. In writing this novel, called "marvellously quaint" by a critic who, he wrote, "subsequently cut me dead" (100), Seth opted for a very tight, rigid structure, that of the sonnet, to explore the vagaries of love, the complex interplay of human relationships against the dazzling background of contemporary California, the epitome of fashionable modern life. It was a daring decision, revealing great self-confidence and assuredness on the writer's part, which possibly only an outsider, an Indian feeling at home in a different world, could feel free to make. What Seth achieves in this remarkable, paradoxically innovative work is the balance he succeeds in maintaining between a sympathetic understanding of the human predicament: lack of communication between people though they are involved in a love affair; the anguish of loneliness in a world promising happiness or at least contentment and self-realization; the difficulties of the artist who dares to defy contemporary fashion and the impositions of the critics, the precariousness of human life against a glittering background of prosperity and glamour and a virtuoso style reminiscent of Alexander Pope, the Byron of *Don Juan* and the Pushkin of *Eugene Onegin.*

How can I (careless of time) use
The dusty bread moulds of Onegin
In the brave bakery of Reagan?
The loaves will surely fail to rise
Or else go stale before my eyes.
The truth is, I can't justify it.
But as no shroud of critical terms
Can save my corpse from boring worms,
I may as well have fun and try it.
If it works, good; and if not, well,
A theory won't postpone its knell. (101)

Basically the plot revolves around John, a middle-class, ordinary young man, the typical representative of the well educated, relatively well-to-do American yuppie who suddenly feels himself sinking in a slough of despair. Encouraged by an old friend of his, he places an ad in the local newspaper, and after several misfired attempts, he finds a suitable companion, the charming, intelligent lawyer Liz Dorati, who comes from a down-to-earth wine growing family. Their relation seems to be proceeding on the best of terms, so much so that they are investigating the possibility of buying a house, "a sedate Queen Anne Victorian" (126) building, slightly ludicrous but as Liz remarks, with "potential," when disaster strikes with the mock heroic battle of Charlemagne, Liz's cat, who resents the presence of John, the intruder who dared to

> breach the bounds of his domain,
> Usurp his realm, or, to be cruder,
> To rape his solitary reign (132)

Shortly after this, during a family reunion for Thanksgiving, in a burst of jealousy John leaves the lady and gives up his dream of a rewarding life with someone to love, plunging once more into depression until he re-establishes relations with Janet, a former lover, an artist of Japanese origin, only to lose her in a stupid, banal car accident. The book is cleverly constructed, juxtaposing John's need for love with the attitude of Phil, Liz's new perspective husband who bluntly considers passion "a prelude to disaster" (244) but decides to marry her because every human being needs a companion, somebody to rely upon. Still the book ends on a poignant note with John finally realizing the importance of his tie with Janet, the sculptress he had found and loved again, deeply regretting his and her failure to express their feelings, preferring "the insulation / Of casual conduct, light and bland" (292). It is only very slowly and painfully that he finds the strength to face and accept his past, drying his tears and clearing his throat, possibly giving new meaning and sense of direction to his life. He has been invited to become Liz's child's godfather; and this birth somehow compensates the awareness of his fragility, faced with the deaths of so many people connected with him: Janet, Mrs Dorati and the doctor Matt Lamont with his wife. *The Golden Gate* is in other words not only a brilliant portrayal of bright and articulate middle-class people, a text in which the author can display his skill to ironically describe the radical chic attitude of many intellectuals, the glib style of much criticism, which cuts to pieces the artists who do not conform to what is considered valid and fashionable, but it also reveals the deep humanity of its author who beyond a glittering surface perceives the pathos of the human condition.

Having seen Seth's development and career so far, it seemed quite natural that he would put himself to the test of writing another novel, this time in prose, steeped in the European tradition of Tolstoy and George Eliot. It is a family saga set in India in the early 50's, shortly after Independence and the drama of Partition, when the country was going through not the pangs of birth, but the painful lessons of learning to adjust to a new political and social situation, when epochal decisions had to be made in high places while families on a humbler level were deciding the future of their children. There are therefore two planes in the novel, the public and the private ones, which often intertwine provoking different reactions. What one admires is the ample sweep of the book, the writer's ability to create a group of solid, "rounded" characters whose destinies are somehow interlocked. In addition, the reader soon learns to appreciate Seth's capacity to keep the whole thing under control, never losing sight of the various threads running through it, even though the whole action is set in motion by a simple, well-defined motif; a mother's wish to find a suitable boy for her daughter, Lata Mehra, a nice, well brought up Hindu girl. The Mehras are in one way or another connected with the Kapoors, whose head of the family is Minister in the imaginary state of Purva Pradesh; the Khans, still a powerful Muslim family in Brahmpur; and the sophisticated Chatterjis living in Calcutta. Through the various vicissitudes of the three clans, involving the destinies of old and young family members, but also of humbler characters (servants, peasants, stewards, shoemakers, administrators) the reader can also participate in the drama of the political struggles which took place before the general elections of 1952, in the explosion of communal riots due to fanatic elements both on the Muslim and the Hindu side, in the petty intrigues of university life. In a revealing passage Seth, in the words of the young intellectual Amit Chatterji, defines his ideas about the composition of the novel, similar to performing a raag:

> [...] first you take one note and explore it for a while, then another to discover its possibilities, then perhaps you get to the dominant, and pause for a bit, [...] and then the more brilliant improvisations and diversions begin, with the main theme returning from time to time, and finally it all speeds up, and the excitement increases to a climax. (394)

Or else he can compare the process to a banyan tree, with its complex structure of roots and intertwining branches, always, in other words, a living thing offering a vast number of possibilities to the artist who chooses this flexible, intriguing form of expression. Yet, in spite of the broad canvas the writer has decided to work upon, Seth manages not to lose sight of his original theme—finding a suitor for a marriageable girl—against the background of the vast panorama of Indian life among the affluent middle class of the north. And he also manages to fuse in the crucible of his art, motifs and topics already present in the fiction of other important writers of the Asian subcontinent. The infatuation of young, charming but somewhat naive Maan Kapoor for the fascinating singer and courtesan Saeeda Bai should remind us of a similar situation described in Ahmet Ali's *Ocean of Night*; the moving account of the harsh life of the *chamars* and landless labourers in the villages make us think of Kamala Markandaya, while the corruption and intrigues of political life are strongly reminiscent of the bitter novels of Nayantara

Sahgal. If the book was written with a European readership in mind, these descriptions of a complex social reality including various well-known religious festivities, both Hindu and Muslim, are relevant in creating atmosphere, in providing the exotic flavour so dear to the Western mind, yet actually they are far more important than just this. They are structural elements in the economy of the novel, supplying solid texture, the necessary perspective to individual private events. One of the most successful minor characters is an old nawab, a cultivated old-fashioned person, who divides his life between his rambling house in Brahmpur, now half empty, as his two sons are living a life of their own; his daughter is married; his pugnacious sister-in-law has moved to an apartment near the Legislative Assembly where she is fighting a useless battle against the new law which will take away part of their property, and the so-called Baitar Fort in the countryside. This is a large, complex structure which had once given an impression of grandeur but now shows evident signs of neglect, even in the precious but dust covered library and in the immense dining hall with its large oil paintings of ancestors and the English royal family looking down from its walls, a visible symbol of another era. The Nawab has few illusions about the future of his class: he feels in his bones that it is doomed, that it will not survive the consequences of the Zamindar Abolition Bill, a legislative measure ironically supported by his best friend, Mahesh Kapoor, however sceptical he may be about the real effects of the long overdue land reform. Being a gentleman of the old school, feudal in his outlook on life, he is worried not so much about his immediate family, as his two sons are perfectly capable of taking care of themselves, but about the future of his philanthropic concerns and numerous dependants, for the most part poets and musicians who periodically entertain him and his guests in memorable musical soirées. Fully aware of the situation, he stops struggling, even against the silverfish which are destroying his precious books in the library where he loves to spend peaceful hours reading Lord Macaulay, and Persian and Urdu poetry. Thus it is not by chance that in modern chaotic Brahmpur, one of the best sights is the Bersaat Mahal, the palace of the old rulers, set in the midst of beautifully arranged gardens, "a filigreed jewel box of white marble, its spirit compounded equally of extravagant dissipation and architectural restraint" (98), "something of abstract and final beauty" (167). In spite of the slight suspicion that Seth may be pulling the leg of the reader taken in by his great cleverness and exceptional technical bravura, I think he sincerely sympathizes with the pathos of the situation, the decay of a former ruling class who contributed in no small way to creating the great and complex civilization we all admire.

If with the Kahns the novelist can indulge in an elegiac tone which may remind us of Ahmet Ali and the Attia Hosain of *Sunlight on a*

Broken Column, one notices a very different attitude towards other people, starting with the delightfully impossible Mrs Mehra, prone to emotional outbursts, exceedingly fond of sweets and gossip, a tender-hearted busybody. She is a character very much in the tradition of mothers in the comedy of manners; but much more intriguing are the portrayals of the members of the other families, less easily definable, but all very much alive in these pages. Seth can be ironic but there is also a vein of human kindness which makes us see the good points of people who are far from being perfect, like Mahesh Kapoor, the honest, sincere politician totally devoted to his difficult job, incapable of understanding his quiet, deeply religious wife, content to look after her family, to follow private prayers in her *puja* room, to tend her beautifully kept garden, an important symbol of order in the novel. She is a simple, inelegant woman deeply mourned by her husband and her son Maan only after her death, but a very positive personality, the moral centre of the book, quietly moving among people who tend to be motivated mainly by love of power and domination.

According to David Myers[1] what Seth wanted to do in *A Suitable Boy* was to emphasize the theme of the "epic renunciation of the passions," not only in amorous relations but also in politics and religion, an assumption already present in *The Golden Gate* but which returns more forcibly in this book. At the beginning of the novel we see Lata falling in love with Kabir, a good-looking, well-read fellow student, who reciprocates her instinctive attraction for him. They meet various times (at the university, in cafés, at incongruous literary soirées), and a couple of times they even succeed in spending some romantic moments afloat on the river, looking at the perfection of the Barsaat Mahal. But Kabir is Muslim and thus cannot be accepted by Mrs Mehra who must find another man for Lata, the suitable person she will eventually discover and whom her daughter will marry at the end of the long novel. It will not be an easy task as Haresh Khanna, the perspective husband, is altogether a different personality from the "sensitive, even vulnerable" Kabir. Older than Lata, belonging to a humbler family, he is ambitious and anxious to succeed. He is not an intellectual, working as he does for a firm producing shoes; he does not dress stylishly and is not refined in manners; but is a likeable person who will take good care of his wife and acquire a position in society, the perfect representative of the 'new' Indian. As Lata tells her friend Malati, "when I'm with Kabir, or even away from him but thinking about him, I become utterly useless for anything. I feel I'm out of control—like a boat heading for the rocks—and I don't want to become a wreck" (1298). This is the real reason behind her decision to accept Haresh's proposal, in spite of her brother's snobbish perplexities: marriage is too serious an involvement to risk following the dictates of the heart and the body, as many of Deshpande's heroines had found out to their own cost. Even if the main theme of the book is actually a love story, this is so enmeshed in a panoramic view of certain aspects of Indian life that it could be compared to an historical novel of our times, although for some critics it is only "a technically proficient blockbuster novel that seeks (and inevitably fails) to encapsulate a deliberately exoticised India."[2]

There is a charming story about Seth on a hot summer day finding respite in the cool rooms of a friend. Here he started writing a collection of animal fables following a well-documented Indian and European tradition. He called it *Beastly Tales from Here and There*, a remake of stories coming from different sources, written in verse and characterized by an inventive use of the rhyme. They are witty and amusing, combining a subtle perception of animal characteristics with pregnant references to human virtues and vices, managing to make them relevant to the contemporary context. A splendid example of such ability is provided by a 'new' fable, created from scratch, "The Elephant and the Tragopan" where Seth indulges in serious ecological discourse, the destruction planned by man of beautiful Bingle Valley, the habitat of a great variety of animals, who feel obliged to oppose such a project. It is an exhilarating story which disguises a very real problem under the cloak of a mock heroic fable, following the Horatian exhortation to the poet to tell the truth but with laughing accents. In their confrontation with the mayor of the town, the incongruous couple of the elephant and the small bird are exposed to the state of affairs in the human world where, "The operative word is Votes, / And next to that comes Rupee-notes" (117). Even if the murdered Tragopan becomes a fetish for the good people of Bingle who suddenly become aware of the possible dire results of human intervention, the author refuses to give a positive end to the tale, leaving readers to draw their own conclusions because in a truly post-modern mood, "This is a tale without a moral" (129) even if one could think of some "quasi-morals" which might be found useful.

In Seth's work the role of both Indian and Western music has always been important, but it is in his last novel, *An Equal Music*, that it becomes the core of the text, the fulcrum of the whole plot which develops around it. It is also a passionate love story, but one without a happy ending; still the book offers a faint hope at the end, because when everything else fails what is most important is "to live from day to day and to hear such music—not too much, or the soul could not sustain it—from time to time" (381). Set in London, with a group of English musicians as protagonists, this first person narrative is about people passionately involved in performing music, who have formed a string quartet. It is a small, almost claustrophobic world, the opposite of the panoramic image of India we found in Seth's previous novel. The main theme, Michael's frantic search for Julia, a pianist he left in Vienna ten years before, a woman lost, found and lost again, can be seen as a contemporary variation of the always popular motif of the search, the quest, particularly felt in the Romantic period. In fact it is very much a story of today, taking place in drab contemporary London, where impecunious artists live in small studio apartments or in the grey anonymity of Archangel Court, like Michael, the main character, a lower-class boy, originally from the North, who through sheer will power and a couple of favourable circumstances, manages to fulfil his dream, becoming a highly considered violinist, playing in professional groups. If one can see the usual touches of humour when dealing with his friends and fellow musicians, one cannot help noticing a deeply felt pathos in the destiny of Julia, an exquisitely talented pianist, who is slowly becoming deaf. There is drama, there is the necessary tension but also the great solidity of the background against which the story develops: concert halls and rehearsal rooms in London and in Vienna, the world of dedicated and often neurotic artists but also of agents, critics, and instrument makers. Quite remarkable in this respect are the pages Seth devotes to Venice, a place most often associated with love and death, with love and betrayal, as in Henry James's *Wings of the Dove*. Having finally found Julia, Michael will spend with her a few, too few, memorable days in the city. It is a momentous time, full of highly strung emotions, like playing together in the deserted church of La Pietà, the church of Vivaldi. Arriving in Venice, they do not stay in the most obvious parts of the city, the ones favoured by both Venetians and tourists, but at Sant'Elena, a former island at the far end of the lagoon, facing the Lido, "green, and suburban, and full of families and dogs" (259) while a major scene, the prelude to Julia's farewell, takes place in the Scuola di San Giorgio degli Schiavoni, where they are first fascinated by the scene of the warrior attacking the dragon against a desolate foreground of half eaten corpses, loathsome animals, then by those of other saints, until the last, culminating experience of looking at Saint Augustine in his study, his face turned towards the window, his pen poised in his hand. It is a magic moment of suspension, the saint seeing a supernatural light and hearing the voice of Saint Jerome announcing his death. In the typical spirit of the author, what strikes Michael in particular is the small dog looking at the saint, "his gorgeous, impeccable, polite, adoring, curly-haired white dog, than which there is nothing more perfect or more necessary in this room, or in Venice, or the world [...]. The painting is unimaginable without you" (278). The novel, in spite of its wealth of technical detail about musical pieces, about the problems of performing not as soloists but in the close formation of a quartet, is engrossing, less flippant and more mature than Seth's previous works, revealing in a different context the same concern for the human condition, the choice one often has to make between passion and a more balanced acceptance of less lofty but possibly more rewarding ideals. It seems that the writer, insisting on the reasonableness of certain decisions both in the East and the West, among sophisticated modern Californians, middle-class Indians, and English quartet players, is really convinced of the soundness of this conviction, which lies at the base of his novels so far.

Such a statement takes us back to the point from which we started: can the author be considered an Indian writer, considering his way of life and his two novels which have nothing to do with his country of origin? This may seem to be a moot point, living as we do in a world where more than ever before national identities are often difficult to define, people move, borders, at least for some intellectuals, collapse. What characterizes this truly cosmopolitan writer is his extreme liberty in moving effortlessly between different worlds, absorbing what suits him from different sources in order to create something new which finds an immediate response in his readers. In other words, although his work is rooted in his tradition as well as in deep concern for finding an equilibrium between the urge of passions and a rational, positive choice which will not be destructive to the order of society clearly reveals, Vikram Seth should be appreciated as an artist above the limits of 'belonging' to one country or another. He dares to be different, to absorb what appeals to him from various literary experiences, to express serious convictions through an innovative use of well-established stylistic forms. Often amusing, never boring, one is very anxious to see what his next development will be, in what direction he will decide to move, reinventing himself as he has done in the past.

Notes

1. David Myers, "Vikram Seth's Epic Renunciation of the Passions: Deconstructing Moral Codes in *A Suitable Boy*," ed. R.K. Dhawan, *Indian Literature Today* (New Delhi: Prestige, 1994) 79-102.
2. Graham Huggan, *The Post Colonial Exotic. Marketing the Margins* (London and New York: Routledge, 2001) 76.

A VIKRAM SETH BIBLIOGRAPHY

Primary Sources

Fictional Works

The Golden Gate. A Novel in Verse. London: Faber, 1986; Paperback edition: Faber, 1987.

A Suitable Boy. London: Phoenix House, 1993.

An Equal Music. London: Phoenix House, 1996.

Non-fiction

From Heaven Lake. Travels through Sinkiang and Tibet. London: Chatto and Windus, 1983; Paperback edition: Penguin Books India, 1990.

Poetry

Mappings. Calcutta: Writers Bookshop, 1980.

The Humble Administrator's Garden. Manchester: Carcanet, 1985.

All You Who Sleep Tonight. London: Faber, 1990.

Beastly Tales From Here and There. London: Phoenix House, 1993.

The Poems, 1981-94. New York: Penguin Books, 1995.

Article

"Forms and Impressions." *London Review of Books* 29 Sept. 1988.

Secondary Sources

Books on Vikram Seth

Pandurang, Mala. *Vikram Seth: Multiple Locations Multiple Affiliations*. Jaipur and New Delhi: Rawat, 2001.

Essays

Dowling, Gregory. "'Allow the Poem to Breathe': Vikram Seth and the Onegin Stanza." *Africa America Asia Australia* 13: 137-49.

Jha, Ashok K. "Vikram Seth: *The Golden Gate* and Other Writings" *Recent Indian Fiction*. Ed. R.S. Pathak. New Delhi: Prestige, 1994. 54-70.

Myers, David. "Seth's Epic Renunciation of the Passions: Deconstructing Moral Codes *A Suitable Boy*." *Indian Literature Today*. Vol. I: Drama and Fiction. Ed. R.K. Dhawan. New Delhi: Prestige, 1994. 79-102.

Piciucco, Pier Paolo. "Elizabethan Influences in Vikram Seth's *A Suitable Boy*." *Studies in Indian Writing in English*. Eds. R. Mittapalli and P.P. Piciucco. New Delhi: Atlantic, 2001. 158-69.

15

Shashi Tharoor

TABISH KHAIR

> Filled with subtlety, grace and beauty, [...] *Riot* takes on a range of topics fusing life, art, history, class and culture into a vibrant novel about communalism in the wake of the Babri Masjid demolition[1]

enthuses one reviewer of Shashi Tharoor's most recent novel, *Riot* (2001), in the serious pages of *The Book Review.*

> An outrageous feast, spilling over with myths, rhymes, tales of ancient treachery and wisdom, and tales of modern foolishness and heroism. [...] An ambitious and often eloquent retelling of India's recent history [...] [with] modern and ancient drama woven into this wildly original extravaganza[2]

wrote Edward Hower in *The Chicago Tribune* about Tharoor's first novel, *The Great Indian Novel* (1989).

These two quotes amply display the range of Tharoor's novelistic interests and the epic extent of his ambitions as a novelist. They also suffice to stand in for the positive reviews that Tharoor has generally received—though, lately, more so in the West than in India; reviews that have firmly established him as one of the most prominent of Indian English writers. As is obvious, it is superfluous to try and encapsulate all of Tharoor's interests and achievements in one paper, partly because they would exceed the space available and partly because an academic paper is *not* the place to simply praise or criticise a writer. The main concern of an academic paper should be the bid to understand the writing and/or to relate it to wider tendencies in literature and society. As such, instead of presenting a reticulated summary of Tharoor's novels or a narrative bouquet of his many achievements, I intend to examine his three novels within the larger framework of Indian English literature and Indian nation-formation.

Here, the latter (Indian nation-formation), as Tharoor has himself stressed in various articles and interviews, should not be simplistically defined in religious, linguistic or ethnic terms. However, as I have noted in a paper forthcoming in the *The Journal of Radical Philosophy* (USA), modern nation-formation and nationalism/s involve class-based attempts at imposing or resisting various bourgeois hegemonies, and in this context Tharoor's novels make for fascinating study.

The modern novel, as the carrier of the ambivalences of sections of the bourgeoisie, assumes a slightly different accent in 'post-colonial' space. One of the things that start sounding a bit different is the novel's relationship to the nation. A number of critics have implicitly or explicitly traced the complicity of literary studies and 19th and early 20th century novels in the "project of nationhood."[3] This implicit or explicit endeavour can be traced in very different ways in, say, the novels of Jane Austen and those of Bankim Chandra; that is, in different ways throughout what I will term 'colonial' space and times. In colonised countries, in particular, the project of nationhood—having come late into fruition and being largely opposed by the colonising presence—would sometimes be more of an explicit issue in novels than it would be in colonising countries. Though this claim should be qualified by an awareness of Frederic Jameson's sweeping generalisation of Third World novels as allegories of nationhood and Aijaz Ahmad's pertinent critique of it.

In post-colonial space, the project of nationhood loses some of its urgency, the nation not only having become a reality but, at least for some, a rather disappointing one. As the much-quoted Urdu poet (Faiz Ahmad Faiz?) put it,

Yeh daagh daagh ujaala, yeh shab-guzeeda sahar
Woh intezaar tha jiska, yeh woh sahar to nahin.
Yeh woh sahar to nahin, jis ki aarzoo lekar
Chalé the yaar ke mil jaayegi kahin na kahin [...]

(Rough transcreation:
"This dawn's banner subverting night,
Seaming it from the cusp of earth
And sky, has a different light:
It doesn't herald the promised birth.")

However, in a language like English this disjunction of nationhood from novelness (to employ a Bakhtinian term generally) assumes an exaggerated twist in a country like India. English predicates a certain relationship to the nation and the novel in India. The obvious relationship of privilege, for English is spoken by less than 3 per cent of the population of India, but (as Harish Trivedi puts it) "it is this tiny minority which is the privileged, prosperous, decision-making new ruling caste of the country."[4] The less obvious relationship of the transparency (or lack of it) of dialogue in those novels that are based in India, especially when they move out of English-knowing circles.[5] The even less obvious relationship that exists, or does not exist, between

English and other Indian languages, a matter complicated by the very late introduction of English in the subcontinent and its position of international prestige.[6] The almost invisible relationship (though overshadowing all the other relationships) that the bourgeois novelist has with English, which is obviously the language of those classes of the national bourgeoisie which are most widely (and thinly) smeared across the length and breadth of the Indian nation, and which is at the same time the most obviously *cosmopolitan* of all Indian languages and, as such, carries with it old and new *critiques* of the project of nationhood.[7]

Shashi Tharoor's first novel, *The Great Indian Novel*, predictably negotiates this particular terrain, though with uncommon style and fluency. It uses the rough outline of *The Mahabharata* to present a parable of the politics of Indian independence and post-independence until immediately after the Emergency years. This involves Tharoor in a bit of rewriting of history, and he constantly adopts a sceptical stance towards the more simplistic of nationalist and socialist discourses of nationhood that prevailed in those decades. However, this scepticism is itself predicated upon a certain inevitability of *nationness*, so much so that *The Mahabharata* is literally translated into *The Great Indian Novel*. This easy equivalence of the 'Bharata' of *The Mahabharata*, which in no way corresponded with 'Bharat/India' as it is today, with the politico-geographical entity of modern India plays into the hands of certain bourgeois Hindu-nationalist discourses, which see nationhood as descending in more or less direct genealogical order from the ancient classical past. Hence, the very re-examination of the discourses of nation-formation that informs Tharoor's narrative in *The Great Indian Novel* is presumed upon a *greater* givenness of nationhood.

In *Show Business* (1992), a similar ambivalence is imposed by Tharoor's language and class-induced cosmopolitanism and his, again, language and class-induced inability to avoid the enabling narrative of bourgeois nationness. Here, however, the interplay is much more complex and less obvious. It can be best highlighted with reference to the central business of the text—show business, or, more exactly, Bombay films.

The narrative basically follows the struggling-actor-to-dying-star years of Ashok Banjara, a character obviously modelled on the cine star of yesteryears, Amitabh Bachchan. Not just the character, the story of Ashok Banjara's life closely parallels what the public has come to know of the life of Amitabh Bachchan (the only major exception relating to the father-son angle). Obviously, this involves not only various forays into the 'real life' of Banjara and others around him, it also occasions incursions into various kinds of reel life. For example, fictionalised screenplays are often offered as full chapters. These are films that

Banjara acted in and they serve two main purposes: 1. to offer a taste of Bombay films and the film world and 2. to comment tangentially on the real life of Banjara.

Of course, Banjara's story probably differs at many levels from Bachchan's: this is a matter hard to ascertain and, anyway, one should not expect simple verisimilitude in a work of fiction even if that work is based on some real life character or event. The point of my criticism is not reliability, authenticity or verisimilitude, but an examination of the pattern, if any, in the narration of a particular person/place/time and whether this pattern reveals something about the novel. It is, therefore, more interesting to examine not the overlap between Banjara and Bachchan but the narration of the Bombay film world in *Show Business*. This is interesting particularly because the cosmopolitan English-speaking bourgeois has a particular relationship of scornful fascination to Bombay films, as is also obvious in Rushdie's *The Satanic Verses*. However, while making this sweeping remark, one also needs to add the qualification that a particular writer's attitude to Bollywood is partly an individual-ideological choice: a cosmopolitan 'Indian English' writer like V.K. Mina provides a less reductive and less superior reading of even the Bollywood elements of the Bombay film industry.[8]

The Bombay film industry is just as pan-Indian as the Indian English fictional world. Bombay films—especially the purely commercial and 'formula-based' ones (henceforth referred to as Bollywood masala films)—are seen across India.[9] In this sense, they are a bit like English, which is spoken across India. However, while English-speaking people make a thin smear on India, Bollywood-fans form a thick crust that enfolds India from Kashmir to Kanyakumari. The media of the two also differ: Bollywood films falling more into the oral traditions of vernacular narrative[10] and Indian English fiction, in spite of all Rushdian claims to the contrary, falling into the high-chirographic tradition of elitist narratives (English today, Persian earlier on, Sanskrit even further back). This difference is reflected, for instance, in the very different relationships that Indian English novels and Bollywood masala films have to the English language.

At least from the 1970s onwards, when the coming of VCRs took the middle and upper classes largely out of film theatres, Bollywood masala films have been largely aimed at what is unkindly called the hoi-polloi and, more kindly, the masses. This means that actors like Dharmendra, Jeetendra and Govinda, who do not come from an elitist English-medium background, have not hidden or not managed to hide their lack of Babu fluency in English. However, while the fluent-in-English Babus have held this lack in general ridicule, the masses have identified with it: the epitome of it perhaps being the famous drunken scene in *Sholay* where Dharmendra tries to comically impress the villagers by speaking pidgin English. Fluency in English is, more often than not, a characteristic of the villain in Bollywood films,[11] while pidgin English is put to largely comic or satirical uses by the hero *in India.* The comedy or satire, however, does not emanate from the character's inability to speak fluent English, but either the supposedly comical nature of English itself or the social pretence that speaking English is supposed to reveal. Even actors, like Amitabh Bachchan, who come from elite Babu backgrounds, have mostly tried to assume screen personae where English is either absent or presented as an acquired language—the persona of a villager, a coolie or a poor, struggling student, for example.

Indian English novels, however, have a very different attitude to fluency in English, and this applies even to Rushdie, as I have shown in my book (Khair 78-126, 265-97). More simply, Indian English novels tend to use broken English to depict a flaw in the character: even in the plausibly 'anglophone' court scene of a socially-committed narrative like Rohinton Mistry's *A Fine Balance*, the good lawyer speaks correct English and the bad lawyers speak broken English. This is also noticeable in the very first section of Tharoor's *Show Business*, where Mohanlal, the spineless director, and Gopi Master, the ludicrous dance director, speak bad English, while Ashok Banjara and the sage and experienced Abha Patel converse in good English (*Show Business* 8-20).

Keeping in mind this implicit class-contradiction between Indian English novels and Bollywood masala films and the fact that both operate over the same 'territory' of 'national' space, it is not surprising that Indian English novelists often adopt a stance of fascinated repulsion towards Hindi films *in general.* However, this stance is difficult to sustain in the actual world of Hindi films, which can be of many different kinds. Many of the commercial stars of Bollywood—including Amitabh Bachchan, on whose career Ashok Banjara's story seems to be based—have acted in films which were not just of the Bollywood masala kind.

In *Show Business*, however, this diversity does *not* come through. Tharoor needs to reduce all the screenplays and films on offer to Bollywood masala films, though Bachchan's early films (*Namak Haram, Anand, Mili,* even the pakora-western *Sholay,* hardly conformed to standard formulas of the time). This reduction is predicated upon Tharoor's narrative. It is only through such a reduction that the cosmopolitan Babu can narrate Bombay films without abandoning the grounds of his ironic cosmopolitanism and his identifying distance from the other 'national' space of 'Bombay film' fans. Many other kinds of Bombay films—the parallel cinema or even the refined commercial films of film-makers like Gulzar or the social comedies of Hrishikesh Mukherjee—do not necessarily have the pan-Indianness of

Bollywood masala/formula films. It is the Bollywood masala film that is based on an equivalence of units within the nation: it reduces entertainment and message to the common denominator, leaving out all that does not fit the bill. Bollywood masala films appeal to the 'nation'; other kinds of Bombay films may appeal to different sections of the populations of India, thus dividing up the nation into discrete units. It is typical of the ambivalences of cosmopolitan Babu discourses that Indian English novels need the *Bollywood masala film* in order to narrate the *Bombay film industry*, even to such an extent that the complexities of the film industry are all reduced to the dominant but by no means singular Bollywood masala component. This is what happens in *Show Business*, even though one has to add that, within this artificial and ideologically-significant circumference, Tharoor offers an entertaining description of the Bollywood masala element.

In his latest novel, *Riot*, Tharoor confronts one of the issues central to contemporary India: sectarian or "communal" riots between mostly, but not only, Hindus and Muslims in India. Again, the very definition of a communal 'riot' assumes the nation: the people involved in the riot are depicted, at least in (Babu *or* non-Babu) bourgeois accounts, as Muslims and Hindus. Muslims and Hindus, it need hardly be pointed out, are pan-national categories.

Until the 19th century, when the British introduced useful and simplified population censuses, most Indians did not think of themselves primarily or only as Hindus or Muslims. In fact, when asked to choose between the two by colonial census takers, some Hindus and Muslims are said to have hesitated: they had considered their identities on other linguistic, caste-based, ethnic and even 'religious' lines. As Jürgen Osterhammel puts it (also echoed by one of the main characters in Tharoor's novel) "the notion of 'Hinduism' as a clearly identifiable 'world religion' whose doctrines can be neatly summarised was alien to pre-colonial India."[12] While Islam might appear to have slightly more defined 'world religion' characteristics, in actual fact many pre-colonial Muslims (at least in South Asia) did not see themselves merely or only as 'Muslims' (Bayly; Habib; Rizvi).

So while communal riots, per definition, assume certain pan-national categories, the occurrence of communal riots also questions the idea of the nation-state (however defined). In simpler words, 'Hindus' and 'Muslims' fight each other assuming the pan-national identities of Hindus and Muslims, but they also fight each other in a bid to redefine or even implicitly or explicitly question the very basis of the nation-state. Or at least that is how the Babu-bourgeoisie sees it, for the Babu-bourgeoisie sees these conflicts in largely pan-national religious/communal colours. 'Communal,' in this case, means the pan-national communities of Hindus and Muslims.

The reality, in spite of increasing ossification of the categories of 'Hindu' and 'Muslim,' might be different in many ways. It can be argued that communal riots have their roots in a number of different causes—linguistic, personal, ethnic, caste-based, political and, above all, economic—and that it is only in the process of the 'communal riot' that the *pan-national* categories of 'Hindu' and 'Muslim' get evoked, reactivated, reworked and reified. As such, when the Babu-bourgeoisie worries about 'communal riots' in purely or largely 'religious' terms, it is worrying about the existence and problems of the nation, but it has already accepted pan-national categories for the articulation and conceptualisation of its worry.

It is not surprising that Tharoor's concerned examination of the anatomy of a largely fictional riot is constructed on the basis of the pan-national categories of 'Muslim' and 'Hindu.' Being the alert writer that he is, Tharoor does problematise these categories—by introducing, for example, various 'other' reasons for the murder of the American welfare worker and student, Priscilla Hart. It appears that Priscilla Hart was having an affair with the District Magistrate, Lakshman; that she had been threatened by the husband of a Muslim wife whom she was trying to help achieve a better life etc. However, these explanations, it has to be noticed, are personal explanations. They might help explain why Priscilla was the eighth casualty of the communal riot. They do not explain how and why the communal riot took place—even the nature of the riot is posited at the pan-national level of Hindu-Muslim confrontation. Tharoor engages with this confrontation with much perception—offering, in the process, a reasoned critique of Hindu nationalism and Muslim communalism as well as providing a convincing portrait of the role of the district administration in controlling or failing to control communal riots. But his discussion remains presumed on the pan-national categories of 'Hindu' and 'Muslim' even when he shows some awareness of the historical construction of these (and such) categories.

This 'nature' of the communal riot in bourgeois and Babu-bourgeois discourses has to be kept in mind. What it proves is the point that I have made with reference to Tharoor's earlier novels: the Babu-bourgeois criticism of certain versions of the nation (or nationalism) is itself presumed on a greater givenness of nationhood. This ambivalence often makes for a rather superficially descriptive narrative. This aspect of Tharoor's novel is a consequence of the pan-national, sceptic-of-some-nationalisms stance that the narrative voice assumes. It should not be seen as only and simply an attempt to get across to an American audience, as Giti Chandra does in a harshly critical though perceptive review.[13]

Giti Chandra does have a point when she accuses *Riot* of a "separate agenda." She goes on to note that the novel

> is written primarily with an American audience in mind. This, at least, would seem to be the rationale behind giving the bulk of the narration over to the American characters: Priscilla Hart, the social worker who comes to India and is killed in a riot; Rudyard and Katharine Hart, parents of the dead Priscilla Hart; and Randy Diggs the reporter who comes to India to do a story on her death. (Chandra 6)

While conceding Chandra's point, I would like to argue that the problem of the predominance of American voices in the novel has other and deeper roots. These roots also help us understand the other problem noted by her—that Indian characters, with the exception of the DM (District Magistrate) Lakshman and the (partly) SP Gurinder Singh, have been greatly simplified and stereotyped in *Riot.* The problem is language, or rather the problem of narrating a country in English when 97 per cent of the population of that country does not speak English. This, however, is *not* to dismiss English as a genuine language of communication and creativity in India, but to acknowledge the fact that writing in English poses different problems than writing in, say, Hindi, Urdu or Punjabi.

Let us consider the evidence first. This is what Ram Charan Gupta, reactionary and manipulative Hindu fundamentalist politician, says to an informant towards the end of the novel:

> How very interesting, young lady [...]. My, you are thorough. Very diligent of you [...]. You are a good girl, Kadambari [...]. Here's a little something for your trouble. No, that's all right, my dear. I insist. (*Riot* 257)

To anyone used to other Indian languages, what comes across first of all is the crystal-clear Englishness of the sentence construction and the phrases in the extract above. "My, you are thorough," "No, that's all right, my dear," "I insist"—these are all extremely, shall we say, *English* English expressions. One may even claim that they are *English* English in a canonical, textual manner. But all of Ram Charan Gupta's previous conversations or effective monologues—entire chapters at times—have been prefaced with the legend "translated from Hindi" (*Riot* 52, 120). The reason for this legend is given by the American journalist Randy Diggs in his notebook:

> Met local Hindu chauvinist leader to check out the politics behind the riot. Man called Ram Charan Gupta[...]. Spoke only Hindi, but I suspect understands more English than he lets on. (*Riot* 51)

The point to be noted is that Gupta, who is not fluent in English (if he speaks it at all) has to be portrayed as using a certain kind of

English English when he tips his informant later in the novel. The sinister, oily, patronising, well-in-control politician that Tharoor wants to etch comes across only when this sleek, nuanced, controlled *English* English, which Gupta does *not* speak, is foisted on to him.

The fault is not as much Tharoor's as that of English in India. People like Gupta do not speak English or do not speak English under most circumstances. What this means is that just as English remains limited in its attempt to narrate some non-English-speaking realities, the English of characters like Gupta lacks the various registers which can be found in the English of characters, Indian or American, who employ the language regularly and extensively. In short, the American characters are *needed* in the novel to make English a more natural medium of narration. It is easier to depict *all* classes of Indians speaking/trying to speak English to Americans or to have a translation incorporated into the narrative by way of the American presence. It is only when two non-Babu Indians have to communicate directly—as is the case of Gupta and his informant—that the limitations of English as a language of novelised narration in India stand exposed. It is also this that explains why so many of the Indian characters come across as wooden or stereotyped to Giti Chandra. Tharoor is at his best when narrating characters like D.M. Lakshman or S.P. Singh, who share an elite Babu education and are fluent in English. Not only do they employ English extensively, they are also capable of various registers in their use of English. The non-English-speaking or non-Babu middle class characters (who speak English out of compulsion, not choice) are partly reduced to standard types—like Shankar Das the project director—because of their inability to claim visibility and complex narratability in English.

Here it is necessary to recall that Tharoor's most acclaimed work, his first novel, *The Great Indian Novel*, partly succeeds in narrating 'India' by using a family of colonial princes and great teachers—who can be assumed to speak English—as its main vehicle of narration. In *Show Business*, Tharoor again uses characters from Babu backgrounds, though this is also the novel in which he comes closest to addressing the relationship of English to other languages and its class situation in India. He does so largely in the promising character of Pranay, but the exploration is not pressed to the point of any genuine insight.

However, the predominance of American characters in *Riot* can also be linked to another vital issue, and one that again highlights the ambivalences of nationness that I am concerned with in this paper. As mentioned earlier, the Babu-bourgeois view of the communal riot is not only based on pan-national categories, such as 'the Hindu' and the 'Muslim,' the 'communal riot' also threatens the national bourgeois conceptions of nationhood. When it comes to the more international members of the bourgeoisie—let us say, cosmopolitan Babu-bourgeois writers—communal riots also do violence to their central belief in *humanity*, in *human* rationality. Not only are such cosmopolitan citizens at best faint believers in any kind of *activist* religion, they might even be sceptical of essentialist or extreme forms of nationalism (as we have seen in the case of Tharoor). The communal riot, even when it does not threaten their notion of the nation, threatens their idea of humanity and humaneness. The communal riot, defined religiously, is the most 'irrational' manifestation of post-colonial India that the cosmopolitan bourgeois vision can be confronted with. The presence of Americans as the people who try to understand a communal riot in India, thus, stands for this cosmopolitan Babu-bourgeois bewilderment in the face of the 'irrational.' Both the American characters and the cosmopolitan Babu-bourgeois narrator/writer look upon the communal riot from a cognitive distance that is just as great, as shocked, as incapable of a real understanding of it all. The irrational bursting out, as in E.M. Forster's caves (and it is, therefore, natural that the ghost of *A Passage to India* should visibly and invisibly stalk the pages of *Riot*), poses a problem that remains as insoluble for both the American characters and the cosmopolitan Babu-bourgeois narrator/writer.

Consequently, Priscilla Hart's murder also remains unsolved.

Here, Tharoor is finally forced to take recourse to that common device of the bourgeois novel, unresolved doubt or aporia. Priscilla Hart might have been murdered by the angry Muslim husband of a woman whose cause she had championed, or due to the manipulations of the Hindu nationalist, Ram Charan Gupta, in order to strike at her lover, D.M. Lakshman. Or she could just have been "in the wrong place at the wrong time." Anyway, the matter is left shrouded in unresolved doubt or aporia.

Elsewhere, I have examined how the use of aporia serves narrative purposes, such as the possibility of narrating subaltern agency in a non-hegemonic way in Amitav Ghosh's exceptional novel, *The Calcutta Chromosome* (Khair 302-31), as well as enabling the Babu-bourgeois writer to avoid facing the contradictions in her/his ideological framework. For example, the aporia at the end of R.K. Narayan's important novel, *The Guide*, is partly necessary to enable the narrator/author to avoid having to choose between the discourses of rationality (traditionally appropriated by the 'West') and those of irrational 'faith' (Khair 340-43). Such a choice has to be avoided so that the Babu can continue to occupy his in-between space—between 'Western rationality' and 'Eastern faith,' in this case—for it is in this space that the Babu identity is most clearly constituted. But of course occupying this space ambivalently also means not being forced to face the contradictions of such a positioning: that is, not having to choose between 'rationality' and 'irrational faith' or even effectively contesting this binary opposition and/or its juxtaposition on the East-West axis.

In Tharoor's case, the aporia seems less significant at first glance. It seems to have to do with the murder of a character only. But if one reads this murder against the backdrop of the riot, one sees a deeper and more troubled picture. What we cannot decide is whether Priscilla Hart died as a consequence of a communal riot or a personal vendetta. It does not really matter whether she was murdered by a Muslim husband or a Hindu nationalist: both these options are motivated by personal grievance and vendetta. However, if she was killed because she was simply "in the wrong place at the wrong time," that is during a communal riot, then we have opened up a Pandora's box of questions. For then the focus is on the 'communal riot,' as a public event, an event that arose in a particular phase of history and that cannot be explained merely at the personal level. The focus, in other words, moves to the unresolved Capitalist-nationalist contradictions that lie behind and cause 'communal riots' in India, and even the definition of such violence in certain pan-nationalist 'communal' (rather than, say, economic) terms. It also moves the focus to the very notions of nationness that enable the narration of a novel like *Riot*, even when it sets out to criticise and sensitively explore various kinds of nationalism. Circumventing the problems of such a change of focus within the bourgeois framework, the ultimate aporia in *Riot* leaves the matter suspended between the personal and the public. This enables the reader to access the unresolved contradictions in the ideologies of the cosmopolitan Babu (contradictions that also *enable* a particular narration of India) in the safer bourgeois form of *ambivalences* of nationness.

Notes

1. Shelley Walia, "Fictional Representation of the Past," *The Book Review* 25.10 (Oct. 2001): 34-35.
2. Accessed and quoted from the author's official homepage.
3. See for instance Firdaus Azim, *The Colonial Rise of the Novel* (London and New York: Routledge, 1993), and G. Jyotsna Singh, *Colonial Narratives/Cultural Dialogues* (London and New York: Routledge, 1996).
4. Harish Trivedi, *Colonial Transactions: English Literature and India* (Manchester: Manchester UP, [1993] 1995) 20. On the other hand, it should also be noted that 3 per cent of India means a number much higher than the population of most European countries: 30 million.
5. Tabish Khair, *Babu Fictions: Alienation in Contemporary Indian English Novels* (Delhi: Oxford UP, 2001) 98-126.
6. Aijaz Ahmad, *In Theory: Classes, Nations, Literatures* (Delhi: Oxford UP, [1992] 1996) 250.
7. The 'cosmopolis,' it need hardly be pointed out, marks a space of tension within the nation: it seeks to exceed the nation, by definition.
8. V.K. Mina, *The Splintered Day* (London: Serpent's Tail, 1999) 14.
9. Actually, they are seen across most of Asia, many parts of Africa and, until recently, regions of East Europe.
10. As phrased in her abstract, Nayar's paper "extends previous analysts' tracings

of the 'oral residue' that unconsciously marks literature into the realm of visual media, positing that there are very clear characteristics of oral performance and orally-transmitted narratives ('the oral epics') operating within, and indeed formatively shaping, the popular cinema of India. These include not only broad psycho-dynamic characteristics of orally-based thought, such as aggregative rather than analytic elements, and a conservative-traditionalist rather than experimental mindset, but as well specific devices and motifs common to orally-based storytelling—from the use of clichés and the portrayal of gross physical violence, to the significance of the verbalized oath, the reliance on "heavy" characters, and the acceptance of—in fact, *preference for*—formula.

11. Even 'villains' like Ajit, whose command of English did not achieve cosmopolitan Babu fluency, assumed screen personae that were supposedly cosmopolitan and fluent in English.
12. Jürgen Osterhammel, *Colonialism* (Trans. from German by Shelley L. Frisch) (Princeton: Markus Weiner Publishers and Kingston: Ian Randle Publishers, [1997] 1999) 98.
13. Giti Chandra, "For American Eyes Only," *Biblio: A Review of Books* 6.9-10 (Sept.-Oct. 2001): 6-7.

A SHASHI THAROOR BIBLIOGRAPHY

Primary Sources

Novels

The Great Indian Novel. London: Viking, 1989; New Delhi: Penguin Books, 1989.

Show Business. New Delhi: Viking, 1991.

The Five-Dollar Smile and Other Stories. New York: Arcade Pub., 1993.

Riot. New York: Arcade Pub., 2001.

Secondary Sources

Essays and Articles on Shashi Tharoor

Balaswami, P. "'The Presence of the Past': Shashi Tharoor's *The Great Indian Novel* as Historiographic Metafiction." *Indian Literature Today* (II). Ed. R.K. Dhawan. New Delhi: Prestige, 1994.

Choudhury, M.K. "The Eternal Present: Shashi Tharoor's Story of India." *Recent Indian Fiction.* Ed. R.S. Pathak. New Delhi: Prestige, 1994.

Karunakaran, Supriya. "Games the Novelists Play: the Subversive Rebellion of Vikram Seth in *The Golden Gate* and Shashi Tharoor in *The Great Indian Novel.*" *Fiction of the Nineties.* Eds. Veena Noble Dass and R.K. Dhawan. New Delhi: Prestige, 1994.

Tripathi, Vanshree. "Polysemy at the Dead End: Shashi Tharoor's *The Great Indian Novel.*" *Recent Indian Fiction.* Ed. R.S. Pathak. New Delhi: Prestige, 1994.

16

Vikram Chandra

ANDREW TEVERSON

Vikram Chandra is the author of two published works; a novel entitled *Red Earth and Pouring Rain* (1995) and a collection of short stories, *Love and Longing in Bombay* (1997). He is currently "in the last arc of" a second novel set against the backdrop of the Bombay criminal underworld and featuring the police detective, Sartaj Singh, who made his debut in the short story, 'Kama,' collected in *Love and Longing.*[1]

Chandra's published works to date share a number of preoccupations: they both exhibit a self-conscious fascination with the mechanics—and the magic—of storytelling, they both promote the tolerance of 'messiness' in narratives and in ideas over the demands of rigorous systematisation, and they are both set, at least in part, in India, and engage with Indian political, historical and social experiences Whereas *Red Earth* treats its themes on an epic scale, however, allowing its narrative to range across three continents and three centuries, *Love and Longing* offers five stories and a frame narrative that concentrate upon the relatively ordinary lives of a handful of individuals in Bombay. *Red Earth,* as a result, becomes an enormous ragbag of a novel that spills, with abandon, over its own edges, whilst the stories of *Love and Longing* are concise and localised vignettes that suggest the dynamism and diversity of the city through a careful and alchemical process of narrative distillation.

Because of the size and scope of *Red Earth,* and because of its many intertwined tales and interchanged narrators, it is almost impossible (and indeed is self-defeating) to encapsulate the plot; broadly speaking, however, it has two principal narrative strands: one in which Sanjay, an eighteenth century poet reincarnated as a monkey with human consciousness in the late twentieth century, tells of his and his brother's adventures in India prior to and after the establishment of the British Raj; and one in which Abhay, a young man who has recently returned to India after a college education in America, tells of a road trip he and his friends took across the States in the mid-1980s. Interwoven within these two broad frames are further tales, many and various, that include an account of British public school life in the early Victorian period, a rite-of-passage tale told by a strip-club dancer in late twentieth century America, and various fictionalised accounts of the lives of historical characters involved in the mercenary wars that fragmented India in the eighteenth and nineteenth centuries.[2] All of these stories are narrated as tales within tales within tales and work to give *Red Earth* an epic *depth* as well as an epic *breadth*. When we hear the tale of George Thomas ('Jahaj Jung' or 'Warlike George'), for instance, we are not only transported across time to the last decades of the eighteenth century and across space to the court of the Witch of Sardhana, we are also sunk several frames deep—since George Thomas tells the tale to the Witch of Sardhana, the tale of which is being narrated to Sandeep by the mysterious woman in the clearing, the tale of which is being relayed by Sandeep to the men of the Ashram where he is resting, the tale of which Sanjay, in monkey form, tells to the growing crowd in the maidan, the tale of which Vikram Chandra tells to us, his readers, in the novel *Red Earth and Pouring Rain*. The impact of this kind of narration upon the reader can be unsettling: faced by a labyrinth of frames within frames and stories within stories, s/he starts to believe, like Reinhardt the Sombre confronted with the sublime enormity of the Indian conception of the age of creation, that s/he is trapped in a "never ending series of peregrinations that [seem] to go nowhere" (114) and that cannot be escaped. Unsettling the reader, however, is not Chandra's sole—or even primary—aim in producing such a vertigo inducing form of narration. More constructively, Chandra is also using the trope of infinite narration to encourage the reader to "luxuriate in [...] curlicues" (24), and, in so doing, to resist the arbitrary demands for 'straightforwardness' that various characters, including Reinhardt the Sombre, voice in the novel. The narrative structure of *Red Earth*, in this capacity—with its ability to incorporate a pyrotechnic diversity of styles (from epic to bathetic to comic to tragic) and of modes (from prose form, to dramatic form to epistolary form to journal form)—operates as a kind of performative rejection of the Enlightenment demands for homogenisation in thought and art current at the time in which the novel is set and still exhibited (in the name of science and reason) a quarter of a millennium later when Sanjay starts to tell his tale in modern India.

This resistance to rationalist or Enlightenment narrative ideals, implicit from the start in the form of *Red Earth*, is given specific thematic focus when the English publisher, Markline, gives Sanjay a copy of Aristotle's *Poetics* and tells him that it "is the origin of all that's good in literature" because it "applies the principles of science to the art of the poet, and thus brings the realm of imagination under the clear light of natural logic" (335). Sanjay, dutifully, reads the *Poetics* and decides that, whilst it represents one possible system of belief or "*darshana* of the world" it depends upon a number of questionable assumptions: firstly, that there is value in "evoking one feeling from the beginning to the end of the construction, as if unity could be said to be defined as homogeneity," and secondly, that the function of literature is to evacuate or empty out emotion "as if the end purpose of art was a sort of bowel movement of the soul" (332). Sanjay, accordingly, rejects Aristotelian theory in favour of the set of ideas about aesthetic form he has received from the "fragmented discourses" of his uncle; ideas that celebrate polyphony and heterogeneity in literature, and that are embodied, metaphorically, in the all-incorporating knot that his uncle and his father, Ram Mohan and Arun, are constructing in their garden when the reader first encounters them: a knot, according to Arun, that has become so complex that new strands need only to be brought close to it to be sucked up and attached (143). This knot, the reader assumes, symbolises the traditions of classical Sanskrit and Indian aesthetics, practised by Ram Mohan and Arun as poets, and can be regarded as a kind of visual antidote to the antiseptic Aristotelian aesthetic promoted by the Europeans. It is all the more resonant, however, for the fact that it is a reconstruction of the Gordian knot which Alexander the Great, when challenged to untie, cut through with a single swipe of his sword. Alexander, of course, was a pupil of Aristotle's, and in expressing his contempt for 'knottiness' or 'messiness' he is adapting his master's aesthetic to suit a more heroic demeanour; in the hands of Alexander the Great (or Alexander the Butcher), however, the Aristotelian demands for cleansing and clarity in the field of aesthetics become slightly more sinister, for when Alexander talks of catharsis, as he does to Sanjay out of the pages of the *Poetics*, he means cleansing, not of the emotions alone, but also of ethnicities, ways of life and competing *darshanas*. The Aristotelian demand to create unity and suppress diversity in the arts is shown, in this way, to be the structural basis of the imperialist desire to subdue peoples and to suppress cultural difference, and in validating the aesthetic theories of Aristotle, British colonisers such as Markline are, consequently, revealing their covert Alexandrine colours. They too, as Sanjay comes to realise, want to hack at the glorious knot of civilisation until "half the world, half the world with its animals and trees and festivals and gods and philosophies and books and wars and loves, more than half the world [is] made insubstantial and nothing" (341).

It is tempting to argue, especially since the narrative form of *Red Earth* is derived from narratives of non-western origins such as the *Mahabharata*, the *Ramayana* and the *Arabian Nights*, that Chandra, in employing non-unitary, oleaginous narrative forms, is promoting a tolerant and inclusive 'eastern' viewpoint over an intolerant and exclusive 'western' one. To some extent this may be the case; throughout the novel Chandra implies that acceptance of the multiple and the paradoxical is a constitutive aspect of Indian philosophical and theological traditions, whilst the tradition of rationalism and materialism that has dominated thought in Europe and America since the Enlightenment has resulted in a desire to simplify and to rationalise: "to kill everything in [...] search [of] beauty" as Sanjay expresses it (528). To suggest that Chandra is doing nothing more than pitting East against West, however, would be to ignore at least three features of his writing: the constructive use that he makes of aesthetic devices and precedents from the European and American tradition of novel writing, the sustained critique he makes of religious and political intolerance within India—which reaches its climax with the terrorist bomb that maims Saira—and the fact that the narrative collections he uses as a precedent for his apparently 'eastern' mode of narration, such as the *Arabian Nights*, have long been beloved of writers in the 'western' narrative tradition such as Jorge Luis Borges (a writer whom Chandra greatly admires)[3] and John Barth (who was Chandra's teacher when he studied creative writing at Johns Hopkins University). What Chandra is resisting in his use of non-unitary forms, in fact, is neither peculiarly eastern nor peculiarly western, but can be both: it is the desire that Sanjay realises towards the end of the novel is overwhelming "everything else": "that there should be only one idea, one voice, one thing, one, one, one" (615). The narrative form of the *Nights* in this context becomes useful to Chandra, not because of any specific cultural allegiances it may have, but because it has been used to express resistance to such unifying drives in diverse cultural contexts. As a narrative that has roots in Sanskrit storytelling traditions it may be used as an example of the resistance to Enlightenment thinking *avant la letter*; as a collection that has been employed by postmodern writers in their quest for non-teleological and non-totalising forms of tale telling it can also be used as an example of resistance to Enlightenment thought *après la deluge*. Both traditions reject the Enlightenment ideal of rationality and clarity in narrative form and both can become allies in the same war; thus when Markline expresses his horror of (and his fear of) traditional Indian narration, he is also, although he does not know it, revealing the horror he would feel if he were to light upon the kind of novels some of his countrymen would be writing two hundred odd years later in which:

> Plots meander, veering from grief to burlesque in a minute. Unrelated narratives entwine and break into each other. [...] Metaphors [...] call attention to themselves, strings of similies [...] go from line to line. [...] Characters die, only to be reborn again. Beginnings are not really beginnings, middles are unendurably long and convoluted, nothing ever ends. (335)

The assault upon the Enlightenment desire for homogenisation conducted throughout *Red Earth*, comes to reflect one of the novel's general philosophical positions: that (as Chandra puts is elsewhere) human beings, in order to be free, must be prepared to "give up nothing, and swallow everything" ('Cult'). In *Red Earth* this philosophy of incorporation comes to have specific implications for the ideas of nationhood and national form implicit in the epic mode Chandra is employing. Traditionally, the epic narrative reflects (and validates) the nation of which it sings, both in terms of content, as a recitation of historical victories and daily rituals, and in terms of form, as a reflection of the ideal shape that the nation might take. *Red Earth* fulfils this formula to some extent—by giving us a heroic account of the events that resulted in the formation of modern India, and by giving us, in the words of the novel, "accumulated stories" that become "the stories of a nation made up of many nations" (299)—but it also rebels against the formula; firstly by giving us a problematised account of heroic victories that foregrounds their destructive and violent effects upon the nation(s) in which they are waged; secondly by refusing to fulfil the conventional epic promise, which is also the promise at the heart of Enlightenment conceptions of nationhood, that there will be a point at which the various strands in the Gordian knot of nationhood will *add up* to a totality. Chandra's representation of nation, in fact, far from offering the conventional epic song to nationhood in which *the many become one*, can be regarded as a fictionalised embodiment of the idea that (in Homi Bhabha's words) "the time for 'assimilating' minorities [and all community groupings] to holistic and organic notions of cultural value has dramatically passed" (175) and must be replaced by a more performative idea of community in which social contradiction can become part of the concept of nation without being absorbed into a pre-established idea nationhood. Whilst Chandra's novelistic representation of nation, like the epic, is incorporative, in other words, it does not become, as epics tend to become, assimilative.

This double-handed approach to genre, in which Chandra, whilst seeming to reproduce narrative conventions, also urges his reader to question them, is not restricted to his treatment of the nationalist epic, but can be regarded as a crucial mechanism in all his uses of traditional form. In *Red Earth*, for instance, he also gives us a conventional chivalric romance, complete with a Spensarian promise to tell "of unearthly horrors and epic loves" (23), but he suggests, simultaneously, that the ravaging of India in the course of the mercenary wars that form the backdrop of his narrative represents "the end of all Romance" (42). In *Love and Longing* similarly various genres are adopted in the telling of the stories—we are told a ghost story, a tale of social ambition, a detective story and a love story—but each formula is treated with a degree of creative irreverence. The first narrative, 'Dharma,' is a ghost story in which the ambivalent and slightly disorientating ending does not provide us with a ghost, but with a psychoanalytically inspired interpretation of what ghosts might symbolise. The third narrative, 'Kama,' equivalently, is a detective story in which the detective is not a conventional hero who solves the crime and captures the villain, but a *Noir*-ish thriller hero who solves nothing and is left with fragments of evidence that cannot be built into a system. In such uses of genre Chandra is, to use the words of Angela Carter (another rummager in the rag and bone shop of literary history), "putting new wine in old bottles" so that "the pressure of the new wine makes the old bottles explode" (69): he milks the chivalric romance or the ghost story or the detective story for its narrative power, but, at the same time, distances himself from them, so as not to be seen to be employing 'stock' or 'tired' modes, and so as not to be seen to be complicit in some of the ideological positions that these genres have traditionally been associated with. He is in this sense, also like Carter, using genre to investigate the "social fictions that regulate our lives" (69)—transforming the Orientalist romance of Indian wars in order to challenge its implicit affirmation of the 'rationality' and legitimacy of the 'civilising' mission of the European colonialists, or re-orientating the detective story in order to question the assumption embodied in many crime thrillers that it is possible for the detective to, as William Spanos puts it, "reveal [...] the whole and by so doing raise the reader above the messiness" (83). In a spirit that might also distinguish Chandra's approach to genre from Carter's, however, he presents his transformation of traditional modes, not as a violent and iconoclastic assault upon literary precedents and their ideological baggage, but as a gentle "meditation" on narrative formulae that, in some instances, such as that of the ghost story, he regards as "very ancient and venerable." "I hope each of the stories works as an affectionate caressing of the contours of the received form," Vikram Chandra told Kevin Mahoney in interview, "but I hope none of them offer the expected and comforting solutions that have become the conventions of the respective genres."[4]

The challenge to expectations that this gentle but persistent revisionary approach to genre produces in *Love and Longing* is designed, in part, to unsettle the habitual modes of thinking indulged by the reader. However, it is not just the complacent attitudes of the reader that become a target of disruption in the collection, but also those of Ranjit Sharma, the narrator of the frame narrative to whom the storyteller, Subramaniam, tells his tales. This protagonist, an employee of a software company, makes his first appearance in the collection as a busy, self-important sceptic, who talks and does not listen, who judges by appearances (failing to notice the respect with which others treat Subramaniam), and who, when his friend Ramani talks of a house that no-one will buy because it is deemed to be haunted, dismisses the subject with knee-jerk rationalism:

> "What nonsense," I said. "These are all family property disputes [...]." I spoke at length then, about superstition and ignorance and the state of our benighted nation, in which educated men and women believed in banshees and ghouls. "Even in the information age we will never be free," I said. I went on and I was particularly witty and sharp, I thought. I vanquished every argument with efficiency and dispatch. (2)

In this context, the leitmotif with which Subramaniam's starts each of his tales, 'Listen,' seems less a request for the computer programmer to open his ears, and more a command that he attend to others in order to learn more about himself. Each of the narratives told, moreover, are not only entertainments designed to while away the hours in the Fisherman's Rest, but also lessons, for Ranjit's benefit, in the value of understanding others, and of considering possibilities that he has not previously entertained. This is nowhere more apparent than in the first narrative, 'Dharma,' in which Jago Antia's double haunting, by the ghost of a leg that he lost in the 1971 war between India and Pakistan, and by the ghost of his childhood guilt over the death of his brother, are shown to be the result, not of inexplicable and absurd superstitions, but of his refusal to confront his emotions and his memories. Jago, we discover, has attempted to overcome the limitations of his body and believes that he "defeated his flesh" (6) when he amputated his own leg without anaesthetic, likewise he has attempted to "cut off" his recollections of childhood, repressing "the poisonous seep of memory" (21) associated with his brother's death for which he was partly responsible. The memories, however (of the body and of the mind) although they are repressed, or *because* they are repressed, return, in distorted and uncanny forms to haunt him and it is only when he is able to confront his ghosts, naked and alone, and recognise that his feelings were 'lost,' that he is able to exorcise them and be free.[5] Since we are all repressed in some way, and since we are all in denial, Subramaniam implies (looking directly at Ranjit) "we're all haunted by [ghosts]," whether we recognise them as such or not. (3)

One of the focuses for critical discussion of *Love and Longing*, unsurprisingly, has been Chandra's use of Sanskrit titles for the tales: 'Dharma,' 'Shakti,' 'Kama,' 'Artha,' 'Shanti.'[6] In some circles these titles have proved a source of discontent for readers. When Chandra gave a reading from the collection at the New Delhi British Council in 1998 he was taken to task by Meenakshi Mukherjee, Professor of English at Jawaharlal Nehru University, for using Sanskrit words "to signal Indianness in the West" (Chandra, 'Cult'). Initially, in the reading, Chandra defended his choice of titles by arguing that he wanted "to see how these principles—Duty, Gain, Desire—worked their way through ordinary lives" ('Cult') but in an article written two years later for the *Boston Review* entitled 'The Cult of Authenticity' he offers several more arguments in defence of his titles, all of which engage with the more fundamental critique he believes to be implicit in Meenakshi Mukherjee's objection: that representations of India by writers working in English tend to be *mis*representations intended to commodify Indianness for Western consumption.[7] Chandra's principal argument in this eloquent and extensive essay rests upon a belief, central to his fiction, that there is no 'correct' or 'authentic' mode of representation, and that many different modes of representation can do justice to an experience in many different ways. "Life, or at least the life I live, is very messy indeed" Chandra notes (in an argument that should throw further light upon the celebration of aesthetic 'messiness' in *Red Earth*) "[...] it is very very common for a person to speak one language at home, use another on the street, do business in a third, and make love in a fourth" and fiction, he suggests, should be broad enough to accommodate that linguistic diversity. Chandra does not deny, in making this argument, that English, as a language, remains (in a satisfyingly ironic turn of phrase) "the *lingua franca* of power" or that learning English will not, for the Indian, be a painful process comparable to swallowing (in imagery strongly reminiscent of *Red Earth*) a "poisonous metallic mass" that "will cut your throat and linger in the skin like a blue bruise" ('Cult'). He does, however, suggest that, since English is one of the languages that "is an inextricable thread in the texture of everyday [he lives] in Bombay and in India," and since English in India, as a "living language," is no longer the English of 'London fogs and Surrey dews,'[8] it is now a legitimate, if not an innocent, mode with which to represent Indian experience. This attitude is summed up by Chandra in a very resonant and suggestive rhetorical outburst: "What a mean economy of love and belonging it must be, in which one love is always traded for another, in which a heart is so small that it can only contain one jannat, one heaven" ('Cult').

This observation, with its clear echo of the title of *Love and Longing* can tell us at least two important things about the collection. Firstly, it emphasises the lexical similarity between the Longing of the title and 'belonging,' and alerts us to the possibility that the meditations on love and longing in the collection are also meditations upon the yearning for incorporation into some kind of greater whole, whether social, cultural or national. Secondly, the overall sense of the observation, that we cannot achieve the illusion of wholeness without trading one love for another, reminds us that such incorporation can only be attained if we are prepared to abandon some of our passions. This provides us with a key to the nostalgia of the stories: they are narratives that derive a certain mournfulness from the characters feelings of alienation, of loss, of their hunger for a oneness and of their yearning for security, but they are also narratives that tend to celebrate that mournfulness, because it involves a simultaneous recognition that we will always be multiple beings, and that we should not try to achieve wholeness by sacrificing difference and diversity, but should accept our fractured, impermanent, inconsistent states and revel in the possibilities that this abandonment throws up. This is a message that Chandra reminds us of directly at key points in the novel, once when Sartaj Singh, the collection's most poignant yearner, having dealt, throughout the story, with a fundamentalist religious group who demand a return to "a perfect past of virtue and strength" (137), plunges, in the last lines of the story, into the furious and far from unitary life of the city; and once, in the collection's closing lines, when the narrator searches in the city not for heaven (as a symbol of completion) or its opposite "but only life itself" (257). In both cases the characters come to an acceptance that life cannot be reduced—that "culture," in the words of Frantz Fanon, "abhors simplification" (174)—and that the multiplicity (the love and longing) of life is itself its primary value. In both cases, furthermore, it is the multi-cultural and multi-accented urban centre of Bombay that becomes the definitive locus, and the most elaborate symbol, of the capacity to exist amidst the diversity of experience without attempting to surmount or transcend it. The city of Bombay, in this sense, can be seen as a cultural location that is equivalent to the nation of India as it is represented in *Red Earth,* since both geographic localities become a means of representing culture as a kind of *performance* that can never be totalised or finished. Whereas *Red Earth,* with its promise of infinite intertwined narratives, attempts to resemble the national community in *all* its prodigious complexity, however, and so becomes a kind of metaphor of disseminated nationhood, *Love and Longing,* with its select narratives snatched out of the fugue of city life, offers itself as a fragment of a community that is infinitely larger and so becomes a kind of metonymy for a whole that, paradoxically, can never be completed.

It is this celebration of messiness, of plurality, of mingling, more than anything else, that binds Chandra's works to date together: both reject unitary explanations of existence, in favour of plurality—and both engage in a passionate plea for tolerance of indeterminacy, difference and perplexity. In some respects, this celebration of the hybrid and the indeterminate make it possible to regard Chandra as a postmodernist writer whose work exhibits, at the level of plot and at the level of text, a Lyotardian incredulity towards meta-narratives, and a correspondent desire to revel in small, contingent narratives, that provide a shape and a structure but do not pretend to be natural or eternal. This postmodern aspect of Chandra's fiction, however, should not blind us to the simultaneous critique that Chandra also makes of certain varieties of the postmodern, particularly those varieties that celebrate hybridisation without an adequate historical conceptualisation of how the state of cultural hybridity came into being. Culture, for Chandra, may be messy, but the mess is always historical and always has material consequences.

The most obvious instance of Chandra's critique of a-historical postmodernism comes with the description of the neighbourhood in which Amanda's parents live in *Red Earth*: a Sears catalogue version of "another century England" in which wealth and privilege has assured that all styles are available and all cultural moments interchangeable, and in which William James can offer the neo-colonial argument (appropriate to his neo-colonial job as a practitioner of corporate law for oil companies) that "the British Raj had been good for India" (415). This suggestion, coming as it does at the end of a novel that has engaged in a detailed historical examination of British imperialism, reveals that William James, like the prince and princess who gaze from a painting in his dining room, practices "a grand condescension that [takes] no notice of history" (409). It also alerts the reader to the fact that any considered evaluation of cultural interaction, if it is not to sound facile and simplistic, as James's does, must take account of the material, economic and political conditions in which that cultural interaction takes place.

Perhaps the most subtle and pervasive critique of facile postmodern affirmations of cultural hybridity, however, comes—not in any individual scene of the novel—but in the work's title, *Red Earth and Pouring Rain*; a phrase that reveals Chandra's ambivalent attitude to valorisations of commingling concisely. In one respect, this title reinforces the celebration of hybridisation conducted throughout *Red Earth*, for the Tamil poem it is taken from is poem in which love is praised for its capacity to transcend the boundaries of kin and caste and mix that which would not usually be mixed: "What could my mother be / to yours?" asks the singer

What kin is my father
to yours anyway? And how
did you and I meet ever?
But in love
our hearts have mingled
like red earth and pouring rain.[9]

When these lines in celebration of commingling are spoken in *Red Earth*, however, they become ironic, since they are put into the mouth of a prostitute who has just been paid for sex by Hercules Skinner, and who is now talking to his high-caste, mixed race sons who have entered her hut. The 'love' that she speaks of, in this context, may bring together classes and races that would not otherwise meet; but it is not a 'love' that occurs because of the benevolence of either group, or because there is a desire to destroy the boundaries that keep people apart. It is a 'love' that occurs because one class of superior wealth is able to exercise power and dominion over another. Thus the 'union' of Hercules and the prostitute, whilst in one sense bringing together, is, in another sense, reaffirming radical separation. The implications of this verse for the processes of colonial hybridisation resulting from the occupation of India by the British (and embodied in the Anglo-Indian characters Sikander and Chotta) are unmistakable: this too, Chandra is suggesting, is not a 'happy' process, by which barriers are broken and people come together and live in peaceful cohabitation—it is, on the contrary, a result of violent occupation, supported by inequalities in social and financial power—and it will result, not in the eradication of boundaries, but in their intensification. Whilst this process of hybridisation is recognised as productive in some respects, therefore, its initial presentation as an idea by the prostitute, reminds us that the need for Indians to accommodate English language and English culture was not a voluntary one resulting from a natural affinity, but an involuntary one resulting from force and manipulation. Just as the prostitute uses the verses ironically, as a means of empowering herself, therefore, Indians should use Englishness and its legacies (Shakespeare, Printing, Cricket) ironically, self-consciously and subversively, as a means of marking it out as their own territory and their own property. In this way, the colonial history of English will not be forgotten, as Chandra has argued in interview, but Indians, having "paid the price," can claim the language as theirs:

> Sanjay swallowed English. It has travelled through his flesh. He has been transformed by those little metal letters, and he has transformed the language they spell out. So, enough. I use English. It is mine. (Teverson)

Notes

1. Andrew Teverson, "Interview with Vikram Chandra." Due to be published in *Wasafiri*, 2002 or 2003.
2. Many of these narratives and characters are inspired by a biography of James 'Sikander' Skinner that Chandra found in a library whilst at Columbia University. The events recounted by Sikander in his letters to Sanjay in *Red Earth* (441-46, 448-54, 461-69) follow the events of the biography of James Skinner (1774-1841) with some fidelity; although Chandra is careful to question the validity of this frequently Anglicised account of the Indian mercenary wars by having Sikander indicate the partiality of his selection of events: "What is this narrative Sanju?" he asks at one point. "I don't know why I pick these moments for you, can you see a connection?" (446). Historical, if melodramatic, re-tellings of the lives of James Skinner, Benoit de Boigne, George Thomas and The Witch of Sardanah, amongst others, can be found in Dennis Holman's biography *Sikander Sahib* (1961).
3. Chandra cites 'Borges-bhai' as an ally in his fight against the 'Ministry of Permissible Language' in 'The Cult of Authenticity.'

4. These quotations are taken from an unpaginated on-line interview with Kevin Mahoney and can be found at www.geocities.com/SoHo/Nook/1082/vikram-chandra.html.
5. "If psychoanalytic theory is correct in maintaining that every affect belonging to an emotional impulse, whatever its kind, is transformed, if it is repressed, into anxiety" writes Freud "then among instances of frightening things there must be one class in which the frightening element can be shown to be something repressed which *recurs*" (363). Chandra, in interview, concedes that this story "could be amenable to a psychoanalytical reading" but he also points out that "psychoanalysis has learnt much from fiction" (Teverson).
6. No adequate translation of these terms can be provided because they represent concepts or systems of philosophical thought that have no immediate parallel in English. *Dharma* can be variously translated as 'duty,' 'law,' 'obligation' or 'proper action' (217); *Shakti* is a name for the goddess Devi, and represents "the active, consuming female principle in the universe" (331); *Kama* involves the recognition that "the pursuit of love and pleasure" is one of the legitimate 'ends of man' (254); *Artha* is "the science of profit or material gain" (234); and *Shanti* means—in all its simplicity and complexity—*peace*. For a fuller explanation the reader who is not already familiar with the concepts should consult the text from which these brief descriptions are taken 'The Hindu Way of Life' by V. Raghavan and R.N. Dandekar in *The Sources of Indian Tradition* edited by Ainslie T. Embree.
7. To compare Chandra's summation of Mukherjee's position with her own statement of the argument see 'The Anxiety of Indianness: Our Novels in English.'
8. I take this phrase from an eloquent essay by Gurcharan Das, which argues a similar point. See "A Novelist's Faith," 3.
9. Chandra notes in the acknowledgments that he has taken this poem by Cempulappeyanirar (meaning, literally, The Poet of *Red Earth and Pouring Rain*), from *The Interior Landscape* translated by A.K. Ramanujan. The poem as it appears in this anthology, however, is rendered slightly differently.

A VIKRAM CHANDRA BIBLIOGRAPHY

Primary Sources

Fiction

Red Earth Pouring Rain. London: Faber, 1995.

Love and Longing in Bombay. London: Faber, 1997.

Published Excerpts from Forthcoming Novel

"Eternal Don." *The New Yorker* 23-30 June, 1997: 130-41.

"Siege in Kailashpada." *The Picador Book of Modern Indian Literature.* Ed. Amit Chaudhuri. London: Picador, 2001. 563-81.

Non-fiction

"The Cult of Authenticity." *The Boston Review.* Feb./March 2000. 22 June 2001 <http://bostonreview.mit.edu/BR25.1/chandra.html>.

Secondary Sources

Articles

Ganapathy-Dore, Geetha. "The Storyteller's Voice in Vikram Chandra's *Red Earth and Pouring Rain.*" *Commonwealth* 19.1. 102-10.

Kaur, Charanjit. "*Red Earth and Pouring Rain*: A Study in Dislocation and Assimilation." *The Postmodern Indian English Novel*. Ed. Viney Kirpal. New Delhi: Allied, 1996. 215-22.

Interviews

Indian Express Newspapers. "Face Off with Vikram Chandra." 8 July 1997. 22 June 2001 <www.expressindia.com/ie/daily/19970708/18950693.html>.

Mahoney, Kevin. "Interview with Vikram Chandra." 1998. 22 June 2001 <www.geocities.com/SoHo/Nook/1082/vikram-chandra.html>.

Teaism Magazine. "Interview with Vikram Chandra." *The Rediff Special*. 25 April, 1998. 22 June 2001 <www.teaism.com/about/chandra.html>.

Wordsworth Books. Interview with Vikram Chandra. 1998. 22 June 2001 <www.wordsworth.com/www/epresent/chandra>.

Teverson, Andrew. Interview with Vikram Chandra. Due to be published in *Wasafiri* 2002 or 2003.

17

Arundhati Roy

NANCY ELLEN BATTY

As of the writing of this essay, Suzanna Arundhati Roy has given the world but one major fictional work: her first novel, *The God of Small Things*. However, the novel has proven to be no "small thing." Released after a bidding frenzy that resulted in a lucrative contract with HarperCollins, *The God of Small Things* received Britain's prestigious Booker-McConnell Prize in 1997. Since achieving this phenomenal literary success, Roy, who trained as an architect, has turned her attention to political activism and commentary in India, her international literary celebrity always ensuring a wide public forum for her opinions. In one of her essays, Roy has objected to the sharp distinction made between her political activism and her literary writing, arguing that, while "*The God of Small Things* is a work of fiction, [...] it's no less political than any of my essays."[1] In fact, Roy has repeatedly hinted at the possibility that she may never return to writing fiction.

If, like American writer Ralph Ellison, Roy leaves us with only one complete, novel-length work of fiction, her reputation in the literary world will rest solely on the basis of the critical reception of *The God of Small Things*. Although it is too early to predict whether Roy will prove to be a literary "one-hit wonder," no critic who attempts an assessment of her work at this point in time can forget this simple fact. While it is possible for a single, "great" novel to earn for its author an enduring place in the literary canon, one cannot predict whether *The God of Small Things* will achieve the kind of universal critical approval earned by, for example, Emily Bronte's *Wuthering Heights* or Ellison's *Invisible Man*. Canons are made, not born, and it would be a foolhardy literary critic, indeed, who attempted such a prognosis. However, like each of the examples above, *The God of Small Things* is daring and technically innovative, as well as deeply flawed, and it may be, perhaps, that these are precisely the requirements for greatness when an author's fictional oeuvre is so limited.

These comparisons to major (non-Indian) canonical writers are neither gratuitous nor specious. They are, rather, strategically deployed in an attempt to offer an approach to *God of Small Things* that aims to mitigate some of the negative criticism that followed its initial success. While *The God of Small Things* is undoubtedly a remarkable first novel, the publicity it has received since winning the Booker Award has burdened it and its author with incommensurate attention, as initially lavish praise has at times given way to disaffected carping. Some critics have suggested that the novel's style is too lush and that its plot risks evoking pathos or even bathos, focusing as it does on an emotional manipulation of small children that amounts, arguably, to abuse. Notoriously, a former chair of the Booker Award Committee, Carmen Callil, publicly called the novel "execrable."[2] Critic Imu Ibrahim labels the novel's plot "trite" and acknowledges that Roy exploits "exotic" raw material, while praising the novel for its "brilliant negotiation of an indigenous Indian English."[3] However, even Roy's use of language has been criticized for being overly poetic and derivative, in its insistent wordplay, of Salman Rushdie's work.[4]

Some of these complaints may, on the surface, have merit. The novel's style is at times dazzling, but at other times it seems merely "overwrought"[5]: one early literary critic suggests that "the author [is] sometimes carried away by the exuberance of her style and effects."[6] Moreover, a single work whose plot features the physical and emotional abuse of children, a child's tragic death by drowning, and a doomed inter-caste love affair, even leavened with Roy's deft, ironic touch, playful language, and intricate structure, does risk the triteness of melodrama. And, in spite of Roy's polite, but frequent protestations to the contrary, there is no question that Salman Rushdie's work has left its mark on her prose, as it undoubtedly has on the work of many writers, Indian and otherwise.

Automatic comparisons to Rushdie, with the implicit suggestion that the novel's style is representative of a certain type of Indian writing, have resulted in a rather parochial view of the work. Such characterization, in fact, has led to the charge that the novel panders to the west's desire for exotic narratives from the former colonies and, therefore, that Roy and her novel are complicit with the European demand for what Graham Huggan terms "Indo-chic."[7] Roy has resisted this reading and this label, her rejection of the Rushdie comparison and the label "magic realist" perhaps most symptomatic of her anxiety about the blinkered reception of her work. However, while Roy rejects what she calls the "lazy" comparison of her work to that of Rushdie, she welcomes comparison to a novelist she claims never to have read:

> Yes, I'm compared to Faulkner the most. But I've never read Faulkner before! [...]. I have, however, read some other writers from the American South—Mark Twain, Harper S. Lee—and I think that perhaps there's an infusion or intrusion of landscape in their

> literature that might be similar to mine. This comparison is not that lazy, because it's natural that writers from outside urban areas share an environment that is not man-made and is changed by winds and rivers and rain. I think that human relationships and the divisions between human beings are more brutal and straightforward than those in cities, where everything is hidden behind walls and a veneer of urban sophistication.[8]

Startlingly, without having read Faulkner, Roy apprehends one of the most elemental themes of his work: "the brutal and straightforward" "divisions between human beings" that are magnified in an agrarian setting with a long history of racism. But, while Roy alludes to frequent comparisons of her work to that of William Faulkner, and while the novel's structure is recognizably Faulknerian (Updike 156), there has, thus far, been no sustained analysis of this intertextual relationship. Nor has there been a serious consideration of the *particular* Gothic elements and themes of Roy's novel that link her work more closely with the literature of the American south than with British Gothicism.

Approaching *The God of Small Things* from a wider perspective than that of Indian or British writing acknowledges the extreme permeability of cultural borders in the late twentieth century, and in particular the increasingly global domination of American. Roy's novel is densely allusive: critics have identified and discussed the most obvious allusions in the novel, references to a range of cultural and literary texts. Less explicit, however, are allusions to novels such as Dickens's *Great Expectations*, but also Twain's *The Adventures of Huckleberry Finn*, Lee's *To Kill a Mockingbird*, and Toni Morrison's *Beloved*, all novels that employ Gothic conventions. If we enlarge our notion of the Gothic to consider its style and themes, we can see that Roy's lush prose and her handling of the motifs of incest and what might arguably be termed a form of "miscegenation" invoke, more specifically, comparisons to southern U.S. writers such as Faulkner.

To call *The God of Small Things* an instance of the Gothic is not meant to diminish it as "mere" genre fiction, nor does invoking the southern American Gothic in particular represent a refusal of the novel's geographic specificity. Recent serious work on non-British Gothic reinvigorates our notion of this genre. Redefining the Gothic as "an impulse rather than a literary artefact,"[9] Robert K. Martin and Eric Savoy liberate the genre from its national, British origins and outré trappings and call attention to the subversive role it plays in diagnosing and defining a nation's cultural symptoms. Citing Anne Williams's claim that the Gothic is "'an intersection of grammar, architecture and psychoanalysis'" (6), Savoy suggests that "the gothic registers a trauma in the strategies of representation as it brings forward a traumatic history toward which it gestures but can never finally refer" (11):

> Paradoxically, the various kinds of trauma represented by the gothic [...] constitute both a return and a loss, and the gothic might be broadly conceptualized as a cultural ritual of inscribing the loss of coherent ego formation, the negation of national imaginary, and the fragmentation of linguistic accountability. (11)

Roy's novel clearly registers such displacements in its linguistic fragmentation, but especially in its structure and in its plot, rife, as the latter is, with losses and returns (even "re-returns").

However, Roy domesticates the Gothic by focusing on a central, enduring Indian cultural trauma: the issue of the caste system, and, more particularly, the plight of Untouchables. The novel, while full of incident, circles around—haltingly "gestures" toward—one brutal, unspeakable trauma: the state-sanctioned murder of the Paravan Velutha, and the impact of his death on an already fragile and therefore vulnerable family unit, particularly the two small children, friends of Velutha, who are forced to participate in this horrifying adult drama. If, as Louis S. Gross argues, "the Gothic quest ends in the shattering of the protagonists' image of his/her social/sexual roles and a legacy of, at best, numbing unease or, at worst, emotional paralysis and death,"[10] we can see how readily Roy's novel conforms to the pattern of Gothic narrative.

Examining *The God of Small Things* from the perspective of Gothic literature not only allows us to reexamine and refute some of the harshest criticism levelled against it, but, more importantly (because more positively), it sheds enormous light on some of the novel's most controversial aspects in ways that render the novel not less relevant to the Indian milieu, but, ironically, even more so; not less relevant politically, but, indeed, as Roy herself would insist, much more so.

Like William Faulkner, Roy has forged her literary universe in *The God of Small Things* out of experience and from her own "postage stamp of native soil." Roy was raised in the city of Ayemenem in the predominantly Christian, Marxist-dominated Kerala province in southern India where the novel is set, and its main character, Rahel, shares similarities in background to the author. In *The God of Small Things*, Roy tests and judges her society, in a setting as historically overdetermined as Faulkner's Yoknapatawpha county, by the way it reacts to those who violate its codes. Threaded like beads through a highly intricate structure that I shall describe later, the essential plot of the novel focuses on the struggle against the vestiges of conservative, patriarchal control in a society that pays only lip service to radical change, a society that remains at its core stubbornly traditional in its values.

The events of the central plot occur over a very short period of several weeks in December, 1969, and are viewed primarily through the eyes of seven-year old twins, Rahel and her brother Esthappen. The preternaturally close twins—they are said to share "a single Siamese soul" (40)—live with their mother, Ammu, on the sufferance of their mother's brother, Chacko, the twin's great-aunt, Baby Kochamma, and their grandmother, Mammachi. Ammu's disgrace is not only that she married outside the faith against her parents' wishes, but that she subsequently left her abusive and alcoholic husband and was forced to return to the protection of her family, where Chacko rules both home and business—the Padma Pickle Factory—with a distracted, benevolent tolerance that only underscores his absolute male privilege.

In what is a supreme irony, and clearly indicative of a double standard in the family, Chacko's status as head of the household is unchallenged despite his own divorced status. It is, in fact, the visit of Chacko's recently widowed, but still idolized, British ex-wife, Margaret, and their daughter Sophie, that inaugurates tragedy. On the day that precedes this visit, the family's car is delayed by a workers' demonstration, at which various members of the family are surprised to see their loyal employee, Velutha. The memory of the family's humiliation by the mob will later play a role in Baby Kochamma's vindictive reaction to learning how impertinent, to her way of thinking, Velutha really is. Later that day, Esthappen, unbeknownst to anyone but his sister Rahel, with whom he seems to have an extrasensory connection, is sexually molested by a vendor at the cinema where the family has gone to see *The Sound of Music*. The juxtaposition of this particular movie with the vile act of exploitation alerts us to the precarious order within this seemingly jovial family: Estha learns that "(a) *Anything can happen to Anyone*" and "(b) *It's best to be prepared*" (186); in short: "Things can change in a day" (156). These insights will, as well, play a significant role in the subsequent tragedy.

Indeed, these events reveal the fragility of the Ipe family bonds. In the days that follow, the disaffected and lonely Ammu begins an affair with her childhood acquaintance and her children's' best friend, Velutha, a Paravan, but also, significantly, a Communist, whose skills as a tradesman have made him almost indispensable to the Ipe family. When the affair is discovered, Ammu is locked in her room, prevented from coming to the support of her lover or from providing comfort to her children, who are additionally stung by their mother's initial, reckless dismissal of them as the cause of all her problems, "the millstones round my neck" (240). Sophie Mol drowns when she runs away with the distraught twins. Velutha, falsely accused of rape, then of kidnapping and murder, is tracked by the police and beaten severely in front of Rahel and Estha. Ultimately, Velutha is tortured to death by the police after Estha has been forced by his great aunt to lie, ostensibly to protect their mother, by identifying Velutha as his kidnapper. Velutha is also betrayed by his party leader, Comrade Pillai, who cynically understands that there is more to be gained politically by betraying than by protecting an Untouchable from prosecution, particularly in a case involving sexual impropriety.

The results of Ammu and Velutha's affair are cataclysmic. Chacko, almost deranged by the death of his beloved daughter, sends Ammu away and "returns" Estha to the twins' dissolute father. Rahel is nominally kept at the family estate, but is ultimately sent away also, to boarding school. After immigration to America and a failed marriage of her own, Rahel comes home to Ayemenem when she hears that Estha has been "re-returned" to the decaying family estate, now occupied only by Baby Kochamma and the household servant, Kochu Maria, Chacko having immigrated to Canada. The twins' mother has long since died, alone and destitute: she dies at 31, the age of the twins at their poignant reunion, "a viable, die-able age" (88). Estha has become a silent wanderer; and Rahel, in a desperate effort to re-establish a connection, breaks "the Love Laws" (311) by committing an act of incest with her brother.

Reading the heightened sentiment in *The God of Small Things* as an instance of the contemporary Gothic is to read its excesses politically, in terms of an abject response to powerlessness in a coercive, restrictive society. Teresa Goddu argues that, as a form "that articulates objection," the gothic "serves as a primary means of speaking of the unspeakable" and of "register[ing] cultural contradictions."[11] In choosing to register these cultural contradictions by charting a course between the Scylla and Charybdis of miscegenation and incest, Roy suggests not only the tragic dilemma of those whose desires fall outside the officially sanctioned "love laws" of their society, but also the illogic and inhumanity of these laws themselves. Although these violations of normative codes, particularly the crossing of caste lines, may be seen as revolutionary only at the personal level, the transgressions of those who are politically weakest in Roy's novel are punished severely, one might even say out of all proportion. A heavy, inevitable, sense of doom, one of the hallmarks of Gothic literature, is persistently foreshadowed for Ammu and her children. Roy's novel locates trauma in "the prohibition of female autonomy in the Gothic, in the families that people it, and in the society that reads it."[12] Thus, the act of incest can be seen as both a final act of defiance *and* a pathetic repetition of the initial family trauma that seeks to master and cancel its effects. As in Faulkner, there is a certain, albeit defeated, logic, as well as revenge, in turning toward one most like oneself (in this case, a non-identical twin) in a society that so neurotically polices the "color" line in an attempt to ensure racial purity.

The novel gains much of its emotional power by juxtaposing the waning innocence and playfulness of the seven-year old twins against the adult Rahel's brooding sorrow and sense of "emptiness" (21) and Esthappen's pathetic wandering and muteness. In exploring the issue of the twins' misplaced guilt over events of the past, Roy's novel exposes the vulnerability of children who are used as pawns by the desperate and self-centred adults to whom their lives have been entrusted. Much like Faulkner's Benjy, Quentin, and Caddie Compson, Rahel and Esthappen are uncomprehending victims of social rules they have had no hand in creating. What saves Roy's novel from descending into the type of bathos that such helplessness and its abject remedies would imply is her adept handling of structure and point of view, through which, miraculously, joy and redemption are allowed fleetingly to emerge, if not prevail.

Roy credits her background in architecture with the inspiration for the novel's intricate structure. She has claimed that "writing is like architecture" in the sense that "there are design motifs that occur again and again" (*Salon* Interview). Repetition and recursion do, indeed, structure the novel. It begins with the return, from New York, of thirty-one-year-old Rahel and her reunion with Esthappen, from whom she has been separated for twenty-four years. The first lines of the novel carefully establish the Gothic mood with words like "brooding," "gorge," and "[D]issolute"; alliterative phrases such as "suffused with sloth and sullen expectation"; and references to oppressive heat and humidity The atmosphere that greets Rahel upon her return to Ayemenem project Rahel's mood and foreshadow the tragic events of 1969 that are about to be related. The description of Rahel's ancestral home, Ayemenem House, most clearly hints at the menace just barely concealed beneath the surface of things:

> It was raining when Rahel came back to Ayemenem. Slanting silver ropes slammed into loose earth, plowing it up like gunfire. The old house on the hill wore its steep, gabled roof pulled over its ears like a low hat. The walls, streaked with moss, had grown soft, and bulged a little with dampness that seeped up from the ground. The wild, overgrown garden was full of the whisper and scurry of small lives. In the undergrowth a rat snake rubbed itself against a glistening stone. (4)

This paradigmatic passage suggests the way that perspective will be managed in the novel: physical descriptions are imbued with metaphysical conceits; surface impressions give way quickly to what is animate and concealed beneath the landscape; and inanimate objects are frequently animated through personification. Through such techniques the reader discovers the layers of teeming corruption that seethe beneath the damaged, essentially frozen, lives of the twins, Rahel and Estha.

In the first few pages of the narrative we learn, but only in telegraphic form, about the major events that have produced this effect, events summarized earlier. However, we must read the intricately threaded discourse of the entire novel to discover how these events are connected, what tragic sequence of mishaps has led Rahel to suffer an unhappy, emotionally disconnected life and Estha to withdraw so completely and, it would seem, irrevocably, into his own mind. At least two time-lines are thus woven throughout the novel: short, chronologically ordered chapters describing Rahel's present attempts to break through her twin's silence are interspersed with the more chaotic relation of the events of the past.

In the early chapters of the novel that are set in 1969, the painted hands on Rahel's toy watch are described as being perpetually frozen at ten to two. Our image of the twins is likewise arrested in shorthand metonymical descriptions of their physical characteristics: Rahel's "Love-in-Tokyo" fountain of hair and Estha's "beige and pointy shoes" and "Elvis puff" (37). Our narrator, a third person omniscient narrator closely, but not exclusively, focused on the experiences of Rahel, is quite explicit about the necessity for returning to this particular, traumatic moment in time and subjecting it to close examination:

> In a purely practical sense it would probably be correct to say that it all began when Sophie Mol came to Ayemenem. Perhaps it's true that things can change in a day. That a few dozen hours can affect the outcome of whole lifetimes. (32)

Before Rahel and Estha can move forward in their lives, they, or at least she, must confront the horror that was precipitated by this past moment.

But while the novel is primarily concerned with the immediate causes of the 1969 tragedy and in tracing its later effects, the structure is actually much more complex than this description would imply. Cecile Oumhani comments that Roy's structure is "a vertical representation [of events] [...] reminiscent of [...] Homi Bhabha['s] [...] [stairwell] metaphor [...] of cultural hybridity."[13] Layered upon the two time-lines, the moment of telling and the moment of trauma, is also a broader family and social history. The narrator acknowledges that "to say it all began when Sophie Mol came to Ayemenem is only one way of looking at it":

> Equally, it could be argued that it actually began thousands of years ago. Long before the Marxists came. Before the British took Malabar, before the Dutch Ascendancy, before Vasco de Gama arrived [...].
>
> That it really began in the days when the Love Laws were made. The laws that lay down who should be loved, and how. (33)

In this way, the story of the twins' lives is embedded in a much larger, recognizable historical context, much as Faulkner links the destiny of his characters to a long history of dispossession in the southern U.S. in works such as "The Bear" and *Requiem for a Nun.* In the case of Roy's novel, this context is the unique political history of Kerala as well as the broader national one of the caste system and imperial rule. Tirkhankar Chanda points out that Roy blurs the boundaries "between fiction and history" through the use of significant dates, notably 1869 and 1969, "dates associated with the consolidation in Kerala of Christianity and Communism which together form the sociohistoric backdrop of the novel" (42). However, even the reader unfamiliar with these milestones quickly becomes aware of exactly what is at stake in the "sociohistoric" milieu of the text.

This sedimented history includes an important Gothic feature: an inherited family curse. In a move strongly reminiscent of a structural motif in Rushdie's *Midnight's Children,* Roy's narrator locates the source of the twins' family's problems in an ancestral quirk and portent. Like Aadam Aziz's broken, bloody nose, the moth discovered by Rahel and Estha's anglophile, Imperial entomologist grandfather, but named for someone else, acts throughout the narrative as a trope for disappointment and despair:

> [...] Pappachi's Moth was held responsible for his black moods and sudden bouts of temper. Its pernicious ghost—gray, furry and with unusually dense dorsal tufts—haunted every house that he ever lived in. It tormented him and his children and his children's children. (48)

The disappointment of the moth becomes a type of shorthand for the family's dysfunctions and tragedies: Pappachi's uncontrollable rages and physical abuse of his wife; Baby Kochamma's unrequited love for a local priest; Chacko's self-conscious anglophilia and misplaced loyalties; Ammu's unrestrained passion for a man she knows she must not touch, let alone love; the flight of confused children and the drowning of a beloved cousin. The stage upon which the events of 1969 are played out, watched over by a "maleficent" portrait of Pappachi hanging in Ayemenem House's drawing room (50), is already replete with the portents of disaster. It is, in a word, always already haunted.

Viewed in relation to the obvious motif of haunting, Roy's insistence upon the architectural metaphor for the novel's structure also provides one of the strongest hints of the novel's Gothic allegiances. Most strikingly, the plot revolves around two central houses in the novel—the Ipe's ancestral home, Ayemenem House, and a vacant house abandoned by the British. Both houses are literally and figuratively haunted in the classic Gothic sense. As we have already seen, Ayemenem

House has become, by the time of Rahel's return, a decrepit ghost of its former self:

> Filth had laid siege to the Ayemenem House like a medieval army advancing on an enemy castle. It clotted every crevice and clung to the windowpanes.
>
> Midges whizzed in teapots. Dead insects lay in empty vases [...]. The only things that shone were the giant cockroaches that scurried around like varnished gofers on a film set. (84)

The ultimate ruin of the ancestral home, while entropic, not fiery and cataclysmic, like that of Poe's House of Usher or Faulkner's House of Sutpen, is equally symbolic of hereditary sin and the oblivion that is always its ultimate punishment in the Gothic novel. Rahel and Estha are the ghostly presences who try to cancel the ancestral sin by committing another that is even more venal, still looking, perhaps, for "punishments that fitted their crimes," not "ones you spent your whole life in, wandering through its maze of shelves" (309).

The abandoned building across the river from their home that Rahel and Estha call the "History House" is the other haunted house in the novel. The young twins seek shelter here after running away from home, and it is here that they witness the "justice" meted out to Velutha and learn "how history negotiates its terms and collects its dues from those who break its laws" (54). But this house is also said to be haunted by the ghost of an "Englishman [Kari Saipu] who had "gone native" [and] had shot himself through the head" (51). Before their ill-fated encounter with the actual house, Rahel and Estha believe it to be the one their Uncle Chacko refers to as the "History House," by which he means the edifice of a European history from which Indian subjects are barred: "But we can't go in [...] because we've been locked out" (52).

The twins' confusion about the History House, mistaking a literal building for a figuration of the colonized, barred mind, is perhaps the best clue to Roy's handling of point of view in this novel. While the focal character throughout remains Rahel, events of the novel are related from an omniscient point of view that allows access to the inner thoughts of most of the major, and even some of the minor, characters in the novel. Through the use of free indirect discourse, occasional lapses into stream of consciousness narrative, and frequent recourse to wordplay, Roy manages to capture the immediacy of perception from a child's point of view, using its juxtaposition against the impoverished and often cynical interior lives of the adults to condemn the latter's self-interested actions. But there are aspects of experience that seem to be barred even from this omniscient narrator, as the narrative, like Pappachi's moth, circles around, falters against, seems to be attempting to postpone, the relation of major, traumatic events. Rahel (and, with her, the reader) is "locked out" of certain experiences, just as she is, initially upon her return to Ayemenem, barred from access to the thoughts of her brother, with whom she had shared a seemingly telepathic relationship in their youth:

> In those early amorphous years when memory had only just begun, when life was full of Beginnings and no Ends, and Everything was Forever, Esthappen and Rahel thought of themselves together as Me, and separately, individually, as We or Us. As though they were a rare breed of Siamese twins, physically separate, but with joint identities.
>
> Now, these years later, Rahel has a memory of waking up one night giggling at Estha's funny dream. (5)

As adults, long separated, "Edges, Borders, Boundaries, Brinks and Limits have appeared like a team of trolls on their separate horizons." (5)

However, Rahel's return to Ayemenem, following closely upon Estha's "re-return," seemingly ignites the latent telepathic capacity in both of them:

> It had been quiet in Estha's head until Rahel came. But with her she had brought the sound of passing trains, and the light and shade and light and shade that falls on you if you have a window seat. (16)

It is not just Ayemenem House and Kari Saipu's House that are haunted: so also are the minds of Rahel and Estha, and the narrative itself serves as a kind of exorcism of the trauma of the past, as it does, for example, in Faulkner's *Absalom, Absalom!* As the twins slowly regain their connection with each other, the story of their shared experience in the past takes shape in chronological narrative form, albeit taking leisurely detours through other lives, other personal histories. Surprisingly, however, this reconstruction of events does not end with either of the most poignant and painful events in their shared lives as children: the brutal beating of Velutha or the twins' parting at the train station when Estha is "returned" to his father. In fact, Roy delivers a structural double-punch when, immediately following the narration of the latter scene, in the penultimate chapter of the novel, Rahel and Estha's estrangement is consummated in an act of incest that is described as an expression not of lust, but of "hideous grief" (311).

Ultimately, we discover just what is barred from the omniscient narrator's mind, and what has prevented the adult twins from transcending the horrors of the past. Surprisingly, rather than the trauma of violence or of separation, it is the recognition of the pleasures of the flesh—the *jouissance* of Ammu and Velutha's physical passion—

that the narrative refuses until the last possible moment. Indeed, it is as though the act of incest awakens the brother and sister to a comprehension of the depth of feeling in their mother that led to her forbidden affair. In a brief episode that follows the description of the incest, the narrative voice relates a pleasurable memory of the twins' mother saying good night to them: before her mother leaves the room, Rahel calls out to her a line from *Kim*: "*We be of one blood, Thou and I*" (312). Her words release a flood of intense, complex feelings in Ammu:

> Ammu leaned against the bedroom door in the dark, reluctant to return to the dinner table, where the conversation circled like a moth around the white child and her mother as though they were the only source of light. Ammu felt that she would die, wither and die, if she heard another word [...].
>
> As she leaned against the door in the darkness, she felt her dream, her Afternoon-mare, move inside her like a rib of water rising from the ocean, gathering into a wave. The cheerful one-armed man with salty skin and a shoulder that ended abruptly like a cliff emerged from the shadows of the jagged beach and walked towards her.
>
> Who was he?
> Who could he have been?
> The God of Loss.
> The God of Small Things. (312)

In her most brilliant structural move, Roy defers until the very last chapter of the novel the narration of a pivotal prior moment, an episode describing Ammu and Velutha's first sexual encounter that is startling in its lyrical intensity, its immediacy, and its joyfulness. This is a moment that stands in stark contrast to what we have just witnessed: the total and humiliating defeat of both of its participants. The scene gains much of its power from the fact that, unlike most of the events of the novel, its telling is not only displaced chronologically, but is not foreshadowed. Moreover, coming as it does immediately following the shock of the twins' incest, it is almost entirely unexpected. The sureness with which Roy delivers this surprising, joyous coda at the end of an otherwise tragic novel paradoxically both underlines and undercuts its pathos; more importantly, its boldness and originality belie her literary ingénue status.

Brenda Bose argues that, in spite of its focus on personal lives and transgressions, *The God of Small Things* is not apolitical, as some critics have asserted. Rather, Bose suggests, Ammu's act of loving Velutha, at considerable personal risk to herself and her family, is both courageous *and* political:

the politics of the novel is contained in the subversion of [...] shame and defeat through the valourization of erotic desire. To lunge, knowingly and deliberately, for what one must not have—for what will result in shame and defeat—is to believe that the very process of the pursuit would render the ultimate penalty worthwhile.[14]

It is precisely this—both the deliberateness and the political "rightness" of the act by which their mother puts her family's happiness at risk—that the ending of the novel permits Rahel, and thus the reader, not just to see, but, in being caught unaware, to experience. Above all else, the narration of this scene elicits forgiveness for what has seemed until that moment to be unforgivable: not the breaking of "Love Laws," but the breaking of children's hearts. The novel leaves us with the question: was their mother's forbidden love worth the price paid for it? But the novel answers its own question with the lyrical intensity of its final chapter, and the promise of its final word: "Tomorrow" (321). The "history lesson for future offenders" (318) is, ultimately, not the lesson of death and separation, but the reminder that hope resides in moving forward and cherishing personal freedom above all else.

Bose argues that Roy's novel goes beyond what John Updike calls the Faulknerian historical sense of "shame and defeat" (cited in Bose, 70) to celebrate the deliberate choices of those "who desire (and perhaps, die for it)" (70). However, Roy's own transgressions—of form and of content—make even more sense when we consider them within the tradition of the American Gothic, a genre whose themes and subjects she has artfully repatriated to the landscape and situations of southern India. Some of Roy's artistic choices, while they have not brought her shame and defeat, have nonetheless brought to her a measure of disapproval—from literary critics, from certain citizens of Kerala, from those who feel her work is counter-revolutionary. While only time will tell whether the novel will survive its detractors, *The God of Small Things* remains an intelligent *tour de force* worthy of its Gothic predecessors.

Notes

1. Arundhati Roy, "The Ladies Have Feelings, So [...] Shall We Leave It to the Experts?" *Power Politics* (Cambridge: South End Press, 2001) 11.
2. Dan Glaister, "Popularity pays off for Roy," *The Guardian* 14 Oct. 1997.
3. Huma Ibrahim, "Transnational Migrations and the Debate of English Writing in/of Pakistan," *ARIEL* 29.1 (1998): 37.
4. The entire gamut of critical response is well represented in a 1999 collection of over forty essays on Roy's work, *Arundhati Roy: The Novelist Extraordinary*, ed. R.K. Dhawan.
5. Updike, John, "Mother Tongues: Subduing the Language of the Colonizer," *The New Yorker* 23 June 1997: 159.

6. Tirkhankar Chanda, "Sexual/Textual Strategies in *The God of Small Things*." *Commonwealth* 20.1 (1997): 38.
7. Graham Huggan, "Consuming India." *ARIEL: A Review of International Literature* 29.1: 253. Others might argue that the strongest criticism has come from either critic Aijaz Ahmad, who is scathing about Roy's portrayal of Communism in Kerala, or Sabu Thomas, a Kerala lawyer who has sued Roy for obscenity. The very fact that Roy's novel can be accused by Euro-American critics of pandering to current literary fashion, by progressive Indians of being anti-Communist, and by a conservative lawyer in her home state of being obscene, gives some indication of the unstable and untenable position that the novel occupies.
8. *Salon* Interview with Arundhati Roy. 30 Sept. 1997. http://www.salon.com/sept97/00roy.html. Accessed 18 Nov. 2001.
9. Eric Savoy, "The Face of the Tenant: A Theory of American Gothic," *American Gothic: New Interventions in a National Narrative*, eds. Robert K. Martin and Eric Savoy (Iowa City: U of Iowa P, 1998) 6.
10. Louis S. Gross, *Redefining the American Gothic from Wieland to Day of the Dead* (Ann Arbor: UMI Press, 1989) [1]-2.
11. Teresa A. Goddu, *Gothic America: Narrative, History, and Nature* (New York: Columbia UP, 1997) 10.
12. Michelle A. Masee, *In the Name of Love: Women, Masochism, and the Gothic* (Ithaca: Cornell UP, 1992) 12.
13. Cecile Oumhani, "Hybridity and Transgression in Arundhati Roy's *The God of Small Things*," *Commonwealth* 22.2 (2000) 87.
14. Brenda Bose, "In Desire and in Death: Eroticism as Politics in Arundhati Roy's *The God of Small Things*," *ARIEL: A Review of International Literature* 29.2 (1998): 70.

AN ARUNDHATI ROY BIBLIOGRAPHY

Primary Sources

Novel

The God of Small Things. New York: Random House, 1997.

Collections of Essays

The Cost of Living. New York: Random House, 1999.

Power Politics. Cambridge: South End Press, 2001.

Screenplays

In Which Annie Gives It Those Ones, *Electric Moon*.

Secondary Sources

Selected Books about Arundhati Roy

Dhawan, R.K., ed. *Arundhati Roy: The Novelist Extraordinary*. New Delhi: Prestige Books, 1999.

Selected Articles on *The God Of Small Things*

Ahmad, Aijaz. "Reading Arundhati Roy *Politically*." *Frontline* 8 Aug. 1997: 103-08.

Bose, Brinda. "In Desire and in Death: Eroticism as Politics in Arundhati

Roy's *The God of Small Things.*" *ARIEL: A Review of International Literature* 29.2 (1998): [59]-72.

Chanda, Tirkhankar. "Sexual/Textual Strategies in *The God of Small Things.*" *Commonwealth* 20.1 (1997): 38-44.

Hai, Ambreen. "Bapsi Sidhwa's *Cracking India.*" *Modern Fiction Studies* 46.2 (2000): 379-426.

Huggan, Graham. "Consuming India." *ARIEL: A Review of International Literature* 29.1: [245]-58.

Ibrahim, Huma. "Transnational Migrations and the Debate of English Writing in/of Pakistan." *ARIEL: A Review of International Literature* 29.1 (1998): [33]-48.

Jones, Sonya L. "The Large Things of Arundhati Roy." *The Literature of the Indian Diaspora: Essays in Criticism.* Ed. A.L. McLeod. New Delhi: Sterling Publishers, 2000.

Nair, R. Hema. "Remembrance of Things Past: A Reading of Arundhati Roy's *The God of Small Things.*" *CIEFL Bulletin* 9.2 (1998): 49-56.

Oumhani, Cecile. "Hybridity and Transgression in Arundhati Roy's *The God of Small Things.*" *Commonwealth* 22.2 (2000): 85-91.

Updike, John. "Mother Tongues: Subduing the Language of the Colonizer." *The New Yorker* 23 June 1997: 156-61.

Wood, James. "The God of Small Thing." *The New Republic* 29 Dec. 1997: 32-36.

18

Synopses of Novels

The authors' initials, given in square brackets after each synopsis, are as follows:

AFG: Alberta Fabris Grube
AT: Andrew Teverson
BN: Basavaraj Naikar
DM: D. Maya
FD'S: Florence D'Souza
GK: Geoffrey Kain
JJ: Jasbir Jain
JT: John Thieme
NB: Nancy Batty
NS: Nandini Saha
NTK: Neil Ten Kortenaar
PB: P. Balaswamy
PPP: Pier Paolo Piciucco
RR: Ragini Ramachandra
SA: Silvia Albertazzi
SC: Sarbani Chaudhuri
SR: Sridhar Rajeswaran
TK: Tabish Khair
UB: Usha Bande

Across the Black Waters (Mulk Raj Anand, 1940)

Lalu and his companions complete the long voyage in the ship and reach Marseilles. These poorly paid and highly esteemed soldiers do not know where exactly they have to fight. Then they are ordered to march to the newly erected tents. After a few days the troops are transported to Orieans and then to Flanders. Lalu, Uncle Kirpu, Daddy Dhanoo and other sepoys get into the train and reach Rouen, where they see wounded soldiers. Finally they reach Lillers, via Calais. Then they are taken to the trenches where they notice bullets coming whistling over their heads. Now each moment seems to Lalu to be his last. He suddenly gets frightened by seeing eight corpses. Lalu struggles eagerly through the ditches, keeping as close to Havildar Lachman Singh as possible. When they reach the location, Havildar Lachman Singh, Uncle Kirpu, Daddy Dhanoo, Lalu and others adjust their rifles unto the holes in the sandbags. But the expected offensive does not come for many days. Then on a rainy day orders come for the sepoys to attack the enemy. They rush forward. There are clouds of smoke and rain. Lalu feels confused. In the two way firing many sepoys and Tommies fall dead. The orders come to 'turn back.' They go to new trenches. Lalu fires round after round as he is intoxicated with a passion for-violence. When they are allowed some rest, they discover that out of 750 soldiers, only 250 are left.

One night when Lalu and other sepoys have a dip in a brook, Lalu happens to meet a boy Andre and his sister Marie and likes them. The farmer and his wife also treat Lalu with affection. Lalu's intimacy with Marie creates sexual jealousy in Jamedar Subah Singh. But in the subsequent firing and counter-firing, Lalu's left leg is hit by a bullet and he is captured by the Germans. [BN]

All About H. Hatterr
(G.V. Desani, 1948)

This is a Rabelesian account of the life of H. Hatterr, the illegitimate son of a European sailor and a Malay woman, whose quest for truth takes him to diverse sages across India who dupe, bully, harass and mislead him in various ways. A "fifty-fifty of the species," Hatterr's racial, cultural, religious hybridity and alien locale mark him as an outcast and an 'everyman' and invest him with the resilience of the truly marginalised. Lustfully pursued by washerwomen and frenzied religious heads, entangled in lawsuits by charlatan money-sharks, serving as a human food-bowl to a lion in a circus, jailed, beggared and de-clothed by impostors, and many more such "assaults below the belt" notwithstanding, he bounces back every time with or without the help of his quotation-spewing friend and admirer, Banerrji. Hatterr's indefatigable jest for life is matched by his irrepressible language: ungrammatical, idiosyncratic, colloquial, replete with ingenuous coinage and literary archaisms it generates a joyously impure 'creative chaos.' The seven chapters with their rigorous sub-divisions, 'Digest,' 'Instruction,' 'Presumption' and 'Life-encounter,' recording Hatterr's transactions with the seven sages fail miserably to check the linguistic heteroglossia and are meant to fail so that the hedonistic, seamless abundance of life-experience is thrown into high relief. Stylistic and generic borders are crossed with impunity as autobiography, picaresque, fantasy, grotesque, and even a solemn 'defence' of Hatterr's narrative by his self-appointed counsel Yati Rambeli jostle together in a carnivalesque assertion of human existence to produce a unique literary work that defies all classification. [SC]

And Some Take A Lover
(Dina Mehta, 1991)

This novel is set during India's Nationalist struggle and apart from gender issues deals with how the Parsis, a Colonial elite, resolved the conflict between old loyalties to the Raj and new loyalties demanded by the Nationalists. Roshni, the female protagonist in this novel tries to come to terms with the new reality but is held back by her family who still bear allegiance to the old order. Her fascination with Gandhi's message is further enhanced by an attraction towards Sudhir, a

Gandhian. Sudhir however rejects her as he feels she is too Westernised and urbanized to be a fit helpmeet for him in his grassroots work in rural India. Sudhir deliberately marries an untouchable girl to convince Roshni of his seriousness in ending their relationship. Such a move was also part of Gandhi's agenda of integrating the lower castes into the Hindu mainstream.

Roshni also suffers another blow when she loses her English friend, a girl who she had known at college. This girl had become involved in a spy ring and Roshni too is drawn into it. Alone and hurt, Roshni seeks solace in the arms of a Parsi man, the husband of an old friend. He turns out to be a dominating, selfish person and takes Roshni's preciously guarded virginity in a rather clinical, uncaring fashion.

As a result Roshni is now torn apart by several guilts—of having had a sexual relationship before marriage, of having betrayed the trust of her conventional family and finally of not having been able to measure up to Sudhir's idealistic standards. The novel ends on Roshni disentangling herself from her lover and becoming more involved in anti-British espionage activities. However, what is ambiguous is whether she has moved into autonomous female spaces or is still caught in the interstices between a departing empire, imminent decolonisation and a demanding patriarchy. [SR]

Apprentice, The (Arun Joshi, 1968)

Son of a Gandhian revolutionary, martyr for independence, young Ratan moves to Delhi to seek employment. After a hard initial period, he finally finds a temporary job as a clerk at the Department of War. His skills, as well as his instinct to please his superiors, secure him a permanent job. Ratan's ambition soon wells up and in a corrupt system he gradually loosens his rigid morality. Once he has become officer, he accepts a bribe from Himmath Singh, a shady businessman, to clear a stock of substandard weapons. This he does while his nationalist feelings are fired up during the Indo-Chinese conflict.

Unknown to him, malfunctioning armaments are sent to the front and cause the death of many Indian soldiers. Before the case becomes known, a corrupt minister hands Ratan to the police to demonstrate his own extraneousness to what has happened. Charges against Ratan are not supported by material evidence, though; Ratan refutes all allegations and is released from prison.

His childhood friend, the Brigadier, is back from the front and Ratan meets him in a dejected mood. He later learns that his friend has deserted and is to be court-martialled, unless proof emerges that the weapons he was using were defective. Ratan is flabbergasted. He first decides to save his friend and declare his wrong but then he temporises. In the meantime, the Brigadier commits suicide. Ratan's final encounter with Himmath Singh, whom he intends to kill at first, leads him towards repentance instead. Humbleness becomes his driving force and this is why every day, before going to his office, he goes to the temple and wipes the shoes of the congregation. [PPP]

Azadi
(Chaman Nahal, 1975)

A three-part novel, *Azadi* narrativises the trauma of post-independence partition of India. Set in undivided Punjab of Western India, the first section 'Lull' traces the humdrum life of the mixed Hindu-Muslim community of Sialkot, a town ultimately bequeathed to Pakistan. Bibi Amar Bhati's tenants, some Hindus, others Punjabis, engage in petty bickerings, friendships and intrigues with a firm sense of belonging. Affinities across religious, political and gender divide, like those between Kanshi Ram and Chaudhuri Barkat Ali, between adolescent Arun, Munir and the socialist British sergeant Bill Davidson, between women of various ages and stature (Nur, Sunanda, Madhu) and Arun are charted alongside distinctions based on class, culture and profession. 'Storm' documents the overnight transformation of this settled community into refugees, their uprooted life at the camp, traumatic journey across the border and 'resettlement' in an alien country, ironically designated as their 'true' home. The effects of partition—riots, displacement, savagery and political insensitivity—are reflected in the topsy-turvy realignment of personal relationships. Docile Ghani Khan seethes with an incomprehensible hatred against his benefactor Kanshi Ram, Arun boldly declares his love/lust for the servant-girl Chandni, domesticated wives replace men as bread-earners. Collective and individual demons come alive as simple people turn into marauding rapists and Hindu-Muslim men alike enjoy the vicarious pleasure of viewing naked women paraded on the streets. The rigorously unsentimental style of reportage adopted by the author accentuates the tales of cowardice, heroism and plain survival where the worst victim is inevitably, humanity itself. [SC]

Bachelor of Arts, The
(R.K. Narayan, 1937)

The plot centres on Chandran, a young man living with his family in Lawley Extension of Malgudi, preparing to graduate with his degree in history from Albert Mission College. Chandran is a bright and respected student, and we witness his successes, first in academic debate, then in the examinations that conclude his college experience. As a student his life is quite focused and regimented, but following graduation he wallows for a time, having no specific ambition or objective and entertaining a vague notion that he may go before terribly long to study in England. His days of post-graduation drifting are disrupted one day when he sets his eyes on Malathi, a 15-year-old girl in a bright green sari, wandering along the banks of Sarayu with her younger sister. Chandran becomes immediately obsessed with her, discovers where she lives, begins to frequent the lodging of his poet-friend Mohan who lives across the road from Malathi, and before long makes it clear to his parents that he wishes to marry this girl. His parents, learning of the family's background, do not feel that it would be a positive move for Chandran, materially, although the girl is of the same caste. Chandran becomes frustrated and impatient, and his father agrees to pursue the issue with the girl's father. Because their horoscopes are ill-matched, however, Malathi's family refuses, and Chandran is devastated, angered by what he perceives to be silly convention and superstition, becomes ill, recovers, then leaves for Madras "for a change."

After a short stay in Madras, Chandran becomes more depressed and disillusioned and decides to become a sanyasi. He spends eight months in this role, wandering about the countryside, before he decides it is time to go home. Believing that he has realized that love is illusion and determined to banish all thought of Malathi from his mind, Chandran secures a position as agent with the Malgudi branch of a Madras newspaper, throwing himself energetically and effectively into his work. Eventually his mother encourages him to consider another prospect for marriage; though he does not believe in love, he feels that marriage may not be such a terrible arrangement, and he wishes to appease his parents. When he views the young woman, Susila, he is love-struck again, and considers Susila a divine creature, far superior to Malathi. Listening to his mother talk of fate, tradition, and love, he waits for the horoscopes to be read: they suggest an auspicious match, and the two are married. [GK]

Baumgartner's Bombay (Anita Desai, 1988)

The protagonist is a German who has sought refuge in a slum near the Taj hotel in Bombay. He bears the memories of the atrocities of Nazi Germany and the nostalgia of a family life dominated by his affection for his mother. The mother's letters and the unfulfilled longing for a peaceful family life are his treasures. The only friend Baumgartner finds in Bombay is the fat, utterly human ex-cabaret dancer, Lotte. He gives shelter to a young boy who finally murders him for the few tarnished silver trophies he possessed. [DM]

Bend in the Ganges, A (Manohar Malgonkar, 1964)

Very rarely does a novel stand on the sheer strength of history even if the detailing is done with an irrefutable fidelity to events.

Manohar Malgonkar's *A Bend in the Ganges* is anything but thus inclined, for barring a general consonance to certain events in the Indian struggle for Independence, there is little else of the laborious penchant for chronologising events which in themselves may do for sufficient documentation, but never make a literary text. In fact the use of the word text by itself is inappropriate since the book's merit lies in the beauty of a simple story well told from a subject position, but one well tempered by the larger political other. Consequently it has no pretensions to exotic points of view, new-fangled narrative techniques, complicated plot structure and/or complex characterisation.

This is the story of two young men that happens during the years when India was in the final stages of its struggle for independence from the British colonial yoke. Gian is an ardent Gandhian, Debi-dayal is a revolutionary—called a terrorist by the British. There is also Singh another undercover revolutionary who is actually a Muslim called Shafi. This brings in the Hindu-Muslim solidarity strand—a solidarity that was to be soon destroyed. There is also a central woman character—Sundari. She is Debi-dayal's sister with whom the idealistic Gian falls in love.

A family feud leads Gian to commit a murder which results in his transportation to the notorious cellular jail on the Andaman islands, which is where Debi-dayal too is sent when his links with the Japanese army are uncovered. In opposite camps in the jail, the men are freed when the Japanese take over the islands. Back in India they try to put the horrific violence they have witnessed and initiated behind them and lead ordinary lives. Violence however continues to haunt them in the form of the bloody carnage that accompanied the simultaneous decolonisation and partitioning of India.

The novel thus poses extremely important questions regarding the Gandhian philosophy of non-violence and wonders how effective it was in changing the nature of men, or whether it merely suppressed the inherent brutality in human beings, to have it spew forth its venom at the first available moment in history. [SR]

Big Heart, The
(Mulk Raj Anand, 1945)

Seth Gokul Chand the *chandri* of utensil sellers' community belonging to *Kasera* brotherhood, establishes a factory in partnership with Lala Murli Dhar, the headman of the *thathiar* coppersmith brotherhood. Lala Murli Dhar's ambition to elevate his family of the *thathiar* caste to the higher sub-caste of *Kaseras* forces him to ignore the welfare of his own community. Consequently most of the *thathiar* youths are not absorbed by the new factory. As the factory begins to produce most of the essential items required by the villagers, the *thathiars* fail to get piecework for making utensils. They are thrown out of their hereditary profession and are rendered jobless. The machine deprives them of their livelihood. At this juncture, Ananta, the coppersmith, the man with a big heart enters. Having visited Bombay and Ahmedabad, and participated in the Gandhian freedom struggle, he has returned to his hometown, Amritsar. He has brought with him a young widow Janaki and been living with her. As he fails to get a job in the factory of Gokul Chand, he tries hard to unite the coppersmiths into a union and fight for their cause. But his efforts are frustrated by the dissidents and by his friends who do not approve of his liaison with Janaki.

One day the hot-blooded *thathiar* youth Ralia takes a few companions to the factory and begins to destroy the machines. The police sub Inspector comes upon the scene a bit too late. When all others are watching Ralia's wanton destruction of machines, Ananta takes courage and tries to reason with him. In the ensuing struggle, Ralia strikes Ananta's head against a broken machine and kills him. Thus in the very process of helping his brethren, Ananta, the defender of machines is crushed between the machine and the oppressed craftsmen. [BN]

Binding Vine, The
(Shashi Deshpande, 1993)

The Binding Vine has in Urmi a woman narrator-observer, bereaving the death of a daughter and as she tries to cope with her loss, she relives the past, looks afresh at her relationship with her mother and her husband and begins to explore the gender positions.

Two other narratives are embedded in this main narrative. One is the story of her dead mother-in-law Mira, which she recovers through her diaries and poems, a story of obsessive love and a loveless marriage and the other is the brutal rape committed on Kalpana by her own uncle, aided unknowingly by both her mother and aunt. This also repeats the story of the aggressive male and the woman who doesn't want him and problematises the conflict between male desire and a woman's right to her body.

As Kalpana lies unconscious in the hospital and the news of the rape rather than punish the rapist result only in defaming the girl, the callousness of a patriarchal society comes in for criticism and Urmi begins to think about her own relationship with her husband whom she loves and yet recognizes the desire which Bhaskar can arouse in her.

The novel moves towards a new self-awareness, even as Sulu, the rapist's wife, commits suicide. In doing so it crosses class and generational boundaries and explodes stereotypes. It also scrutinizes gender relations, love, romance and sexuality locating these categories within patterns of real life as well as myth. [JJ]

Bombay Duck
(Farrukh Dhondy, 1990)

Farrukh Dhondy's *Bombay Duck* is a typical Diasporic text that indulges in nostalgia, is full of time warps and tries to re-possess and re-write histories—personal and political—from a distant space. It is also a Parsi text in which Dhondy tries to write in the history and culture of his demographically challenged community.

The duck in the title as all good Bombaywallahs know is not actually a fowl but a fish peculiar to the waters of the Arabian Sea around the island-city. Dhondy adds to this etymological confusion by saying that it is actually a misspelling of Bombay Dak—Bombay Mail.

There are also other fantastically named characters in the text—one of the narrators himself goes by the name Xerxes Xavaxa, whose name harks back to the Imperial Iranian past of the Parsis already in a 1300-year-old diaspora in India itself.

The book opens with the first narrator, Gerald Blossom, aka Ali Abdul Rahman, who is a British Black. Like Xavaxa, Blossom too is displaced by European colonization. The story told here is that of a team of British actors, under the direction of David Stream, who go to India to perform his version of the *Ramayana*. This is a tongue-in-cheek reference to Peter Brook's *Mahabharatha*. The performance kicks up a furore in conservative Hindu circles, as the characters of Ram and other Hindu icons in the production are played by an international cast—Ram by a Black man and Lakshman by a Chinese. There are riots and finally the Indian actress who plays Sita is killed. This raises questions of identity in an increasingly global milieu and that of ownership of culture—what the protesting mob calls *sanskriti*.

The second part of the novel is narrated by Xavaxa and is focused on Xavaxa, who born in Pune (Poona), like Dhondy, goes to Cambridge as a student and then becomes a substitute teacher in England. This section, like other Parsi novels, details what make Parsis unique even in diaspora and what constitutes their ethno-religious identity. This section also raises questions about intolerance, authoritarianism and insensitivity towards 'the other' in a postcolonial world. [SR]

Bubble, The
(Mulk Raj Anand, 1984)

Krishnan Chandar Azad, the protagonist of the novel, participates briefly in the Gandhi movement and goes to jail. His pro-British father beats his mother for Krishnan's anti-British and nationalistic activities. Then Azad goes to the West on a philosophical quest. A naïve poet from the 'Ocean of Nectar' undergoes the many torments of loneliness and self-exile. But he unexpectedly meets a beautiful girl Irene, step-daughter of a scientist, Professor Rhys. Azad is inspired by Irene to become a novelist, to celebrate 'love at first sight,' to experience

Laila-Majnu like sexual-spiritual passion and emotional tension. When Irene goes back to her native Ireland, away from her orthodox mother, to work with Maud Gone in the liberation movement, Azad tries to channelise his pangs of separation by conversing with eminent writers and thinkers in Bloomsbury like E.M. Forster, Leonard, Virginia Wolf, J. Krishnamurthi, Bertrand Russell and others. [BN]

Bye-bye Blackbird
(Anita Desai, 1971)

The novel projects the problem of cultural alienation and ethnic discrimination suffered by an Indian immigrant in England. The plight of Adit is typical of the colonized visiting the land of his former masters with nostalgic longing for the colonizer's land which he has come to regard with love and longing as a second home. Adit's situation is problematic because of his marriage to Sarah, an English lady. The ethnic prejudice of the English man comes heavily down on them—Adit, the coloured "wog" who has chosen England as his home and Sarah, the English lady who has married the brown Indian. Culture shocks that encounter them in their life together, are endured by them. A few days' stay at Sarah's parents' house makes Adit realize the cold animosity of the British towards him and he takes the decision to leave England for his own homeland. Sarah in her earnest desire to save her marriage decides to accompany the 'blackbird' to India. [DM]

Calcutta Chromosome, The (A Novel of Fevers, Delirium and Discovery)
(Amitav Ghosh, 1988)

The story seems to originate by chance. The Egyptian computer archivist Antar, living in a New York of the future, while working on his computer accidentally localises the identity card of a former colleague of his who had disappeared, the Bengali clerk Murugan. All traces of him had been lost in the summer of 1995 when Murugan, overcome by an irrepressible urge to prove a strange malaria theory of his, had embarked on a solitary mission in India. Murugan, a bizarre character, was famous as a world expert on the Nobel Prize winner Ronald Ross, the American bacteriologist who had discovered the antidote to malaria in 1898. The Bengali clerk suspected that the medical discovery still adumbrated a mystery he was resolute to unearth: instead of conducting experiments in his Calcutta laboratory, Ross himself may have been the object of a parallel experiment run by a secretive organisation, possibly led by Ross's sinister laboratory sweeper Mangala. To Murugan it looks like as though she had controlled all the stages of Ross's search. Unknown to the scientist himself, a dangerous opposition between science and counter-science was taking place. Antar's hunt for Murugan and Murugan's hunt for Ross therefore question directly the mysterious aims behind this subversive group. Past, present and future tales blend into a heterogeneous continuum. Thanks also to the crucial help and collaboration of some female characters, in particular Urmila who is close to Murugan and Tara to Antar, the mystery is uncovered: the "Calcutta Chromosome" appears to be the project led by this organisation and meant to allow its initiates to reach immortality through interpersonal transference. [PPP]

Cat and Shakespeare, The (Raja Rao, 1971)

This slender novel is in many ways a logical sequel to *The Serpent and the Rope.* If the earlier novel concludes with the hero's longing to go to Travancore, the succeeding one begins with the hero's actual arrival there. Raja Rao's metaphysical preoccupations thus continue even in this work which is at one level a "tale of modern India" (its sub-title) and at another a "metaphysical comedy" as Raja Rao himself chooses to call it.

This first person narrative has Ramakrishna Pai, a brahmin as its narrator. Married to Saroja, he has two children Usha and Vittal, whom he has left behind in Alwaye to work as divisional clerk in Trivandrum. His friend and neighbour Govindan Nair, also a married man with a son by name Sridhar plays an important role in the life of Pai.

The whole work is steeped in complex symbolism. The image of house building for instance is pervasive. It doesn't take long for the reader to realize that Pai's deep desire almost assuming the form of an obsession to build a house, a house of three stories is highly symbolic, as anyone with even a slight acquaintance with Hindu philosophy will immediately recognize its correspondence with the three states or *gunas* it propounds, namely *Tamas, Rajas* and *Satva. Satva* being the highest and almost unattainable by ordinary people, it is but natural that a sensitive man like Pai with a philosophical disposition should aspire for it. In fact, his friend Nair strongly encourages him to realize his dream. The character of Govindan Nair himself adds much to the fascination of this unusual tale. Nair always talks of the kitten and urges his friend to follow the ways of the kitten and be led by the Mother Cat. The Cat here represents the Feminine Principle which accounts for its presence in the title that has intrigued many. As for Shakespeare his presence is invoked because the whole world here is envisaged as a "Ration Shop" in the same way that Shakespeare himself conceived of the world as a "stage." Hence the observation, "Shakespeare knew every mystery of the ration shop." The ration office, the ration card, the accounts, the scale are all loaded symbols. The crux of the novel hinges on this symbolism, an understanding of which is imperative for a proper understanding of the complex theme itself.

Interestingly it is the non-brahmin Nair who explains *Brahman* and similar profound truths to the brahmin Ramakrishna Pai and not the other way round making the reader wonder if this is not the novelist's way of hinting at the failure of the brahmin in modern India to keep up his traditional values. Consequently it is Shantha, the Nair woman (with whom Pai has developed a relationship), who knows how to *give* that is extolled and not Saroja, his legally wedded wife who knows how to *take* and is always interested in supervising rope-making, meaning she is lost in a world of illusions ("rope" evidently symbolizing "illusion").

The Ration Shop plays a crucial role in the story. This is where the cat is brought one day and Nair teaches his colleagues to revere it and surrender themselves to it, for it represents the Absolute. It also becomes an agent of redemption for Bhoothalinga Iyer who dies when he physically comes in contact with the cat.

The greatest achievement of this little novel is the author's courage in making the cat, generally considered an unclean and unholy animal, a symbol of the highest Reality matched only by his other singular accomplishment, namely, the technique of evolving a language of incredible simplicity to convey profoundest truths. [RR]

Chessmaster and His Moves, The (Raja Rao, 1988)

Considered to be Raja Rao's *magnum opus, The Chessmaster and His Moves* is in many ways a continuation of *The Serpent and the Rope*. In its spiritual concerns and metaphysical preoccupations and in its glorification of the Feminine Principle, the novel comes very close to its predecessor. In the bare outline of the story as well as characterization, particularly of women, the two works bear an astonishing degree of similarity.

The protagonist Sivarama Sastri like Ramaswamy has lost his mother early in life and is confronted by a sense of emptiness. Thus begins his search for the Mother Principle that carries him through many vicissitudes. He, a mathematician goes to France on a French Government scholarship to work in the Institute for Pure Mathematics in Paris. He falls in love with a young French actress by name Suzanne and their intimate relationship is the focus of attention in the early part of the novel. But in course of time Suzanne drifts away from Sivarama to Michel and Sivarama himself turns to Mireille, a married woman and a mother. Mireille is an intelligent woman, an art historian researching in art history. What with her unmistakable beauty to boot she can entice the young man Sivarama who feels the world to be subliminally real with Mireille by his side. But even this relationship cannot last long, for fundamental differences in their very outlook on life come in the way. He is subsequently drawn to Princess Jayalakshmi Devi (Jaya in short), largely because of her interest in abstruse matters who in many ways recalls to our minds Savithri of *The Serpent and the Rope*. The novelist's adoration of the Feminine Principle finds its supreme expression in the exaltation of these two characters. That both of them are highly idealized is of course very much in evidence. Sivarama's admiration for this Rajput princess is total and unconditional. But he cannot consummate his love, for Jaya is a married woman. Hence his relationship with all three women peter out. And he turns inward to find an answer to his private sorrow, transforming his struggle into a metaphysical exploration in the process. The answer he finds is, "Marriage is marriage that never takes place" (700); "The not-two alone is marriage [...] so there is indeed no marriage" (701). Sivarama's search for the Absolute is the stuff of this most ambitious novel described as the first part of a trilogy.

Breathtaking in its sheer sweep and range of concerns, the novel with its deeply engaging meditations on numbers; zero vs infinity; dissolution of contradictions and similar matters pertaining to the self/Self concludes with Sivarama's preparations to return to India, the "Mother of us all," who would "protect us with her vast filigree pallo." The wheel comes full circle when resting his head on Uma's bosom he feels a sense of being "home." [RR]

Circle of Reason, The
(Amitav Ghosh, 1986)

The Circle of Reason begins in Bengal with the recently orphaned Alu's arrival at the home of his uncle, Balaram. Balaram is a passionate believer in his own particular brand of Reason, which combines superstition and nineteenth-century scientific discoveries and the first part of the novel is centred on his efforts to eradicate disease by disinfecting the whole of his village. These efforts bring him into conflict with his neighbour, Bhudeb Roy, and their feud ends with the accidental killing of Balaram and his followers.

Suspected as a terrorist, Alu, who has been trained as a master-weaver, escapes first to Kerala and then by boat to the fictional Middle East oil state of al-Ghazira. He is pursued by the bird-watching police detective, Jyoti Das. In al-Ghazira, Alu is associated with the brothel-keeper Zindi and the group of women in her charge, with whom he has made his voyage there. When a huge commercial complex collapses, Alu is buried in the rubble, but is rescued days later, emerging as the champion of a communal life-style that links Balaram's campaign against germs with a belief that money is the root cause of society's ills.

Forced to flee from al-Ghazira, Alu once again travels westwards, this time to Algeria, along with Zindi and the prostitute, Kulfi, who dies there of a heart attack. Kulfi's cremation convinces Alu he should return home. Jyoti Das has caught up with him, but no longer has any intention of arresting him. The novel ends in a mood of reconciliation, with Das deciding to migrate to Düsseldorf and asking Alu and Zindi, who will return home via Gibraltar, if he can accompany them on the first leg of their journey. [JT]

City and the River, The
(Arun Joshi, 1990)

The Great Yogeshwara recounts this sad tale to his disciple, the Nameless One, in order to explain who he is.

The story is about a city by a river, under the rigid control of the Great Master. Following a disturbing dream, interpreted as a harbinger of problems by the Astrologer, the dictator resolves to strengthen the grip of his rule. He surrounds himself with a group of ambitious sycophant ministers and tries to win the boatmen's sympathies; these represent the other pole in the city, the poor ones who still live according to old traditions and who have made an alliance with the River. Since they are not spellbound by the Great Master's cajoling, stronger measures are needed to make them submit.

The Great Master adopts various atrocious strategies to harass the boatmen. Imprisonment, torture and death—sometimes arbitrary—are meted out to those who dare oppose the regime. Entire quarters of barracks are bulldozed to make room for grand avenues; furthermore, disturbed by the songs played on the banks of the river, the ruler orders the boatmen's instruments be destroyed with futuristic weapons.

The River rebels, though, and in a week of heavy rains it wipes out the City. Of the old City nothing remains: a new City is built on the ruins of the old one and the same forces return again under new names. The Nameless One, child of the deluge and the only survivor, represents the element of continuation. [PPP]

Clear Light of Day
(Anita Desai, 1980)

Bim, the protagonist of Clear Light of Day is a middle aged college lecturer living in Old Delhi with her retarded brother Baba. She has been burdened by the responsibilities of a consumptive brother, an alcoholic aunt and a retarded brother after the death of her parents. The younger sister snatched the opportunity to escape when Bakul, an officer in the diplomatic service proposed marriage. Raja, the poet of the family recovered from his illness and went to Hyderabad where their neighbour Hyder Ali Sahib had fled in the days of the communal riots preceding independence. Raj got married to Benazir, Hyder Ali Sahib's daughter, virtually effecting a partition in the family. Dr. Biswas who looked after all the ailing members of the family proposed to Bim, but she did not accept the proposal. She resented the fact that those who had made their nests, never remembered her or shared the burden of Baba. The story begins with the visit of Tara and Bakul to Bim's house which triggers off memories of their childhood together and the contrast in their character. Tara tries to make up for past mistakes and remove the bitterness in Bim's mind towards Raja. Raja's daughter is getting married. At the end of the novel we find Bim forgiving Raja with the enlightening revelation that they are all part of her and she cannot be happy without them. The life of the Misras, their neighbours, is also connected to their story. [DM]

Coffer Dams, The
(Kamala Markandaya, 1967)

The Coffer Dams revolves round two central issues: the necessity to build a forward-looking, industrialized India, at the national level; and the efficacy of the relationship forged between two individuals from two different backgrounds, at the personal level. Other themes like East-West encounter, man-woman relationship, the tension between technological power and nature, and tradition and modernity woven dexterously into the plot, remain at the periphery. The plot concentrates mainly on the construction of the dam, with the sub-plot dealing with Helen-Bashiam relationship.

Howard Clinton, an engineer with the Clinton-Mackendrick Company undertakes the construction of a dam in South India. He faces innumerable hurdles: the ravages of nature, the impossibility of taming the turbulent river, the hostility of Krishnan and the skeptical attitude of the Indian workers after the two accidents. But, Clinton is a man of "iron will" who surmounts all the difficulties and the work progresses satisfactorily. Clinton is so engrossed in his work that he neglects his wife who feels lonely and unhappy. Gradually, she becomes friendly with the tribals, identifies with them and by and by she comes closer to Bashiam, a tribal crane-operator on the Dam. Humane and compassionate as she is, she objects to her husband's British superiority complex, his highhandedness in dealing with the Indians, and his insensitivity towards human suffering. Helen enjoys the "fullness of life" in her relationship with Bashiam but she tosses between her love and her responsibility as Clinton's wife. When Clinton comes to know of the affair, he deliberately lets Bashiam operate a defective crane. Bashiam meets with an accident and becomes a helpless cripple while Helen returns to Clinton as she wakes up to her social and marital responsibilities. Bashiam returns to his tribal village realizing the futility of a relationship that cannot be enduring. [UB]

Come Up and Be Dead (Shashi Deshpande, 1993)

A mystery story, located in a girls' school, *Come Up and Be Dead*, opens with Kshama Rao, a woman with determination and grit, being appointed the headmistress. She also has a dependent brother who is not entirely 'there' and she sends for her cousin Devi to come and help with the housekeeping and the brother. Of the several narrative voices of the novel, Devi's is the main one. She also plays the amateur detective, who finally unravels the mystery.

Several things seem to be going wrong. A young fifteen-year old girl Mridula dies in what appears to be suicide, another girl stops coming to the school. Mridula is found to be pregnant. A teacher resigns and wishes to take her daughter away. There is an atmosphere of fear and uncertainty. The headmistress half-crazy brother dies in a staged accident but in actuality he has been murdered. One of the teachers Mrs Raman is strangulated with her own scarf. A murder attempt on her daughter Sonali is thwarted by Sharmila who is attacked in her own turn.

The truth begins to dawn on Devi and as she rushes to reveal everything to the Inspector the doctor, Girish Varma, insists on escorting her, makes her his captive and threatens her with death when she is rescued by the Inspector. The doctor is the murderer and part of a call girl racket. The headmistress, who had resigned, is rehabilitated. [JJ]

Company of Women, The (Khushwant Singh, 1999)

Mohan Kumar, a millionaire running a successful export business in New Delhi, is not successful in his married life. When Mohan returns with a coveted degree in business management from Harvard University, USA, his father sincerely arranges an alliance with Sonu, the only daughter of a fabulously rich businessman. Sonu, Mohan discovers soon, is a spoilt, egoistic and ill-tempered woman, who can not relish her separation from her doting parents. Mohan has an insatiable sexual urge and has had countless sexual encounters with willing women during his stay in the US; he had been initiated into unbridled sexual activity by an ebony beauty named Jessica Browne and also had an unusual encounter with a middle aged Pakistani, Yasmeen.

Mohan's conjugal life turns out to be an enforced one and produces a boy and a girl. Sonu dislikes Mohan's father and indirectly compels him to opt for an ashram life in Haridwar, despite his deep attachment with his grandson. The irrepressible Mohan beds Mary Joseph, the nurse for Sonu, sowing the seeds of discord in their married life. Their marriage of thirteen years is broken up when Mohan's father dies unattended at Haridwar.

Mohan feels free and elated and launches on an audacious plan to indulge in sensuous pleasures, as he believes that "lust is the true foundation of love." Responding to his advertisement in the newspaper seeking women companions, different types of women make their entries and exits—Sarojini Bharadwaj, a college professor from Haryana; Molly Gomes, the free spirited masseuse from Goa; Susanthika Goonathilleke, the Sri Lankan diplomat. In between these affairs, he finds an outlet for his passion in Dhanno, the dusky servant maid. Even though he enjoys the company of different women so continuously and so arduously, soon age takes its toll. He loses his appetite for women; however, during a visit to Mumbai, he takes a housewife-prostitute and in return contacts the HIV virus. Within a year his end comes and he spends his last moments reciting the Gayatri mantra and reading the *Bhagavad Gita*. [PB]

Comrade Kirillov
(Raja Rao, 1976)

Comrade Kirillov is about a South Indian brahmin called Padmanabha Iyer, introduced to the reader as Comrade Kirillov, fiercely loyal to the Communist ideology. Leaves the Indian shores for America and later England to preach theology and fulfil his destiny. Marries Irene, a Czech woman and begets a son whom he calls Kamal. He has visions of a "classless society" where "no man will be master of another," where the only God is the common man and where the only worship is the party meeting. He visualizes such a state of society for India and is optimistic that it will come one day as it already has to China. With his faith in "the new Humanism" that his party stands for, he is hopeful of ushering in better days for the country's hungry and houseless millions. He loves India ardently but is outwardly critical, savagely critical of everything that is Indian, whether it is her literature or metaphysics, politics or theology, Mahatma Gandhi or Kalidasa or Tagore. As he sets supreme store by logic which he calls his religion, he cannot stand any sentimentality that Indians are notorious for!

Understandably the book is replete with references to Hitler, Stalin, Lenin, Churchill, Soviet Policies, Marxist mannerisms, wars, revolutions, working classes and trade union meetings. Yet Kirillov is a strange paradox. He has his "superior metaphysics" allright just as Communism itself has a "metaphysic." He wouldn't let anyone talk ill of Gandhi though he himself may judge him harshly, similarly wouldn't like Irene or anyone to criticize the country either. But with his "ecclesiastical look" or query, "what do you know?" simply silence them. He may decry all outward forms of worship, "all this God-God business" but many times he himself would, "close his eyes and go into profound meditation."

As the Indian struggle enters the international arena it is a great, a very great day in the history of India. Comrade Kirillov now becomes Mr. Padmanabhan Kirillov and a much sought after authority on India's place in the war effort and his manuscript on Indian struggle is bought by a publisher and hailed as a great document for international understanding. Gandhi is now given his right historical place. It is one of the greatest days in Kirillov's life as well.

This is how his Indianness comes through, in fact, manages to "break through every communist chain." Irene's Diary appended to the work reveals the other side of Kirillov more fully, his interest in philosophy, in the Indian theory of the word in particular, in *Mantrasastra* and *Sphota* and the word principle involved in its four different stages. Which only goes to suggest how Kirillov, the "sadhu of communism" does rise above the "Occidental veneer" afterall to show his true Indian self. [RR]

Confessions of a Lover
(Mulk Raj Anand, 1976)

Krishnan, the protagonist is a brilliant young boy who tries to seek solutions in the seemingly nightmarish world of the changing political life. He tries to maintain a balance between his life and the environmental pulls. He takes delight in reading poetry. He comes under the influence of Dr. Mohammed Iqbal, a poet-philosopher who initiates him into the world of poetry. When he goes to London, Krishnan finds himself in self-imposed exile, leaving the comforts of home and the affection of his Indian friends. Deeply imbued in his narcissistic self-absorption, he finds it difficult to come out of his solipsistic circle. [BN]

Coolie
(Mulk Raj Anand, 1936)

Munoo, the protagonist of the novel, is an orphan boy of fourteen years of age. Though ill-treated by his Uncle Daya Ram and aunt Gujri, he remains happy in his native village of Bilaspur. But his Uncle Daya Ram finds him old enough to earn his livelihood, forces him to leave the village and go to the town. He makes Munoo walk miles and miles barefoot without giving him any rest. In Sham Nagar, Munoo is employed as a domestic servant of the sub-Accountant at rupees three per month, with the understanding that the amount should be paid not to him but to his uncle. The Babu's wife, Bibiji treats Munoo like an animal. When Munoo makes a petty mistake, Baboo Nathoo Ram slaps, strikes and kicks him mercilessly. Munoo, therefore slips out of the Baboo's house at night, runs down the hill and reaches the railway station. He enters a compartment of the train and sleeps on the floor under the bunk of a passenger named Seth Prabha Dayal who owns a pickle factory. He takes pity on Munoo and takes him to his place Daulatpur and employs him in his pickle factory. But unfortunately Prabha Dayal experiences heavy losses in his business and becomes a pauper. Munoo, therefore, leaves the factory and becomes a coolie in the Grain

Market of Daulatpur and a porter at the station. One day he happens to meet an elephant trainer in a circus and becomes his servant for fetching water. Munoo requests the elephant trainer to help him to go to Bombay when the circus party will move to that city. Accordingly, the elephant trainer helps Munoo to go to Bombay secretly in a goods wagon.

Munoo manages to get a job as a coolie in George White Cotton Mills at the rate of Rs. 25 per month. Munoo lives in a hut and endures all the exploitation and atrocities committed by their employers. But soon there arises a misunderstanding between the employers and the labourers. But the labour meetings are cleverly converted into Hindu-Muslim riots. Sensing danger in the situation Munoo runs away from the factory. As he runs up Malabar Hill to escape the hectic police action, he is knocked down by the motor car of an Anglo-Indian lady, Mrs Mainwaring. She feels pity for the wounded boy and takes him to Simla. A women of vast pretensions and no morals, she employs Munoo as a servant in her house at Simla and makes him pull her in a rickshaw up and down the road. Munoo gradually grows weaker, catches tuberculosis and dies. [BN]

Cow of the Barricades, The
[The Policeman and the Rose]
(Raja Rao, 1947 and 1978)

Between *The Cow of the Barricades* (1947) and *The Policeman and the Rose* (1978) lies a yawning gap of three decades. Though they belong to two distinct periods and as is rightly observed, even categories, yet what brings the two together is not merely are they both Collections of Short Stories but also have between themselves many stories in common like 'The True Story of Kanakapala, Protector of Gold,' 'In Khandesh,' 'Companions,' 'The Cow of the Barricades,' 'Akkayya,' 'The Little Gram Shop' and 'Javni.' The new additions in the latter publication include 'Nimka,' 'India—A Fable' and the title story 'The Policeman and the Rose.'

The Stories in the earlier Collection demonstrate the writer's social concerns and preoccupations which he shared with other writers of the period when they had to contend with thorny issues such as poverty, backwardness, social and religious dogma, denial of rights and equal opportunities to all, conservatism of the upper castes, exploitation of women, victimization of the weak, oppression of the untouchable, etc, etc. The humanistic and the compassionate side of the writer comes through in his poignant portrayals of human suffering in stories like 'Javni,' 'Akkayya' and 'The Little Gram Shop' finding their culmination in 'Nimka,' a very mature story belonging to the later phase of Raja Rao's creative career. The transition from the first three stories to 'Nimka' is obvious in the very handling of his material, for though woman is still a victim and a symbol of pain and suffering, she exhibits a rare capacity for not just acceptance, but even transcendence. The other stories like 'The Cow of the Barricades,' 'India—A Fable' and 'The Policeman and the Rose' are all symbolic and anticipate the maturer Raja Rao. There is a mix of fantasy and metaphysics in these stories and at times the symbolism tends to be quite private and complex calling for much hard work on the part of the reader. But what is certain is that the evolution of a major novelist is at work here.

In language, style, sensibility and vision these stories pave the way for the later Raja Rao. Though they are themselves (barring a few) the products of an "apprentice to his craft," they contain unmistakable evidence of promise; of a potentially great writer. [RR]

Cry, the Peacock
(Anita Desai, 1963)

Cry, the Peacock deals with the emotional incompatibility in the lives of Maya and Gautama. The death of the pet dog Toto brings to the surface the hypersensitivity of Maya which makes the death of the dog an unbearable tragedy and the insensitivity of Gautama for whom it is an everyday event to be dealt with practically. Maya fails to understand how Gautama can dismiss things which appear as calamities to her, with cool indifference. He is equally blind to the beauty of nature that thrills Maya. Maya feels alone and totally alienated from her husband and broods over the childhood encounter with an astrologer who had told her that within four years of her marriage either she or her husband would die. Maya gradually moves towards neurosis, and her fear of impending death is intensified by the cry of the peacock which seems to be a bad omen. Finally she conceives the idea of killing Gautama, and makes herself believe that Gautama, who is impervious to the beauty of the colours and forms of nature, would not mind dying. One evening she leads him to the terrace, inviting him to enjoy the beauty of the moon and pushes him down to certain death. As Gautama's mother and sister await the arrival of Maya's father from abroad, they hear Maya laughing and talking in her madness upstairs and finally her mother goes up and we hear a scream as Maya too falls from above to the tragic end of her neurotic existence. [DM]

Dark Holds No Terrors, The
(Shashi Deshpande, 1980)

The Dark Holds No Terrors is about the homecoming of Saru for the first time since her marriage to Manohar, against the wishes of her parents. She has just learnt of her mother's death who had been ill for the last two years and has had ample time to forgive and forget. But she did not summon her daughter to her deathbed, revealing a much deeper estrangement which Saru has always sensed. The mother has always held her responsible for the death of Dhruva, Saru's younger brother.

Saru is a doctor, married and has two children. At this particular moment her marriage is also going through a crisis. Her husband, unable to take her success in his stride has turned sadistic and subjects her to physical violence. Working through the parallel narratives of her childhood and her adult life the novel explores the various dimensions of family life and the compulsions which govern it.

On her return she finds that her father has fallen into a routine and there is another student Madhav, who is living with him. Madhav acts like a buffer between the father and daughter but later during Madhav's temporary absence they find the courage to talk to each other and go over the past in order to work out the sense of guilt which possesses them. This helps Saru to get over the terrors of the dark and exorcise her ghosts. The novel ends on a note of reconciliation with Saru deciding to discuss her marriage with her husband. [JJ]

Dark Room, The
(R.K. Narayan, 1938)

A work with a scarcity of Narayan's later lightheartedness and comic irony, the novel focuses on Savitri, the traditionally devoted wife and mother, much loved by her children and who serves as the pillar of her home. Her husband, Ramani, is portrayed from the opening pages as self-absorbed, distracted by or obsessed with his insurance business, strict with his children, and showing only passing or obligatory attention to his wife—although we learn that he had been passionate in their early relationship. Complication and suspense enters the narrative when the business Ramani works for decides to hire a woman (and Ramani is "all for" efforts to improve women's social status), and an attractive/enchanting (and jaded) woman named Shanta Bai is given the job. Ramani becomes entangled in an affair with Shanta Bai and after one of his long nights out, Savitri angrily confronts him, presents him with an ultimatum, gets no results, and walks out. Finding herself alone on the street and feeling she has nowhere to turn (he even "owns" the children), she attempts to drown herself in the river Sarayu.

After she is fished out of the river by a villager named Mari, Savitri reluctantly agrees to be taken by his wife, Ponni, to the village. In contrast to Savitri, Ponni is a sharp-tongued, tough and domineering woman, who nonetheless immediately becomes Savitri's protectress. Determined to accept nothing that she has not earned, Savitri resists food and shelter offered by the villagers, who then manage to find her a job maintaining a small local temple. The temple priest is a manipulative and exploitative old man, and Savitri discovers that she is unable to cope with the harshness and loneliness of her location and employment, admits defeat, and returns to her family. She moves immediately into her previous role and patterns of behaviour, accepting her lot but reflecting that "a part of me is dead." [GK]

Darkness
(Bharati Mukherjee, 1985)

In this collection of twelve short stories, despite their gloomy sounding title *Darkness*, Bharati Mukherjee mentions (in her introduction to the volume) her desire to widen her vision as a postcolonial immigrant writer in "a movement away from the aloofness of expatriation, to the exuberance of immigration." Thus, she seeks to step beyond backward-looking nostalgia towards a bonding with her new host community, with an attempt to overcome "the ever-present fear of failure and betrayal," in a deliberate celebration of "fluid identities."

The stories portray a double-pronged dynamics where danger and disappointment appear side by side with a hopeful determination to adapt and make the best of difficult circumstances, featuring immigrants mainly from the Indian sub-continent in North America. Various ethnic and political currents come together in "The World according to Hsu" where political unrest creates a backdrop of violence as Graeme Clayton and his Czecho-Indian wife, Ratna, holiday from their Canadian university and media jobs in an island off the coast of Africa. Amidst worries about racist attacks on Pakis in Toronto, news of a coup on a nearby arhcipelago (in the southern Indian Ocean) and snippets from an article from *Scientific American* on the theory of continental collision, Ratna finds herself feeling at home while sipping French red wine, surrounded by Indians and Europeans and a motley of languages and dialects.

Similarly in "Nostalgia," Dr. Manny Patel, a psychiatric resident at a state hospital in Queens, married to a white American woman named Camille, or in "Tamurlane," a tandoor chef named Gupta at Mumtaz bar-b-q in Toronto, whose legs had been crippled in a subway accident, and in "Visitors," Vinita Kumar in her expensive condominium home in New Jersey, take risks and have to make devastating choices as they do their best to survive in their new lives. [FD'S]

Day in Shadow, The
(Nayantara Sahgal, 1971)

The Day in Shadow, Nayantara Sahgal's fourth novel, has a strong autobiographical note. The journey of Sahgal's earlier heroines ends for Simrit in divorce. This divorce has left her both emotionally and financially drained. When the novel opens Simrit is in Delhi and is desperately trying to put the pieces of her life together in this husband-centred world and to gain financial independence.

Her one support comes through Raj, a member of the Parliament and a Christian by faith. He encourages her to think on positive lines and is astonished how easily she has been duped by her husband into signing a divorce agreement which cripples her and holds her in bondage even as it pretends to set her free. The novel critiques Hinduism and the centrality it gives to the idea of woman as Devi. *Storm in Chandigarh* had focused on the *Gita* and the hidden passivity in the concept of karma. This novel focuses on the Hindu tolerance of brutality which limits the possibility of change.

Simrit's husband Som is a ruthless person, dealing in ammunition supplies and obsessed with the idea of masculinity. For him the daughters don't matter, it is only the son who is important and whom he lures away from his mother with promises of wealth, indifferent to the building of any sensitive, emotional relationships. The novel ends on a positive note with Simrit deciding to face her new life squarely and fight the injustice inflicted upon her. [JJ]

Death of a Hero
(Mulk Raj Anand, 1961)

Maqbool, the protagonist of this novelette, is a young poet of the National Conference. In the late October of 1947, when the raiders from Pakistan have advanced to Baramula, he flees to Srinagar to consult the leaders of National Conference Volunteer corps. They advise him to go back to Baramula in order to rally the people to fight against the Pakistani invaders. As he gets near Baramula, he feels tired and spends the night in a field by making a cave out of some hay. When he hears the distant rifle and machine gun fire, he walks towards Baramula and sees the Presentation Convent being burnt. Soon he comes to know that Baramula is completely in the grip of Pakistanis and that they are filling their trucks with loot. He feels it safe to meet Muratib Ali. Muratib Ali's factory is looted and burnt by Pakistanis. Maratib Ali advises Maqbool to run away from there to save his life. Maqbool is surprised and shocked to learn that his trusted friend and lawyer Ahmed Shah and Ghulam Jilani have joined the pro-Pakistanis. He is further shocked to see Ghalam Jalani and Ahmed Shah conspiring with Khurshid Anwar, an official of the invading army. When Maqbool is about to be arrested by Khurshid Anwar, he is helped by a woman-servant Ibil to escape from there in the guise of a woman in *burqua*. When Maqbool reaches home, he is again chased and captured by the Pakistani invaders. He is brutally treated, summarily tried and shot dead. Ahmed Shah orders his soldiers to tie the corpse to a pole, write the word 'kafir' on his shirt with his own blood and place it for the people of Baramula to see.

The next day, when the conquering Indian troops enter Baramula, they see the dead body of Maqbool Sherwani tied to a wooden pole. They search his packet and find a letter written by him from the prison cell to his sister, Noor. It reveals the truth that conscience is the real source of poetry. [BN]

Delhi
(Khushwant Singh, 1989)

This vast, erotic and documentary book does not have any plot of any type nor does it have any unifying pattern. The narrator is the alter-ego of the author and describes his love/hate relationship with the city of Delhi and Bhagmati, his hermaphrodite mistress. Both are ugly, repulsive, unhealthy, yet to him eternal, fascinating and quite enjoyable. The paradox cannot be explained in short lines and hence this "novel." The chapters are presented under the loose structure of some kind of inter chapters dealing with Bhagmati, everyone of them followed by a historical account. Some kind of chronological order, however, has been maintained in the presentation of stories of individuals who have made Delhi.

'Musaddi Lal' is the tale of Hindus' travails under the Muslim emperors of the 13th century and also about the long and hideous power struggles among the heirs of Sultan Ghiasuddin Balban, Alauddin Khilji, Qutubuddin Mubarak Shah and Ghiasuddin Tughlak. 'The Timurid' narrates the gory conquest of Delhi by the Mongolian King Timur after a battle with Delhi's ruler Mahmud Tughlak in 1398 in which anywhere between "50,000 to 500,000" Hindus were massacred. The account of how a Sikh holy man was hanged to death despite the attempt of a group of untouchable Sikhs to save his life is dealt with in 'The Untouchables.' One of the famous emperors of Delhi was Aurangzeb, and the infamous tale of his ascent to the throne of Delhi in 1666, the year Shah Jahan, his father died, is told in the chapter 'Auranzeb Alamgir: Emperor of Hindustan.' Emperor Nadir Shah of Iran also came to conquer Delhi, which he did in 1739; much blood was shed on the battlefield as well in the riots against the invader on the streets of Delhi before the Shah was satisfied and left with large quantities of the loot. After the story of a poet and lover called Meer Taqi Meer, the historical events of 1857 in which the British men and women were killed during the rule of Bahadur Shah Zafar are told in disconnected narratives. Next follows the account of how modern New Delhi was built by white architects and Sikh contractors. The next chapter is the fictional account of the holocaust of partition and how millions of Hindus and Muslims were dispossessed of their homes and how the culture of violence and hatred took the precious life of Mahatma Gandhi. The last Bhagmati chapter deals with the ageing of the narrator and the assassination of Mrs. Indira Gandhi which witnessed the backlash of the massacre of the Sikhs. [PB]

Desirable Daughters
(Bharati Mukherjee, 2002)

Mukherjee's most recent novel (2002) bears a title that seems like a retort to Vikram Seth's best seller,

A Suitable Boy. It is made up of twenty chapters divided unequally into three parts. Four narrative threads overlap and are woven together.

There is the tale of a child bride in East Bengal in 1879, who was forced to marry a tree and remain celibate in her father's house, since the groom selected for her died of a snake bite on the very day fixed for their nuptials.

There is the story of the three beautiful and talented Bhattacharjee sisters who grew up in their Ballygunge family home and attended the Loreto House convent in Calcutta in the 1960's.

There is the narrative of the youngest Bhattacharjee sister, Tara, who is also the first-person narrator throughout, in her life as a married woman, a mother and a divorcee in San Francisco, California, in the 1980's and 1990's. This is completed by exchanges with her second sister Parvati, established in Bombay, with her eldest sister Padma, established in Upper Montclair, New Jersey, and with her ageing parents who have retired in Rishikesh, in the foothills of the Himalayas. Tara's ex-husband, Bishwapriya Chatterjee, a computer industry tycoon, and their adolescent son Rabi, are also important centres of attention in Tara's narrative.

The fourth narrative thread introduces an element of mystery and suspense into the novel. It concerns an enigmatic character who presents himself as Christopher Dey, the illegitimate son of the eldest Bhattacharjee sister, Padma, and whose existence had been hushed up by the family over 25 years. The investigations of a Sardarji police officer of the San Francisco Police Department reveal that there was indeed a bonafide Christopher Dey but that he was murdered and his place taken by a terrorist criminal of the powerful Dawood gang, based in Bombay and Dubai, with tentacles reaching all over the globe.

The juxtaposition of these four narrative threads results in a moving and absorbing novel about the dilemmas and crises faced by diasporic Indian families as they adjust and adapt to constantly changing circumstances. [FD'S]

Difficult Daughters
(Manju Kapur, 1998)

The search for individual identity is intertwined with the search for national identities in this sensitive novel by Manju Kapur. Straddling Lahore and Amritsar, two neighbouring towns which complemented each other till the Partition tore them apart, this is the tale of three generations of women struggling to comprehend and shape their own lives—the prodigiously fertile Kasturi whose energies are consumed by the trauma of successive childbirth; her expatriate divorcee granddaughter and Virmati, the protagonist who links the two as daughter to one and mother to another. Virmati's death paradoxically initiates her daughter's exploration of the past to 'communicate' with and thereby exorcise her mother. Forced into 'mothering' her siblings because of Kasturi's interminable pregnancies, Virmati's suppressed desire to rebel and reach for her own sky finds an outlet through an all-consuming passion for the much-married Professor, a family tenant. Released from the shackles of home, Virmati's new life revolves round her studies and the Professor, in short the grooming of a new Virmati. The process both releases and binds her, as against the backdrop of the imminent Partition of the country, her own life is partitioned and realigned. Her married life with the Professor likewise entails humiliation, grit and occasional happiness. Kapur's impartial, de-glamorised, realistic yet sensitised narration illustrates how women's quest for independence is an unheroic journey of pain, isolation and even selfishness and can only be partially successful in a patriarchal world. [SC]

English, August: An Indian Story
(Upamanyu Chatterjee, 1988)

Catering to a Western audience with a glossary of Indian terms appended to it, *English August* is the story of Agastya Sen (anglicised as 'August'), the son of a Governor of Bengal, uprooted from the elite, jet-set society of the metropolis and sent to the backwaters of Madna as a young IAS trainee. Linguistic, cultural and social barriers, which Agastya makes little effort to transcend, turn him into a pot-smoking, masturbating recluse, shut off in his Rest House room and yearning for release from boredom. Nothing in the ugly but thriving Madna interests Agastya—the local community, the corrupt officials, their heavily decked gossip-mongering wives, their unendearing brats. A semblance of communication is struck up only with those who do not belong—the perpetually inebriated singer-engineer Shankar, the cartoonist Sathe basking in the wealth of his hotelier family, Gandhi who has his hands severed by the tribals because of his illicit relationship with one of their 'loose' women, and even the consciously Americanised Bhatia, whom he had completely ignored in college. Their common bond is their utter contempt for the unsophisticated, uncivilised humdrum existence of Madna and its surroundings and an abiding sense of their own innate superiority. Seen through the cynical, disinterested eyes of the self-obsessed Agastya, the hinterland of India becomes shorn of beauty, variety and ultimately humanity. The saving grace of this well written novel is the equally unrelenting portrayal of Agastya—a self-obsessed, spoilt, rich boy insensitive to everything except his own ennui. [SC]

English Teacher, The
(R.K. Narayan, 1945)

The novel focuses on Krishna, a young lecturer at the Albert Mission College in Malgudi. He is dissatisfied with his work, seeing that he is merely doing what is expected of him by running hordes of pupils through a less than satisfactory encounter with English writers such as Shakespeare and Milton. His disaffection at work transfers seeps into other aspects of his life, and he faces the truth that he is living in a void. He does have a wife and a baby daughter, but they live removed from him, in the village—until Krishna receives a letter from his father urging him to locate a house, set up a home, and prepare to live together as a family. Krishna throws himself into the hunt for a house, then into the preparations. Narayan thus emphasizes the growth of Krishna's love for his wife (by arranged marriage), Susila, and their daughter, and illustrates the way in which love and family grow to fill the emptiness seen in Krishna at the beginning of the novel.

The novel takes a sharp turn when Susila contracts typhoid, her health steadily fails, she slips into a coma, and dies. Her courage and Krishna's desperation are vividly depicted, as are her funeral preparations and public burning. Following Susila's death, the novel traces Krishna's dedication to his daughter, as well as his efforts to establish contact with his wife's spirit. Through the efforts of a medium, Susila's presence becomes more and more pronounced, and in the end Krishna experiences a (short-lived) fusion with her personality that leaves him satisfied. [GK]

Equal Music, An (Vikram Seth, 1996)

Michael Horne is a youngish musician living in London who is second violin in the Maggiore String Quartet. Ten years earlier, when studying in Vienna, he had had an intense love affair with a pianist whom he had abruptly left in a moment of crisis. One day he seems to recognize his former lover on a bus unfortunately going in the opposite direction. At this point a frantic search for her begins as does another for the score and a recording of Beethoven string quintet in C minor, Opus 104, Virginia, a friend of his, has mentioned to him. After a successful concert he actually meets Julia again and begins to see her fairly regularly. He soon finds out that she is married, that she has a son but also that she is going deaf. In the midst of his renewed love affair with Julia, they fly to Vienna to give a concert at the famous *Musikverein*. At the last minute Julia agrees to play with them as she has been asked to replace the original pianist who has fallen sick. After the concert during which Michael had unexpectedly been unable to continue playing and manages to go thanks to his lover's help, they all go to Venice where the couple enjoys some beautiful hours in the magic atmosphere of the city. But after a painful scene in San Giorgio degli Schiavoni church, Julia decides to go back to her family. Michael, having read Julia's tender letter to her husband, attacks her violently both physically and verbally. Back in London he withdraws from the quartet. It is only after hearing her playing a piece of Bach's 'Art of the Fugue' at a concert that he realizes that more important than anything else is music, music which can transcend all human understanding. [AFG]

Family Matters
(Rohinton Mistry, 2002)

Set in Bombay in recent years, the story deals with the problems concerning the caring of an elderly father in two branches of a Parsi family. 79-year-old Nariman Vakeel, who suffers from Parkinson's disease, lives with his stepson and stepdaughter, both single and in their forties. Living together is very difficult, because the young people cannot forget how Nariman neglected their mother for the sake of a former lover. Actually, Nariman's marriage was an arranged one: compelled by his parents to break his long lasting affair with a Christian woman, he had accepted to marry a Parsi widow with two children. Of the marriage a baby daughter, Roxana, was born. After his wife's death in tragic circumstances which will be revealed only at the end of the book, and his daughter's marriage, he had been left alone with the two stepchildren. When Nariman breaks his ankle accidentally, he is moved to Roxana's. Here he has to share a two-room flat with her, her husband Yezad and two children. Yezad's meagre salary is not enough to satisfy the demands of a bedridden old man, and Roxana's physical and mental health is badly affected by the hard work. Yet Nariman's stepdaughter refuses to take her stepfather back, taking this situation as an opportunity to take revenge for how her mother was treated. Only after her accidental death, can Nariman go back to his own large apartment, this time together with Roxana's family. But it is already too late: Yezad, who looked for comfort in religion, has become a Parsi fundementalist. His children resent the change of environment, and Nariman dies soon afterwards. [SA]

Fasting, Feasting
(Anita Desai, 1999)

The novel has two parts; the first section focuses on the story of Uma, the eldest daughter in a middle class family who has been backward in studies, average in looks, suffers from epileptic fits and though married, has no marriage "to show." Her younger sister Aruna, on the other hand, is smart, intelligent and beautiful and gets the kind of partner she aspired for. Arun, a late arrival in the family, and the much-longed-for son, is watched over by father and mother and given no moment to spare till he passes all the entrance examinations and goes to America for higher studies. Uma has to toil for the parents and put up with their tantrums and is never allowed a moment of privacy for herself. Mira masi, an aunt who has chosen a spiritual way of life wanders from one holy place to another and considers Uma too as the beloved of God.

The second section focuses on Arun's plight in America where his father finds a home to stay as paying guest and the hostess Mrs. Patton feeds Arun raw vegetables which she thinks is the diet of vegetarians. The loose family ties at the Pattons' shock and dismay Arun. Mrs. Patton's over solicitousness becomes embarrassing to him and as soon as the holidays end, he leaves the home after presenting to her the packet of tea and the woollen shawl his parents had sent for him. [DM]

Financial Expert, The
(R.K. Narayan, 1952)

A sort of King Midas tale (that is, a tale of "be careful, or you just might get what you wished for"), the novel centres on the character of Margayya, a man of high ambition and limited imagination or skill whose great obsession in life is the possible accumulation of money and whose firm belief is that money is the principal, almost mystical power in life. As the novel opens, Margayya is engaged in his meager business of lending money to and assisting clients—chiefly poor, illiterate villagers—to secure loans from the Cooperative Bank, for a percentage of the received loan; Margayya's "office" is beneath a banyan tree, directly opposite the bank, and he operates entirely out of a small, easily transportable trunk. Desperately anxious to improve his own very shaky financial situation, he visits a temple priest hoping for some guidance. The priest encourages him to undertake a forty day puja dedicated to the goddess Lakshmi. Just when Margayya is beginning to suspect he has been hoodwinked by the priest—and as his business has certainly not improved during his extended absence—he is approached by a "sociologist" named Dr. Pal who extends to Margayya the opportunity to buy from him and publish a book he has written for the general social welfare. The text, "Bed-Life, or the Science of Marital Happiness," is a *Kama Sutra*-like text focused on specific techniques of sex. Margayya spends what little he has and then proceeds with publication, sharing profits with the printer, the book appearing under the safer title *Domestic Harmony*.

Margayya begins to make a considerable sum of money rather quickly, although he becomes concerned about stagnating sales and, to a lesser extent, the possible stain on his family name and the impact this may have on his son, Balu. Eventually Margayya sells his publishing rights to his partner, the publisher, and uses his accumulated wealth as investment to further his private "banking" interests, with Dr. Pal acting as an agent. As his wealth continues to swell, his difficulties with his son, whom he has largely neglected, simultaneously increase. As rooms in Margayya's home fill with cash, his health declines and his relationship with Balu deteriorates further to a critical point (due also to Dr. Pal's insidious involvement with Balu). In a moment of righteous rage, Margayya assaults Pal and violently confronts Balu—and this becomes the incident that precipitates the sudden, dramatic end of Margayya's fortune. Investors withdraw their money, Margayya declares legal insolvency, and events return to their starting point, with Margayya clinging to his newborn grandson, then deciding to take up his trunk again and return to the banyan tree across from the Cooperative Bank. [GK]

Fine Balance, A
(Rohinton Mistry, 1995)

Set in India in 1975, in an unnamed city by the sea, during Indira Gandhi's State of Emergency, the novel is the story of four people: a young widow called Dina, two tailors who help her in her sewing shop and a student renting a room in her apartment. In the first 250 pages, we learn about the previous lives of the four characters. In Dina's family a tyrannical brother dominated the household after the death of her father and consequently her mother suffered mental illness. A widow after only three years of marriage, Dina strives to be independent, in order not to go back to her brother's house, where she is treated like a servant. The two tailors, Ishvar and Omprakash, had their dwellings burned down by the government because of their attempt to rise out of their caste; the student, Manek, comes from a difficult family situation. Starting from reciprocal diffidence, the four characters learn friendship and compassion among every possible hardships. They will keep on going despite the tragedies happening in their lives and in the lives of their friends. Forced vasectomies, amputations, loss of work and dwelling are among the misfortunes which befall them, while around them their acquaintances are tortured by the police, commit suicide out of sheer hopelessness, are hanged to the branches of the tree and so on. Mistry follows the destinies of all these outcasts and underdogs until the assassination of Indira Gandhi in 1984. [SA]

Fire on the Mountain
(Anita Desai, 1977)

Fire on the Mountain tells the story of three lonely beings, trapped in their own islands of loneliness. Nanda Kaul, the Vice Chancellor's wife has chosen the house on top of a mountain in Carignano in the village of Kasauli, as her shelter away from the disturbances of family and society. Life with the Vice Chancellor who always loved the Mathematics Professor, had been a long ordeal with only the duties and responsibilities of her position without any love attached to it. Now that the Vice chancellor was dead and the daughters settled, she preferred to live like a recluse without any disturbance from anywhere. Then comes a letter announcing the arrival of her great granddaughter Raka. Though she resents this intrusion into her private world, there is no time to prevent her arrival. Raka turns out to be more of a lonely being than her great grandmother and has an instinctive abhorrence for human company. The third woman Ila Das is a village social worker and a childhood friend of Nanda Kaul. She is invited for tea at Nanda Kaul's and she speaks of the hostility of the villagers towards family planning and prevention of child marriage. The novel ends as Nanda Kaul collapses on receiving the news that on her way back home Ila Das has been raped and murdered. Raka comes to the window to announce to her grandmother that she has set fire to the mountain. [DM]

Foreigner, The
(Arun Joshi, 1968)

Sindi, born in Kenya and an orphan at the age of four, has spent some years in the U.K. before moving to the U.S. and receiving a degree in engineering. Here he meets June Blyght, a pretty and good-hearted American girl, and they soon get engaged. Their affair is seriously threatened by the behaviour of Sindi, who seeks total detachment from all bonds. As a consequence, June gradually shifts to Sindi's friend Babu Khemka, another Indian student who seems to be much more insecure and in need of all the sincere affection spontaneously pouring out of her. June's generosity proves vain with him too, and, shortly before her marriage to Babu, she realizes how wrong this move could be. A flirtation she has with Sindi enrages Babu who leaves home and dies in a car crash. June dies too, while trying to abort Babu's child. Sindi decides to go to India.

In Delhi Sindi meets Babu's father and sister Sheila who are affectionately drawn to him. Mr Khemka, an affluent and unscrupulous industrialist, employs him in his office, while Sheila frequently asks him about her brother. Shortly afterwards, Mr Khemka's corrupt economical empire crumbles under police inspection and Sindi is irritated on discovering his boss's shady manoeuvring. While Mr. Khemka is doomed to end up in jail, Sindi finally opts for involvement and tries to save his boss's financial empire from bankruptcy to stop many people losing their jobs. In the final scene, he has tea with Sheila who has become increasingly fond of him. [PPP]

From Fear Set Free
(Nayantara Sahgal, 1962)

From Fear Set Free is Sahgal's second autobiographical work and covers the decade of the fifties. It can be read as a work about value formation and the struggle for independent womanhood as it explores the meaning of freedom for the personhood of women.

It also offers an account of her whirlwind courtship and later the romantic marriage to Gautam Sahgal, the birth of two of her children, one in America where her mother was India's ambassador and the other in Allahabad in Indian conditions, her life in Bombay, Kanpur and Delhi and her experiences of setting up home in the multi-cultural, multilingual society of India.

The account of the political life of the young democracy, the growing disillusionment with idealism, the struggle to sustain values, is interspersed with a sensitive and often humorous depiction of human relationships. The work pays homage to the idea of "nirbhaya" to be without fear and extends the meaning of political freedom to personal categories.

Together with her earlier memoir, this details her family history and provides an insight into the Nehru family history, her own parents' marriage, Indira Gandhi's marriage, and the challenges that the newly independent country faced. There is also a strong undercurrent of Gandhian thought. Told with a sense of wit and irony, it presents a wealth of social history of the fifties and the cultural changes which were rapidly taking place with the anglicised India claiming its share of power. [JJ]

From Heaven Lake. Travels through Sinkiang and Tibet
(Vikram Seth, 1983)

The book is a travelogue based on notes and photographs Seth took on a trip from Beijing to his home in Delhi using a rather unusual means of transport, that is hitchhiking. Getting lifts in trucks of various description he meets a number of interesting people from different walks of life. As he speaks Chinese he is able to communicate with them and get a close view of their difficulties and problems. He travels through the desert region of Sinkiang, and the eastern part of Tibet until he reaches Lhasa. From the capital, where he admires the fascinating historical buildings which had survived the ravages of the Chinese occupation and the harrowing experiences of the Cultural Revolution, he goes through more familiar Nepal, stopping over in Kathmandu, where he rests for a couple of days, before reaching his final destination. [AFG]

Fury
(Salman Rushdie, 2001)

Malik Solanka, a Cambridge professor famous for having designed the dolls that perform in a British television series about famous philosophers and scientists, has abandoned his wife and son and fled to New York. He is afraid ever since he found himself standing above his sleeping wife and child with a knife. The fury within himself is also found in the great city, where it rages beneath every surface. No one anywhere is satisfied. Solanka suspects that he himself may be responsible for the brutal murders of wealthy and beautiful women that shock the city, but it turns out that their rich boyfriends are killing them. The modern fury also has worldwide repercussions in the murderous wars being fought everywhere on the global periphery, notably in Lilliput-Blefescu, an island country resembling Fiji. Solanka's life is defined by three women he loves or has loved who represent the three Furies of Greek mythology: Eleanor, his second wife and the mother of his beloved son; Mila, who helps him establish a new creative brainchild, an imaginary world in several dimensions on the internet; and Neela, the most beautiful woman in the world, committed to revolution on Lilliput-Blefescu. Solanka is haunted by his childhood at Methwold's Estate, in Bombay, where, we eventually learn, he was sexually abused by his stepfather. That is the origin of his own personal fury. At the end Solanka is once again without a woman to love but at least he makes a claim on his son Asmaan. [NTK]

Gauri (or, The Old Woman and the Cow)
(Mulk Raj Anand, 1960)

Panchi, the protagonist goes to Piplan Kalan village and marries Gauri who is gentle like a cow. Gauri's stepmother Laxmi asks her to be like Sita in her husband's home. After the marriage Panchi continues to stay with his guardians like uncle Mola Ram and aunt Kesaro. But Kesaro, because of her deep attachment to Panchi, tries to brainwash him against Gauri and makes him believe that Gauri is a bringer of ill luck, famine, drought and poverty. Taking the role of a ruthless mother-in-law, Kesaro continues her hate campaign against Gauri and maligns her in so many ways.

Panchi and Gauri start living under the care of a potter of the village and a Muslim friend Rafique Chacha. Panchi and Gauri come closer. But their harmonious relationship is spoilt by Kesaro who poisons Panchi's mind by highlighting the evil stars in her horoscope and by falsely accusing her of adulterous relationship with Rajguru. Suspecting his wife's chastity, Panchi kicks Gauri out of his home.

Gauri returns to her parents' home sadly and helplessly. But her uncle Amru takes her to Hoshiarpur and sells her as a wife to the aged Seth Jai Ram Das. She refuses to have sex with Jai Ram Das. When she has acute fever Jai Ram Das brings Doctor Mahindra to treat her. She is then, admitted into Dr. Mahindra's hospital for treatment. After she recovers from fever, she refuses to go to Seth Jai Ram Das's home; and wishes to be restored to her first husband, Panchi.

In the meanwhile Panchi realizes his folly and returns to Piplan Kalan to take back his wife. When he learns that Gauri is not at her parents' home, he takes Laxmi and Amru to task. Laxmi grows nervous and goes to Hoshiarpur along with Adam Singh. They trace Gauri in Dr. Mahindra's Hospital and bring her back. Thus Panchi and Gauri are reunited and happy.

But their happiness does not last long. Kesaro, Rakhi and the villagers indulge in gossip about Gauri and refer to her as a prostitute from Hoshiarpur. Again Panchi's mind is filled with suspicion and he begins to ask her to confess her 'sin.' But Gauri who is chaste refuses to convince the brainless husband and walks towards Dr. Mahindra's Hospital to lead an independent life. [BN]

Glass Palace, The (Amitav Ghosh, 2000)

The novel covers a long period of time, from the end of the 19th century, when the last Burmese king was defeated and exiled by the British, to the late 90's when Burma, now called Myanmar, became independent but was suffering under a military dictatorship which had put Aung San Sui Kyi under house arrest. It is a family saga involving three generations of Indian and Burmese families, living through a century of portentous events. Rajakumar is a poor Indian orphan from Chittagong who ends up in Mandalay. Not only does he survive but also, through strong will power and sheer capability, manages to become a rich man trading in teak, and to marry the girl he has been in love with since boyhood, Dolly, a trustworthy maid of former queen Supayalat. In his successful career he has been greatly helped by Saya John, a contractor from Malacca, brought up by Catholic priests but now living in Burma. The close relationship between these two men is further cemented by the next generation. Rajakumar has two sons, Neel and Dinu; Saya John is the father of Matthew who, back in Burma, starts a rubber plantation with his American wife, Elsa, by whom he has two children, Alison and Timmy. Another important character in the story is the Indian Collector in Ratnagiri; his wife Uma has one nephew, Arjun, and two nieces, Manju and Bela. Manju will marry Neel, live in Rangoon and give birth to a child, Yaya, who after the deaths of her parents during the Japanese occupation, will be brought up in India by Uma's family. Arjun, an officer in the Indian army, will eventually join the INA and fight against the Japanese, before being shot at the end of the war. There are many deaths in the novel as well as many political changes: the old generation eventually disappears; the Indian Collector, left by his wife, commits suicide; Alison, while trying to escape from the Japanese forces, kills herself. Countries which were part of the British Empire become independent, while great changes occur in their economic set-up. Among the people whose stories are told in the book only Dinu and Yaya survive, the first active in his Glass Palace photographic studio in Rangoon, the second a mature lady who at a certain point in her life starts "to write this book—the book my mother never wrote." [AFG]

God of the Small Things, The (Arundhati Roy, 1997)

In the year 1967, fraternal twins Rahel and Esthappen experience a series of tragedies that will forever scar their lives, tragedies that are inaugurated by the family's reaction to their mother's brief, passionate affair with an untouchable man. Years later, Rahel returns from a failed marriage in America to her ancestral home in Ayemenem, hoping to reunite with her shattered brother and find a way to deal with their horrific past. Roy sets her story in her home province of Kerala, a region in the south of India where Christianity and Communism co-exist with much more deeply ingrained values and social customs and practices. Using Gothic techniques and an intricate structure that belies her ingenue status, Roy gradually reveals, mainly through the eyes of the seven-year-old twins, the events leading up to the tragedy. At the same time, she exposes the corruption, hypocrisy, and inadequacy of the adult society around them. In the end, the novel condemns society's treatment of those who break its "love laws" and celebrates the passion for which so many innocent people were made to suffer. The novel, which won the Booker Prize in 1997, is characterized by Roy's playful use of language in representing the speech and thoughts of children, its use of a wide range of allusions to both Eastern and Western cultural texts, and its frank approach to sexuality. [NB]

Golden Honeycomb, The (Kamala Markandaya, 1977)

The Golden Honeycomb is a historical novel in which Kamala Markandaya concerns herself with the fate of princely India; she recasts the life of the palace, the intrigues within, the British attitude without, the national awakening and its impact on the princely states and the final triumph when India attained independence. The story is set in the State of Devapur and deals with the saga of almost a hundred years of Bawaji Raj family.

Bawaji I, the people's king of Devapur is deposed for his nationalist allegiance. In 1870, Bawajiraj II, and later Bawaji III become the kings. But both remain puppets into the British hands. Bawajiraj III is given the best of English education to ensure that he becomes the mouthpiece of the colonial powers. As a ruler, he proves ineffective, and devoid of pride and is contemptuously called an "expensive cipher" by his people. Bawajiraj's son Rabi, born of his mistress Mohini is a contrast to his father; he has a high sense of self-esteem and national pride. During the Delhi Darbar, young Rabi feels humiliated on seeing the abject servility of his father bowing before the Viceroy. Rabi experiences the affection of the common man when he is injured during a mill-workers' strike in Bombay and is looked after by Jaya, a mill-worker. Resentment spreads in Devapur when Bawaji III raises an army to fight for the British during World War II. Winds of change blow with the national awakening and the Maharaja realizes that the state is no longer his domain, and that Mohini, Usha and in fact all his people are with the masses. The moment of triumph comes when India attains Independence. [UB]

***Golden Gate, The. A Novel in Verse* (Vikram Seth, 1986)**

The narration revolves around a group of typical Californian professional people. John, the main character, is going through a difficult period. He is sitting alone in his apartment on a Friday night, when everybody is supposed to enjoy himself in good company. Following the advice of Janet, a former lover of his, he puts an ad in the local paper in order to find a possible companion. After several negative experiences with women he cannot connect with, he believes he has found the right person in Liz Dorati, a brilliant lawyer. His friend Phil is also having a difficult time: having resigned for moral reasons from a well-paid job, he lives alone with his son Paul, as his wife has left him and moved to New York. Liz and John decide to throw a party and invite various friends including Phil who, having had too much to drink, finds himself in bed with Ed, Liz's brother, a Catholic homosexual. In spite of the problems caused by Liz's cat resenting the presence of a man in the house, things seem to be proceeding well between her and John and they are thinking of settling down and buying a house. But the situation explodes during the Thanksgiving celebrations when John finds and reads a letter to Liz written by Phil, who had been briefly arrested during a pacifist demonstration. Seeing the growing friendship between Liz and his friend, in an outburst of jealousy John leaves Liz. At this point Phil and Liz quite unexpectedly decide to marry. John is dejected and starts going with prostitutes but it is a frustrating experience. Having met his old friend Janet again he becomes her lover, in what he thinks is only a casual relationship. Only when she dies tragically in a car crash does he realize the depth of his commitment to her. Full of regret for what he had not been able to tell her, John is prostrated by grief: haunted by his memory of Janet, he finds the will to survive when asked to be the godfather of Liz's and Phil's child, a tangible proof of life continuing, after the deaths of both Janet and her friends, the Lamonts. [AFG]

***Great Indian Novel, The* (Shashi Tharoor, 1989)**

Shashi Tharoor's first novel, *The Great Indian Novel*, is divided into eighteen books, many of them with titles that display the intertextuality of the book: titles like 'Midnight's Parents' and 'A Raj Quartet.' The novel itself presents a modern rewriting of the ancient Indian epic, *The Mahabharata* (literally 'Great India'), which is turned into a parable of modern India. The book is dictated by the cantankerous old politician, Ved Vyas, to Ganapathi, the scribe. It narrates the story of the fight for independence of Hastinapur, led by the saintly and shrewd Mahaguru Gangaji (Mahatma Gandhi), his famous Mango March (Salt March) and "the birth of Indian democracy as the result of the passionate coupling of a blind Nationalist [Jawaharlal Nehru] and a British Vicereine [Lady Mountbatten]." Other crucial characters are Karna (Md. Ali Jinnah), the Muslim leader who calls for and achieves the partition of the country, and Pandu the Pale (Subhash Chandra Bose), who seeks Japanese support to liberate India. This phase of intricate family politics leads on to the post-independence fight for position between the Pandavas and Duryodhani (Indira Gandhi), the only 'Kaurava' who makes it into *The Great Indian Novel* from the pages of *The Mahabharata* where Duryodhan had 99 brothers. Written with much panache and humour, which however stops short of satire, the book (combining lucid prose with public school-type light verse) is not only an important first novel but a significant landmark of 20th century Indian English fiction. [TK]

Grimus
(Salman Rushdie, 1975)

The young American Indian, Flapping Eagle, having drunk an elixir that confers longevity, spends 777 years crossing oceans in search of his sister Bird-Dog, who has been kidnapped by Grimus, and in order to find an antidote to agelessness. The demonic figure Nicholas Deggle shows him how to drown and thus to enter a new dimension, that of Calf Mountain, which is Grimus's home. Deggle schemes to use the young man to carry out his revenge against Grimus who had banished him for trying to break the Stone Rose, the source of his power. Grimus denies the plurality of dimensions and insists, falsely, on a single one. His name is an allusion to the Simurg, the king of the birds who lives on Kaf Mountain in the *Conference of the Birds*, a twelfth-century religious poem by the Sufi mystic Farid ud-Din 'Attar.' The Simurg is a symbol of mystic unity: thirty birds successfully make the journey to find him and his name means "thirty birds." Virgil Jones, who has no desire for Grimus's power himself, serves as Eagle's guide up the mountain. Halfway up Calf Mountain, the people of the town of K come under the baleful influence of the Stone Rose, but are able to survive by steadfastly denying that Grimus even exists. Flapping Eagle is tempted to join them, but his presence introduces an element of instability that leads to his ostracism, and he must continue his journey. This actually fits in with Grimus's intentions for he longs to die and wants Flapping Eagle, his double, to be his successor and thus to preserve his power. In the course of their struggle, Grimus and Flapping Eagle are so subsumed into each other that they become indistinguishable. In the end, however, Eagle refuses to take over Grimus's tyrannical spiritual machinery, Grimus is destroyed, and Eagle and his lover, the prostitute Media, escape Grimus's dimension by making love. [NTK]

Ground Beneath Her Feet, The (Salman Rushdie, 1999)

Rai Merchant, born in Bombay the same year as the author, narrates the story of Ormus Cama and Vina Apsara, his rock musician friends who, in a universe parallel to the familiar one described by history, made it big in the West as part of the Indian invasion of popular music in the early seventies. Vina was born Nissa Shetty in America, of a Greek-American mother and an Indian father, but raised by relatives in Bombay. Ormus is the son of Sir Darius Xerxes Cama, a Parsi anglophile, and the stepson of Sir William Methwold. Ormus hears in his head all the classics of rock music before they make it to the radio. Eventually, he moves to England and is able to use his peculiar instinct for the spirit of the times to write his own songs. He and Vina form the immensely successful rock band VTO. America, the home of rock and roll, is the inevitable destination of all three friends, Ormus, Vina, and Rai, now a famous news photographer. Both Rai and Ormus are both hopelessly in love with Vina. She dies in an earthquake in Guadalajara, Mexico, on Valentine's Day 1989. Earthquakes are the faultlines dividing the world of the novel from other worlds, notably the worlds of history (the world of readers) and of myth (the source of creative energy and imagination). After her death Vina is worshipped around the globe as a goddess, more loved even than Princess Di. Ormus, like a later-day Orpheus, thinks that, through the power of his love and his music, he has brought Vina back from the dead in the figure of Mira Celano. He loses Mira, and is murdered himself. [NTK]

Guide, The (R.K. Narayan, 1958)

Using a narrative strategy of juxtaposing passages of flashback against passages set in the present, Narayan tells the story of Raju who, as a boy, did his best to avoid studies and spend his time helping his father to sell sweets at their small shop alongside the new railway in Malgudi. During his spare time in his father's shop, Raju reads the scraps of newspaper used to line shelves and wrap items, and from these—as well as from the talk of the many people along the platform—he gains his true education. When Raju is asked questions about some of the local sites by tourists arriving in Malgudi by train, he feels compelled to answer them; sometimes his answers are accurate, sometimes not, but what matters most to him is the apparent need to satisfy their curiosity. The next logical step for him is to take tourists to some of the local sites himself, and in this way Railway Raju (as he comes to be known) establishes his reputation as a guide. People ask for him when they arrive, his reputation growing over time.

The narrative takes a decisive turn when a man named Marco and his wife, Rosie, arrive in Malgudi. Marco is a scholar interested in the paintings in local caves, while Rosie privately asks Raju to take her somewhere she can see a snake charmer. As Rosie watches the charmed cobra, she emulates its movements in dance, and Raju sees at once that she is a skilled dancer. Although Rosie is estranged from her husband and he refuses to allow her to dance, Raju is able to encourage her commitment to classical dance, satisfied to do nothing but watch her practice, and wins her over as his lover. Soon he becomes Rosie's (now known as Nalini) manager, organizing tours for her, and becoming wealthy from her fame. Raju eventually lands in jail after forging Rosie's signature, and he loses a tired and disaffected Rosie/ Nalini in the process.

When he emerges from prison, Raju takes refuge in an abandoned shrine, where he is mistaken as a holy man by the local rustics. Consistent with his character, he simply adapts to the role in which he finds himself, staying put primarily because food comes to him without effort. Before long, Raju is forced into a fast, however, through confused circumstances, and in the process of apparently attempting to end a feud between villages and, then, to end the terrible drought, Raju experiences a significant change in character. The novel ends ambiguously, and the reader cannot be certain whether Raju dies and whether rain actually comes to the village. [GK]

Handful of Rice, A
(Kamala Markandaya, 1966)

A Handful of Rice is based on the theme of hunger and poverty, exodus from the villages to the towns and a search for identity that is lost forever in the impersonal atmosphere of the cities. It recounts the story of a young man Ravi who leaves his native village and suffers in the city; but at a broader level it is the sad account of all those innocent villagers who fall into the trap of criminals and undeserving underground dons and are initiated into the world of crime.

The protagonist, Ravi, leaves his village in the hope of getting some employment in the city. There he comes into contact with Damodar, a criminal, under whose direction he starts stealing. Once, while escaping a chasing policeman, he lands into the household of a tailor. He is detected, beaten and admonished. Next day, he comes back to fix the window bars he had displaced the other night. His good heartedness captivates Apu, who offers him a job as an apprentice to him. Ravi accepts it just because it would give him an opportunity to be near Apu's young daughter, Nalini. After a brief courting, he marries Nalini. Day to day life becomes difficult for Ravi and his growing family. The irony is that while he struggles with want and poverty, Damodar flourishes by corrupt means. Ravi is pained to see how Apu's value system and code of conduct is meaningless in a world of greed, dishonesty, and black-marketing. Burdened with further responsibilities after Apu's death, he goes to Damodar for help who rejects him as a "gutless" fellow. In desperation Ravi joins the rioting mob but he cannot loot even a 'handful of rice' as his personal values do not allow him to take to lawless means. [UB]

Haroun and the Sea of Stories (Salman Rushdie, 1990)

The great story-teller, Rashid Khalifa, also known as the "Ocean of Notions" and the "Shah of Blah," has lost his story-telling powers, and his son Haroun must get them back. Butt the hoopoe leads Haroun to his journey's end on a moon called Kahina, where he meets Walrus, ruler of Gup and controller of the Sea of Stories. The people of Gup are at war with Chub and its wicked ruler Khattam-Shud, who is poisoning the Ocean of the Streams of Story with his factory-ship because stories represent a world he cannot control. Haroun and his allies win the day, release the Sea of Stories, and restore his father's story-telling abilities. Haroun's mother who has run away with a neighbour at the beginning of the story is reconciled to his father at the end. [NTK]

Holder of the World, The (Bharati Mukherjee, 1993)

In this expertly constructed novel made up of four parts, the first-person narrator, Beigh Masters, is an assets researcher, born in New England in 1950. Her narrative has two threads, one about her own 20th century research and stumblings on traces of a distant female relative from the 17th century, and the second, about the adventures of this seventeenth-century character, Hannah Easton (1670-1750). The text is set in New England at first, then in England with Hannah's adventurer husband Gabriel Legge, in Southern India where Gabriel Legge operates as a mercenary freebooter dealing with Indian merchants and officials of the English East India Company, then between the camps of a rebellious Hindu Raja and the all-powerful Emperor Aurangzeb, while the widowed Hannah undergoes many adventures, and finally back in New England where she is reunited with her mother Rebecca Easton, a few years after the ruthless Salem witches' trial.

A heart-rending love affair between the rebellious Hindu Raja and the New England Salem Bibi results in the birth of a black-eyed, black-haired daughter named Pearl Singh, born "somewhere in the South Atlantic" during the Salem Bibi's long voyage home in 1701. The title, *The Holder of the World*, is perhaps ironic since it refers to an ornamental symbol of power Aurangzeb had suspended over his throne: a golden globe with a lion nuzzling a lamb on one side of it, crowned with a large diamond known as the Emperor's Tear, the whole contained within a golden replica of Aurangzeb's hands.

Mukherjee's tale deliberately belies the pretentious claim that anyone power can ever completely seize control over all the empires in the world. [FD'S]

I Shall Not Hear the Nightingale
(Khushwant Singh, 1959)

The events described in this novel relate to 1942-1943, the years during the Second War and just before the Indian Independence, focusing on a Sikh family in Punjab. Bhuta Singh, the District Magistrate, as a member of the old guard, is a very obedient servant of the British Government. He misses no chance to show his loyalty to the British and is also proud of it. His young son, Sher Singh, however, is opposed to the British rule and wants to oust them from India. With that objective, he has formed a revolutionary group of young boys, whose bravado does not pitiably match their wisdom. The Deputy Commissioner, John Taylor, learns about their misadventures through informers and waits for chance to take action.

Buta Singh's wife Sabhrai is highly religious and loves her son, Sher and daughter, Beena, yet runs her family on strict discipline. Beena is attracted towards her friend Seetha's brother, Madan Lal, the cricket hero and a member of Sher's rebel group. Sher is not interested in sex, driving his young wife Champak to fantasies and extra-marital sex when she happens to be together with the unscrupulous Madan Lal in Simla. Buta Singh is ignorant of his son's treasonous activities and is shocked to learn that Sher has caused the death of an informer. Under the Deputy Commissioner's instructions, the police arrest his son and keep him under custody to find out, by coercion and threat, about the other members of the group. A mortified Buta Singh refuses to help, but Sabhrai prays in the Gurudwara through the night and inspires Sher to be courageous and not betray his comrades. Since no witness could be found, the police have to release Sher Singh, who becomes a hero instantly. A victory procession takes him home; however, his mother is dead and not available to "hear the nightingale anymore." Her death creates more sympathy for Buta in the District Commissioner's mind and Mrs. Taylor offers to raise a monument in memory of his dead wife. [PB]

Ice-Candy-Man
(Bapsi Sidhwa, 1988)

This is the tale of the partition of India told by an outsider Lenny—an eight-year-old Parsee girl with polio residing in Lahore. Her deformity notwithstanding, she lives a more than full life straddling two complementary worlds—her own social circle with parents, younger brother Adi, Grandmother Rodabai, Mini Aunty, Cousin, neighbours *et al* and Ayah and her mixed coterie of admirers identified by their professions rather than their names or various religious allegiances. The adult world around her is viewed through a child's canny shrewdness as she absorbs the happenings around her—Rodabai's constant bullying of Mini, Ayah's deft handling of her suitors, Muccho's inexplicable violence against her daughter Papoo, the Cousin's and her own discovery of her adolescent body. The raucous ribaldry of this fulsome world is rudely shattered by the holocaust of communal violence. The narrative of a torn nation is recounted forcefully through the trauma and bewilderment of personalised experiences. Individual tragedies collectively set up a collage of fragmented India as each one is implicated in partitioning the lives around them. Lenny's parents bicker over the 'other woman,' a drugged Papoo is 'married off' to a cynical dwarf, Ranna's family is betrayed by their trust in their motherland, Lenny's innocent truth unleashes a riotous mob over Ayah, the Ice-candy-man's 'love' for Ayah turns her into a *kothewali* (prostitute) and him into a half-crazed pitiable wretch. Sidhwa's present tense, seriocomic narrative underscores human inability to fathom or direct its own violent energies. [SC]

If I Die Today
(Shashi Deshpande, 1982)

One of Deshpande's early novels, *If I Die Today* is a suspense story which has a hospital as a main setting. One of the doctors employed there has to play host to a friend's brother who is terminally ill. Guru, this patient is an ascetic and a philosopher and invites easy confidences, but as these confessions are made, he is keen that they be made open and truth be faced. He indicates this through casual references and mention of secrets known only to him.

Gradually the early feeling of trust and awe leads to an uneasy feeling of suspicion and fear and guru, who dies in his sleep is actually murdered. Another murder follows close on this, that of Tony who is found dead in shallow water. Everybody suspects everyone else, children are sent away and fear stalks the land. One day the Dean is missing and there is general panic. Then Ashok is attacked as he is walking home with his wife Manju, who is the narrator-observer of the story and whose relationship with her husband is also under stress.

As the mystery deepens, scandals are unearthed, confessions are made and the pieces of the puzzle put together. The murderer is none other than the Dean's unmarried sister, Vidya, who is abnormally possessive about him. This disclosure destroys her emotionally, the Dean resigns and leaves and life slowly comes back to normal in the hospital. [JJ]

In an Antique Land
(Amitav Ghosh, 1986)

The book is based on the author's personal experience when he spent several months in Egypt in the 80's doing research in social anthropology. Intrigued by a casual reference to a slave in a letter to

Abraham Ben Yiju, in Mangalore, published by S.D. Goitein in his collection of medieval documents found in the Geniza of the Ben Ezra synagogue in Cairo, Ghosh decides to pursue the matter, vaguely referred to, finding out more about the slave and his master. Yiju was a Jewish merchant, a member of the international community. Born in Tunisia in the 12th century, he lived in Cairo, Aden and Mangalore in South West India before returning to Cairo where he probably died. By concentrating on the micro-history of a minor figure, Ghosh wishes to highlight the complexity of the Mediterranean medieval world, where Jewish holy men were honoured in Muslim Egypt, documents and letters were written by the Jewish community in colloquial Arabic but in Hebrew characters. By interlocking his vicissitudes among poor Egyptian villagers, (including a final clash with the police), with those of Yiju and his Indian slave Bomma, the writer emphasizes the absurdities of today's rigid border divisions compared to the fluidity of the medieval world where people sometimes could move more freely than today. [AFG]

In Custody
(Anita Desai, 1985)

Deven, the college lecturer is frustrated by the emptiness of his life when he is asked to interview the famous poet Nur. Deven thinks that this is the breakthrough he has been waiting for all along. When he goes to Nur's house, he finds the poet's privacy is invaded by guests, relatives and friends who have kept him in custody. Deven finds it even difficult to tape-record his poems. After severe struggle, he finds to his dismay that there is no clarity in the recorded interview. Meanwhile there is pressure from the college and from the magazine editor for whom he was doing the job. An enlightened Deven returns to the drab reality of his life and to his long-suffering wife Sarla. [DM]

Inside the Haveli
(Rama Mehta, 1977)

While upholding the conventional values of a traditional Indian family, Rama Mehta also chooses to sensitively describe the clash of modernity with conventionality. Married at the tender age of nineteen to Ajay Singh, a teacher at the University, Geeta arrives in Udaipur from the carefree world of Bombay, to face the stifling life behind the 'purdah' in Sangram Singhji's marble haveli. Through the mournings and celebrations, the description of the discriminatory lives in the different segments of the haveli is given: the men's apartments, the 'zenana' or the women's apartments, and the servants' quarters. Though the feudal system has long been abolished, people like Sangram Singhji and his relatives in the other havelis, continue to maintain the system in their homes. Thus when Geeta wants to send Sita, a maid's daughter, to school or when she takes classes for the maids and their children of the other havelis, there is a lot of resentment. Realising the change in time, both Bhagwat Singhji, Geeta's father-in-law, and Ajay Singh, support her in her endeavours. Even though she is furious at first with the idea of her thirteen-year old daughter getting engaged, she eventually comes round and agrees that it is in the child's best interests. In the almost fifteen years of life that is described here, Geeta learns to respect and love the quiet pride, strength and warmth that lies behind the reticent behaviour of her husband and his family. She too eventually earns everybody's love and their respect for her convictions. [NS]

Jasmine
(Bharati Mukherjee, 1989)

Born in a Jat family in rural Hasnapur, in Punjab in 1966, Jyoti is the seventh child in a family of nine. She marries Prakash Vijh at the age of fourteen, after her father, a Lahori landlord forced to relocate to Jullundhar District during the Partition Riots, suddenly dies following upon a brutal attack by a bull. A whole series of further upheavals marks the unfolding of this novel that opens with an epigraph on the new geometry of a tangled universe from James Gleick's *Chaos.*

On being widowed at the age of 16, Jasmine Vijh pursues her deceased husband's goal of migrating to the USA, despite his untimely death in India under the bullets of a Sikh terrorist. All on her own at the age of 17 in this foreign land, she moves from Florida to New York, where she goes from the Indian ghetto in Flushing to the select university neighbourhood of Claremont Avenue. She then decides to shift to Iowa because of fears of crossing the path of Sikh terrorists in New York. In Baden, Iowa, Jasmine meets the banker Bud Ripplemeyer and becomes Jane Ripplemeyer in the American middle West. 18 months later, after having adopted a young Vietnamian refugee named Du, Bud is crippled when he is shot by a local farmer, furious at Bud's bank having refused him a loan. Despite the crisis, Jane Ripplemeyer manages to keep the household together for two years, after which a new set of upheavals puts her on the road again. This time she feels sure (despite the fact that she is expecting Bud's baby), that she has found the great love of her life as she sets out for California with Taylor Hayes and his adopted daughter Duff.

Against a backdrop of tragedies and setbacks, this novel seems to be an optimistic declaration of belief in the unlimited capacity of human beings to constantly reposition the stars of their lot on earth. [FD'S]

Journey to Ithaca
(Anita Desai, 1996)

The Italian Matteo journeys to India on a spiritual quest accompanied by his German wife Sarah who hardly shares her husband's urge for spirituality. The quest leads Matteo from one guru to another and Sarah is exasperated and takes to drugs and becomes sick. Finally Matteo reaches the Mother's ashram and realises that he has found his guru. He dedicates himself to her service to the resentment of Sarah who lives in the quarters with her children and avoids all contact with the mother. With the birth of her second child she leaves for home. When the novel begins, we find Sarah summoned to nurse a sick and emaciated Matteo suffering from hepatitis. Sarah wants to prove to him that the Mother is just an ordinary woman, who was once a dancer and even lived with a man. To collect evidence about the Mother's past, Sarah first goes to Alexandria and then to Paris and back to India, where the Mother (Laila)'s restless quest for God had brought her. It is a transformed Sarah who comes back to the Mother's ashram only to find the Mother dead and a heart-broken Matteo gone to the Himalayas. Sarah's journey has to continue. Ithaca is never reached, but it is the journey itself that matters. [DM]

Kanthapura
(Raja Rao, 1947)

Raja Rao's maiden novel which created a sensation in the early 60's deals with an authentic portrayal of village life as narrated by Achakka, a simple village woman. She recounts "the sad tale of her village," with episode following episode in a breathless way.

Kanthapura which lies in the province of Kara, high on the Ghats, is a small, humble and obscure village, hallowed however by rich local history or *sthala purana* which says that in times past Goddess Kenchamma not merely came down from the heavens to slay a demon that was ravaging the land but even settled down to protect the people. Their implicit faith in this village Goddess is such that all life centres round Her. The village has a complex caste structure and the people of each community carrying on trade customary with their caste are allotted a particular quarter to live in and life goes on at a leisurely pace amidst births, deaths, marriages, festivals and consecration ceremonies. What one encounters in the early stages of the novel is a picture of harmony and community life at its best, for be it a festival or a wedding, the whole village is involved and a sense of kinship established. The village affairs are managed by important people like Patel Range Gowda, a veritable "Tiger" to the villagers and prominent upper caste Hindus like Zamindar Bhatta, the first brahmin of the village. There are also many other notable characters like Rangamma and Waterfall Venkamma and educated boys like Moorthy and Dore who are vividly etched in our minds. But life is not destined to move at this quiet pace for long what with the sudden and dramatic advent of Gandhi and the Freedom Movement which ruffles the calm and placid tempo of life in this back-of-beyond village.

The impact of Gandhi is such that initial criticism and prejudice notwithstanding, more and more villagers overcome by a patriotic fervour respond to his call for *Swaraj* and rally round him making many a sacrifice in the process. Thanks to Moorthy whom the rustics regard as "our Gandhi," the now famous and historic campaigns such as the non-violent non-co-operation movement, the civil disobedience movement and the Salt Satyagraha gather momentum and elicit people's such whole-hearted support that the Freedom Movement becomes a *mass* movement with patriotism filling the air. Pulsating accounts of picketings, lathi charges, imprisonments and police brutalities reconstruct the entire period with a sense of immediacy. The most notable thing is even the simple women-folk of Kanthapura unflinchingly throw in their lot with the political movement as they resolve to fight the Red Man and his sinister designs, at any cost.

The exploitation of the coolies on the Skeffington Coffee Estate by the Red Man's Government with all its attendant horror and ignominy makes the chapter a harrowing tale of violence and brutality. But such their loyalty to a cause and such their devotion to the Mahatma the people of the village rise like one man making endless personal sacrifices in the process. One is not sure, though, what the positive outcome of all this suffering and sacrifice is at the end, when the whole village is deserted and there is "neither man nor mosquito" in Kanthapura. But that the common folk put up such a brave fight at all in the first place and saved their honour and self-respect is the chief redeeming feature of this struggle. In this sense Kanthapura is India in microcosm, because what happens in Kanthapura might have happened anywhere. [RR]

Karma Cola: Marketing the Mystic East

(Gita Mehta, 1993)

Wanting to find the answer to a casual question, Gita Mehta found enough material to write a book about the oft misunderstood term 'karma.' She does a brilliant job of not only tracing the story of the quest for 'karma' but also analysing the marketing of the East as well as the after effects of such interactions that thus take place. The work is a satire on the misconceptions of the West about Indian philosophies, thought and religion. The author mercilessly deals with the naïve westerner in their search for peace or the hypocritical Indian guru who has helped to commodify Hindu religion and philosophy, thus gaining in the bargain. With journalistic precision the author describes the fate that meets undoubting young girls who travel across nations to India in their quest for a 'guru.' The author carefully delineates the long history that ensued in the 60's and the 70's when the first batches of hippies landed on the Indian shore and popularised the 'Hare Rama Hare Krishna' cult. She mentions the influence of this exodus on figures like the Beatles, Hollywood stars and also the lost student. The author also exposes the evil effects that such an interaction between the East and the West has had on Indians. Some of the greatest evils have been the widespread use of drugs and the problems that arise due to large numbers of foreigners taking shelter and misusing the hospitality of poor villagers. [NS]

Lament on the Death of a Master of Arts
(Mulk Raj Anand, 1938)

Nur, the protagonist, is a young man and a tuberculosis-patient. He has passed his Master degree. He is bed-ridden. He has not been able to get a job in spite of being a postgraduate degree holder. He is insulted by his father, relatives and friends. As he has no future, he makes a philosophical search into the past. In the afternoon, his death wish triumphs over his desire to struggle. He lost his mother when he was only five. He dreaded the punishment given by his teachers. His father's insistence that he should say his prayers irritates him. When his grandmother comes and offers him tea and enquires about his condition, he loves her but he dislikes her as she allowed his father (her son) to marry again after his (Nur's) mother's death. Then his old schoolmate, Gama, now a *tanga*-driver visits him. They discuss the uselessness of the modern system of education. Nur tells Gama how his father wants him to apply for admission to all Government services one after another as he places too much reliance on his Master degree. Then Nur's mother-in-law, wife and her aunt visit him and wail and cry. Nur's physician, Captain Pockkanwala, and I.M.S. Officer comes there. He examines Nur and advises him not to excite himself. Nur is alone in his room. Within a short time, his whole form is numbed and he breathes his last. [BN]

Last Labyrinth, The
(Arun Joshi, 1981)

With his father's death, Som Bhaskar, a 25-year-old from Bombay, inherits a fortune, marries Geeta, and becomes the head of a number of companies.

Everything goes smoothly until he meets an impractical businessman from Benares, Aftab Rai, and his woman, Anuradha, a mysterious creature who irresistibly attracts him. The couple lives in a haveli, a labyrinthine building in old Benares which provides the bizarre setting of the novel. Som's pursuit of Anuradha is relentless: the protagonist even starts buying shares in Aftab's company to humiliate his rival. Yet, when Som seems to have definitively won Anuradha, he has a terrible stroke: his doctor K. expects him to die at any moment but he unaccountably survives.

As he recovers, though, Anuradha refuses to meet him again without providing further explanation, and this infuriates Som, determined more than ever to purchase Anuradha's remaining shares of Aftab's company. His search for the lot left takes him to a temple on the mountains where this seems to have ended up: it is here that he finally discovers that Anuradha's shares have been left to the temple's deity. In order to save Som from death at the time of his heart attack, Anuradha had in fact vowed to sacrifice her love for him. He does not accept this mystical explanation and promptly heads for Benares where Anuradha, accompanied by one of Aftab's men, mysteriously vanishes in the labyrinth on her way to a temple. [PPP]

Leave It To Me
(Bharati Mukherjee, 1997)

This novel contains a prologue, followed by three parts, of which the second is the longest, and an epilogue. It is recounted by a first person narrator, Debby di Martino, alias Devi Dee, who is also the protagonist. It is the tale of an adopted child in search of her biological mother and father. The prologue presents a village story-teller in Devigaon, west of Delhi, recounting to wide-eyed children the age-old myth of Devi, the slayer of the Buffalo Demon, usurper of the throne in the kingdom of heavenly beings. This female redresser of cosmic wrongs can be associated with the Greek mythological figure of female vengeance, Electra, who kills her mother and her mother's usurper-lover, in order to safeguard the memory of her murdered father. In the first part of *Leave it to Me,* Debby di Martino takes wing from her foster parents' home in upstate New York, has a love affair with a Chinese-American serial blockbuster maker, Frankie Fong, in Saratoga Springs, and then decides to move west in search of herself, and of her biological parents. The second part is set in San Francisco, California, and presents Debby in her new incarnation as Devi Dee through all her encounters and adventures as she continues her search. Starting with a few sparse details, pieces of the puzzle fall into place quite by chance. Devi meets her Bio-Mum Jess Du Pree, who runs a Media Escort agency with the eponymous name of Leave it to M.E., through a movie producer friend, Ham Cohan, who also becomes her protector. In the third part complex triangles of desire and violence overlap as a mysterious female writer-guru named Ma Varuna emerges, reveals her/himself to be Devi Dee's Bio-Dad and takes the novel to its apocalyptic climax. In the Epilogue, Devi Dee is alone on board the house boat Last Chance in the bay of San Francisco, after a mega-earthquake has struck, cutting the boat free of its moorings, amid flames and sparks. [FD'S]

Love and Longing in Bombay
(Vikram Chandra, 1997)

Love and Longing in Bombay is a collection of five short stories, bound together by a frame narrative in which an elderly man named Subramaniam tells tales to the habitués of the Fisherman's Rest just off Sasoon Dock in Bombay. The stories are re-narrated by one of Subramaniam's auditors, a young computer programmer named Ranjit Sharma.

Ranjit Sharma suffers from some unexplained heartache and is initially suspicious of anything that does not accord with his 'information-age' philosophies. As Subramaniam works his magic, however, Ranjit becomes more receptive and a warmth develops between the two men. The final tale of the collection, 'Shanti' represents the culmination of their friendship, since it is an intimate story of Subramaniam's own youth, told in Subramaniam's flat with Ranjit as the sole audience member.

The first four stories of the collection are genre pieces that challenge the expectations of the reader. 'Dharma' is a ghost story in which the protagonist is haunted by memories of his youth and by the phantom of a limb that he lost in the 1971 war between India and Pakistan; 'Shakti' is a tale of ambition in which a manipulative but likeable heroine conducts 'drawing room warfare' against a rival; 'Kama' is a detective narrative in which the crime is never solved; and 'Artha' is a story of love, work and money—in which a homosexual computer programmer loses his partner to a covert underground organisation. [AT]

Man-Eater of Malgudi, The
(R.K. Narayan, 1961)

Nataraj, a printer in Malgudi, enjoys a solid reputation in the community as a small business operator and also entertains a regular cluster of visitors/loiterers at his shop each day. His rather predictable, mundane existence is disrupted when the huge and blustery Vasu arrives, a dictatorial man of nearly impossible strength (having received special training from a renowned circus strongman) and great bravado. Because of orders he places with Nataraj, the two become more entangled than Nataraj would prefer, and before long Vasu simply moves in to the abandoned upstairs room of Rajan's shop. Vasu is a taxidermist, and he returns almost daily with fresh kills from his hunts in the nearby Mempi Hills. His room becomes his taxidermy studio, and soon the smell of decaying flesh, chemical vats, etc.—not to mention the steady flow of prostitutes and other disreputable women—becomes a neighborhood issue, not just a source of anguish for Rajan who finds himself unable to remove his vile "guest." Before long Vasu suggests that he has plans to shoot a beloved temple elephant during a procession, planning to sell its legs as umbrella stands. Nataraj is convinced that Vasu is a demon and he sees himself as thrust into the role of protector/redeemer, having to intervene and thwart the killing. Suspense mounts as the two men's wills oppose each other, and the novel ends with Vasu inadvertently destroying himself prior to carrying out his planned sacrilege. [GK]

Matter of Time, A (Shashi Deshpande, 1996)

A Matter of Time is a story of three generations, a women-dominated family and a house. The house is 'Vishwas,' Sumi's parental house belonging to her mother's family to which she returns with her three daughters when her husband Gopal walks out on her. Her parents, Shripati and Kalyani live on separate floors having become estranged when their only son, a mentally retarded child had strayed away from the mother during a journey.

Divided into three parts, "The House," "The Family" and "The River," the novel is a fine study of the complexity of human relationships and traces the matrilineal inheritance analysing the different ways in which women have worked for their freedom. While Sumi's mother pleads with Gopal and Sumi's daughter Aru threatens her father with legal action Sumi, herself remains neutral. She lets him go and begins to look for a job and a house so that she can be on her own.

Several things happen. Family members jump in to advise, help, negotiate and restore normalcy. They also build up the past through memory and recollection. Shripati begins to relate to his granddaughters and the girls find young men interested in them. Sumi herself goes through the experiences of other people's loss, finds a job, writes a play and discovers herself from under the layers of wifehood. But the novel does not end on a note of reconciliation, instead both Sumi and her father die in a scooter accident and Gopal continues with his ascetic withdrawal. [JJ]

Middleman & Other Stories, The (Bharati Mukherjee, 1988)

This later collection of eleven short stories includes characters from a wider range of countries than Bharati Mukherjee's earlier collection of short stories, *Darkness*. Here, they hail from India, Afghanistan, Iraq, Vietnam, the Philippines, Sri Lanka, Nepal, Trinidad, and Italy. The movement in this volume is four-ways, with downsides and upsides for the immigrants as well as for their host country—thus not only are they forced to transform themselves, but they inevitably transform the land of their adoption as well.

In the eponymous story "The Middleman," an Iraqi Jew, named Alfred Judah, finds himself in an unnamed Latin American country in between two successive revolutions. Between shady arms dealers, supporters of revolutionaries and other counter-revolutionaries, he realizes that even survival hinges on luck and uncontrollable factors. In "Fathering," a Vietnam vet named

Jason is reunited in Rock Springs, USA, with his daughter by an anonymous bar girl from Saigon. He is divided between his American girlfriend Sharon and his insecure little daughter Eng, who is tormented by memories of physical suffering and a belief in amulet cures. Jason finds himself playing the rescuing hero in an imaginary scenario in order to reassure and "save" Eng from her torments. In "The Management of Grief," the sorrow and disorientation of bereaved relatives of the victims of an Air India jet that crashed off the coast of Ireland, are contrasted with clumsy attempts by Canadian government officials to provide them with bureaucratic assistance.

The linking thread that runs through all these stories is a pervasive restlessness and optimistic energy to remake lives from shattered pieces, despite heavy odds and setbacks. [FD'S]

Midnight's Children
(Salman Rushdie, 1981)

Saleem Sinai, who was born at the exact moment of Indian independence, is handcuffed to history: his genealogy and his life parallel the story of modern India. His grandfather, Aadam Aziz, a Western-educated doctor, marries Naseem Ghani, a traditional Muslim woman in Kashmir in 1917. They move to Agra, where they raise a family of two boys and three girls. One of the daughters, Mumtaz, after a failed marriage to the poet Nadir Khan, marries Ahmed Sinai, a leather merchant, and they move to Delhi where Mumtaz, now Amina, conceives a son. After arson destroys Ahmed Sinai's leather warehouse, the family move to Bombay where they buy a house from William Methwold, a colonial returning to England. There the son Amina conceived is switched at birth with the son of a poor Hindu woman who dies in childbirth. Saleem, whose biological father is Methwold himself, is raised in Methwold's Estate, while Amina's biological son, called Shiva, is raised in great poverty and becomes a thug and a gangleader. Saleem discovers that all who were born, as he and Shiva were, in the first hour of independence have magical powers. He himself has the power of telepathy and the Midnight's Children hold conferences in his head. After a series of humiliating accidents, Saleem discovers he is not the birth-child of Ahmed and Amina, loses his telepathy, and moves to Pakistan. There he falls in love with his sister, Jamila Singer, whose singing has earned her the title of the Voice of Pakistan. In the Indo-Pakistani War of 1965 Saleem loses his family and his memory. Unable to remember who he is, he fights as a dog on the side of Pakistan in the Bangladeshi War of 1971, becomes disillusioned with war, and descends into the nightmarish world of the Sundarbans jungle, where eventually he recovers his identity. Saleem's story is not over, however: he returns to Delhi and marries another child of midnight,

Parvati, who has had a son by Shiva. Saleem and the other Midnight's Children are hunted down and castrated by the Widow, Indira Gandhi, and by Shiva, now a major in the army and her henchman. Chastened and much diminished, Saleem retires with his infant son to a pickle factory run by his former ayah, where he spends his days writing his story. Each day he completes a chapter and each night he reads it to Padma, one of the workers in the factory, whom he agrees to marry at the end of the novel. He fears, however, that he will disintegrate before the marriage takes place. [NTK]

Mistaken Identity
(Nayantara Sahgal, 1988)

Mistaken Identity is a narrative of the turbulent years 1929-30 of Indian history and brings together the various ideological positions and strands. Nayantara Sahgal works through the consciousness of a male narrator Bhushan, a young princeling, is arrested at midnight during a train journey, under the mistaken impression that he is a revolutionary. The prison cell where he is housed is shared by Bhaiji, a Congress worker and his two disciples, and communists like Comrades Yusuf and Iyer.

This prison cell represents a mini India incorporating the different religious and political positions. Bhushan, as he narrates his lifestory to his cellmates, and as the bizarre trial takes place in the court begins to realize how truth and reality work through multiplicities. His love for Razia had caused two Hindu-Muslim riots, his poetry is perceived as rebellious, the play he helped Scylla put up is termed subversive. His obsession with Razia and the imagined suffering he has foisted on her comes to a sudden end when he finds her happily married. But the theme of inter-religious marriage is sustained in another way when his mother, the Rani marries Comrade Yusuf and he marries his daughter.

Concentrated in time and place, it opens up in various ways and works through both humour and fantasy to address issues of ideology, politics, gender discrimination, the imperial power, the colonial stand and the events of the thirties. The trial ends as bizarrely as it had begun and the accused are acquitted. [JJ]

Moor's Last Sigh, The
(Salman Rushdie, 1995)

Moraes Zogoiby, called the "Moor," tells the story of four generations of his family line as he sits in a prison tower in Andalusia. Forced to write the story by his captor, Vasco Miranda, a painter and former lover of the Moor's mother, he makes the story as long and convoluted as possible in order to delay his death. The Moor is the heir to a successful spice business and to deadly family feuds in Cochin. His mother is the artist Aurora Zogoiby, of the wealthy and troubled Goan Catholic da Gama family, his father Abraham Zogoiby, a Cochin Jew.

Through his father's side Moraes claims to be descended from the Jewish lover of Boabdil, the Moor who surrendered the Alhambra to Ferdinand and Isabella in 1492, the year the Moors and the Jews were both expelled from Spain. The love affair of Aurora and Abraham, first consummated atop a pile of spices, defies the wishes of their families. They move to Malabar Hill in Bombay, where Abraham eventually becomes the head of a drug and prostitution syndicate, and they have four children, three daughters and a son: Ina, Minnie, Mynah, and Moor. Aurora becomes India's greatest living painter. Her paintings of family secrets, especially the Moor paintings that feature her son, are also allegories of India. The Moor is subject to a malady that makes him age prematurely: his body is already full-grown while he is at school, and he approaches old age long before his time. He also has a deformed hand that serves as a deadly weapon. Eventually he becomes a hitman for another of his mother's alleged lovers, the Hindu fundamentalist leader Raman Fielding, and for his political movement, Mumbai's Axis, a satire of Bal Thackeray and the Shiv Sena. As political violence wracks Bombay: Aurora, whose annual dance atop a tall building had been her celebration of creativity and defiance of the gods, falls to her death; her paintings are destroyed or stolen. She has hidden the identity of her murderer, her husband Abraham, under one of her paintings. [NTK]

Morning Face
(Mulk Raj Anand, 1968)

Krishnan Chander, the protagonist moves with his family to his hometown Amritsar, the nectar-city that proves to be a 'City of Dreadful Nights.' There also Krishnan is unhappy to know that people are superstitious. He is also angry at the British oppression of Indians. His mind is beguiled with serious questions about life. He seriously begins to question the existence of God, the caste-consciousness of Indians and the inferior status of women in Indian society. Krishnan's boyhood is characterized by a rationalistic interrogation of all the traditional values and evils. But he receives much love from Devaki, Shakuntala and Mumtaz (his brother's mistress). To resolve his mental conflict, he tries writing verse, reading Dickens, Thackeray, Tolstoy and Gorky and writing fiction. [BN]

Mr. Sampath, The Printer of Malgudi
(R.K. Narayan, 1949)

Contrary to the title, the novel centres on the character of Srinivas, the sole writer/editor of *The Banner*, a small newspaper dedicated to social commentary, focusing especially on issues such as the penury of landlords, the problems attending development, etc. After drifting from job to job, and under pressure from family to establish himself, Srinivas leaves his ancestral home and heads (alone, temporarily without his wife and child) for Malgudi to launch his publication. In need of a printer, he is introduced to Sampath, and they begin a reasonably successful business venture. Dedicated to his readers, highly conscious of publishing deadlines, intent on offering thoughtful writing, Srinivas becomes so deeply absorbed in the paper that he nearly forgets his own family, who later seek him out in Malgudi and move with him into the house he shares with four other families.

The Banner's publication is halted when Sampath's staff walk out on strike, and Sampath quickly shifts professions, becoming engaged as a partner/director in a local film studio, with Srinivas following as screenwriter. In a subplot, a young artist named Ravi has been talking with Sampath for some time about a young woman he has been obsessed with, but who has moved away from Malgudi—but who may now have returned. Ravi does not know her name, but he entrusts to Srinivas a beautiful sketch he has made of her, hoping he might help him to find her. Coincidentally, the film's lead actress (Shanti) looks strikingly like the woman in the sketch—Ravi is convinced of it—but Sampath suggests it is not possible. Like Ravi, Sampath becomes obsessed with her (nearly ruining himself and his family) and, in a bizarre sequence, Ravi swoops down on the movie set, kidnaps Shanti, destroys as much of the film equipment and props as he can, is captured, and then lapses into incoherent insanity. Srinivas agrees to care for Ravi until he might improve, Shanti runs away, Sampath is left deflated, the film ends in ruin, and Srinivas—after experiencing a "cosmic" vision of life, eternity, oneness, and his own virtual insignificance, resumes writing *The Banner*—in partnership with another printer. [GK]

Nectar in a Sieve (Kamala Markandaya, 1954)

Nectar in a Sieve can well be called a novel of continuity and change, the story of rural India of the early 1950s struggling with the forces of tradition and modernity, rapid industrialization and the exodus to the cities. It is also the tale of hunger and poverty and the sufferings of the landless farmers encountering the onslaught of nature in the form of droughts and famine, floods and storms.

The novel is a first person narration from the point of view of Rukmani, the female protagonist, married to a tenant farmer, Nathan. Rukmani gives birth to her first child, a girl but the craving for sons increases their family to a large size. Life is not easy for the couple with so many mouths to feed and the scanty crop failing year after year. After the tannery is opened in the village many young men, including Rukmani's sons prefer to join as labours instead of slogging in the field. Two of their sons leave for Sri Lanka, one goes to a city to become a domestic servant, two die—one in a clash and the other of malnourishment, and one remains in the village to work as a Compounder with Dr. Kenny. As if the existing troubles were not enough, Ira's husband sends her back to her parents because she cannot bear children. In desperation and hunger, Ira is compelled to sell her body for money; she gives birth to a sickly child; but is satisfied because the slur of being a barren woman is washed off. After the landlord evacuates his tenant farmers, Nathan and Rukmani decide to go to the city to their son whom they cannot locate and they road-workers. Nathan dies of fever and debility and Rukmani goes back to her village with a street urchin, Puli, a leper boy she has picked up out of pity. The novel shows human endurance and is a tribute to a woman of insurmountable courage. [UB]

Nine Moods of Bharata
(Mulk Raj Anand, 1998)

Krishna Chandar Azad, the protagonist of the novel embarks on a pilgrimage in search of meanings and resolutions of the contradictions, which had plagued him throughout his childhood and adolescence. He is guided and inspired by Mahatma Gandhi's injunction that we should always remember the suffering of those who are the most in need. The twenty-two-year-old Krishnan has returned from England only recently. He accompanies the former World War I German internee—a seeker of a different kind—of art treasures and photographs for future sale who is inclined to thievery whenever the opportunity arrives.

The young Krishnan, accompanied by a guide who happens to be an outcaste, enters the Ajanta caves. In the painted universe of the caves, he intuits all the nine *rasas* (or aesthetic sentiments) mentioned by Bharata in his *Natya Sastra*. In those paintings, Krishnan finds reflections of everything he has been observing throughout his life. Then his confrontation with the Jataka stories, those age-old folk tales in which the Buddha, as *bodhitsattva* in previous lives, reveals his compassionate nature in many diverse forms, the tales which had already sustained the people for centuries. [BN]

Nowhere Man, The
(Kamala Markandaya, 1972)

The theme of East-West encounter, which Kamala Markandaya has been tackling in her earlier novels, becomes more pronounced and pervasive in *The Nowhere Man*. It is, in a way a novel of confrontation rather than of reconciliation. The protagonist, Srinivas, who migrates to England never feels at home and remains a dangling man all his life. The conflict between the traditional Indian way of life that Vasantha represents and the English ways that her sons identify with becomes conspicuous in this work.

The Nowhere Man is the story of the suffering of Srinivas, his uncertainties and the prejudices he faces in England. A South Indian Brahmin, Srinivas migrates to England to escape the harassment at the hands of the British officers in India because of his family's association with the freedom struggle. In England, Srinivas follows a bohemian way of life while his wife, Vasantha, remains a typical Indian. Their two sons—Sheshu and Laxman, born and brought up in England, identify completely with the country, thus distancing themselves from India. When the boys leave home to join the army, Srinivas feels desolate. Vasantha and Sheshu's death, followed by Laxman's callous attitude further aggravate his misery. Lonely and uncared for, Srinivas finds solace in the company of Mrs. Pickerings, a divorcee and former nurse. They soon realize that they need each other and Mrs. Pickerings moves into Srinivas's house. Troubles multiply as Laxman objects to Mrs. Pickerings' presence, Srinivas contacts leprosy and the neighbours turn hostile. Everybody shuns him and when Fred sets his house on fire, the distraught old man is scorched to death inside. Srinivas had received affection and understanding from some of his British acquaintances and friends but unfortunately, that could not give him a sense of belonging; he remained a rootless, alienated man all his life. [UB]

On the Ganga Ghat
(Raja Rao, 1989)

On the Ganga Ghat is a Collection of 11 short stories with Benares acting not merely as backdrop but as the "final resting place on earth," for character after character feels irresistibly drawn to this sacred city. No story has a separate, individual title, for one story follows another in succession like the waves of the mighty river Ganga, all striving to fulfil their destiny. Like the perennial flow of the river, life too moves on in an endless procession and that is the reason why the stories are merely numbered. The novelist himself states in a brief *Preface* to the work that "these stories are so structured that the whole book should be read as one single novel." And it has but one theme which is, emancipation from the flux of life. And for an Indian what better place than Benares where Mother Ganga flows to wash away the sins of mankind. In this sense does Benares become a metaphor for transcendence as Byzantium for Yeats. So all roads lead to Benares. And Benares is the real hero of this novel judging by the way it impinges upon the consciousness of people. Indeed the whole novel is a reiteration of the truth, "Home is Ganga Ghat" in artistic terms.

But the work which primarily discusses philosophical matters also abounds in sensuous descriptions of "life's multiple riches" in fascinating detail suggesting eloquently how even this author with a penchant for the abstract *can* be concrete when he wants to. A master craftsman that he is, he can render even the mundane things of life with exquisite art and make his writing pulsate with the joy and vigour of everyday life. He can re-create the past and the present with a rare degree of intimacy and infuse his narrative with lively episodes and memorable characters. There is a generous sprinkling of delightful humour too.

The highpoint of the work however is the way Mother Ganga, a physical presence to begin with, is transformed ultimately into *Jnana Ganga*, Knowledge that flows as Ganga. [RR]

Painter of Signs, The
(R.K. Narayan, 1976)

The narrative focuses on the relationship between Raman, a thirty-something sign painter, and Daisy, a militant government servant working across the country to improve upon the nation's family planning efforts. Raman is focused on the aesthetics of his own craft, while the loveliness of various women around him is not lost on him, either. He meets Daisy when she solicits his services to paint a sign for her headquarters in Malgudi. Raman is strongly attracted to her, and he struggles against this attraction, feeling it is absurd for him to be drawn to a woman whose obvious passion is to avert conception. Nonetheless, he quickly agrees to accompany Daisy as she invites him to join her—as a painter of family planning slogans in the villages—on extended travel into the surrounding countryside. The power of his attraction to her overcomes him when, one night during their travels, he decides to ignore his inhibitions and make love to her, even if it must be done by force. Daisy manages to evade him just prior to his planned assault, and they return to Malgudi estranged—with Raman fearing that she will go to the police. Before long Daisy visits Raman in his home and their intimate romance begins to develop, evolving to the point of their planned marriage. When Raman announces to his aunt, his longtime caregiver, that he is going to marry, his orthodox aunt decides that she will leave on a long—and final—pilgrimage, determined to end her days in Benares. Raman becomes increasingly crestfallen and increasingly uneasy about the change in his life, recognizing the love and commitment of his aunt over the years and questioning Daisy's level of commitment to him and her ability to become more self-effacing. In the end, after Raman's aunt has left, Daisy rather abruptly ends their relationship, deciding that she must give herself instead fully and fiercely to the crusade for population control. [GK]

Paro: Dreams of Passion
(Namita Gokhale, 1984)

The novel starts off from a middle class milieu in Bombay. The narrator, Priya, is the elder daughter and the sole earning member of a middle class family who works in a private firm owned by B.R. Her love for and her physical relations with her boss B.R. do not bear fruit and she gets married instead to a budding and eventually a successful lawyer named Suresh. B.R. has in the meantime got married to Paro. Her marital life in Delhi gives Priya the chance to live her dream by socialising in the upper classes. Her dreams of such a life is manifested through the character and life of Paro. She comes in contact with Paro for the second and a longer period in Delhi. Soon Paro becomes a part of Priya's fantasies. The novel then centres around Priya and her sexual fantasies and Paro's sexual exploits. Paro is the insecure character who flits from one relationship to another in search of love and financial security. She is probably meant to signify that strength which Priya never found herself to be equipped with, namely the courage and dint to live one's life on one's own terms. Paro, in spite of several unsuccessful attempts to kill herself to attract attention, eventually succeeds. Priya, though she manages to muster enough courage to defy her husband in wanting to get her personal diary published, at the end reconciles and returns to him. [NS]

Plans for Departure
(Nayantara Sahgal, 1985)

Plans for Departure is a polito-historical novel focusing on the events between 1912-1918 but moving to and fro to capture the flow of history and encompassing more than three generations and various different political positions.

The observer eye is of a Danish woman, Anna Hansen, who on the eve of her marriage to Nicholas, an Englishman, decides to come to India and work out for herself the meaning of life. She takes up the position of a secretary with Sir Nitin, a scientist, and joins him in Himapur, a small hill town tucked away in the foothills of the Himalayas. The plans for departure are of several people—Anna and Sir Nitin, Stella Brewster who leaves her husband, a liberal in favour of Pryor who is an imperialist; Lulu Croft, the wife of the American missionary, who wants to leave her husband but is probably murdered before she can do that, and of the British, who can now read the writing on the wall with the Indians demanding freedom.

The novel works around several mysteries and character analyses. Anna is deeply impressed by Tilak's stand, imprisonment and following and sees in this a parallel with Tulsidas's (the writer of *Ramayana* in the spoken language of the people) obsession first with his wife and then with god. The ending is located in a free India with Anna granddaughter Gayatri and her husband Jason working on the mysterious processes of Indian history. [JJ]

Pleasure City
(Kamala Markandaya, 1982)

In *Pleasure City* Kamala Markandaya sees some of the old themes in a fresh light: the encroachment of Western science and technology on the remote life of Indian villages, the East-West relations which are no longer based on inequality in independent India and the necessity to bring in change.

The novel is set in a coastal village of post-independent India. A pleasure resort named 'Shalimar' is to be constructed near the village, for which AIDSCORP a transcontinental consortium gets the contract. The story begins with the hard life of the fisher folk and the fate of Rikki. After foregrounding the tale thus, the author turns attention to Rikki and Tully relationship. Rikki, a young orphan boy, has an artistically oriented temperament shaped by the old missionary couple in their school. Mr. Tully, the Director of AIDSCORP, besides working with the Shalimar project, is interested in renovating Avalon, a deserted castle nearby built long ago by his grandfather. Rikki and Mr. Tully engage wholeheartedly in this venture and Avalon gets a new lease of life. The author dwells on the close ties that forge between the two men despite the basic cultural and social differences. Mr. Tully is the director of the AIDSCORP and the son of the consul who once ruled the people of the area, while Rikki is a poor, orphaned fisherman. As the construction work completes and the 'Pleasure City' is in its final stages it is time for Tully to leave. Rikki who had once accepted his tragic fate stoically feels desperately lonely on Tully's departure. [UB]

Possession
(Kamala Markandaya, 1963)

Kamala Markandaya once again looks at the East-West question in *Possession*, but from a different angle this time. She moves away from her earlier stance of portraying village life in transition and concentrates on spiritual India versus material England. Critics read the novel as symbolic, with Val standing for India and Lady Caroline representing the colonial power holding India in its octopus grip.

Valmiki, a poor village lad, tends cattle on the desolate mountainside. He is ridiculed and discarded as a demented, good for nothing fellow. But, Valmiki is an inborn artist. He draws masterly motif on the rocks and is patronized by a Swami. It is here that Lady Caroline spots his art and is struck by its spontaneity. She pays a good amount to Valmiki's impoverished parents as his price and takes him to England. For her, Val is one of the showpieces she has brought from India to show off her artistic tastes to her aristocratic society. Irrespective of the comforts and accolades, Val's art does not flourish in captivity. Caroline holds him as her protégé, restricts his natural desire for the love of a young girl and exploits him sexually. Finally, disillusioned and nauseated by the restrictive atmosphere, Val decides to go back home, to the Swami whose benign presence has always been conducive to his art. Caroline follows Val to India, to the cave of the Swami. The denouement comes when she fails in her attempt to buy Val from the Swami with the lure of monetary power. Too egoistic to accept defeat, Lady Caroline remarks at the end of the novel that Val would soon have sense and return to her folds. [UB]

Prison and Chocolate Cake (Nayantara Sahgal, 1954)

Prison and Chocolate Cake is the first autobiographical account by Nayantara Sahgal, written as early as 1952-53 and recounts the experiences of her growing-up years from 1943 to 1948. At the age of sixteen Nayantara and her elder sister both left for the States in order to continue their studies and returned in 1948 to a free but divided country as Pakistan was carved out of India in 1947. This was also the period when she lost her father.

The years in America were full of surprises and also an exposure to a celebrity status on account of being Nehru's nieces. There were several moments of fun and laughter as well as of embarrassment. But despite the difference in cultures there was a tremendous amount of goodwill. Though the narrative covers five years, it moves, through memory and recollection, to include childhood memories of a family of several generations, the freedom struggle, the visits of many political leaders and the awe-inspiring presence of Gandhi.

The work takes it title from a childhood association of prison with chocolate cake. Her earliest memory of her father going to prison goes back to a time when she was three and the police came to take him away. On that occasion the family was having chocolate cake. One of the characters from this memoir goes on to develop as Anna Hansen of *Plans for Departure*. [JJ]

Private Life of an Indian Prince (Mulk Raj Anand, 1953)

The Maharaja of Sham Pur is the protagonist of the novel whose full name is Victor Edward George Ashok Kumar. He wants to please his British masters even by his 'impressive' name in which East and West merge. He wants to safeguard his little crown. He has had his college education at the chief's college, Lahore where he has formed his (Shelleyan) motto of never being confined to a single woman. He has a first class scandal with Miss Bunti Russell, daughter of Captain Russell. He has a nymphomaniac mistress in Ganga Dasi. He is so unwilling to accede his Kingdom to the Indian Union. The activists of *Praja Mandal* protest against the misrule of Victor.

Victor welcomes the foreign guests and arranges for a hunt of panthers. Ganga Dasi who has captured the Prime Minister Popatlal Shah is also seen in bed with Kurt Landauer. Victor wants to kill both of them, but controls himself. His American friends leave for Delhi without helping him. Then Sardar Vallabhbhai Patel sends for Victor and orders him to sign the papers for the accession of Sham Pur to the Indian Union. Victor returns to Sham Pur crestfallen and is shocked to learn about Ganga Dasi's elopement with Bool Chand. He literally cries and wails for having lost his mistress, Ganga Dasi. After the accession of Sham Pur to Indian Union, the Maharaja is advised by the Administrator, to take a holiday in Europe. So Victor flies to London along with his physician Dr. Shankar and Captain Partap Singh. After reaching London, the Maharaja tries to seduce a shop girl named Miss June Withers. But he can never forget his Ganga Dasi. He begins to talk and act like a mad fellow. He is called by India Office to return to India to give evidence in the case of Bool Chand's murder. But on the way the Maharaja behaves so foolishly in the aeroplane, that he is admitted into the lunatic asylum at Poona. On hearing the tragedy of Victor, Maharani Indira, the real but neglected wife of the Maharaja comes to look after her husband. [BN]

Red Earth Pouring Rain (Vikram Chandra, 1995)

Red Earth is a wide-ranging epic novel that incorporates diverse narratives into a single, flexible frame. The narratives are initiated when a young man, Abhay, returning to India from America, shoots a white monkey that lives near his parents' house. The monkey is not killed, but the force of the bullet causes it to remember its previous incarnation as Sanjay, a poet born in eighteenth century India. Yama, Lord of Death, realising that there has been a complication, arrives to reclaim Sanjay, but Sanjay makes a deal with Yama, that enables him to live if he can entertain a crowd with stories for a certain time each day.

Sanjay starts typing his tales, which are relayed orally by his human hosts to a crowd that gathers in the Maidan. He is not able to sustain his narration for the length of time allocated by Yama, however, so Abhay agrees to supplement Sanjay's tales with stories about his own experiences on a road trip across the United States. The narrative of eighteenth century India thus becomes entwined with a narrative of late twentieth century America.

Initially Sanjay's narratives are based upon the lives of various historical figures such as Benoit de Boigne and James 'Sikander' Skinner who were involved in the mercenary wars that raged in India in the eighteenth century and resulted in the establishment of the British Raj. Since Sanjay outlives his contemporaries by magical means, however, the stories also extend to encompass the Mutiny of 1857 and the murders committed by Jack the Ripper in Victorian London.

Abhay's narrative focuses upon his relationship with an American college girl, Amanda, and the novel comes full circle when we realise, that it was his frustration at the break up of this relationship that caused Abhay to shoot the monkey in the first place. [AT]

Relationships: Extracts from a Correspondence (with E.N. Mangatrai)
(Nayantara Sahgal, 1994)

Relationships brings together the letters written by Nayantara Sahgal and E.N. Mangatrai to each other during the period 1964-1967, a period when he was posted in Kashmir and she and her husband were in Bombay. This developing friendship and understanding was the cause of much social criticism and the final breakdown of her marriage and lead to an internal conflict whether there was any possibility of friendship between a man and a woman outside the bond of marriage. From several points of view, this can be viewed as a transgressive act and requires a tremendous amount of courage not merely to talk about it but also to share the process with others.

These were also the years immediately following Nehru's death and a great deal of politics finds place in the letters, revealing the working of a nation's mind as it began a fresh search for a perspective and an identity.

The letters record the beginning of a relationship which went on to be the basis of a long term one, continuing right up to the present, even if in itself it was subversive of society's sense of propriety, and besides reflecting on marriage, freedom and social attitudes, also attempts to redefine individual freedom and virtue in feminist terms. [JJ]

Rich Like Us
(Nayantara Sahgal, 1985)

Rich Like Us is a novel set against the background of the political emergency imposed by Indira Gandhi in 1975, the then Prime Minister of India. Nayantara Sahgal works through two alternative narratives of women of two different generations, race and situations, Rose, the second wife of a businessman, dislocated from Punjab on account of the partition and now lying paralysed, and Sonali, a civil servant, educated abroad and brought up in Gandhian India, child of a Kashmiri mother and a Maharashtrian father.

Sonali is the first casualty of the Emergency as she refuses to finalize a shady deal despite political pressure. Posted out, depressed and shocked, she falls ill and turns to the memory of her father, who has recently died, for moral and emotional support. As she goes through his papers, she unearths his diary with an account of his grandmother committing sati, and newspaper cutting reaching even further back to the public debate on the issue. For generations women have suffered and Sonali and Rose both are oppressed in their own way.

Rose's stepson, Dev is busy withdrawing huge sums from his father's bank by forging his signatures. Another character is

Ravi Kachru, Sonali's Colleague and friend who is with the power wielders. In the end Rose is killed and a crippled beggar is the only witness to this heinous crime, who is whisked away to safety by Sonali and Kachru is now appreciative of her stand. [JJ]

Riot: A Novel
(Shashi Tharoor, 2001)

This novel is, so to say, sandwiched between two halves of a news item in *The New York Journal*, describing the death of an American woman during a riot in a small town in North India. Following up this novelistic device, Tharoor writes the rest of the novel largely in the form of excerpts from the diaries, notes etc. of the main protagonists, many of them American. This makes for a relatively fast pace and, at least in the first half, a gradual build up of suspense that almost has the reader committing the crime of what-happened-nextism, so roundly and (to my mind) unfairly deplored by Rushdie's narrator in *Midnight's Children*. The novel basically tells the story of 24-year-old American research student, the idealistic Priscilla Hart who is killed during a riot on the last day of her stay in a small town in India, where she has been involved in family planning and social welfare work. This involves the return to India of her divorced parents, in a bid to put together the life and death of their daughter, the notes of an American journalist sent by *The New York Journal*, the secret story of Priscilla's love affair with the District Magistrate (DM) Lakshman as well as the gradual build up of communal tension in the days following the *rath yatra* that marked the rise to power of the Hindu-rightist, *Bharatiya Janata Party*. [TK]

Road, The
(Mulk Raj Anand, 1961)

The people in the village of Govardhan produce plenty of cattle milk and large amount of vegetables. But selling them to their city, Gurgaon, is a big problem as there is no transportation facility. To solve this problem the Government decides to build a road connecting Goverdhan village and Gurgaon City. When the work on the road is started the villagers are very happy and dream of economic prosperity. Bikhu, the protagonist and other untouchables get a chance to work in the road construction. But the landlord, Thakur does not tolerate the idea of Bikhu and other untouchables drawing wages equal to caste-Hindu labourers. The caste-feelings soar up. The upper caste Hindus refuse even to touch the stones carried by the untouchables. But the village headman Dhooli Singh, inspired by the Gandhian reformist philosophy, decides to treat the untouchables as children of God or *Harijans*. But the infuriated landlord Thakur Singh instigates the village priest to excommunicate Dhooli Singh. The landlord's son Sanju who is a merciless 'goonda' burns the huts of the untouchables. Dhooli Singh's son Laxman who is in love with the landlord's daughter Rukmani, joins hand in the arson organized by Sanju against the untouchables. But Dhooli Singh takes pity on the untouchables and decides to help them rebuild their huts. He allows them to occupy his own house till their huts are built. But his wife gets furious to be polluted by the untouchables in her house. When the Government authorities come to know the practice of untouchability leading to a number of problems, ban untouchability legally. Hence the construction of the road is resumed temporarily. Finally when the road is ready, Bikhu instead of going home at Gurgaon follows the road and reaches Delhi where there is no caste or outcaste. [BN]

Roots and Shadows (Shashi Deshpande, 1983)

One of Deshpande's early novels, *Roots and Shadows* is the story of Indu, a motherless girl, brought up in a joint family, a girl who has moved away from the usual pattern of behaviour. She has done well in studies and, much against her families wishes, has married a man from outside her caste.

The novel opens with her coming home after a period of ten years on having been summoned back by her great aunt Akka who is on her death bed. The rest of the novel is about the sprawling family, its rebels, dependants, exploiters and supporters and the family intrigues, politics, frustrations and expectations. Naren, a distant relative is another rebel and an outcaste and Indu feels a certain empathy with him. Indu's own father, a journalist, is a permanent traveller and almost an outsider.

The two events which upset all norms are the bequest which her great aunt leaves Indu, making her the sole heir and the adulterous and almost incestuous relationship that develops between Naren and Indu ever so briefly. Mini, her cousin's marriage to an older person is another issue which juxtaposes romantic expectations with the ground reality of everyday life.

The house is sold, Mini chooses the marriage and Naren dies, perhaps on an accident, but it could also be a suicide. Indu gets back to her home and husband with a strong sense of realisation that her earlier rebelliousness had only been a half measure, and that she needed to recover herself. A step in this direction is her decision to do serious writing rather than indulge in market oriented journalism. [JJ]

Satanic Verses (Salman Rushdie, 1988)

Gibreel Farishta and Saladin Chamcha, who represent two kinds of immigrant, fall to earth after a terrorist bomb destroys Air India flight 420 above the English Channel. Saladin, the son of a wealthy businessman sent to public school in England, is determined to be more English than the English. He marries an upper-class Englishwoman,

Pamela Lovelace, without realizing that she is marrying him to escape the very stereotype that attracts him. Known as the Man of a Thousand Voices and a Voice, he provides the voices for television programmes and commercials. Gibreel, on the other hand, has no desire to become English but wants to "tropicalize" London. He is famous as a star in Bombay "theologicals," but has lost his faith. He has journeyed to England in search of Alleluia Cone, his former lover. Gibreel develops a halo and Saladin sprouts horns. Because he looks like the devil, Saladin is arrested and mistreated by the police. He escapes and goes into hiding at the Shandaar Café, a restaurant and rooming house run by Mohammad and Hind Sufiya. Saladin, jealous of Gibreel's angelic success in London, internalizes the devil and resumes his human form. He then conspires, Iagolike, to arouse Gibreel's jealousy and drive him insane. A mark of Gibreel's growing insanity is that his dreams leak into his waking life. He dreams of returning to seventh-century Arabia, to a town called Jahilia (Ignorance), based on Mecca, where a prophet named Mahound, a derogative term for Mohammad, founds a religion much like Islam. In the dream Gibreel takes on the role of the archangel who dictates the Quran to Mahound on Mount Cone. Gibreel's revelation does not come from Allah but is forced from him by the force of Mahound's personality. In a brothel called The Curtain twelve prostitutes take on the names of the twelve wives of Mahound and the satiric poet Baal, who is hiding in the brothel, marries them all. Gibreel also has two twentieth-century dreams, one of the Imam, a figure like the Ayatollah Khomeini in exile in London, and the other of a girl called Ayesha who wears and eats nothing but butterflies and convinces all the members of a village to go on pilgrimage on foot to Mecca across the Arabian Sea. Gibreel eventually goes mad and kills himself, but not before he has killed Alleluia Cone by pushing her from the roof of Everest Villas in Bombay. Saladin returns to India with his Indian lover, Zeenat Vakil, and is reconciled with his father, Changez. [NTK]

***Serpent and the Rope, The* (Raja Rao, 1960)**

The Serpent and the Rope said to be a largely autobiographical novel is the "sad and uneven chronicle" of a south Indian brahmin called Ramaswamy who becomes an orphan having lost his mother Gauri at the tender age of four. It is significant that the theme of homelessness should be treated at both personal and cosmic levels in the novel with a remarkable degree of perceptiveness. Crying poignantly for her the protagonist seeks the Mother Principle in all things he sees. His father marries twice again. The second one also having died, Rama now has another step-mother whom he regards as his own mother and who interestingly reciprocates his feelings with love and warmth.

Rama leaves for France at an early age to pursue his interests in History and Philosophy, particularly the Cathars and Albigensian heresy; meets Madeleine, a French woman, five years his senior who teaches History at the university, falls in love, marries, has a son Pierre Krishna who sadly enough dies when he is hardly seven months old. Madeleine never recovers from his death nor the subsequent birth of a still-born child which leaves her completely shattered compelling her to turn to Buddhism for solace. But more than Buddha's compassion it is the intellectual brilliance of Buddhism that appeals to her.

The relationship between Ramaswamy and Madeleine also brings to the fore an ever-recurring theme in Indian-English fiction, the theme of East-West encounter which lends a depth and a dimension to the novel, for nowhere else has this subject of East-West confrontation been handled either with such detachment and objectivity or maturity and understanding. Madeleine goes as far as a European woman can go to participate in Rama's life, but apparently it is not enough and despite Rama's most civilized and magnanimous gestures towards Madeleine, the marriage fails. What hurts more is Madeleine's approach to the whole issue of divorce and legalities. Most marriages in the novel are failures (except perhaps the symbolic marriage between Rama and Savithri), as no marriage has been an ideal one, in the Upanishadic sense, as revealed in the dialogue between Yajnavalkya and Maitreyi.

For the sensitive, introspective hero, there is no way out except to go to Travancore, seek his Guru and obtain the vision of Truth. The novel which begins with the theme of homelessness ends on the same note, with Rama's poignant realization that he has no country, no climate, no home to go to. But for Rama, for whom life is a pilgrimage, it has now come a full circle, culminating in his search for a Guru.

This highly sophisticated novel with an intellectual hero, with cerebral as well as spiritual concerns is also a celebration of the Feminine Principle, a preoccupation with the novelist which continues in succeeding works as well. The novel is also distinguished for its remarkable use of tradition reflected in myths, legends, history, philosophy, religion and metaphysics drawn from both the East and the West. [RR]

Seven Summers
(Mulk Raj Anand, 1951)

Krishnan Chander, the protagonist is an impetuous and mischievous child growing up in the cantonment of Mian Mir where his father is a respectable Head Clerk. Krishnan is petted and fondled by his parents and relatives. The unexpected death of his younger brother Prithvi gives him a jolt and an awareness of the mystery of death. When the family moves to Nowshera cantonment his inquisitiveness increases. He is sent to school, but he finds out that his school is a jail and his teacher, a jailer. When he visits Delhi with his father, he gets lost for a while. Meanwhile he goes with his mother to Dasaka where he gets the first glimpses of lovely and serene country life from which he returns perforce to Nowshera owing to a quarrel between his mother and aunt. Krishnan is a supersensitive and highly inquisitive boy who reacts to the world with intense feelings of joy and sorrow. [BN]

Shadow Lines, The
(Amitav Ghosh, 1988)

The story depicts the touching events which bring a middle-class Hindu family from Calcutta—refugees from East Bengal—to cross path with the Prices, from London, in a period of time which spans three generations. History, including the two world wars, Indian independence and the 1964 riots in Bangladesh, emerges as the real setting and driving force of the stories being told.

The two families and their respective destinies mirror one other and trace a criss-cross network of encounters on colonial and postcolonial maps: Mr. Tresawsen, in the novel the Price's progenitor, travels extensively through Asia before settling in Calcutta, while the young narrator's cousin, Tridib, a fascinating and mysterious character gradually securing a central role as the plot unfolds, goes to London for his postgraduate studies and is there during the war.

Women play also crucial parts in the stories: Ila, the narrator's pretty cousin, moves to London to become the emancipated woman she always dreamed of being, marries Nick Price, but sadly discovers how wrong this choice is. In a parallel way, May, Nick's elder sister, accepts Tridib's passionate invitation to India because she` is secretly in love with him. Their much-awaited for affair, however, fails to concretise because of the tragic death of the young Indian, who sacrifices his life in an extreme effort to save the incautious English woman.

Another character at the heart of a number of crucial episodes is Th'amma, the narrator's grandmother. Starkly opposed to Ila, providing an alternative model of female emancipation independent from the Western canon, she appears to be a stern widow, a sort of a family dictator, resolute in defending the traditional morals that she had taught in her long career as a teacher first and as a school-director later, until almost the end of the novel when her long-suppressed wish to re-unite her family, divided by past quarrels and present geographical boundaries, demonstrates her hitherto unsuspected emotional vulnerability. [PPP]

Shame
(Salman Rushdie, 1983)

Omar Khayyam Shakil, the putative hero, is a watcher, a voyeur, and not a participant in events. Born on his grandfather's deathbed in a labyrinthine mansion called Nishapur in the border town of Q, he is the bastard son of an Englishman born to one of the three Shakil daughters, Chhunni, Munnee, and Bunny (they never reveal which one). He spends his first 12 years imprisoned in Nishapur but then escapes. The core of the narrative is an allegory about contemporary Pakistani politics. Ali Bhutto and Zia ul-Haq appear as Iskander Harappa, Omar Shakil's libertine companion, and Raza Hyder, a Puritan fanatic under the sinister influence of Maulana Dawood. Raza is commander-in-chief of the army under Iskander, the prime minister, but somewhat to his own surprise, he leads a coup. Iskander is subsequently charged with corruption and murder for which he is sentenced to death. Iskander's wife depicts her husband's many excesses and crimes in eighteen embroidered shawls, but his daughter, Arjumand, the Virgin Ironpants, worships him as a martyr and dedicates herself to his memory. Political and sexual repression give rise to the Beast which possesses Sufiya Zinobia, the severely retarded daughter of Raza Hyder and Bilquis Kemal, taking her over in a kind of spiritual rape. Dr Shakil has fallen in love with her and married her, but is unable to control her increasing violence. She represents the true collective spirit of Pakistan. In the end Raza, Bilquis, and Omar flee to Nishapur. Bilquis dies of fever, the three Shakil sisters kill Raza in a gruesome fashion, and Sufiya tears Omar, her husband, limb from limb. [NTK]

Show Business
(Shashi Tharoor, 1992)

This is the story of Ashok Banjara, "product of the finest public school in independent India, son of the Minister of State for minor textiles," who seeks and gains superstardom in the Bombay film industry. Divided into six sections—predictably ranging from 'Take One' to 'Take Six'—the novel brings in a number of voices. These are not only the voice of Ashok, who is (it becomes clear later on) lying in hospital, critically injured, but also the voices of those who have known him for better and worse—Pranay, the villain who loved and loves the woman Ashok Banjara married, controlled and was often unfaithful to; Kulbhushan, Ashok's disapproving father, who is a rather clean politician; Mehnaz Elahi, Ashok's lover; Ashwin, Ashok's brother etc. Each of the sections, except the last one, also contains the fictionalised screenplay of one of Ashok's films—which serve to comment on the other parts of the section and the Bombay film world as well as mark or dissolve (as the case may be) the borders between the real world and the reel world. Serving as a backdrop to an assortment of interesting characters, these screenplays help highlight the never-ending and self-centred fantasy that, as Ashok realises lying paralysed in hospital after an accident on the sets of a film, has transformed his life into a gaudy, compelling lie. This book, written with humour and fluency, is different from Tharoor's first novel primarily for the plurality of novelistic voices that it introduces. [TK]

Situation in New Delhi, A (Nayantara Sahgal, 1977)

A Situation in New Delhi is a novel of Nayantara Sahgal's middle phase. It opens with Michael Calvert learning about the death of Shivraj, an Indian political leader whom he has always held in great regard. Michael, who is also a family friend, journeys to India and plans to do a book on Shivraj. What follows then is an account of Devi, Shivraj's widowed sister's political role, her emotional loneliness and her struggle for survival in the harsh political environment.

Living under the shadow of two dead men, her brother and her husband, she seeks support in her relationship with Michael and the sensitive, poetic and idealistic Usman, the Muslim vice-chancellor of Delhi University. The parallels between personal lives and political situation are stressed and the narrative also encompasses the generational conflicts through introducing several young people who represent different attitudes and classes. Devi's own nineteen-year old son, Rishad has turned a Naxalite out of disgust with the inequality of the system. But the violence he advocates destroys him as he dies in a bomb blast. There is also his girl friend Suvarna Priya (Skinny), and Madhu, another student, who Immolates herself after she is raped. Contrasted with these is Pinky, the daughter of a wealthy household with not a single idea in her head.

The novel, though written before the emergency, anticipates in an uncanny manner its imposition as it captures the class war and the power struggle of the period alongwith all its frustrations and hopes. [JJ]

Small Remedies (Shashi Deshpande, 2000)

Small Remedies has two parallel narratives which interact at several points reflecting on loss, estrangement and bereavement. Madhu's son, Adit, dies in a bomb blast and in order to help her to cope with her bereavement, friends ask her to write a biography of a well-known musician Savitribai Indorekar, who at one point was their next-door neighbour and whose daughter Munni had been Madhu's friend. Munni has also died in the same bomb blast.

Madhu realizes that there is a deliberate erasure of motherhood in Savitribai's life. Also in order to pursue her art she has had to sacrifice her marriage and take on a Muslim lover. Munni was the child of this union and her whole life had been a denial of this. This act of reconstructing Savitribai's life also enables her to analyse her own past more sharply—her father's mistress, Munni's adult world, her own husband's possessiveness, her motherless existence, the surrogate family which her aunt Leela provided her, her mother's marriage defying parental authority—all these lead her to review her life more dispassionately and learn to accept its losses along with the gains.

She learns to redefine truth and reality and relate to her hosts, who she discovers are related to her, and as Savitribai nears her end, Madhu is compelled to examine the nature of romance. The novel explores a host of issues, relationships, bereavement, creativity and its relation to the self, and ends with a reconciliation between Madhu and her husband Som. [JJ]

Socialite Evenings
(Shobha Dé, 1988)

Declaredly an autobiography, but recurring to continuous emotional upside-downness, as is customary in soap operas, *Socialite Evenings* follows Karuna's arrival in society and her frenzy to reach status.

Coming from a Maharashtra village, young Karuna is a pretty and ambitious girl, hostile to her traditional family and allergic to their expectations of her. Her friendship with the sophisticated Anjali, who introduces her to the flashy metropolitan attractions of Bombay, is of paramount importance for Karuna who soon starts modelling—a fact which, once discovered, enrages her parents—and determines to make her way and experience life.

From this point on, the entertaining, glittering, silly Bollywood world is fully exposed through Karuna's contacts and experiences. The neurotic Anjali, married to a wealthy man constantly looking for young girls, encouraged by the proud Karuna, divorces her husband and marries the well-off and polygamous Kumar, but is disappointed when she later finds out that he is a closet gay. After various exciting incidents, the assertive Karuna also marries the wrong man and is caught in the paranoia of crosswords and newspaper chess. Nonetheless, this does not prevent her from meeting the effervescent, shoe-fetish Ritu, the Naxalite but affluent ad agent Krish, the powerful Varun, eager to ruin other people's reputations, and entire crowds of movie stars, businessmen, fake Babus, show-business editors and directors, who pullulate in this colourful but vain world.

In the end, Karuna goes to live alone in rented lodgings. She first works as a theatre actress and ad film writer, then, encouraged by her new lover Ranbir Roy, starts typing the story of her life to be filmed as a documentary. [PPP]

Some Inner Fury
(Kamala Markandaya, 1955)

Some Inner Fury is set against the backdrop of India's freedom struggle highlighting the theme of

East-West encounter. While some Western educated Indians side with the British, there comes a strong countering force from the nationalists. Between these two opposing forces is placed the story of love and death, awakening and sacrifice.

The novel dramatizes the story of Mirabai (a Western educated young woman), her anglicised brother, her British friend and lover Richard, on the one hand, and the Indian nationalists Govind, Premala, and Roshan Merchant on the other. The focus, however, is on Mira who loves Richard intensely but who has the spirit to reject him for her country. As the events go, Kitsamy belongs to a well to do Brahmin family. From Oxford he brings home with him an English friend, Richard. Mira and Richard become friendly. Kit is thoroughly anglicised and his wife Premala, a quiet, simple Indian girl remains a misfit in Kit's social circle. Mira visits Madras when Kit is posted there where she meets Roshan Merchant, the nationalist journalist whose work interests her. She and Premala go to a village with Roshan to see a school coming up. Here, the course of life changes for both: Premala, who gets involved wholeheartedly in social service, and Mira, who meets Richard after three years. Their friendship is renewed and an exciting world of love opens up before them. Mira's cousin Govind is fully wrapped up in the freedom movement and takes to violent activities. During a violent incident, the nationalists blow off the school building in the village; Premala is caught within and is charred to death. Kits rushes to the spot but is killed by a flying knife. Hickey's false testimony implicates Govind in the murder. Mira realizes that truth means nothing even in the court of law as against the words the Englishman. Disillusioned and angry, she decides to join the nationalists leaving Richard behind. Her patriotism wins over her personal sentiments. [UB]

Storm in Chandigarh
(Nayantara Sahgal, 1969)

Nayantara Sahgal's third novel, *Storm in Chandigarh*, locates itself in Chandigarh the joint capital of Punjab and Haryana. In the background are the two Chief Ministers Gyan Singh and Harpal, men cast in two different molds, and in the foreground is the narrative of Saroj and Inder and their marriage which is passing through a crisis. Several other relationships like the one between Jit and Mara, Inder and Mara, Vishal and Gauri open out other dimensions of man-woman relationships.

The characters are finely portrayed and the emotional aspects worked out in detail. Saroj's sensuality, Vishal's Brahminism, Jit's tenderness and consideration, and Inder's self-righteousness, all project authentic portraits. The novel continues to explore some of the themes projected in her earlier novels, like the complexities of marriage, its related morality and freedom as well as the right of women over their bodies, Inder victimizes Saroj for having had a pre-marital relationship, ignoring the fact that she loves him, while he himself is guilty of adultery. Male aggression brutalizes sexual relationships. *Storm in Chandigarh* criticizes the abnormal premium placed on virginity and seeks to redefine both masculinity and femininity.

Finally Saroj decides to leave Inder.

The political parallels are also intricately worked out with men like Harpal, Vishal and Jit representing feminine qualities and Gyan Singh and Inder the masculine ones. The novel lends itself to a reading on this basis facilitating a Gandhian use of femininity just as it foregrounds the injustice of patriarchal value structures which oppress women. [JJ]

Strange and Sublime Address, A (Amit Chaudhari, 1991)

This first novel by Amit Chaudhari is written in a minimalist style that Chaudhari has since made his own. There are no great flourishes, no drum rolls or exuberance in this text. It is all very quiet and low-key here if not sublime.

A Strange and Sublime Address narrates the experiences of a young boy Sandeep who goes to Calcutta one summer to spend time at his maternal uncle's—Chhotomama—house. Here he finds life moving at a slower pace and to a different rhythm from what he had been used to at his parent's home in Bombay. An only child he was the centre of his parent's life and subconsciously resented this focus. In Calcutta, in a large joint family, he experiences for the first time sibling bonds and the joy of being left to himself, even in a group. The close ties within the family give him a feeling of being rooted which he did not have in the nuclear family in Bombay.

The text also foregrounds the city of Calcutta. This is Calcutta of the 1970s, a mega city but still warm and caring. Each locality—*para*—had its own identity sense and neighbours knew one another and did not display the indifference exhibited by the residents of most big cities. The *addas*, the *Pooja* rituals and other Calcutta specials are also detailed. There is no linear narrative here, but a series of episodes that happen to and around the little boy. In the shorter second half of the novel, Chhotomama's illness becomes an excuse for the rallying of the clan and family gathers around in a 'communal ceremony' and talk flows around the sick man of son's jobs and daughter's marriages. The book thus becomes a celebration of everyday life lived within the sometimes stifling, but in times of crises comforting, confines of the family. [SR]

Strange Case of Billy Biswas, The (Arun Joshi, 1971)

Romi, the witness narrator, is an Indian student in the U.S., and close friend of Billy Biswas, son of an Indian judge, a lively and brilliant student of anthropology living in New York. Romi is fascinated by Billy's sense of freedom and the acuteness which emerges in his relationships with other people but is particularly evident in his dialogues with Tuula Lindgren, a young Swedish psychiatrist and Billy's close friend.

On their way back to India, Billy takes up an academic career while Romi chooses the Indian Administrative Service. Contrary to expectations, Billy's engagement to Meena, a pretty westernised Bengali girl, gradually leads the protagonist to moodiness and lack of interest in life. Following a crisis, they marry, much to Romi's surprise, and he finds out that ordinary matrimonial life makes the situation still more stifling for him, until one day, while searching in the wilderness, he vanishes. Attempts by the police to trace him prove vain and a few years later the case is finally disposed of. It is only ten years later that he surfaces again. As a District Collector, Romi is surveying a forest area when Billy, in a loincloth, suddenly pops out and recounts his story to his astonished friend.

Stifled by civilization, Billy started a new life in the wilderness; he has a tribal woman, a new family, and has become the priest of a primitive civilization. Allegedly, he is endowed with strange magical powers. Despite contrary indications, Romi cannot keep the secret and a huge manhunt, led by Billy's father and Meena, is soon started. In a desperate attempt at escape, Billy kills a constable before he finally falls, shot by a policeman. [PPP]

Such a Long Journey
(Rohinton Mistry, 1991)

In Bombay, in 1971, Gustad Nobel is a Parsi bank clerk and a family man. He has two children, Sohrab, a university student, and Roshan, nine years old, and a loving wife. His life is shattered when he receives a letter from an old friend, Major Jimmy Billimoria, requesting him to receive a package for him. This letter does not only plunge Gustad at the core of a complicated political situation, but is itself harbinger of disaster. His son leaves home after quarrelling with him over the young man's refusal to go to the Indian Institute of Technology. His daughter falls ill. The municipal government requisitions the land where his apartment stands in order to widen a road. And last but not least, the contents of Billimoria's package put at risk Gustad's job at the bank. During the chaotic times of the Bangladesh war, family order is disrupted and Gustad has to find a new way to look at reality and cope with the outside world. [SA]

Suitable Boy, A
(Vikram Seth, 1993)

Mrs Mehra, a middle class widow, wants to find the right husband for her daughter Lata, a student at Brahmpur University, where the girl has met Kabir, a fellow student with an appealing personality who she soon falls in love with. They see each other on various occasions and even manage to spend a few romantic hours on the river, where they kiss and embrace. The problem is that Kabir is Muslim and so unacceptable to Mrs Mehra who must look elsewhere for a "suitable boy" for her daughter. The 'search' for a possible husband intertwines with events related to three families variously connected by marriage or friendship. Savita Mehra has just married Pran Kapoor, a college teacher engaged in a long term struggle to improve his position; his sister Veena is the wife of Kedarnath Tandon who is in the "shoe business"; their father, Mahesh Kapoor, is Revenue Minister in the state of Purva Pradesh, an exacting occupation as political struggle is rife before the general elections of 1952. Arun Mehra is married to Meenakshi Chatterji, daughter of a judge who lives in Calcutta; the old ruling class is represented by the Khans, in particular by the Nawab Sahib of Baitar. After several failed attempts Mrs Mehra seems to have found a suitable man in Haresh Khanna, a Hindu of a different background, older than Lata, financially independent and also working in the shoe industry. Lata, who had been courted by a young intellectual poet, Amit Chatterji, will eventually marry Haresh, not out of respect for her mother, but convinced it is the right choice for her. An important element in the well-structured plot is the devastating love affair between Maan Kapoor and the courtesan Saeeda Bai which ends almost tragically with the boy trying to kill her and his rival Firoz Khan. He is arrested and risks a severe sentence, but at the last minute is saved, thanks to the noble behaviour of Firoz and Saeeda who give a favourable but false report of what had happened, thus clearing Maan of the charge. The book ends with Lata beginning her married life, leaving for Calcutta where she will live, while unhappy Kabir remains alone in Brahmpur. [AFG]

Sunlight on a Broken Column (Attia Hosain, 1961)

Taking the title from T.S. Eliot's 'The Hollow Men,' Attia Hosain describes the life and times of the Indian independence and the partition. The trauma and anguish for lost glory and happiness, and the readjustments that followed in the changed world is described in a delicately moving manner. The narrator Laila is the orphaned daughter of a Muslim *taluqdar* family of Lucknow. Through Laila's cushioned life in her grandfather's house amidst her aunts and several attendants, the transition from the feudal life to the 'hollow' life of being a member of a minor Muslim population left in India after the partition, is poignantly depicted. The social and political situation of pre and post independence is finely interwoven with the portrayal of the characters and their inter-relationships. The innumerable number of cousins and relatives that Laila spends her growing up years with are a part of the wider world where Laila meets and discusses politics with friends in college. Asad's participation in the movement, Laila's choice of getting married to someone of her choice, Zahra's refusal to accept Asad and settling down rather in a comfortable marriage with the choice of her guardians, are the various shades of human characteristics of the patriarchal world that the author presents in the novel. The freedom movement, the end of the rule of the *taluqdars*, the partition, and the after effects of all these incidents on the lives of the people are deftly presented in an engrossing way with much intelligence and grace. [NS]

Swami and Friends
(R.K. Narayan, 1935)

Narayan's first published novel, a largely episodic narrative, establishes his penchant for humour, as well as his ability to build suspense and evoke a range of emotional response from his reader—all through the experiences of his protagonist, ten year old Swaminathan. The novel focuses on Swami's experiences in school, the central significance in his life of his small circle of friends, their often humorous ways of interpreting the seemingly inscrutable ways of the adult world, and the emotional pain that comes with the separation of close friends at a young age.

By no means slow, Swami is nonetheless not so motivated as a student as his stern father would prefer (comparable to Narayan's own experience from childhood), and is instead much more passionate about the daily affairs of his friends and, above all else, the game of cricket. When Swami leaves the Albert Mission School after his turbulent experiences with the school's headmaster and transfers to the Board High School of Malgudi, he has no better luck—particularly after he does all he can to avoid the late afternoon drill sessions so that he can attend the practices of the newly formed Malgudi Cricket Club (so named by Swami and his friends) in preparation for their showdown with rival Young Men's Union club. After an altercation with the headmaster, Swami runs away, becoming lost along unfamiliar roads in the Mempi Hills, collapses from exhaustion late into the night, and is rescued by a passing cart driver. By the time he is restored to his family, the cricket match has ended—and so, apparently, has his friendship with his domineering friend Rajam, captain of the M.C.C., who has been counting on the contributions of Swami, his star bowler. Rajam unexpectedly must move away and, after a period of not speaking to one another, Swami goes to the train station to bid Rajam farewell, only to see him open his mouth as if to speak to Swami as the train lurches and heads off down the tracks. [GK]

Sword and the Sickle, The
(Mulk Raj Anand, 1942)

When World War I ends in 1918, Lal Singh, a prisoner of war in

Germany is set free. He returns to India. As he goes to Lahore cantonment by Bombay Peshawar Mail, he is full of hope that he will be given a medal, promotion and some land for his meritorious service to the Sarkar. Hope envelops him with happiness. But after his meeting with Peacock Sahib at the cantonment, Lalu's hope and happiness are ruined as he is accused of seditious behaviour in the German prison camp and is demobilized without the promised gift of land. He returns to his village, where he is shocked to know about the death of his mother two years ago and the auctioning of his home and land by the Machiavellian machinations of the moneylender Chaman Lal. As he has nowhere to go, he accepts the hospitality of his friend Gughi, now a bus driver, and stays with him. One evening, when Lalu is alone in Gughi's apartment, the landlord's daughter Maya, now a widow, visits him and narrates how she has been waiting for him. She promises Lalu that she is prepared to go anywhere with him.

Professor Verma meets Lalu and offers him the job of organizing *Kisan Sabhas*, on behalf of the count of Rajgarh, Kanwar Rampal Singh. Lalu elopes with Maya reaches Rajgarh, where he reacts very strongly against the cruelty of landlordism. Comrades Lal Singh, Ram Din, Nandu, Gupta and twenty evicted peasants take the dead body of Chandra to Allahabad. But on the way the dead body begins to stink. They therefore offer it to Mother Ganga. Then Lalu succeeds in meeting Mahatma Gandhi who invites him and other peasants and untouchables to a dinner at Motilal Nehru's place. Lalu leads the peasants in their revolutionary activities, but is ultimately forced to surrender to the soldiers. When he and the peasants are in the jail, he learns the news that a son is born to him on Maya. [BN]

Tales from Firozsha Baag (Rohinton Mistry, 1987)

A collection of short stories set in an apartment complex in Bombay. The stories describe middle class life among the Parsi community and the problems of their everyday life. Three of them—"Squatter," "Lend Me Your Light" and "Swimming Lessons"—deal with problems of migration. [SA]

Talkative Man (R.K. Narayan, 1986)

A compulsive talker/storyteller, Talkative Man (TM, for short) tells us the story of his having told to his friend Varma the story of his encounter or involvement with Dr. Rann, a mysterious draper man (3 piece blue suit, fully out of place in Malgudi) who appears one day in Malgudi claiming to be from Timbuctoo and currently engaged in a project for the United Nations. Rann first entrenches himself in the waiting room of Malgudi railway station, causing extreme anxiety for the station master who is concerned with the regulations (and for his reputation) and wants Rann out. TM manages to force Rann out, only to have him become an intractable "guest" in his own house a lodger he eventually adapts himself to.

A large and domineering woman, claiming to be Rann's "one true" wife (of many lovers and perhaps additional wives) shows up in Malgudi, hunting for Rann, whom she claims abandoned her and thus hasn't seen in years. Rann struggles to avoid her, while TM serves as both the semi-enabler for the woman and a somewhat flimsy shield for Rann, with whom he is intrigued and somewhat enchanted. TM discovers in Rann's room, however, a series of letters from women all over the world, all abandoned and seeking some sort of compensation.

After Rann's wife returns to Delhi from Malgudi, having failed to locate her husband, Rann develops a relationship with a seventeen-year-old girl TM has known since her infancy. As information comes to TM regarding Rann's plans to elope with the girl, he feels it urgent that he intercede; he sends a telegraph to Rann's wife in Delhi, who then rushes down to Malgudi and virtually kidnaps her husband in order to return him to "the prison of domesticity." As the novel ends, however, we learn that Rann has abandoned her again (after two years) and is somewhere on the prowl. [GK]

That Long Silence
(Shashi Deshpande, 1988)

That Long Silence is a novel which works through a woman narrator, Jaya and is a novel in four parts. The central event is the inquiry which is being conducted against Jaya's husband, Mohan on a charge of misappropriation. In search of temporary anonymity, they move out of their Churchgate flat to Jaya's flat in Dadar located in a much poorer locality. It is this return which sets of a whole process of recollection, memories of childhood, poverty, deprivation, the silent suffering of women and the way they have coped with their problems, Jaya's own relationship with Kamat, a man very different from Mohan.

But it is not necessarily that women are seen as victims. Mohan's own insecurities also come through very powerfully and as to how the need for social respectability and financial security have been two motive forces which have guided his conduct and have lead to a deliberate forgetting of his origins.

While the first part is about the inquiry, the two central parts focus on the past and as they analyse relationships also comment on the patriarchal impositions on women to the extent of cramping their space. The fourth part however brings the family together with Rahul, their missing son, back home and a telegram from Mohan informing them of having been absolved of the charge. The strength of the novel lies in its use of time and space in its effort to get beneath the surface realities and to articulate the silence of the feminine world. [JJ]

This Time of Morning (Nayantara Sahgal, 1965)

Published in 1965, *This Time of Morning*, Nayantara Sahgal's second novel, reviews the coming of new political affiliations in India. The novel opens with Rakesh returning to India after a foreign posting and reflecting on the Indian situation. Two narratives run parallel, one the story of changing political values, manipulations and bureaucratic workings and the other the story of Rashmi's love life, her unhappy marriage which is on the verge of collapse, her relationship with Neil Berenson, Rakesh's one-sided love for her and the whole question of relationships.

Both, Rashmi and the nation are facing a conflict between tradition and modernity. And this is represented by the split right through the political thinking. The problem is that the choice is not one in terms of either/or but it is more complex for each has its good points. It is also not a matter of generations. Kailas Vrind represents Gandhian ideas, but Kalyan Sinha, his contemporary, overrides all personal qualms. And Rashmi who believes in human goodness is not willing to be sacrificed to a loveless marriage in the name of tradition.

The crisis of Rashmi's life is placed against the background of her parents, Kailas and Mira, marriage based on accommodation and understanding. Several other couples are also there to reflect the complexity of human relationships. A novel about secular and liberal values, it reflects a Nehruvian India and captures the game being played in the corridors of power and ends on a non-conclusive note with the search for self still going on. [JJ]

Thousand Faces Of Night, The (Githa Hariharan, 1992)

Weaving tales of women from Hindu mythology, Githa Hariharan narrates the struggle of various women in this novel. On getting married to Mahesh, chosen by her mother, severing all her ties with America, Devi finds herself trapped in a marriage devoid of love and companionship. Her sole companion is her father-in-law who tells her mythological stories about the strength and endurance of women with the sole intention of how important it is to be a good wife and a good daughter-in-law. Dissatisfied with her marriage Devi elopes with Gopal. However this relationship too does not last long. In contrast to Devi's directionless quest for an anchor in life, is the story of Sita—Devi's mother. Sita gives up her passion for music to concentrate all her energies on her husband and daughter. Just as she prunes the plants in her garden, Sita determinedly spruces up the lives of her daughter and husband. The story of Mayamma is of a woman who has to suffer the tortures of all—husband, mother-in-law and son. She finds respite only when she runs away to take shelter with Mahesh's family. Apart from these are stories of other women, like

Mahesh's mother Parvati, Gauri and Annapurna, who either choose to escape from marriage or suffer for being a woman. The novel ends on a positive note with Devi returning home to the tune of her mother playing the veena again, intending to start life afresh. [NS]

Tiger for Malgudi, A
(R.K. Narayan, 1983)

The novel's central character and narrator is the tiger Raja who, in his early days, was proud to be regarded king of the jungle, preying on weaker animals, and enjoying the fear he instilled in other creatures around him. When Raja's wife and cubs are killed by hunters, he begins entering the village at night, making off with livestock, and contemplating revenge against the villagers. He is captured by Captain, director of the Grand Malgudi Circus, who takes it upon himself to train the majestic animal. Raja's will is molded by Captain's as Raja realizes that he will not be provided for unless he succumbs. Captain relies on his whip and electronic prod a bit too often, however, and one day after being stung Raja tears off Captain's head. Raja escapes to the streets of Malgudi, and panic ensues. Everyone having gone into hiding, the Master enters upon the scene and suddenly, mysteriously, gains immediate control over the animal. Under Master's influence, Raja comes to understand that his instinctive, often violent ways will have to change. The tiger reaches the point of feeling revulsion with himself after having killed another animal, then limits his food intake, and eventually adopts a vegetarian diet—at this point Master leaves him, after committing him to a zoo for the remainder of his days, so that he may bring pleasure to others. [GK]

The Tiger's Daughter
(Bharati Mukherjee, 1971)

This novel, made up of four parts, is recounted by a third-person narrator. It presents the trajectory of the protagonist, Tara Bannerjee-Cartwright, the only daughter of a Bengali Brahmin tobacco industrialist (known as the Bengal Tiger). Tara returns to her native Calcutta after a seven-year stay in the United States, where she has studied English Literature and married an American. However, she does not find the peaceful, familiar Calcutta of her childhood, having herself become hyper-sensitive to the poverty, squalor, industrial unrest and frequent political demonstrations of the city. She is also keenly aware of the indifference and smug maliciousness of her privileged circle of friends and family. She begins to doubt and question the soundness of the Brahminical order of life, religion and society.

A number of key scenes through the text highlight the fragility of a decaying traditional way of life. The visit to Tara's widowed aunt who fans incense around her clubfooted daughter's feet in the hope of a cure, Tara's mother's bhajans with the servants' children, a British Council debate on the abolition of English in India, the unmarried Joyonto Roy Chowdhury observing street destitutes amidst rats and roaches from his rambling Park Street apartment, a charity carnival organised by the Calcutta Chamber of Commerce in a former Maharaja's palace, a visit to funeral pyres by the river, a picnic at the Bengal Tiger's factory guest house, a visit to a derelict estate taken over by needy squatters, a holiday excursion to the quaintly old-fashioned Darjeeling, all seem to follow in arbitrary sequence. However, the restrained violence that links all these episodes reaches its paroxysm in the final scene where a rioting mob attacks and kills one of Tara's childhood friends, while she watches helplessly from inside another friend's car. [FD'S]

Time To Be Happy, A
(Nayantara Sahgal, 1958)

A Time to Be Happy is Nayantara Sahgal's first novel and represents India of the fifties against the backdrop of the freedom struggle. It is a novel which works through polarities and juxtapositions of opposing lifestyles, political and moral beliefs and political leanings with the pro-British and westernised views contrasted with the Gandhian ones.

Primarily a narrative of two families, the Shivpals and the Sahais, the male narrator's own family constitutes a third factor as three different generations intermingle, exchange confidences and seek help from each other. A gradual shift marks the attitude of the anglicised classes as they move towards more indigenous modes of thinking. And the handful of Britishers who have stayed on in various executive positions also respond in a more favourable manner to indianization. These changes reflect the shifts in power.

It is a youthful novel, voicing the spirit of young India and studying both cultural inheritance and power relationships. There are several sharply etched characters like Ammaji, Sohan bhai, Lakshmi, and Govind Narayan. Several issues are problematized—construction of a nation, Hinduism, rituals, the theory of Karma as the characters work out their own solutions.

Another issue which was to surface again in her later novels is the issue of a second marriage. This is further developed in *Mistaken Identity* and *Rich Like Us* and needs to looked at from that perspective. Loveless marriages which fall apart for reasons of ideological basis are another theme. These reflect the cultural division caused by the colonial situation. But the narrative despite its serious problems is a positive one. [JJ]

Train to Pakistan, A
(Khushwant Singh, 1954)

The year is 1947 and the Indian subcontinent is just about to be partitioned. Having been uprooted from their homes, millions of Hindus from Pakistan and Muslims from India are in flight and a million lives have been lost.

Mano Majra, a small village on the border of Pakistan, has been an island of peace. Sikhs and Muslims have been living there in peaceful coexistence for many centuries. The only Hindu is Ram Lal, the moneylender. The story begins with a group of dacoits striking terror at Ram Lal's house and shooting him down. Jagat Singh, known as Jugga, the village bad man, is in love with Nooran, a Muslim beauty. Hukum Chand, the Magistrate, a typical public servant in his indifferent to the problems of the people, seeks pleasures using his authority. The next day the police arrive at Mano Majra to investigate the murder of Ram Lal and drag Jugga to police custody. The same day, Iqbal Singh, a Western-educated communist arrives to work for the social uplift of the common people. Iqbal is also arrested, since the police suspect him to be a Muslim terrorist.

A 'ghost train' arrives at Mano Majra, causing a big sensation. It carries corpses of Hindus, fleeing from Pakistan. This creates a sense of terror and unpredictable violence among all the sections of the village. The Sikhs start suspecting the local Muslims, and the Muslims begin to cower in terror. Hukum Chand decides to evacuate the Muslims from the village to avoid bloodshed. Nooran is with Jugga's child now and is sent to the refugee camp. Meanwhile, some misguided Sikh youth plot to avenge the death of their people in Pakistan.

Jugga and Iqbal are released from the lock-up at this crucial stage. When Jugga searches for Nooran, he learns about the plot to kill Muslims entrained to Pakistan. In a rare show of selfless courage, Jugga foils the plan to dynamite the bridge as the train carrying Muslim refugees is about to cross it. Even as he saves innocent women and children from certain death, including his beloved Nooran, he gets crushed by the train. [PB]

Trotter-Nama, The
(Allan Sealy, 1988)

Allan Sealy's first novel *The Trotter–Nama* is at one and the same time both Postmodern and Postcolonial. The Postmodern/ Western elements manifest themselves as micro-narratives, juxtaposition of time and space, inter-textuality, self-reflexiveness, mixing of genres, rapid changes of register and all the other techniques available to the Postmodern novelist. An Anglo-Indian, Sealy has dedicated his book to "the Other Anglo-Indians" and in the tradition of minority discourses, tried to re-possess and re-write the history of this community disowned by both its progenitors—the Europeans as well as the Indians. Like many other Postcolonial texts *The Trotter-Nama* draws upon Oriental narrative techniques—in this case that of the "Nama," used by the Mughal Emperors of India who had their lives and reigns encapsulated in eponymous Namas—such as the *Akbar-Nama.*

The Trotter-Nama is of epic proportions and using the device of the narrator Eugene Aloysius Trotter—the Chosen Trotter—tells the tales of seven generations of Trotters and ranges across continents and centuries. These tales are not told in a chronological order but jump back and forth in time and are interspersed with delightful digressions on 'the crocodiles of Hindoostan' and several instructive tracts ranging from 'how the gypsonometer is made' to 'how suspense is made.'

The novel opens with the balloon flight of Justin Aloysius Trotter—the Great Trotter—in which he is killed. The body is never found, having landed in the Ganda Nala that separates the Trotter's domain, Sans Souci, from Nakhlau (Lucknow). The corpse of the Egg Brahmin which transmogrifies in death to become the Trotter, is buried instead. Justin's only son Mik (Kipling's Kim), born of his Muslim wife Sultana, ushers in the Anglo-Indian strain in the family. Now a litany of well-known and not so known Anglo-Indians flow through the text, in their own identities and disguised as so many Trotters—the poet Henry Derozio, the Hollywood actress Merle Oberon. Their identification with and alienation from India, their arrogance and their vulnerabilities are detailed in this novel which is in the ultimate analysis a quintessential hybrid text—both Western and Indian—just like the Anglo-Indians themselves. [SR]

Trying to Grow (Firdaus Kanga, 1990)

Firdaus Kanga's autobiographical novel *Trying to Grow* depicts the life and times of a handicapped Parsi boy growing up in Bombay. The first person suffers from osteogenesis imperfecta. This illness gives the protagonist brittle names and his nickname Brit. His growth is stunted by his disease and he is confined to a wheelchair.

Brit lives in Bombay with his typically anglicised and at the same time impacted by India parents, Sam and Sera and elder sister Dolly. He faces his handicap and the insensitivity of family, friends and strangers regarding it with wit and humour. As he grows up in the city of his birth he develops a crush on Cyrus, which has homosexual overtones and subsequently inherits his out-grown girlfriends Amy and Ruby. Brit's narrative makes the reader realise that the handicapped also have feelings and sexual urges like other people.

This novel also centrestages the Parsi identity and how in postcolonial India it took on the hues of the majority community. So Brit's mother Sera in spite of her Betty Garble legs and prominently displayed pictures of the British Royal family, has an immense faith in Hindu holy men and takes her son to a *Baba* in search of a cure for his brittle bones. The text also takes in the biggest problem facing the Parsi community—that of decreasing numbers. The demographic downturn is due to several causes such as late marriages and Parsi girls marrying outside the community and their offspring then not being admitted to the religious fold. Brit's sister Dolly is unmarried at thirty and her mother is not worried about this situation. The one time she tries to arrange a marriage for Dolly ends in a fiasco and the girl finally marries a Muslim doctor from New York. Her family is at first shocked by her decision but then accepts it with some reluctance.

Brit however is unfazed by this marriage as he is by most things that life has thrown at him and takes it on board with his usual equanimity—making this book a celebration of human resourcefulness under the most trying circumstances. [SR]

***Two Leaves and a Bud* (Mulk Raj Anand, 1937)**

Gangu, the protagonist of the novel, travels to Assam. His journey is aranged by Buta, the Sardar and coolie-catcher of Macpherson Tea Estate of Assam. Gangu, along with his wife Sajani, daughter Leila and son Buddhu goes to the Tea Estate in Assam. Gangu has a secret doubt that he has been deceived by Buta. After a week of hard labour in the Estate, Gangu is disappointed to receive less than 8 annas per day as wages for his entire family of four labourers. In his village he used to earn 8 annas per day by working on the landlord's land. Then within a week of employment in the Tea Estate, Gangu becomes a victim of malaria. Then the fever catches his wife Sajani also. The coolies become panic-stricken. The Medical Officer of the Tea Garden. John de la Harve promptly visits Gangu's hut, examines Sajani, and sadly declares that she is dead. Gangu's sadness is aggravated by the worry that he has no money to buy a red cloth and to make a bamboo hearse. Unwilling to borrow money from the *Sahukar*, Gangu approaches the Babu of the Estate, Shashi Bhushan Bhattacharya to talk to the Manager in 'angrezi' and a loan from him. When the Babu takes Gangu to the Manager, the letter grows furious, kicks Gangu and asks him to get out of his premises.

Gangu leaves the place deeply chagrined and humiliated. The next day he requests Buta for a loan, but Buta comes up with all sorts of excuses. Then Gangu goes to the Bania desperately and borrows 20 rupees from him for the cremation of his wife. In order to repay his loan, he pleads with Doctor John de la Havre to recommend a patch of land to be given to him for cultivation. Soon Gangu is given a strip of land in which he cultivates rice. But as luck would have it, the rice crop is ruined by the torrential rains.

Ruggie Hunt, the assistant planter aged 22 is notorious for his womanization. He gives a strip of land to those coolies who offer their wives or daughters to him for satisfying his lust. The sexual jealousy among the coolie women causes a big stir leading to a murder. The situation becomes uncontrollable. When Doctor John de la Havre represents the coolies, he is dismissed from service by Ruggie Hunt. The coolies' demand for justice is mistaken for a mutiny by the authorities who, therefore, seek the help of R.A.F. bombers to attack the coolies. The frightened coolies scatter away in different directions. The mutiny is crushed and life returns to normalcy.

One day Reggie Hunt happens to cast eyes on Gangu's daughter Laila and feels sexually attracted by her. He, therefore, asks her to come to his bungalow. But Laila slips into her hut. When Gangu comes on the seen, Reggie Hunt is frustrated and indiscreetly fires thereby murdering Gangu. In the subsequent trial conducted by Mr. Justice Mowberley and a jury of seven European and two Indian members, Reggie Hunt is declared as not guilty on the charge of murder and discharged. [BN]

Two Virgins
(Kamala Markandaya, 1973)

In *Two Virgins*, Kamala Markandaya explores the conflict between the old and the new, the traditional and the modern and the rural and the urban ethos by juxtaposing the two differing attitudes of the two sisters—Lalitha and Saroja. The novel, though considered a weak link to the fictional chain of Markandaya's oeuvre, highlights some of the problems that the country was facing during the period of transition. It is dangerous, the author seems to suggest, to be lured by the urban glitter without understanding the pitfalls of the glamorous new world.

Two Virgins is told from the consciousness of Saroja, the younger sister. Lalitha and Saroja are spirited young girls, pulsating with life. They imbibe the traditional values from their parents but are also exposed to education, which opens up new vistas for them. Saroja is simple, plain and timid, while Lalitha is pretty and bold. The stories of love and sex recounted in hushed tones by the women folk tickle the fancy of the growing girls but they remain within the traditional limits. Once Miss Mendonza introduces Lalitha to the city she relishes its freedom and eagerly embarks on adventures. A self-seeking tout, Mr. Gupta lures her to the film world and Lalitha, with flagrant disregard of all sane counsel, falls into his trap. He takes advantage of her innocence and spoils her. She dies when she realizes her folly and the disrepute and ruin she has brought on her family. Although Saroja too feels attracted by the mysteries of sex, she is demure and cautious; she remains away from its lure as she has seen her sister suffer. An obedient and well-behaved girl, she forms a contrast to her outgoing sister and is appreciated for her conventional approach. [UB]

Unotuchable
(Mulk Raj Anand, 1935)

Bakha the protagonist is a sweeper boy of eighteen years of age who is chidden and ordered by his father to clean the public latrines. He starts his work just out of the bed without even having a little hot water to warm his throat. After completing five rounds of cleaning the latrines, he returns home with the hope of getting something hot to drink. But there is no tea and not even water. Hence his sister Sohini takes a pitcher and goes in search of water. Luckily she brings some water without waiting for long and prepares the tea. Bakha drinks tea and feels happy. When Bakha wants to buy a packet of *jalebis* the confectioner throws the packet, like a cricket ball, for Bakha to catch. Being an untouchable, Bakha dare not touch the confectioner. Bakha enjoys eating the sweet. In this excitement he forgets to call out "Posh, posh, sweeper coming" and inadvertantly touches Lalla on the road and therefore harshly scolded and cursed by the latter. Lalla slaps Bakha and runs away from there. Now Bakha realizes his social position and the wickedness of the caste ridden Hindu society. He continues to sweep the temple courtyard. When he goes near the entrance of the temple, he is cursed by the brahmin priest. He is also angered to learn from his sister Sohini that she is molested by the priest when she was cleaning his house. He feels furious and wants to retaliate, but yet remains helpless due to his low status in the society. This bitter experience ruins his happiness even when he participates in a hockey match, a country walk and a wedding. In the evening he listens to a lecture by Hutchinson, the Salvation Army Missionary and finds three solutions to his problem: one, he may become a Christian, two, wait for the social change due to Gandhiji's efforts and three, he may put his faith in the water-closet about which the positivist poet has talked. The flush system may remove scavenging and untouchability from the Indian society. He thinks of everything he has heard and returns to his mud-walled hut, with a desire to tell his father about the Christian Missionary's suggestion of conversion, Gandhi's idea of social reformation, of the clever poet's suggestion about the flush system. [BN]

***Vendor of Sweets, The* (R.K. Narayan, 1967)**

Jagan, the sweet vendor, sees himself to be a disciple of Gandhi, carrying on and living a life committed to the principles espoused by the Mahatma: he has written an unpublished work on natural diet and nature cure, he regularly reads the *Bhagavad Gita*, he spins cloth for his clothes, meditates on (and often repeats) various moral principles and proverbs, etc. On the other hand, Jagan is every inch the businessman, thoroughly immersed in the rhythms and rituals of his own business activities, motivated by profit, sometimes manipulating the financial records, always conscious of economic strategy. Steeped as he is in the affairs of the world and the life of his own community, Jagan decides, in keeping with Hindu tradition, to spend the last period of his days in seclusion, in retirement from the world—in this case to assist a stonemason in carving a transcendent image of the goddess. His decision to retreat is motivated, however, by the frustrations and deterioration of his relationship with his son Mali who has returned from a university in the United States (having studied creative writing) accompanied by his Korean-American girlfriend, Grace); Jagan is also motivated to withdraw by the deterioration of his own house and by the emptiness he experiences following the death of his wife. Since Jagan is an ambiguous character, the reader is left with an image of a man who adheres to particular traditional spiritual practices (because he feels that he should) and one who slips away because he feels defeated, unable to negotiate the tensions between cultures and generations suggested by his relationship with his son. [GK]

Village, The
(Mulk Raj Anand, 1939)

Lal Singh, the protagonist and the youngest son welcomes his father Nihal Singh when the latter reaches Nandpur station after selling cotton and maize at the town of Manabad. He accompanies his father in his homeward journey. The seventy-year-old father curses the Devil like train, curses it as the sign of the arrival of the age of darkness and speaks of the advantages of going by bullock carts. He is sad that the cotton and maize he sold did not earn enough to even to pay the rent that was due.

Lala (or Lal Singh) strikes the earth with the newly mended hoe, but his mind is preoccupied with the Fair at Manabad. He wipes his perspiration and feels annoyed with his religion, which enjoins on its followers to wear long hair. In the evening, as directed by his father, Lal Singh goes to the Mahant and offers the gifts to him. Then he joins his two friends, Gughi and Churanji and travels in a hayladen cart to the fair, where he loses sight of his friends. Left alone and hungry he goes to a Mohammedan shop and eats some curry. Then unaware of the sacrilege he is committing, he enters King George Vth Haircutting and Shaving Saloon and has his hair shorn. When he returns home, the situation suddenly becomes tense. His father grows furious and slaps and strikes him mercilessly for violating their religion by having his long hair cut. Hardit Singh, the elder son of the landlord blackens his face, whereas Arjan Singh, the priest of the Sikh temple lifts and sits him on a donkey thereby insulting him publicly. Lal Singh escapes from the humiliation with great difficulty. After this shocking event, Lalu keeps a low profile in his house.

Now Lal Singh's family is busy preparing for the marriage of his elder brother Dayal Singh, Lal Singh happens to meet Maya, the landlord's daughter whom he had seen in the bullock cart ride earlier. Both of them play with each other quite innocently. But the landlord grows furious to observe them in their playful intimacy and drags his daughter away. The next day the police Havildar Nipoo Singh comes to Lalu's' house and arrests him on the charge of theft. Lalu realizes that the charge is fabricated by the landlord to punish him for playing with his daughter. So he runs away from there and reaches Manabad where he joins the army to escape arrest.

Lalu and other recruits are taken in the evening by the Karachi Mail to the 68th Rifles of Ferozepur. Though a Sikh by birth, on account of his short hair, Lal Singh is enlisted as a Hindu Dogra. The new recruits undergo intense training. The capricious and bloodthirsty drill instructor Lance Naik Lok Nath dislikes Lalu from the very beginning. He slaps and insults Lalu for the slightest mistake during the drill. As against the cruelty of Lok Nath, Lalu receives compassionate treatment and affection from Kirpu, the orderly of the Subedar Major, Daddy Dhanoo and Havildar Lachman Singh. After five months in the army, he receives a telegram about his father's illness and goes from Ferozepur and reaches home. His father is treated by a Muslim medicine man. After the expiry of his leave, Lalu touches his father's feet, seeks his blessings and leaves the village. His father asks him to be brave. He reaches Ferozepur and learns that the war has started between England and Germany. When Lalu and his companions wait for their turn to enter the ship, Lalu receives a telegram about the death of his father. Tears trickle down his cheeks. After being consoled by Uncle Kirpu, Daddy Dhanoo and Havildar Lachman, he shrugs his shoulders and runs along the decks towards the sepoys. [BN]

Village by the Sea, The (Anita Desai, 1982)

The awakening of a remote Indian village under the impact of industrialisation is pictured through the story of a poor agricultural family. The young Hari struggles to feed the family consisting of an alcoholic father, a sick mother, and two sisters. The little plot of land they own cannot yield enough to feed them all. News spreads in the village that a factory is going to be set up in the village and their land will be taken away for the factory. Hari joins the demonstration against this and reaches Bombay. There he finds a job in a restaurant and though oppressed by the crowded atmosphere of the city, he feels happy to be earning money. The *panwallah* in the next shop also teaches him to repair shops. The de Silvas who went to the village for the holidays help Hari's sisters to take their mother to the hospital for treatment. She is admitted there and the father stops drinking and stays there to look after his wife. The girls work for the de Silvas and make enough for themselves.

Hari comes home for Diwali with plans of starting a poultry farm in their little plot of land and setting up a watch-repair shop when the factory comes up. The mother is brought home and the novel ends with hopes of a better future in store for them. [DM]

Voices in the City (Anita Desai, 1965)

Voices in the City tells the story of artists who migrate to the city in search of recognition and better prospects, only to realize the sordidness and brutality of city life.

Different artists and their plight form the theme of the novel. Nirode, the central character is a sensitive artist who cannot mingle even with friends and feels totally alienated. The other artists are different. David is a man of positive faith, and Dharma, even though equally disgusted with this world, wants to create a world of his own. The city of Calcutta creates a sense of claustrophobia in Nirode and he wishes to kill himself. His sister Monisha also comes to the city with her husband and feels suffocated in the joint family living in a crammed house in the city. Unable to cope with city life and the emptiness of her own life spent in buying things from the bazar and cooking, Monisha commits suicide.

Unlike her brother Nirode, Amla wanted to be a commercial artist, but after she started modelling for Dharma, she is totally transformed. Dharma too starts taking interest in the life around him, instead of escaping totally into his own ideal world of beauty. [DM]

Waiting for the Mahatma (R.K. Narayan, 1955)

As the title suggests, the novel focuses on the influence of Gandhi—in this case, within the Malgudian context. When Gandhi speaks to a gathering in Malgudi, the orphaned young man Sriram is in attendance and, while he is moved by Gandhi's message, he is much more entranced by Bharati, one of the young women followers of the Mahatma who line the dais. Before attending the Congress rally, Sriram is initially warned by his grandmother about the destructive elements of Gandhi's campaign, especially his focus on overcoming untouchability and his apparent indifference to getting people into violent confrontations with police. Sriram becomes drawn into Gandhian activism only through his passion for Bharati; in order to be closer to her, he becomes one of the satyagrahi. Ironically, his physical passion (which he scarcely keeps in check) and his love-obsession (which hardly qualifies as *swaraj*) lead him, ultimately, to become serious in his commitment to self-denial, self-control, and a deep sense of service. While Gandhi plays a central role in the novel, Narayan does not offer a politicized narrative, only a depiction of the Mahatma's reception in Malgudi; the Sriram-Bharati love plot runs parallel to the Gandhi plot, and ultimately they become fused. [GK]

Where Shall We Go This Summer?
(Anita Desai, 1975)

The heroine is a sensitive woman who finds city life so oppressive and hostile that she doesn't want to give birth to the fourth child in her womb. Her husband Raman cannot understand the growing discontent of his wife, inspite of the material comforts and luxuries he has provided. The trivial incident of a crow's death or the petty quarrel between the ayahs in the presence of the children that they are supposed to look after, are enough to upset Sita for days. Sita decides to go to Manori, the village in which she had grown up under the care of a father who was a guardian to the whole village and seemed to have magic powers to cure illnesses. Though he is no more, the house is being guarded by a paid watchman and Sita thinks that the magic aura of the place would enable her to retain the child in her womb so that it does not have to come into this hostile world full of noise and cruelty. Sita arrives at the old house without any modern amenities with her children and soon becomes totally disillusioned. Nothing remains of the father's powers and even the memories of the father that come back to her now, necessitate a change in the glorified image. The children find it extremely difficult to adjust to the surroundings and are anxious about their own studies and finally when Raman arrives at the bidding of his daughter, Sita is ready to go back with him to the city and to cope with life. [DM]

Wife
(Bharati Mukherjee, 1975)

This novel is composed of three parts and is recounted by an omniscient third-person narrator. The first part is set in Calcutta and is centred on the gulf between the dreams, fantasies and aspirations about marriage of 20-year old Dimple Dasgupta and the compromises of her arranged marriage in actual fact with 29-year old Amit Basu, a mechanical engineer who had already applied for immigration to Canada and the US. References to Sita, the ideal wife of Hindu legends are contrasted with Dimple's attempts to be a modern and intelligent spouse.

The second part is set in the Queens area of New York and follows the first few months in the lives of Dimple and Amit Basu after their arrival in the US. Thus begins Dimple's adaptation to the American way of life—with the community of Indian expatriates in New York, various dinner gatherings and parties, and exposure to American shopping, advertisements, consumer-oriented magazines and TV shows. Again a disturbing gap between life's promises and actual experiences is highlighted.

In the third part, the Basu couple moves into a sublet flat in Manhattan and Dimple ardently smooth domestic life seems to fall apart as she undergoes culture shock and psychic dislocation. While her fantasy world feeds on television talk shows and soap operas, she has increasingly upsetting dreams, imaginings and yearnings. The inner violence in her personality reaches a climax when she mixes up the violence of TV scenarios with her own actions in a savage act of murder.

Thus, Bharati Mukherjee blends two themes—the upheavals of migration and the unresolved dilemmas of a modern woman—in this carefully constructed novel that operates through a series of deft touches and well-observed details. [FD'S]

World of Nagaraj, The **(R.K. Narayan, 1990)**

Nagaraj is a carefree man in his fifties who has a considerable inheritance, having divided his father's wealth with his brother Gopu. Gopu took his father's lands, livestock, and homestead in the countryside outside of Malgudi, while Nagaraj lives on in the expansive family house in Kabir Street, Malgudi, together with his wife and mother. Nagaraj visits a handful of familiar places and people around Malgudi each day, and although he has no need to work, he assists his friend Coomar, the sari salesman, with his account books and accepts no money for his labours. Nagaraj is obsessed with a plan to write his "magnum opus" on the sage Narada, in English, feeling that the work would be beneficial for readers everywhere. The problem is that he does not know enough of the Narada lore himself, nor does he know well where to locate it. A considerable portion of the novel, then, is given to Nagaraj's ruminations and frustrations regarding his grand ambition and his repeatedly aborted efforts to get the great project off the ground.

One of the principle obstacles to what he perceives to be the smooth path to his writing comes with the arrival in his home of his nephew Tim. Having become disgusted with life in the countryside and becoming fed up with the abuse directed at him by his father and by the local schoolmarms, Tim packs his trunk and returns to Malgudi to live with Nagaraj and his wife Sita, who have no children of their own. Nagaraj's dreaminess and lack of structure are not conducive to Tim's well-being and, although Nagaraj enrols Tim in the Albert Mission junior college, Tim drops out and begins wandering for much of the day, everyday, and eventually becomes a regular at the rather disreputable club, Kismet. Gopu learns of his son's disintegration and returns to chastise his brother and straighten out his son. Tim agrees to marriage, and Gopu arranges a match with a Delhi girl named Saroja who is particularly fond of playing the harmonium—which proves yet another hindrance to Nagaraj's composing his great literary work. Before long, Tim and Saroja leave Nagaraj's house and become fixtures at Kismet together, he a bartender and she a performer.

Gopu returns to Malgudi again to take his son home, but Tim refuses to see him. Considering the whole affair a disaster, but with quiet returned to his home, Nagaraj is encouraged to finally get his *magnum opus* under way. However, at novel's end, Tim and Saroja return abruptly to live with Nagaraj and Sita—Saroja bringing with her an even larger (and louder) harmonium—and Nagaraj sees his literary prospects as perpetually receding. [GK]

CONTRIBUTORS

Alberta Fabris Grube is Associate Professor of English at the University of Venice. In 1969 she published a book on Henry James and France and since then she has written extensively on the relations between Europe and the Oriental world and on Indo-Anglian literature. Her most recent work is *I due volti dell'India. Essays on Anglo-Indian literature and Indo-Anglian literature.*

Andrew Teverson has a doctorate from London University in the field of contemporary fiction. He is currently lecturing at Goldsmiths College, and working as an editor for a web-based Literary Encyclopaedia. He has published articles on the sculptural work of Anish Kapoor and the fiction of Kazuo Ishiguro, Angela Carter and Salman Rushdie.

Basavaraj Naikar, born 1949, began his teaching and research career at the Post-Graduate Centre of Karnatak University at Gulbarga and is presently a Professor of English at Karnatak University, Dharwad. In 1996, he was awarded D.Litt. from the International University at Los Altos, California, U.S.A. He is a bilingual writer, in Kannada as well as English. Among his translations, we should mention his *Beowulf* in Kannada. Likewise, he has published critical works and translations like *Sarvajna: The Omniscient Poet of Karnataka, Critical Articles on Nirad C. Chaudhuri, Musings of Sarvajna, Shakespeare's Last Plays: A Study in Epic Affirmation, The Folk-Theatre of North-Karnataka* in English. His reviews and research articles in Kannada as well as English have been published in various regional, national and international journals. *The Thief of Nagarahalli and Other Stories* was short-listed for the Commonwealth Fiction Prize for the Best First Book from Eurasia in the year 2000.

D. Maya is Reader and Head of the Department of English, at Govt. College for Women, Thiruvananthapuram, Kerala. She took her Masters and doctoral degrees from the University of Kerala. She has several years of teaching experience and several research students working for Ph.D. under her guidance. She has authored a book titled *Narrating Colonialism* and has contributed articles to leading literary journals and books. Her area of specialisation is Indian English fiction. She has presented papers at various national and international seminars.

Florence D'Souza is a lecturer in the English Department at the University of Lille 3 in France. Her thesis was on French travel writing on India in the second half of the eighteenth century. She has published several articles on the postcolonial creations of Indian writers in English.

Geoffrey Kain is a professor at Embry-Riddle University in Daytona Beach, Florida (USA), where he teaches world literature, postcolonial studies, and interdisciplinary humanities. As contributing editor he has published *R.K. Narayan: Contemporary Critical Essays* (1993) and *Ideas of Home: Literature of Asian Migration* (1996), both with Michigan State University Press. He has also published chapters and essays on a number of South Asian writers, including Bharati Mukherjee, Bapsi Sidhwa, Rohinton Mistry, Himani Bannerji, Prafulla Mohanti, and others.

Jasbir Jain, Emeritus Fellow, University of Rajasthan and Director IRIS, is currently working on a project on the Post-independence Novel in India 1947-2000. She has authored several books, the most recent are *Attia Hosain* and *Contextualising Modernism: the Novel in India 1880-1950.* Two recently edited volumes are *Gender and Narration* and *Films and Feminism.* Jain has travelled extensively and has taught abroad.

John Thieme is Professor Emeritus of English Studies at South Bank University, London and previously taught at the Universities of Guyana, North London and Hull, where he was Professor of New Literatures in English. He has published extensively on postcolonial writing, particularly Caribbean, Canadian and Indian literatures. His books include *The Web of Tradition: Uses of Allusion in V.S. Naipaul's Fiction* (1987), *The Arnold Anthology of Postcolonial Literatures in English* (1996), *Derek Walcott* (1999) and *Postcolonial Con-Texts: Writing Back to the Canon* (2001). He is currently working on a book on R.K. Narayan and a glossary of postcolonial studies. He is Articles Editor of *The Journal of Commonwealth Literature*, General Editor of the Manchester University Press Contemporary World Writers Series, Consultant and Contributing Editor of the Literary Compendium of *Pears Cyclopaedia* and Editor of the postcolonial sections of the electronic *Literary Encyclopedia* (www.LitEncyc.com) and the *Annotated Bibliography of English Studies.*

Nancy Ellen Batty teaches International and American literature at Red Deer College, Alberta, Canada. She has published essays on Salman Rushdie, Toni Morrison, and William Faulkner, and she has recently co-edited an issue of *ARIEL: A Review of International English Literature.*

Nandini Saha is Sr. Lecturer, Dept. of English, University of Kalyani, West Bengal, India. Recently registered for a Ph.D. on John Fowles.

Areas of specialisation are: Nineteenth and Twentieth century fiction, and Women's literature.

Neil ten Kortenaar teaches African, Caribbean, and South Asian literature at the University of Toronto at Scarborough. He has published articles on Midnight's Children.

P. Balaswamy is Chairman of the Department and Professor of English at Pondicherry University, India, where he is engaged in post-graduate teaching and research. His doctoral dissertation dealt with the element of allegory in John Steinbeck's early novels. Even though American Literature is his thrust area, he has a keen interest in such subjects as Translation (translated *Sembaruthi* a classic of modern Tamil fiction into English), Indian Writing in English and Commonwealth Literature. He visited Re Union Island (France) as a Visiting Professor at the University of Re Union, during November-December 1997 and delivered a series of lectures on Indian Fiction in English. Most of his publications are on American Literature and Indian Fiction in English. He has visited the United States twice to attend International Conferences.

Pier Paolo Piciucco is a lecturer at the Department of English, University of Turin. He has collaborated with the Italian academic institute CSAE (Centre for the Study of Literatures and Cultures of Emerging Areas) and for them has edited and translated into Italian a bilingual volume of short stories by Indian writers entitled *Feminine, Plural.* For Atlantic Books he has already edited four books dealing with various aspects of Indian literature in English. *The Two Souls*, his first monographic work, a theory of Black South African theatre, was published earlier last year.

Ragini Ramachandra was educated at the Universities of Mysore, Bangalore and Utah. Twice gold-medalist, she was also the recipient of National Merit Scholarship, Fulbright Scholarship and UGC Fellowship. She is currently Professor and Head of the Department of English at A.P.S. College, Bangalore University, Bangalore. She has authored a full-length book titled *Literary Criticism: An Enquiry into its Continuity and Vitality* (1989), and contributed to *The Encyclopaedia of Post-Colonial Literatures in English* (Routledge). Member, Cambridge Society, Cambridge, U.K., she is also co-editor of *The Literary Criterion.* Her major interests include Indian Literary Criticism, Indian Aesthetics and Indian Responses to Shakespeare.

Sarbani Chaudhury is a reader at the Department of English, University of Kalyani. Her publications include *Shakespeare and the Discourse of Protest* [1994], *The Merchant of Venice — a Work Text* [2000], *Re-presenting Shakespeare* vols. 1 and 2 [2002] and *Undergraduate Syllabus: Perspectives and Possibilities* [2002]. She is also the Indian correspondent for the world Shakespeare bibliography published annually by *Shakespeare Quarterly.*

Silvia Albertazzi is Professor of New Literatures in English and Head of the Centre for Postcolonial Studies at the University of Bologna. She has been studying English Postcolonial literatures since 1978, when her book on Indo-English fiction, *Il tempio e il villaggio* was published. Among her volumes we can mention: *Il sogno gotico* (1980), *Il libro dell'egoismo* (1983), *Introduzione a Lawrence* (1988), *Bugie sincere. Narratori e narrazioni 1970-1990 (1992), Il punto su: La letteratura fantastica* (1993), *Translating India* (1993), *Nel bosco degli spiriti* (1998). In 2000 she published the first comparative study of postcolonial literatures and theories to appear in Italy, *Lo sguardo dell'Altro.* With the members of the Centre for Postcolonial Studies she is now carrying on a project of study, analysis and discussion of English, French, Portuguese and Spanish Postcolonial literatures, in a comparative and historical perspective.

Sridhar Rajeswaran studied at the Universities of Madras and Bombay. His doctoral work dealt with postcolonial perspectives on the poetry of W.B. Yeats. His post-doctoral area of research and specialization are the Poetry of W.B. Yeats and Ireland, Postcolonial Theories, Race-Class-Caste-Gender studies and Modern Indian Drama in English. His essays have been published in reputed academic journals and critical anthologies in India and abroad and has presented papers at international conferences in Britain, Germany and Austria. As a creative writer and literary critic he has lectured in various Universities in Germany and France. Till recently, Dr. Sridhar was Assistant Professor in English Literature at the University of Hodeidah, Yemen.

Tabish Khair is associate professor in the Department of English, Aarhus University, Denmark. He is the author of *Where Parallel Lines Meet* (Penguin, 2000) and *Babu Fictions: Alienation in Contemporary Indian English Novels* (Oxford UP, 2001) and a number of other books. His novel, *The Bus Stopped,* is scheduled to be released soon.

Usha Bande is a fellow, Indian Institute of Advanced Study, Shimla, working on a project on the subcontinental women writers. Earlier, she was on the faculty of English under the Himachal Pradesh University, Shimla. Her Ph.D. is on the novels of Anita Desai which she explored using Karen Horney's psychological tenets. She has worked on the novels of William Golding and has recently completed a major research project on Indian Short Stories by Women, funded by the UGC.